SHADOWS IN THE WATER THRILLER BUNDLE

BOOKS 4 - 6

KORY M. SHRUM

All rights reserved
Copyright © by Kory M. Shrum
ISBN: 978-1-949577-66-2
Cover design by Christian Bentulan
Editing by Toby Selwyn

TIMBERLANE
PRESS

SHADOWS IN THE WATER THRILLER BUNDLE

AN EXCLUSIVE OFFER FOR YOU

Connecting with my readers is the best part of my job as a writer. One way that I like to connect is by sending 2-3 newsletters a month with a subscribers-only giveaway, free stories from your favorite series, and personal updates (read: pictures of my dog).

When you first sign up for the mailing list, I send you at least three free stories right away.

If giveaways and free stories sound like something you're interested in, please look for the special offer in the back of this book.

Happy reading,

Kory

CARNIVAL

SHADOWS IN THE WATER BOOK 4

1

Lou sat in the dark of the car, low in the seat so that she could not be seen through the window. She relied on the shadows to conceal her as they always did. Her eyes remained fixed on the front door of 1882 Cherry Lane. It did not open.

She checked her watch again, the face illuminating as she rotated her wrist toward her. It was 9:49.

He was cutting it close. Maybe Jeffrey Fish wouldn't visit the grocery store tonight. Maybe he would stay home and pretend he was a good boy.

Lou knew better.

The front door swung open, momentarily revealing a brightly lit living room decorated in mauve. A boy zoomed a red airplane in the air above his head. Then a man stepped into Lou's line of vision and the boy was gone.

Fish stood on the porch in the cascading light. His mouth moved and Lou could hear the low drum of his voice, though his words were indiscernible across the street. The porchlight haloed his soft brown hair, loaning him a deceptively angelic appearance.

When the woman came to the door, wringing her hands in a check-ered dishcloth, Lou sat up. She hadn't seen the wife before and was more than a little curious. The woman was pretty, with a round face and bright eyes. Her full cheeks made her look younger than she was.

Do you know about him? Lou wondered, searching her face. *Do you even suspect, maybe only in the back of your mind, that you're sleeping with a monster?*

Lou didn't think so, as the wife leaned forward and accepted the kiss her husband planted on her cheek.

With a bounce in his step, Jeffrey descended the porch and marched briskly to the waiting black SUV.

The little boy with the red airplane briefly reappeared before his mother closed the door.

Lou slid back down in her seat as the SUV's taillights flicked on.

She watched the vehicle reverse from the driveaway and head east, driving away from Lou's hiding place. The engine was disturbingly quiet—electric maybe? At the end of the road, the car paused at the four-way stop. When she saw the right blinker turn on, she smiled.

"Show me your real face," Lou whispered. *Show me what you really are.*

Her bones thrummed with excitement. She sat up and wrung the steering wheel with both hands.

Please.

Instead of turning on the car and following Fish through the moonlit streets of Mount Vernon, Lou took a breath and let the darkness swell around her. She closed her eyes, feeling it envelop her in its totality. When she couldn't hold her place any longer, she slipped.

The world dematerialized. A sensation like cold silk slid over her skin, and then she was through. The frosty interior of the car was replaced by the chilled brick wall under her bare hands. Her nails scraped against the concrete grout.

She pushed away from the wall, leaving the parked car half a mile away. It wasn't her car, after all. She'd only used it as a convenient hiding place while scoping the Fish residence. Boosting a car certainly wouldn't have worked in her favor anyway. Police involvement only complicated things. She'd leave the cops to King.

Lou had her own way—a *better* way—of tracking this man.

Lou surveyed her surroundings. She stood in the deep shadows collected beside the grocery store's western wall.

It protected her from a bitter midwestern wind, but already her skin had begun collecting frost from the air. Her cheeks and mouth grew cold. Water pooled in the corners of her eyes.

The parking lot had only five cars in it. Unsurprising, since the store closed at ten on weeknights. She surveyed the lot and the line of trees encroaching on it.

Her eyes remained focused on the road, searching, waiting, for any sign of Fish.

At 9:54, the black SUV swung into the parking lot, bouncing as it cleared the yellow speed bump, and took the empty space closest to the door. The engine clicked off. The lights died.

Fish jogged across the parking lot, the collar on his jacket slapping lightly against his throat.

I could take him now, Lou thought, her restlessness rising up in her again. *I could step out of this alley right now and just grab him.*

But her curiosity was too great. She wanted to know if she was right.

Fish made it into the store unharmed. Lou sighed and leaned against the brick. Nothing to do now but wait. Not that Fish had actually come for groceries.

Sure, he would pick up whatever menial item his wife had sent him to retrieve, some last-minute necessity like bread for their son's lunch tomorrow.

But if Lou was right, Jeffrey Fish wasn't here to shop. He was here to hunt.

A mother and daughter exited the store four minutes later. The kid blasted music in her headphones so loud that Lou could hear it even from her hiding spot. They drove a red Corolla off the lot, reducing the cars to four. Three guys carrying a case of beer each appeared next. After putting the beer in the trunk, they took possession of a silver Volvo.

Jeffrey Fish returned with a small paper bag tucked into the crook of his arm. He climbed into his SUV, but didn't drive away.

"What's wrong? Did you forget something?" Lou whispered mockingly from the dark.

Six minutes later, she appeared.

A young woman, brunette with an angular face and dark eyes, stepped from the store. She held the green apron that all the grocery employees wore in one hand and had a canvas bag slung over a shoulder.

Well-behaved women rarely make history was printed in block white letters across the canvas tote. She stuffed her apron inside it and rummaged for her keys. The lights of a blue Honda flashed.

Jeffrey Fish visibly tensed in the front seat of his SUV.

"You like that?" Lou whispered. She licked her chilled lips.

And what would you think if you knew you were the one being watched right now?

Lou saw only his chest and a slender white hand on the steering wheel. A shadow cut across his jawline, hiding his face. But Lou knew hunger when she saw it.

It was in the way his hand opened and closed on the wheel as if aching to reach out and take what it wanted. The way his chest rose too quickly in short, tight breaths.

She knew hunger.

She had her own.

Behind the wheel, the girl turned on her car, adjusted her rearview mirror, and reversed out of the lot.

For a moment the SUV only sat there as the Honda's taillights grew smaller and smaller.

You can go home, Jeffrey, Lou thought. *Take a shower. Brush your teeth. Make your son's lunch. Fuck your wife.*

But when that slender white hand finally turned the key in the ignition, he didn't head in the direction of home.

Instead, he turned right onto the main drag, following the blue Honda's trail.

Lou smiled.

She took a deep breath and pressed her back to the brick wall. The cold seeped through her leather jacket. She enjoyed it, feeling that rough grit brush against the back of her knuckles before letting the darkness overtake her again.

Groundlessness. Weightless freefall. And then the world was made real. Earth formed beneath her feet. The grocery store was gone but the night had not changed.

Her hand grasped the bark of a thick tree trunk. She lost her footing on the enormous root sloping down into the soil, but regained it, digging her boots into the dirt. Old trees were good cover. The shadows beneath the thick branches were complete.

Lou regarded the house across the street. It was a farmhouse in a cul-de-sac with two big picture windows punched in front. This configuration gave Lou the impression of a worried face. The light was on, illuminating a covered porch and the swing hanging to the left of a turquoise door. The paint looked fresh even if the rest of the house sagged.

After ten minutes, Lou checked her internal compass. But there was no pull, no inner wisdom saying she'd gotten it wrong, that she was needed somewhere else. Not that she couldn't imagine all manner of ambushes. Maybe Fish had decided to rear-end the girl. He'd pretend to be a concerned and apologetic citizen, before dragging her off the shoulder into the woods.

Headlights appeared at the end of the road, and Lou's patience was rewarded. The blue Honda swinging into the paved driveway didn't have any dents. The young brunette climbing from the driver's side looked unharmed, if tired from her day.

She was already inside the house when the SUV rolled up and parked on the opposite side of the street.

Lou's side—mere feet from her hiding place beneath the tree.

I'm right about him. I know what he is. That means he's fair game.

She could slip into the dark of his car, wrap her hands around his throat and pull him—well, anywhere. She'd take him to her dumping ground, to the lake half frozen with winter, a place of endless night. She would put a bullet between his eyes and watch the light click off.

Or maybe she would play with him first. Maybe she would let him fight her, just so she could enjoy breaking him.

When it was over, and Jeffrey Fish could no longer prey on the women of this world, she would drag his body into the water and—*No, Louie.*

It was King's words in her head. The bothersome private detective had somehow become one of four voices that now polluted her mind. And it rose, principled and insistent, even now.

We are playing a different game this time, he had said. *This game has rules.*

Lou sighed, her breath fogging white in her face.

They were playing a different game all right. And Lou wanted to know how much time they had left on the clock.

How long could Fish go before he *had* to kill? Once Lou herself had taken nearly two months off of killing and it had nearly killed *her*.

She hadn't been able to sleep. She'd eaten only when necessary.

She'd used her body like a punching bag, offering herself up to any half-cocked asshole stupid enough to take a swing.

Was Fish's hunger the same?

Did it make his skin itch the way Lou's sometimes did? Did it feel like cold fingers sliding into his skull, obliterating all thought, replacing all rationality with a single, desperate need? Did it prevent him from sleeping, or sitting still? Did it make him reach for a gun, just to hold it as he paced the floor—or was that only her?

His charade of normalcy worked well enough. Hadn't that been her first thought when she'd seen him in the Huntington Park playground two days ago?

His son had been swinging on the monkey bars while Fish had pretended to read a novel. He'd turned the pages after the appropriate pauses. He'd kept his head tilted down as if carefully regarding each page.

He'd presented himself as the picture of suburban acceptability in his pressed dress shirt and khakis. He had clean fingernails and a washed, shaven face. The mothers watching their children had regarded him with mild interest. No suspicion had creased their faces. One had asked him about the book.

How well you disguise yourself, Mr. Fish, Lou had thought, knowing he couldn't have seen the words on the page.

And what was he thinking now? As he sat in his dark car, watching the house, what was he feeling? Deciding?

Inside the house, an upstairs bedroom light clicked on, illuminating a white closet door and the foot of a bed. The girl was in pajamas now, her hair pulled up off her face. It was red and shining, freshly scrubbed. She wore glasses. She bent to plug in her phone, connecting the charger to the small device.

The light clicked off.

The driver's side door of the SUV opened, and Lou dropped into a crouch.

Two shining leather shoes stepped out onto the street. The heels ground into the pavement. She slipped around the side of the tree to get a better view.

Jeffrey was halfway across the street, standing in the moonlight. His shirt shone, wrapping him in a spectral glow. His chest was visibly heaving as he stared up at the dark window. His fists were clenched at his sides. The shirt fluttered in a light breeze.

No, he was *trembling*.

Go in, Lou begged silently. *Go in and try something. Come on.*

Her palms itched. She licked her lips, shifting her weight from one foot to the other.

It was as if she was watching her hunger grow in proportion to his.

With a grimace, Fish grabbed a fistful of his hair and pulled, as if yanking his whole body back to the car.

He grunted and changed course. He threw himself behind the wheel. The door slammed loudly.

The SUV hooked a U-turn in the dark street. The tires squealed.

Lou watched the vehicle go, the red taillights like hungry eyes in retreat.

The bedroom light clicked on again, showing the young woman framed in the backlit window. She was also watching the taillights fade into the distance.

This is a different game, King had said.

A game that Lou hoped wouldn't get this woman killed.

2

———

Robert King parked his '98 Oldsmobile by the curb outside the row house. Police crawled the lawn and sidewalks like a parade of oversized ants, going in and out of the door with clear plastic bags in their fists.

"Stay here," he told the dog sitting upright in the passenger seat. Lady, a regal Belgian Malinois, blinked her brown eyes at him. "I'll whistle if I need ya."

King swung his large body out of the car and crossed the patchy lawn. He waved at the officer guarding the door to get her attention.

"Mr. King, you can't be comin' around here." Clarice McGee's voice was stern, but she gave him a toothy smile, revealing the large gap between her two front teeth. "Do I have to chase you off again? You come to the station and ask your questions. Those are the rules."

"Dick called me in for a consult," King said. He shifted his weight to the hip that wasn't throbbing and pulled his hands out of his pockets. He held them up in surrender. "I wouldn't be here otherwise."

It was true that in the fourteen months since he'd opened his PI office, the Crescent City Detective Agency, he'd crossed paths with the local PD often. Follow-up questions and points of clarification could be handled over the phone, but sometimes King needed to see the scene of a crime to make sense of a report. He had to track witnesses to see if he could catch them contradicting their own statements, and if he'd seen something for himself, it was easier to note where the witness had gotten it wrong.

The police didn't care much for a meddlesome ex-DEA agent poking around unless they were the ones who'd hired him—and sometimes they were. But mostly it was private clientele, including lawyers and even the DA, who called on him to stick his nose where it didn't belong.

"Robbie!" Detective Dick White's voice was deep and robust. "Get in here."

With another apologetic shrug, King angled himself under the yellow tape.

Clarice let him pass, but didn't bother to hide her eyeroll. King would've been hurt had he not seen the smile tugging at the corners of her lips.

King followed Dick down the narrow hallway. Officers turned sideways to pass each other, angling their bodies carefully as to not touch the walls where hidden fingerprints or evidence might remain.

The smell of sweat and cigarettes was strong. Yet neither of these strong scents could mask the putrefaction growing stronger the closer they came to the back of the house.

The hairs in King's nose burned. He knew what he was going to find even before Dick opened the last door on the left. He swung it wide, hearing it bounce off the wall behind it.

King's breath hitched. He reflexively covered his mouth and nose with his hand.

"I should've warned you," Dick agreed. "But you've seen worse with the DEA, right?"

King managed a nod, but he couldn't tear his eyes away from the scene on the bed. It was true that the DEA encountered plenty of murder crime scenes. But since he'd left the agency, the only dead bodies he'd seen had been those that Louie Thorne—his dead wife's niece—tended to leave in her wake. It was admittedly quite the body count. But Lou was cold, methodical. She killed as a means to an end.

But this...*this*...

A woman was splayed on top of the covers, a stiff and scratchy patchwork of fabric. King wasn't sure what color the blankets had been at the start of their life, and it no longer mattered. Now they were soaked in blood.

Her silk negligee was a festoon of crimson splatters from neck to groin. Her eyes were rolled up into her head, her mouth still partially ajar. Two of her upper teeth were gold, and her lower lip had a hoop ring looped through it.

One of her legs had been partially severed, above the knee.

The mangled mass of meat and white bone poked through—King looked away.

The second body was that of a man slumped against the wall. His clothes were mostly clean. But the wall behind his head was splattered with brains and blood from a gun blast.

Dick was chattering away. "He stabbed her thirteen times then shot himself in the mouth. It looks like that happened *after* he tried to cut off her leg."

"Christ," King said. The woman's toes were painted a bright aquamarine. It clashed with the rest of the room, and King's eyes just kept coming back to them. "I didn't work homicide. There better be a good reason you called me here."

Because making him look at something like this for no reason would've been a sick joke.

"Oh, right." Dick turned to the closet covering the wall opposite the bed. "At first we thought it was just a domestic dispute. A crime of passion. But then we found this."

Dick opened the closet and King whistled.

Part of the plaster had been cut away to reveal brick after brick of cocaine. They were piled on top of each other like a secret hidden wall within the wall.

King scratched his chin. "That's a lot of dope."

"There's more."

"How much more?"

"It's behind every wall." Dick gestured at the house around them.

"*What?*" King laughed, unable to believe it.

"*Every* wall," Dick insisted. "Every cut we've made, we've found it piled up from floor to ceiling. It's way too much for a humble couple living a quiet life in the The Big Easy, don't you think?"

"It's too much even for heavy dealers."

"That's what we thought. The knife had the man's prints on it, but now we're wondering if maybe the woman was tortured to get him to talk. It's still possible he offed himself out of guilt for not saving her. Or maybe the mysterious third party hurt the woman, then shot the man before framing him. Either way, we're hoping if we learn more about the drugs, we'll learn about these two. Right now, we don't have anything on the man at all. No name. Not even a wallet with a driver's license in it. The woman is Rita Cross. She owns the house and works as a hairstylist in Treme. But she isn't married and doesn't have this guy's name on even the utility bills. So who the hell is he?"

King whistled. A second later, someone—probably Clarice— yelped. Then Lady was in the room, looking up at King expectantly.

He gave the dog the sign to search the house for evidence. With a delighted yip, she put her nose to the ground and started in on her work.

"Damn smart dog," Dick said.

"Yeah."

"Where'd you get her from?"

"The NYPD. I'm friends with a guy up there. They said that she was perfectly trained as a dual-purpose dog. The department's original plan allowed for the recruitment of six dogs. Then a budget cut revised it down to four. They decided to keep the males and let the two females go. I was able to convince my friend to sign over ownership of Lady in exchange for reimbursing their expenses."

"Budget cuts, man. So, she's from New York?"

"Europe, actually. Demand for these dogs is so high right now, nine out of ten of these dogs are imported."

"You're lucky to get her," Dick agreed.

"Damn lucky. Except my French is shit."

Dick snorted. "Excuse me?"

"She learned her commands in French. And my pronunciation is no good. It's why I prefer the hand signals. She listens better to Mel."

"I didn't know Ms. Mel spoke French."

King shifted his weight, trying to abate the ache in his lower back. It snuck up on him these days if he stood for too long. "She's got that Creole background."

Dick laughed. "Of course she does. Well, I'll send what we've got about the house, the drugs, and these two to your office. Piper's usually quick getting back to me."

"She is," King said. "But she'll be in and out for the next two weeks. Carnival."

"We're spread pretty thin ourselves."

King had suspected as much. The flood of tourists also meant a flood of police force in the Quarter. Probably another reason why calling in a local PI seemed so attractive, if manpower was thin.

Dick gestured to the hallway, and King was relieved for permission to leave the room. It was the painted toes—those damn aquamarine toes—that he kept seeing.

Dick closed the door behind them.

Lady barked twice and King looked at the ceiling, tracking the sound.

"She got something?" Dick asked, his hand still on the bedroom doorknob.

"Let's see." Though he had no doubt. Lady really was a damn good dog. He'd only had her for eight months, but his affection for the animal was unlike any he'd had for a pet before.

King mounted the stairs, following the sound of Lady's instructive yips.

He found her at the top of the landing, her paws on the base of an open window.

"What have you got?" King asked her, ignoring the worsening ache in his lower back as he crested the stairs.

Lady hopped out the window onto the sloping roof. She scratched at the shingles.

"That isn't going to cave in," Dick said supportively. "If you think you can squeeze out of that thing."

King was able to squeeze through the window with much effort, collapsing onto the shingles with an undignified *harrumph*. His back was definitely talking to him now. He saw a Vicodin and a long nap in his future.

Dick laughed behind him.

"I don't see you coming out after me," King called crossly as he pulled himself up.

Lady's paws framed a splatter of blood about a quarter in size and another beside it no bigger than a dime.

"Good girl," King said, and gave the dog an affectionate scratch behind the ears. He reached into his coat pocket and found one of the treats he kept there now. He never knew when he would need to reward Lady for her work, so it was just easier to keep his pocket stocked.

Lady lapped the treat from his hand.

"What is it?" Dick asked, his head hanging out the window, giving the impression of a guillotine about to come down on the back of the man's neck.

"Blood," King said, resisting the urge to touch the tacky surface with his finger. "Call someone up here to collect it."

3

———————

Melandra had just closed her loft door when the telephone rang. Her hand hovered above the handle.

"No, *nuh uh*," she said, shaking her head. She was supposed to have turned over the open sign on the front door of her shop four minutes ago. She wasn't taking calls right now that would set her back even further.

She was late because she'd overslept—and she *never* overslept. But she'd tossed and turned much of the night due to the unbearable din of the street outside her window. It was Carnival in New Orleans, a time when an already restless French Quarter fell into a fever pitch of revelry.

Two weeks, Mel reminded herself and her splitting headache. *Two weeks and this will all be over...*

Mel, being the light sleeper she was, found this part of the year to be wretched—even if her sales did quadruple as the tourists flooded the Quarter. It seemed everyone wanted their fortunes told and their pockets filled with voodoo trinkets.

Money aside, it had still been dawn before the ruckus quieted and she'd finally been able to doze off.

The phone rang again. Melandra turned her key in the lock with a huff.

Nobody called her landline these days anyway, except old friends and telemarketers. If the former, they could leave a message on the answering machine that she'd had since 1999. If they were telemarketers trying to sell her a time-share condo in Florida, they didn't need to bother with the message.

Melandra adjusted her shawl around her shoulders and backed away from the door despite the small knot forming in her stomach. She descended the metal staircase that bridged the two loft apartments above Madame Melandra's Fortunes and Fixes and the occult shop occupying the first level.

Her bangles clanked noisily against the rail. She surveyed her domain.

The shop was quiet, wrapped in the long gray shadows of morning. She glanced at her watch. 10:05.

Outside the storefront window with the decal of her business logo printed on its front, a bike messenger whizzed by. He rang his bell twice to alert a woman crossing the street. Otherwise, the area was quiet. No doubt the drunks would be back in the streets by noon, after a late, boozy brunch, taking full advantage of the city's open container law.

God, she hated Carnival.

Head buzzing and eyes burning, she unlocked the front door. She pushed it a little to make sure it would swing, then flipped the sign from *Closed* to *Open*.

Her bangles continued to jingle on her wrist as she moved about the shop, preparing for a fresh onslaught of customers looking to kill the hours until the sun went down and the next round of debauchery began.

She checked that all the candles were forward facing, labels out. She untangled the glittering beads hanging from a hook and straightened the crooked *5 for $1* sign. The Carnival masks were fussed over as well, a few turned toward the window to catch the eyes of passersby.

She checked her appointment book, knowing she would be busy

well into the night, and guessed where she might squeeze in her food and bathroom breaks.

The back-to-back readings she didn't mind. Using her gifts was one way to channel her own restless energy and gave her a real chance at sleep. For once, exhaustion would work in her favor.

Lastly, once the rest of the shop was ready, she lit incense—deciding on myrrh today—and two candles: one for Mother Mary, another for St. Jude.

She considered these unconscious choices for a moment and wondered if they were a warning. That knot in her stomach hardened a bit more.

Her gaze softened on the candles' flames, and the room dimmed around her.

Almost, she thought as she felt the world disappear. *There.* Something was coming through all right. A dark shape. A shadow. Perhaps a woman walking toward her? Or a man...?

The shop phone rang, high and strident. Goosebumps rose on her arms.

She turned from the flickering candle flame, listening to the sound. There was something about its tone she didn't like.

Bad news, she thought. *It's felt in the bones.*

She answered on the fourth ring, knowing already it wasn't a customer. She gave the standard greeting anyway, in case she was wrong. It wouldn't be the first time, especially on as little sleep as she'd had the night before.

"Madame Melandra's Fortunes and Fixes."

"Mel!" Her name came out in one long sigh of relief. "God above, why are you so hard to get ahold of? I thought you'd done changed your number on me."

"Janie?" Melandra leaned a hip into the glass counter, either for support or in relief. She couldn't be sure. It wasn't that she wasn't happy to hear from her cousin. It was only that she couldn't shake that feeling nipping at the back of her neck.

This wasn't an expected call. No birthday or holiday today. *So why now?*

"Everything all right up there?" Melandra ventured.

"Oh, me and the girls is fine, *yeah*. Not that you'd know. Your ass ain't been back here in...what?"

"Six years," Melandra said without hesitating. She wasn't one for guilt trips. "Funny thing is, I hear cars travel both ways. Like money."

Melandra had sent money to all her family when they asked for it.

Janie knew this. Her tone turned saccharin sweet. "Hey now. I know, I know. It's just so hard with the girls in school. And they got so many *practices*. You wouldn't believe. Band *practice*, cheerleading *practice*, math team *practice*—whatever the hell that is."

Melandra felt the knot in her stomach tightening. The longer her cousin prattled on nervously, the more worried she became.

"If everyone is all right, then why you callin' me, Janie?" Without meaning to, she heard her own accent deepening, spreading out. It always happened when she spoke to her people back home.

There was an audible pause as Janie licked her lips. "Now don't get mad. I didn't have to call you and tell you nothin', but that wouldn't be right. I wanted to call. I *wanted* to. You *remember* that now."

A hard stone dropped somewhere deep inside her. The worrisome turning of Melandra's stomach gave over to full nausea. And then all at once she knew the truth. "Terry is out of jail."

Janie clucked her tongue. "Now how'd you know that? Damn, I swear, you're just like Grandmamie, ain't you?"

Her pulse roared to life in her ears. The room moved on a tilt. She reached out, found the countertop and seized it.

"You there?" Janie asked. "Melandra!"

"I'm here," Mel managed despite her tightening throat and the panic pressing in on her, compressing her vision. All the spit had left her mouth. She licked her lips futilely, finding them parchment dry. "When did he get out?"

"I don't know. But he was here three days ago. He visited his momma out at that home. She don't even know him, got Alzheimer's and all that. But he went and seen her anyway. He also went to see his girl."

"Alexis?"

"Yeah, his kid, but she didn't want nothing to do with him. She's married with a big house and two little ones. When the hubby flexed on his ass, he left without putting up much of a fight. *Big* surprise. He ain't done nothing for that girl. And she's a good 'un. She got her schoolin' and got a good job. She don't need no dog like him around."

Melandra grabbed hold of the back of her neck. It ached now. It was as if the muscles there were being squeezed by a large, unforgiving hand.

"He came around here too, asking 'bout you."

No, her mind said. *No, no, no.*

Janie kept speaking, unaware of the way Melandra's world spun around her. "I didn't say nothing, mind you. Not a damn word. But Tommy went and opened his big fat mouth like he always do."

Melandra eased herself into the chair before her legs gave out beneath her.

"Tommy got to talking about how everyone was faring these days— you know how he likes to shoot the shit. Big ol' lips just flappin' in the wind. He got around saying you were doing well down there in The Big Easy. That you had yourself a nice little shop in the French Quarter and wasn't hurting for no money."

No, no, no, no. Her mind was screaming now.

"I'll have you know that after Terry left, I slapped Tommy upside his damned head. I said, 'Why'd you go and tell him all that for? He don't need to know her business.' And he's like, 'He's her husband.' And I'm like, 'On paper. Not in any of the ways that matter.' I swear he's as smart as a box of rocks, that man."

Mel was on this side of hysteria when a sharp, uncompromising voice cut through her consuming fear.

Get ahold of this. Get ahold of this right now. Don't you lie down when there's a snake in the grass. I raised you better than that.

This was her grandmother's voice. And though Grandmamie had been long in her grave, Mel could've no sooner shut off this voice than cut off her own hand.

She straightened on the stool, adding steel to her spine.

"How did he seem to you?" Melandra said. Her voice wasn't perfectly steady, but that was all right. She was asking the right questions again, and that's what mattered.

"Like Terry," Janie said. "He's lean now. Before, ya know, he had a bit to him, but now he looks like one of those dogs that Bubba Rick fights out off Longfellow Road. And he got…"

She faltered.

"Tell me," Melandra said. "You called to tell me, didn't you? So tell me."

"I don't know." Janie sounded sincere. "I don't know what it was, but there was something about him. Something about him had changed, you know?"

"Twenty-five years in prison will do that to you," Melandra said.

"Yeah, maybe. Maybe that's it. But there was something about him. It was just a feeling, but I don't know. Shit. I just wanted to call you."

"Thank you for that," Melandra managed. She wasn't feeling particularly grateful, truth be told. She felt like the world had just served her a giant pile of shit and demanded she eat it.

"Well, I gotta be gettin' off here, but you call me, all right? If you need me. Cars *do* go both ways. I know it."

"Yeah, all right," Melandra said. "Thanks for calling, Janie. I mean that."

And she did.

The moment the call ended, Melandra dropped her phone onto the counter. She put her face into her hands, taking deep, desperate breaths.

Three days. Three days. Her mind repeated it over and over again. *He's been out of prison for three days.*

And it took no time at all to get to New Orleans, did it?

Why didn't he tell me he was getting out? Why—But she knew.

It was just like Terry to sneak up on her like this, and she had no doubt he was heading her way. If he could get a car, hitch a ride—and didn't he have enough friends left to manage it—he could be down here…now.

He could be here now.

With shaking shands she searched her robes for her tarot deck. *Grandmamie's* tarot deck. It reminded her of the way she used to search her pockets for cigarettes when her nerves were really bad, back when smoking had been the only way to relieve them.

A ghostly moan circled the shop, and the flickering lights startled a scream from Melandra. Another high-pitched scream met it, the sounds twining.

"Christ!" Piper exclaimed. Her hand went to her chest. "What the hell? It's just me."

Melandra's hands shook all the harder.

"What are you doing?" Piper crossed to her, letting her backpack slip off her shoulder and hit the floor. Her face pinched with confusion. "Mel, what are you doing?"

"I can't find my damn cards. I can't find them!"

"They're right here." Piper pointed at the wrapped bundle on the glass, a rectangle of black velvet tied neatly with a piece of red ribbon.

Melandra didn't even remember removing them from her pocket, but she must have. She must have reached for them while she was still talking to Janie.

Her hands shook so badly as she unrolled the cards that they spilled from the wrapping.

"Help me," she begged. She offered the cards to Piper with shaking hands. "Help me!"

A calm came over the girl. It surprised Mel. Usually if someone acted hysterical it induced hysteria in others. Piper seemed to grow calmer, more patient in direct balance to Melandra's outburst.

That's from dealing with her junkie mother, Mel thought distantly with that part of her still in control of itself. *She knows what to do when the world is unraveling.*

Piper held Grandmamie's cards in her hand—something she'd never been allowed to do before—and the look of awe on her face told Melandra she was well aware of it.

"What's happened?" Piper licked her lips. She tucked her blond hair behind her ear with her free hand, the cards grasped in the other. The silver rings on her fingers caught the light from the chandelier, sparkling. There was a small mole on her right thumb, and Mel found herself focusing on that. Right now, she'd take *anything*.

"Mel?" Piper asked gently. "What do you want me to do?"

"A three-card spread."

Piper shuffled the cards without having to be told. Over and over again they rolled between her nimble fingers while Mel grappled with the terror writhing inside her.

Get on top of this, Grandmamie said. *Get high so you can see that damn snake.*

Piper held out the deck, offering it to Melandra.

Mel closed her eyes and exhaled slowly. She knew that old deck so well she couldn't pick its cards with her eyes open. Every crease, every worn edge—she knew what they were. And if she was going to do this right, she had to blind herself to what she *thought* she knew.

Grandmamie, she prayed. *Help me.*

A feverish chill ran down her spine.

Melandra's fingers traced the cool edges of the cards. The feather-soft grazing of card after card after card, until a tremor of electric fire sparked in her fingertips. Then she pulled that card, laying it on the countertop only to begin trailing her fingertips over the rest of the deck.

Tick, tick, tick, tick... Her fingernails caught on the edges.

Another spark, a rush of heat up into her hand, and she pulled that card, too. The heat only deepened when she moved to the next card, so she pulled it as well. Just to be sure, she traced her fingers over the deck once more. But there was no heat on this pass.

The cards were chosen.

Melandra opened her eyes.

Piper gathered up the chosen cards. "You want to flip it or me?"

"You can do it," Melandra said. It didn't matter.

Now that her eyes were open, Mel knew which cards lay before her. Every crease and blemish was recognizable, even when the cards lay face down.

Piper caught the end of the first card—the one representing her past—and flipped it over. A man—half goat, half human—stared up at them with soft brown eyes. His head was cocked like a bird's, quizzically with a hint of a mischievous smile playing on his candlelit face.

"The Devil." Piper looked up from its worn image to Mel's face.

"Go on," Mel said. She sounded composed now, far more composed than she felt. Though her lips were still brutally dry, the desiccated skin rasping together as she spoke.

Piper turned over the second card—this one representing her present circumstances—and saw The Wheel of Fortune. "A second major arcana card. This is some fated shit."

"The next one is major arcana too," Mel said calmly. She knew that slight crease on the upper edge, that place where the black background had been worn away to show a bit of the card stock beneath.

Piper flipped it over. Upon seeing the face, she shifted uncomfortably. "Death."

Devil. The Wheel of Fortune. Death.

Sometimes the bills just come due, Grandmamie said. *They just come due.*

She clasped her hands so they would not shake.

"Mel, seriously. What the hell is going on?" Piper tapped the cards, looking from the ominous images up into Melandra's face. "This looks...serious. Like, are you—"

Mel interrupted her speculation. "Don't you worry about it. It's my concern, not yours."

Piper seemed not to hear. She was tapping the Death card. "Is this Lou?"

"No, I don't think so," Melandra said. Then with more certainty, "No, not this time."

Mel was relieved to find that the steel in her spine was holding. At least enough to get her out of this damn store.

"I'm going back to bed," Melandra said, gathering herself up with all the strength she had.

"We just opened."

"My head hurts, and I didn't sleep well last night. You run the shop until I come back down, okay?"

If Piper wanted to argue, she swallowed those protests as Mel mounted the stairs to her apartment slowly, aware that Piper's eyes were fixed on her back.

That's why Mel kept her head high and her steps measured.

It wasn't until she closed her apartment door and collapsed against it that she allowed herself to cry.

4

———————

Piper stared at Mel's apartment door for a long time after it snapped closed. She'd never seen Mel so upset before. She considered the woman's personality synonymous with *cool and collected*. Hell, just last year they'd been kidnapped by Russian mobsters and Mel had acted like it was an inconvenience rather than a very possible ending to all their lives. An *inconvenience*.

"What the hell just happened?" she whispered to the empty store.

Piper realized now as she gathered up the cards that she'd built Mel up in her mind. Up until this moment, the woman had been almost godlike. She'd idolized nearly everything about her: her independence, her business savvy, her take-no-prisoners attitude, the way she saddled up and handled whatever arrived on her doorstep like a woman with a pen and a to-do list to obliterate. Given Mel's proximity to King and Louie, this to-do list might include anything from dirty cops to murderous criminals—oh, and let's get another case of Nag Champa in by Wednesday.

She was amazing.

But the woman who had risen from the stool just now had been *shaking*.

Mel—*shaking*.

"What the hell just happened?" she whispered again. She flipped through the cards, trying to make sense of what she saw. She lifted the first closer to her face as if to read it better.

The Devil.

This could be read any number of ways, of course. It could be self-deception. Or it could be a literal person who messed with someone's head or got people into trouble. Either way, it was definitely viewed as a negative force. Piper was pretty sure that Melandra had asked for a past-present-future spread, though she couldn't be certain. There were a lot of ways to throw down a three-card spread. But assuming this was a past-present-future reading, did that mean someone from her past was coming back around? Was this person going to fuck with her?

Piper considered the card beside The Devil—The Wheel of Fortune.

She often thought of The Wheel of Fortune as the karma card.

Change. *What comes around goes around.*

This notion melded with her interpretation of The Devil. A troublesome person coming back around for...what, exactly?

It didn't explain the blind fear that she'd seen in Mel's face or the way that she'd practically fled from the shop with all that bullshit about a headache.

Okay, maybe she had a headache, but Piper wasn't stupid. What had scared her? What could stress her out so badly to trigger a migraine? They'd survived shootouts, and what in the world could be worse than a mob boss threatening to kill them all while a gun was pressed to her head?

Piper sighed and lifted the third card.

Death.

Her thumbnail traced the dark hood covering the bleached-white skull. In all honesty, this card used to freak Piper out. That was before she'd come to associate it with Louie. That was a pretty morbid outcome on its own, wasn't it? She wasn't supposed to look at a card and think, *Oh, hey! I think my good friend Louie is going to get up to some shenanigans again. Better check on that girl.*

She did want to check on Lou. It had been a couple of days since she'd heard from her. Carnival week had sort of washed over them like a tsunami wave, carrying all of them out to a sea of sleepless nights and harried days. King had cut her hours back as much as he could so that Mel could get the extra support in the shop. But this chaos would continue until the first Tuesday of March.

She sighed, regarding that whitewashed skull again, noting that it resembled a mask. Carnival. Masks. People pretending to be what they aren't...Lies masquerading as truth.

Secrets surfacing.

In essence, the Death card was another card about change. Lying beside The Wheel of Fortune and The Devil, it suggested some serious shifts in Mel's life.

If Piper was being honest with herself, it had been a quiet year. Oh, she'd been busy as hell with her two jobs, moving into her new apartment, and resuming classes—all while trying to hold together something that looked like a social life.

But busyness aside, the year had been blessedly free of drama. As long as she ignored the guilt-laden texts from her mother.

Regardless, this spread certainly suggested their momentary peace was coming to an end, because while it hadn't been for her, Mel was family.

Mel was *family*.

Whatever the hell was about to go down, Piper wasn't going to let her face it alone.

"It was fun while it lasted," she murmured, turning the cards over as if the images offended her.

The lights in the shop flickered and the chandelier moaned, but Piper didn't notice either, still engrossed in that terrible memory of Mel shaking as she demanded Piper read her cards.

She was so afraid. So, so afraid. But of what?

"Why can't people just tell me what's going on? God, use your *words*," Piper groaned.

"As a rule, people are poor communicators."

Piper's gaze snapped up and her heart dropped. All the air left her in a single *whoosh*.

Dani smiled, pushing her hair behind her ear and flicking her eyes down. "Hey."

"Hey," Piper said reflexively. "What are you doing here?"

And why do you look so damn good?

Dani was wearing a low-cut white blouse that contrasted against her skin. Her jeans were tight to her hips. Her dark hair was longer than Piper remembered and fell over the front of her gray woolen coat. The diamond solitaire hanging from a thin, almost invisible wire kept drawing Piper's eyes to her chest.

"The sign says open," Dani said with a half-smile. "Have my reading skills deteriorated?"

Piper bristled. *Don't come in here and act cute with me.* "I thought maybe you came by to pretend to be into me again—you know, so you could milk me for another story."

Dani wrinkled her nose. "Yeah, I did that, didn't I?"

Piper settled onto the stool. *Act cool,* she told herself as she tried to strike an indifferent pose. *Just play it cool.*

"So are you here for a story?" Piper asked, tapping her fingers on the glass.

"No, I have some information for King." Dani pressed her lips together.

"Do you?"

"He's working on a case for the assistant DA."

"I know," Piper scoffed. She knew about every case coming across their desks.

Dani shifted her weight. "I'm just delivering the goods he asked for."

Piper felt like someone had punched her in the guts. "What?"

Dani shrugged. "I went by the office to drop it off, but it's locked up. His cell phone is turned off, so I thought I'd see if he was here."

Piper's mind was trying to wrap itself around these details.

Not only was King still in contact with Dani, maybe he'd been in contact with her *all year*. And *how* hadn't Piper known?

"He was called in for a consult with the NOLA PD this morning," Piper managed, feeling a little better that she knew *something* Dani didn't.

Dani extended an envelope toward her. "I can leave the information with you."

"If it's so top secret, how do you know I can be trusted?"

Dani snorted. "Take it."

Piper didn't, and Dani put the envelope on the counter with a sigh. Piper looked at it, then up at Dani. "I'm sorry, *how* is this the first time I'm hearing about you working with King?"

"Because I've been avoiding you." Dani pushed her hair behind her ears again.

Piper laughed. "Why would you avoid *me?*"

Because I was the one who visited you in the hospital every day after you got tortured. I was the one that asked Lou not to kill you even though you were going to run your little journalist mouth about her to the press. And I wasn't the one who pretended to fall in love with you just for some stupid information.

"I feel pretty shitty about what I did."

Piper scratched the back of her head. "Well, it was a shitty thing to do, so..."

Dani's cheeks flushed.

The overhead chandelier moaned, flickering again.

It was the door chime, announcing the arrival of six very hungover-looking women. They were bleary-eyed and yawning.

Piper greeted them as her job required before turning her gaze back to Dani.

"Listen, I'm sorry I didn't call you back." Dani spoke softer now that they weren't alone. "I should've, but I...I have my reasons."

The pitiful fact was that Dani was as beautiful as ever, and Piper was the first to admit that beautiful girls were a personal weakness.

Against her will, something inside Piper softened. "I'll give this to King."

She reached out and took the envelope, moving it to her backpack on the floor.

"Thanks. I know it's safe with you." Dani turned, took a few steps toward the door.

That's it, I guess, Piper thought. *Am I just going to let her go?*

Before she could decide, Dani whirled back around. "Do you want to have dinner sometime?"

The words came out in a single rush.

Piper snorted. "Dinner?"

I was sucking your face off in that closet last year, we shared a near-death experience together, and now you want to act like we've just met?

"I want to talk more about everything that's happened—well, after Dmitri—but you're busy right now and I need to get back to *The Herald* anyway. We could do a drink if you'd rather—"

"Dinner's fine," Piper said as the chandelier moaned again. Three more customers stumbled across the threshold, laughing. And so the rush began.

Dani glanced at the customers. "How about The Praline Connection, tomorrow night? Eight o'clock?"

"Okay."

"Please come," Dani added with a sad smile, backing toward the door.

Before Piper could reply, two of the girls approached the counter, blocking Dani from view.

Piper plastered on a grin that she didn't feel. "Just the skull candles today? And a voodoo doll keychain! Excellent choice."

She glanced at the door one more time as she accepted the customer's credit card, but Dani was already gone.

5

———————

Lou sat up in bed. Only it wasn't her bed. She ran a hand over the coverlet and surveyed the room. Before her was a large window, rounded at the top, reaching all the way to the floor. The curtains covering it had been pulled apart, framing the Arno River. Guessing by the light, purple in its iridescence, it was nearly twilight in Florence. Laughter carried up to the room from the streets outside.

There was a small desk against the wall—no note on it—and then the bed she sat in, which was pinned between the stairs leading to the lower level of Konstantine's apartment and the bathroom on her right. All was quiet except for the noise carrying up from the city itself.

She was alone.

She ran a hand over the covers beside her again, as if trying to divine the answer to the question circling her mind. *Was he here when I slipped into his bed?*

It had happened a lot this year—her tendency to lie down in her bed, in broad daylight, with every fluorescent bulb in her apartment turned on just in case—and still wake up in Konstantine's bed.

Her ability to shift through shadows had always been dependent upon the darkness itself. She couldn't transport herself in daylight.

That was a fact. So why hadn't she been able to keep herself in her own bed?

Or maybe it's not about the light at all, a little voice chided. *Maybe it's about being where you want to be.*

Another curiosity, apart from waking in Konstantine's bed four or five times a week, was the way he received her.

He never woke her.

He never wrapped himself around her body or kissed her. He simply let her sleep.

In the fourteen months that this game had been going on, when she had awoken to find him there, he would smile. Only then would he reach out and place a hand on her hip or speak softly to her—never before she woke.

And she couldn't help but wonder why.

She pulled back the covers and found she was still wearing the clothes she'd had on when scoping Fish the night before. Black cargo pants and a black t-shirt. She crossed to the bathroom, splashed cold water on her face, and used his comb to smooth down her hair. Running his comb through her hair felt strangely intimate.

Far more intimate than anything they'd done in the last year.

She placed the comb on the sink and met her gaze in the mirror. Dark hair, dark eyes. Not unlike the grocer girl that Fish had followed home.

I'm your type, Fish, she thought. Not only in her coloring, but also in her jawline.

One step through Konstantine's closet, and she found herself in a cathedral.

It wasn't Padre Leo's cathedral. The old man had named Konstantine as heir to his dark empire, and his exiled son, Nico, had blown it to pieces. This church, though not as opulent, was its replacement.

What had Konstantine called it? *Sufficient.*

He'd used this word more than once, and Lou simply didn't understand. It was beautiful.

The ceilings rose far above her head, with stained glass filtering the light through the chapel.

The floor, columns, and walls were all old stone. She could spend years tracing each intricate carving with her finger and not take in every detail, every inch of art.

Better still was the silence that hung in the air. Hundreds of years had hollowed out the place, and left it cold, sacrosanct. Just how she liked it.

Sufficient.

Soft voices echoed through the shadows.

Lou traced the exterior of the room, following the familiar sound of Konstantine's voice.

When she stepped around the last column at the end of a long row, Konstantine himself sprang into view. Twilight filtered through a window above him. The way the light hit his dark hair gave the appearance of a halo, reminding Lou instantly of Fish and how he'd looked as he leaned forward to kiss his wife.

Was Konstantine any different than Fish? Lou thought so.

While it was true that the *capo dei capi* had his own body count, and had admitted to torturing when necessary, for Konstantine it was never about the kill.

It wasn't about revenge or feeding a hunger. It was about furthering an aim. His actions served an ambition that he wished to see to fruition. And even then, violence was a last resort.

But what about Lou? She had no underworld empire to secure or grow. She no longer had a family to avenge. All she had was her hunger, the hunt, and the kill.

Surely that made her more like Fish than Konstantine, didn't it?

Lou circled the chapel, watching Konstantine issue orders to the men gathered there. Twelve of them were strewn about the pews. They asked questions—all in Italian, of which Lou knew very little—and Konstantine responded, gesturing as he spoke.

Though she didn't understand the context of the Italian, she liked his voice. Its easy roll rumbled in her chest in a way that reminded her of her father. His voice had also been deep.

Women's voices trailed across the face and ears, but Konstantine's vibrated through her body. The soft bass vibration of a favorite song.

He turned toward her suddenly, looking in her direction, though Lou was certain he couldn't see her in the shadows.

Still, a smile tugged on his lips, and after only a few more minutes of instruction, he sent the men away.

He watched them go, hands in his pockets. His back was to her.

When they were alone, he spoke. "Ciao."

He faced her, still relaxed. He crossed to her with an easy smile on his face. But he stopped just short of where the light became darkness. "How did you sleep?"

"I seem to like your bed better than mine," she said.

His smile deepened. "I am not complaining."

He gestured toward the pews. "Did you understand what I was saying just now?"

He was trying to see her face, she realized. She stepped from the shadows into the edge of the light.

His smile softened.

"No," she said. "Your English is much better than my Italian."

"We're preparing for *Carnevale*," he said. "We've been invited to visit an associate in Venice. I was giving instructions for our visit and what should be done here in my absence."

Lou's attention pricked with excitement. "Are you expecting to be ambushed in Venice?"

It had been a long time since she'd murdered a bunch of gangsters. Her hunts were one or two at a time these days, a markedly slower pace than what she was used to. She wouldn't have minded the chance to stretch herself.

Konstantine laughed. "Sorry to disappoint you, but no. Vittoria and I have known each other for a long time. I don't expect her to betray me."

"An old friend, huh?"

Konstantine reached for her. She stepped forward, allowing him to touch her.

"If only that were jealousy in your voice," he lamented. "I would be thrilled."

It was her turn to laugh. "Why?"

"Jealousy means possessiveness. It means you consider me *yours*. Nothing would make me happier."

Here they were again, skirting the unspoken. They'd done this dance for fourteen months. Konstantine would circle around the issue, clearly trying to discern what she wanted from him—how much she wanted—and Lou would duck away from the questions. Or she would make a joke.

As she was about to do now. "I came to collect you from Nico, didn't I?"

"You came to kill me yourself."

She looked away, aware that his hands were still on her forearms, his thumbs running over her skin.

"And how long will you be in Venice with *Vittoria?*"

He pulled her closer until their bodies touched, hip to hip. When he spoke, she felt his breath on her hair. "A few days. We have contracts to negotiate and she's very stubborn. I suspect that she won't make it easy."

Lou was tall enough that her chin was at his neck and collarbone. She placed a sudden kiss there, already inhaling the scent of him before she realized she was doing it.

His arms wrapped around her instantly, reflexively, holding her against him.

And she returned the embrace. Had they done this before? Simply stood there and held each other? She didn't think so.

Her heart began to speed up in her chest.

Lou pulled her gun.

She pointed it at the man crossing the cathedral. He froze, midstep.

Konstantine didn't release her when he spoke. "I would never creep up on her if I were you, Stefano. That's how you get a bullet in the head."

Lou was certain Konstantine spoke English for her benefit.

If Stefano was worried about being shot, he hid it well. He was the picture of composure now, with his shoulders relaxed, his head slightly cocked.

"Buonasera." He slid his gaze from Louie to Konstantine. *"C'è una chiamata per lei. È urgente."*

"You've got a call," Lou said, catching the gist of it.

Konstantine squeezed her once more before reluctantly letting her go. "Will I see you later?"

His unbridled hopefulness made her smile. She shrugged. After all, it wasn't that she was consciously choosing to come to Konstantine's bed. "Maybe."

He bent and placed a kiss on her throat, almost the same place where she'd kissed him.

"Until then."

With a stiff nod to Louie, Stefano turned and followed on his master's heels.

Lou lowered her gun, watching them disappear into the bowels of the church.

KONSTANTINE WAITED UNTIL THEY WERE ALONE IN THE LONG hallway that led out of the church before he voiced his concern to Stefano. "You enjoy interrupting us."

"*Quella stronza ti distrae*," Stefano said beside him. *That bitch distracts you.*

The words sent red-hot fury through Konstantine's body. He whirled and seized Stefano by the collar. He threw a punch into the man's jaw, feeling the bone creak under his knuckles.

Stefano's head rocked back, his shoulder hitting the wall hard. The breath left his lungs in a *whoosh* felt across Konstantine's neck.

"Never call her that again, or I will put a bullet between your eyes. Do you understand me?" Konstantine's hand burned and his chest heaved with anger. "*Hai capito?* Speak of her as if she were *my wife*."

When Stefano didn't answer, Konstantine slammed him against the wall again.

Stefano rolled his eyes up to meet Konstantine's. "*Ho capito*."

Konstantine released him with a shove.

"But it's true." Stefano touched his jaw with a grimace. "She distracts you, and you don't even care. It should have been you to pull a gun on me. Admit it. You didn't even hear me."

Konstantine hadn't. He'd been thinking of his body against Lou's, and marveling at how natural it had become to hold her after so many years of longing for it. They hadn't consummated their relationship—and he hadn't pressed her because there was a terrible certainty in his heart that the moment they did, she would leave him.

"I'm in my own house. What do I have to be afraid of?" Konstantine asked, rolling his neck.

Stefano pushed off the wall. "Did you learn nothing from Nico? Nothing at all?"

Konstantine remembered the ambush. The alarm raised as his own men were slaughtered from within. Mutiny had been part of Nico's strategy. He'd turned half their gang against Konstantine. But Konstantine had methodically culled all traitors from his ranks since that night.

Of course, that meant bringing new men into the Ravengers, men who did not share a history with Padre Leo, or Konstantine himself. Men who might be more loyal to the money he put in their pockets than to Konstantine himself. For that reason alone, it didn't pay to be lazy with his own security, did it?

Stefano was not one of those men, which was why Konstantine listened. Stefano was like a brother. A tempestuous little brother who often touched a nerve, true. But his loyalty could not be questioned.

"You didn't even hear me," Stefano repeated, cursing.

"I have a lot on my mind," Konstantine said, straightening.

"Of Carnevale?" Stefano asked with an arched brow.

It was a generous offer, because they both knew he hadn't been thinking of Carnevale. Konstantine remembered the way Lou had looked the night before, when she'd appeared in his bed.

He'd gotten home late. Preparing to leave Florence for even a few days proved to be a monumental task. Coordinating crews, supplies, procuring a suitable gift for Vittoria, and all while overseeing the day-to-day operations of his organization, had kept him up until well past midnight. It was nearly one in the morning when he'd arrived and stumbled up to his bedroom, too footsore to change into his bed clothes.

His bed had been empty when he'd stripped down and put on loose pants, leaving his chest bare. Then, as he was brushing his teeth, a peculiar feeling had overcome him, like a change in the pressure between his ears.

He stepped from the bathroom, toothbrush still in his mouth, and there she was, curled into his pillows as if she'd been there all along.

She hadn't even awoken when he bent to pull the covers over her.

He was careful not to disturb her when she slept, for fear she might disappear like a mirage. It was enough for him that she was beside him—that whether she was willing to admit it to herself yet or not—she was choosing him, slowly, night after night. It was the surest sign of progress he had.

He wanted that to continue.

And just now, in the cathedral, she'd openly walked into his arms.

His heart hitched.

"You must admit she has made things much safer for us," Konstantine said. "After Nico and then Dmitri, our rivals won't even look at us crossly."

"Because they think she's a devil you've sold your soul to in exchange for all the power you have, and that if they hurt you, she will hunt them down and eat their children."

Konstantine smiled. "I don't care why they are afraid, the result is the same. No one wants to challenge me."

And it was true. They had already feared her before Konstantine had crossed her path—whispers of a woman who killed criminals in the night. It frightened them how she could appear and disappear without a trace. But then they'd believed she was a curse on the Martinelli family. It was his father's men, shipments, and sons she was murdering—mostly. But that shifted with Nico, with his complete and utter obliteration, and now no one understood whose side this mysterious woman was on. Only that if they came for her, or for Konstantine, they would die. They needed only to look to Nico's and Dmitri's mistakes to see the truth of that.

It had helped that the underworld had already greatly feared Nico and Dmitri. How much worse Lou must seem to them, when she could destroy their nightmares so easily.

"It doesn't matter what they believe. I'm safe with her," Konstantine insisted.

Stefano sighed. "That you think this scares me."

"I cannot spare you that burden," Konstantine said, stopping

Stefano with one hand. He inspected his friend's jaw. He wiped away a smudge of blood with his thumb before lightly slapping Stefano's cheek.

Stefano resigned himself to this. "At least *she's* paying attention. And I don't think she'll let anyone else kill you."

Konstantine shook his head and smiled. "No, I believe she wants that honor for herself."

"And what about the times when you're not with her?" Stefano asked, stepping from the shadowed hallway into the courtyard leading to Konstantine's private offices.

Konstantine spared him an affectionate smile. "That's what you're here for."

6

———————

The chime above the agency's door dinged, and King lowered his copy of *The Herald* to see who had entered.

"Okay!" Piper called out, tossing her red backpack on the floor. "You've got some explaining to do, *sir*."

King reached for his mug. He tilted it to his lips and found the coffee cold. He grimaced.

Lady's tail thumped against the floor. Piper acknowledged this with an affectionate pat on the dog's head, but didn't take her eyes off King.

"Seriously, you better fess up."

"It would help," King began, pushing back his chair and crossing to the coffeemaker, "if you gave me an idea of what you want me to confess to."

Piper threw an envelope down on his desk. King recognized it as one of Dani's assembled info packets. "Confess to the fact you've been working with one *Daniella Allendale* behind my back!"

He topped off his coffee, the carafe clattering back onto the burner. "I wasn't doing it behind your back."

Her mouth fell open as she gazed up at him from the floor where she squatted beside the dog. "How could you?"

"By telephone. Though sometimes we meet in person."

"Be serious!"

King laughed. "She's an investigative reporter. It's what she does."

"*I* get you the details you ask for."

King took a long sip of his coffee, trying to cool it with his inhale alone. Sensing that there was an accusation in this somewhere, King placed his bet. "It's not like I think she's better than you at the job. But sometimes we need extra hands. You *know* this."

And it was true. King couldn't comfortably have taken on any more cases if he'd wanted to. He'd turned down three spouses seeking to confirm infidelity this week alone. With his aching back, he couldn't imagine hiding in bushes, climbing trees, or hobbling after husbands and wives in this cold weather anyway. But that wasn't the point.

Piper threw up her hands, her face getting redder with every word. "I don't understand how I didn't know. I'm involved in *every* case that comes through here. You've never *once* mentioned her. You never asked me to call her to confirm something. You never sent me to pick something up or mention where your source info came from. *Why?*"

"I didn't realize I was supposed to," he said. Frankly, he was doing his best to keep his nose out of Piper's business. "Lou has been working with her too. Hasn't she said anything?"

"What?" Piper's outrage spiked. She collapsed to her knees. *"Are you kidding me?"*

Lady saw this dramatic display as an opportunity. She rolled onto her side, offering her tawny belly.

The door at the end of the office opened and Lou stepped out, closing it behind her.

The room was nothing more than a storage closet, pitch black and empty, but Piper had jokingly put a name plate on it that read *Ms. Thorne*, as if it were an actual office.

Lou froze as soon as she took in the scene. "What's wrong?"

"Traitors!" Piper said, pointing at Lou and then King. "Both of you."

Lady pawed Piper's hand, reminding her about the belly offer. Piper began to absentmindedly rub the dog's stomach.

King sipped his coffee again. "Piper wants to know why we didn't tell her Dani has been part of our investigations."

Piper scoffed. "Damn right I want to know."

"I thought you didn't want to talk about her," Lou said.

Piper placed a hand on her chest. "When did I say that?"

Lou pushed her mirrored sunglasses up onto her head and frowned. "I asked if you've seen Dani, and you said, 'I don't want to talk about her.'"

"I was *joking*."

Lou arched a brow, bending down to give Lady a good scratch behind the ears.

Piper sighed and folded her arms across her chest. "So what have you guys been doing with her exactly?"

"It isn't like we've been having secret sleepovers and not inviting you," King said. The urge to add cream and sugar to his coffee rose, but he batted the temptation away. He was trying to keep his diet clean until Fat Tuesday. He'd promised himself a box of paczkis if he could manage it.

"Okay. Fine. But I don't like it when you guys don't tell me things." Piper openly pouted now. "It makes me feel like I'm not part of the team."

King laughed. "What are you talking about? Of course you're part of the team."

Lou was watching the girl with a curious expression. Then she said, "She asked me about you."

Piper visibly perked up. "Really? What did she say?"

"How's Piper."

Piper inched forward. "And what did you say?"

Lou shrugged in her leather jacket. "I said you were fine."

King didn't understand the look of disappointment crossing Piper's face.

Lou's frown suggested she didn't either. "Was I supposed to say something else?"

King crossed the office, skirting around the puppy pile, and took his seat behind his desk once more. "Honestly, we just ask her to make phone calls or fact-check for us."

Piper stood from the floor, brushing invisible dirt off her knees.

"Speaking of phone calls, Planned Parenthood called me back to let me know my STD tests were clean."

She scowled at Lou.

"Why did you give them this number?" King folded the paper again and placed it on the corner of his desk, out of the way. He was searching for a coaster for his coffee. Maybe he would find it faster if he weren't trying to sip his coffee at the same time.

Lou shrugged. "I used Piper's name to get an STD test."

King choked on his coffee. Neither of the women seemed to notice.

"It was smart going to the Baton Rouge clinic. They would've recognized you here." Piper clasped her hands behind her head. "And I'm all for protecting your anonymity, babe, but now my sex history is all messed up. Do you know how long it took me to convince them I don't need birth control?"

"Why don't you need birth control?" Lou asked, deadpan.

"Do you know how lesbians have sex, Louie? Do you need a diagram?"

Lou's lips twitched. "Maybe."

"Why are you worried about being clean?" King asked. Then, as if hearing the words that had just come out of his mouth, "None of my business, is it?"

He found a coaster from Richard's Crab Shack and put his mug on it.

"It's not a sex thing," Piper said. "I convinced her to get the tests because she's always fighting these guys with open wounds. They bleed. She bleeds. It's just cross-contamination. Don't make that face. This is a good thing! It took me two months to convince her to get these tests."

"Congrats on your bill of health." For some reason King was relieved.

"Yeah," Piper agreed. "But that doesn't exonerate you from keeping Dani a secret. I feel like you've been cheating on me."

Lou reached out and placed a hand on the back of Piper's neck. Piper's face reddened by three shades, but her shoulders visibly relaxed.

"Okay," Piper said finally, as if Lou had spoken. "Yeah, I'm being dumb."

King watched them smile at each other. Lou slowly took her hand off the back of Piper's neck, and it gave him the distinct impression he'd missed something.

A strange warmth spread through his chest. *Lucy would love this*, he thought. Lou with a friend her own age would've made her happy beyond belief. Not that she'd believed her niece incapable of friendship. But how often had Lucy expressed in those last months of her life that she'd worried about Lou being alone?

If she isn't connected to anyone, what will she do once I'm dead, Robert? She'll only have her revenge. I don't want that for her.

King had done his best to assure his wife that he would look out for Louie after she was gone. But watching Piper and Lou together now, both playfully rubbing down the dog on the floor, King knew he'd had no part of this, not really.

King turned over his watch and realized what time it was. "Aren't you supposed to be at the shop?"

Piper quit baby-talking the dog and shrugged. "Mel told me to go home."

"Wasn't it busy?"

"Yeah, and she spent the morning in bed with a headache. But when she got up she told me she had it covered and sent me home."

Interesting. "She seems okay to you?"

She shrugged. "Don't you need me to do something around here?"

King saw hesitation flutter across her face. He could press harder about Mel or he could drop it. Maybe it was nothing but her lingering insecurity about Dani. He made a mental note to check in on Mel later, just to be sure. To Piper he said, "You got homework?"

"That's the thing about asynchronous online courses, man. I can do my work whenever I want, and no, I'm caught up for this week. I worked ahead thinking I was going to be too busy during Carnival."

King pointed at the empty desk across from him. "I'll send you the witness reports for the Henderson case. Can you get them organized by timeline for me?"

"*Can I?*" she huffed.

King let this slide, understanding that he could expect more of such comments until Piper forgave him for this Dani blunder. "And then I'll have you make some phone calls."

"Sure you don't want *Dani* to make the calls?"

King tilted his head.

"All right, all right." Piper gave Lady one last pat, retrieved her bag from the floor, and crossed to the desk.

Lou stood, tugging at the end of her leather jacket as if it had ridden up. She met King's gaze. "Any updates for me?"

He gave her a quick once-over, hoping he wasn't being obvious.

But she looked good. Her face had more color these days and the bags under her eyes were gone. He suspected that she was finally getting some sleep after months of insomnia.

Not that he could judge. Lucy's death had laid him to waste too.

For a month after her passing, he'd slipped back into his drinking habit, his shitty eating, and deep depression. It had taken him months to get back on the horse of clean living.

Melandra had taken such good care of him in the wake of Lucy's death. He wasn't exactly sure what he would've done without her insisting that he eat, sleep, and take a goddamn shower.

He hoped he could repay her one day.

The detective agency had also helped. Work had always been his preferred form of escapism. Between that and a renewed mission to look after Lou—the last piece of Lucy left on this planet—King had managed to cobble together a decent reason for living, as old and tired as he was.

He opened his desk drawer and grabbed the napkinned bundle resting between a stapler and a wad of rubber bands. He unwrapped the bologna and cheese sandwich he'd packed that morning and leaned back in his chair.

"Both the videotapes and the witnesses you delivered were crucial to closing the Wilkins case. It was pivotal. We won it."

Lou didn't even acknowledge the praise.

King took a big bite of his sandwich. He spoke around the lettuce filling his cheeks. "How'd you get Charise to talk?"

Lou did smile now, a gentle tug on the right side of her lips. "Trade secret."

"The jury lapped up her story. The guy's going to jail for at least twenty years, and that's with parole and good behavior."

"They should kill him," Piper said without looking away from her laptop. "Eighteen little girls walled up in his basement. Christ. But *no*. Just because the judge thought he was a 'good Christian man,' they let his ass go. So freaking gross."

"I might pay him a visit," Lou said with a sinister smile. This one reached her eyes.

King imagined her stepping from the shadows and wrapping her fingers around Devaroe's throat. A squat, middle-aged man with a hooked, warty nose, no doubt he would squeal like a pig at the sight of her.

"Speaking of crazy bastards, did you get rid of Miller?" Piper asked.

Lou answered without turning around. Her eyes remained on King. "Two days ago."

Piper shuddered, making her chair creak. "Good. I can sleep better knowing that guy isn't out there doing God only knows what."

"Bothered you, did he?" King asked between bites.

Piper gave him a disgusted look. "He hunted blond women." She paused in typing long enough to point at her own hair. "Tortured them for days in his soundproof apartment, and then when they died from the torture, he fucked their corpses. Sometimes for *weeks*. Hell yeah I'm glad he's dead. I just don't understand how he was allowed to go free in the first place."

"Hung jury," King said, sucking mayo off his thumb.

"Because of his girlfriend's testimony. How could she lie like that?"

"Maybe she loved him."

Piper scoffed. "If I found out my partner was sexing up corpses, that would be a hard pass for me. Thank you, *next*."

"He had a corpse in his apartment when I took him," Lou said, sliding her shades back down on her eyes.

King started. "Did he?"

"*No way.*" Piper gaped over the top of the computer.

"I left the front door open so it would be noticed. The smell should annoy someone."

King opened his web browser and did a preliminary search. "The story hasn't broken yet. You should tell Dani. She'd love to be the one to drop that bomb."

Piper made a noise behind them that sounded suspiciously like a repressed scream.

Lou pivoted away from Piper and mouthed *I already did* for King's eyes alone.

Aloud she said, "I found a new target."

King glanced up from his computer. "Really? Using your compass thingy?" He made a circular motion over his chest.

King would be the first to admit he didn't fully understand what Lou called her compass, only that it was somehow connected to her ability to travel through the dark. In a way, it made sense to him that if Lou couldn't see where she was going, she would *feel* places instead. But it wasn't only limited to places, was it? She could also target people or even ideas, including *Where is a serial murderer?*

"I've been following him for a few days. He's good at hiding in plain sight, but he's definitely a target."

"What do you know so far?"

"His name is Jeffrey Fish. He lives in Mount Vernon, Ohio, with a wife and son."

"How'd you get his name?"

"I went through the mail in his mailbox."

"That's a federal offense," King said, but he was impressed. "Anything else?"

Lou stood and slipped two fingers into the back pocket of her jeans. She pulled out a folded square piece of paper and handed it over to King, who leaned forward to retrieve it.

He sank back into the office chair, brushing crumbs off his lips. He unfolded the piece of paper and first read the plate number and address for Fish off the upper corner. But below that was a photocopy of a driver's license.

He read aloud, "Jennifer McGrath."

"She works at a grocery store near his house," Lou explained.

"And he's stalking her?" Piper asked. She came around the desk to look at the photo. "She's pretty."

King frowned at the photocopy in his hands. "How did you get a photocopy of her driver's license?"

"I took it from her purse while she was sleeping."

"And just hop-skip-jumped to a Kinko's or something?" Piper marveled. "Damn, you're cool."

The corner of Lou's lips tilted up.

"I told you no contact," King said. Realizing that he sounded like the petulant father he most certainly was not, he sighed. "If she knows she's being followed she could panic. Or at the very least, she could tip him off by acting differently. Or Fish could see you."

Lou wasn't smiling now. Her hard stare made the hairs on his arms rise.

"Women aren't stupid," Lou said. "Most of them."

"Yeah," Piper added companionably. "We are actually much better at staying alive than men are, thank you very much."

"We're talking about human behavior, and we talked about this..."

Boy had they talked about this. King had tried every line of reasoning his mind could conjure to control Lou's happy-go-lucky trigger finger. True, it had been her idea to hunt serial killers who'd escaped the system. She wanted to bring retribution to the men who thought themselves apex predators above the law.

And Lou had been damn good at it, with that unnatural gift of hers combined with an unshakable aim.

But catching her prey alive wasn't Lou's natural inclination, and they both knew it. It just wasn't how she liked to do things. And the learning curve had been steep. She'd eliminated six killers before she got the hang of "due process."

She crossed her arms, King's first real sign of trouble. "Fish is alive, and he hasn't seen me."

King shifted in his seat, trying to ease the pressure in his hip. "We just need him to fuck up. That's all. And this will help us get a better sense of what's going on and develop a connection between them." He held up the photocopy of the woman's driver's license. "Thank you."

He and Lou had begun a dangerous game—two games, actually.

One hunt was tailored for men like Jeffrey Fish. These men could still be prosecuted. They could be convicted of their crimes, and those convictions could let parents and spouses and children rest easier knowing justice was served.

But then there was the other hunt. When a monster didn't qualify for the prosecute file, King considered him for the *execute* file.

He'd grappled with that a lot at first. Who was he to sentence men to death? Who was he to decide who deserved a one-way trip to La Loon—Louie's dumping ground?

He convinced himself that his candidates were only men like Miller —who had a high chance of reoffending and had somehow escaped retribution. By taking care of the men the system had freed, they were saving lives.

Weren't they?

"Guys like Devaroe and Miller have beat the system. There's no way to make them pay for what they've done. So they're fair game. But someone like Fish—there's still a chance to make it right," he said. He sounded defensive to his own ears. "Who knows how many women he's killed and families he's destroyed? We're doing this for them."

Lou sighed. "Miller was the last one from the list you gave me. Who else have you got?"

You need something to hold you over, he thought. *Fine.*

He opened his desk drawer and removed the insert. His fingers searched the bare metal bottom beneath. After a moment of groping he found a folded-up piece of paper.

He pulled it out and—feeling a little like a drug dealer—extended it toward her across the desk. She took it, opened it up, read the names. She said nothing. She only slipped the sheet of paper into her back pocket, where the photocopy of McGrath's license had been moments before.

Then she lifted the slate gray urn from the edge of his desk and smiled.

"I miss her," King said, falling back against the chair. "So shoot me."

He brought Lucy to work with him every day.

"Don't tempt me," Lou said. Without the smile, King couldn't tell if she was joking.

"I think it's sweet," Piper said, typing away. "Nothing wrong with wanting to keep Lucy close. I like to think she watches over us."

Lou turned the urn in her hand as if reading something. But King had inspected that container enough to know there were no words on it.

She returned it to the desk without comment.

"Be careful out there," King said, sensing the imminent goodbye.

But Lou lingered.

She turned to face him, squaring her body. "If Fish makes a move before we get this so-called evidence, I won't hesitate. I'm not going to let her corpse be the evidence we need for a case."

King opened his mouth to protest, but stopped.

Lou was already opening the storage closet marked *Ms. Thorne* and stepping inside. The door shut with a ringing finality.

Piper caught his eye across the room. "Don't look at me, man. You know she does whatever the hell she wants."

A feeling of unease grew in King's stomach. "Yeah, she does."

7

Mel turned counterclockwise in the storeroom again, glancing from her makeshift list to the shelves. The closet smelled like old cardboard and incense. At the back of the room was a black safe with silver embellishments. It stood as tall as she did.

She lifted a box from the shelves and counted the remaining sugar skulls. She scribbled on the list. They were burning through their inventory—not that Mel was complaining. It was good that sales were high. It only meant that she would have to place another order today and pray it arrived in time. Slipping the pen and paper into the folds of her skirt—they had hidden pockets that she'd sewn in herself—she flicked off the light and exited the storeroom.

The store had a few more patrons than when she'd entered. Piper was showing two men the selection of Fortunes and Fixes hoodies, holding one against the taller man's chest.

Several girls crowded around the incense stand, slipping long sticks into their plastic bags. Another couple were fingering the beads, chatting excitedly to each other about having survived Bourbon Street the night before.

Oh my god, she walked four blocks before she realized her skirt was tucked into her panties!

He puked for three hours. I swear to God, I thought he was dying.

There's a reason they call them hurricanes.

Mel was about to circle the shop with the perfunctory "Finding everything all right?" when the two young men shifted, revealing someone else.

This man was browsing the t-shirts in a lazy, languid way. The manner in which he held his body caused a knot to form in Mel's gut. Her heart dropped like a stone in a well.

It's my imagination, she begged.

But she watched the man, lean and wiry, move across the shop, watched the girls with their cache of incense step aside so he could cross to an adjacent shelf.

Mel absorbed everything about him. The light denim button-up shirt, the acid-washed jeans. The tan belt and matching scuffed shoes. His curling dark hair hanging under his leather cowboy hat. A crow feather protruding from that hat. The fishhook earring in one ear and the bone choker with turquoise accents encircling his throat.

All of it was familiar, but it was the way he stood, the way he held himself that she knew best.

Her heart kicked against her ribs painfully, fear rising high in her throat.

Run! her mind screamed. *Run up to your apartment, lock the door, call the police. And then what?*

Then what?

"Terrence." She meant it to be a cold acknowledgment, but her voice came out in a desperate rasp. "What are you doing here?"

His fingers froze on the Papa Legba statue, the smile already pulling into place before he turned to face her.

"Melandra," he said, and tapped the brim of his hat. His eyes raked down her body lasciviously. "Nice place you got here."

She drew her shawl tight around her. "Get out."

It was hard to put the full force of her anger—and her fear—into her voice while trying to keep it low. She glanced nervously at the customers around her. Piper held a hanger in one hand while one of the men tried on a hoodie. They were turned at such an angle that Piper wouldn't be able to see Melandra in her periphery.

"Is that any way to talk to your husband?" Terry drawled softly. His voice rasped like sandpaper. "Not that you've treated me like a husband for some time now."

Fresh horror chilled her bones. The last sliver of her hope, of her wishful thinking that somehow this was all a horrible, terrible dream, slipped through her hands like sand.

"I haven't gotten a visit in, what? Twelve, fourteen years? And you stopped sending money two years ago. Thought I'd just up and die without it, I reckon."

She'd clung to the wish that he wouldn't seek her out at all. After all, maybe prison really could change a man. He certainly *looked* changed. He was leaner now. A wolf-thin shape of his former self, but far more muscular. He'd been a scrawny terror of a boy when they'd met and had grown into a wiry man. Now it looked like the lanky man —all elbows and knees—had put on about fifty pounds of muscle.

"Did you forget about me in there? Did you forget about your own husband?" Terry licked his lips and hooked his thumbs into the waistband of his jeans. "Or did you think we were all paid up?"

"I don't owe you shit!" she hissed. Her bangles jiggled as she jabbed her finger at him.

She caught the stare of a young woman coming around the candle display. *Damn*, she thought. *I'm being too loud.*

Or not loud enough, her thoughts countered.

"Come on," Terry said. His smile hadn't faltered. "We had an agreement. You write the checks. I keep my mouth shut."

"In hell," Melandra groaned, forcing a smile at the woman lifting a candle from the shelf.

The register dinged behind her. Mel glanced over her shoulder and saw that the men were committing to the hoodies after all, along with a fistful of lighters.

A cool hand wrapped around hers.

Reflexively, she jerked back, yanking away.

The hand only clamped down harder. Closing on the wrist until pain shot up Melandra's arm. "Easy now."

"*Don't* touch me." She tried again to free her wrist but he held fast.

"Now, now," he said, pulling her close. "Don't want to cause a scene, now do we? That's bad for business."

She could smell his aftershave, splashed generously along his neck and collarbone. The heady scent made her stomach turn.

Don't panic, she told herself. *You're in control here.*

"From what I can tell by this *lovely* establishment you've got here, you haven't been paying me nearly enough for the burden of keeping your secret. But that's all right. We're going to make up for lost time, aren't we?"

Mel couldn't quite get enough air into her lungs. The room was darkening at the edges. It felt like he was leeching all her strength from her body with his grip alone.

"There we go," he said softly into her hair. "There's the girl I know."

"Mel?" a voice called out. It was strong enough to pull her back from the edge of hysteria.

The hand around her wrist released her immediately. Mel stumbled back as if pushed.

Piper placed a hand on Mel's shoulder, turning her. "Hey, are you okay?"

"I'm fine."

Piper regarded Terry. "Can I help you with something?"

"He was leaving," Mel said, meeting his gaze.

"Was I?"

Piper was already squaring off as if preparing to fight this man. Melandra was certain her bravery and scrappy attitude were due to the fact that she had no idea how dangerous Terrence Lamott was.

The chandelier moaned overhead, and the enormity of Robert King crossed the threshold. A second later, a cool snout was pressing itself into Melandra's palm.

"Security is here." To Terrence, Piper said, "See yourself out, buddy. Or he'll help you out."

Terrence drew himself up and took King's measure.

A low grumble echoed through the shop. Melandra had a moment of wondering if the heat had kicked on before realizing Lady was growling.

This stopped King in his tracks, and he glanced down at the dog. "What is it?"

"Some jackoff here is being—*Hey.*" Piper cut off mid-speech. "Where did he go?"

Melandra scanned the aisles. She pulled back the curtain on her reading room and found it empty. Out on the street, she thought she glimpsed an oil-black crow feather sticking out of a leather cowboy hat. But she blinked and it was gone.

The cold snout pressed into her palm again. "*Ma grande.*"

The Belgian Malinois leaned her weight into Mel's legs.

"What did I miss?" King asked, his face pinched with confusion.

"Some asshole was messing with her," Piper said. "He ducked around those shelves when you came in."

"Language," Melandra said. She was trying not to tremble all over. "We have customers."

She pointed at the counter, where the women were waiting to buy their incense and candles. Piper slinked away.

"You okay?" King asked. His gaze was heavy and assessing.

"I'm fine."

"You don't look fine," King said, frowning at her. "Who was the guy?"

"No one."

King arched a brow.

"Someone I used to know," she said. "Please drop it."

"Okay."

"I'm just stressed." She wasn't sure why she felt like she had to defend herself.

King looked around the shop. "Let me take care of things down here. Take a break. Go lie down or something. Take Lady with you. She loves a good nap."

Mel looked to the window once more, expecting to see Terrence framed in the glass, watching her like a tiger through its bars.

But the sidewalk was full of tourists, walking, laughing, gearing up for the oncoming night.

And a headache was forming behind her eyes again. "Just for a couple hours."

To the dog she said, "*Allez*."

She mounted the stairs to her apartment with only one wish in her heart—that this was the end of it. That Terrence had had his say and would leave her be now.

She knew better.

8

____

Lou stood in front of the ramshackle bar on the outskirts of Colcord, Oklahoma. There was only a blinking yellow light at the four-way stop regulating the town's non-existent traffic. A lone building, the bar itself, was surrounded by a gravel lot on all sides. Apart from the dark and sloping landscape behind it, there was nothing else on which to fix the eye for as far as Lou could see. Only two cars sat in the lot, a black Ford pickup and an old white station wagon that had a ring of rust outlining the wheel well.

Lou unfolded the piece of worn paper from her back pocket and read it once more in the moonlight.

Ricky Walker.

Lou smiled at the period punctuating the name, as if King had made it a point to seal the man's fate with that small mark.

Is this what you are now? a small voice asked as she folded up the paper and slipped it into her pocket. *A hitman?*

It wasn't Aunt Lucy's voice or her father's. It was that new cold voice, an unforgiving version of her own.

She suppressed a bitter laugh. She wasn't hunting and killing these men for King. She wasn't fulfilling some old grudge for him. Likely King had never even met these men. He'd heard of their stories secondhand, done his research, and earmarked them for death because his beloved justice system had failed to do so. And she knew King well enough to know his conscience weighed on him far more than hers ever could. He would not have signed anyone's name to a letter of execution unless he was certain of their crimes.

Ricky Walker, for example, had raped and murdered four boys. DNA evidence submitted at his trial proved he'd committed the crime. There were even eyewitnesses to the abductions of the last two kids. Still he'd been let go.

No. Lou wasn't doing this for King. He was handing over these names the way a zookeeper fed meat through the bars of the tiger's cage. He was trying to placate her, domesticate her, and she knew it.

And how do you feel about that? the cold voice asked. *Do you want to be domesticated, kitty kitty?*

It's not like that, she thought crossly. After all, wasn't King only doing what Lucy had asked of him? Lucy, her benevolent Buddhist aunt, got her way even in death.

Lou's ease with death, with killing, had never sat well with Lucy.

Lou understood that some creatures of this world were simply predators and she was one of them. She was part of an ecosystem, an elaborate dance of checks and balances. A tiger would never feel guilty for the meat it ate. Lou felt no guilt for the lives she took.

At the very end, Lucy understood that. If killing only very bad men helped King sleep at night, and feel as though he were upholding a promise to his dead wife, then fine.

Lou could play along—within reason—though she'd learned not so long ago that *bad* and *good* were relative. A system built for justice and equity could be polluted with cutthroats. An underground network built upon rule-breaking and exploitation could offer liberation.

And who taught you that? Konstantine?

Rolling her shoulders as if to relieve them of some unseen burden, she crossed the parking lot and stepped into the bar. Some whining country music played. At first, Lou thought the place was empty. But then she saw the bartender perched on a stool, looking up at a television mounted above the bar. It played a boxing match between two fighters Lou didn't recognize.

The man watching the television sat hunched, his paunch of a stomach hanging over his belt. His t-shirt had ridden up on his belly, revealing a hairy patch below the navel.

"Ricky Walker?" Lou asked.

The bartender didn't even look at her. He just pointed a thumb over his shoulder. "He's back there. Three sheets to the wind."

Walker sat in the last booth on the right. His head was down on his arm. He snored softly. A glass full of half-melted ice sweated in his grip. His short, gnarled nails had black grime beneath them. His stubble was mostly gray.

She slid into the booth and regarded the man. The smell wafting off of him was acrid, like a mixture of piss and sweat.

He's sick, she thought. *He's sick as hell.*

She wondered if she could smell it because of her time with Lucy. Her aunt's illness had had a stench too. It was like Lou could smell the body souring, going bad like old meat.

"Ricky Walker?"

No answer.

She kicked his leg under the table.

He harrumphed and drew himself up, fixing his bleary eyes on her. He squinted in the low light before pinching the bridge of his nose. "Hi. How you doing?"

"Are you Ricky Walker?" she asked again.

"Yeah, that's me." He lifted the glass mechanically and then frowned when only ice hit his lips. "Do I know you?"

"No."

He shook the glass, rattling the ice. "Chuck!"

Chuck slid off the bar stool with a grumble and brought a bottle with him. He took Ricky's empty glass and filled it to the rim. "Another Walker for the Walker. A drink for your lady friend?"

"No," Lou said.

It was no matter to Chuck. With a shrug, he slinked away, taking the bottle of Johnnie Walker with him. He had eyes only for the boxing match.

"How long?" Lou asked.

"Seven inches," Rick said, and snorted. It echoed in the glass. "But it's what you do with it that counts."

Lou smiled. It was a promising answer. She liked it when they were mean. "Cirrhosis?"

He drew long and deep on his drink. He sat it on the table with a *humph*. "Alcoholic cardiomy—cardiomy..."

"Alcoholic cardiomyopathy?" Lou offered.

"My heart's failing. It's swollen, or some shit like that. Hey, are you from the clinic? Come out here to tell me to stop drinking again? It won't work. I told y'all it's all I've got. That and the dreams. I ain't getting my heart rate up or whatever you said. I'm chilled, all right? *Chilled* as ice."

He shook the glass at her, the ice clinking against the sides as if to emphasize his point. Whiskey sloshed over the rim onto his thumb. He brought it to his mouth and sucked it.

Lou said nothing as he tipped the glass back and drank the remainder in one go. When there was only ice left, he groaned. "Chuck!"

Chuck didn't come. He was cursing at the television.

"It's all I've got," Ricky said again. His slurred murmuring seemed for his ears only. "And the dreams. I got the dreams too."

That's more than some, Lou thought. "Do you want to dance, Ricky?"

The man lowered the glass and sucked his lips. He smirked at Lou, which could have been interpreted as unabashed lust if the gaze had not been so unfocused. Lou doubted he could see her at all.

"You're not really my type," he said with a low laugh. "But you'll do."

He slid from the booth as she did and followed her to the dance floor—if that's what the space could be called. In reality, it was the simple open area between two sections of tables, with the jukebox resting against the wall.

The fluorescent lights from its frame warped and spread like a prism across the surface of Lou's sunglasses, and Ricky squinted. The ice tinkled in his glass as he sauntered toward her, a leer on his lips.

"Yeah, you're mighty pretty," he said, sucking his teeth.

"For a female?" Lou returned as Ricky slid one arm around her waist.

He stiffened.

"Or for an adult?" She clamped onto him, pinning his arm against her leather jacket, letting it rest where the top of her pants and belt met.

She didn't need to get him into a corner. The bar was already dark enough.

A STRANGE PRESSURE POPPED BETWEEN THE BARTENDER'S EARS THE moment before the sound of glass breaking rang out. He turned away from the match on the suspended television. Ice and glass fragments spread across the middle of the floor. It sparkled in the jukebox's shifting lights.

"Goddamn it, Ricky," he said, climbing off the stool and grabbing a white towel. "You're paying for that glass."

Chuck stooped over the mess and began to gather up the shattered pieces. He turned to the adjacent booth, expecting to see the couple there, but it was empty.

Maybe they went to the bathroom. Or maybe they snuck out the back for a blowjob.

Just as well. Chuck was tired of the guy's shit anyway. So what about the booze and the glass? If Walker thought he could dine and dash, he was mistaken.

The joke's on you, Chuck thought. Ricky had left his credit card behind with his tab.

THE WARM REPRIEVE OF THE BAR WAS SACRIFICED ON THE ALTAR OF total night. Lou's boots shifted, adjusting to the hard-packed earth forming beneath her. A chorus of toad song sprang up around them. Something in the tree above spread its wings and took flight. Its considerable wingspan kicked up the air around them, blowing the hair back from her face.

Ricky seemed totally unaware that the bar was gone and that he stood in unadulterated darkness.

Lou could pull her gun now, put a bullet between Walker's eyes and be done with it. He would never know what hit him.

That would be too easy, she thought. *Merciful.*

No. Let Ricky Walker see the horror of La Loon with his own eyes. Let him see what waited for men like him.

"Can you swim?" Lou asked.

"Yeah, I can fucking swim." Ricky's hands were trying to get under her leather jacket, searching for her tits. But he was having trouble with the unyielding material. His breath misted white in her vision, fogging the mirrored sunglasses she wore even at night.

"Good," she said, stepping backward into cold water. It sloshed over the rim of her boots, wetting her socks. No matter. How many times had she done this? Walked fully clothed into this lake, a body—sometimes living, sometimes dead—in tow?

She continued into deeper water, and like a puppy Walker followed her, planting a sloppy kiss on her throat as he moved forward. With a wave of revulsion, she fisted his hair and yanked it back.

The water had reached halfway up her thighs, inching toward her pelvis, when his fingers finally managed to get under her leather jacket.

His eyes widened the moment he found the guns in their holsters.

"What the fu—"

Lou latched onto the man, grabbing him hard enough to pull him off his feet.

Then she fell. Straight back into the cold water, slapping its surface hard. Walker coughed in surprise as the water hit his face. But they were already sinking into its dark depths, already passing from his world into Lou's. There was no going back.

Like the shadows, the water gave way for Lou.

It seemed to wrap itself around her, entwine itself with her body until the murky depths gave way to red waters. The cold to warmth.

The moment Lou knew the transfer was completed, she pushed for the surface, bringing Walker with her.

She released him and started up the clumsy embankment until she was on the barren shore.

Walker stood in waist-deep water, stunned. He regarded the violet twilight sky with its twin moons. The abnormal mountains in the distance, so monumental as to look like a watercolor backdrop spread for decoration only. The strange yellow hue they projected on the red waters of the lake surrounding him.

"I don't understand," he said, turning full circle in the shallows. "Am I having a flashback or something?"

"Highly doubt it."

He waded to the water's edge, where the black foliage met the patina of Blood Lake, named so—unimaginatively, Lou admitted— because of the color of the water.

He grabbed a palm-sized leaf and began to inspect it. "I ain't never seen anything like this."

"You want to die in the water?" Lou asked calmly. She was trying to shake the water out of her boots. She'd never gotten used to the awful way her saturated socks squished between her toes. "Or on land?"

"No," he said.

A roar echoed through the valley. The rumble was so deep it shook Lou's core.

Lou smiled.

Walker, on the other hand, had most certainly pissed himself. "The fuck was that?"

"I call her Jabbers," Lou said plainly. She opened her leather jacket, trying to flap some of the water off its surface. She'd treated it twice to protect the material from her bouts to La Loon, but that didn't mean she wanted to let the water set in.

"Jabbers?" Walker asked, wiping the water from his face nervously.

"Like the Jabberwocky," she said. "Have you read *Alice in Wonderland?*"

"I don't read."

"No," Lou said companionably. "I suspect you were too busy raping children."

"What?" The first real note of fear seized Ricky's features.

Then Jabbers emerged from the forest and turned his terror complete.

"My god," he said. He staggered back as the beast drew herself to her full height. Lou thought she was at least nine feet tall, maybe twelve. "Oh my god, no. I'm sorry. I'm so sorry."

Lou snorted. "Sorry for what?"

"For what I did to those boys. For what I did to my momma. For—for that money I stole and—and anything else I can't think of right now. I'm sorry for everything. Please take me back. Take me back and I'll make up for it with every minute of my life. Give me more time. Please. *Please.*"

His begging confused her. What did Ricky believe? That she was some Angel of Death? Some demon who had brought him to hell for his punishment, and if he only repented, confessed, he could be delivered from evil?

The serpentine creature cast a cursory glance at Lou as if also confused by the man's pleas.

"He's all yours," Lou said, waving her on.

The scream hadn't even fully formed in Walker's throat before Jabbers was on him. One foxlike pounce and her widening jaw snapped shut over his neck, severing the head from the body cleanly.

Then she had a leg between her teeth, dragging the rest of him onto shore.

The beast purred affectionately, rolling its eyes up to meet Lou's over its dinner.

"Yes," Lou cooed, patting it on the head in much the same manner that she'd scratched the Belgian Malinois earlier in the day. "I missed you, too."

9

____

Piper exhaled slowly, aware that her arms and chest were buzzing with nervous energy. She stared at the laptop on her kitchen counter in front of her. She shifted her weight on the stool as if this would alleviate some tension. It didn't.

Piper read the address off her phone again as if she hadn't eaten at this soul food place a hundred times before. Recognizing this for the nervous tick it was, she sighed and forcibly put her phone on the counter. She had twenty minutes to get to the restaurant where she and Dani were meeting for dinner.

Dani. Dinner.

It's just dinner. It's not like you're proposing to the girl who totally ghosted you.

Against her will, her mind replayed last January, when Dani had walked into their lives.

All the make-out sessions in Mel's storage closet. The way Dani's eyes had shone in the light the night they watched Henry's drag show in a Bourbon Street bar.

The way she'd looked in the hospital bed, black and blue after surviving Dmitri's quest for information about Lou. The way she'd laughed when she'd shown Piper her finger reattached to her hand.

She'd been so sure that Dani was into her, and she'd never misread a girl before. The fact that she'd been so off the mark had shaken her confidence.

What the hell am I going to say?

"It's dinner. Just a meal. Maybe a drink," she told herself again. "Calm down."

She bit her lip for focus and reread the discussion board post in her Intro to Policing class. It was due at midnight, so she had better finish it before going to dinner. She reminded herself how important salvaging her GPA was. It had dropped from 3.5 to 2.8 in the semester when her mother had been at her worst. Piper had to get a 4.0 in this class—and every class from now until graduation to pull it up again.

The sharp image of her mother in the dark, dingy room, smoke hanging in the air as track marks ran up the interior of her pallid arm, sparked in her mind.

She blinked, pushing the thoughts away.

Not my circus, not my monkeys, she reminded herself. *I'm building my future now. Come on. Focus.*

If Lou could have her whole family slaughtered when she was a kid and grow up to be this badass that the whole criminal world fears, you can write a freaking discussion board post. The teacher doesn't even read them. Just post something already!

She opened her textbook and reread a section before referencing it in her post. She added the citation at the end and—*send.*

She checked the clock on her phone. Fourteen minutes.

Piper slid off the stool and snatched her puffy black coat off the hook by the door. It took a minute to find her keys and wallet, and she stuffed them into her pockets along with her phone.

The stairs leading from her loft down to King's office were dark, so she moved carefully, one hand on the wall until she reached the bottom.

The agency was awash in moonlight along the bare wooden floors. The ruckus of the tourists laughing on Royal Street echoed softly through the room, sliding over the bare desks and empty chairs. After double-checking that she'd locked her apartment doors, she locked the office door behind her as well. If someone tried to break in—a disgruntled client or someone looking to sabotage evidence—there was no guarantee they wouldn't ransack Piper's apartment, too.

People were assholes. Better safe than sorry.

Pulling her coat around her against the chilly night, she stepped into the throng of partygoers. The scent of alcohol and weed hung in the air. A woman's robust laughter broke open around her.

Piper did her best to push on. The crush of bodies flooding the Quarter slowed her progress. What should've been a quick twelve-minute walk took her twenty minutes. When she arrived, she was late.

"I'm looking for someone. She might be here already," she said to the hostess, holding the collar of her coat down to be better heard. She caught herself licking her lips, yet another nervous tick, and refrained.

"That her?" the hostess asked, pulling the pen from her hair and pointing it at a table a couple of rows back.

Dani sat alone. She looked elegant with her hair swept up off her face and a wine glass in hand. She gazed wistfully out the window beside her, watching the people pass. If Piper hadn't known better, it looked like Dani was going to cry.

Piper tapped the hostess stand. "Yeah, thanks."

Gathering the last of her bravery, she crossed the restaurant and pulled out the wooden chair opposite Dani's.

Visible relief washed over the girl's face the moment the chair screeched across the floor. Dani sat up straighter. "I was starting to think you weren't going to come."

"Sorry." Piper shrugged out of her coat. She hung it off the back of her chair. "I remembered a homework assignment at the last minute, so I wanted to turn it in. Then the crowds slowed me down."

"You're back in school?" Dani asked, her hands wrapping around the stem of her wine glass.

Piper spread her hands on the table. "Yeah. I'm taking classes at Delgado. Once I get my GPA up, I'll transfer somewhere."

"How in the world do you have two jobs, go to school, and still sleep?"

Piper snorted. "Who said I sleep?"

They shared nervous laughter.

When it died away, Piper said, "I take my classes online. At this rate, it'll take me about three years just to get the criminal justice associates."

"That's still great!" Dani's enthusiasm seemed forced. "I mean, you're so busy. You can only do so much."

Piper nodded. She was glad to be back in school and knew she was doing her best, but she was keenly aware that Dani already had her degree and years of work experience. It was hard not to feel like she was behind.

"So, criminal justice." Dani had been watching Piper's face as she talked. When their eyes met, Dani flicked hers away. "You want to be a cop?"

"I was thinking law, actually. You can do a lot with a law degree. Even join the FBI."

Dani nodded, reaching for the wine bottle in the center of the table. Piper noted it was out of her reach and nudged it forward. When their fingers brushed, a blush spread across Dani's cheeks.

Piper clasped the back of her neck, rubbing it. "I don't want to be in a courtroom or anything. But I really enjoy the investigation part. Due process. All that. I'm learning a lot working with King at the agency."

"What about tarot reading?"

"That's fun too," Piper said. "But it's not a career. No health insurance, you know?"

Piper snorted at her own joke. She also noticed that Dani did not. She seemed a million miles away as she tipped the bottle over to refill her glass. Piper didn't miss that she filled it to the rim. So much for a six-ounce serving.

"What about you?" Piper asked, hoping to shift the focus away from herself. "You still at *The Herald*?"

She felt stupid as soon as she'd asked. They both knew she knew Dani was at *The Herald*.

Dani drank deep from her glass, making a sound that could be taken as a *yes*.

"I mean, are you happy there?"

"I liked the promotion," Dani said.

"Right. I saw—" Piper cut herself off from saying *I've been reading your paper all year, following your stories and looking for your picture.* That seemed too desperate. "You were promoted to assistant editor, right?"

"They offered me a permanent column, but I really like investigative reporting. I don't want to do lifestyle pieces or give advice. Who am I to give advice?"

A nervous laugh escaped her.

Piper noted all this distantly. Her attention was on Dani's finger, trying to see the scar where Dmitri had cut it, taking it as a trophy. But the candlelit room didn't offer much light.

Dani caught her staring. "There's not much of a scar. I got lucky. Well, kind of. PT was a bitch."

She bent her finger to demonstrate that its mobility was still restricted. It could only fold down half as far as her other fingers.

"I've learned how to type without it." Dani, who'd been sliding down in her chair, straightened again. "It slows me down when it stiffens up."

The waitress appeared in her white-and-black ensemble, apron tied around her waist. "What can I get y'all tonight?"

"Fried chicken with mustard greens," Dani said reflexively.

"Same," Piper parroted. "And cornbread."

"Anything else to drink, hon?" She looked up from her notepad.

"Can I get a wine glass?" Piper flicked her eyes up to meet Dani's. "Assuming you don't mind sharing."

"Another bottle then?" the waitress asked.

Dani nodded. "Thank you."

The waitress left them alone, initiating another stretch of awkward silence.

Piper watched Dani gaze out the window for a long time. She saw the dark circles under her eyes and the sunken look of her cheeks.

She's lost weight. Too much weight.

"How's the shop?" Dani asked.

"It's crazy during Carnival. But staying busy is good. Mel gets stressed when there's not enough money coming in." It was Piper's turn to feign enthusiasm. When the bottle of wine and fresh glass appeared, she was able to busy herself with that.

"I bet. And probably no shortage of drunks. And assholes."

Piper thought of the man who'd harassed Melandra. Despite the stupid feather in his hat and the bone choker tied around his throat—both of which Piper thought were pretty cool—she hadn't liked the look of him.

"There's always assholes. Assholes come cheap."

Dani laughed suddenly, her voice echoing in the wine glass.

"What?" Piper asked.

"Cheap."

Piper half-smiled. "Are you drunk?"

"I had a bottle of wine before you got here," Dani admitted, sliding her glass onto the table as if realizing holding it might be a bad idea.

"You drank a whole bottle of wine in eight minutes?"

Dani pulled up her sleeve to reveal a silver watch. "I've been here since seven."

"Why did you come so early?"

"I thought sitting here would help my nerves." Dani pressed her lips together, searching Piper's face, as if unsure of what else she should say.

"Why were you nervous?" *Oh yeah, let's pretend I wasn't freaking out too. Not one bit.*

Dani dragged her hands down her face. "I wanted to apologize to you for ghosting you last year. I should've at least called or sent a letter or something. What I did was wrong—on so many levels."

A letter. Piper smirked. *What is this, World War Two?*

"I realize I never explained what happened, so it must've seemed especially shitty to you."

"I'm just...confused. One minute we were hot and heavy. The next I'm at your bedside in the hospital every day, and when you're released, I can't get you to even return a text."

Dani chewed her lip. "I didn't want you to think I stopped talking to you just because the case was over—"

"You were doing your job." Piper shrugged and hoped it looked nonchalant, because she felt anything but. The ache in her chest was building. "I get it. I'm also a workaholic."

"No, see. *Ughhh.*" Dani pulled at her face again. "You weren't just a job."

"Look, you don't have to say that—" Piper's voice broke off the moment she met Dani's eyes.

They were bright with unshed tears. Her lower lip trembled and she broke the gaze first, looking away to the big picture window beside them and the street beyond it.

"You weren't just a job," she said again, looking apologetic. "At least, not by the end of it."

Piper reached for the wine bottle. "Then it's even more confusing why you'd stop talking to me. It seems like you talked to everyone *but* me. I mean, *Lou?*" Piper clicked her tongue. "Lou was going to kill you and dump your body...wherever she dumps bodies. How was it easier to talk to *her* than me?"

Dani laughed. It was a choked, miserable sound.

A couple at the adjacent table glanced over, curious.

"Come on. Don't cry," Piper said, shifting in her seat. "People are going to think I'm being mean to you."

Dani brought her hand to her eyes, delicately dabbing at her lashes. Mascara came off on her fingers. "I'm sorry."

"Don't be sorry, just tell me what happened." Piper took another long drink of wine. In case whatever Dani said next turned out to be horrible. That was the thing about asking for the truth. You couldn't be mad if someone gave it to you.

Dani was clearly mustering up the courage to speak. She licked her wine-stained lips, staring down at her clasped hands on the white linen tablecloth.

"I don't know where to start," she admitted, sniffling. "And it just sucked that I was super into you and then I fucked it up. You've got no reason to trust me."

"I might if you told me what happened. Start with when you left the hospital." It was the last time Piper had seen her.

The waitress appeared with two plates. "Here you go, honey." She set a plate of steaming fried chicken down in front of Dani. "And one for you too, sugar. Everything look all right?"

Piper made a show of looking the plate over. "It looks amazing, thank you. Can I get some butter for the cornbread?"

"Sure. And hot sauce for the chicken, sweetheart?"

"Yes, ma'am." Piper accepted the bottle of hot sauce pulled from the waitress's apron.

"And you, baby?"

"It's perfect, thanks." Dani spoke without looking up.

As if sensing the mood of the conversation, the waitress excused herself.

"When I left the hospital, I didn't sleep for twelve days."

Piper paused in unwrapping her fork. "What?"

"It took me a while to figure out that it was the apartment keeping me up. That's where they got me—Dmitri and his guys." Dani flicked her eyes up as if to gauge Piper's reaction. "That's where they...That's where they started in on me."

She lifted a fork but seemed unable to take a bite yet. It hung loosely in her grip.

"After two weeks, I had a breakdown, because apparently not sleeping makes you crazy. They tried putting me on sleeping pills but I started sleepwalking, so I quit that. I used all my vacation time and moved back home for a while, until I could find a new place to live. I couldn't be in the apartment anymore."

"Of course not." Piper couldn't even live in the same house as her stoned mother and dope-dealing boyfriend. She understood the way the walls of a place could close in on someone, hang like an atmosphere, pressing against her chest until she couldn't breathe.

"I couldn't tell my parents what happened because they would've made me quit the paper. But the longer I tried to ignore the trauma, the worse I got. It was almost a month after I left the hospital that I went into therapy and was diagnosed with PTSD."

Of course you were, Piper thought. *How the hell could you not have PTSD?*

"My therapist advised that I slowly try to reconnect with the people involved, to get a better sense of my triggers. We started by going back to the places where it happened together and walking through these mental exercises. It was...*awful*. It took me five months before I got up the courage to reach out to King and let him know I was still interested in working cases for him if he needed the help. It was seven months before I managed to say a word to Lou."

Piper cut into her chicken. She had questions—of course she did. But Dani wasn't even looking at her. She had a million-yard stare, replaying the story in her head, and Piper knew better than to interrupt the momentum now. Her questions could wait.

"Every time I heard their voices, I *knew* the pain was about to come."

"King and Lou?" Piper asked around a mouthful of chicken.

Dani put her fork down. "You have to understand that your voices were the ones I heard that night. In the garage. After Dmitri...after he did the worst of it. Then I blacked out and you were there. I was scared and in pain and it was your voice in my head."

My voice triggers your PTSD. Ouch.

"I think my brain got confused. It began to associate all of you—King, Lou, Mel, everyone involved that night—with danger. Even a text message from you or King would trigger a panic attack."

"So it's somehow worse with *me* than with King, Lou, or Mel?"

Dani's face crumpled. "I know. I know and I'm *so* sorry. I think it's because I cared about you the most and because I was already feeling so shitty about trying to use you to get the story. Whatever it was about you, I couldn't see you. Seeing you, talking to you, any contact at all would've reminded me that it was real. It wasn't a dream I could just put behind me. And I was more than a little embarrassed that you'd seen me that way. I mean, I'd pissed myself—"

"You were *tortured*," Piper whispered. "Of course you pissed yourself."

Dani held up her hand. "Don't. I don't want to go into details, okay?"

"Okay."

"I just wanted to apologize for my shitty communication skills," Dani said, meeting her gaze for the first time since she'd begun to cry. "And I need you to know that I didn't stay away because I didn't like you."

Piper sat back against her chair. "That's what it felt like. You got the story you wanted and then you disappeared."

"I know," Dani said. "I know, and I'm sorry."

Piper looked at the steaming chicken on her plate and tried to muster her appetite.

"Why did you reach out to King first?"

"My therapist told me that sometimes working can help with PTSD. She thought focusing on the job I love would be one way to get back in the game. She asked me, 'Are you going to let one asshole destroy your dream of being the best damn investigative reporter you can be?' And I was like, 'No. No, I'm not.' Because I love it. It's all I want to do. So I finally returned King's texts and started helping him on cases."

Piper thought, *But you had no reason to reach out to me.*

She arched her brows. "And Lou can give you the 'big break' case of your career, sooner or later." To this, Dani said nothing.

"I like you, Piper," Dani said softly. "Every time I walk through Jackson Square I'm hoping that I'll spot you there at your table. I'm also terrified that you'll be there."

Piper's heart seemed to swell in size, pushing against the base of her throat.

"I've given up on the idea that we could be something more," Dani went on. "Good relationships are built on trust, and you have no reason to trust me after what I did. And I'm still so messed up, I couldn't offer you a decent relationship anyway." She searched Piper's face. "But I'd be *so* grateful if we could just learn how to be friends."

Piper stared into the wine glass as if she could use it to divine her future.

Dani fidgeted in her seat, drawing her arms across her chest. "Say something. Please."

"*Only* friends?" Piper smiled, twirling the glass on the table. "I never pegged you for a quitter, Daniella Allendale."

And for the first time that night, Dani truly laughed.

10

———————

Waterlogged and dripping, Lou pulled herself from the cold lake. She stood on the embankment, trying to catch her breath. The night sang to her. Nightjars trilled. A fox yipped in the distance. Something splashed in the lake. A fish? She wasn't sure. She saw only the ripples spreading across the moonlit surface.

Her skin and hair itched. She remembered the affectionate way Jabbers had dragged her thick white tongue over bloody knuckles and up the side of her neck. She could smell the monster's breath in her hair. She was filthy and longed for a hot shower.

But before she could do that, she wanted to check on Fish. The situation with Jeffrey could turn at any time. No point in showering prematurely in case she needed to take care of him tonight.

Lou hated washing her hair too much.

She stood in the dark, shaking the water off her leather jacket. She flapped her harness, checking to make sure the guns were fine.

Her chilled hands pushed away the strands sticking to her face and lips. She wrung out her hair and sighed, inwardly willing her compass to life.

Fish, she thought. *Where is he tonight?*

She wondered if she would find him on the prowl. Maybe he'd be loitering around the grocery store again, but to no avail. The girl wasn't working tonight. Lou knew this because she'd slipped into the manager's office and checked the posted schedule. Now that she had the woman's name, it was easier to do such things.

And Lou trusted her compass. How many times had it whirled to life inside her, screaming the alarms, *Lucy! King! Piper!*, when it was time to act. This didn't mean that Jeffrey wasn't up to no good. After all, Lou noted the feeling of unease settling within her. Like a coil of snakes, it slithered in her guts, somewhere deep and unseen.

Locking in on Jeffrey's location, she said goodbye to her nighttime paradise and shifted through the shadows once more.

The cacophony of a thriving nature was replaced by silence.

Lou felt the cold cement under her hands and realized she was against a concrete wall. There in front of her, spotlighted as if on stage, was Jeffrey, his back to her.

Too close, she thought. *I'm too close.*

But this was the last pocket of shadow in Jeffrey's garage. Against one wall was a long worktable, laden with tools and the small lamp responsible for spotlighting Jeffrey's shoulders.

He wore his pajamas. A bizarrely mundane matching set, both the top and bottoms composed of soft blue and white stripes.

Your wife buy you those? Lou found herself marveling at the strange regularities of suburbia. *Here was a killer. Here he was working in his two-car garage, on a quiet Midwestern street, in his soft pajamas.*

She almost laughed at the sight of Fish bent over the table in concentration.

At least Lou never tried to hide what she was.

Then she saw the blood.

It dripped from his right forearm onto the concrete floor. Lou shifted, trying to get a better look, and her shoes squeaked on the concrete.

Jeffrey whirled. His eyes frantically searched the dark. But he could not find her in the shadows. With his back angled in the light, Lou had a better sense of the situation. In his left hand was a straight-edge razor. Around his right arm, above the bend of the elbow, was a leather strap tied tight. On the forearm itself were six vertical lines. The first three were crusted black with dried blood. The three above it, as if he'd moved up the arm toward the fold, were bright crimson and oozed along the curve of his forearm, dripping onto the table.

The utility lamp illuminating his pale arm added a theatrical quality to the scene. His lower jaw jutted forward and his chest heaved with his labored breath. The whites of his eyes shimmered as he stood there, listening. Waiting.

Is this what you do to quell your hunger? Lou remained still in her pocket of shadow. *Does it bring you back from the edge?*

She knew the pain couldn't fulfill him.

Lou herself had tried that trick in barroom brawls and petty fights. She'd invited any man willing to take a swing to have a go at her. But even the best of split lips or scuffed cheeks hadn't scratched that itch within her.

Nothing short of the actual kill would do.

An unexpected swell of pity washed over her. She had never in all her years of hunting felt pity for a target before.

Was it his wounded expression?

Was it the way he cowered to his desires, clearly owned by them?

He ripped the strip of leather off his arm and threw it back into the case on his wooden workbench. He wiped the blade and spilled blood with a navy blue mechanic's rag before tossing both into the box as well.

His back was to her as he rummaged for something. When he produced a thin roll of gauze and began to wrap his wounds tight, she realized this must be a longstanding ritual for him, these nighttime cuttings.

And what do you tell the wife and kid, Jeff? Kids ask questions. How do you explain the gauze? Is his daddy clumsy in the garage?

He slammed the lid down on his box. He reached overhead and drew the utility light close. The combination lock on a safe sat illuminated in the light. Lou watched him twirl the dial left and right, enjoying the *tick, tick, tick* of the spinning dial.

He placed the toolbox inside the safe and pushed the door closed. He tugged the handle and spun the dial.

Can't be too careful, can we?

Fish didn't seem to think so as he threw one more nervous look over his shoulder, then crossed the garage, past the parked cars, and into the house.

For several minutes Lou stayed where she was. She was no fool. Fish could throw on the lights, trapping her in the garage. He might've only pretended to go up to his bed, waiting to lure her from her hiding place.

But when she heard water running through the pipes above, she suspected Fish was washing up for bed.

Lou crossed the garage silently, stooping down beneath the wooden workbench just as Fish had done minutes before. She brought the utility light down with her and illuminated the lock. The combination had been easy to see and memorize.

Inside the safe, she found not only the plastic bin containing his "toys" but a stack of photographs beneath it.

Lou flipped through the photographs one after another.

They began innocently enough. A woman tied to a chair. A woman naked, blindfolded. These could be mistaken for light BDSM photographs, just a bit of couple's play.

But then the blood came and the anguished expressions on the women's faces—at least eleven, by Lou's count—told Lou these were not consensual sex games.

Anger sparked along her spine.

It seemed that it wasn't enough for Fish to stalk, hurt, and murder the women he wanted. He clearly enjoyed documenting the experience as well. More than one photograph immortalized his dick buried to the hilt, but he'd photographed the rest of his process as well, from the time he took them, through their torture, until their deaths. Most of the photographs were of the deaths.

Do you have a favorite moment, Fish? Let me guess. I bet the police could guess too. Maybe I should show them these photographs. Would you like that?

King's strident, angry voice overrode her pulsating anger. *Don't take anything! Even if it's proof, you can't take it. It would be inadmissible in a court of law if it's obtained without a warrant. Put it back.*

All the pity she'd felt for Fish while watching him self-harm was gone.

She wanted to have a nice, long, and uninterrupted session of her own. See how much of this she could reenact.

Boots shifted gravel on the other side of Fish's closed garage door.

Lou froze. She waited, holding her breath, until she heard it again —rocks shifting under someone's weight.

Lou did her best to wipe down the photographs and put them back under the toolbox. Then she shut the safe and gave the lock a spin.

She regarded the two tracks of boot prints on the garage floor left by her soggy steps.

They'll dry before morning, she told herself, hoping she was right.

The gravel shifted again, and this time so did Lou. The cement wall at her back gave and opened onto the cold night. Lou was across the street now, not far from the parked car she'd used as sanctuary earlier that week.

She bent beneath the hedgerow framing an adjacent property and searched the Fish family's driveway.

There, where the rock retainer wall gave way to the open drive, someone stood. Lou moved to the left, trying to get a better view despite the hedge's jutting branches. A gap appeared and Lou leaned in.

It was hard to tell if the person was a man or a woman. The form was slight, which initially suggested female to Lou's eye. But then she thought of the dock full of Hong Kong heroin dealers she'd dispatched seven months ago. They had been as short—or shorter—and their bodies even leaner.

This observer was taking photographs of the Fish residence with a large-lens camera. He—or she—wore black gloves, black jeans, and black boots, and a hoodie was pulled up over the head.

Then as suddenly as they came, they started down the walkway again, casting glances at the house as they passed.

Who are you? Lou wondered, watching the person go. *Who are you?*

She heard their staccato steps cut up the sidewalk, around the corner, and then they were gone.

. . .

Lou was more than ready for a shower. The grit in her hair only intensified the itching and her feet had grown so cold in her boots that she could barely feel them. Cold, wet socks were the bane of her existence. She pressed open the closet door, expecting to find her warm and welcoming St. Louis apartment awaiting her. Only it wasn't her apartment on the other side of the door.

Konstantine's bed was neatly made, with his sweats thrown over the covers. The shutters on the arched window were closed, but moonlight filtered through the cracks, giving the bedroom a ghostly glow.

This is getting ridiculous, she thought. She chided her inward compass. *Do you even know where I live anymore?*

She was about to step into the closet again, redirecting herself home, when a sound caught her attention.

Water splashed against tile and the low, melodic tone of a sultry tenor reached her.

She stepped from the closet and to the bathroom's open door. Steam hung in the air like low clouds, but it wasn't thick enough to obscure the view of the naked man in the shower.

Konstantine's back was to her. It was stained red from the assault of the shower. His right arm was covered in tattoos from shoulder to elbow. The black ink was beaded with hot droplets.

I wanted a shower. A shower is what I'll get.

She checked the GPS watch synced with her new location. It was after four in the morning. She wasn't sure if Konstantine was starting his day or ending it.

It didn't matter. Lou unlaced her boots and worked her wet, clinging clothes off her body. When she opened the shower door, a hand shot out. She ducked, snatching the wrist.

"Does this mean I can't join you?" she asked, rolling her eyes up to meet his.

His gaze raked over her naked body. Goosebumps rose on his skin.

The tension in his body vanished. "I didn't realize it was you."

Obviously, she thought. "If you don't want me to join you—"

He reached out for her, seizing her with both hands, and pulled her into the hot stream.

"Late night or early morning?" she asked.

"I'm just getting home. But preparations for Venice are complete, and we leave in two days."

"I don't think you want me to touch you yet," she said, adding distance between them even as he moved in.

"I can always wash again." He leaned into her, tucking his lips under her jawline and caressing the skin where the neck and jaw met. Lou tipped her head back to allow it.

He pulled back and frowned at the pink water swirling down the drain. "Are you bleeding?"

"It isn't blood," she said. She didn't have any of Walker's gore on her. "I call it Blood Lake for a reason. The waters are red."

He gathered a handful of her wet hair and brought it to his nose. "You smell like sulfur."

"That's La Loon too," she said, letting her hands rest at last on his hip bones. She squeezed him, loving their hard edges.

"Perhaps it *is* hell then," Konstantine said, giving her a devilish smile to match. Lou had noticed, in the passing months, that this smile always came to his lips the moment she put her hands on him. "Doesn't hell smell like sulfur?"

Lou tilted her head back again, letting the hot water assault her scalp. "You're the good Catholic boy. You tell me."

"May I?" he asked. She opened her eyes to see him closing the lid on the shampoo bottle.

She redirected the shower head so that the water hit her upper back instead of her hair. When Konstantine's fingers touched her scalp, delicious warmth ran through her. She wasn't entirely sure if it was the hot water or the massage. He paused to pick something out of her strands. Seaweed? Algae? She had no idea.

She found herself leaning her body against his.

"You're like a *gatta*." He laughed softly. "*Meow*."

So domesticated, the cold voice whispered.

It was gone the moment he put his hands on her stomach, walking her back into the water's stream. His fingers moved clean water through her hair. His torso brushed hers. Their hips slid against one another, the tops of their thighs brushed.

Lou relished every point of contact.

"What do you do next?" His breath was on her ear, and it tightened muscles low in her stomach.

"Conditioner?"

He surveyed the bottles on the ledge.

"You know," she said, smiling up at him. He had only a few inches on her. "I *do* know how to bathe myself."

He didn't hide his smirk. "Why would you when I am here? I'm always at your service."

She saw the gooseflesh rise on his arms and chest.

"You're cold," she said.

He rubbed conditioner between his palms before pushing his fingers through her hair. "It's worth it to share the shower with you."

"Come here."

"Don't you want to rinse?"

She pulled him into the hot water. Her hand trailed down the front of his body, over his abdomen. Her finger rested on the small divot beneath his navel.

"I let my conditioner set. What should I do in the meantime?" She rolled her eyes up to meet his, still tracing his Adonis belt.

"You're my guest," he began, his voice notably dropping an octave. "I should entertain you."

She didn't miss the tight set of his shoulders or the way he slid his gaze away.

He's already preparing for rejection, Lou thought. *And why shouldn't he? I've turned down every advance for over a year.*

It wasn't that she hadn't reciprocated attention. She'd ground her body against his. She'd given him blowjobs, hand jobs, and let him see her naked more times than she could count, but she hadn't let him between her legs.

Part of her was curious as to how long she could get away with it. Another part simply hadn't cared. She'd always been able to gain pleasure from topping her partners, often more pleasure than from the sex itself.

But this resignation in his hazel green eyes now, this anticipation of defeat...

No. That won't do.

Lou kicked the bottles off the wet ledge and propped her foot there.

She leaned her weight back against the wall, giving Konstantine a look to match the blatant invitation.

He gulped visibly. He looked down as if unable to control himself. Then he met her gaze again. "Are you sure?"

She arched a brow.

He didn't make the mistake of asking her twice.

When his fingers brushed her wet sex, she slid her arms around his neck, trapping him against her. Part of it was to help her balance, part of it was simply to ensure the compression she desired.

Konstantine didn't mind providing it.

He began with the clitoris, letting the slow heat build until her mind lost track of its thoughts. It was if the steam around them filled her head, suppressing and obscuring everything except the feel of his chest against hers, his lips on her throat, his hand between her legs.

She gave herself over to it.

KONSTANTINE PULLED BACK, SEARCHING HER FACE. HE WANTED TO look into her eyes the moment he slid inside her.

They were closed in concentration. A delicious blush had spread across her cheeks.

When her brown eyes finally opened, meeting his, he relinquished her clit and plunged into the hot center of her. Her eyelashes fluttered. Her mouth opened in a soft pant.

The moan that slipped between her lips vibrated through him.

It was as if a cord was cut inside him. His limbs felt heavy and weak, all the tension leaving the line. Yet he built a steady rhythm.

He noticed every shift in her body, every response to his tender probing. When she moaned into his ear his desire exploded. His erection grew so hard it hurt.

He wanted to lay her down somehow. He wanted to taste her. But the shower wasn't big enough.

He knelt instead, his back and heels pressed against the shower door. He was too large to be in the bottom of the shower, but that didn't stop him from nosing his way between her legs and finding her clitoris with his tongue. She trapped his hand in place, making her request for dual stimulation clear. Once he returned his hand to its original task, she released him and cupped either side of his head encouragingly.

He continued like this, with his mouth and his hand in synchronicity, despite the fact that the water was turning cold against his back.

She fisted his hair the second before her whole body tightened. The sounds coming from her throat were more of a whimper than a moan.

Her legs shook when she released his head, and for a moment she stood there trembling against the wall.

"Are you—"

"Shut up," she said.

Konstantine obeyed, and after a minute or two, she took his hand and slipped it between her legs again.

11

————

Mel moved the brown grocery sack from one arm to another, trying to alleviate the weight in her arms. Her mind was trying to puzzle out dinner. *Takeout or a nice and easy chicken salad?*

It was hard to focus. It wasn't the chilly air, which she usually attributed to clearer thinking. It was that gnawing feeling that hadn't left her since the day Terrence walked into her shop.

She'd hoped King had scared him away, or even Lady—as Terrence had always hated dogs.

But she knew that she hadn't seen the end of him, and that was what weighed on her.

She felt eyes on her back and turned.

A man stepped out of the adjacent corner market with a pack of cigarettes in one hand and a lighter with the price tag still on its plastic casing in the other.

Speak of the devil.

She stopped dead on the corner, facing him.

Better than having him at my back.

"Melly," he said in mock affection. His thin smile appeared. "Fancy seeing you here."

"This is my shop," she said, gesturing at the *Madame Melandra's Fortunes and Fixes* sign. "As you damn well know."

"I think you mean *our* shop," he said with a wicked smile. He tapped the soft pack of Marlboros against the heel of his hand.

"*Our* shop," she spat. She almost threw her groceries down on the sidewalk.

"We're married. According to God and the State of Louisiana, what's yours—"

"I'm about to give you what's *yours*," she said, and here she did stoop and lean the grocery bag against the storefront.

Don't let no man undo you. Grandmamie's voice rose like a tidal wave. *You're better than this.*

That sharp rebuke defused her anger.

"You can't loiter here," she said. "Pick any other convenience store in the Quarter, or in all of New Orleans for all I care. But you can't hang around here."

He cupped his hands around the end of the cigarette, letting his gaze hold her own. They stood like that, on opposite sides of the street, staring for almost a full minute as Terrence drew on his cigarette. He broke the gaze first, tipping his chin up and blowing thin gray smoke into the sky.

"You wouldn't believe the things people would do for a cigarette in prison. But not me, because I had a good little wife who sent me money when she was asked. Do you know *why* she sent me money? Because she didn't want to be in prison either. And why might I *protect* her? Because not only was she my wife, but she was more use to me on the outside."

A sly grin spread across his face. He slid his hands into the front pockets of his jeans and crossed the street to her.

"But if she's no use to me, maybe I shouldn't keep her secrets no more. What do you think?"

Mel tried to steady her breath. "I swear, if you—"

He shoved her into the front of her shop, his hand at the base of her throat.

And there he was, the Terry she knew and remembered.

"You'll *what?*" he growled. "*What* could you possibly do to me? You can't tell me where I can and can't go. I'm free now. No thanks to you."

Smoke from his cigarette stung her eyes.

As if realizing how this must look, he released her. He stood back, tugging at the bottom of his white t-shirt. He touched his bone choker self-consciously, as if *he* had just been the one with a hand on his throat.

He bent, lifted her grocery sack off the ground and thrust it into her chest. She wrapped her arms around it reflexively.

"I asked around about your friend, *Mr. King.* I know you're not together, and I know he's a cop. Why you makin' friends with the po-po, Melly? Does your po-po friend know what you did?"

Mel's heart knocked in her throat.

Terrence smiled. "I didn't think so. Or you'd be in jail yaself right now." He flicked the ash off his cigarette. "I'm glad the two of you aren't together. I wouldn't take too kindly to another man touching my wife."

"I'm not your wife," she said. She wanted to throw the sack in his face.

Pull yourself together. Come on. Pull yourself together. He knows how to get a rise out of you. That's all he wants, to get a rise out of you. Push back or he'll just take more ground.

"I don't remember signing no divorce papers," Terry said, sucking his teeth. "I wonder why that was?"

Because I was hoping you'd rot in that place. That if I just forgot about you, you'd disappear like the damn nightmare you are.

"Get the fuck out of New Orleans, Terry. This is the last time I'm telling you."

He laughed, opening his mouth to pinch the tip of his tongue. He removed a piece of tobacco stuck there. "I ain't leaving unless you give me my due. You don't want me around, fine. But a new life costs money, and you're already several years behind in your checks."

She unclenched her jaw, trying not to grind the enamel to a pulp.

"Don't you remember your promise?" he said, feigning a pout. "Or do promises not mean anything to you now you're a big-time bitch?"

Mel saw the courtroom the way it had looked decades ago, how

Terry himself had looked in his orange county jumpsuit, his hair inside its black do-rag. The look he'd given her when the officers pulled him from his seat and dragged him through the doors out of her life.

Why had she even gone to the damn trial? More importantly, why had she gone to see him on that first visitation? If she'd stayed away, if she'd never seen him at all, maybe she'd be free now—truly free.

But she'd gone because of the photographs.

Across from him, where he sat with his shackled wrists on the table, she'd told him about the search warrant. How the day after Terry was slammed onto the floor of their trailer so hard the dishes rattled in the cupboards, the police had returned with a warrant. They'd torn the house apart, taking no care to replace the cushions removed or fix the rugs lifted.

Mel could do nothing but stand in the middle of the living room, one hand clasping her opposite elbow, and wait until they were done.

Her heart had quickened when she'd seen the uniformed officer marching toward her.

"Do you know what these are?" he'd asked, thrusting the photographs at her.

She'd hoped he hadn't noticed the tremble in her hands as she'd taken them.

The first photograph was of the red Firebird. A dent—a very *human*-shaped dent—curved the grill of the car. Across the paint was something drying—blood? Brain? She couldn't be sure. The other photographs were the same. Every conceivable angle documented the damage to the car. Why had Terry taken them? It couldn't be for an insurance claim because they didn't have car insurance. They couldn't afford it. That's when she'd known it was evidence.

"Well?" the officer asked impatiently. He ran a hand through his buzzed blond hair.

She licked her lips. "I don't know what they are."

"You don't know what they are?" He snorted derisively.

"Photographs," she said.

"Is that all they are?" he pressed.

It took everything Mel had to look up from the photographs,

tearing her eyes away from the blood-crusted dent, and meet the officer's eyes.

"I don't know," she forced out.

He snatched the photographs from her hand and marched away with them. On her front porch, he slipped the photographs into a clear plastic bag.

"So they have the evidence now," Mel had told Terry during that first visitation.

He'd grinned at that. "They won't know what happened unless *I* tell them."

Horror had rocketed through her then.

"You don't want me to tell nobody, do you?"

"No," she said.

"Good." He'd leaned back in his seat and sucked his teeth. "You're a good girl, and here's what my good girl is going to do for me."

She was going to stay married to him, and she was going to send him money. In exchange, he was going to keep her secret.

What had happened when she'd protested? When she'd insisted that she didn't have that kind of money to send him every week?

You'd better find it, he'd said. *Find it or I'm going to tell them what you did. I'm going to tell them you killed somebody, and they'll put you in here right next to me.*

It wasn't until four or five years into her payments that Mel realized her mistake. If only she'd never visited, or if only she'd walked away and had never sent her first payout—then it would've just been her word against his.

But she'd paid, and she'd kept paying—and only a guilty person would do that.

I'll tell them I paid because he's my husband, she thought.

And wasn't that why she'd let the marriage stand? It was all she could do to keep that fail-safe in place should he turn on her and bite the hand that feeds.

But she was tired of it. She was tired of the lying, tired of the stress, of handing over the money she worked so hard to make to this asshole who didn't deserve a dime of it.

Most of all, she was tired of the guilt eating her from the inside out.

"You remember," he said. Sly confidence filled his face again. "You remember what really happened that night on the old town road outside Baton Rouge. And you remember your promise to me and to God."

Mel heard the sudden squeal of brakes and smelled the burning rubber. She recalled the splatter of rain on the car's windshield and hood. And the unmistakable sound of crying.

"Don't you want to make up for what you did? For all this freedom you've got out here?" Terrence considered the burning cherry of his cigarette carefully. "I'm thinking a hundred grand will set me up just fine. Get me out of your hair...for a while."

"There's no way in hell," she said with a bitter laugh. "Even if I had that kind of money I wouldn't give it to you."

He sucked his teeth, drawing himself up to his full height. "Sell the shop if you have to, call in favors, I don't care how you get it. Give me the money or get used to seeing my pretty face right here, day and night, for the rest of your life—if you're lucky. If you're not lucky, maybe I'll stroll on down to the po-*leece* station and make a report. I'm a good, reformed citizen now. Maybe I've got something to say."

He flicked his cigarette onto the sidewalk and ground it out with the heel of his boots.

"Since I'm a nice guy, I'll give you a day to think about it." With a wink and a tap of his hat, he started off down the sidewalk toward Royal Street.

For a moment, Mel could only stand there with her sack of groceries in her hand.

A hundred grand, she thought. *No way in heaven—or hell.*

But even as she thought it, she heard the rain falling on a windshield and a woman crying softly.

12

Piper knew it would be a busy night the moment she unfolded the card table and twin metal chairs in Jackson Square. There was no shortage of fellow palmists and tarot card readers, so she hoped bathroom breaks weren't out of the question.

Just a couple hundred bucks, she told herself as she opened the backpack between her feet and dug out her cards and donation box. *Then I'll pack up and get some sleep.*

A desperate shiver ran through her body at the idea of falling into her warm bed for a good night's rest. She'd only managed five or six hours the last few nights, and it was catching up to her.

But she also knew better. Piper had never been able to walk away from the chance to make money. It was true that King was letting her rent the apartment above the agency for a pittance and that her wages between her two official jobs with King and Mel had allowed her to put back more money than she'd ever had.

It also helped that she wasn't trying to pay her mother's bills anymore.

A pang of regret shot through her at this thought. That happened whenever she imagined her in that dark and dingy house off the canal with her druggie boyfriend and a coffee table covered in dope, needles, and who knew what else.

That's not your problem, she thought. *It never was your problem.*

Yet sometimes she shot up in her bed in the dark, heart pounding with an all-consuming belief that it had happened. That her mother was finally dead. But she wasn't, and Piper was finding a way to live with that—in the limbo of loving someone she couldn't help.

It wasn't like she didn't have plenty to be getting on with.

She had herself to feed, tuition to cover, her own rent and utilities. Now that she was back in school, she also had her grades to worry about.

It's going to be okay, she told herself. *If only you'd get more sleep.*

Piper unwrapped the cards, feeling the cold cardstock slide out of the black silk into her dry palm. She returned the scarf to her back-pack and moved the donation box to one side, propping it open with a little sign.

Tarot and palm readings, donation only.

She hadn't even gotten comfortable in her chair when her first customer—a forty-year-old woman with thick black eyeliner and a streak of gray through her box-red hair—sat down.

"Can you do me?" she asked.

How much? Piper thought, but had the good sense not to make the joke aloud.

"Tarot or palm?" she asked, and just like that, she was off.

Piper was six readings in before she had a chance to count the money—$103—and bring out the water bottle from her bag. She drank half of it in one go.

Two teenage girls with perfect white teeth and ripped jeans came to the table. The blonde placed two fingers on the table's edge and opened her mouth to speak, but a husky, masculine voice came out instead. "This bitch is closed."

Piper lowered the water bottle and found a glorious drag queen standing on the other side of her card table.

Henry, a longtime friend, stood in six-inch stilettos and a golden brassiere. His ass was—as her mother would have put it—tight enough to bounce a quarter off of, and expertly framed by the fishnet hose pulled over it.

The hand on his hip had been recently manicured and the long nails gleamed like honey in the square's streetlights. His other hand was wrapped possessively over the back of the metal chair, preventing either of the girls from sitting down.

"But—" one of the girls began to object, a deep crease forming between her eyes.

Yet one look from Henry sent them both scurrying deeper into the square.

Piper grinned. "Don't frighten the children, H."

"I didn't come all the way down here in my Louboutins to be stopped by some teenage horndogs."

Piper laughed. "Splurging for Louboutins now? Wow, your dances at Wild Cat must be paying well these days."

He settled down into the folding chair and crossed one leg over the other. "I thought I'd find your skinny ass here. I was starting to think you were avoiding me."

He pushed out his rouged lower lip.

Piper offered her hands across the card table. "Sorry, man. I've been so busy."

He clasped them briefly, giving them a squeeze. His nails grazed her wrist. "I know. So I thought I would come and see you for once. You're always coming to see me, aren't you? I'm sure I owe you."

Piper withdrew, settling back against the chair. In truth, a short mental break wasn't totally unwelcome. "It's good to see you."

Henry tilted his head and batted his lengthy eyelashes. "I know." He flashed her a roguish smile. "Now, tell me what the hell you've been up to."

Piper gave him the condensed version of her life—investigation, case building, criminal justice classes, day-to-day at the shop, and the status of her apartment, finishing up with the special hell that was Carnival.

"God, don't I know it," Henry said, gesturing at the rambunctious crowd of drunks around them, covered in beads and plastic masks and ridiculous hats. "Let's hole up in your apartment until it's over."

"You have an open invitation," she promised.

She hadn't made the invitation earlier because one Miss Louie Thorne had a tendency to pop out of dark corners unannounced whenever she pleased, and Piper hadn't been ready to explain that phenomenon to anyone.

"At least you aren't ignoring me because you're shacking up with some girl."

Piper took the money out of her donation box, wrapped it up, and tucked it into the bottom of her backpack. "There's no girl."

"No one on your radar at all?" Henry asked, arching a painted brow. "You haven't seen a girl for days? *Months?*"

Piper noticed his shift in tone and frowned at him. "I had dinner with Dani last night. First time I'd seen her in over a year."

She searched his face as she said it, confirming her suspicions.

"But you knew that, didn't you?"

"I'm friends with Tyriqua." When Piper didn't register the significance of the name, he said, "The hostess who seated you told me she'd seen you come in."

"You've got spies in the Quarter." Piper snorted, shuffling the cards absentmindedly. "Why am I not surprised?"

Henry, like Piper, had lived in New Orleans all his life.

"I haven't seen you, is all. I needed to know you weren't dead in a ditch or had fallen into prostitution."

Piper grinned. "Since when do you have a problem with prostitution?"

"I don't. I love prostitutes." He clasped his hands around his knees, glancing around the square. "It's kind of cold out here. You just sit out here all night?"

"Not all night. Just until I make my personal quota."

He's pretending not to care much about Dani, but in a second he's going to ask—

"So what's going on with Dani anyway?" he asked.

Piper smiled. "Who?"

Henry rolled his bedazzled eyes. "The journalist who used you for a story and then decided she likes you—probably because you laid her better than she'd ever been laid in her life—and now wants to kiss and make up."

Piper felt the heat rise in her face. "We didn't have sex."

Henry arched his brows again. "That speaks volumes all on its own, doesn't it? Piper, heart-slayer, *didn't* bed a gorgeous woman who wanted it? *Damn.* The world must be ending."

"You're reading too much into it." Yet Piper wondered why her heart was knocking strangely in her chest.

"Hmmm," he said, unconvinced, and let his gaze slide out over the square again. Piper followed his lead, noting the lit lamps, the crowds chattering. People standing around with their cups of booze or hot drinks. A brass band was tuning up to begin their set. The square echoed with laughter and the chatter of dozens of overlapping conversations. One girl holding a hurricane glass looked ready to puke in the shrub beside her.

Henry pointed at the other tables clustered around. All of them were full with a few hosting lines.

"You ever get your own cards read?" he asked.

"No. I don't have time for that."

He checked the clock on his phone, then, seemingly satisfied, reached across the table. He waved his manicured nails. "Hand them over."

Piper laughed. "What?"

"The cards. Give them to me. I'm going to tell your fortune."

She drew them back instinctively. "You don't know how to read cards."

"No, but you do. You pick them and I'll turn them over and you can read them for yourself."

She wanted to argue that it wouldn't actually be him reading the cards, but his face was so determined she laughed and gave up the deck.

It was incredibly difficult to read one's own fortune, even if someone else volunteered to do the flipping and shuffling. Everyone had a self-view, and self-beliefs always got in the way of seeing a situation objectively. That's why it was better to get someone else's interpretation.

"This should be interesting," she said, unaware that she'd folded her arms over her chest.

Henry watched her with a devilish grin as he shuffled the deck. "Do you have a question?" he asked in a mock fortune teller voice. It was over the top, dramatic, and actually went well with his drag queen persona. The wide eyes helped.

Piper giggled. "Let's just do a Celtic cross."

"Ah, yes," he said, remaining in character.

Piper laughed, her knee accidentally bumping the table. It rocked. "You can stop shuffling. Spread them out for me so I can pick ten."

Henry did as he was told, and Piper took her time thumbing through the deck. She only picked the cards that made her hesitate, the ones she kept coming back to.

When she had all ten cards removed from the deck, she moved the pile over to one side and handed the ten to Henry.

"Keep them in order, like that," Piper instructed. "Just flip one at a time."

He nodded gravely. Piper wondered if maybe he would do a fortune teller skit of some kind for his next drag show. Surely there was a song that would work for it. Didn't The Rolling Stones also have a song about a fortune teller?

Despite his long, elegant nails, Henry flipped the cards easily, one at a time, putting them down where Piper instructed him to.

"Look at all these cups," he said, batting his eyes at her. "I wonder what they mean?"

She refrained from rolling her eyes. "The cups suit usually has to do with love and relationships."

"Oh," he said in mock surprise. "Imagine that."

"I thought you didn't know anything about tarot."

"I know a little. Enough to know this is all about *love*." He tapped The Ace of Cups. Then he plucked one card off the table and held it up at her accusingly. "The Lovers? Come on now."

He tapped The Queen of Wands.

"What about this one?" he asked.

That's Dani, she thought. "A strong, independent, and passionate woman."

Henry arched a brow. "A reporter, perhaps."

And Piper couldn't argue. The cards she saw spread before her had every indication of a new and promising love. One that, given enough time, could bloom into complete fulfillment. A soulmate connection. But it wasn't a straight shot to happily ever after. There were obstacles —big ones—that would slow down progress.

A shiver ran down Piper's arms.

He laid another card down and then frowned. "This one looks less cheerful."

It was the Five of Swords. Ill-gotten gains. Victory through deceit.

"It's a card about double-crossing someone," Piper told him.

"She did double-cross you." He pulled the card close to better see the artistic detail.

"Yeah," Piper agreed. But the positions of the cards also mattered. This betrayal was in the future, not the past. In fact, it was just on the horizon.

Henry threw down the cards, giving Piper a minute to look them over.

There was the promise of romance, but on the fringe cards something darker lurked. *Keep your eyes open,* her intuition said. *Keep your eyes open for what's going on around you. Something is happening right under your nose.*

But she couldn't be sure if that was about Lou, about hunting killers, or her work at the agency. Or if maybe it was about her mother. Or maybe Mel, who she'd been thinking about on and off all day. The way her hands had shaken. That man in the bone choker...

Pay attention to what? she wondered.

"Just talk to her," Henry said at last, misreading her troubled expression. "I'm sure she's sorry. So she got a little short-sighted in the face of her ambition, but I think an ambitious woman is exactly what you need in your life. You should give her another chance."

"Why?"

"Because I can tell you're super into her, and I can't let you walk away over something as stupid as her doing her job."

Piper gathered up the cards, unable to shake the worry knotting in her guts.

Pay attention...to what...

"Earth to Piper." He clapped his hands.

"Okay, okay. I'll text her," she agreed, shuffling the cards to clear them of her own energy.

"Good," Henry said, loving when he won.

He reached into his golden brassiere and fished out a folded $20 bill. He threw it into Piper's donation box and leaned forward coquettishly.

He placed his chin in the palm of his hand. "Now, do me."

13

Lou dreamed. A white t-shirt. Red blooming through cotton as she was lifted by strong, sure hands and thrown into waiting waters. The ghostly face of retribution emerged from the dark like a Carnival mask. A gun turning its black eye on her.

Pop! Pop! Pop!

With a gasp she sat up in bed. Her heart knocked against the base of her throat, making it difficult to breathe. The back of her neck was soaked with sweat. When she wiped at her forehead, she found it wet too.

She slowed her breath. She counted the gold fleur-de-lis emblems embroidered on the green blanket stretched over her legs.

Green and gold.

Konstantine's bed. She turned and saw him sleeping on his back. The sheet cut across his abdomen as his bare chest rose and fell slowly. One hand was tucked under his head, the other in the waistband of his pants.

She clasped her hands behind her neck and squeezed. It had been a long time since she'd dreamed of her father's murder.

What had triggered it now? Why should the terror of that night—a decade and a half behind her—rise up now?

She slid from the bed as quietly as she could, looking for her clothes. They were still soaked from her time with Ricky Walker, but she didn't need to wear them. Konstantine had given her a pair of gray sweats and a large white t-shirt that hung off one of her shoulders.

You're dry. You're safe. So why the dream?

She didn't want to leave the clothes behind. She grabbed them in both fists and turned to the bed once more.

Konstantine continued to sleep, but Lou had a sneaking suspicion that he was pretending.

Why? So she could sneak off without explanation?

The shadows softened and stretched around her. They thinned for her as they always had, offering her passage.

Say something. Anything, she thought. *Tell him goodbye. Give him a kiss.*

Konstantine's apartment fell away, and in its place her own apartment formed around her.

The old-world charm and sounds of a languid canal were exchanged for the bright city lights of downtown St. Louis. The Gateway Arch, illuminated at night, stood guard over the Mississippi River. Lamp posts and skyscrapers twinkled like trapped fallen stars.

Her bed was as she'd left it, unmade. Its downy comforter was rumpled and bathed in moonlight. Lou admired the skyline for a moment longer before crossing to a laundry basket and tossing in her soaked clothes.

Gauging by the color of the sky, she'd only slept a few hours after falling into bed with Konstantine. Her GPS watch said it was just past three in the morning here.

It was too early to pester King or check on Fish again. She could hunt. But she was tired. Her head buzzed and her eyes felt like they had sand in them. She fell onto her mattress and pulled her comforter over her body.

You're going to bed? Then why did you leave Konstantine at all? You could've slept in his bed as well as yours. Hell, his bed is more comfortable.

That much was true.

Lou suspected it was because Konstantine had a proper frame, headboard and all, whereas she had only a mattress on the floor.

But that didn't explain the restlessness that filled her.

It made her legs itch and palms ache. She turned onto one pillow, fluffing it. When that provided no relief, she turned onto the other. She removed the comforter, then added it again.

She slid her hand into her pillowcase, searching for...

There.

She retrieved the 5x8 photo from the pillowcase's cotton folds and held it up to the moonlight.

Her father smiled down at her. His hair was wet with ocean water, his eyes bright with his laughter. Lou, no more than eight at the time, was tucked under one of his muscular arms.

She wondered if she would have forgotten his face—as she had her mother's—if not for this photo.

Jack Thorne. He was young when he was murdered by the mafia—by Konstantine's family.

The dream pressed in on her again, a white shirt soaking through with blood. The *pop-pop-pop* of gunfire. Angelo's phantom face.

"Stop it," she whispered to the dark. *You didn't even see him get shot.*

The moment that Angelo had burst through the back gate one late summer night in June, her father had lifted and thrown her into their pool, knowing the waters would save her.

How often had Lou wondered if, had he simply jumped into the water with her—if only to shield her body with his own—he might have survived. Perhaps she would've been able to take them both away.

But Lou hadn't been able to successfully carry anything through the dark with her until she was older. That was probably why these fantasies of saving her father were so few and far between these days. No matter how she turned the memory—and hadn't she turned it every way imaginable?—it always came out the same.

Jack Thorne had made his choices. And Louie had been left to live with them.

So why the dreams? she wondered, looking at the swirled patterns in her ceiling.

Lou knew her mind well enough to know when it was signaling something to her. It was trying to bring something up from its murky depths into the light of Lou's awareness.

But the message wasn't yet clear to her, and forcing it wouldn't make the revelation come any faster.

Finding the pillows flat and the comforter suffocating, Lou stood and stretched. She checked the time again.

4:08.

She got a drink of water. She placed the empty glass on the counter.

Without consciously deciding to, she let her apartment dissolve around her once more. The granite countertops and water-stained glass faded from her view. In its place, a shadowed bedroom rose to meet her.

Coarse carpet formed under her feet. In front of her, a queen bed sat center stage in a small bedroom. Beneath a purple comforter, a blond head poked out. Lou traced the outline of the bed, noting the closed laptop and textbooks covering one side.

She moved these to the floor, lifted the comforter, and slid in.

The girl woke immediately.

"Lou?" Piper raised her head. She blinked and wiped her eyes.

"Yeah."

"What's wrong? Did—"

"Everything's fine," Lou said to counter the girl's rising alarm.

"Oh." Piper's frown deepened. "You okay?"

"I couldn't sleep."

Piper lifted the sheets, frowning. "Whose clothes are you wearing? No, don't tell me. You smell like *man*."

Lou snorted.

But Piper's humor didn't hold. "Seriously, are you okay?"

"I'm fine." Lou tucked the pillow under her head. "Why are you looking at me like that?"

Piper propped her head in her hand. "I don't know. It's dark in here, so I can't see your face really well, but you look...weird."

"Thanks."

"I mean, your face is fine, but you look upset. Did you have a bad hunt or something?"

Lou thought of Walker's last pitiful screams before Jabber's milk-white maw wrapped around his throat.

"No," she said.

Piper finally lowered her head to the pillow, fluffing it for added height. "So there's nothing you want to talk about? No feelings you're dealing with? No explanation as to why you smell like some Italian dude and are clearly wearing his clothes, but you just climbed in bed with a lesbian in the dead of night? *No?* Everything is *perfectly* fine, is it?"

"I'm fine," Lou said, noting her own defensiveness.

Piper snorted. "I'm not sure if you're aware, but you *do* have emotions, Lou-blue. Like everyone else. Maybe you want to check in on them once in a while."

Lou thought of the dream again. Of her father's startled cry before he lifted her into his arms and threw her into the family pool—even if it was to save her life. "I had a bad dream. That's all."

As soon as she said it, she felt stupid.

Piper's face softened. "What kind of bad dream?"

"The night my parents were killed."

Piper sat up, exhaling. "Why are you dreaming about the night you lost everything? Did something scare you?"

"No."

Piper was undeterred. She lowered her voice conspiratorially. "Are you sure? What did you do tonight?"

"I went to the bar and got Walker—"

Piper clucked her tongue. "*No.* What did you do with *Konstantine?* Did you have sex?"

"No."

"No, I guess having sex wouldn't send you running to my bed in the middle of the night." She broke into a huge grin. "*Or would it?* Was it *bad* sex?"

"No." Lou gave her a dangerous look.

Piper only laughed. "Oh man. You're killing me. Listen, you just need to listen to yourself. Figure out how you feel. That's what I'm trying to do."

Lou frowned. "With who?"

Piper put one hand under her head and snorted. "Freaking Dani. I mean, why does she have to be so beautiful and intelligent. And have you seen her hands? They're so pretty. And she kisses like—"

Lou sat up in bed. "Do you want me to leave? It sounds like you need to be alone. Or I could go get her."

Piper elbowed her under the covers. "Don't even joke about that. Besides, you're the one who *didn't* have sex and then decided to come sleep with a lesbian."

Lou elbowed her.

Piper folded, protecting her ribs. "Don't worry. I'm not going to let you do what I do in these situations."

"What do you do?"

"Run off and sleep with someone else. That's how I roll."

Lou only frowned harder.

"Seriously, ever since Dani showed up, I've been thinking about calling my ex about twenty times a day. I know, I know. It's not healthy. Unless you're here for some distraction too, because if you *are...*"

Piper puckered up and leaned in for a kiss.

Lou pushed her off, smiling.

Piper continued making dramatic kissy faces until Lou had the pillow pressed firmly over her face. After a momentary struggle, Piper tapped out.

Once the laughter had died and they'd settled back down to their own sides of the bed, Piper spoke up once more.

"Listen. We are smart, capable women. We'll conquer this bullshit. At least we aren't psychopaths."

"I murder people."

"Yeah, but you've also got some empathy. Lady loves you, and dogs are never wrong." Piper adjusted her head on her pillow. "You're worlds apart from trash humans like Jeffrey fucking Fish. Oh, do you want to know what I found out about him today?"

Lou turned on her side to face her. "Yes."

"In high school he worked part time in a cemetery. Two cemeteries, actually, that were side by side. One for people, one for pets. It looks like he was there for about a year before he got fired."

Lou's compass stretched out through space and time, locking on

Fish. But there was no immediate thrum of danger. No doubt he would make his move soon, but at least for tonight, the beast was still caged.

"Can you guess why he got fired?" Piper asked, rolling on her side to face Lou.

Lou thought of the photographs again. The glossy sheen capturing the pain and fear on the women's faces. Their tear-stained faces. The spit drying on their lips and chins from so much screaming.

"No," she said.

"He was caught digging up the graves. Digging them up so he could look at the decomposing bodies. What a freak!"

Lou thought of the grocer standing in her bedroom window, face scrubbed for the night. She didn't want her to become another photograph in Fish's collection.

She couldn't let that happen.

Piper placed a hand on Lou's arm. "We'll stop him before he hurts that girl. You're amazing, and I'm going to help you get the evidence you need. We've got this. But first, we have to sleep."

Sleep, Lou thought, and worried she wouldn't be able to manage it in this bed either.

But she was wrong.

14

———————

King reached into his fridge and grabbed the cold neck of a soda bottle. He twisted the cap off with the end of his shirt and threw it into the sink. The first deep gulps were delicious, even if they did burn his throat.

He'd left the office for a mid-day lunch. It was a perk he enjoyed as the boss with the added convenience of living around the corner from the agency.

With a satisfied sigh, he put the soda down and unwrapped two leftover steak enchiladas. He removed the aluminum foil before popping them into the microwave.

That's when he caught Lady's steady gaze. She was too proud—or well trained—to outright beg, but King was no fool.

"Oh, all right." He reached into the cabinet beside his stove. He drew out a long rawhide bone and held it in front of her snout. "Will this do?"

She closed her jaws around the bone, her tail swishing gleefully behind her as she took her prize over to the rug. She stretched long, her hind legs thrown out behind her.

With seconds left on his lunch, King's phone rang. There was no number, which was enough to tell King exactly who was calling. "King here."

"Good evening," a man said. The lilting Italian accent gave his words a melodic quality. "I have the information you asked for."

"That was quick." King's enchiladas beeped. He grabbed a plate from the cabinet and dumped them from their wax carton onto the plate before fishing through a drawer for a fork.

"What's for lunch?" Konstantine asked, obviously having heard the microwave ding.

"Mexican." King found his fork and shut the drawer. "So what can you tell me about those drugs?"

"They were mine," Konstantine said plainly.

King's fork hovered above the enchiladas. "Really?"

"Yes," he said with a hint of amusement in his voice. "But I didn't make the kill personally, if that is your next question."

King saw Rita Cross's slack jaw and one gold tooth. His stomach soured.

He'd never be so bold as to outright accuse the Ravengers' kingpin of murder, but King also wasn't stupid. There was no doubt in his mind that he had blood on his hands. Perhaps not as much as Lou personally, but enough.

"Why were they killed?"

"He was stealing the drugs, and she was in the home when they came for him."

He says it so matter-of-factly.

"And where is the man responsible? Do you know?"

"I'm afraid that if you go looking for him, you will not find him," Konstantine said.

King sank onto his sofa, placing his plate on the coffee table in front of him. He put his soda on a Margaritaville coaster and threw his fork onto the plate. The anger building inside him made the enchiladas less appealing.

"Convenient." He consciously unclenched his jaw. "Did you see the handiwork yourself?"

"No."

"It was brutal. The woman..." He lifted his fork and put it on the plate again. "It was bad. Did you tell them to kill her?"

"No. I do not condone violence against women. And daily operations of my territories aren't my responsibility. I do delegate that."

Daily operations. *Christ.* King dragged his hand down his face, trying to clear the image of the fly landing on Cross's toe.

"When a man steals from our organization, as Shawn Mince did, there are consequences, Mr. King. If the consequences aren't severe, more people would steal, don't you agree?"

King marveled that a world as lawless as the drug trade relied so heavily on order, but it made a certain amount of sense. In the Ravengers, Konstantine might be CEO. His managers weren't going to ask him to discipline an employee who'd stolen a stapler. King supposed he had bigger problems to contend with.

"So his name was Shawn Mince and he was stealing the drugs from the Ravengers?"

"Given the quantity found, it seems that he was taking them for a long time."

"Why did he keep them rather than sell them?"

"There was likely no opportunity for him to sell without being discovered. He tried and was caught."

"So your manager handled the problem?"

"Manager?"

"Drug mule. Lackey. Local boss. Whoever is in charge here in New Orleans. This guy discovered that Mince was stealing and he made an example of him."

"Yes."

King patted his pocket, looking for his notebook and pen. "Any chance I can get the name of the guy who cut up Rita Cross? He deserves to be taken in, don't you think?"

Konstantine's voice crackled across the line.

"You there?" King checked the bar strength on his phone. Damn dead spots. "Hold on. You're breaking up."

King stood, glancing at the urn.

"Keep an eye on that, would you?" He motioned toward his lunch.

King opened the French doors and stepped out onto his balcony.

The cold February air nipped his cheeks and ears. He flipped up the collar on his coat, realizing now that he'd never taken it off, and checked the phone again.

"You still there?"

"I'm here," Konstantine replied, his voice clear as a bell.

"I want his name."

"I cannot give you a name."

King wrapped a hand around the balcony. Red pressed in on the corner of his vision. "I suppose this is about the drugs. It's a lot of drugs to lose."

"Did I lose them?" Konstantine asked.

King heard the smile in his voice.

Then he realized this wasn't about the drugs or the murder.

King leaned a hip into the balcony. "Do you own the *entire* NOLA PD or just a few of the officers?"

"You're confusing me with Dmitri Petrov, Mr. King. I am not in the business of owning anyone."

"So the cops just take all the drugs out of the house, pack them up, and what, ship them to your local supplier?"

Konstantine said nothing.

King opened his mouth to dig deeper—he wanted the name of Rita Cross's killer, damn it—but a man on the street below caught his eye.

He was tall, lean, with a bone choker tight across his throat. His leather hat had a crow feather protruding from its left side.

King first noted the lack of a coat. True, it was warmer in New Orleans than, say, Chicago, but one didn't walk around bare-armed even in the crowded Quarter. Not in February.

In the light from the convenience store window, King thought he could make out the hazy outline of a prison tattoo. But it wasn't clear from where he stood.

The man was watching Madame Melandra's Fortunes and Fixes with a hungry expression that King didn't like one bit. As if sensing eyes on him, the man looked up suddenly and met King's gaze.

The smile that spread across his face, a scarecrow's smile, made the hair on the back of King's neck rise.

"The fact remains that a woman was killed. Brutally," King said, but the anger in his voice had cooled. "Forget about the drugs for a second and think about her."

"I assure you that the man responsible for her murder will be handled. I cannot control the actions of every man I employ. I can only make my *sentiments* known."

So your guy makes an example of Shawn Mince and then you make an example of your guy, King thought. It was a stark reminder, should King have made the mistake of thinking Konstantine was only a diplomat.

A low growl made King look down. Lady's nose was stuck between the balcony's slats. If King didn't know better, she was following the man with her gaze.

"Yeah, he looks like trouble," King agreed, giving the dog a pat on the head.

"Excuse me?"

King turned back to the conversation. "If you can't give me names, I guess we're done here."

"I regret that I cannot help you in your investigation. But I assure you the man has been punished."

Tell that to Rita Cross.

"Is there anything else I can do for you, Mr. King?" Konstantine said.

King searched the swelling crowd for the man with a crow feather in his hat. "Actually, there is one more thing you could do."

15

———

Someone knocked on the door. Lou turned toward the sound, toothbrush in hand. Her foaming mouth frowned. This was the second time in twice as many years that someone had knocked on her apartment. Her instinctual response was to run. Simply step into her converted linen closet and disappear.

Instead she crept toward the front door.

The last time someone had come, it had been a law firm courier, delivering letters from her dead aunt. But Aunt Lucy was in her grave —or urn, so to speak—along with her parents. There wasn't anyone left to send letters. And Lou had never given her address to anyone else.

She looked through the peephole. A woman with a bouquet of flowers and a blue denim hat stood on the other side. *ABC Florists* was stitched into the cap's bill with red thread.

Tired of waiting, the woman put the vase on the floor, wedged the card between the jamb and frame, and left. Lou waited until she heard the stairwell door clank closed before she opened the door.

The card fell face down onto the industrial carpet. Lou picked it up along with the vase.

Her first emotion: *annoyance*.

Lou carried the flowers inside. *Why would he bother?*

Lou appraised the gift. It was a strange vase. Large and wooden with intricate carvings on its sides. The explosion of garden roses, carnations, pink lilies, alstroemeria, baby's breath, greenery, and a few flowers Lou didn't recognize on sight.

Then a phone began to ring.

Lou cocked her head, locating the sound before lifting the vase. Taped to the bottom of the vase was a burner flip phone. She let it ring while she rinsed her mouth in the kitchen sink.

Lou answered on the sixth ring, certain she knew who was calling. "How did you figure out my address?"

"Do you like the flowers?" Konstantine countered.

"*How* did you get my address?" Because Lou had been careful, long before Konstantine had taken it upon himself to scour the world on her behalf, to keep her whereabouts untraceable.

"The law firm who manages your father's estate and trust have a list of properties. Five are located in your area. I used internet maps to figure out which one was you. Only one fit."

When she'd let him heal in her bed after Nico's assassination attempt, he would've seen the skyline for himself. Who else had been in this apartment? Lucy, King. She should've known the view was a liability.

"You don't know what I like," she said plainly, even as she leaned in to smell a gorgeous peach garden rose.

"No?" His voice was full of amusement. "Did I get the flowers or the colors wrong?"

She didn't humor him with a reply, but inwardly she thought, *Color.* These blooms were too soft and feminine. She preferred deep reds and purples.

"Perhaps you'll like what's in the box better? Can you figure out how to open it?"

She frowned at the arrangement. "There's no box."

"The vase," he said after some hesitation.

She traced the whirls etched into the wood, feeling for any loose seams. One small node, and another shifted slightly under her finger-tips as she passed over it. She went back and pressed them again.

One then the other, and when that did not work, both at the same time.

Something clicked. The wooden panel slid away.

Lou removed the pistol. It was a standard Hi-Power Browning. She palmed the walnut grip and noted the adjustable sights.

"They discontinued these," Lou said. "How did you find a new one?"

"Almost new," Konstantine corrected. "Very gently used."

Lou was certain that guns were never *gently* used but didn't argue. She appreciated the weight of the Browning in her hand.

"There are two," Konstantine said. "The hammers have been replaced to prevent them from biting your hand."

"Do you think I don't know how to hold it?" Lou inspected the wooden vase again and discovered the second secret panel.

"No," he said. Then after a short pause, he added, "What do you think?"

That I guess you do know what I like.

Lou had heard something in his voice then. But he'd covered it so quickly she couldn't be sure.

"I think...I'd love to see what you can fit in a box of chocolates."

He laughed at her joke, but it was too tight. It wasn't the easy vibrato that she enjoyed.

When the laughter died away and the silence stretched itself long, Konstantine said, "When will I see you again?"

Was that what this gift was about?

She hadn't returned to his bed since the night in the shower. She hadn't slipped there by accident—at least, not that she was aware—not even to say hello.

Maybe that was what she heard in his voice.

"When do you go to Venice?" she asked instead.

"Tonight," he said. "For three nights at most. Vittoria..."

The hair rose on the back of Lou's neck at the way he said her name.

"She's *very* challenging," he said with a tender laugh.

"Have a good trip." She regarded the beautiful pistols in her grip, preparing to end the call.

"Wait, Lou."

Lou put the phone to her ear again. When she thought he wasn't going to say anything else, he finally added, "I hope I see you in Venice."

Lou decided to take the Browning pistols with her to check on Fish. She crossed to her kitchen island and unhooked a small latch tucked beneath the lip of the counter.

The side sprang free and Lou descended the steps into its darkness. Even years after building this room, it still smelled of sawdust and soft pine. She breathed deeply, loving the scent.

She found the string overhead on the first try and pulled, illuminating her hidden storeroom.

Guns lined the shelves neatly. A belt of grenades hung from a hook on the wall, as well as her father's service vest. She touched it tenderly, without realizing she'd done so, as she reached out for a box of 9mm bullets. She loaded both Brownings.

She considered the weaponry lining the shelves but decided the guns would do.

It was early in the day, which made it harder for her to move around. But daytime also meant less chance of serious trouble. A flamethrower, grenades, or heavy artillery of any kind simply wouldn't be feasible.

Night was easier.

Upstairs, with the island sealed again, Lou put the Brownings in her shoulder holster. She placed one on each side. It was true she was ambidextrous when it came to shooting. She'd trained hard on both sides of her body, but she favored her right. She slid the leather jacket on, covering the guns, and added her mirrored sunglasses as a finishing touch.

Stepping into her dark linen closet, she breathed a nervous sigh. Even after all this time, after more than fifteen years of hunting men, she still got excited. It didn't even have to be the killing moment. The stalking, the watching—all parts of the chase were enough.

No one else would notice the electricity in her fingertips, or the way her heart sped slightly in her chest. But she did.

She was most herself when in search of something. There was no denying it.

She leaned against the bare wall, smelling the cedar sachet she'd thrown in the bottom of the converted closet. She reached out and touched the rough wall, feeling wood grain pull at her fingertips. Her nails caught on the end of a brace, one of the four that used to hold up shelves before Lou removed them.

She closed her eyes, focusing on that compass inside her. She willed it to hone in on Fish. After a moment of cool darkness, a sense of floating in black waters, the tug came. A pin was dropped in the map of her mind and she felt the currents of those waters shift direction like rounding a river bend.

She let go of her hold on the world, parting the shadows around her, and slipped through. When Lou found herself in the solid world again, her little closet had expanded by three or four times its size.

The only light in the room came from beneath the crack in the door. Lou stepped toward it, groping at the wall until she found a light switch.

A bathroom sprang into view. A single toilet beside a safety bar was in the left corner behind her. Adjacent to that sat a white sink beneath a mirror. Smeared soap creased its corners.

Lou pushed the door open a crack.

It was a hallway full of shuffling bodies. Teenagers opened and slammed lockers. Books were shoved roughly into backpacks.

In the sea of bodies, Lou spotted Fish. He stood a head taller than most of the teens. They parted around him like water around a boulder.

Surveying him there, shoulder to shoulder with a brunette girl, pointing out something in the textbook she held open in her palms, Lou understood why her compass had selected this bathroom.

Light from the hall's windows struck him in all directions. It sprang from open classrooms and the fluorescents beating down from above. There was no way she could've gotten closer to him.

Fish reached forward to turn the textbook's page. Lou didn't miss the way his shoulder brushed the girl's. Nor did she miss the nervous smile that reflexively crossed the student's lips.

Even from where she hid in the bathroom, Lou saw the gauze peeking out from under his light purple dress shirt.

What do you tell them, Fish? she wondered. *Oh, that? It's nothing. I cut myself working in the garage.* Or perhaps to his little wife, *I've been pretending to make your kitchen island for six months so that I have an excuse to stare at my precious photographs. It's better than slitting this pretty girl's throat, isn't it?*

How many monsters simply walked the world as this man did? Hidden in plain sight, in classrooms or offices or marital beds.

Fish licked his lips, laughing at something the girl said. Lou understood the look in his eyes and was certain that she was one of the few people in the world who knew it for what it was. Hunger.

You're playing with your food, Fish.

Lou's head throbbed. Her fingers itched to pull her gun. She became hyperaware of a thunderous pulse in her throat and her own gnawing hunger in her guts.

She wanted him. She wanted to take him right here and now to her own special place. She wanted to hurt him, watch him cry, watch him beg.

We're playing a different game, King had said.

Lou hoped Fish was about to lose.

There were signs he might. His polished edges were wearing away, visible in the deepening dark circles beneath his eyes. His once clean and clipped nails had been recently chewed. The thumb in particular looked savaged, the cuticle red and pulled back.

Does anyone else see these things? Or is it only me? And then, *He's trying. He's trying to hold himself back.*

And who was she to judge? Hadn't she been pacing her apartment just an hour before?

Do you think his craving is stronger or weaker than yours? a voice asked. It sounded suspiciously like Aunt Lucy's voice of reason. Aunt Lucy's kind patience was enough to tug at her heart. It was enough to stunt the hunger building inside her. And it was typical of Lucy to bring compassion to any moment like this. *Do you like how it feels when you're that restless?*

The crack through which Lou surveyed Fish's world suddenly widened.

A teenager in hot pink pants stepped back, surprised.

"God, lock the door!" the girl huffed. Her bright eyeshadow creased with her scowl. As her eyes roved Lou's body, the scowl only deepened. "This is the *handicap* bathroom, lady. Are you even—"

Lou pulled the door shut but didn't lock it. Instead, she hit the light switch and was gone.

16

————————

A sharp voice pulled Mel from her thoughts. "Mr. Rushdie can see you now."

A receptionist with bushy eyebrows regarded Mel over his computer. His gelled hair was slicked back from his face and his gaze was indifferent at best. Mel wondered how long this one would last, as it seemed that Rushdie had a new receptionist every time she visited the cramped little office downtown.

Mel rose from her seat in the waiting area and threw a nervous glance at the three fake plants against the far wall before reaching the mahogany door at the end of the room. It opened before her fingers could clasp the handle.

"Ms. Durand." The balding man extended his liver-spotted hand toward her. "Come on in now."

"Thank you for making the time to see me." Melandra sidestepped through the narrow doorway into the cramped office so that the lawyer could close the door behind her.

The desk sagged with stacks of file folders one on top of the other. Some stacks looked quite precarious, on the verge of tumbling onto the floor. The filing cabinets behind the desk, all as tall as she was, looked no better. Some of the drawers didn't even close. Tabs protruded from them at unkempt angles like crooked teeth.

"I understand you want some legal advice about your business and husband." Rushdie shuffled past her, his head half-tucked like a turtle's. One of his shoulders hiked up, giving him an uneven walk just short of a hunchback.

"Please sit down," he said when he came around the desk and found her still standing awkwardly in the middle of the room, wringing her hands. "We're all friends here."

Mel forced a smile and obediently perched on the edge of one of the stiff chairs.

Rushdie seemed to sense that further encouragement was needed. "Why don't you tell me what's on your mind?"

She licked her lips. "My husband"—*God*, she loathed to say the word—"just got out of prison, and now he's here in New Orleans."

"Is this a happy reunion?"

"No," Mel freely admitted. "No, not at all."

"You've seen him?" Rushdie was searching the papers on his desk, looking for something.

"A few times. He's been trying to...harass me into giving him money and says he is entitled to part of my business because we're married."

Rushdie settled on a piece of paper, lifting it closer to his bespectacled eyes. "Is this the gentleman you came to me about in ninety-nine?"

"Yes," Melandra said. Though she thought the word *gentleman* was a gross and inaccurate description for Terry.

"He was already in prison then?" He eyed Melandra over his thick spectacles. His mouth hung open in a heavy pant.

"Correct."

"And your little shop is something you built while he was in prison."

Mel tried not to stiffen at the patronizing "little shop" comment. Maybe it wasn't much to this guy, but she'd worked hard to get her business off the ground and keep it off the ground.

Rushdie leaned back in his chair. "I remember you cancelling the divorce proceedings in ninety-nine, but if you've changed your mind and want to pursue divorce, we can certainly begin those proceedings now. And we can make the case in court that you're a good, hard-working woman who doesn't deserve to give half her livelihood to such a man. It helps that he was in jail for so long. It will be easier to paint the picture of why you shouldn't have to share. But Ms. Durand, they're going to ask why you didn't divorce him sooner."

Of course they'll ask, and what the hell am I supposed to say?

Rushdie arched his brows. "Did you still love him, perhaps?"

The attorney's slow, southern drawl gave the impression of mock sympathy.

Mel straightened. "No."

Rushdie nodded as if he'd expected this. "All right. Did he threaten or coerce you into staying? He has the history of violence against you, does he not? And let me be honest here. Even if that's not the story, we might want to embellish, if you know what I'm saying."

Mel wasn't sure how much Rushdie remembered from the murder trial that eventually led to Terrence's incarceration. So she briefly retold him the story.

She began with the affair, with the hickeys on his neck and finding his parked car outside Sholanda's trailer on many a night when Terry said he'd gone to the bar.

What she *didn't* say was how she'd gone to the trailer herself one morning. After she'd waited in the gravel drive for fifteen minutes, working up the courage to knock, Sholanda had opened the door first. The woman had known perfectly well who Mel was. She'd offered her sweet tea in a plastic tumbler and waited until Mel managed to ask in perfect calm, "Do you love him?"

Sholanda said that she did.

"Even though he did that to you?" Mel had pointed at the black bruise spreading across Sholanda's right cheek.

"Even so," the girl had said. And Mel felt like she'd never understood another person so deeply in her life than she had in that moment.

And Melandra—God forgive her—didn't mind the affair.

For one, she was no longer the target of Terry's drunken assaults. Years of being forced onto the mattress or struck across the face, shoulders, and back had slowed from every day, to weekly, to monthly, until nothing at all. He still took her money. He still pawned anything of value that she didn't carefully hide away. But that felt like such a minor insult after everything else.

Mel left Sholanda's trailer that day without having drunk the tea, and it was the last time she saw the woman alive.

A year later, Terry beat the girl to death. She'd been four months pregnant with his child.

To all this, Rushdie only shrugged. "Has he hurt you since he's got out of prison?"

Mel shook her head. Though she thought of the snarl on his face as he'd thrown her into the wall outside her shop and the way he'd grabbed her wrist before that.

Rushdie sucked his teeth. "Too bad. But we can still make all the arguments. It's really just a matter of how well we prove your virtue and his indecency. The good news is that he's got quite the track record of indecency. We only have to hope that he doesn't try and play the *reformed* card."

He reached for the cigarettes on his desk.

He paused, rolling his hound-dog eyes up to Mel's. "Do you mind?"

"Not if you give me one." Mel's bangles clanked on her wrist as she reached forward.

Rushdie grinned. "Why yes, of course. I think my office might be the last public place in the whole state of Louisiana where smoking is allowed."

Mel smiled, accepting the cigarette offered.

"Here now," he said, coming out of his seat with the lighter in one hand.

Mel leaned forward, letting him light the end of her cigarette.

Something about the scene reminded her of Grandmamie's porch. Of some hot summer day, or at least, it seemed like all her days in the parish bayou were hot summer days.

She'd just finished collecting the chicken eggs as she was told to do, dumping them carefully from a faded apron into a basket by the front door.

"You missed one," Grandmamie had said from her place on the

porch step. She'd pointed a crooked finger at a patch of high grass in the yard. "There."

Of course, her grandmother was right. Grandmamie was always right.

"After supper you make sure those chickens end up back in the coop now. Latch that door tight." She flicked her ash. "I've seen them racoons running around here. And a fox too. Can't have them eating our girls, now can we?"

Mel had been watching the thin gray smoke rise from the cigarette between the old woman's fingers. "What are them like?"

"What are what like?" Grandmamie asked. Her dark eyes narrowed. She glanced at the cigarette. "This?"

"Yeah. You're always smokin' them. Do they taste good?"

Grandmamie laughed. It was a dry, cracked sound, like leather left out too long in the sun. "No, they don't taste good."

"Then why you smoke 'em?"

"Because I'm stupid. And stupid people do stupid things."

"Can I try it?" Mel said.

"You want to be a stupid person too?" Grandmamie cackled. Her eyes regarded Mel in that steady, sure way of theirs. "If I let you take a puff, will you promise not to smoke them ever again?"

"What if I like them?"

"Do you *promise?*" Grandmamie grinned. "Yes or no, girl?"

"All right," Mel said, already sensing some sly trick to the promise. Grandmamie had had a way of running her crooked fingers through her short gray curls when she was up to mischief.

Mel came forward, leaning to take her promised puff on the cigarette.

Grandmamie clucked, snatching it back. "Don't wrap your whole damn mouth around it like that. Just a bit of lips. Heaven."

Frowning, Mel tried again, feeling her braids slide over her shoulder as she leaned forward. The plastic beads clinked together.

She inhaled and felt the white-hot burn of the smoke hit her throat. It spasmed, giving over to ragged coughs.

Grandmamie smiled her slyest smile yet.

"That's....*awful,*" Mel managed between choked gasps.

"Remember that next time you want one. They'll kill you. Turn your insides black. Make you cough until you hurt. Stain those pretty teeth yellow."

Mel tried to nod, to say she understood, but she couldn't stop coughing. Tears streamed from her eyes.

Finally she realized the sound stinging her ears was her grandmother's laughter.

"You knew it would hurt me." Mel wiped at her eyes and spat on the ground. "So why you'd let me do it?"

"Ain't no use telling you something once you get it in your head. You're just like me that way."

Mel remembered the regret and weariness in Grandmamie's eyes when she'd said that. But there had also been tenderness Mel didn't understand until she was much, much older. Years after Grandmamie had died, and Terry had gone to prison.

"You're doing that thing you do," Mel had said, straightening. She pushed her braids back from her face and glared at her grandmama. She spit on the ground again, hoping that would get the taste out of her mouth. It'd been like eating dirt.

"What's that thing I do?" Grandmamie paused to pluck a piece of stray tobacco off her tongue. Mel mimicked her, thinking maybe that was how she got rid of the taste.

This only made her grandmother laugh harder. "You ain't got no tobacco in your mouth. Show some sense."

"You're the one letting fourteen-year-olds smoke!"

Grandmamie gave her a warning look. While she had always been kind and patient, backtalk was not tolerated. "What's 'that thing I do'?"

"Where you is tellin' me somethin' and not tellin' me somethin' at the same time."

"I suppose I am." She flicked her ash again, watching it fall onto the porch step before wiping it away with her sandal. "Come over here and hear the truth then. You're old enough."

Whenever Grandmamie had treated her like an adult, Melandra had never been able to resist it. Now, looking back, Melandra suspected that Grandmamie was well aware of this fact.

Grandmamie had rummaged in her black purse, the one they'd gotten from the $1 bin at the Salvation Army. She'd pulled out a slick deck of cards wrapped in black cloth.

"You know my cards will be your cards one day," Grandmamie said, holding her cigarette between her lips. It bobbed as she spoke. "I'm going to leave them to you when I die."

Mel hadn't been able to imagine a world in which her grandmother, as battle-worn as any general, could *die*. Yet Grandmamie was dead three years later.

"Why me?" Mel had dared to ask. Grandmamie had despised compliment-seeking all her life, and in a way, Mel knew that this question could be mistaken for such.

But Grandmamie only arched a clever brow. "Why not your aunties Simone or Adele? Or your cousins? Maybe you think I favor your mother over my other children?"

It was true that Melandra had been the only child of Grandmamie's eldest, Melva. But Melandra didn't think that made her a favorite. In fact, Melandra would've bet a great deal of money—had she had any— that the only thing Grandmamie carried in her heart for Melva was heartache. And all five of her cousins were little. The closest to her in age—Janie—was only seven.

"I want to give you these because you're the only one like me." Grandmamie snuffed out her cigarette in a glass ashtray resting on the top step and gave her a hard look. "I think you know what I mean by that."

Of course Melandra knew.

"But let me tell you a secret," Grandmamie said, leaning close and leveling Mel with a stare that would straighten any spine. "We may have a lot of vision, we may see a lot of what other folks don't, but we've also got a big ol' blind spot right here, you hear me?"

Grandmamie had touched her heart.

"Shuffle them."

Grandmamie handed over the cards then. Mel was impressed by how big they were in her hands, and how heavy, and did as she was told.

"Now flip over the top three."

Again Mel obeyed.

Grandmamie clucked her tongue. "The Devil. Justice. Death. You go in deep with a bad man when you're young. Not even twenty, by the looks of it. And you stay in deep with him for most of your life. Only death gonna get you out."

"No, I won't. I won't *fall* for nobody."

Grandmamie spared her a sad smile.

Mel stood up. "You said the tarot is a guide, not a sentence."

"Your life is your own."

"Then I won't choose no devil." Melandra stamped her foot down on the wooden step so hard the ashtray bounced.

Grandmamie gathered up the cards and tucked them back into her purse. "Maybe you can break the cycle, but every Durand woman I can think of, as far back as I can know, has been stupid about love. Sometimes I think we're cursed."

And like every other instance in Mel's life, Grandmamie had been right. If only Mel had remembered the conversation the day Terry pulled up in his red Firebird.

Rushdie spoke, yanking Mel through the decades, back to the warm and cramped attorney's office. "Bottom line is, don't let men like that scare you, Ms. Durand. If he ain't got nothing on you, you have nothing to worry about. He's got no case."

Mel saw his Firebird parked in Grandmamie's driveway. She saw the black dress she wore the day of her grandmother's funeral as she stepped out onto the porch to greet him.

She heard the squeal of brakes, felt the car rock on impact.

But he does have something on me, Mel thought bitterly. *He really does.*

17

———

Lady placed her heavy snout on King's knee. He looked away from his laptop and regarded the sad, desperate eyes. "Need a walk? Er, *promenade?*"

She sat back on her heels and shook her head. King knew this to be *yes*.

He regarded the case file he'd been annotating. It was as good a place to pause as any. "All right. I could use a break too."

He wouldn't mind a coffee and maybe even a snack. The afternoon slump was getting to him. Usually he powered through with a short nap, but since Piper had been working at the shop today, he hadn't wanted to walk away from the office. But a short thirty minutes or so would help his productivity and carry him until five or six.

"Come on then."

King closed his laptop, locked it in his industrial desk, and checked his coat pocket for his keys and wallet. Confirming he had all that he needed, he stepped out of the Crescent City Detective Agency and into the Quarter's crowded streets. He bumped shoulders immediately with a tall man holding a plastic container of booze.

The reveler looked ready to say something to King until he turned and took in the full size of the man standing before him. Then Lady began to growl.

"You all right?" King asked with a cocked eyebrow.

"Yeah, I'm all right." The man turned away to rejoin his friends.

To King, who was doing his best to remain sober these days, Carnival was a particularly trying time. It wasn't just that alcohol in the Quarter spiked—it was that the flush of open drunkenness left him feeling like the only sober guy at the party. It was a feeling he'd never enjoyed.

"I'm going to need that paczki now," King muttered to himself. "A nice powdery one with raspberry filling. What do you think?"

Lady had wandered forward to squat beside a trash can.

King had his coffee twenty minutes later and was feeling more alert. He'd even forgotten the ache in his lower back, which had been aggravating him since the weather turned cold back in November.

He was standing outside the French Market, watching girls in Carnival masks haggle with a merchant about the price of a shoulder bag, when Mel appeared. She stepped out of a bank with a stack of empty deposit bags in her hand, pulling the door closed behind her.

"Hey," King said, smiling. There was a certain pleasure in seeing a friendly face he hadn't been expecting. He crossed the walkway to her. "Bank run?"

"I've only got Piper until two. Thought I'd handle it before she left for the agency."

King had forgotten about that. It was past 1:30 now.

"Can I walk you back?" he asked. He thought he smelled cigarettes on her hair, which was strange. King knew she didn't smoke.

"Sure." But she didn't start walking. Instead she bent to scratch Lady's ears. Her bangles rolled forward on her wrists, creating a beautiful musical melody that King deeply enjoyed.

Lady pressed her head into Mel's hand.

"*Ma grande,*" Mel murmured. "*Tu es une bonne chienne, non?*"

Lady's tail thumped against King's leg.

King harrumphed. "I would be jealous if I hadn't gotten Lady for the both of us."

After Dmitri Petrov and his goons came to King's apartment and abducted them, he'd decided it was definitely time to invest in a guard dog. But Lady was becoming more pet than working dog.

King would be lying if he said he wasn't a little lonely on the nights Lady slept in Melandra's apartment. He often found himself glancing at the empty dog bed, knowing that Lady probably preferred Mel—who let her sleep in the bed.

Mel snapped her fingers, and Lady fell into step beside her as they began their stroll back toward Royal Street.

From the corner of his eye, King took Mel's measure. He saw the deep purple beneath her eyes that she'd tried to hide with makeup and her dry, dehydrated lips, which she kept chewing nervously.

"You been sleeping okay?" King asked. He pretended to be more interested in his coffee than her.

"No. I'll be glad when Carnival is over."

She took a step to the right to let a group of teens pass.

King scratched the back of his head. "We'll get a short reprieve before St. Patrick's Day."

"I don't mind the short festivals," Mel said. "It's when they carry on for weeks like this. The Carnival and Christmas sprints are what do in my old bones."

King laughed. "If you're old, what am I?"

She shot him a warning look, even though she was at least fourteen years his junior.

King spotted a tall man leaning in a doorway, a cowboy hat perched on his head. It wasn't *that* man, but it was close enough to remind King what was really bothering him, buzzing like a fly in the back of his mind.

"I've been seeing a guy hanging around the shop," King said. He'd turned his chin just enough to watch her expression without giving himself away.

Her face tightened. "Oh yeah?"

"You know him? Because he seems to know you."

Mel clasped her opposite elbow. "I know him."

"Who is he?"

"Not someone worth talking about."

Jackson Square broke open in front of them. The line from Café du

Monde cut across their path, snaking around the artists selling paintings and trinkets perfectly sized to fit into one's carry-on bag. A saxophone whined out of sight.

"Is it the same guy that came into the shop? The one who was giving you trouble?" he asked.

He enjoyed the click of Lady's nails against the stones, even over all the other noises threatening to drown it out.

"I'll handle him," Mel said. "You're busy enough."

"I've always got time for my friends, Mel."

Again her face tightened, and King struggled to understand what he was seeing. Anger? Remorse?

Even as they crossed onto Royal Street, he was none the wiser. The truth of the situation remained just beyond his reach. He grasped for it once, twice, but found only darkness.

His agency came into view.

"Is it serious?"

Mel whirled on him, and now he had no doubt that it was anger on her face. "I told you, I'll handle it."

Lady's ears flicked back against her head.

"Okay." King stopped in front of his door. "Message received. I'll stay out of it."

"Thank you."

"But I'll see you tonight, right?" King asked, sensing that their time together had ended.

Mel frowned. "For what?"

"RuPaul's show is on."

Her eyes pinched closed. "Actually, I'm going to bed early, if it's all the same to you. See if I can't get a few hours before the drunks really get going."

It *wasn't* all the same to him, but he wasn't going to say so. "Sure. I'll record it."

When Mel turned away, presumably to return to her shop around the corner, King called after her, "Take Lady."

When Mel looked ready to refuse, King added, "She misses you."

This earned him a small half-smile. To the dog she said, "*Suivez.*"

Lady didn't have to be told twice. She took off after Mel in a happy trot.

King stood outside his door with his cooling coffee in his hand and watched them go. He didn't like the sinking feeling in his chest. He didn't like it at all.

18

———————

Piper glanced at the wall clock and saw she had fifteen minutes left before the shop closed. There was only one shopper left, two if she counted the man behind the purple curtain getting a palm reading from Mel. With such a thin crowd, Piper thought it was safe to start her closing routine.

She couldn't break down the drawer or count out the money yet in case the girl in the Care Bear t-shirt wanted to make a purchase, but that wouldn't take her long. There was the sweeping and glass cleaning, the restocking of shelves, and forward-facing the merchandise. She completed each task quickly and efficiently, but her mind wandered.

Piper had texted Dani as she'd promised Henry she would do—only to receive radio silence. Nada. Even after all that talk about "I'm sorry I ghosted you"—it seemed like she was doing it again.

But why? She thought the dinner had gone okay despite the initial awkwardness.

Piper put the glass cleaner under the counter and picked up her phone for the hundredth time that day. Zero messages.

She frowned. "I mean, I can't *make* her hang out with me," she muttered. "She's the one who said she'd missed *me*."

She put her phone down and sighed.

Speaking to no one, she added, "I've made myself *perfectly* available. If she really wanted to talk, she would've said something. Or maybe the dinner was just about getting some guilt off her chest for lying to me in the first place. God, why are people so difficult. Use your words, people."

A polite cough interrupted Piper's rolling monologue.

She looked up and saw the girl in the Care Bear t-shirt holding a twelve-inch Pillar of Love candle.

"Girl, *same*." The girl gave Piper a sympathetic smile and handed the candle over for purchase.

WITH THE DAY'S MONEY LOCKED IN THE SAFE TO BE DEPOSITED tomorrow, Piper turned off the lights and locked the doors. Melandra had excused herself after her last reading, walking up the stairs to her apartment with Lady on her heels.

Another woman who won't talk to me, Piper had thought, watching her go. Her pensive silences and distant looks hurt to watch only because Piper knew no amount of prying would get Mel to open up and let her in on the situation.

Piper picked up her phone and texted a number she knew by heart.

Pick me up.

A pressure formed between her ears seconds later and then popped.

Lou stepped from the shadows beside the rack of hoodies and into a beam of moonlight. It cut across her face dramatically, highlighting her lips.

"That was quick." Piper slid her phone into her pocket.

"It seemed urgent."

"No danger," Piper clarified, grabbing her backpack off the floor. She stopped short of admitting she felt lonely. "For me, anyway."

A sharp tug on her heart strings made her look down. Piper prided herself on the fact that she was the go-to for all her friends. When they ran into trouble, they called her. And Mel was dealing with something and wouldn't even talk to her about it. It hurt. It hurt in the same way it had hurt to know that King and Lou had been working with Dani behind her back.

Is it because I'm younger? she wondered. *Is this some sort of age prejudice here?* Because Piper could do stuff. Hadn't she proven that already in all the close calls they'd faced together?

"What do you mean?" Lou asked.

"Mel's dealing with something and won't speak up about it. You think I'm easy to talk to, right?"

Lou only blinked at her. "Yes."

Piper sighed. "I mean, you don't talk much, but that's not the point. Why wouldn't she tell me what's going on?"

"She hasn't told King anything either. If she had, he'd have told me to watch her."

Piper pursed her lips. "Good point."

She'd seen King come through the shop just before eight that evening. He'd stopped and said hello to Piper, asking how she was doing. Then he'd glanced at the purple curtain and asked, "She back there?"

When Piper had said she was, that had been the end of it. King hadn't looked worried or afraid. He hadn't asked any questions.

"Where did you want to go?" Lou rested the cuff of her leather jacket on the counter. Piper appreciated that she didn't put her fingers on the glass she'd just cleaned.

"What are you doing tonight?" Piper asked.

"Hunting Fish."

Piper snorted. "Gonna need a pole for that?"

Lou didn't even smile.

"Okay, bad joke. But when the world finds out what a monster he is, he's going to wish he had a better last name." Piper adjusted the pack on her back. "So you're busy? No chance we can hang out?"

She could go down to Wild Cat if she wanted to. She'd drink with Henry and their friends and dance all that pent-up energy off until collapsing into bed before dawn.

But she wasn't in the mood to drink, and the bars were less fun during Carnival anyway. That many bodies made talking and dancing nearly impossible. And there was always that one person who hadn't put on enough deodorant, ruining it for everyone else.

Lou pushed her sunglasses up on her head. "You can come with me."

Piper's heart stuttered in her chest. "Come with *you?* To *stalk* a serial killer?"

Lou's lips quirked. "I won't be getting that close."

Piper felt the stupid grin spread across her face. "Hell *yeah* I want to go with you. You've never taken me into the field before. I wanna see what you do."

"You'll have to be quiet, and you can't yell if I move us suddenly."

"Control my vocal chords. Got it." Piper snorted. "That's not the first time a woman has asked me to do so."

Lou arched an eyebrow.

A blush spread across Piper's cheeks, and she averted her gaze first. "Never mind. Let's do this. How long will we follow him?"

"Maybe hours. Maybe thirty minutes." Lou slid her glasses back down over her eyes. "Do you need anything before we go?"

Piper tapped the pack on her shoulders. "I should dump this off at my apartment. Then I'll be ready to go. Listen." She leveled Lou with a stern look. "I've seen the cop movies. I know stakeouts are serious business. I won't be loud or stupid."

"I trust you." Lou's lips twitched with a smile as she reached out and wrapped a hand around Piper's wrist.

LOU KNEW THERE WAS A RISK IN BRINGING PIPER ALONG. IT WAS true she'd only planned to watch Fish from a distance tonight. She also wanted to check on Jennifer McGrath and make sure she was still alive and kicking. And Lou would be lying if she said she wasn't curious to appraise the state of Fish's hunger. The carved arm and ragged nails she'd seen earlier suggested that feeding time was near. But how long could he hold out? Apart from cutting himself, what other methods did he use to beat back the ravenous beast inside him?

Lou wanted to know.

But things could always go wrong on a hunt. Piper was smart and resourceful. Lou herself had been impressed by her survival instincts more than once in their short acquaintance. But tonight she was Lou's responsibility.

You're bringing her along. You keep her safe.

Lou suspected it was the weight of responsibility that caused the strange knocking in her chest after they deposited Piper's backpack on her kitchen counter.

"Oh, let me pee," Piper begged. "It'll only take a second."

Lou stood in the apartment, noting its tidiness and charm. It had high arched windows and hardwood floors. It reminded her a little of Konstantine's loft in Florence's city center.

She pushed this thought away as the faucet in the adjacent room squeaked off.

"Okay," Piper said, wiping her hands on the sides of her jeans. She crossed to the door and turned the bolt, locking them inside the apartment. "I'm ready."

Lou stepped toward her, sliding one hand up the girl's back. She pulled them both through the dark.

Lou's boots settled on solid ground first. Piper's balance tilted, but Lou held tight until she settled on her feet. A relieved little sigh rolled past the girl's lips as Lou released her.

They looked around, trying to figure out where her compass had brought them.

Lou stepped forward, aware immediately of the cavernous space around her. The sound of her boots on concrete echoed in a way only possible with high ceilings.

Lou took another step forward as headlights whipped around an adjacent aisle. It was followed by the recognizable *beep beep beep* of a machine backing up.

A tug on her arm made her turn. Piper pointed at a door on their right. A strip of light shone through the cracks surrounding it as well as one port window high in its face.

Lou exited first, willing to take the brunt of any danger they might intercept in the light.

She understood immediately why her compass had chosen the adjacent storeroom. The grocery store was brightly lit with its overbearing bulbs beaming down from above.

To her left was a dairy case full of stacked yogurts, tubs of cream cheese, butter, and plastic-wrapped cheeses lined up in their individual dispensers. On her right began the cases of milk.

Fish was in front of the milk. He had the door propped open with his hip as he read the label on a bottle of fat-free chocolate milk.

"He *is* a monster," Piper whispered into Lou's ear. "Fat *free?*"

Lou elbowed her slightly, crossing the aisle. Piper followed suit, showing profound interest in a box of aluminum foil on the shelf at eye level. Lou realized they didn't have hand baskets or shopping carts. She pulled a package of napkins off the shelf and held it loosely in her fist.

Piper seemed to have the same idea. "I'll get a cart."

As soon as Piper rounded the corner and disappeared out of sight, something in Lou's chest relaxed. It was one thing to put herself so close to Fish. Even though she knew what he was and what he'd done to at least a dozen women, she wasn't afraid of him. In fact, that self-destructive core inside her, that part that wanted to throw herself from the cliff and see if she could survive the fall, leaned toward Fish like frostbitten hands toward a fire.

But on top of this old, familiar desire to put her hand in the flames was a new and interesting impulse.

Piper wasn't his type. She was the right age, but she was blonde. Lou didn't think Fish had ever hunted or killed a blonde, based on the photos she'd seen. Still, she found herself wanting to keep Piper behind her.

Why did I bring her?

Because Piper had worried her, hadn't she?

The moment she'd gotten the page, a tug in Lou's stomach had caused a jerk of worry in her guts. Once she'd seen Piper for herself, realized it was a social call and not a cry for help, she'd still been left with Piper's sad, lonely expression.

Lou grabbed a box of plastic forks from the shelf and placed them on top of the napkins.

She replayed the last few months in her head as she trailed Fish from the dairy section into the baked goods. He plucked a box of brownie mix from the shelf, and Lou recalled the cake she'd received from Piper last month. It was the second birthday cake Piper had given her. And what had Lou given Piper for her birthday?

Nothing.

She wasn't even sure when it was.

There was nothing she had consciously done to nurture this affection—no gift giving, certainly. Yet Piper had been doggedly kind and generous, sometimes about the simplest things.

She'd given Lou the remote when they'd watched television. They'd sat on Piper's couch watching a show about a serial killer who killed serial killers.

"I feel like you'd connect with this guy," Piper had said, plopping a popcorn bowl into Lou's lap.

They had day trips: San Francisco, New York, Chicago, San Diego, London, Paris, and Kyoto.

Why had she taken Piper? Usually because the girl had made some small remark about wanting to see a landmark or a building, or to eat at a specific restaurant.

Do you know they have a sculpture in Millennium Park that's shaped like a bean? It's called Cloud Gate.

San Diego is supposed to have some of the best beaches.

Have you ever had New York pizza? Real New York pizza?

What's the Eiffel Tower look like at night?

But she had never asked Lou to take her. She'd never expected Lou to use her power—a talent that came as easy to her as thinking. Lou had *wanted* to show her.

They'd been friends for almost seven months when Lou learned that Piper had never actually left the city except for a spring break vacation to Panama City her junior year of high school and another vague trip about which Piper had left out a great many details, except that she'd driven her friend Henry out of state to visit his sister.

If there had been a particular moment or gesture that had created this friendship, Lou had missed it. Now it was simply here, as if it always had been.

"Psst."

Lou jumped, turning away from Fish, who was exiting the end of the aisle.

"Whoa," Piper whispered. "Did I scare you?"

Piper searched her face as she pushed the cart to a stop beside her. "You okay?"

Lou focused on the cart. She was surprised to find it half full. A bag of potato chips, a box of breakfast pastries, two packages of cookies, and a two-liter bottle of soda sat in the bottom of the cart.

Lou arched a brow at her.

Piper smacked her lips. "For *authenticity*. Wouldn't you be suspicious of two people following you with an *empty* cart?"

Lou put her forks and napkins in the cart beside the soda.

"I'll push, you stalk." Piper wagged her eyebrows.

Lou took her time exiting the aisle. She pretended to read the signs as her eyes roved. She spotted the familiar button-down shirt and loafers farther up the center aisle. She started after him, working to close the distance. When she felt like he was within range, she slowed again, pretending to look at an end-cap of pink lemonade in colorful tubs featuring bright summer scenes that didn't match the winter pressing against the store windows.

Fish pushed his cart into checkout line number six, even though it was noticeably longer than both lines four and five. The cashier saw him the moment he pulled into her line and gave him a tight smile.

Fish's spine straightened immediately, as if he was pleased by the attention.

Lou turned to Piper, who was reading the box of breakfast pastries. "Is it trans-fat or saturated fat that's bad for you?"

"Why don't you push the cart over to the bathrooms?" Lou nodded at the sign beside customer service. "I'll be over in a minute."

"Got it." Piper pivoted the cart in that direction.

Fish was now only two patrons from the cashier. Lou decided to grab a magazine off the rack in the checkout line next to his and pretended to read an article about an actor's supposed plastic surgery. Lou looked at the glossy photographs without seeing them. Behind her sunglasses, she flicked her gaze toward Fish, who'd finally reached the cashier.

She watched the exchange.

He was bouncing lightly on his feet as he spoke to her. Excitement? Contained joy? The cashier looked as tired as the first night Lou had seen her. Her makeup hid dark circles, but not the puffiness caused by lack of sleep. As she made change, her gaze flicked up to meet Lou's.

Then it slid away.

Fish pushed his cart toward the exit, and Lou crossed to the bathroom.

Piper was frowning. "I've got something to show you."

"It'll have to wait," Lou told her, and grabbed her wrist, pulling her into the bathroom. "Come here."

The door hadn't closed all the way when Lou flicked off the switch. In a stall, a woman cried out in surprise, but Lou was already pulling them through the dark.

They were in the alley beside the exit. The sharp cold hit her cheeks instantly, and Lou had a passing thought that they couldn't linger. Piper wasn't dressed warmly enough for an Ohio winter.

"We won't stay long," Lou whispered into her ear as Piper began to shiver.

"I'm okay."

The swoosh of automatic doors opening caught Lou's attention. Fish appeared with his shopping cart. *He's practically running to his car*, she thought.

Once the back end of the SUV was open, he threw the sacks into the trunk the way she'd seen a worker throwing bags of dog food onto a pile.

She would have smiled, amused by his desperate movements, but again she felt like she was looking through an opaque glass, seeing only the reflection of herself inside. She didn't like it.

Piper tugged on Lou's sleeve, three sharp yanks, and Lou turned.

She was pointing at a woman, alone with no cart, exiting from the same door Fish had. When she saw that Fish hadn't yet climbed into the driver's seat, her steps faltered. She slowed and veered off to the right. She tucked her chin down as if to hide her face.

Strange behavior, Lou thought, *for someone leaving a grocery store.*

She regarded the red hoodie and slight build and recognized the familiarity.

Fish was already backing out of his parking space and speeding in the direction of his home. Lou searched the compass within her but felt no danger. Maybe he would cut himself tonight. Maybe he'd fuck his wife a little more roughly. Lou was curious to know how he'd handle the aggression bubbling inside him.

"It's too dark to get her picture," Lou said, watching the woman climb into a red Honda and turn the key. She also drove in the direction of Fish's house.

"Good thing I got a picture when we were in the store," Piper said, and gave Lou a devilish grin.

"When you sent me to stand by the bathrooms I spotted her. I saw her when I went to get the cart too, and both times she was watching Fish."

Lou frowned, thinking she'd done a pretty good job of not being too obvious.

"I've got a good one of her face."

Piper handed over her smartphone so Lou could look at the picture more closely. There was something familiar about her—her complexion, her features.

"I've seen her before," Lou said, frowning at the picture. "I'm pretty sure she was outside Fish's house the other night."

"Why would another woman be stalking him?" Piper asked, and Lou had the distinct impression she was asking herself, not Lou. Sure enough, the answers came immediately. "Maybe she's a reporter who's onto him. Or maybe a detective. What do you think?"

Lou was kind enough not to point out that not every person sneaking around was a reporter.

"We'll find out who she is," she said.

"Yeah, we've got recognition programs for that, don't we?" Piper's teeth were chattering.

"Come on," Lou said, and wrapped her arms around the girl. They'd done what they could tonight. "Let's get cocoa."

"I love cocoa," Piper said with a sniff.

"I know."

19

———

King opened the fridge and considered his dinner options. It was after eleven at night, but he was hungry. The shelves weren't entirely bare, but nothing screamed *eat me*. There were the usual suspects, half-used condiments and a gallon of milk. There were two wrapped steaks that he'd planned to grill for tonight's dinner before he'd decided on takeout—drunken noodles with chicken.

He decided on the noodles, vowing to do some proper grocery shopping tomorrow.

Takeout box in hand, he closed the fridge.

Piper and Lou stepped forward.

He squeezed the box so hard the lid popped off. "Christ."

Lady barked in response. The short yap came from Mel's apartment across the walkway.

"I'm fine!" King called, turning his chin toward the door. "It's just Lou."

Piper threw up her hands. "Who the hell am I?"

Since there was no follow-up bark or scratching at his door, he assumed that Mel had shushed the dog.

He regarded the two of them. "Is there not enough shadow in front of my door for you to *knock?*"

"On the balcony there is," Lou admitted, shrugging in her leather coat. King noted his tired face in her reflective sunglasses. He grimaced. "We wanted to see if you were awake."

"And it's cold out there." Piper tossed an empty Styrofoam cup into King's trash.

"Where have you been?" he asked, frowning at the cup. He didn't recognize the logo stamped in red lettering across the compressed material.

Lou pushed her sunglasses up on top of her head. "Fish."

"But plot twist!" Piper pulled her phone from her pocket and pushed buttons wildly. After a moment of delighted humming, she turned the phone so King could see the screen. "Someone is already following him."

King accepted the phone, setting the carton of drunken noodles on the counter. "Are you sure?"

"Totally." Piper pointed at the face, grinning triumphantly. "She was doing what we did. But she had salsa and chips."

King looked up, frowning.

"We found him in the grocery store," Lou clarified.

Piper bounced on her heels. "We had a cart and everything. We were like real detectives. It was *so* cool."

King couldn't help but smile. Piper's enthusiasm was contagious.

"And you found her following him too?" he asked, frowning at the grainy photo. He tried to enlarge it, but that made it worse.

"Yeah," Piper said, coming around to stand shoulder to shoulder with him. "She followed him in the store and then out into the parking lot. Then she got in a red Honda and followed him out of the lot."

"We don't know she was following him." Lou took the carton of drunken noodles and sniffed it. "We stopped tracking them in the parking lot. They could've been heading in the same direction. Or not."

King squinted at the phone. There was something familiar about the face, but he couldn't place where he'd seen it before. He forwarded himself the picture, and heard his own phone buzz on the coffee table in the other room.

"So can you do it?" Piper asked.

King looked up from the photo and found them both looking at him expectantly. He felt like he'd missed something. "Do what?"

"Can you run the photo and find out who she is?" Piper asked.

King shrugged. "I can try, but I don't have access to the same databases that I did when I was active with the DEA. And since Sampson told me to back off, I've tried to stay off their servers illegally. I can call in a favor and ask someone to do it, but you know what they say. Three may keep a secret if two of them are dead."

"Right. Someone might wonder why we're looking into her." Piper bit her lip.

"Why can't you ask Konstantine?" King asked, handing over the phone. "He's far better at finding people than I am. This picture is more than enough for him to get what he needs."

Lou's warm grin evaporated. She turned away, crossing to the balcony door. She gazed out at the light as if suddenly very interested in the raucous celebrations below.

Piper pocketed the phone. "Is this our case or not?"

King arched an eyebrow, hoping Piper would elaborate. But she only shook her head and shoved the carton of noodles into his hand. "Don't let us interrupt your dinner."

King pulled a plate from the cabinet, dumped the noodles onto it, and slid the whole thing into the microwave.

So was there trouble in paradise? Were things not lovey-dovey between Konstantine and Lou? He had no idea what their relationship even looked like, or if it was officially a relationship at all. But she'd saved his life when the whole world hunted him, and he'd turned up when Dmitri Petrov had hunted her.

They could be friends, Lucy's voice chided gently in his mind. *Friends protect friends.*

You haven't seen the way they look at each other, King thought. *I sure don't look at my friends that way.*

The microwave beeped, and King retrieved his noodles and soda and took both to the sofa. "So you've nothing else to report on Fish?" He forked noodles into his mouth.

Lou turned from the balcony. "He's cutting himself."

"If he's cutting, he's trying to numb out."

"Is that common?" Lou asked.

His fork scraped the plate. "As a coping mechanism? Sure. Anything to stave off the craving a little longer. One guy burned his arm whenever he was trying not to kill."

"Did it work?"

King snorted before forking more noodles into his mouth. "What do you think?"

"These records smell like weed." Piper crouched down in front of the stack leaning against his speaker. "Is this where you keep your weed, because man, it's not even subtle."

"How much longer before he caves?" Lou asked.

"Some killers go years without killing. Maybe he'll slip into a dormant period."

Lou turned away, effectively ending the conversation. There was something in the hard set of her shoulders that told King to drop it. He didn't take it personally. If she had a problem, she'd speak her mind. She was too much like her aunt to give him grace for long.

Piper pulled out one of the vinyl records and opened it on her lap. It was Sam Cooke, *Portrait of a Legend.* She fingered the edges. She frowned at him. "Why is this one so much newer than the others?"

"It's a replacement." He scraped the last bite of noodles off his plate into his mouth. "Lou—if I gave you the name of someone—no. Shit. I don't have a name."

Lou turned toward him, clearly intrigued.

King scratched his jaw. "If I said find the man who killed Rita Cross, would you be able to do it?"

She knew what he meant. "Yes."

"Really? That would be enough?"

"When I found Fish, all I was thinking was 'Give me someone who kills women and thinks he's getting away with it.'"

King couldn't hide his surprise. "Huh. That's impressive."

"Who's Rita Cross?" Lou asked.

"A woman who was murdered. Do you..." He searched for a word. "Get any *vibes* about where her killer might be?"

Konstantine be damned. If the killer was around, he deserved to answer for his crimes.

"No," Lou said.

"No what?"

"Nothing is coming up."

King took another drink of his soda, aware that it was way too late at night to be drinking this shit. "What does that mean?"

"He could be dead."

He is being dealt with. Wasn't that what Konstantine promised?

Piper looked up from the record. "How does Mel seem to you?"

King thought of Mel's anger as she told him to back off earlier that day.

"She's okay."

Piper shook her head. "See, *no*. I can't be the only one who sees it. Something is getting to her. When I showed up for work the other day she was halfway to a panic attack about something, and asked me to read her cards. Spoiler, they weren't happy cards. Then that guy came in and was giving her shit."

"The guy with the feather in his hat?" King asked. "The bone choker."

"*Yes.*" Piper groaned. "I don't like him. I think he's The Devil."

Lou had gone so still beside him King had to turn his head to make sure she was still there.

He arched a brow. "Do you mean this literally or—"

"When I read her cards, she drew The Devil. It's a person who screws with you. Gets in your head. You know, a bad person."

"Or it could mean you're lying to yourself," King said.

Piper crinkled her nose. "True. But I think in this case, it's *him*."

King thought of the way Lady had growled, her nose through the slats of his balcony.

"I've seen him around." King pushed away the plate and reached for his soda. "Do you think he's harassing her?"

"Want me to pick him up?" Lou asked.

King snorted. "Not yet, Cujo. We don't know that he's actually the problem."

"I wish she'd just talk to us," Piper said. She slipped the vinyl back into the pile and stood. "Why can't she just talk to us? We're her friends, right?"

King took a long drink and smacked his lips. "Some people like to handle their problems on their own. Mel is one of those people."

"That's stupid. We love her and—" Piper began.

"Are you trying to tell me you're *not* one of those people? Because I seem to remember you standing in the middle of the office with tears rolling down your face, and you sure didn't tell me what was going on."

Piper pushed out her lower lip. "Not fair."

"She knows we're here for her," King said. "If she needs help, she'll ask."

Lou was regarding him with a cold expression that he couldn't quite read. But it made the hair on the back of his neck rise up.

That's big talk coming from you, Robert, Lucy whispered in his mind. And then, *Those in the most danger don't even know how to ask.*

She's a capable woman, King thought. *Nothing is going to happen to her.*

Even to himself, he couldn't tell if he was stating a fact or a wish.

20

―――――――

Mel opened her side table drawer. She shoved aside the notepads, the pens, the sticky notes, the half-used tube of lip balm. She slammed the drawer shut and yanked open the next one.

Lady barked, a sharp, alerting sound.

"*Calme*," Mel hissed.

Lady's ears lay flat against her head.

King's voice rumbled from across the hallway, but then nothing. Whatever he wanted, it wasn't important. But this momentary interruption allowed Mel to look up from her work and see her surroundings for the first time.

Every drawer in her kitchen and living room was pulled open. The cushions on her couch had been lifted and thrown to the floor. The pillows were strewn everywhere.

She'd searched every inch of this apartment. *Every inch.*

Her tarot cards were gone. She had a horrible feeling she knew where they were.

No, she begged. *No, I've just put them somewhere and forgotten.*

They've been in our family since 1804, Grandmamie's voice chided. *Over two hundred years, and you've lost them.*

"I haven't lost them," Mel mumbled, pulling her shawl tighter around her. *And they aren't really two hundred years old.* But even as she thought this, her heart sagged in her chest.

According to Grandmamie's account, the original deck was given to her great-great-great-great-great-great-aunt Josephine Beloit by her mother, Simone, when Haiti won its independence. *We make our own future now*, she was supposed to have said. Who knew if it was true.

As the deck was passed from woman to woman throughout the centuries, it was updated as necessary. If a card was damaged, it was redrawn by its owner's hand. That explained the varied styles spread throughout the generations. Mel was certain that none of the cards in the current deck were original to the deck Josephine received in 1804. But she also couldn't say they weren't.

The Ace of Cups and The Fool, for example, looked older than dirt.

Grandmamie had always insisted that it wasn't the age of the cards themselves. It was that their own spirits had imprinted on the deck, and as long as it passed through their family, it didn't matter if they were touching the exact same card or not.

It's our history in the cards. It's our blood and sweat in these cards, Grandmamie used to say. *We made the magic. Don't forget that.*

"I haven't lost them," she said again, and stepped out of her apartment into the hallway.

Lady moved to follow her, but Mel held up her hand.

"*Restez.*"

Lady whined, the closest thing to an objection Mel had ever heard, but she obeyed. She fell back on her haunches, her ears lying flat against her head.

"I just want to look one more place."

Mel paused outside King's apartment door. She raised her fist to knock but then heard Lou's voice. She hesitated. They were working. She shouldn't bother them. And she'd already shown too much of her distress as it was. If she alerted them now that she'd misplaced her cards, they would only worry more.

They might get involved in the situation she'd worked so hard to keep them out of.

She crept away, trying to keep her footfall silent as she descended the steps into the shop. She checked the cubbies beneath the register. She checked—nonsensically—the register itself. She pulled back the purple curtain and gazed into the nook where she conducted her readings with the full air of *Melandra the Magnificent*, or whatever her customers called her behind her back.

But there were only the two low benches, covered in bright Bedouin cushions, and the wood table resting between. She lifted the extinguished candles as if to find something hidden beneath. She ran her hand along the cushions.

No cards. On neither her side nor the customer's.

She sat down with her face in her hands and pushed back against the tears. "When did he take them?" she whispered. "When did he have the chance?"

It hardly mattered now, did it? It mattered only that Terry had managed to get his filthy hands on them in the first place.

She stepped from the nook and pulled the curtain behind her.

A ghostly face hung in the glass outside her shop door. Its skull-like visage and skeleton grin filled her with rage. Tremors shot down each arm, curling her hands into fists. Without consciously deciding to, she stormed to the door, unlocked the bolt, and pushed out into the chaotic night.

The music rose to a nauseating cacophony. The scents of booze, piss, and fried foods hit her like a physical force, even as the cold February wind seized and tumbled her hair.

"Give them back," she hissed, letting the door fall closed behind her. "You goddamn bastard, give them back!"

Terry's grin only widened. "Give what back?"

She shoved him hard. "Don't bullshit me, Terry! You took 'em. I know you took 'em from my own damn pockets. Hand them over!"

Was it when he'd slammed her against the building? She couldn't be sure. When had she used them last? All her appointments since then had been palm readings, hadn't they? Had she brought out her cards at all?

Lights from the shop windows sparked in his eyes. They shone liquid black.

He smirked, capturing her wrists in his grip. "I don't know what you're talking about."

"You know how much those cards mean to me. *You know.*"

For the first time, she felt herself on the verge of real tears. Whether she was crying from anger, loss, or perhaps both, she couldn't be sure.

His smile spread too wide, revealing too many wolfish teeth. "It's a good trick, isn't it? You pick up a lot of tricks in prison."

She yanked her wrists from his grip and stormed into the throbbing crowd. She batted the drunks aside as she stepped through the streets, searching, looking for—*There.*

"Donny!" Melandra called. She waved at the uniformed officer. "Donny!"

The cop who'd been standing on the corner talking to another officer turned at the sound of his name. His black wool coat brushed his chin but didn't hide his smile.

"I need to report a theft!" She pointed at Terry. "Thief!"

A rough hand seized her upper arm. It squeezed so hard she cried out.

"Shut your mouth, woman," he said. "Shut it *now*. If you tell him a damn thing you'll never see your cards again. I'll burn every single one, you hear me? And once I'm done with that, I'll make a confession of my own. I'll tell them what you did, you hear me? I'll tell them *every-thing*. Then we can rot in prison together."

Melandra remembered the first time she saw Terry in Hokum's Bar and Grill down by the interstate. She'd been only fifteen at the time, but looked old enough that Bill Hokum let her wait tables three nights a week after school. Bill had been a good friend of Grandmamie's, and she'd trusted him to keep an eye on her girl.

On Friday nights, men from the neighboring parish came into the bar and played pool in the back. One evening, a new boy came in with the Henrietta crowd. Mel met his eyes instantly, as if she'd felt him enter the bar.

He'd smiled first, and she hadn't returned it even though the heat in her face was enough to give her away.

Something inside her prayed that would be the end of it.

Forty minutes later, he was at the bar, placing a dollar bill on the counter. "Quarters for the jukebox, miss."

His voice was how she'd imagined it. Smooth bourbon poured into a glass like Grandmamie drank on Sunday nights after church.

She'd made change without looking higher than his mouth.

"You mute or something?" he asked, taking the quarters she'd placed where the dollar had been a minute before.

"No, she just don't talk to strangers," Bob had called from the end of the bar. "Get out of here."

And if only *that* had been the end of it.

But Terry had kept playing pool in the back with his friends. Melandra eventually began talking, and before she knew it, she was hustling half the pool halls in three parishes with him.

If only I'd honored Grandmamie's wish, Mel cursed herself. *If only I hadn't been such a damn fool.*

It was the biggest fight they'd had in her life, the night Grandmamie had demanded Melandra stay away from Terry. *Have you learned nothing from my mistakes? Nothing at all?*

The old woman had hissed. And she was an old woman then, aging for reasons Mel wouldn't understand until later.

When Grandmamie got her pancreatic cancer diagnosis and was given months to live, Mel did finally honor her request. She stopped going to the bar. She stayed with her grandmother day and night until she died just seven months later.

"Don't be a fool," Grandmamie had begged her in one of her last lucid moments.

Not two hours later, Terry was in her driveway in his Firebird, beckoning her to "Come on now. You've had enough of all this."

And she had. For better or worse, she had left with him. She'd never been so desperate to escape anything in her life, not since living in the small apartment with her strung-out mother in Baton Rouge—those dark days before her mother overdosed and her life with Grandmamie began.

She'd used to think those early days with her mother were the darkest of her life. That was only because her time with Terry had not begun. The hustling, the drinking, the vagabond way he liked to crisscross below the Mason–Dixon line. All of it culminating in the worst moment of her life.

"Will you drive?" Terry had asked her.

And though it was dark and pouring rain, and though she'd had a couple of drinks herself, she'd said yes.

Damn her, she'd said yes.

Terrence jerked his hand free of Melandra's arm, and she found herself in the present moment again, surrounded by pushing bodies, with only her pain left to contend with.

"Careful what you say now," Terry spat.

Donny pushed aside the last bodies between them and reached her, smiling. As soon as he saw her face, his smile faded.

"Mel, what's wrong? What's been stolen?"

Mel wrung her hands. She leaned her weight against the brick. "I—"

She turned, but Terrence was gone. He'd faded into the crowd, and with him any chance that she could get her cards back tonight.

She searched the crowd but didn't see him. She couldn't spot the leather hat or that single black crow feather in the sea of laughing, horrible faces. There was no hint of that wild, murderous smile.

It didn't mean he wasn't watching.

"I'm sorry," Melandra stuttered. She forced a smile. "I'm so sorry for calling you over like that, Mr. Edwards."

Donny frowned, clearly taken aback by her sudden formality. "What happened?"

Mel straightened her shoulders and released a slow breath between her teeth. "I thought someone had pickpocketed me."

She let out a laugh. It was supposed to sound relieved, bordering on nonchalant. But it sounded strained and nervous to her own ears. She forced a smile. "But I've got everything on me. So I'm very sorry to have scared you like that."

Donny was still frowning.

Another sharp laugh. "You probably think I'm one of those hysterical women that cry about everything."

"I don't think that." Donny's frown only deepened. He was searching her face. "Are you really okay?"

"I'm fine. I feel stupid for overreacting, but I'm fine."

This was partially true. Mel had never felt so stupid in her life. Stupid for ever having gotten involved with Terrence in the first place.

"Honestly," she said with an air of conspiracy. "I haven't been sleeping well this week. I think it's the noise."

Donny favored her with a polite smile. "That's all of us. *Carnival.*" He gestured at the masked faces around them. The throbbing bodies swayed, drinks spilling over from their cups and splashing on the street.

Mel nodded companionably. "I'm going to try to get some sleep now. Thank you for coming over when I called you. I'm so sorry if I scared you."

The frown was back. "You can always call on us, Mel. Always."

She nodded, making her apologies. *Stupid. Stupid, stupid woman.*

When she reached the door of Fortunes and Fixes, a hand clamped over hers, pinning it against the handle. She wasn't surprised. She'd known he'd stay close.

"You'll get your cards back when I get my money," a voice whispered in her ear.

She jerked her head back. She didn't want his breath on her.

Terrence glared down at her. "You have until Friday to pay me or I'm going to burn them. I swear to God. Just pay me and I'll leave."

"How do I know you'll really leave?" she asked. Because she was more than aware that he could stay. He could stay and haunt her for the rest of her life. What was stopping him?

His skeleton grin was back. So many teeth.

That's how he'd looked that night on a backroad somewhere in west Louisiana. The rain beating down on his head and shoulders as he stared down at the road, his face bright in the headlights as the windshield wipers furiously worked back and forth across the fogging glass.

"Did I kill her?" Mel had asked. "Did I—"

"Stay in the car," he'd said.

And she had. God forgive her, she had.

He released her hand, but not his hold on her, and he knew it. "I guess we'll see, won't we?"

21

———————

King leaned back in his office chair, pressing the phone to his opposite ear. His eyes roved the sunlit office, taking in the coffee station and the red plastic chairs. Piper's laptop was still open, the way she'd left it before stepping out to grab them sandwiches. King glanced at his watch and wondered how long he would have to wait on hold.

"Here it is," Sampson said finally, the line crackling with the sound of movement. Maybe it was papers shuffling or the phone brushing the collar of Sampson's shirt. "Jeffrey Rodgers Fish. Shadyville High School, American History teacher. Sound right to you?"

"That's the one."

"I had to make three phone calls for this," Sampson said grumpily.

"Don't give me that," King said, rubbing his nose. "I sent you the info on both the Robinson and Henley cases yesterday."

"Fair enough." Sampson smacked his lips. "To answer your question, no. He's had no prior charges, but he had two comments on his work record that I think you might find interesting."

King twirled a pen between his knuckles. "I'm listening."

"Two girls at his school have made complaints about him."

The pen stopped twirling. "What kind of complaints?"

"One said he was keeping her after school to do work."

"Sounds teacherly."

"Yeah, but she claims that she didn't need to do the extra work and thought he was trying to get her alone."

"That sounds *less* teacherly."

"Her official statement called him 'creepy.' The school dismissed her claims until her mother got involved. She's a pediatrician, pillar of the community, something like that. They gave the girl an exam and she tested out of his class and into the AP course. She graduated six months later. Problem solved. The other girl had the same problem, but her family moved out of state before it was resolved."

This wasn't anything King could use for a bona fide case against Fish. Predatory behavior toward female students certainly counted as part of the habits of murderous sociopaths, but unfortunately something as ambiguous as a student–teacher conflict wouldn't hold in court.

King scratched at his jaw. "Anything else?"

"Yes," Sampson said conspiratorially. "And *this* is more interesting."

"I'm listening."

"One night Fish was stopped by a patrol car."

"What time?"

Papers shuffled on Sampson's end again. "Just past midnight. The patrol car stopped him because he wasn't wearing a seatbelt."

"Careless," King clucked.

"When the officer got out of his car, he realized the back bumper was soaked in what he first thought was mud."

King sat up in his seat. "It wasn't mud."

"Nope. The officer asked him to get out of the car, explained why he'd stopped him, and brought him to the back of the car to show him the blood."

King couldn't suppress a laugh. "What did he say to get out of this?"

"Claims he hit a deer and that it must've been the deer's blood. The cop makes him open the trunk anyway, but there's nothing in there save the tire and jack. A few reusable grocery bags. And the cop can't test the blood right there on the side of the road, so he gives him the ticket and lets him go."

"Seems lenient."

"Especially given the fact that if he'd been a black man, and not just a white guy in a button-down, he probably would've been shot."

King agreed.

"But the best part," Sampson said, "is that Fish traded in that car two weeks later."

"That is interesting. Especially if the blood wasn't from a deer. Were there scuff marks?"

"Yep. Maybe some shoes kicking out?" There was a long pause. "Christ. People are sick."

"Yeah, it gets into your head if you're not careful. But I admit, there's also something stimulating about it."

"Robbie." Sampson's tone was suddenly grave. "I'm worried about your mental health, buddy."

The door opened, and Piper appeared with two paper-wrapped sub sandwiches in her arms. She arched her eyebrows at King's expression, but he shook his head. *Nothing to worry about.*

"I told you. I've got an interest in cold cases. Keeps my mind young."

Sampson laughed. "That's what Sudoku is for."

Piper placed the sub sandwich and his change on his desk before pulling a cold diet soda from their mini fridge. He thanked her with a wink and a thumbs-up.

"Fish has the look, I admit," Sampson said. "But what have you *actually* got on the guy?"

King pulled the tab on the soda, enjoying the crack of the opening can. "We'll find out, won't we?"

The door chime rang again, and a man in uniform crossed the threshold into the detective agency. His black boots thudded heavily against the wooden floor.

"Hey, Donny," Piper said before taking a big bite of her sub sandwich. "What can we do for you?"

The police officer nodded toward King. "I need to talk to him if he's got a minute."

Piper met King's gaze with her lips pursed in question.

Sampson must've heard either the chime or Donny's voice. "You gotta go, I take it?"

"Yeah," King admitted, putting his soda on the desktop. "But thanks for calling and letting me know what you found out."

"Anytime." Sampson ended the call without saying goodbye. It was a bad habit that King had set the precedent for, so he couldn't complain.

King stood and offered his hand. "Hey, Donny. How've you been?"

"Not bad," he replied blandly, barely shaking King's hand.

King knew the local cop as one of the officers who commonly patrolled the French Quarter. For that reason, he was a friendly and familiar face, with his ragged eyebrow scar that bisected his left brow and a small cleft lip scar from a surgery he'd had as a kid.

Piper pulled up one of the chairs so that Donny could sit across from King.

"Oh, it's okay," he protested. "I can't stay long."

And yet he sat down.

"What can I do for you?" King was trying to discern the source of the cop's nervousness. He'd never worked with one of the street cops on a case before, and nor would it make sense that Donny would come to King with information when good law enforcement absolutely required that the chain of command be upheld for all evidence and procedures so that they could pass a conviction in the court of law.

Maybe it was a personal inquiry. God, King hoped Donny's wife wasn't having an affair.

"It's about Melandra," Donny said.

"What?" Piper and King said in unison.

King shot her a look. *You can stay, but be quiet.*

Piper rolled her eyes and made an impatient gesture with her hands. Fortunately, this was done behind Donny's back.

"I was patrolling last night with Ramika, and Mel called out to me. At first she looked, well, I'm not sure how to describe it. Like she was pissed but also pretty scared. She said she'd been robbed."

"By who?"

"That's the funny part." Donny shook his head. "I saw the man who was talking to her. I'd spotted her before she spotted me, actually, but I was working and she was talking to this guy so I didn't think nothing of it. But then I see her coming at me and he grabs her. That's when I knew something was up. But then he sort of disappeared before I got to her."

Disappeared. King's stomach dropped. He thought of the man in the leather hat with the crow feather sticking out of one side and the bone choker stretched across his dark throat. Hadn't he disappeared on King too?

King relayed this description.

Donny sat up straighter. "Yeah, that's him. You've seen him?"

"Yeah," King said, recalling the way the man had rolled his eyes up to meet King's from the street below. "And I've seen him pull the disappearing act."

"By the time we got to speaking, she said she hadn't been robbed and was clearly trying to smooth it over, you know? I didn't want to push it, but what could I do?"

"Nothing," King said sympathetically.

Donny licked his lips and sheepishly met King's gaze.

King leaned forward and grinned. "But you did do something, didn't you?"

"Not officially." Donny flashed a guilty smile. "Between you and me, I might have gone across the street to the convenience store and got the security tape from Larry. I might've also got a match on the guy. I just wanted to know who the hell he was."

"And?"

"The name's Terrence Lamott. He just got out of prison two weeks ago for murder. *And* he's Melandra's husband."

King glanced at Piper and saw her reddening face and working jaw. She looked ready to explode.

Donny rubbed his forehead as if a headache was coming on. "He's on parole, so he can't fuck up or he goes right back in, but that doesn't mean shit."

"People reoffend all the time."

"Anyway, Mel might not want to talk about it, but I thought at least

I could tell you. You live and work so close, you can keep an eye on her."

Donny stood from his seat.

King, sensing the departure mixed in with the apology, reached across the desk and offered his hand. "Thanks for telling me. I appreciate it."

Piper bounced in her seat, making her chair emit tiny desperate squeaks. Both King and Donny glanced her way.

She stopped bouncing. "Sorry."

"If that guy starts giving her any shit, call me." Donny dragged his chair across the room to where Piper had taken it from.

"Will do."

With an apologetic smile, Donny slipped from the office out into the sunlit streets.

Piper was out of her chair before the door fully closed. "Husband. *Husband!* Did you even know she was married?"

"No," King lied, absentmindedly flicking the pull tab on his soda. Because Mel had told him a different story. In her version, she had been married to an abusive alcoholic for many years and then she'd divorced him. It had been ugly, but she had gotten a nice settlement out of it and it had allowed her to buy her shop. The idea she'd lied—felt like she *had* to lie—formed a cold rock in the pit of his gut. "No, I didn't know."

"And he's a murderer! Who *stole* something from her!"

"You need to calm down," King said, but his own irritation was biting at the back of his neck.

"Calm down?" Piper cried. She threw up her hands. "This murderer is harassing her and stealing her shit and she's too scared to even talk to us about it. I will *not* calm down. We have to do something."

"She must have a reason for wanting us to stay out of it," King said. He wasn't sure if he was trying to reassure Piper or himself. A horrible tight sensation had formed below his solar plexus and was growing. The nerves in his arms and legs felt jittery with weakness. *She lied to me. She lied to me.*

Piper crossed her arms over her chest. "She's wrong. She needs us."

Think, King scolded himself. *Think! Why would she lie? Embarrass-ment? Fear? To protect you?*

"And he's a murderer," Piper muttered to herself while pacing. "Mel is married to a *murderer*. And not the good kind like Lou. He's the bad kind of murderer."

"We don't know who he killed or why." King covered his eyes.

"What are we going to do?" Piper asked, coming up on the balls of her feet expectantly.

"Shhh. Be quiet. I'm trying to think."

"Think later. *What are we going to do?*" Piper paced anxiously in front of him. "We *are* going to do something. We have to get rid of this guy. What if she was in witness protection and he found her? We—we have to protect her!"

"Of course we'll protect her," King said.

The problem was King knew Melandra. This omission, though surprising, made sense to him. It also meant that given what he knew about Melandra, she was already protecting herself. And if she was, the question was from what?

Something must've happened. Somewhere in their shared history, something must have happened. *I have to figure out what it was. I need more information.*

It would take a lot of asking. He'd have to talk to her family, his family, old friends. Cell mates and people from his time in prison— because boy, don't people talk in prison. He'd have to go through the husband's records and history. This would take a while, but he had to see the situation clearly—both what was on and off record—if he was going to help Mel.

King lifted his phone, chewing his lip while he considered which call he should make first.

22

———————

Lou was perched on a stool inside the busy ramen house when she felt the tug in her abdomen. Someone was calling for her. It didn't feel like panic or the nerve-singeing ignition of all-consuming fear. But it got her attention. She dipped her chopsticks into her warm bowl of Tonkatsu and glanced at the bustling Tokyo street beyond, trying to get a sense of where the call was coming from.

Japanese, which had always been a beautiful and melodious language to her, filled her ears. It was complete with the exception of two American tourists sharing a table near the back of the noodle shop. Their brash, loud mouths ran as their cameras and shopping bags crowded around their feet.

Another desperate pull, this one a little more urgent than the last.

She did the math in her head. It was almost noon in Tokyo, which meant that it was almost ten in New Orleans.

With a sigh, Lou shoveled as much of the food into her mouth as possible, placed a generous stack of yen beside her bowl, and nodded to the chef on the other side of the counter. "*Dōmo arigatō gozaimashita.*"

Then Lou was walking toward the bathroom in the back, a room so small she couldn't fully extend her arms without brushing the tiled walls on all sides.

No matter. She only needed its momentary darkness, long enough for the shadows to overtake her, wrap her body with their power, and sift her through the underbelly of the world.

A new bathroom formed around her. The smell of cooking meat and smoke was replaced with the rancid burn of alcohol. The voices were all American now, and about twenty times louder than they needed to be as they fought to overcome the Beyoncé track blasting through the unseen speakers. The walls vibrated.

Lou stepped out of a dark corner into the bar itself, and was greeted by a crush of bodies. She spotted Piper right away.

"There you are." Piper stepped forward, flipping one blond pigtail over her shoulder, and hooked her arm through Lou's.

"What's going on?" Lou asked.

"I'll tell you outside. I'm sweating to death in here."

Piper pulled her through the throng of bodies, aware that more than once her guns shifted beneath her leather jacket, pressing into her ribs. If the passersby felt it, they showed no sign.

Because everyone is drunk, Lou thought. *They aren't noticing anything.*

Piper raised her hand and waved to a small throng of girls near the DJ booth. One bit her lip and pouted, giving Lou a ruthless once-over the moment before Piper pulled her from the bar and into the open street. It was twenty degrees cooler outside, but crowd control wasn't much better.

"Are you ditching your friends?" Lou asked.

"Sort of. I invited them out because I'm trying not to think about freaking Dani, or the fact that Mel's *husband* is a *murderer* and out of *prison* and I have an exam in two days that I don't feel remotely good about—"

"Stop," Lou said, pulling her to a halt in the middle of the street. Outside the bar, it was easier to smell the alcohol on Piper's breath. She was well on her way to drunk. "Say all that again. Slowly."

"I mean, Scarlett is nice but I shouldn't be sleeping with one woman when I'm thinking about another one. That's not healthy, man. And drinking and screwing all night has never helped anyone pass an exam." She burped and pressed her fist into her chest. "That I know of."

Lou pushed her sunglasses up on her head. "Tell me about Mel and the husband."

Piper pinched the bridge of her nose. "Oh *man* that burns. Ever burped in your nose?"

"Mel," Lou insisted. "Has a husband?"

"It turns out that creepy guy I don't like is Mel's *husband*. And he just got out of prison a couple weeks ago after being in there for twenty-something years for beating his pregnant girlfriend to death. He's a cheater, woman beater, and baby killer, man. A total trash human."

Lou listened carefully as Piper recounted Donny's story. As some point she realized that Piper hadn't texted her when she'd needed her. Unlike King, who always sent his messages like a page, Piper had relied on the fact that her simple desire to see Lou was enough to summon her.

"You didn't page me. How did you know I'd come?" Lou reached out and steadied Piper on her feet.

"I didn't *know* you'd come. I just hoped."

"And if I hadn't?"

"I would've tried paging you, but I like knowing I can reach you like this." She placed her fingers at her temples and hummed. "I don't know when another Dmitri Petrov is gonna show up. And I'm not going to wait until I'm actually kidnapped—*again*—to make sure the alarm system still works, if you know what I'm saying."

"I won't let anything like that happen again," Lou said. And she was surprised by both the admission and the swell of possessiveness that rose in her chest at the idea of someone hurting Piper.

"Back at you." Piper blushed, looking embarrassed. "But King said we can't kill the husband. Yet. He's investigating the guy or something. But I swear to God, if he puts his hands on her..." Piper rolled her eyes to the sky and pretended to choke an imaginary neck. "I'll kill him."

Lou thought of Fish and the tender way his wife leaned toward him, smiling as she offered her cheek for a kiss. *No*, she thought. *Some-*

times the monsters stay hidden in the dark. "You're certain he's threatening her now?"

"Oh yeah. And *we're* going to do something about it, because she's Mel. She's one of us. We're not going to let some sleaze bucket assho —" Piper bit her lip the moment her eyes fixed on something over Lou's shoulder. She hiccupped. "Oh shit. Be cool."

Lou felt the girl behind her before she stepped into Lou's line of sight. The impulse to pull her gun or turn and seize the person approaching rose in her. But since Piper's expression looked somewhere between apologetic and annoyed, she suspected this would've been an overreaction.

"Hey, P." A girl with curly dark hair came to stand beside Piper. "You heading out?"

"Yeah," Piper said with an apologetic smile. She hiccupped again. "My cousin Lou*ann* is in town for Carnival. I promised to show her around if she visited, so—"

"It's nice to meet you." The girl extended her hand. The attitude shift was palpable.

She's okay with me now that she knows I'm not a threat, Lou realized, and something about the ridiculousness of it—that this girl would view her as a threat for this reason above any other—made her smile.

"Hey," Lou said, and shook the offered hand. Then she adjusted her jacket to make sure it stayed over her guns.

Piper prattled on. "You were having a good time and I didn't want to interrupt and—"

The girl intercepted by placing a hand on Piper's shoulder. "It's fine. We're heading over to Veronica's anyway. Amy wants to smoke. You guys can come if you want."

"No, that's not her scene," Piper said, pointing at Lou. "We'll probably walk around the Quarter then get beignets and coffee. She'll be out cold before midnight."

Lou said nothing.

The girl gave Piper a long, pitiful stare, and then sighed. "Call me later."

"Yeah, sure."

With one last, lingering look, Scarlett followed her friends up the crowded street.

"I'm going to hell," Piper whispered.

With a tight smile, she waved to the departing group one more time.

"I'm terrible. She's probably going to go home and cry about this. I'm the one who invited her out and got her hopes up. Why did I do that? I'm so dumb."

Lou couldn't help but grin. "She'll live."

Piper nudged her hard with an elbow. "Shut up. If Dani would just return my freaking calls I wouldn't be here right now. Besides, you're one to talk, with your Italian stallion drama. Oh, speaking of which, King said he couldn't get anything on the mystery stalker. Her face didn't match any of his data sweeps. He suggests that you ask Konstantine."

Lou slid her glasses down on her face, hiding her eyes.

Piper hiccupped again. "I could come with you to talk to him. I can even do the talking. I'm feeling pretty chatty right now."

"He's in Venice."

"I've always wanted to go to Venice." Piper threw an arm around Lou's shoulder. "Isn't it Carnival there too? How cool would that be to visit *actual* Venice during Carnival?"

Lou glanced up the street at the drunks leaning against buildings and laughing loudly in the streets. The smell of piss hung around them. No doubt someone was relieving themselves against a brick wall.

Piper tugged on her wrist. "Come on. Let's do it. I've got the photo on my phone and we need to know who this woman is and what she wants with Fish. And I need a distraction from a certain MIA journalist."

"You realize it's four in the morning there," Lou said. "Konstantine will probably be in bed."

A sly smile flickered across Piper's lips. "I mean, we need to know who this woman is, so..."

With a resigned sigh, Lou pulled Piper into the deep shadow of a darkened stoop. She leaned her body against Piper's and heard the girl's throat click. But already her attention was sliding away, searching the other side of the world for her intended target.

Something fell into place, and like a current inside her, the waters changed. The pull swept through her. Lou let go, giving herself over to it.

She had been expecting a hotel room. Or maybe a room in a villa, if Vittoria was any kind of hostess.

What she *hadn't* been expecting was a large and opulent ballroom full of swelling music, writhing bodies, and full-costumed regalia.

Her first thought—*It's nearly dawn*—was drowned in the melancholic music of strings. She couldn't see the violins, violas, or cellos, but their twined voices echoed below the cavernous ceilings and the women in busty corsets and ornate masks swayed and laughed. Men in long jackets stood speaking to one another. Pairs danced in the center.

Lou spotted Konstantine immediately. She knew it was him even with the mask.

He had one arm over the back of a velvet chair. His clothes weren't archaic or costumed like the others around him. He wore a simple black suit, perfectly cut to his body, and an open red shirt beneath. His mask was also red, covering only the top half of his face.

He was speaking to the woman beside him, a beautiful blonde with large, radiant curls. Her breasts were pushed up nearly to her chin by the white corset she wore. Her costume resembled a peacock, from the long, willowy feathers protruding from her shimmering mask to the cape and dress filled with those same placid eyes.

Piper stumbled beside her, seizing her arm as she righted herself. "Whoa. Look at this place!"

It was this movement that drew Konstantine's eye. The smile on his lips faltered for a moment, and he touched the woman's arm, excusing himself.

The bodies in the room parted.

"Oh boy," Piper murmured, nudging Lou. "Here he comes. That's Konstantine, right?"

"Why are you giggling?"

"I don't know." Piper covered her mouth. "It's funny. Look at him."

Konstantine stopped just short of her, regarding her through the dark slits of his ruby mask. "Ciao."

Lou raised an eyebrow. "*Ciao.*"

"Is that booze over there?" Piper pointed at a bar on the right side of the dance floor. A man in a black-and-white suit and white plaster mask was behind it, refilling glasses. "I'm going to get a drink."

Something hard pressed into Lou's open hand. It was Piper's phone.

"5567," Piper whispered into Lou's ear. "It's the last picture I took."

"Take this," Konstantine said, reaching behind his head to untie his mask.

"Oooo, okay. Thanks." Piper tied Konstantine's mask over her face and struck a haughty pose, with one hand on her hip. "How do I look?"

Konstantine nodded. If Piper saw it, she made no further reply, already making a beeline for the bar.

"Is she safe here?" Lou asked, watching her weave through the bodies. She noticed that they did not part for her the way they had for Konstantine.

"With her face covered," he replied. He shifted to the right, and Lou followed his gaze. She wasn't surprised to find Stefano there, lurking in the dark. She hadn't spotted him as quickly or easily as she had Konstantine, but she'd known he would be close. Something about the man's possessiveness of Konstantine amused her. The cold look he gave her only made her smile deepen.

Konstantine dragged a thumb across his cheekbone, and Stefano nodded once.

"What does that mean?" She mimicked him, dragging her thumb across her cheek.

"He'll look after her," Konstantine said with a half-smile. "This is neutral territory and no one should cause trouble, but just in case."

"Shame," Lou said. "I'm in the mood for a fight."

She was very aware of his body beside her. He was turned, his feet pointing toward hers, his hands clasped loosely in front of him. And his smell. It was heady. It made her think of a deep wood, an endless forest full of moonlight.

"Yes, I imagine all of this hunting and not killing is a challenge for you," he said, watching her face carefully. "Does it remind you of your days tracking Angelo?"

"Yes," she said, realizing the truth of it for the first time. "Yes, it's like that."

Silence stretched between them. She found she couldn't figure out how to start the conversation.

Just show him the picture. What's wrong with you?

"I thought you'd be in bed," she said.

"The party will continue until dawn."

She nodded, as if this mattered.

"When I saw you, you already had your eyes on me," Konstantine said. Lou admitted, only to herself, that she enjoyed listening to him speak. "How did you know it was me?"

She shrugged in her leather jacket. "You forget how much time I've spent watching you."

"I'm flattered." But he didn't sound flattered. His laugh was tight and tired.

She glanced toward the white peacock, who'd fallen into conversation with another woman. But her gaze slid to Lou every few seconds.

"Is that your hostess?" Lou asked. "Vittoria."

"Yes."

"Will she mind that I've crashed her party?" Lou's eyes slid instinctively to Piper. She was on the dance floor now, swaying with everyone else, pausing only long enough to take a long drink. Several feet away, Stefano lurked dutifully.

"I will explain that you're with me," he said softly. "Though I suspect she knows you can come and go as you please."

If Vittoria isn't the reason for his fatigue, it must be me, she realized.

His low voice interrupted her thoughts. "Dare I hope that you came to see me simply because you missed me?"

He was looking at her now. She felt the gaze on the side of her face.

She lifted the phone, punched in the passcode, and found the app that opened Piper's photos. The last ones were actually selfies of Piper in the bar. Before that, three photos of Lady with her head on her paws. The blurred tail suggested an enthusiastic wag. It was nearly ten photos back before she found Fish's mysterious stalker.

"A woman is following Fish. She's tracking him like I am."

"*Exactly* as you are?" Konstantine asked, eyebrows rising.

"No. She's using more conventional methods. King looked into her but couldn't find anything."

Konstantine opened a text message and sent the photo of the woman to a number he punched in. Lou heard the buzz in his pocket.

He looked at the photo for a long time, before handing the phone back to her.

"Have I offended you?"

Lou met his gaze. "Your heart's still beating. I'm pretty sure I've shot everyone who has ever offended me."

His lips twitched with a smile. "I've only noticed that you haven't come to see me since..."

She arched an eyebrow, wondering if he was going to say it right here in the open. They were somewhat alone in their corner of the ballroom. But Lou had no doubt ears were listening.

"Since the shower," he finished.

"I've been busy." Lou shifted in her leather jacket again. She felt the guns rub against her ribs. It made her feel better, knowing they were close.

"I'm also busy." His eyes traced her jaw before focusing on her lips. "And I still want you in my bed every night. You *sleep*, don't you?"

"Not always at the same time you do." She met his eyes, and an icy wind rolled through her. The wind was of her own making, she knew it. She was steeling herself against...whatever this was. "What do you want from me?"

"You."

The ice hardened in her chest and stomach. Even her limbs grew heavy with it. She looked away first.

"I'll find this woman for you," Konstantine said, slipping his hands into his pockets. "Even if it's only an excuse to see you again."

He bowed his head, rolling his eyes up to meet hers, and then backed away with one hand over his heart. She watched him go with a strange sensation in her guts. It was an ache. Not unlike hunger.

Piper saw Konstantine crossing the floor and bounced over to him.

She was offering the mask, her hands already behind her head, ready to untie it, but he waved her off with a kind smile.

Then Piper was bounding across the room toward Lou.

"This place is amazing! Free booze and free food. They've got a bunch of those little cakes and something that I *really* hope was sausage. Oh, and the ladies! God, there's this one who is *soooo* cute. I don't know a word she's saying, but that's probably for the best, right? Talking is where I usually go wrong. Talking is the worst. That's why I'm a listener. People think it's because I'm sweet but really it's because I'm *smart*."

Lou watched Konstantine take his place beside his host again, and the possessive way she leaned into him while meeting Lou's gaze made the hairs on her arm rise.

"Yes," Lou agreed. "Talking is the worst."

23

Piper sat up in bed and instantly regretted it. The world whirled around her, falling into a tailspin. The room kaleidoscoped out of focus.

"Whoa." She fisted her sheets as if they would stop her whirling. "Man, what did I *drink*?"

Her head throbbed and instantly was made worse by the earsplitting tone. She groaned, fumbling for the device on her side table, desperate to end the Troye Siven "Fools" ringtone as quickly as possible.

"Hello," she croaked. Her tongue scraped over her teeth like sandpaper. She tried to clear her throat. "Hello, hi?"

She saw the glass of water on the side table and the bottle of aspirin. A memory of Lou placing them there surfaced in her mind. That would explain the fact she was still in her clothes and smelled like booze. At least Lou had removed her shoes before dumping her onto the mattress. Had she stayed the night? Piper couldn't remember.

Propped against the glass was a note in Lou's simple print. Squinting, Piper read, *Payback is coming.*

Even with the smiley face at the end, it wasn't a note one wanted to receive from Lou Thorne.

Payback? Payback for what? What did I do?

But then she remembered. She'd promised Lou she would be the one to talk to Konstantine, but at first chance, she left her alone with him in favor of the open bar.

Oops.

"Hey. Hi. It's me." Dani's voice faltered. "Were you still sleeping?"

Something in her tone encouraged Piper to check the time. She pulled the phone from her ear and squinted at the screen. It was almost ten. She was supposed to be at the shop ten minutes ago.

"Oh shit." Piper threw back the covers and seized the aspirin. She tapped four out into her hand and drowned them with the water.

"If this is a bad time—" Dani began.

"No, no." Piper stumbled from the bed to the adjacent full-length mirror. Her clothes were rumpled but passable. She smelled a little like booze, but nothing some deodorant and a couple sprays of body mist wouldn't fix. She would wash her face, brush her teeth, grab a granola bar from the cabinet. If she was quick about it, she would only be about twenty minutes late. "What's up?"

She put the phone on speaker so that she could shoot Mel a text. *Out with Lou last night. Overslept. So sorry. See you in five.*

Piper got the thumbs-up emoji for her trouble.

"I wanted to apologize for not contacting you again," Dani said, her voice echoing through the speaker phone as Piper went into the bathroom and turned on the faucet. "Something came up and I got distracted."

"It's okay," Piper said, fishing a washcloth off the shelf. "I'm glad that you called."

And to her surprise, she was.

"I was hoping that you could come by tonight for dinner at my place. I'd like a chance to explain. Again."

"I close tonight," Piper said, balancing the phone on the ledge above the sink so she could splash hot water on her face. "How do you feel about a late dinner? Ten thirty?"

"It's perfect," Dani said. "I'll text you my new address, okay?"

It wasn't a full minute after the call ended that Piper's phone buzzed. She recognized the small neighborhood north of the Garden

District. If Dani's new place was there, then she was paying at least two grand a month in rent.

"Ouch." Piper whistled, stuffing the toothbrush slathered in paste into her mouth.

When she closed Dani's text, her eye caught on a number she didn't recognize. She frowned at it, opening the text with a press of her thumb.

There was the image of the woman, Fish's stalker, staring back at her.

"Oh shit," she said, realizing what she must be looking at. Her thumb raced over the keypad. *Konstantine?*

A moment later, *sì, piper.*

Piper spit into the sink. *You better not have installed any tracker crap on my phone dude.*

Or what? What was she going to do if he had? Ask Lou to kill him?

She sighed and added, *Just use the photo to find the chick, k?*

I have only the photo.

"Lies," Piper grumbled, scooping water into her mouth from the running faucet. Of course she couldn't say anything. She'd given Lou the phone to begin with, and it wasn't like Konstantine was supposed to memorize the photo with his eyes or something. But the idea of a crime lord with her information, even one on their side, didn't leave her feeling particularly secure.

May I ask you a question?

Piper looked into the mirror. To her reflection she said, "See. This is how it starts. One second you're texting it up with the gangsters, the next you wake up in a whorehouse in Siberia."

About? she wrote, eyebrows raised.

Our mutual friend

She reread the text several times. With each pass, a dropping sensation intensified in her stomach. She knew she was on a precipice here and that it would be so easy to cross over to the other side, a darker, more dangerous side.

"Damn," she murmured, and typed her reply. *You can ask, but I reserve the right to not answer.*

Into the mirror, she said, "She better not kill me for this."

. . .

W̲HEN P̲IPER LOCKED UP THE SHOP AT TEN MINUTES AFTER CLOSING
that night, she expected to see Mel's husband lurking in the streets
outside. But there was no sign of him. Still she lingered at the entrance
until she saw Mel ascend the stairs, Lady on her heels, and disappear
into her apartment. Only then did she take off through the Quarter,
maneuvering through the bodies that stood between her and the St.
Charles Avenue streetcar stop.

She tracked her progress on her phone, the little blue dot of her
position moving as she moved, until she found herself in front of a
pink stucco building with old French windows. In the foyer, there were
four buttons. Piper mashed the one beside Dani's name.

A voice cracked through the speaker. "Hello?"

Piper leaned toward the com. "It's me."

The door buzzed, and Piper was allowed to pass through the locked
inner door. Dani stepped out into the hall, motioning her forward.

God, she's beautiful.

In a wine-colored turtleneck and tight jeans, her dark complexion
seemed to glow.

"Hi." She chewed her lower lip. "Come on in."

Something about Dani reminded Piper of the night before, of the
woman in the peacock outfit who'd been a bit handsy with Konstantine. She'd been curious about the beautiful, busty blonde, especially
since all the eyes in the room seemed to track her and Konstantine.
But Piper had admittedly been distracted by the pretty drunk girl in a
cat mask who kept whispering super-sexy Italian in her ear.

Piper stepped inside the apartment and slipped her shoes off,
leaving them by the door. She just assumed since Dani was in socks
herself that this was the protocol.

But Dani shook her head. "You don't have to do that."

"It's okay." The shoes were already off. Piper wasn't going to put
them back on.

One quick visual inspection of the apartment told Piper she
wouldn't have been comfortable wearing the shoes anyway. It was
immaculate, with twelve-foot ceilings and the rounded French

windows that Piper had admired from the outside. It was an open floor plan, so the dining area, kitchen, and living room were all laid bare. There were two doors off a short hallway, but they were open too. The walls were a cheerful yellow. The ceilings and trim were creamy white.

Something rubbed against her leg, and Piper looked down to find a fluffy British Blue cat blinking large gold eyes up at her.

"That's Octavia," Dani said, stepping forward with a bottle of wine and two glasses. "I call her Tavi. You're not allergic, are you?"

"A bit, but she's fine." Piper frowned at the wine. "I don't want to drink tonight. I had a bit too much last night, if you know what I mean."

Dani put the wine glasses down on the counter and smiled. But the smile was tight. "Did you go out for Carnival?"

"In *Venice*," Piper couldn't help but say it. "I didn't even need a passport. We were only there for like an hour, but still. Being friends with Lou has its benefits."

Dani was nodding, but Piper had the distinct feeling that she wasn't hearing what Piper was saying.

Dani filled her glass of wine to the top. "She was here this morning. She was the one who told me I'd better call you. I was in the shower and she just opened the door and—" A small, nervous laugh escaped her. "She scared the hell out of me."

"Wait, what? Lou got in your shower?"

Payback is coming—is that what she'd meant by that? That she was going to force me to talk to Dani because I forced her to talk to Konstantine? Vicious!

Piper pouted. "If you only called me because Lou made you—"

"No." Dani brought the wine to her lips but didn't drink it. She still held the bottle in the other hand. "No, I wanted to talk to you. She just gave me the little push I needed. I'm just saying that yes, Lou is a good friend to you."

By popping into your shower and making demands?

Piper rubbed her forehead, feeling a headache blooming behind her skull again. She tried to remember the last time she'd taken a dose of aspirin. "I hope she sees it that way."

Dani's brow furrowed. "What do you mean?"

"Uh, I offered some love advice to her beau that wasn't really mine to give."

Hopefully it won't backfire on my ass.

Konstantine had promised not to say a word, and Piper had suggested that Lou's reluctance to accept Konstantine's devotion was probably because Lou had lost the only man she ever loved when she was a child. Even if he hadn't been Paolo Konstantine, brother to the man who pulled the trigger, even if she hadn't been Louie Thorne, executioner to hundreds of men just like him—there was that simple fact. It was true that Lou only felt in control when she had a gun in her hand and that she didn't attach to people because she understood how easy it was for them to disappear. Especially men like Konstantine.

Didn't you almost die just, like, a year ago? she'd asked. *Do you think she's forgotten that?*

Konstantine had conceded the point.

More than once during their text session, Piper had thought, *I'm texting one of the world's most dangerous men. Ruler of the underground. This guy probably tortures people on a Saturday. Life is so weird.*

Dani smirked.

"What?"

"It doesn't matter." Dani drank half her wine in one go. Then she said, "I wanted to apologize. Again."

Piper refrained from tapping her fingers on the glass tabletop. "For?"

"When we had dinner the other night, I know I gave you the impression that I wouldn't disappear again, and then I did just that. I ghosted you *again*. I'm sorry."

Dani searched her face, and Piper realized she was waiting for a reaction. But Piper, perhaps from having such an exciting night before, then a long day at the shop, felt mostly tired.

"It's okay," she said.

Dani grimaced. "Don't do that."

"What?"

"Don't just forgive me like that."

Piper laughed. "It's easy when you don't really care."

Dani flinched.

"I didn't mean I don't care about you. I'm just tired and I have a headache and I'm worried about"—*Mel mostly, but also Lou*—"my people. I'm sure that if you ghosted me you had a good reason, right?"

There. Piper had left it wide open for Dani to explain herself. She waited.

It was clear by the way Dani wrung the wine glass in her hand, the way she put the bottle down on the table, the way she chewed her lower lip, staring at her hands. All of it signaled that she was working up to it—whatever it was—and Piper knew well enough to hold the space.

I wish I had three more aspirin though. Italian booze was no joke. Her head was killing her.

"I didn't call you back because I was in the hospital."

"So you're sick?" *Oh god, cancer? Something worse?* Piper's mind raced.

"Not that kind of hospital." Dani chewed her lip. "I was at the Crescent City Psych Hospital."

So I did trigger an episode, like you thought I would.

"I've checked myself in a few times this year, just a few days here and there—when the episodes get really bad." She licked her lips again, then pulled on her ear. "It's a good thing the hospital has Wi-Fi, right? Otherwise, I probably would've lost my job by now."

The nervous laugh that escaped Dani set Piper's teeth on edge.

Once she dared a glance up, finally meeting Piper's eyes, Dani grimaced harder. "Don't look at me that way. That's exactly why I didn't call you. I didn't want you to see me as this pathetic, broken little doll."

"I don't see—" Piper began, but she didn't get very far.

The words fell from Dani's lips hot and fast. "I wake up in the middle of the night screaming because I think someone is in my bedroom. I couldn't even stay one night in my old apartment because all I could see is *Oh, this is where he tortured me. Oh, here is where they tied me to a chair and punched me in the stomach a million times. Here is where he pulled out a fistful of my hair. Here is where they—*"

She covered her face and began to cry.

Piper stood and slid her arms around Dani's waist.

"It's okay," she whispered into her ear. She placed a kiss on the top of her ear, then her temple. "It's okay."

"Terrible things happen to people all the time. I don't know why I can't get past this."

"Maybe because you were almost beaten to death for information you didn't even have and then the psychopath cut off your finger? I don't think anyone could just *get past* that. You're putting too much pressure on yourself."

Dani didn't seem to hear her. "I didn't want you to see me this way. But I also didn't want you to think I don't care about you. I'm so weak. I thought adversity made you stronger."

"Hey. Don't say that." Piper pulled back, cupping Dani's cheeks in her hands. "Listen, I think it's important to point out that you were strong before all this bullshit happened. Shit like this doesn't make women stronger. It makes everything *harder*. You don't have anything to prove to me. Or the world."

Dani's eyes were bright with unshed tears. Her lip trembled. "You must think—"

"I think you're an amazing, smart, courageous woman who had a really fucked-up experience. And you survived and it's going to take some time to heal. Maybe you'll never heal completely, and that's okay."

"But you're surrounded by strong women. Lou—"

Piper laughed, a tight, bewildered sound. "We can't compare ourselves to *Lou*." *And it isn't like that girl hasn't got her own problems.* "And I've *never* been through something like what you've been through."

Dani cried softly into Piper's shoulder, and Piper held her. There was nothing else to be done. After the sobs died to a quiet mewling, Piper spoke. "What happened to you *happened*. Period. You don't have to justify your pain to anyone, okay? Not me or anyone else. I'm going to say this a million times until you believe me."

Dani pulled back and dabbed at her eyes. "I'm sorry. I stayed away so you wouldn't see me fall apart, and I'm falling apart anyway."

Piper pushed the hair back from Dani's face. "I'd rather see you fall apart than not see you at all."

Dani laughed, a sad, desperate little sound that could be interpreted in a hundred different ways. "You don't mean that."

Piper grabbed both sides of her face, forcing Dani to look her in the eyes. "I mean it. Okay? I mean it."

Dani looked around her apartment as if seeing it for the first time. "Are you hungry? Will you stay the night?"

Piper smiled, unwilling to point out that these two questions were entirely unrelated. "Yes."

24

———

As Melandra's spoon stirred cream into her coffee, her eyes fixed on some point in the distant past. Her bare kitchen wall served as the screen for the theater of her mind. The table creaked under the press of her elbows as she adjusted herself, unable to get comfortable.

The apartment, she realized, was the antithesis of the trailer she'd shared with Terry all those years ago. It had been narrow, stuffed with furniture that had come from the Salvation Army, mostly browns and yellows with tears at their seams. And no matter how hard she'd cleaned its windows, it seemed not enough light had ever filled those small rooms.

She'd spent nearly six years working first shift in a small manufacturing plant to pay for it. On the weekends, she wandered the rooms of that old trailer, doing her best to keep the little place clean. She scrubbed the toilet and the shower and packed up all their clothes to be taken down to the coin-operated laundromat at the other end of the trailer park.

On most days, Grandmamie's voice had haunted her.

Us Durand women are both blessed and cursed, Melandra. You hear me? Blessed with the sight but also blind in the heart. We're destined for bad men, every one of us, and if you fool enough to go an' have a girl child of your own, she gonna be as blind as the rest of us.

Now, decades later, in her beautiful, airy apartment full of light, Mel still remembered feeding quarters into the slot, adding the powdered soap to the machine, and thinking that Grandmamie had been right. Mel had been blinded. By Terry's easy smile. By the way he'd lower his voice and whisper directly into her ear all the things she needed to hear. How he'd lean his hip into her hip and her whole body would soften.

A damn fool, Mel thought, bringing her coffee to her lips. *But at least I didn't have a baby girl.*

When Terry was arrested, and his body was slammed onto the floor of their little trailer so hard the whole place shook, she'd been ashamed of how relieved she felt. How could she be *relieved* to see her husband cuffed and dragged from the room?

She looked over the rim of her coffee mug at the three replacement cards spread before her on her kitchen table. They echoed the long ago spread laid out by her dead grandmother's crooked fingers.

Then it had been The Devil, Justice, Death.

Now it was The Devil, The Wheel of Fortune, and Death.

It was The Wheel of Fortune she fixed her eyes on, a card she'd laid off to one side. The problem with the wheel was that she couldn't be sure if it was turning for or against her. Change for the better, change for the worse. It could go either way.

If it was turning for the worst—what of it? Didn't Mel know, in her heart, that she had it coming? However this shook out, with her dead or in prison, she had it coming.

She had it coming because of what happened in November 1982.

It had been flurrying on and off all day, in that way it did sometimes in Louisiana. No real snow would come of it, but it was enough to make the roads slick and the face and knuckles cold.

By the time they'd left the bar at two in the morning, it had given over from snow to rain. Terry had been in a good mood. He'd won the pool games he'd played, and hadn't gotten caught cheating. Then he'd drunk away half his winnings to celebrate.

"You drive," he'd told her as they stumbled down the steps into the gravel lot.

Mel hadn't wanted to. She'd had two beers herself, and though she wasn't drunk, she was tipsy enough to know it was a bad idea.

He threw her the keys to the Firebird and missed. They hit the gravel at her feet.

"We should call a cab."

"I ain't leaving my car here." He unzipped his pants and began pissing on a bush beside the bar door. "Drive, or I will."

She bent and fished the keys out of the gravel despite the sense of pending dread filling her.

I'd known, she thought. *I'd known something was going to happen and I drove anyway.*

She'd put the key in the ignition, turned it, and pulled out of the lot onto the dark country road. She'd driven slowly, but it hadn't mattered. She'd gotten tired, as she always did with a few drinks in her. The soft sound of rain splashing against the windshield hadn't helped.

Her eyes had closed only for a moment. Then the car hit something, hard. She slammed on the brakes, skidding to a stop in the middle of the road. Each swipe of the wiper blades revealed the rain falling in her headlights and the bend in the road ahead.

Her first thought—*If I'd slept for even ten seconds longer, we would've slammed right into those trees.*

Her second thought—*What did I hit?*

Terry came awake beside her, jolting up in his seat. "What the hell happened?"

"I hit something."

Mel craned her neck, looking behind her. A lump lay in the middle of the dark road. The red taillights gave it a demonic glow. But it had the unmistakable shape of a human body. A small woman? A child?

"Oh god," she whispered. "Oh my god, I hit somebody."

He turned in his seat, looking back over his shoulder into the dark. "Stay here."

He pushed open the passenger side door.

Mel had begun opening her door when Terry grabbed her arm hard, yanking her back into the seat. "Stay here, I said."

First he went to the front of the car, stood in the headlights and inspected the damage while rain pelted his face. He rubbed something with his hand and swore. Then he walked to the back of the car and bent down over the unmoving form.

That's when Mel put her face in her hands and began to cry.

Terry got back in the car, dragging a hand down his face. "Drive."

She looked around, searching the darkness for help, or a witness. She'd seen a light through the trees.

"We can go to that house and call for help."

He grabbed the back of her hair and pulled hard enough to bring startled tears to her eyes. "*Drive*, or I'll pull you out and I'll drive."

And God forgive her, she had driven away from the scene without having to be told twice.

"It was an animal," he'd whispered. "You hear me. It was an animal."

"It wasn't! It—"

He'd slapped her, and that was the end of it.

The next day he took five hundred dollars from her account and the car went into the shop. That was the last they ever spoke of it until he went to prison.

"If I pay him off, he'll just come back. If I go to the police, he'll run. Or he might tell them what happened."

Or maybe he won't give me a chance to confess at all, Mel thought. *He's never liked not getting his way.*

She reached past the three cards and lifted the revolver resting there. She noted its weight in her hand, the finality of it.

Lady placed her head on Mel's leg. A long, mournful whine escaped the dog. Mel cupped one ear with her hand, but her eyes remained fixed on the gun.

"There, now. Everything's gonna be all right."

25

———————

Konstantine woke the moment he felt the weight beside him. He instinctually reached for his gun before the familiar scent washed over him. He relaxed. Turning only his head, he saw the outline of her body.

Lou lay on her back, her eyes closed, her lips slightly parted. Her dark lashes rested on her cheeks. For a long while he only looked at her, watching her chest rise and fall. She was dreaming, and he longed to know what she dreamed of. Killers prowling the night? Drug dealers? His dead brother Angelo with his gun? Her father or mother? Her aunt?

Him?

The familiar stab of rejection shot through him. He ached to reach out and touch her, but to do so would break the spell. Maybe he would never see her again.

Maybe the girl, Piper, had been wrong.

She comes to see you. She's not doing that with anybody else, man.

No. She hadn't joined another man's bed. His constant canvassing of the internet for photos, video clips, or any other trace of her existence *was* in the name of protecting her anonymity, but he did look for other men.

There had been a few, before they'd begun—whatever it was they had now.

But she wasn't sleeping in anyone else's bed, braless. She wasn't taking showers with them or wearing their black sweats. And most importantly, she went to no one else—save the old detective in New Orleans—when she needed help.

It was more than that.

She chooses me when she dreams, he thought, watching her breathe beside him. *What are dreams but our deepest desires?*

Don't rush her, man. She's like a cat. She's going to love you on her terms.

That, at least, Konstantine had agreed with. The girl, despite her American slang, had seemed very wise in her text messages. It contrasted with her sweet, angelic face. She looked like a child when standing next to Lou.

He recalled the way the girl had looked, laughing, hanging off of Lou's shoulder in the ballroom. What a contrast. Lou, somber and imperial. The girl blond, smiling, and infused with girlish radiance. Proserpina in her two forms.

Konstantine traced the line of her jaw with his gaze, down her throat to the small hollow there. He longed to touch it with his lips.

A sound over his right shoulder caught his ear. He turned and saw Vittoria in the doorway. She beckoned him forward.

As silently as he could, he slipped from the bed, pausing to regard Lou once more.

He pulled the door closed behind him.

Vittoria was in a red dressing gown. Her face had been wiped of its makeup, and she looked her age now.

"Mi stavi guardando?" Konstantine asked as she settled into a leather chair. *Were you watching me?*

"I have cameras everywhere in this house."

"I know." Konstantine had wired into her system before ever agreeing to stay at her villa.

"Clever boy." Vittoria grinned. "Imagine my surprise when a woman appeared in your bed. Does that happen often?"

"Why are you speaking in English?" Konstantine asked, and settled into the leather armchair across from her.

"I need to practice," she purred, turning her glass in the light. She flicked her eyes up to meet his. "You didn't answer my question."

"Don't worry about her," Konstantine said.

"I worry about everything that happens in my home. In my city. Italy. The world. To be a woman in this business you have to worry twice as much as the men," she said with a playful pout. "How lucky you were to be born with a dick, *fratello.*"

Konstantine didn't rise to her bait.

"If she can appear and disappear like in the rumors, I wonder what else may be true." Vittoria rose from her seat and crossed to Konstantine. She sat down on his lap, perching on his knee. "*Te la sei scopata?*"

Konstantine frowned up at her. "*Greggia.*"

She laughed. Then in English, "If you haven't, you certainly want to. I see it in your eyes. Do you own her then? Have you made her love you? Is that why she seeks you out in the night like some *vampira?*"

"She doesn't love me." Despite the sinking in his chest, he felt he'd spoken the truth.

Vittoria clucked her tongue. "A shame. With Fernando Martinelli as a father you should be better at this."

LOU WOKE WHEN THE DOOR CREAKED SHUT. THE SMALL SOUND pulled her straight from her dreams. She couldn't remember what she'd been dreaming of—something about a car sinking through red waters and a monster that waited outside its windows to snap her up.

Lou sat up, taking inventory of the room. She was in a high four-post bed. On the right were floor-to-ceiling shutters, latched tight. Dim light squeezed through the slats, cascading over the uneven tiled floor. Against the far wall, an armoire twice her size sagged.

She didn't recognize the room or its furniture. But she knew the smell that lingered on the pillows around her, on the sheets.

Voices carried from somewhere outside the room, and she saw the light under the door. She slid from the high bed, feeling her bare feet press into the cold tiled floor.

At the door, she grabbed the handle and turned it ever so slightly. She held her breath, as if that might somehow dampen the sound.

Fortunately, the door did not creak, and through the crack she could see the large expanse of a living room. A soft fire crackled against the far wall. Framing it were two armchairs facing one another.

Even without the white peacock costume, Lou recognized the woman immediately. She sat sprawled on one of the leather armchairs with a glass of wine in hand. Then she rose, crossed the room, and sat on Konstantine's lap.

The movement obscured her view of his face, of his reaction to the woman. But she saw what he didn't do—push her off, move her away, demand that she stop.

Why should he? she asked herself. *If this is what is required to make a business deal, why stop now?*

Yet there was an intense heat building in her face.

She backed away from the door the way one moves away from the sparking wick of a stick of dynamite. Then through the darkness, she was gone.

26

―――――――

After failing to sleep in her own bed, Lou put on jeans, her guns, and her leather jacket. She grabbed her mirrored sunglasses off the counter and stepped into her linen closet once more.

This really was the only way to deal with a restless night.

The scent of cedar swelled around her, and she pressed her back against the wooden wall.

Through the dark she searched for her target—Fish. And like anyone, Fish had his usual haunts. He went to work at the high school. He favored the grocery near his house. He worked in the garage and took his son to the park.

But Lou's compass didn't direct her to any of these destinations.

When the dark opened around her, she was in the forest. Pine sap stuck to her fingers as she clung to the tree. Her boots settled on dried needles. Clouds moving across the sky dappled the moonlight, causing the shadows to sway and swell like water across the ground.

For a horrible heartbeat, Lou thought Fish might be behind her. Ready for her.

But then she heard a grunt, a small, muffled cry.

The clouds moved and moonlight spilled over Jeffrey Fish's hunched body.

There was no victim. No struggle as she had feared. It was only Jeffrey on his knees, pants down.

She moved closer silently, careful not to betray her approach with a snapping twig or shifting rock. His erection was in his hand as he furiously pumped it up and down. Sweat stood out on his brow as his eyes rolled closed.

Lou could smell the death from here. It wasn't unlike passing roadkill on a hot summer day, mixed with the scent of overturned earth. She didn't need to look into the grave to know what she would see. By the smell of the corpse, she didn't think it was the grocer, who she'd checked on just that afternoon.

She suspected it was someone else. Someone killed recently.

Rage welled within her. She drew her gun before she knew what she was doing.

Shoot him. Shoot him and kick his corpse into this grave and be done with all this bullshit. Broken systems and stupid rules that no one plays by. End it. End it now.

No! This was Aunt Lucy's cry. *Think of the families. Think of the families who'll never know what happened. Who will lie awake at night and pray for news, any news, to get past the horrible limbo of uncertainty.*

Gritting her teeth, Lou raised her boot and kicked out. Fish cried out, falling forward into the grave. She peered in, watching his scramble on top of the corpse.

By the time he managed to spit the soil from his mouth and begin screaming, Lou was already gone.

King woke when his bedroom light clicked on. Lou stood over his bed, scowling at him. He squinted up at her, his heart rocketing in his chest.

"What?"

"He's killed again," she said. The coldness in her voice echoed through his bones.

King sat up, scrubbing at his eyes. "Who?"

"Fish killed someone."

"How?"

"I wasn't there," Lou said in that same flat tone. "I suspect he tortured her then fucked her like the others. He was certainly masturbating over her grave—"

"Christ."

"I want to take him now. I'll keep him somewhere until you can build your case."

King looked at her. Again, her face betrayed nothing. It was better to listen to her voice, which at least gave a hint of the fury raging inside her.

"We can't take him to court if you do that. Him missing will only complicate the case."

She rolled her shoulders in her jacket. It was the first real threat of aggression he'd seen from her. "He *killed* someone and we didn't *stop* him."

King glanced at the urn on the side table. *What do I tell her?*

Reason with her. She's smart.

"Fine," Lou said. "Then let's expose him. I'll take them to the grave where he was jerking off. With his DNA, that might be enough to get the conviction."

"But not enough to tie him to the other cases."

"That's what the photos are for."

"We can't use the photos without a warrant to obtain them lawfully. And we can't get that if we don't have a reason to go into his house. They'll want to know how we know about the grave. We'd have to fabricate witnesses that we don't have or who might lose their cool during cross interrogation. The system requires—"

"Your system is broken," Lou said, and here her face contorted. As much as it frightened King to see it, in a way, it was a relief. When he had no idea what she was thinking in that dark mind of hers, he found it all the more difficult to respond.

"I know you're frustrated. I am too. I didn't want any more women to die either," he said, trying to wipe at his dry, tacky mouth. "But we don't have enough to convict. Not a white high school teacher from suburbia. At the very least we need the DNA."

"*Go* to the grave and *get* it."

King pinched his eyes shut. He wasn't awake enough for this. What time was it? It was just past midnight. He'd barely gotten a single REM cycle before she'd showed up. Now he was likely to spend the night tossing, turning, and blaming himself for a murder they might have prevented if they'd been quicker.

He pinched the bridge of his nose. "It's not that easy. I'm not even an agent anymore. I'm not sanctioned by any agency. I can't just show up in someone's jurisdiction and point a finger at Fish and say he did it."

His ears popped and he opened his eyes.

Lou was gone.

Groaning, he fell back against his pillow. He reached out and found the edge of the urn with his fingers. "I'm doing the best I can," he whispered.

Yes, but is it enough?

27

———————

Dani watched Piper reach into her bag and pull out several items. "You have your toothbrush with you. That's convenient."

"Never know when you're going to need to brush your teeth." She hoped her smile looked easy and not the least bit guilty. She didn't want to mention that she'd packed it yesterday in case she went home with Scarlett. In addition to the collapsible travel toothbrush, her small tin box included a small bottle of face wash, deodorant, hair ties, and clean underwear.

Piper hadn't packed pajamas, but she could sleep in her t-shirt and boxers. The only problem was, as she stood in the doorway to Dani's bedroom with her face scrubbed and teeth brushed, she wasn't sure where she was supposed to sleep.

She watched Dani pull back one side of the sheets and lift a pillow.

"Am I sleeping on the couch or——?" Piper asked. *Don't shuffle awkwardly. You look stupid.*

To Piper's relief, Dani was visibly disappointed. "Oh. You can if you want to."

Piper couldn't suppress her grin. "Or I could sleep here."

She grabbed the other side of the sheets and turned them down.

Dani's cheeks reddened. "Do you want a glass of water? I like to have a glass of water."

"Sure." Piper slipped into the bed and pulled the sheets over her lap. She arranged and rearranged them, trying to decide where they lay best.

Stop it, she chided herself. *Nothing's going to happen. You don't need to look sexy in her bed.*

She'd thought they were heading in that direction with their make-out sessions in the stockroom, before Dmitri almost killed them, of course.

Dani reappeared with the waters and a shy smile on her face. "I hope that no ice is okay."

"It's great. Thanks."

Dani handed the glass over. "You know, I was so nervous about you coming over, but now that you're here I feel so much better. I feel safe—"

The closet door opened and Lou stepped into the room.

Dani yelped in surprise, dropping her water glass.

Lou stopped where she stood, one hand on the handle.

"Christ, Lou!" Piper threw back the covers. "Warn us!"

Dani's hand was over her heart as she stared down at the water on the hardwood floor. "I'm going to get a towel."

She stumbled from the room, out of sight.

"Was I interrupting something?" Lou frowned at the water.

"No. I mean, yes. But not *that*. Man, she's got PTSD from Dmitri— you can't just pop into her bedroom at night like that."

"She's never minded before."

Piper's brows shot up. "Excuse me?"

Dani reappeared and gave Lou an apologetic smile. "I'm sorry I screamed. Usually I feel the ear-pop thing when you show up. Obviously I wasn't paying attention."

Piper swallowed. "Would you say you can count on one hand the number of times you've had chats in darkened bedrooms? I'm just curious."

Dani blotted at the water on the floor. "I wasn't counting."

Piper sucked her teeth. "On one hand or two, would you say?"

Dani refolded the towel. "We only talk about work. Except yesterday when she told me I should give you a call. That was a first."

Two people can play at this game, Piper thought.

She raised her chin defiantly. "Yeah, well, *I've* been texting Konstantine."

Lou smiled. "He's probably scraped your phone of all its data and is tracking you now."

Piper placed a hand on her hip. "You don't know that."

Dani stood with the soaked rag in her hand. "You wouldn't be here if it wasn't important. What happened?"

"Fish killed a woman."

Piper sank onto the bed. "Oh shit, the grocer?"

"No. It was someone else. The corpse was...fresh, but not that fresh."

Piper glanced at Dani. When they'd told her that Dani had been helping them verify details of the case, Piper had imagined that meant Google searches or well-placed calls. She hadn't realized that Dani was so thoroughly entangled in the entire process.

The jealousy made her throat tight. The problem was, she couldn't be sure what she was jealous about. Lou and Dani's working relationship? Or was she feeling left out again?

"So we know nothing about this woman," Piper said, determined to be part of this.

"We don't know it was a woman," Dani said.

"The corpse was wearing a blue floral top," Lou offered. "And we know Fish hunts women."

"What did King say?"

Piper scoffed. "How do you know that she's even spoken to King about it?"

"He's worried about jurisdiction."

Dani frowned. "If the bodies are found, won't that activate jurisdiction?"

"First someone has to discover them."

Piper placed her hands on her hip. "Should I just go make coffee? Or am I included in this conversation?"

They both looked at her. Lou frowned. "Of course you're included."

Dani patted the bed beside her. "Come here. We'll hatch our plan together."

Something about her sweet voice or the way she tilted her chin down ever so slightly when she called Piper closer was enough to soothe that ache in her chest.

Piper settled onto the bed beside Dani. Dani fished a pair of glasses out of her side table and slipped them on.

She caught Piper's eyes. "What? Why are you looking at me like that?"

"I've never seen you in glasses. It's hot. You look like Lois Lane."

"Thanks." Dani blushed. She flicked her eyes up to meet Lou's. "So we need someone to find the bodies. Then what?"

28

K ing pulled the tab on his diet soda and listened to it crack and fizz. With the long week behind him, he settled into his red leather couch and groped for the remote. He hadn't decided what he wanted to do for dinner yet. The grocery shopping hadn't happened as he'd hoped.

He'd pushed to have the last bit of work done before leaving the office at six that evening, hoping for a weekend of no paperwork.

Piper's check was written, tucked into an envelope and slid under her apartment door. He'd wrapped up four outstanding cases, closing out their invoices. He emailed his other clients and gave them updates.

The frantic, high energy of Carnival hadn't helped. All that frivolity in the Quarter seemed to permeate his skin like humidity. He needed this quiet weekend to recharge, even if true rejuvenation wouldn't be possible until after the festivities.

He enjoyed the feeling tremendously. Organization, order, progression grounded his life in a way that few other things could. He still remembered his arrival in New Orleans and those first boozy, restless months. Now he understood how ridiculous the notion had been—that he would simply pass a quiet retirement in a city like New Orleans.

Whether or not he'd known it at the time, he'd come to the city to drink himself to death.

He'd told himself that it was to relax and enjoy the lively atmosphere. He was half convinced it was for the food and for the bars. That should've been his first warning sign. He could've chosen a golf community in Florida or even a beach house in North Carolina. But no, he'd chosen one of the most crime-ridden cities in the US.

Why would he do that unless he was secretly hoping to either work or get himself into trouble?

King glanced at the bouquet of flowers on his coffee table. A rich spray of orange, yellow, and pink blossoms rested in the green glass vase. A card stuck up from its center, perched on its plastic pedestal.

Thanks for everything. Until next time – Beth

His eyes slid to the urn sitting beside it. "Oh, come on. It's not like that."

Beth McMiller was the assistant DA. The flowers were a thank you for the critical evidence King had provided in an attempted murder case. It was only footage from a laundromat across the street from the crime scene.

Immediately King felt foolish to be explaining—to an urn—why he'd received flowers from another woman, but the lack of reply was worse. The feelings that welled up and overtook him were *much* worse.

Lucy didn't give a damn about who was or wasn't sending him flowers, because Lucy was dead.

Lucy was dead.

And though he'd been living with this reality for over a year, it hit him again. A horse kick to the chest and he folded over, putting his head in his hands.

He began to cry.

I just miss her, he thought. *It's fine to cry. I just miss her.*

So he let himself cry while the television rambled on about gas prices, political scandals, and an earthquake in Ecuador that had left over a hundred people dead. He cried because he missed Lucy's face, her voice, and the brief, beautiful summer they'd had together. But he cried harder about what he couldn't remember, and the years they hadn't had.

He wasn't sure how long he went on like this, letting the sweet, heady scent of the flowers perfume this dark, secret moment. He probably would've gone on most of the night like that if he hadn't heard the word *graves*.

He looked up, sniffling. The television screen blurred through his tears.

He blinked and dabbed at his eyes. He mashed the volume button on the control, turning it up louder.

"This is the second grave discovered in the area today. Both contained the bodies of young women between the ages of eighteen and thirty."

A male reporter with a large mole beside his left eye continued to stare solemnly into the camera lens.

"The body found here in Ridgeway Park was nearly three miles from the nearest road. The grave was discovered when a resident birder left the trail in search of an oriole. The birder's dog discovered a disturbed patch of earth. Within moments, the witness realized just what his dog was digging up."

The camera angle widened, and for a moment King saw a patch of road and the police cars parked in a long line between two barricades.

When the camera swept forward one more time, King's breath hitched. He sat forward, moving toward the edge of his seat.

On the side of the road, beside the news van, King saw a woman that looked suspiciously like Dani speaking to another reporter. In fact, he was so certain that was who it was, he would've put $500 on red.

I wonder how Dani got all the way to Ohio, he thought bitterly. *Way to force my hand, kid.*

And Fish's hand. Without a doubt, King knew the discovery of not one but two graves would incite Fish to react. He just wasn't sure what that reaction would be.

If Fish was the vainglorious type, he might turn himself in, confess to the crimes, and bask in the limelight of a highly publicized trial. If he was more desperate, hungrier, he might instead go on a killing spree. If he felt as though he had little time left to slake that dark desire within him, he would use his final free hours to gorge himself on his favorite prey. Or similarly, he might disappear or lay low in hopes that he could continue to hunt once the danger had passed. Many killers had dormant periods. There was no reason to think that Fish wouldn't see that as a viable option for himself.

Whatever happened next, the fact remained that Lou had changed the rules of the game and King had better prepare for it.

He stood and crossed the living room to his cell phone, which lay connected to its charger. He pulled the cord out of the phone and entered his passcode. He hoped Lou would be quick about answering his page.

But before he could type in her number, the phone rang in his hand.

He hesitated, thumb hovering over the green acceptance button flashing on his screen. He didn't recognize the scrolling number. While it could be a telemarketer, it could also be someone important. He decided to take the gamble and answered the call before it could go to voicemail.

"King speaking."

"Robert King," a man said.

"Yeah, that's me."

"It's Assistant Deputy Dayton Richardson with the Baton Rouge PD. I was told to call you about the inquiry you made earlier this week."

King took the phone over to his armchair beside the record player and sank into it. "I'm listening."

He let his fingers trail absently over the worn covers of his records while the man spoke. He listened for a long time, only interjecting a clarifying question when necessary. When the call ended, he sat back in the chair.

The news had moved onto a commercial for auto insurance. King only distantly noted this, his mind turning over all that he'd just learned about Melandra and her husband.

He stood, punching the first of many numbers into his phone. "So much for a quiet weekend."

29

───────

Lou stood in her apartment, staring out at the setting sun. Her plain white t-shirt and Konstantine's sweats hung loosely from her body as she sipped her coffee. It didn't matter if it was seven at night. It was morning somewhere. Maybe not in St. Louis, New Orleans, or Italy, but somewhere, and coffee drinking was really just a signal for her brain to start its day.

After a very long night in Ohio, she'd fallen into bed around noon and had slept for six straight hours.

The Mississippi River blazed in her eyes as she sipped the warm coffee, rotating her shoulders to relax them the best she could.

She was only halfway through her coffee when her watch buzzed. She took another sip. When it buzzed a second time, she wasn't surprised. She expected King to be livid about the graves. By now, the story would have broken on most of the news channels.

Except it wasn't King's number on the screen. It was Florence.

Konstantine.

Her stomach turned. The coffee turned bitter on her tongue, and suddenly the brilliant orange blaze she'd been enjoying just a moment before burned too bright.

She put her coffee on the counter and picked up the Browning pistol. She walked halfway toward the linen closet before turning back and grabbing the coffee. She cradled it against her chest as she pulled the closet door closed. Two heartbeats and she'd crossed an ocean.

Rough tile formed under her bare feet. A winter breeze slid along her skin. She was in Konstantine's apartment. The sight of him in his tight jeans and a black turtleneck hardened something inside her, as if she were preparing for a physical blow.

He poured himself a glass of wine. He spoke with barely a glance at her. "Can I offer you a glass of prosecco?"

She lifted her coffee. "I'm all set."

He came into the living room, holding his wine glass in his right hand. He regarded her for a long moment, and under the weight of that stare she felt the itch inside her grow. She didn't want to stay. In fact, she half-turned, stepping toward the shadows from where she'd come, but then Konstantine spoke.

"I know who your stalker is."

She stopped, turning back.

He settled behind his desk and turned on the lamp. His wet hair shone in the light. It had been pushed back from his forehead, framing a beautiful square face that he'd shaved. But it was his green eyes she kept looking at.

"Her name is Diana Dennard."

He turned his computer toward her so that she could see the photographs on the screen. Two sat enlarged, side by side. The photo on the right was the woman Lou recognized. Thirty-something with round blue eyes and blond hair. The photo on the left was her as a child, crooked teeth and a shy smile. An abundance of freckles sprayed across her sun-kissed nose.

"I believe I know why King recognized her."

"Why?"

"She was in the news," he said. "Her parents reported her missing in 1995. They were convinced she was kidnapped after school. There were witnesses saying a man in a blue Acura pulled up to the sidewalk and that she got into the car with him. She was gone for nine weeks."

Nine weeks is a long time, Lou thought. *A lot can happen in nine weeks.*

"When she came home, she said she'd run away. That seems to be the end of it."

"So why is she following Fish?" Lou asked, unable to hide her curiosity. She placed her coffee on the desk and perched on its edge.

"I've tracked her movements and can tell she's been in the area for over a year. Before Ohio, she was in Pennsylvania."

None of this told Lou why the woman had an interest in Fish.

"Is she police or something?"

"No. Even in the deep organizations, I found no mention of her. She uses aliases for her purchases. I know of at least four that I can track purchases to in the last twelve months. She should be more careful. She could go to prison for a long time, given how many credit card scams she's run."

He was watching her face expectantly. Maybe he was expecting payment for this work.

"Anything else?" she asked.

He sat back in his chair and brought the prosecco to his lips. "No."

A natural lull filled the space between them. Lou found it unbearable. She stood and took her coffee with her.

"Do you want me to keep digging?" he asked.

"Yes. Thank you," she said, and stepped toward the shadows.

"Why did you leave?" he asked. "When you saw us together?"

Lou froze halfway across the room.

"Vittoria had a camera in my bedroom. She has cameras in all the rooms, actually. I knew this before I visited. I'm not surprised. But I recorded her footage anyway, just to see for myself."

Lou eased her shoulders away from her ears and turned back. "It sounds like you don't trust each other."

"That is how it is with my family." He met her gaze over the rim of his wine glass. In the shadow, his green eyes looked nearly black. "I cannot even trust my own sister."

She felt her stomach clench. She knew by the smile on his face that her body had betrayed her.

He set the glass down and laced his fingers behind his head. "Yes,

Vittoria is another of Fernando Martinelli's bastards. There are many more than you know, not just those you've disposed of. But Vittoria is the only other one who is, as you say, still in the family business."

Lou suddenly couldn't decide what to do with her coffee cup. She lifted it, looked at it, considered where she might put it down.

"Why do you look disappointed that she is my sister?" Konstantine asked.

Lou shrugged. "It would have been easier."

"What would have been easier?"

"If you were fucking another woman. It would be easier for me."

He sat upright in his chair. For a long time he only regarded her with his unflinching gaze. Then he shook his head, as if to rid himself of an unpleasant thought. He said, "I hate disappointing you, but this one you'll have to live with. I have no intention of having other lovers."

"*Lovers.*" Lou snorted.

"Girlfriends. Women. Whatever you want to call them."

"Even if it meant I'd actually fuck you?"

His eyebrows rose. "You have to understand that since I was a child, I've been this way."

She tapped the Browning impatiently against her thigh. "Principled?"

He looked up through his eyelashes at her. "When I want something, nothing less will do. I would rather work harder for the thing I want than substitute it for something that cannot compare."

The shadows around her softened. It would be so easy to give herself over to them, to slip through the dark without so much as a goodbye.

"Will you speak to her?"

Lou stilled. "What do I possibly have to say to Vittoria?"

"Diana Dennard," he said. "Will you ask her why she's following Fish?"

"If I get the chance."

He rose from the desk, leaving the prosecco behind. He crossed to her slowly, as one might approach an animal ready to run.

"What are you doing?" she asked.

He laughed softly. "I was going to ask you to come closer, but I know better. I'll come to you."

He stopped just short of her, aligning his body with hers so that their hips were only centimeters apart. His lips grazed the side of her face.

"I missed you," he whispered. "I was sad to find you'd gone when I returned to the bed."

"You didn't seem sad," she said, thinking of the way Vittoria had draped herself over him. It hadn't seemed sisterly, in Lou's opinion.

"Vittoria can be boorish and immature, but she isn't stupid. She won't make an enemy out of you just to entertain herself. Her survival instincts are far too high. Besides, I believe she is like your Piper."

"Piper," she corrected. He'd pronounced it like *pepper*. "What do you mean?"

"*Lesbica.*" His eyes traced the side of her neck. "She prefers women to men. Perhaps *I* should be the one who is worried."

"You're assuming I'd hurt someone for you."

"You made a good example of Nico."

Her eyes fixed on the scar on Konstantine's cheek, a gift from Nico.

He leaned forward until she could feel the heat of his body wafting toward her. He smelled like the prosecco and some sort of earthy soap.

"I missed you," he said again, and the back of his hand brushed hers. It was part question, part invitation.

When she didn't immediately move away, he clasped her hand and pulled her to him.

He bent his head and kissed her neck. First it was the barest brush. Another question. He moved up her throat to her jaw to her lips. He kissed more deeply when she didn't refuse him. She enjoyed the taste of wine on his lips.

"I am sure you've just woken up." He put his chin on her shoulder. "But I'm exhausted."

"I'll let you sleep," she said, and took a step back.

"Stay."

She wanted to count the vertebrae in his lower back, trace them with her fingertips. But she realized she was still holding her coffee and the Browning pistol.

"Stay until I fall asleep?" he asked, as if already sensing some concession must be made. "Please?"

She held up the gun and the coffee. "I'm bringing these."

30

Mel pulled back the purple curtain and stepped into the shop. It was cooler in the store than it had been in the tiny space with its burning candles and heady incense. The woman whose cards Melandra had just read sniffed twice as she stepped around her.

"Take care now," Melandra said. It wasn't meant to be a menacing remark, and yet the woman burst into fresh tears, exiting the shop as one would flee a fire.

Piper looked up from behind the register and arched a brow. "That bad, huh?"

"Her husband is cheating on her."

Piper pouted her lips. "Ouch."

"With her sister."

"God, why do you tell them stuff like that?" Piper laid down the pen she'd been using to furiously scrawl at their ongoing to-do list.

"I didn't. I only told her that things weren't going well at home."

Melandra hadn't had the heart to tell the woman a lot of things. That not only was her husband cheating on her with her sister, but that her sister was pregnant with his child. That would be what hurt her most, as it had been clear to Melandra's inner eye that the woman had longed to have children of her own, and after years of trying and failing had not been able to carry a child to term.

What would happen to them once the child was born? Melandra could only wonder.

Mel braced herself for a question she'd been expecting. But it didn't come. She'd done her best to hide the fact that her cards were gone. She'd scheduled only palm readings for the walk-ins, letting Piper do the card readings. For those who'd insisted on cards, she'd used an old deck that she'd kept on display for customers.

If Piper had noticed the display cards were gone, she hadn't said anything.

You should be used to hiding things and keeping secrets, she chided herself. *Aren't you full of them?*

Piper tapped her pen against the notepad. "All I've got left to do is clean the front door glass and call the Hamway distributor again about the masks. They still haven't come."

"I'll do it," Melandra said. Her bangles jingled as she reached for the pad and pen, plucking them from Piper's grip. "You can go. Don't you have a test tomorrow?"

"Yeah, but it's online. As long as I finish it by midnight, I'm good." She pulled her cell phone from her pocket and read the time. "I've got twenty-six hours to take it. Plenty of time."

"Maybe you want to study," she suggested.

Get out of here. Melandra's stomach knotted as she noticed the time. *He's going to walk through that door any minute now.*

"Mel." Piper's voice was low and strained. "If you were in trouble, would you tell me?"

Melandra searched the girl's face. "No."

A surprised laugh squeaked out of her. "At least you're honest."

Melandra forced her own smile, but it felt false on her face. The cheek muscles were too tight. They resisted.

"I know you think I'm just a kid."

"Who said that?"

"I'm trying to say"—Piper flicked her eyes up to Mel's—"that I love you, okay? And if you needed something, *anything*, I'm here for you. And so is King. And Lou. But *me* especially."

Mel understood then, with perfect clarity, that Piper knew about Terrence. Maybe she didn't know who he was or what he wanted, but she sensed the danger. Likely it wasn't only Piper but King and Lou who knew as well. If they knew, that meant she didn't have much time to resolve this on her own. They would step in, and she couldn't have that.

This was her burden. Hers alone.

Melandra placed a hand on Piper's shoulder. "Don't you worry about me."

A shaky breath escaped the girl, but the deep worry darkening her face didn't recede.

"Go home," Melandra said finally, removing her hand. She took the pen and notepad. "I'll handle the rest."

At first Melandra thought Piper was going to resist, put up a fight, demand to stay until the shop was locked up, or maybe escort Melandra up the stairs to her apartment door.

Instead she grabbed her phone. She bent and seized her backpack from the floor and hefted it onto one shoulder.

She frowned at Mel. "I'll check in tomorrow."

"Good luck on your test." Melandra followed her to the door.

Piper stepped out into the night. The smell of fried food from the convenience store across the street greeted them. It instilled a craving for egg rolls and orange chicken in Mel's gut. Add to it a nice side of white rice.

The icy wind gusted, pulling tears from Piper's eyes. "Night."

Melandra locked the door behind her and followed her as far as the picture windows allowed. When she was out of sight, Melandra stood in the dim shop, considering her options. She wasn't going to clean the front door glass or call the distributor. Not tonight.

Her phone rang.

Her heart skipped a beat in her chest and her stomach twisted. The sudden urge to empty her bowels filled her. She looked down at the ancient cordless phone beside the register as if it were a beast come to life. Each trill echoed louder and longer, until it made her think of a rabbit Grandmamie had once killed.

"We gotta eat," the old woman had said. It had screamed as she'd pulled it from its wired hutch.

Melandra answered on the fourth ring. "Madame Melandra's Fortunes and Fixes."

"Do you have my money?" he asked in lieu of saying hello. Terrence had always been an impatient man.

"And if I don't?"

"Don't fuck with me, woman. I will go to the police and tell them the truth. I'll tell them what you did."

"Maybe I want to go to prison." What was meant to be a joke came out remarkably calm. *I meant that*, she realized, surprised. *At least in prison, I'd know I was paying for what I did. Then this guilt wouldn't be able to grow inside me like a cancer, poisoning all my days. And he wouldn't be controlling me anymore.*

Terrence laughed, but there was no humor in it. It was an irritated, bitter sound, punctuated by a sucking of teeth. "Only a dumb bitch would say that. Clearly you ain't ever been in prison."

Melandra said nothing.

"Listen to me," he began. "Either you bring me what I ask for, or I'm going to come to that shop and take it, you hear me? I'm tired of playing around."

She pulled once on the locked door then mounted the stairs to her apartment as he ranted.

She found it dark and quiet. Lady was with King tonight. She'd insisted that King take her, suspecting this very moment would come.

Terrence laughed, and Mel heard the real pleasure in it. "Oh yes, I'm going to enjoy reeducating you, woman. You know, I learned a few tricks in prison, too. I know how to do more than just slap a bitch around now. You wanna find out what I learned?"

Melandra's eyes fell on the duffel bag on the kitchen table. It was little more than a shadowed outline in the pale moonlight filtering through the window. She turned on the light and crossed to the table.

"After I beat you so bad you can't walk, I'll leave you one good eye so you can see me burn every one of your mamie's cards."

Melandra opened the bag. At the very bottom were the bricks.

They filled one half of the bag. On top of that lay a coil of rope as thick as Melandra's wrist. Lastly, the revolver she'd had since '78 sat tucked into a loop of the rope. She counted the divots marking each chamber.

What would Terrence do when he realized the duffel had no money?

On the table beside the bag were her instructions to King, including the power of attorney for him to dissolve and reallocate her assets per her instructions.

King was a good man. He would do what she asked of him. She'd done her best to apologize for this burden. She was sorry to ask King for this last favor, but she trusted him.

"You hear this?" Terrence asked. The sound of ripping paper crackled through the line. "That's them cards right there. You hear it?"

"I have the money," she said, in what she thought was a convincing panic.

In truth, she felt almost nothing. It was funny how her mind had blanked, shut down in the face of his threats. Had it always been this way when he'd tormented her? Or was this a new development? She couldn't recall.

"I'll bring the money down to the canal," she said. "There's a little plaza by the Julia Street station. Be there in twenty minutes."

"I'll be there in fifteen," he said fiercely. "And if you don't have my money I'll be turning what's left of you over to the police."

She lifted the gun from the bag and felt the weight of it in her hand. The metal was strangely warm, as if alive. It was ready. And so was she.

"I'm on my way," she whispered as her hand tightened on the revolver.

"Good." She heard Terry's smile through the phone. "I'll be waiting."

31

Piper brought the two mugs of coffee over to the sofa and sat down beside Dani. She placed one of the steaming mugs into Dani's hands.

Dani barely managed a thank you before Piper returned to the subject at hand. "I'm just saying there's a lot that can go wrong."

"Yes," Dani said, before bringing the mug to her lips and blowing.

Piper chewed her lip nervously. "Lou has many, many talents, but she doesn't really specialize in trying to keep the bad guys alive, you know?"

"I know," Dani said, following her with her gaze.

Piper was pacing her living room again, unaware that she was doing so. "What if he stabs her or shoots her or something because she's trying not to hurt him?"

"I'm pretty sure she's been stabbed and shot before," Dani offered, doing her best to keep her voice level, steady, in order to balance out Piper's obvious concerns.

Piper huffed. "Yeah, I guess she's kinda indestructible. No. See, *that's* what we start thinking, and then *bam*, she's going to get seriously hurt. Maybe even die. That's how the universe is. It doesn't want you getting too cozy, thinking you know things."

"Will you sit down beside me?" Dani asked.

Piper stopped pacing. She crossed to the sofa with her coffee mug and sat down beside her once again.

Dani placed a hand on her knee. "We did everything we could. All we have to do right now is wait."

"Oh god, then there's Mel!" Piper exclaimed. She put her coffee on the table and began pacing again. "What are we going to do about her murderous husband? That guy is just as much of a monster as the dudes Lou hunts. No wonder she was so calm when that dirty cop pointed a gun at her."

Or when Dmitri Petrov's men threatened to shoot her in the head. Piper had caught herself from saying these last thoughts aloud at least, realizing that Dani didn't want to be reminded of Petrov.

"King's working on that," Dani said from her place on the sofa. "Piper? You're doing it again."

Piper stopped pacing. "Sorry."

"Come sit down."

Piper sank onto the sofa for a third time and sighed. "Sorry. I'm sure me freaking out isn't helping your PTSD. I'm just so worried about everyone and I feel like I'm not doing enough."

Dani reached across the sofa and put her hand on top of Piper's.

A cool chill skittered across Piper's skin. She licked her lips compulsively. After several beats of agonizing silence, Dani broke it first.

"This is better," she said, placing her mug on the coffee table and turning toward Piper.

Piper settled against her sofa cushions. "Me sitting and shutting the hell up?"

"No." Dani cocked her head playfully. "Freaking out. *Together.* It's better than doing it alone."

Piper's heart swelled in her chest. It seemed to double then triple in size.

"Piper," Dani began, glancing first at her hands before flicking her eyes up to meet Piper's. Then she laced their fingers together. "Can I kiss you?"

Piper only managed to swallow against the knot in her throat. "For real?"

"No ulterior motives. No secrets. Just kiss you."

I think it's the only thing I've wanted for like fourteen months, Piper thought.

She shrugged. "It might be cool."

Dani mimicked her. "Yeah. Cool."

"Really cool."

"Absolutely cool."

"Would you mind if I just—"

"Please."

Piper was across the sofa before permission fully passed Dani's lips. She kissed her once, twice, and somewhere between the third and fourth kisses the flurry of lips devolved into one long, continuous make-out session.

Piper pulled back, breathless. "Should I keep going?"

"Yes." Dani's kisses fanned across Piper's cheek to her neck and down to her collarbone. "Assuming that's what you want."

"I like this. This is nice." Piper swooned, heat flooding her head.

She pushed Dani onto the flat of her back against the sofa and bent to kiss her again. But she hesitated. "Wait, is this too much too soon? Aren't you—"

A deep blush had filled Dani's cheeks. She came up onto her elbows, trying to snare Piper's lips. "I'm okay. I'm really, *really* okay."

"Are you sure? I don't want to trigger—"

"Piper!" Dani exclaimed, grabbing the girl's shirt and pulling her back down. "Shut up and kiss me."

32

———————

Lou waited until Konstantine's breathing slowed to a steady rhythm. He lay on his back, his face turned toward her. His eyes were closed and moonlight collected in his dark lashes as his chest rose like a cresting ocean wave. The woodsy scent she'd come to associate with him—amber and sandalwood—surrounded her. It was on his clothes and hair, of course, but also on the pillows and sheets.

On her.

She couldn't explain why she'd agreed to stay, or why she'd propped her back against the headboard and drunk her warm coffee until he'd drifted off to sleep. She couldn't explain why it was sweet—the fact he slept so well beside her.

He trusts you, her father's voice said in her mind. *Do you trust him?*

That was the question. And why did trusting him matter? It was more important that she trusted herself. She knew there was nothing he could do to her that would break her.

That should be enough.

With her eyes, she traced the light cutting across his cheek, down to his lips. They rested slightly open, with a hint of teeth between them. She wanted to kiss him.

Hell, if she was being honest with herself, she wanted to do a lot more than kiss him.

She knew herself well enough to know she wouldn't disappear once they'd crossed that final threshold, as she had with every other man in her sexual history. She would keep fucking him. And if she did...

Then what?

She leaned toward his lips, moving in to seal that mouth with her own, when a shocking jerk reverberated through her body. It was like catching a fishhook in her navel. It yanked hard through her abdomen, sending electric sparks up her spine.

Her back arched with a sharp inhale.

Konstantine's eyes opened instantly. "What's wrong?"

Her eyes pinched closed. Lou searched the darkness. Her compass whirled wildly, trying to fix on a space and time. The frantic, desperate pull was unquestionably urgent.

Who? her mind begged. *Where?*

Piper? No.

King?

"Louie," Konstantine whispered. His cold hands touched her burning face. "What's wrong?"

The compass latched onto its target at last.

"It's Fish." She pried open her eyes. "I have to go."

"Take me with you," he said, still cupping her face.

She managed to get the coffee cup back to the nightstand, surprised she hadn't spilled its contents all over them both.

"No," she said. "Call King."

Konstantine's irritation was clear. She'd scared him. "And tell him what?"

"Fish is hurting her. We need to move now."

"Where are they?"

"At her house."

"How can you know that?" Konstantine was on his feet. He bent to remove his phone from its charger.

How could she explain it to him? That once she'd been in a place, knew its smell, its taste, she could recognize it as well as a face she'd seen before. And even if she could articulate the experience for him, now wasn't the time. The darkness pulled at her skin, her body, her face, like a torrential river. Its current was hell-bent on carrying her to where she needed to be.

"He's at McGrath's house." She turned her head, glancing at him from the side of her eye to make sure he was listening. "Tell him."

Then she let the darkness take her.

She opened her eyes and found herself in a kitchen, holding the Browning pistol she'd taken with her to Konstantine's.

Outdated checkered tile ran from wall to wall. The kitchen looked ransacked. The cabinets stood open. A stack of pots had been pulled from their resting place and thrown across the floor. A drawer had been yanked from its track. Forks, spoons, and butter knives were strewn like confetti. They sparkled in the moonlight pouring through a kitchen window. Sugar packets littered the counter and floor. Two chairs had been turned on their sides.

It was the blood that stopped Lou in her tracks.

A large splash lay on the tile, soaking through a few of the sugar packets. It had turned half of the white paper a dark red. Then a trail began. It dripped toward the living room. Lou followed it to the base of some stairs.

A woman screamed. The sound echoed through Lou's spine, sparking electricity through her arms to her fingertips. Two shadows swept over the white walls above. Lou took the stairs two or three at a time. The blood had soaked into the carpet at the top. A new trail formed from this landing into the bedroom at the end of the hall. Lou placed a hand on the bannister, listening for a moment to make sure she knew where the sounds of struggle were coming from.

Definitely from the bedroom straight ahead. The door itself confirmed this.

It hung at an angle, with splinters jutting from the busted handle. McGrath must have locked herself in the bedroom to buy time. Fish must have busted through the door shortly after.

A lamp flew past the open door and shattered against the wall. Ceramic shards and lightbulb glass rained down on the carpet.

Then Fish was there.

He rounded the bed, hair in disarray. His chest was heaving like a wild dog's and his body was hunched as if in hunger. He was *snarling*. The sight of him like that—more beast than man—stunned Lou.

Perhaps because it was so different from the drug lackeys she so often hunted. Different from the fools like Walker who went quietly, ignorantly, to their own deaths. She'd seen this level of maniacal animalism only a few times—in Dmitri Petrov most recently, as he demanded that she account for the murder of his son. Before that, it had been Nico, who'd wanted Konstantine's complete and utter destruction for inheriting the wealth and power he'd believed belonged to him.

But those outbursts, those demands for retribution, had made sense to her.

Fish's made no sense. Logically, McGrath owed him nothing. She had never wronged or hurt him. How could he look at her as if he *deserved* her life? As if he *deserved* her pain?

When he rounded the bed out of Lou's sight, Jennifer screamed.

The fear in the cry cut through Lou's confusion and sharpened her awareness to this single moment in time. She pulled her gun and pointed it. She remained hidden in the hallway, but her shot was clear. All she had to do was pull the trigger and spill his brains all over the wall.

Take him alive. We need him alive. We need him—

"Fuck." Lou lowered the gun and rushed into the bedroom.

Jennifer stood in one corner with her arms out as if bracing herself against both walls. Her chest heaved. Her eyes were wide and frightened. An overturned lamp gave her face a severe, ghostly appearance.

Her eyes flicked from Fish to Lou only a second before Lou seized him.

She grabbed a fistful of his hair and pulled him back through the dark.

Not to La Loon—though *oh* how she longed to do it—but instead to the kitchen, putting distance between the murderer and his target.

The jarring outdated kitchen tile reappeared. Her bare feet squeaked against the floor as she released Fish, shoving him forward into the cabinets. A butter knife shifted underfoot.

He hit the edge of the counter hard. All the air left him in a surprised *oomph*. When he turned, he lost his balance. His black sneakers slid on the sugar packets. His arms pinwheeled as he struggled to right himself, kicking one of the pots into a corner.

His struggle gave Lou time to slip the gun into her waistband and free her hands.

Once he was able to right himself again, Fish saw her for the first time. His eyes roved her body, taking in the oversized sweats and t-shirt. Her bare feet and disheveled hair.

Lou expected the usual questions. *Who are you? How did I get here?* Instead, Fish charged her.

She sidestepped him easily, and as she did, brought her elbow down hard on his shoulder.

He screamed and hit the far wall with the full force of his momentum. Pushing off the wall, he grabbed an overturned chair and hurled it at her. She ducked, feeling it pass over her head, stirring a slight breeze before crashing behind her. He lifted a second chair, and this one didn't sail past as cleanly. One of its legs clipped her shoulder, spinning the chair off in a new direction. It hit the counter and broke off a leg. Both pieces clattered to the floor.

Fish used the moment to charge again, hoping to catch her in the squatting position. But before he reached her, Lou sidestepped into the shadow created by the kitchen table.

The world disappeared and reappeared, offering her a more secure position in the doorway between the living room and kitchen.

He only looked for her for a moment. Then he was at the drawers, ripping them open, tossing contents on the floor. When he didn't find what he wanted, he moved on to the next drawer.

What does he think is happening? she wondered. Then, *He's not thinking. He's gone feral with...what? His hunger? His need to feed or cause pain? What?*

And he wasn't the only one. Lou felt that part of herself—the ravenous, insatiable part—burning with a longing, a deep ache throbbing through her entire core. She wanted to pull her gun. She wanted to shoot him and see his head knock back as if punched the second before his brains sprayed out behind him in a delicious final release.

She wanted his blood on her hands, on her lips. She wanted to see his anger turn to fear as she hurt him—slowly, deliberately.

He might have thought that he could return to McGrath, that he could finish this game, but Lou had no intention of letting him out of this kitchen.

She stepped into the light, giving him a target.

He snarled, fresh fury overtaking his face.

With his newfound knife, he slashed at her. She folded her elbow, deflecting the blow, but his immediate reverse thrust caught her upper arm. Fresh, hot pain cut cold across her flesh.

It burned, igniting an indignation that bordered on humorous.

Lou pushed this away, focusing on the glinting blade coming toward her. He'd folded it against his arm.

He struck at her throat, but missed and nicked the collarbone.

Blood soaked the front of her shirt.

She lifted Fish off his feet and slammed him into the kitchen table. It didn't crumple as she thought it might. The wood only creaked, miraculously withstanding the blow. She drove her elbow into his forearm with such force that the knife dropped from his hand and clattered to the floor.

He howled, groping for her hair. He managed a fistful and yanked hard. Lou saw stars, but more than that, a rage unfurled inside her. She *hated* having her hair pulled. She hated it worse than a punch to the jaw or ear. She hated it worse than being stabbed or kicked in the guts.

Before she could fully articulate the rage, or understand why it had been so immediate and all encompassing, she'd pulled her gun and pressed it under Fish's chin.

Lou's scalp burned. She pushed the gun into Fish's chin harder, until a small sound of panic escaped him. His hands trembled on either side of his head.

That hungry hand inside her writhed. It opened and closed within her, desperate.

We need him. We need him. We need—

Lou screamed, a berserker's battle cry, and brought her gun across Fish's jaw hard, rendering him unconscious.

The man went limp on the table.

Red and blue lights splashed across the bare kitchen wall.

Lou checked on Fish once more before crossing the living room to the window. There were the police, and no surprise, a news van. It must've been Dani's doing. But across the street was a shadowed figure, lingering under the tree as Lou herself had done weeks before.

"Are you okay?" Lou called out to Jennifer.

"Yeah," she replied weakly. "Is it over?"

"The police are here. Come let them in."

As soon as Jennifer's steps resounded on the stairs, Lou was across the street, standing under the thick darkness cast by the old tree's limbs.

"Did you enjoy the show?" she said into the woman's ears.

The woman jumped, turning toward Lou's voice.

She took one look at Lou and whistled. "You look like shit."

Lou glanced down at the ruined shirt.

"Are you responsible for this circus?" The woman gestured toward the house. "It's a pretty quick response for the police *and* the media."

The front door opened and police crowded in, pushing past Jennifer, who held the door open. She was shaken and unharmed. Lou felt—*relief.*

The news crew crowded the porch, ready and eager for the goriest of details.

"Why were you watching him?" Lou asked.

"For the same reason I suspect you were," she said, staring at Lou again. "How did you get here so fast? Were you sleeping inside the house?"

"We should have coffee and talk about it."

"Why should I meet you for coffee when you can't even answer the questions I've already asked?"

"You could try asking better questions," Lou replied.

Diana snorted, pushing the hood back from her face. She took an unflinching appraisal of Lou's appearance. "Maybe you'll want to clean up first. You look like Carrie had a slumber party and it went *all* wrong."

Lou touched her throat and found it was still bleeding.

Diana glanced at the house again, at the police crawling over it like ants. The yellow tape was going up. The news crews were pushed back.

Jennifer, with her hands wrapped around her body in the perfect mimicry of a victim, answered an officer's questions.

"Yes to coffee. Only I'm not going to tell you where. Let's see if you'll just turn up like you keep doing. Don't keep me waiting."

Diana started down the sidewalk. She didn't walk to one of the cars parked on the street, nor to one of the houses. Instead, she hopped over a low stone wall and disappeared into the adjacent field.

Lou watched her go.

She stood in the shadows a long time. Long after Fish was dragged from the house in handcuffs. Long after McGrath was wrapped in a blanket and tucked into the back of an ambulance for safekeeping.

She stood there until the hunger inside felt manageable again.

Only then did she peer through the darkness, directing her inner eye to hunt for Diana Dennard.

33

Lou stopped at her apartment long enough to clean and patch her wounds. After throwing away the ruined white t-shirt, she changed into jeans, a black t-shirt, her boots, and glasses. At the last second, she decided to put on her father's vest under her shirt.

It wasn't an entirely rational decision. Would Dennard really try to kill her in the open? She didn't think so. Yet Lou knew it was best to trust her instincts even when they didn't make sense.

So the vest went on.

Her compass delivered her to the edge of a parking lot.

The lot was unpaved, gravel shifting under her boots. It had only six or seven cars, lined up along the front of the Susie-Q's all-night diner. It looked like an old-fashioned airstream camper, but longer, with a proper door and windows.

Diana Dennard was sitting in the booth that aligned with the second window on the right.

Lou crossed the lot and pulled open the door. Show tunes featuring a lot of brass greeted her. Diana saw her immediately.

"How did you do it?" She looked at her watch as Lou slid onto the opposite bench.

Lou raised her eyebrows, signaling a desire for clarification.

"How did you know where I was? This is some deep-state shit. Are you FBI? CIA?" She held a steaming coffee mug with both hands. "You've got access to the city's cameras or something?"

"Does this place have cameras?" Lou asked. She didn't see any.

"So you don't work for anyone?"

"I don't work for anyone."

It was true enough. No one wrote her a paycheck. Though she did work with people, didn't she? That fact was becoming more and more clear to her.

"You're like me then," Diana said, almost in disbelief. She scoffed, looking away toward the window. When she caught sight of her reflection, the loose blond ponytail and dark circles under the eyes, she scowled. "I was wondering how many of us there might be. Vigilantes, prowling the night, finishing off the assholes of the world."

Vigilante. It wasn't the first time Lou had heard the word, but she'd never used it in conjunction with herself. And it had never occurred to her that there might be other women like her, out there hunting killers.

As she watched Diana turn her mug in her hands nervously, she realized, perhaps arrogantly, that it had never occurred to her that another woman would be up for the job. Not an ordinary woman, anyway—one who was bound to a time and place. Would Lou have pursued Martinelli if she hadn't had her abilities?

Yes. But she might not have gotten as far.

She'd learned to fight and shoot, but she knew what her real advantage was.

"Were you pursuing Fish for personal reasons?" Lou asked, aware that Dennard didn't want to look her in the eyes. It unnerved people to see their own faces reflected back in her glasses. She often wore them to mess with King for that very reason.

But now, she removed her glasses, folded them, and placed them on the table.

Yet the woman stared into her coffee. "No. I knew what he was and that Jennifer was in danger. That's her name, right? I found it in a tax record from two years ago."

Lou didn't want this to be an endless conversation, and she loathed small talk. "Do you hunt these men because of what happened to you in 1995?"

Diana's eyes flicked up to Lou's. "You really want the story?"

Lou said nothing.

Diana opened her mouth to reply, but the waitress appeared in her old-fashioned white apron with a menu under her arm. "You keep multiplying. Can I get you something?"

"Coffee," Lou said, refusing the menu.

Tense silence hung between them until the waitress left and returned with a mug and a coffee pot. They watched the cup fill.

"Cream or sugar?"

"No."

Then they were alone again.

"Poor little Diana Dennard's origin story. It seems unfair that you know who I am and what I do and I don't even know your name." Diana's cold gaze appraised her again. "If Fish wasn't a menace to you, why take him out?"

Lou said nothing.

Diana scoffed. "Fish is a *breed*. You understand that, right? A *species*. Men like him think they can prey on women and get away with it. Someone needs to change their mind about that."

"What happened in the nine weeks you were missing?" Lou asked.

Diana pushed her coffee mug away. "Give me your name and I'll tell you."

"Lou."

"Lou what?"

Lou shrugged. "Just Lou."

Diana smiled. But before the expression had a chance to fully settle onto her face, it hardened again. "One of my father's friends rolled up to my school one day, telling me that my dad wanted me to ride home with him."

Lou's stomach clenched.

"So I get in his car. I put on my seat belt. I listen to him because I know my dad loves this guy and trusts him. Even though I wanted to walk home with my friend and I knew we were going the wrong way, I still stayed, quiet and obedient like the good little girl I was raised to be. That's how they get you. They count on the fact we've all been raised to be good little girls."

Lou lifted the coffee to her lips. It didn't hide her furious, working jaw.

"Anyway, this so-called *family friend* locked me in a soundproof shed for eight weeks." Diana squinted. "I don't really need to describe what happened in the shed, do I?"

"No."

Diana's cheeks had reddened and her jaw was tight. It was several minutes before she spoke again.

"When I escaped, I spent a week in the woods behind a pizza place trying to decide if I was going to kill myself or run away. I knew better than to tell my father what his *friend* had done to me. He wasn't going to turn him in. Adults don't listen to kids, and even at twelve I understood that. But I also couldn't let the bastard win. I was too damn pissed. A week in the woods drinking flat soda and half-eaten pizza fished out of a dumpster will do that to you."

Lou didn't smile at the joke.

Diana didn't seem to notice. "So I went home. I told them I'd run away. I can't even remember what bullshit reason I gave them, and they didn't really care. When the *family friend* came over to congratulate my father on my safe and sound return, I *smiled* at the bastard."

"How?" Lou couldn't imagine smiling at Martinelli after all he'd taken from her.

"I wanted him to think he'd won because I had *plans*. I'd spent weeks making these plans. I wasn't going to screw them up."

Lou drank her coffee and said nothing.

Diana, emboldened by the silence, leaned forward over the table.

"One night I went to his house where he lived with his perfect family. I rang the doorbell. When he answered, I told him I thought I'd left something in the shed. Would he come out and check for me? You should've seen the excitement on his fucking face. It was disgusting. So I went to the shed with my father's pistol and I waited for him. He came in. He shut the door behind him. Then he said something I'll never forget. He said, 'I knew you'd be back.' He already had half an erection pushing through the front of his fucking khakis. He still had that erection after I shot him, too."

They both fell silent as the waitress approached again.

"Thirsty, weren't you?" She smiled at Lou.

Lou accepted the top-off, forcing her lips to mimic the smile. "Thanks."

Dennard waited until the waitress was out of earshot before speaking again. "I've been hunting bastards like him ever since. Serial rapists, women killers, abusers. Anything to do with children and women, really. I happened upon Fish because—" She seemed to catch herself.

"How do you find out about them?" Lou asked, hoping to coax her into talking more.

And she was curious as to how she managed to find the men. She didn't think this woman had an inner compass that responded to *Take me to a serial killer.*

"I have an internet forum where women can report offenses anonymously. A lot of them report stuff that the cops have dismissed. I came here because a woman reported her sister missing. Because the sister had a history of drug use, the cops said she was probably just holed up in a drug den somewhere, but the sister insisted she'd been sober for two years. I chose to believe her."

She paused to take a sip of her coffee.

"So I came to town to check it out, interview witnesses and all that jazz. I found out that the last time she was seen was at a coffee shop, and *who* followed her out of that coffee shop three weeks ago?"

"Fish."

Diana smirked. "I'm well versed in stalker behavior. I should be an expert by now, after doing this for twenty years. And it looks like I was right. I'm glad I stuck around even though I didn't catch him before he hurt the sister. I have a feeling she's in one of the graves they found the other day. Did you see that on the news?"

Lou shrugged.

"Yeah. You've probably been too busy to catch up on the news," Diana said with a suspicious smile. "Did you have anything to do with that story breaking open by chance?"

Lou lifted the warm mug to her lips.

"I'm disappointed that you let him get arrested though. What happens if he's released? All he needs is the sympathy of some judge calling him 'a good family man' or 'a man with values' or some shit like that. It happens all the damn time."

Lou didn't like hearing her fears voiced back to her. She pushed her coffee cup away.

"Do you always give them over to the authorities?" Diana asked.

"No."

"Maybe you're not FBI then." Diana grinned. "And what will you do if he goes free? You have a protocol for that?"

"I'll handle it," Lou said, and wasn't sure why she suddenly felt so defensive. It had been something about the comment regarding the broken system. It wasn't that she disagreed. After all, the system created men like Senator Ryanson and Chaz Brasso, the DEA agent who'd betrayed both her father and King. But it also created men like King. Surely this woman knew that it wasn't so easy to tell the bad guys from the good guys.

"And how do you *handle* it, Lou?" Diana spun her mug anxiously between her palms. "Do you work alone or with a team?"

Lou didn't answer.

Diana held up her hands, palms out in surrender. "All right, all right. You're not interested in sharing trade secrets. But I'll admit I'm very curious about you. I was camping out at the house tonight, wondering when Fish was gonna make his move. They always do eventually. So imagine my surprise when he pulled up, went inside, started up on her, and then *bam*. You were in the house! *What?* I didn't even see you come in. How did you get in?"

Lou recalled the destroyed kitchen. The glass, broken chairs, and those ridiculous sugar packets thrown about like Carnival confetti. But it was the blood on the floor that made her temperature boil.

"If you were there, why didn't you step in?"

Diana leaned back against the booth and shrugged. "I didn't want to act prematurely."

Hot anger ripped through Lou. "What?"

"Situations like that make women strong. Jennifer will always feel more powerful, more capable now, because of what she went through. I wasn't going to let him kill her, but I also didn't want to rob her of the fight."

Lou's fingers itched for her gun. Her desire to pull the Browning and put a bullet between this woman's eyes was immediate—and it frightened her. She'd never wanted to shoot a woman before.

Diana spoke, unaware of the emotions rolling through Lou. "Women are strong, so much stronger than anyone gives them credit for. We are *survivors*. Every single woman you've ever met has survived something. But many of them forget it. I just want them to remember what they are."

This woman is crazy, Lou thought. *More than a little crazy.*

Look who's talking, a voice chided.

Diana scoffed. "I suppose you view yourself as some kind of white knight. You ride in and save the damsels before even a hair on their pretty little heads falls out of place. But women don't need to be saved. They need to pick up the sword."

Lou didn't identify with the label *white knight*. When she'd hunted Angelo and his brothers, it had never been about saving anyone. She'd simply wanted the men who'd murdered her father to pay.

But how could she explain that to Dennard?

"I don't think women need to be tested to prove they're strong," Lou said.

Dennard wrinkled her nose. "How feminist of you."

A sudden jerk hooked through Lou's navel. White-hot heat rippled through her core, climbing up her throat. She knew instantly who was in danger and how little time she had.

Mel.

The surprise of it must've shown on Lou's face, because Diana stiffened.

"What?" she asked, glancing behind her as if expecting a monster to appear.

"I have to go." Lou slid out of the booth, grabbing her sunglasses off the table. She finished the coffee in a single go.

"Another damsel in distress?" Diana regarded Lou with a look that couldn't exactly be described as friendly.

Lou threw a $5 bill on the table.

"Until next time then, *Lou*." Diana sat back, stretching her arms along the top of the booth.

Lou had no time to worry about what such a malicious smile meant. *Mel* had no time at all.

So without a goodbye, she stepped out of the diner and into the night.

DIANA WAITED UNTIL LOU DISAPPEARED INTO THE TREES surrounding the diner's parking lot before taking her empty coffee mug and the $5 bill, slipping them both into her bag.

34

———————

With the duffel hanging heavy at her side, Mel limped from the streetcar stop into the station. Because of the hour, it wasn't crowded. A group of teenagers stood together smoking, laughing too loudly at a joke a redheaded boy made, complete with pantomime. A girl with a laugh like a horse's high whinny overtook all the others.

Mel's arm ached by the time she reached the end of the station platform and stepped out into the adjacent plaza. A water fountain equipped with lights changed the water from red to blue to green, and there, against a concrete wall overlooking the Mississippi River, stood Terrence. His head was bent as if in prayer as he cupped a hand around his cigarette.

She switched the bag to the other arm and limped forward. She closed the distance until there was only twenty feet between them.

He turned at the sound of her approach. His eyes slid from her face down to the bag in her hand. He frowned. "That sure looks heavy. You better not have given me a hundred grand in dollar bills."

The wind blew in off the water and pushed Mel's hair back from her face. It pulled water from her eyes and iced her cheeks.

"Where are my cards?" she asked, dropping the bag at her feet.

He slipped his hands into his pockets and stepped forward. This moved his face into the light of the adjacent streetlamp, adding an orange glow to his cheekbones and chin. It also added fire to his eyes.

"I think I'm going to hang on to them," he said, looking at her from under the brim of his hat.

"You said—"

"I know what I said. But if I'd known you would've parted with your money so easily, I would've asked for more."

Mel's anger rose inside her, uncurling like a viper in her guts.

"So here's what we're gonna do," he said, taking another easy stride forward. "You pay me, you get a *few* cards. Pay me more, you get more. Maybe you'll get all your cards back in, oh...twenty years."

She clenched her teeth, gathering what was left of her sanity. *Don't lose it now. See this through.*

"Think of it as alimony."

"My cards—"

"You shouldn't have lost them if they meant so damn much to you."

Mel bent down toward the large duffel at her feet. She unzipped it and looked inside.

"You won't ever stop torturing me, will you?" she asked softly.

"Why would I stop when I enjoy it so much?"

She exhaled slowly. "That's what I thought."

Mel stood and pointed the gun at her husband. She cocked the revolver, saw the loaded chamber slide into place.

Terry stilled. Every muscle in his body tensed like a stag sensing danger. His mouth parted ever so slightly in surprise.

"Don't look so shocked, Terry," Mel said, adjusting her grip on the gun. "You've given me little choice, haven't you?"

Terrence's face twitched almost as if he were working to keep a snarl suppressed. When he spoke, his voice bore the false geniality that she'd always despised.

"You ain't gonna shoot me. Shooting a man is different than clipping one with a car and leaving him to die."

"Is it?" she asked without inflection. "I'm sure it's all the same in the eyes of God."

Terrence must've thought she meant to do it, really meant to put a bullet in his heart and be done with him. His eyes widened. His hand began to lift, extending toward her. A *no* formed on his lips.

But it was too late.

Mel pulled the trigger.

35

Good police work meant following the rules. But King understood that in order for the right thing to happen, sometimes lying was necessary.

As soon as he terminated the call with Konstantine, who had more than a little irritation in his voice, King noted distantly, he decided *now* was one of those times. Lying was suddenly *very* necessary.

"Christ." He threw back his covers and hobbled across the room to a dresser drawer. He lifted a stack of sweaters and found the two burner phones he kept hidden there.

He dialed the non-emergency line in Fish's county. That was the only way he could be sure to get the police in that area.

"Knox County Police, how can I help you?"

"Yes, hello!" He added as much panic to his voice as he could manage. "There's a man attacking a woman. Right inside her house! I can see it from the street."

"Where are you located, sir?"

King rattled off McGrath's address. "I'm out here walking Lady"—he glanced at the dog sitting erect in her oversized bed, watching him with alert eyes—"and oh god! He's chasing her! Please send someone! He's going to kill her!"

King hung up the phone. He hoped that would be enough to get someone to the house. He knew ending the call so quickly might make it seem like a prank.

"How did I do?" he asked Lady. The dog rose from her bed and walked toward him expectantly. "No, it's okay. I know I said your name, but I wasn't calling you. You can go back to bed."

She turned several circles on her large cushion before settling down again.

King went to his own bed with the burner phone still in his fist.

His original plan had been to call the Ohio Bureau of Criminal Investigation and say that he'd taken up investigating cold cases in his retirement. One such cold case had led him to Jeffery Fish. He'd hoped to already have that evidence in place when he approached the OBCI, but that would never work now. His anonymous tip was the best he could do.

Please go to the house, he thought. *Please. If you don't, Lou is definitely going to kill him.*

His feet rested on the little rug beside his bed. His socks sank into the white shag. The roar of Carnival raged outside.

What else can I do? He massaged his forehead. *Damn it, Lou.* She must've known blowing his cover would incite Fish to act like this. He racked his brain. *What else can I do?*

The good news was that now Fish had openly attacked the woman, they should be able to obtain a warrant to search his home. This assumed he was captured at the scene and Jennifer McGrath lived to tell the tale. If Jennifer was able to give a statement claiming Fish had been hunting her for the weeks leading up to the attack, it would give a judge enough probable cause to issue the warrant.

King groaned and dragged his hand down his face. He fell back against the bed and tried to consider his options for pinning Fish to the mat. Minutes bled into each other. His mind wandered. He was almost asleep again when his ears popped.

"Get up," Lou said.

King jumped, making the bed creak. Lady yipped.

His hand went instinctively to his chest. "Shit."

"Mel' s in trouble. We have to go. *Now.*"

"What?" But King pushed off the bed and stumbled to the dresser again. He grabbed a shirt out of the top drawer and searched for a pair of jeans to pull over his boxers. "How do you know she's in trouble?"

Lou twirled her finger in the air. He understood this meant her compass had told her.

No doubt it had also told her about McGrath's close call with Fish.

"Do you think it's Terrence?" he asked, forcing his second leg into the jeans.

"It won't matter if you don't *hurry up*."

"Okay, *okay*." He wanted to ask her about McGrath and Fish and learn how the situation had played out. But apparently now was not the time.

"Did the girl make it?" he asked.

"Yes, and they arrested Fish." Lou scratched Lady behind the ears.

King slipped the burner phone and his cell phone in his pocket, just in case he had to make more calls tonight.

"Ready?" Lou asked.

"Stay. Er, *pas...pas bouger*," King said to the dog, and Lady whined.

"Sorry, girl," Lou said as her hand fixed on King's arm. "We'll be back."

The darkness gathered around them.

What the—? King's mind sputtered.

Had it ever happened like that before? Lou had always stepped into the shadows—as Lucy had—and passed through them like a thin gossamer curtain to wherever lay on the other side.

But this, whatever had just happened, had been almost like she'd called the shadows *to* her.

The darkness pooling in the corners of his bedroom and beneath his bed had seemed to stretch toward them, overtaking her.

You're imagining shit, he warned himself. *You're tired, you're up past your bedtime, and you haven't slept properly since Carnival started up. Get ahold of yourself.*

But he couldn't shake the image of the darkness cutting across her pale face. She hadn't moved. She hadn't moved, but the shadows had. He was sure of it.

Pressure doubled, tripled in his head, squeezing it in the imaginary vice he detested so much. The floor, which was no longer a floor at all, dropped out from underneath him. His stomach dropped with it. For a moment, his old claustrophobia reared inside him.

He was squeezed, twisted. This continued until the moment when he felt he might fall into complete panic—what a hell of a time to have a panic attack—then the world finally, *blessedly* opened up.

Sidewalk sprang up under his feet, jarring him forward. Lou held fast to his arm, unmoved by his momentum. She held him in place until he righted himself.

"God, I hate that," he said. He clasped the back of his neck.

Lou wasn't looking at him. Her eyes were searching the plaza. King realized they stood under an overhang, in the dark of a pavilion. During the day this was the seating area of the Living La Vida Lobster Bar and Grill. King noted the absurd plastic lobster looming above the tables.

"What's he saying to her?" Lou asked, pressing one shoulder into a pillar.

King squinted across the pavilion, focusing on the man in the leather hat with the crow feather protruding from it. Across from him stood Melandra. Lou and King were too far from the pair to hear their conversation. King noted only the low drone of their voices.

"What do you think is in that bag?" King asked. "It looks too heavy to be a payoff. See how she's leaning?"

"What do you want to do?" Lou's shoulders tensed under her leather jacket.

King knew what she was going to say before she even asked.

"Can I—?" she began.

"No," King said, thinking of the first conversation he'd had that evening, before the story of Fish had broken.

"There are no families in this case," Lou said. "No one needs to know what happened so they can sleep at night. Melandra will know what happened. Isn't she the only one who matters?"

I found the camera footage, the cop had explained. *You can see everything.*

"I need the guy alive for other reasons."

Lou looked at him through her damned mirrored sunglasses. How the hell did she even see through them at night?

"I'll explain later. But for now, don't kill him," King said. "Please."

Lou was obviously disappointed. Her shoulders slumped.

King couldn't worry about that. "I'll call the police and tell them where we are."

He had an uneasy feeling about that duffel bag, and his gaze kept sliding between it and the husband. King hoped he was wrong.

He removed his cell phone from his pocket and dialed 911 for the second time that night. There was no need for the burner. He hoped his clout and reputation in the city would actually help them now.

"911, what's your emergency?"

Mel pulled a gun.

"Shit," Lou and King said in unison.

"Go," King said, and the shadows overtook Lou before he'd even finished pronouncing the word. "Go, go, go!"

This time he was sure of it—that the darkness had in fact moved *toward* her, enveloping her and blotting out the orange lanterns circling the riverwalk and pavilion. She hadn't stepped back into it as he'd often seen her do.

She'd called the darkness. Had she even noticed?

"Hello? 911, what's your emergency?" a woman said.

"Yes, hello," King began, moving toward the tables. A cat hissed and ran out from underneath one of them. It bolted toward the restaurant and the cluster of trash cans to the left of the door. Once it was safe between two cans, it looked back over its shoulder at King appraisingly.

"I want to report an armed robbery in progress. I'm in the Julia Street station plaza. My name is Robert King."

"We have a car in the area, Mr. King," the responder said blandly. "We can get someone to you quickly. Are you in a safe place?"

King opened his mouth to answer. That was when the shot rang out.

. . .

Lou stepped from the shadows of the closed pavilion with its discarded napkins and crumpled receipts tumbling in the icy winter breeze rolling off the river. When the world reformed around her, she was standing between Mel and her husband.

It hadn't been the exact spot she was aiming for, but the darkness must have been thickest where their bodies' shadows overlapped on the stone. And she certainly hadn't meant to turn her back on the man, who in her core Lou understood was dangerous.

But that's where she found herself nonetheless.

Lou had only a millisecond to note Mel's gasp of surprise, register her widening eyes. It seemed like the gun jerked at the last second, rolling slightly away from its target.

Then the whip crack of a gunshot rang out.

And Lou knew something was terribly wrong. *Terribly* wrong.

The force that slammed through her body staggered her.

A hot-cold sensation ran through from her head to her toes. It began as ice water, rolling down her spine and the back of her legs. Her flesh tingled.

Then the water suddenly heated, filling her with a feverish, hot sensation that seemed to stand the hairs on her neck and arms on end.

There was a moment of blissful ignorance before the pain came. It bloomed bright and biting at the base of her throat.

She reached up to touch her neck, half believing that she wouldn't find it there. But her fingers found flesh. Blood pumped against her hand.

A wave of dizziness crashed over her, and her knees buckled.

"Oh god. Oh god. Oh god."

Lou wasn't sure who was speaking, but she wanted them to shut up. The pounding in her head had escalated to a tumultuous thunder that obliterated all thought with its battle drumbeat.

She couldn't think. She barely saw the cold pavilion under her palms. The blood was dripping from her throat onto the stones beneath her, soaking her hand.

The black pool spread out. It was like a lake opening up just for her. If she wasn't careful, she would fall right through—maybe to La Loon.

Or maybe to a darker, wilder place.

"Lou." A hand touched her back. A white-hot hand that made her feel weak all over. She wanted to knock it away. She thought she might have shrugged, but she wasn't sure. Her arms were losing feeling, tingling the way they do when waking from sleep. And they were no longer obeying her commands.

"Lou!"

The greedy hands turned her over, rolling her onto her back. She stared up at the industrial gray sky, smoky white clouds full of diffused orange light sliding by, uninterested in her petty drama.

It was King staring down at her. "Fuck. Lou! Lou, can you hear me? No, she'll choke. Roll her. Lou?"

"Stop shouting," she said, or tried to say. Her throat couldn't quite find enough air to force into her lungs. The pain radiating through her right shoulder was unbearable.

"Give me your shawl," King said. "*Give it* to me!"

"I'm *trying*!"

Something rough pressed against Lou's throat, intensifying the pain. Someone was screaming. Distantly, she wondered if it was her own voice.

"I'm sorry," King said. "But we've got to compress this. You're losing blood too fast."

His shadowed face only darkened, giving a hint of features she no longer recognized.

I'm going to black out, she realized. *Any minute now I'm going to lose consciousness and—*

Someone was tugging at her chest. The familiar ripping sound of Velcro crackled in her ear. She reached out to stop the rough hands from finishing their work.

"I have to take them. I'm sorry. You can't go to the hospital with these on. And you're *going* to the hospital, you hear me?"

The vest fell away and suddenly her chest expanded, finally able to pull in a full breath. It wasn't smooth, and she didn't like that whistle-wet sound in her ears. But without the vest and shoulder holster, she did find it easier to breathe.

Still, exhaustion pressed against her brain. The warmth promised sleep. A blessed, relaxing release if only she—

Someone shook her until her eyes opened. "Lou, listen to me! The police are here. You have to go. New Orleans General Hospital, do you hear me? New Orleans General! *Go! Now!*"

Red and blue lights danced across his face. The strange strobing effect intensified her dizziness and the dreamlike quality that had been pulled over the world.

"*New Orleans General.* Now!"

Come on, she told herself. Come on. *Who is in control here?*

Drawing deep on her reserves, she reached out for the darkness around her. *Come on*, she begged. *I can do this.*

She coughed to clear her throat and instantly regretted it. The pain spiked in a way that made her scream again—and now she was sure it was *her* screaming. Such a strange sound. Had she ever screamed like this before?

Before she could answer her own curiosity, she was falling, falling through the black.

King stared at the blood on the paving stones where Lou had been just a moment before. His heart was racing. The blood was on his sleeves, on his hands. He wondered if it was maybe on his face as well.

It's too much, he thought. *Oh god, it's too much blood.*

Had the bullet cut her carotid? He couldn't be sure. It'd been hard to see the wound clearly in the dark. The hole, before he'd covered it with his hands, had looked a little low for that. Maybe it had only torn through the shoulder. But he could be wrong. God help him, he could be *wrong*.

Please let it be the shoulder and not the neck, he begged. He wasn't sure if he was praying to a god—any god—or Lucy herself.

Not the neck. Not the neck. Let it be the shoulder. Not the neck, not the—

Because if it was her carotid, she was dead.

Mel was crying softly beside him. On her hands and knees, she rocked back and forth beside the duffel bag.

"Check him and make sure he's alive," King said, pointing at the unconscious husband.

After the gun had gone off, and the husband had been distracted by Lou's sudden materialization from nowhere, King had taken the opportunity to throw a right hook across the man's jaw, dropping him before he got the bright idea to run for it.

He'd hit the ground like a sack of bricks.

But King had had no chance to evaluate his handiwork because Lou had collapsed, making a strange noise he'd never heard before. *Like an animal dying, like an animal dying...*

Then he'd seen the blood. *So much blood.*

"Mel," King said. He squeezed the woman's knee hard enough to bruise. "See if he's still alive. Before the police get down here."

King heard car doors shut and the low pounding of police boots crossing the station. He stood and grabbed the duffel bag without fanfare. He bent and picked up the gun without pausing his stride. At the edge of the pavilion, he threw the bag over the rail. It splashed, sinking into the black water below. Next King emptied the bullets from Mel's revolver and tossed them into the canal, followed by the revolver itself. Then his own burner phone, because why not take care of all of it at once?

He ran over to the restaurant. The cat, thinking he was back for another go at his tail, hissed and scuttled farther into the dark.

"Sorry," he muttered, already imagining what Lou must think of having her weapons thrown away. He shoved her gun and vest into the trash bin. "You can look for them later."

If she lives.

She's going to live.

On the left side of the restaurant was a fountain that sprayed water into the sky.

He plunged his hands into the icy water. He rubbed them vigorously, trying to wash Lou's blood from his skin and sleeves.

King could do nothing about the pool of blood left on the pavilion. Hopefully, they would not ask.

That was here when I arrived, King practiced in his mind. *Who knows what this asshole did before we showed up...Maybe he hurt someone. He looks like a dangerous guy.*

When King returned to Mel she was still on her knees, crying.

Please let Lou make it to the hospital, King begged as the flashlights swept the pavilion, fixing on the three of them at long last. He waved to get the officers' attention. "We're over here!"

"I killed her. Oh my god, I killed her," Mel wailed at his feet, her face still buried in her hands. King reached down and pulled her to standing.

"Lord in heaven, I—"

"Shut up," he said. "Let me do the talking."

36

Lou fell against the brick wall, coughing. Blood sputtered down her chin. It was a disgusting feeling, but it was hard to care much about it in the face of the unbearable pain shooting through her bones. Every time the weight in her head shifted forward or back, a new explosion of pain ricocheted through her, threatening to knock her unconscious with its ferocity.

Why am I at the grocery store? She'd been aiming for New Orleans General Hospital like King had instructed. But here she was, sliding slowly down the brick wall. Her leather jacket scraped along the face, no doubt scuffing the black hide.

Who gives a fuck? Who gives a fuck about your stupid jacket? her mind asked. *You're dying.*

And she was. She could feel it. She was too cold. Way too cold for even a February night. Her teeth chattered and her face felt frozen.

Then the wall ended and she fell forward, suddenly unable to support her weight.

On her knees, she looked around. *Anybody*, she thought. *I'll take anybody.*

Only it wasn't the parking lot of the Ohio grocery store. She was looking into the back of an ambulance. Its doors were open with a pristine white bed waiting inside. It was lit with the bright fluorescents overhead as if showcased for her.

Come on in, it said. *Come on in and lie down.*

She wanted to. Her body felt so weak and exhausted. Her heart raced in her chest, in her head. She just wanted to lie down. And here was a bed.

She tried to stand, but before she even got a knee out from under her, hands grabbed her shoulders.

"I'm sorry, miss, but you can't be back here," someone said.

She screamed as the hand brushed her wound. Mel's soaked head-scarf fell from her throat to the pavement beneath her. Blood sprang forth, the stream renewed.

"Whoa, *fuck*. Bernie! Bernie! Get your ass out here!"

Those relentless hands moved her and she screamed again.

"I'm sorry," the voice said. "I'm so sorry, but I have to touch you."

Just let me lie down, she begged as the white bed swam in and out of her vision. *Just let me lie down.*

And that was the last thing she remembered.

For a long time there was only darkness. Cold, indifferent darkness. That was okay. Because for Lou, in a way, the darkness was as familiar as a childhood bedroom.

She walked around in it, feeling as one always does when they return home after a long time away. There was something here, waiting for her. It had been waiting patiently for a long time. But it would have to be patient for a little while longer. For now, she needed to rest.

While she slept, she dreamed.

She dreamed of La Loon.

She stood on the banks of Blood Lake, listening to the water gently lapping at the shore.

In the water was every man she'd ever brought to the dumping ground. Hundreds of them, almost shoulder to shoulder, covered the lake's patina. They floated face down in the water. Their clothes billowed around them with the air trapped inside, ballooning the fabric. They almost looked like cheap blowup dolls.

It didn't matter that Lou had seen many of these men devoured or torn apart by the creature that ruled this world. They were whole now.

None of this had to make sense, she understood. This was metaphorical. She was trying to understand the message. That was all.

So she counted the bodies. She noted how they lay, sprawled face down in the water.

She thought, *It's because the lake is hungry too. It consumes what it can from our world because it is so hungry. It's hungry like me. It's hungry like everyone.*

And like everyone, it has to eat.

She watched the bodies float until a slow, gentle breathing filled her ears. She reached out and placed a hand on the beast's reptilian head.

It was Jabbers. Her scaled skull felt cool under Lou's fingers. She traced the familiar ridges with her fingers. She cooed under her hand.

She dragged her steaming white tongue up Lou's arm. It smelled the blood dried to her shoulder and neck.

"You can eat me," Lou said to the beast. "I think I'm dead now too."

KONSTANTINE WOKE TO HIS PHONE RINGING.

On the third ring he realized it wasn't his business phone. It was his private line.

He threw back the covers and grabbed the phone.

"Hello?" he said in English, knowing of only a few who might call this number.

"Hey. It's Robert King." It was the New Orleans detective. "I'm at New Orleans General Hospital, and after this I need to get back to the police station, so I've got to make this quick."

King spoke rapidly, relaying what needed to be done.

"The Julia Street station plaza. Yes," Konstantine confirmed. "Yes, I'll take care of it."

"There's more," King said. "It's Lou."

Konstantine listened, doing his best to understand the detective despite the thunderous pounding of his heart.

When King was finished, Konstantine took a slow, deep breath. "I'll come right away."

37

Mel shifted in the plastic chair, trying to ease the cramp in her lower back. These chairs were a special kind of torture. Mel was certain they were manufactured in a factory specifically for interrogation rooms like this one.

"Just a while longer now," Mr. Rushdie said beside her. He'd been feeding her this platitude since eight that morning, when they'd first arrived to give their statements. That was over six hours ago.

"Is that right?" she asked without expecting an answer.

The man rubbed his humped back and sighed. "You'll be back in your own bed before the night is through. I promise. Can I get you anything to drink?"

Mel shook her head. She didn't believe they'd let her leave so easily. Terry would have no choice but to rat her out. The photographs might be long gone, but the fact was, she wanted to confess. She wanted this to be over. It wasn't living, what she'd been doing all these years. It couldn't go on like this.

If they gave her the chance to confess, she would. It was all she wanted to do.

It was the only thing that was *left* to do, really. She couldn't mention shooting Lou without exposing her identity, but she could confess to the hit and run.

And she was going to do it—she really was. If someone would just come back into the room and take her damn statement.

Then I can die with a clear conscience.

She rubbed her face one more time, groaning into her palms.

"Just a while longer," Mr. Rushdie said placidly beside her. "Just a while now."

That's how these interrogation rooms work. They leave you in here so long you go crazy. You'll confess to anything just to get out of here.

"Now when they come back," Mr. Rushdie said for the fourteenth time, "you gonna let me do the talking, all right? We're gonna—"

The door opened and a large black man in a buttoned-up white shirt stepped into the room. His hair was cropped close to his head. In his arm was a stack of folders. His sleeves were rolled up past the elbows, and his holsters could've been mistaken for suspenders at a glance.

King came in behind him, pushing a small television on top of a metal cart. Below it was the oldest VHS she'd ever seen.

King looked worse for wear. It wasn't only the dark, puffy circles under his eyes or the new gray growth that had sprouted on his jaw overnight. It was also his stride. He hadn't seen his bed yet, and it showed.

"I'm sorry to keep you waiting, Ms. Durand. It took us longer to find a TV cart than we anticipated. And nineteen people were injured in a shootout in the Quarter, so everyone has been running around like headless chickens." The officer went to the other side of the table. He extended his hand. "I'm Dick White. Robbie here has told me only good things about you—"

"Sir, let me stop you there." Mel held up her hands. She couldn't bear compliments in the face of the confession she was about to make. "I need to get some things off my chest. I—"

A hand clamped down on her shoulder. The fingers dug into the flesh of her collarbone with such sudden ferocity that she almost cried out. The words dried up in her mouth.

"Dick's been working *real* hard on this, Mel. We had to go back forty years for these tapes," King said, bending his face down to look into Mel's eyes. "I think you should listen to what he has to say before interrupting him."

"No need to rough her up," Dick said with an uneasy laugh. "We aren't going to play good cop/bad cop here."

Forty years? Did that mean Dick already knew about the hit and run? Did they already have evidence of her crime?

Mel searched King's wide eyes and took the hint. "You go first."

"You'll get to say your piece," Detective White promised, settling into the plastic chair opposite her. To King he said, "Plug that in over here. There's the socket."

King pulled the cart over into the corner and wedged the plug into the wall. He angled the TV so that Mel and her attorney had a clear view.

"Good," Detective White said, rubbing his nose. "I hardly know where to begin! We've got so much to cover. You've had an exciting night, Ms. Durand. We're glad you're all right."

Mel followed King's suspicious movements with her eyes. She knew something was going on here, but she hadn't gotten a handle on it yet.

"Where's Terrence now?" Mel asked, thinking this was the safest entry point into the conversation.

"He's over in county, in a holding cell." White turned to King. "You want to give her the rundown, or shall I?"

"After you," King said, with a smile that could almost be taken for joviality. To Mel, King arched his eyebrows. It seemed to her that this meant, *Keep your mouth shut and listen. It'll be better for both of us.*

Detective White shuffled his folders until he fixed on one from the middle of the pile. He opened it, reviewing the top page.

"We've got your statement from last night—" he began.

"And it's absolutely clear that Mr. Lamott is guilty of extortion," Mr. Rushdie inserted.

"Yes, it is," the officer agreed.

"But that doesn't excuse my behavior," Mel said.

Mr. Rushdie moved to drown out her words with his own. "Melandra, I would advise you not to—"

"Listen to your lawyer," King interjected with a pointed look, seemingly unaware that he himself was interrupting the man.

Detective White looked from Mel to King to the lawyer. He arched a brow. "Should I continue or do y'all need to talk about something?"

"Please, continue," Mel said, doing her best to gather her reserve.

"Terrence Lamott *has* been charged with extortion as well as intimidation, harassment, and theft of property. This violates his parole, of course. We also have Robbie's testimony and Piper's, and also Donny's —who you approached in the street one night, if you recall. We also have some footage from the convenience store across the street that shows him shoving you against the wall outside your shop."

King's jaw flexed.

"When we got the warrant to search his apartment we found your cards, which we believe he was holding ransom in exchange for money in addition to the violence he was inflicting on you."

"Are they okay? My cards?" Mel asked, sitting up in her seat. Its unbearable stiffness was temporarily forgotten.

King pulled a black bundle from his coat pocket and pressed it into her hands. "Piper says they're all there except The Devil."

She began to cry. Someone rubbed her shoulders.

"Is it irreplaceable?" King asked.

Mel lifted her face. "No. I can replace it."

It was about time for her to add her own card to the deck anyway. Every woman over the generations had had to do the same. It felt right that The Devil should be hers.

"Extortion carries a twenty-year sentence, even without the parole violation and the extra charges laid against him," King said. "You'll never see him again."

"Assuming you will testify," Detective White said.

"Of course I'll testify," Mel said. That was the least she could do. Hell, she was ready to testify against herself.

"Now, don't make any promises yet," Mr. Rushdie said. "My client—"

"I'll testify," Mel said. "Can I testify even if I'm in jail?"

Detective White laughed. "Why would you be in jail?"

Mel was certain that even if she'd somehow passed a statute of limitations for the hit and run, even if no one had ever come forward for it or made the crime known, and therefore she could receive no punishment—at the very least she would get attempted murder. She'd put bricks and rope into a duffel bag, for Christ's sake. She'd taken them down to a river with a gun.

It was true that she'd only intended to scare the hell out of Terry and not actually kill him, but that hardly mattered now. She'd *fired* the gun. Someone *was* shot.

"In the plaza—" Mel began.

"Ah, yes. King is the one that hit him, not you."

"The blood—" she tried again.

"What blood?" Detective White asked. He looked to King. "You break the man's nose or something?"

"My client is tired," Mr. Rushdie interjected. "We've been here all day and—"

King leaned in and whispered in Mel's ear, "There was no duffel, no gun, no bricks, and no rope. And if you're wondering, there are no tapes from the plaza security cameras either."

Mel searched his eyes. "*What?*"

"I spoke to a friend. He's more Lou's friend than mine, but he took care of the footage. There's nothing to pin on you." Then aloud, loud enough for the squabbling White and Rushdie to hear, "We have more than enough to convict Terry for extortion."

You could not say anything, her mind suggested. *You can go back to your life, to your shop. You don't have to give everything up.*

"No," Mel said, wiping at her face. "No, I have to say something."

Both Rushdie and King looked stricken.

King held up his hand, and it filled Mel with sudden anger. *No.* She would not be deterred, damn it. She was sick of living with the guilt of that night. Of closing her eyes and seeing the rain pelting the window of Terry's red Firebird. Of seeing Grandmamie's anguished face when Terry pulled up in the driveway.

Don't be a fool.

"Please let me show you something," King said, going around the table to the TV cart. He pressed eject on the machine, looked at the tape, and put it into the VCR once more. Then, as if he didn't believe she could keep her mouth shut, he said, "Just give me a minute to show you one last thing, and if you still have something to say, I'll be the first to hear you out. I promise."

He lifted the remote from the cart and pressed the buttons until the television flickered on.

King rewound the tape, explaining as he went. "In May of eighty-one, Dustin Malone submitted a complaint to the county commissioner, to the state patrol, to the mayor—hell, he complained to just about anyone that listened that they needed to add speed signs and a speed trap to his road. He said that twice cars had been racing by too fast and had clipped his farm dogs. There had been three crashes on that curve. Because nobody listened to him, he installed these cameras on the edge of his property. He recorded the road for sixteen months, hoping to gather enough evidence to take the state to court over it."

Mel's heart knocked in her throat.

"I don't see how this is relevant—" Mr. Rushdie began beside her.

King stopped the tape, watched for a second, rewound it, and played it again. "Here we go."

Two seconds…three…and Mel's chest was so tight she couldn't draw a breath. She started, physically *jumped* in her chair, when the red Firebird rolled into the frame from the right side of the screen.

Mel leaned forward, searching both sides of the road for her victim. *Where? She must be—*

There was no one.

A fox, low to the ground, shot out from the trees away from Malone's property line and into the road. Its lithe body was momentarily lit by the headlights of the approaching Firebird. The fox hesitated, sinking back onto its heels, but it was too late. The tires struck the animal on its right side, rolling it under the car and onto the pavement. It tumbled to a stop in the glow of red taillights.

The car screeched to a halt.

The passenger door opened and a much younger Terry—the way she often still saw him in her dreams—stepped out into the rain. He went to the front of the car, bent down, and inspected the grill. Then he went to the back of the car and saw the fox. He nudged it with his foot.

King bent close to Mel's ear and whispered, "You didn't hurt anyone, Mel. He lied to you so he could control you. You hear me? The bastard *lied*. Then he bragged to his jail buddies about it."

"But I saw..." *I didn't kill anyone. I didn't kill anyone.*

"You might have been drunk or scared or tired. Or maybe it was late, I don't know. But you didn't kill anyone. You *didn't*. He *lied* to you," King whispered.

She covered her face with her hands and began to sob.

"Can we have a minute?" King asked, and Mel was distantly aware of dismissing her attorney.

Then they were alone in the questioning room.

Forty years of regret...over something that didn't happen. *Forty years, forty years, forty damn years wasted*—her first emotion was raw, raging anger.

Goddamn you, Terry! Goddamn you and your lies!

But she couldn't sustain the anger in the face of such blessed relief.

Her sobs shook her whole body. Strong hands found her back, pressing gently into them.

"I can't believe you were going to shoot him and shove him into the canal," King whispered. A surprised little laugh escaped him.

"I wasn't." She lifted her head, sniffling. She knew she wouldn't have been able to follow through actually taking his life. "I thought if I scared him bad enough he'd leave me the hell alone. The gun only went off because Lou surprised me."

It was over. It was really over. This ordeal with Terry, these forty years of torment, they were really, *truly* over.

She began to cry harder.

"You're all right," King said. He kissed the top of her head. He rubbed her shoulders. "You're all right. You're going to be just fine."

"I'm sorry I lied to you," she said. "I told you I was divorced and—"

"I know," King interrupted, squeezing her shoulder. "It's okay. I'm not mad. It hurt, thinking there was some reason you didn't trust me, but I'm not mad."

"I trust you," she said, sniffling.

And a warm smile broke out on his face. "Good. Because I trust you, too. You're my best friend, Mel."

But part of her couldn't believe she could be so totally exonerated. There was still Lou.

She'd shot the girl. She'd watched her bleed all over the pavilion, the blood bubbling up between her lips as she screamed out in pain.

Mel dragged her nose over her sleeve, trying to clean herself up. *Oh god, Lou.* "How is she?"

38

Lou understood that she was dreaming. Or maybe she was dead. She suspected that both may be the same: dead and dreaming. It was the awareness that one clung to despite the way the world warped around a feverish mind.

Lou was in her parents' house—or rather, it was the house they'd had when they were still alive. She stood just inside the front door, overlooking the pristine living room with its fluffed cushions and vacuuming marks in the carpet as if her mother had just finished her daily pass. She noted the way the light slanted through its large bay window. It was early afternoon, perhaps even the time when she would have just come home from school.

Lou crossed the living room, half expecting to find her mother any moment, knowing the woman would click her tongue at Lou's leather boots and jacket and the mirrored sunglasses poised on her face.

All the blood...

But her mother wasn't in the living room.

Lou passed the bathroom on the first floor, noting distantly that this was the tub she'd disappeared from all those years ago when her parents began to take her condition seriously. But now it was dry, empty, awash in light.

She regarded it from the corner of her eye, noting how much smaller it seemed, and kept walking.

Her heart flopped in her chest when she did find her mother. She stood in the kitchen, by the stove, dragging a wooden spoon through a pot of something red.

"You're late. Your father is outside waiting for you," she said.

Lou had forgotten how high her mother's voice was. Nasal. Indignant.

Affection welled in her chest for this long-dead woman. It surprised her. Her mother had never been particularly kind or patient. She had not been a loving mother. The closest Lou had gotten to tasting that experience was after she'd disappeared, when she was delivered safely to her mother's arms.

She'd gotten a long, lingering hug then. But that was the extent of Courtney Thorne's love before Martinelli's men shot her.

She won't even look at me.

But then she did. And Lou was stunned by their resemblance. She'd always thought she looked like her father, and she did, but now it was undeniable that she had Courtney's features too. It was the hard mouth and eyes, the sharp cheekbones, and the build of her body. Though her mother had always bleached her hair, and Lou's was dark like her father's.

"Wash your hands. Dinner's almost ready."

Lou didn't wash her hands. Instead she backed away from the kitchen and the woman tending the stove. She strode through the dining room to the doors that would let her out onto the patio.

Time skipped.

She neither opened the doors nor stepped outside.

One minute she was at the glass, looking out at the manicured lawn, at the clusters of daylilies and cone flowers, and then she was outside. She stood beside the pool, looking down into the dancing crystalline water.

The shine was too bright.

Because this is a dream, her mind reminded her. *This is how it is in dreams.*

The old gate creaked, and Lou turned, half expecting to see Angelo

Martinelli again, bursting through the fence with a gun and an all-encompassing desire to end their lives.

But it was her father. He was in a white t-shirt and jeans—his favorite weekend outfit. His dark hair had fallen forward into his eyes as he whistled the tune "Louie Louie" by The Kingsmen.

He was also young, no older than Konstantine. He grinned, his smile catching sunlight. "Lou-blue! I've been looking for you."

The love she'd felt for her mother paled compared to what she felt for him. It had been a drop of blood in an ocean. This was the ocean itself.

She wrapped her arms around his waist.

It's a dream, just a dream, a dream, her mind reminded her.

She didn't care. It felt real enough.

A large hand pressed into her back. He planted a kiss on her forehead. Even how he smelled—though there was something different about it—took her back.

"Come here," he said, motioning her toward the water.

She dug in her heels. "You'll push me in and I'll wake up."

"No, I won't." He laughed, and it startled her to see that she had his smile, as rare as it was for her to show it.

"We don't have a lot of time. Come on," he said.

He crossed to the glass patio table adjacent the pool and sat in a red-and-white-striped beach chair. He pulled something from his pocket.

It was a piece of paper, which he began to unfold with his large, tanned fingers.

"It's not just *who*," he said. "It's when. The *when* is very important. Do you understand? Too soon and it will be worse. Too late and then more damage is done. Timing is everything."

He spread the page flat on the table.

Lou didn't see anything written on it. "It's blank."

Her father laughed, as if she'd made a joke.

"I know it's a lot to take in, but it's about balance. You couldn't have saved Christine, because it wasn't the right *when*."

"Who's Christine?"

Her father's finger went down the page, stopping at a name. "Like this one. You won't be able to stop this one either, but it's okay. It's not your job to save everyone, Lou-blue."

Lou stared hard at the paper, now convinced there were names of people that she couldn't see. Dark shapes began to form on the paper, squiggly shadows, but nothing legible.

"I'm showing you this because I don't want you to beat yourself up about it. You're doing everything you're supposed to do."

He placed a heavy hand on her shoulder, squeezed hard enough for her to feel it through the leather jacket. She didn't give a shit about names on some paper. She wanted to soak in every second with him.

He smiled. "I'm so proud of you. Do you know that? I want you to know how proud I am of the amazing woman you've become."

"I've missed you."

"I miss you too." His smile brightened. "But we'll see each other again soon. Until then, don't forget, Lou-blue. I'm proud of you."

She had only a moment to appreciate the beauty of his face in the lazy summer afternoon before night fell.

It was as if someone had snapped their fingers and sunshine was replaced by moonlight. The pool was lit from within. It glowed, ethereal with steam rising from its surface.

Her father was gone. A woman stood on the first step of the pool. The water rippled from her knees out toward the deep end. Her long skirt floated on the surface.

"I've come to take you back," Lucy said without turning. "You can't stay here. If you stay any longer, that might be the end of it. And there's still so much you can do. You're only getting started."

"Take me where?" Lou asked. She was trying to remember what her father had said, what he'd been doing the moment before. But already it was a memory slipping away from her. The tighter she tried to hold on to it, the faster it bled through her fingers.

"You can trust him, you know," Lucy said, and then she did turn, casting Lou a mischievous look over her shoulder. Lou thought Lucy was talking about her father at first. Then she said, "It might help you to know that he'll outlive you."

Lou left her seat at the table and went to the pool. She stepped down onto the first step beside her aunt.

"Konstantine?"

Lucy regarded the shimmering water. Lou couldn't be sure, but it seemed like the lights inside the pool were getting brighter.

"They'll all outlive you. You won't see anyone else you love die. You've done enough of that."

Lou thought the water in her boots would chill her feet. But instead it seemed that warmth filled them, spreading up her legs into her groin, her abdomen, and climbing.

"Even King?" Lou asked. "Because he's pretty old."

Lucy's smile was beautiful, radiant. She was healthy again, whole, looking the way Lou remembered her best.

Of course, King could drop dead tomorrow, or live another fifteen years.

Lucy turned and gave Lou a look full of so much sadness. She reached up and touched her face, the hand cool.

The lights in the pool brightened more, causing Lou to squint her eyes against it.

"Love them while you can," her aunt said, and Lou clamped her hand over hers to prevent her from disappearing.

When I open my eyes she'll be gone, she knew. *When I open my eyes*—

"Are you ready?" Lucy asked.

Lou didn't have to answer.

Her eyes opened.

She had only one moment of blessed ignorance before the pain made itself known. In this moment, she noted the hospital bed and the shape of her body tucked neatly under the blankets piled on top of her.

She noted the dark, silent television hanging from the wall above. She noted the bathroom, the hint of a toilet shining in the dark behind the ajar door.

Konstantine was in the doorway, speaking to a man in a white coat.

"She's awake," another man said, and Lou's eyes tracked the noise.

It was Stefano, who stood by her bedside.

Both the doctor and Konstantine stopped talking and turned.

That was when the pain came—almost as if summoned by their gazes alone.

Lou groaned, trying to sit up, as if she could escape it by adjusting herself.

"Easy, easy," someone said.

"It hurts," she groaned, and felt like a stupid, petulant child. "It *hurts.*"

"Hold on. Here we go."

In the periphery of her vision, she saw a thumb mashing a little button several times.

"This will help."

Warmth spread through Lou's arm and into her chest.

"Welcome back!" the doctor said, perhaps too enthusiastically. "We almost lost you there!"

"Mel—" Lou began.

Konstantine shook his head and raised his brows. "Let the doctor tell you what happened, and then we can...catch up, *amore mio*. Quickly though?"

The doctor released a nervous laugh. "Of course. As you know, you were shot. The bullet grazed your collarbone and tore through the muscles there. The stitches will have to stay in for a while, and you'll definitely have restricted movement on your right side for, well, possibly forever. We can try PT to regain most of it, but I suspect you'll discover some nerve damage once you begin moving it again."

Lou looked down at her shoulder and saw that her arm was taped to her side and chest.

"You're incredibly lucky," the doctor went on. "Had the bullet been centimeters closer to your neck, it would've severed your carotid and you would be dead. If it had been any lower, it could've shattered your collarbone and punctured your lung. Even a centimeter lower and I wouldn't have been able to dig the fragments out of your lungs. Someone up there must be looking out for you."

Lou saw Lucy standing in the pool, her dress floating on top of the water. Nonsensically, her mind thought, *It's because I was in the darkness. And Lucy lives in the darkness now.*

"How long until she is healed?" Konstantine asked.

"Six months is the soonest for full use of the shoulder," the doctor said.

Konstantine's gaze lingered on his face.

The doctor seemed to take the hint. "I'm sure you want to speak to your wife. So if you'll excuse me. But, uh, if you need more morphine" —he put a small remote control into her hand—"don't hesitate to push this button."

Konstantine nodded toward the door, and Stefano followed the doctor out, shutting the door behind him.

Konstantine pulled the empty chair up to the side of her bed and sank into it. He suddenly looked very, *very* tired.

"Wife?" Lou asked, leveling him with a stare.

"Only family is allowed to access medical information and make decisions on your behalf."

"Couldn't you just hack into their systems?" It hurt to talk. Not only because her neck throbbed but because her mouth was incredibly dry.

"I wanted to be in the room with you." He placed his face in his hands.

Lou closed her eyes. The morphine was pressing at the edges of her brain, making her eyes heavy. She wanted to go back to sleep.

Konstantine's deep voice drew her to consciousness again.

"Do you know how painfully *slow* an airplane ride feels when the woman you love is dying?"

"I've never been in love with a woman. And I don't fly."

His lips twitched. He settled against the back of the chair and sighed. "Would you like to know about Fish or the shopkeeper first?"

"She has a name."

"I know," he said. "But it is difficult for me to say."

"Melandra."

"Yes, but I meant without cursing it. She nearly killed you."

"It was an accident."

"Which is why she is alive and well. King needed only a little help making sure that there was no evidence against her."

Something in Lou's chest relaxed. It was either relief or the morphine was working nicely.

Konstantine continued, unaware.

"Fish has been arrested and charged for murder. He confessed after two days of interrogation. King called this normal, saying he is a megomaniac."

"Megalomaniac." Lou's tongue raked over her dry lips. "Can I have some water?"

Konstantine called out in Italian, and Stefano's face appeared in the hospital door.

"*Acqua, per favore.*"

Stefano disappeared again.

"He loves to do your bidding," Lou said.

Konstantine's lips quirked. "For a very high price."

"How high?" Lou asked. "Because I can fetch water too."

Each sarcastic quip seemed to loosen Konstantine's shoulders, forcing them back down away from his ears.

"His case is going to court, and the families now have a chance at peace. King says this was your objective. So, congratulations." Konstantine adjusted the watch on his wrist. "What happened with the woman?"

"Diana?"

"Yes."

"She told me that she's a hunter like me."

"Is she?" Konstantine rubbed his chin. "This isn't surprising. I can't imagine you're the only woman like this in the world. She must be jealous of your gifts."

"She doesn't know about them."

"I would keep it that way."

Lou tried to find the best position for her head, but no matter how she turned it, she was uncomfortable. "What about Mel's husband?"

"In prison, and the divorce is in process."

The door slid open and Stefano appeared with a Styrofoam cup of water. He delivered it to Konstantine.

Konstantine scooted his chair closer to the bed, angling the straw so Lou could drink.

She scowled at him.

"If you try to hold it yourself you may drop it."

With a stifled cry, she leaned forward and accepted the water.

"You look like you're in a lot of pain. I see it in your eyes."

"You're observant," she murmured between drinks.

He frowned. "Is there anything I can get you? Is there anything you want?"

Lou snorted. "I want to fuck you."

Definitely the drugs talking, she thought distantly.

Stefano exited the room with his eyebrows raised and closed the door behind him.

"I recommend we wait until you're healed."

"You're no fun. Maybe I like the pain."

He cocked his head. "You could have done it before. I made that perfectly clear."

"I didn't want you to fall in love with me."

He laughed. "I love how honest you are when you're high."

She leaned back with a grimace. It was very hard to get comfortable, and she'd begun to itch. Nowhere specific, but all over. Her scalp. Her chest. Her flesh crawled.

"It's too late, you know," he said after trying to help her adjust the pillows. "I'm already in love with you."

"Don't." She scowled. This was not helping her discomfort. "People in love want to get married, they want kids. I don't want any of that."

"Would you believe me if I said I only want to love you? I'm not asking for anything else."

Lou said nothing.

"Is it really so hard to believe? Or do you think you're incapable of love?" he asked, unable to let it go.

"People like me—like Fish—we don't love."

He frowned. "You aren't like the men you kill, *amore mio*. You loved your father, your mother, your aunt. You love your friends."

Lou grimaced, scratching at her chest with the unbound hand. "Maybe not my mother."

He sat back and crossed one knee over the other. "If you don't love me, that's fine. But that doesn't mean you *can't* love."

Love them while you can.

Lou closed her eyes. It was impossible to keep them open anymore. She tried to remember what Lucy was wearing in the dream, but it was fading, and fading fast. Had her feet been in the water? Had it been nighttime? Was the pool lit from within? Lou thought so.

"You scared me," Konstantine whispered.

"I'll keep scaring you," she said, without opening her eyes.

"I'm sure you will."

39

King lifted the paczki from its brown pastry box, delighting in the way the dough gave softly under his touch. When he bit into it, warm raspberry jelly oozed out onto his tongue, and powdered sugar coated his lips. He was in heaven. He moaned with happiness.

Piper snorted beside him, leaning over the black wrought-iron railing. "That good, huh?"

"You want to split one?" Dani asked, looking up from the box.

King wanted to object and claim the entire dozen for his own, but that hardly seemed like appropriate Fat Tuesday spirit. And he hadn't bought the donuts. Mel had.

The four of them were waiting on the balcony, watching the crowds jostle below in anticipation of the upcoming parade.

"Yeah, I'll split one," Piper said, grinning at her. "You pick."

Dani tucked her hair behind her ear. "They all look so good."

"Yes, they do," Mel agreed, crossing and uncrossing her legs from her chair. She readjusted the rectangular card on her clipboard. It was The Devil, in progress. Most of the lean man's face was hidden beneath a tipped hat, but Mel had given him a ghost of a smile.

"It's coming along," Piper said, peering over Mel's shoulder. "It's going to be cool as hell when you add color."

"Cool as hell," Dani snorted, finally selecting a paczki from the box. "Was that an intentional pun?"

She was about to bite into her selected paczki when she frowned, leaning over the balcony. "Someone's here."

Everyone turned.

A black car rolled up to the curb. The driver's side door opened first, and Konstantine stepped out into the throng of people, politely excusing himself as he pushed through. The doors on either side of the backseat opened, and two men stepped out onto the street.

They formed a buffer of space around the passenger side door, but it was Konstantine who opened it.

Piper choked on her bite. "Shit, it's Lou."

"I'll get her," Mel said, rising from her seat.

But Piper, red-faced, was waving her back down. She was through the doors and out of sight before anyone could object.

"That's a Maserati," Dani said.

Mel barely looked up from the card as she bent closer to add another line to the devil's hat.

Konstantine and Lou had disappeared beneath the balcony. The two men climbed into the front seat and drove away.

Mel pulled back, frowning at the card. "Give me one of those," she said, motioning for the donut box.

King pushed the box toward her, only after taking a second donut for himself.

"Look who it is!" Piper called, throwing open the balcony door so that Lou could step through. "Our indestructible heroine!"

The color was back in her face, which pleased King. The last time he'd seen her, she'd been white as a ghost. Her arm was still wrapped tight to her body and her leather jacket was draped over that shoulder. But she was up and moving.

"When I saw you get out of a car I thought you'd lost your powers," Piper said.

Konstantine pulled out a chair for Lou. "There wasn't an easier way to transport us both here without hurting her."

"My shoulder is…tender." Lou pushed her sunglasses up on her head with her good hand before accepting the chair.

"So no piggybacking for a while." King sucked the raspberry jelly off his fingers. "I hope you'll rest."

Lou shot him a warning look.

"That was a nice car you rolled up in," Piper said, and King caught the tonal shift.

"Thank you," Konstantine replied, simply unaware.

"Is it yours or…?" she searched.

"While I am in the city, yes."

Piper pursed her lips. "Cool, cool."

Dani grabbed her hand tenderly and pulled her close. "Finish this."

Piper reluctantly took the half-eaten paczki and stuffed it into her mouth. She gave Dani a suspicious look.

A handful of purple beads flew through the air past their balcony.

"Damn, we forgot beads!" Piper cried. "Be right back."

Lou looked very placid in her seat, watching the crowds below.

King couldn't tell if it was the pain in her shoulder that was subduing her or if something else was on her mind.

Then he remembered something. "I forgot to tell you. We got an ID on the woman whose body you found in the woods—the one we hadn't been expecting."

Lou turned toward him finally, leveling him with her gaze.

"Her name was Christine Haslett."

Lou started as if slapped.

King frowned. "You know her?"

"Did you ever say that name to me before?"

"No."

"Maybe in the hospital while you were visiting me? Maybe someone else said it?"

King shifted his weight. "No, I don't think so. Why?"

Her scowl deepened. "It doesn't matter."

"By the sound of it, Christine was an impulse kill. She'd been walking home from a friend's house when he picked her up. He'd never met her and didn't have any connections to her. It's the kind of murder he would've never gotten caught for. But thanks to you breaking this wide open, her family will get closure. Did you see the families on the news?"

"Yes," Lou said, shifting her body to alleviate the dull throb at the base of her neck. It was her jacket. Why did it feel so heavy? But she didn't want to remove it, given the cold. "I saw the news."

Lou had seen the story break while she was in the hospital. She'd had little else to do in the days before she was allowed to go home. Konstantine had read to her, and when he'd gotten tired they'd turned on the television. A tearful woman had stood at a podium and given her statement to the press. *I'll never get my baby girl back, but it helps my heart to know that this monster will pay for what he's done. There's still justice in this world.*

Lou had felt something as she watched each mother, father, sister, brother come to the microphone and say their piece about Jeffrey Fish. The photographs taken from his home had let them know which of the missing girls to account for even though not all of their graves had been found.

Lou also knew there was a strong possibility that Fish had not photographed all of his kills. So she might occupy her painful, sleepless nights directing her compass to those unmarked graves. She'd take Dani along. Maybe Piper. Together they would figure out how to let the police know about the graves.

"I saw the news," she said.

"I told you closure is important," King said. His attempt at solemnity was dampened by the powder on his lips and raspberry jelly on his face. "You should be proud of yourself for making that possible."

Will they really get closure? Lou wondered. She thought of her father and her mother, whose deaths had been unexpected. She thought of Aunt Lucy, whose death had been expected. There had been no closure in either case.

Not really.

But she let King speak his mind, aware that he was assessing her the way her father used to. She'd scared him. She understood that.

Seeing her bleed out on the pavilion's stones had shaken him, and part of his mind was still wrapping around the idea that she was here.

They'll all outlive you, Lucy had said.

"And when I die?" Lou asked, turning toward him. "How will you find closure then?"

"Who's gonna die?" Piper squeaked. "Not you! I told you. You're indestructible, man."

She felt Konstantine shift in her periphery. Until that moment, he'd been politely engaging Melandra in conversation, asking about Carnival and its role in the city as well as complimenting the tarot card she was sketching.

He punctuated his sentences with affectionate scratches behind Lady's ears, whose tail thumped against the balcony's wooden planks.

Lou knew better. When she'd asked the question, his hand had faltered. His back had stiffened.

Lou pretended not to notice, keeping her eyes trained on King.

"I'll be sixty-one years old this year," King said, wiping jelly from the corner of his lips. "I should be asking you that question."

"Do the men in your family die in their sixties?" Lou asked with a smile. She was doing her best to keep her tone light, teasing. But her shoulder had begun to throb again, shooting up the side of her neck into her skull.

"My dad kicked off at eighty-six. His dad went at eighty-two. I've probably got twenty to twenty-five years if I take care of myself."

"As long as we keep the gun out of Mel's hands, you should be fine," Piper said around a mouthful of donut, sugar falling from her lips.

"No need." Mel covered her face with her hands. "I'll never touch another gun as long as I live."

Piper scoffed. "Never say never. That's how fate gets you."

"How do you feel?" Melandra asked Lou, settling down in the empty chair beside her. She pulled her clipboard to her chest and grimaced as if she were the one in pain.

Lou forced a smile for her benefit. "You're not the first person to shoot me. Not even the tenth."

"You almost died."

"Often," Lou said, turning up the wattage on her smile. "Don't worry about it. It's not bad."

"I think she likes it," Piper said, pointing a donut at Lou's mouth, forcing Lou to open up and take a bite. "If she doesn't almost die once a week, she's bored to tears."

Piper took a bite of donut herself.

"You know," she said around her mouthful, "while you're resting we should do something fun. Like, for spring break we should do a road trip."

"A road trip!" Dani cried, kneeling down on Lady's other side. The dog now had two admirers, and her thumping tail suggested that was just fine.

"I've never been on a road trip," Lou admitted.

Dani and Piper gave each other big, excited grins. "We're doing this."

"We need a playlist."

"And snacks."

"I have the car," Dani said. "And gas money."

"We'll split that. What do you think about Clearwater? Miami?"

"Las Vegas? Or the PCH?"

"Whoa. Go big or go home. I love it." Piper chewed her lip, thinking. "But how much time can we actually get off work?"

"Lou could just—"

"No, we have to drive! That's the point!"

"I just meant one way—"

Lou's shoulder seized up, and she squeezed her eyes closed against it.

Then Konstantine was there with a glass of water and two large pain pills. "I think it's time for these," he said, pressing them into her hand.

She took them both, tipping back the water glass until it was empty. When she handed the glass over, she caught Mel's fraught gaze.

Melandra reached her hand across the table, palm up in question. "Please forgive me."

Lou hesitated, regarding the half-finished devil on the clipboard. He bore a striking resemblance to Mel's ex-husband. The leather hat with a single crow feather. The bent head and fire-filled eyes. The bone choker stretching across his throat. At last she took the woman's smooth, dry hand. "There's nothing to forgive."

"No way!" Piper scoffed. "Doritos are *way* better than Pringles."

"Are you kidding me?" Dani rolled her eyes. "Next you'll be telling me Reese's Pieces are better than M&Ms."

Piper squealed. "*Way* better."

"I *am* sorry," Mel said, pushing her hair back from her face. "*So*, so sorry."

"I'm sorry too," Lou said with a mischievous smile.

Mel's gaze darkened. "For what?"

"For what I'm going to do to your ex-husband the first chance I get."

EPILOGUE
SIX MONTHS LATER

Terrence Lamott lay in his cell, staring at the ceiling. Someone had scratched *suck my big white dick* into the concrete and drawn a crude phallus beside it that looked nothing like, in Terry's opinion, an actual dick. A balloon animal, maybe.

When the nights were long like this and sleep wouldn't come, he liked to count the ways he was going to hurt Melandra Durand. It was his favorite game. He imagined tying her up and pulling all her fingernails off one by one with rusty pliers. He imagined holding her head under water in a shit-filled toilet. He *dreamed* of branding his name onto her tits with a red-hot poker.

All the bitch had to do was give him what she owed him.

Why had that turned out to be so hard?

The pressure between his ears rose suddenly, the way it did in elevators that went up into high buildings. He shook his head to clear it.

When he opened his eyes again, there she was. The devil herself.

"I wondered when I might be seeing you," he said. He sat up on his elbows and regarded the young woman. She wasn't really a woman. He understood that. But she was pretty to look at all the same.

"Sorry to keep you waiting," she said from the shadows.

It was hard to hear her over the ruckus of the prison. All hours of the night people carried on, hooting and hollering, singing, screaming, or laughing.

She stepped forward just enough that her mouth and lips were lit by the lights outside his cell.

"I have a question for you," she said, and now he could see her eyes too. He'd half expected to see them full of hellfire, but they were a soft brown like his momma's eyes. Like his little girl Alexis's eyes.

"What's that?" he asked.

"Why did you lie to Mel?"

He laughed. "*When?* I lied to that dumb bitch every day of her life."

"The night she hit the fox. Why did you tell her she'd killed someone?"

Again, Terrence thought of all the ways he wanted to hurt Melly. After pulling off her nails, he wanted to cut her ears, not all at once, but in little slices. Then maybe he would slit the cartilage between her nostrils, giving her one large one instead of two small breathing holes. Oh yes, he could do quite a bit to her face, he thought.

"I like hurting her," he said, rolling his eyes up to Lou's. "Sometimes it feels good. Hurting somebody."

He thought she might disappear then, leave him on his mattress with the ruckus of this concrete jungle, and only his mad thoughts to console him through the night.

But a wicked smile spread across her lips, and Terry worried for the first time that maybe he'd said the wrong thing.

"I know what you mean," she said.

Then her hands were on him, pulling him into the waiting dark.

DEVIL'S LUCK

SHADOWS IN THE WATER BOOK 5

AUTHOR'S NOTE
TRIGGER WARNING

This book includes descriptions of child pornography and rape. These moments are short and allusive and you can usually see them coming. As an author, I tried to keep the emotion and gravity of the situation realistic to the story without gratuitous embellishment. However, please skim or skip these passages, with my complete support, if they will hurt or bother you.

Kory M. Shrum

*For Uncle Craig,
my biggest fan*

1

———————

Spencer Halliday hobbled down the checkered hallway. The two-inch difference in length between his left and right legs accounted for his gait, but he was determined not to be slowed down by it.

"Where's Diana?" he called out, without stopping. A sheet of paper trembled in his hand as he swung his arms to steady himself.

The woman in leather pants leaning against the wall looked up from her phone.

"Surveillance room." She blew a bubble until it popped, a large pink film spreading across her lips. She licked it away with a swipe of her tongue. "Why? What do you want now, Quasi?"

Only Blair was brave enough to call him this to his face.

No matter. What was she to him anyway? The scent of grass and sweat wafted off of her. Dirt was smudged across her upper arm. Spencer supposed she'd just returned from a raid.

Dirty, disgusting, he thought, his mouth pulling into a sneer. *My Diana would never be so unkempt.*

And Diana was the only one who mattered.

"Diana," he called out. "Diana, I have something!"

He shuffled past Blair without answering, the bald spot on his head reflecting the flickering fluorescents above.

He burst through the closed door and found her in the dark, staring into the blue light of a computer terminal. Her face was scrunched in concentration. This glow made her look like a fresh corpse still tormented by its gruesome death. Her blonde hair, pulled into a severe ponytail on the top of her head, was toned silver.

"What is it?" she asked blandly, a hint of annoyance in her tone.

"Look at this."

"No," Diana insisted. Her blue eyes were made bluer by the glow. "I can't take my eyes off him."

Spencer sucked at his upper lip with his considerable underbite. "But I finally got a match on the DNA results you wanted."

"What DNA results?" she asked, again not looking away from the screen. "How can he smile so much? He smiles *all* the time. *Why? What do you have to smile about, you bastard?*"

Spencer ignored this. Diana often mumbled to herself when concentrating. He continued undeterred. "There's a match for the coffee cup and the five-dollar bill. In New Orleans."

At this Diana did look up. The lines in her face smoothed out. Her eyebrows lifted in surprise. "Really? New Orleans?"

"There was a blood sample collected from"—he looked at the sheet again—"Julia Street station. It's definitely her."

"How recent?"

"March."

"If the blood was collected in March, why am I only now hearing about it?"

Spencer shifted his weight. *No, no.* This wasn't going how he wanted. He'd imagined Diana's joy at the news. He imagined her slipping her arms around his neck and—what?

Biting him maybe.

Or perhaps shoving him against a wall before pressing her tight body into his. Delicious rewards for his efforts.

He shivered at the thought.

But there was no joy. She was scowling at him.

His anxiety spiked electric along his skin. "I don't know. A lag in processing? The NOPD has been understaffed since Hurricane Katrina. Their police force hasn't recovered."

Her reaction made him doubt himself.

Foolish, he thought. *I shouldn't have told her.*

Maybe letting her know about the match would put her on a collision course with the woman. Diana's obsessive mind would make it impossible for her to let such a trail go. He could only hope that Lou was long gone and the trail in New Orleans cold.

Because the Lou woman frightened him. She wasn't to be trusted, especially not with someone so precious as Diana.

But if Diana had learned that he kept things from her—*She'll kill you.*

Desire ripped through him at the idea.

"New Orleans," Diana murmured to herself. "I haven't been there in years."

Spencer shifted uncomfortably against the pressure building between his legs. "Why do you care so much about her?"

"You mean, why do I care about finding someone like me?"

No one like you. Never anyone like you.

Instead he said, "You must've known there'd be at least a few."

"Spencer," Diana began, and the hair on the back of his neck prickled. It was her voice, pitched low. He knew that voice. It promised violence.

She pushed back her seat and stood. She had a hand on his throat before he'd seen her move.

Her heat radiated like the sun across his face and neck.

His mind babbled. *I want I want I want—*

Her eyes were black now, the inner blue cannibalized by the room's shadows. "I want to know who she is and what she has, Spencer. It's obvious she has connections and assets that I don't."

"No," he said, too quickly. His tongue darted out from between his lips. If only he could taste the air like a snake, taste *her*. "No, I just—I just wondered if this is about Winter."

Spencer already knew the answer. For Diana, *everything* was about Winter.

Diana affected a shrug. "So what if it is? Would that matter?"

"No." Spencer didn't like how high and tight his voice sounded. "You're free to—"

Diana tightened her hold on his throat and drove him back. His head hit the cinder block wall, ears ringing.

"I *am* free to do whatever I want. And what I want is for you to find me the best PI in New Orleans."

Her mouth was over his now. *Hot. So hot.* He wondered if those lips could scald him.

"A PI?" he repeated, his dick hardening.

She must've seen the ache in his eyes. With a wicked smile, she slid the fingers from her free hand into his hair and gripped it. Then she pulled so hard tears sprang to his eyes. A small whimper escaped him.

She put her lips close enough to his ear that her words tickled when she spoke. "The best PI in town. Someone who can find her."

"Okay," he mewled, squirming beneath her. His fists opened and closed at his sides. He wanted to touch her, wanted more than anything to put his hands on her body.

But that was not allowed. He was *never* allowed to touch her unless she said *the word.*

"Spencer," she whispered into his mouth.

Please, please, please, he thought. *Please say it. Please say—*

She released him, stepping back out of his reach and taking all the heat with her. "Don't disappoint me."

2

———————

Piper Lynn Genereux rested her weight against the door jamb, watching the six-foot-tall drag queen lean over the sink to peer into the mirror. With steady hands, fake eyelashes were glued and pressed to each eye. The lightbulb overhead hissed, but neither noticed. Piper was mesmerized.

Their eyes met in the mirror.

"You're pretty," Piper said reflexively.

Henry laughed. "Don't sound so surprised."

"I'm not surprised," she said defensively, uncrossing and recrossing her arms. She'd seen Henry in drag countless times. "I'm just saying you've gotten really good at this."

"I've come a long way from plastic pants and Aqua Net, yes," he said. "Thanks again for letting me use your bathroom. My apartment is too small for three queens."

Piper could only imagine how difficult it was for Henry to share a bathroom with his boyfriends, especially now that she was reminded how much work getting ready was for him.

"What time do you go on?" she asked, offering a tissue so he could dab the fallout from his mascara.

"Eleven. I go on right after Mustang Mary," he said. Their eyes met in the mirror again. "Are you coming?"

In truth, Piper had hoped to go to bed early. She hadn't slept well the night before. Too many strange dreams only half remembered. But with Henry's hopeful face pouting at her, *no* wasn't an option.

She rubbed her nose. "Sure. I'll come."

"Will you bring a girl?"

"*A* girl?" Piper snorted. "You make it sound like I have more than one. Dani and I aren't even official. Besides, she's working late. She has a deadline."

"What about the dangerous one? You could bring her instead."

Piper frowned. "I don't have a dangerous girlfriend." *Or any girlfriend.*

Henry removed a glob of mascara from the wand. "Leather jacket. Mirrored shades. Looks like she eats flesh for breakfast and drinks blood for dinner."

Piper laughed. "Lou? She's not a cannibal."

"I'm just saying she's got a man-eater vibe. I haven't seen her in a while. I thought you were into her."

"I was," she admitted. "But now I'm not."

"Because..."

This was dangerous territory. It wasn't that Henry was forbidden to know about Lou. It was that *no one* was supposed to know about Lou.

"It's not like that," she said. "We're friends."

"Just work friends?" he asked, adding stick-on jewels beneath his eyes.

"More than that," she said. He'd seen Lou pick her up from the bars. Work friends don't do that. Nor did the word acquaintance work after all that had happened between them.

Lou had saved her life. And she loved her. At first she'd been certain it was an intense romantic love. Now she knew it was deeper than that.

Best friends? she wondered. *Is she my best friend?*

"How much *more?*" he asked, rummaging in his makeup bag.

"You're such a perv. Nothing is going on. We're just close."

"I mean, without a doubt, Dani is gorgeous, but I'm trying to understand why you passed on Lou."

Lou passed on me. "She's way out of my league. So is Dani, but at least that seems like a mountain I can climb."

Henry snorted at the innuendo. "I know what you mean. There was this hot barista at Starbucks."

"Poydras or Canal?"

"Poydras. He was thick as hell and had this amazing butt."

"You're quoting Todrick Hall again," Piper said.

He didn't seem to register this comment. "But then I started talking to him and found out he's a double finance and plant biology major at Tulane. He wants to revolutionize the coffee industry and create a coffee with negative emissions that will save the planet while we *drink* it." Henry scoffed. "Definitely not the barista I thought he was."

Piper saw the popped button on his sequined bodice. She tried to refasten it. "What kind of barista were you hoping for?"

"The kind who only works for beer money, I guess."

Piper had no idea what any of this had in common with her and Lou. "Well, good thing you already have two boyfriends."

"I'm always shopping for my third."

The button finally snapped into place. "I'm aware."

"And now you have a hot girlfriend and you and Lou are disaster friends," Henry said, dabbing on foundation where he'd over wiped.

"What? No."

"You work together at the detective agency, right?"

Piper couldn't even imagine Lou managing the register at Madame Melandra's Fortunes and Fixes. "Yeah, but—"

"Your job is to hunt criminals, catch bad guys, clean up messes. It's all drama, drama, drama. Didn't Dani end up in the hospital?"

"That was more of a journalism accident." A complete lie, given that a Russian mob boss had cut off her finger and had beaten her half to death.

Henry arched a brow. "Sounds disaster-y to me."

"Stop saying that."

"It's not a bad thing! It just means that your relationship is based on drama, rather than, I don't know, a shared love of churro sundaes or boy-hunting."

Piper scoffed. "We're real friends."

Though admittedly, there are a lot of bodies, she thought glumly.

"It's just that people like us, with shit parents, we tend to have certain types of relationships. We attract the drama. It's hard to make real connections with people. Disaster friends come and go. That's okay. It's as it should be. That's all I'm saying."

I don't want Lou to come and go.

"We aren't disaster friends," she said again, lip stiff. "We connect."

Henry arched a brow at her hard refusal. "Okay. Whatever you say, sis."

Lou threw the dusty towel into the hamper and observed her gleaming apartment. She'd cleaned it top to bottom for the second time that week, and considering her minimalist style and near-nothing possessions, this was...

Ridiculous, she thought. *I'm losing my mind.*

She was no less restless than when she'd begun the project six hours ago. All that scrubbing and organizing hadn't expelled any of the energy itching along her spine. What had she hoped to accomplish?

Perhaps nothing, but she'd run out of options. Her guns certainly hadn't helped.

She'd begun with those, of course. She'd drawn the curtains and pulled her entire arsenal from the myriad of hiding places tucked around the apartment. She'd disassembled, cleaned, and reassembled each gun carefully. She'd counted ammunition. She'd sharpened her blades and rewrapped fraying handles. She'd repacked her medical kit and made fresh rags.

Still, she couldn't settle. She needed to *do* something.

I need to hunt.

Her shoulder twinged. The stab of pain slid up the side of her neck like a knife.

It was a reminder that even cleaning was a gamble.

Her shoulder refused to heal, at least not as quickly as Lou wanted it to. When the bullet had grazed her collarbone, the doctor had warned her it would be at least six months before she could use it.

Be grateful the bone didn't shatter.

"Grateful," she murmured, and sank onto the edge of the mattress pressed beneath the windows.

Behind her, the St. Louis night was vibrant. The illuminated arch stood like a starlet on the riverway carpet. Headlights from boats swept the moonlit waters. A half-moon hung tilted in the sky like a spotlight.

Her hands smelled like bleach. *For all the wrong reasons*, she lamented.

What had she done before, when the restlessness was this bad? When she was a moment away from pulling the skin off her body with her bare hands?

She grabbed her leather jacket off the kitchen stool and stepped into the converted linen closet.

Once upon a time it had shelves for towels. The shelves had been removed to make room for her body.

Now it smelled like sawdust from her recent sanding, another desperate, itinerant task. When her fingers brushed the wall, they came away powder-soft, a thin film coating them.

She pulled the door closed and darkness swelled. It slid over her face and hands, along the side of her throat, and pooled at the back of her neck. It was like a cat rubbing against her.

She surrendered to it.

The world thinned, a gossamer curtain falling away into nothing but pitch. A compass, unseen but felt, whirled inside her. It searched for a location to latch onto, two points to align in the dark.

Something snagged, and the sense of weightlessness evaporated and gravity returned.

Lou stepped from the shadows toward the sound of voices.

"I'm thinking of Todrick's *I Like Boys*," a gruff voice said.

"I love that song," Piper said, shifting her weight against the door where she leaned. "Such a bop. It'll be fun to dance to."

The kitchen was dark and quiet, as well as the open living room adjacent. At the start of a hallway was the lit bathroom where Piper stood, ankles and arms crossed.

She turned away from the light of the bathroom toward Lou, as if sensing her arrival. Then she did a double take, eyes widening.

She stepped away from the frame and slammed her index finger against her lips.

"What?" the gruff voice asked.

"I thought I heard something," Piper said. She made a frantic knocking sound with her hand.

Lou understood, lifted her hand, and rapped against the closed door beside her.

"Coming," Piper called. She opened and closed her front door, her eyes never leaving Lou's face. "Hey, Lou-blue. So nice of you to *drop in.*"

A bedazzled head popped out of the bathroom, looking like an exotic bird checking to see if the coast was clear of predators. His face sparkled.

Lou remembered this one. *Henry*, she thought. Or was it Harry?

"Oh hey," he said. "We were just talking about you. Are you coming to the show tonight?"

Piper looked as interested in this answer as Henry.

"I have work," Lou said. To Piper, "I came to see if you wanted to join me."

"Ohh," Henry said with a dramatic gasp. "Fun crime-fighting stuff? Are you going to *cuff* someone?"

He waggled his eyebrows.

Piper let out a nervous laugh. "We aren't cops, H."

"Well, either way, duty calls. Do you care if I finish up here and lock up after I leave?" he asked.

"You're assuming I'm going to go. What about your show?"

"Pfft. Girl, you've seen me shake my ass a million times. You're not missing anything. Go save the world."

"Grab a coat," Lou said quietly.

"What's that?" Henry poked his head out of the bathroom.

"Good luck with your show," Lou said, pitching her voice louder.

He smiled and tilted his head. "Thanks, girl. Have fun with the handcuffs."

Piper grabbed a coat off the back of the kitchen door and forced her arms through the sleeves. As they stepped into Piper's stairwell and shut the apartment door behind them, Piper made a show of stomping on a few of the stairs, but they never reached the floor below, which opened onto King's detective agency.

Instead, Piper felt an arm hook around her waist the moment before she was jerked through the dark.

Piper might have been disturbed by this, the sense of compression and falling, if she hadn't traveled in Lou's special way many times before.

When the world reformed around them, it revealed a pine forest. The smell of sticky sap, pungent and thick, saturated the air. The air was also noticeably cooler, which explained Lou's insistence on a jacket despite the ninety-degree weather holding New Orleans hostage.

"Oh, wow." Piper sucked in a deep breath. "It smells like Christmas up in here."

Lou was looking at the GPS watch on her wrist. The screen illuminated her face green and created deep shadows beneath her lips and nose.

Moonlight shifted through the clouds, giving Piper the impression of spirits wandering between the creaking trees.

"Not that I don't love coming to the forest in the middle of the night, but, uh, what are we doing here? The creep factor is *quite* high right now."

"We're looking for a body."

"Oh, that's nice. I feel better already," Piper deadpanned. "What body?"

"One of Fish's."

The mere mention of the serial killer they'd captured five months ago brought the situation into clearer view. This wasn't the first time she'd been invited to a find-a-murdered-body dig-along. In fact, they'd uncovered fourteen bodies more than the thirty Jeffrey Fish had confessed to since his arrest in March.

Piper's suspicions were confirmed when she saw the two shovels propped against the tree, their blades glinting. And the sight of the shovels told Piper two very important things.

First, Lou was going crazy and running out of ways to self-soothe. That explained why she smelled like bleach.

Second, Piper needed to do the digging.

Lou stepped carefully through the low-lying ferns until she seemed to settle on a spot. She checked her GPS watch again.

Something cried shrilly overhead, thrashing the branches as it passed.

Just a bird, Piper told herself. *Maybe a bat.*

"Where are we?" she asked.

"Ohio. The Zaleski State Forest." Lou grabbed a shovel. "It's here. Beneath me."

"*No.*" Piper knew better than to question Lou's amazing abilities, one of which meant she could find anything she was looking for. What she objected to was the shovel in Lou's hand.

"No," she said again, pulling at the shovel. It didn't budge.

"Okay, so you're still stronger than me, but I don't need to tell you that shoveling will destroy your shoulder, do I? Do you remember what happened last time?"

Because of course there had been a last time. Lou insisted on trying to dig up every body they found and it never ended well. Lou's stubbornness seemed as infinite as her high tolerance for pain.

"Maybe I can do it this time," Lou said.

"And maybe you'll keep on being wounded for the rest of your life. I know this is hard for you, but please just wait until the full recovery time is up and you get the doctor's approval, okay?"

Lou relinquished the shovel and Piper stumbled back.

Damn, she's strong.

Lou looked away. "I should get Dani to help you."

"Don't bother. She's got an editorial deadline." Piper put the tip of the spade into the earth and pressed hard with the heel of her sneaker. The earth broke open easily. Maybe it'd been raining.

Lou dropped into a crouch a few feet away.

Piper didn't mind shoveling with an audience, but twenty licks in she asked, "I'm in the right spot, correct?"

Lou gave a nod barely registerable in the dark. If the moonlight hadn't been abundant, Piper would be digging blind.

She was sure the canopy cover helped keep the forest cool, and there was a light breeze. She could hear water somewhere in the distance, and smelled it too. A nearby river or stream likely cut through the woods.

And yet despite the coolness, a thin line of sweat formed on her brow and the back of her neck as she labored.

The wooden handle turned in her grip, growing slicker. The muscles in her back were already talking to her. Her hands began to ache.

Lou seemed to pick up the thread where she'd dropped it. "We need Dani to report the body. She's the one with the media contacts."

"If we find a body you can just send Dani the coordinates. These journalists need almost nothing to follow a lead, man. They're like bloodhounds."

Piper was about two feet down when she asked, "Where'd you get the shovels?"

"I borrow them from a ditch digger in Alabama."

Were ditch diggers still a thing? "He knows you're borrowing his stuff?"

"No. And I put them back in a slightly different place each time."

"Don't do that!" Piper said, pausing to wipe her face. "Poor guy will think he's losing his mind."

Then she thought glumly, *Maybe we're all losing our minds.*

She was three feet down when she asked, "We do stuff, right?"

Lou's face was unreadable in the dark. Part of her cheek and jaw had collected moonlight, but her eyes were invisible.

"I don't understand the question," Lou said.

"Do we do stuff?"

"Can I have an example?" Lou inched forward into the moonlight, revealing the rest of her face.

"Do we hang out, go to the movies—you know, *stuff?*"

"We've had pizza in New York."

"Yes!" Piper said. "Though that was a lunch break in the middle of the Bennigan case."

"We went to that party in Italy," Lou added. "You got drunk."

Piper frowned. "It was a mob boss party. We went so Konstantine could get the name of that stalker for you."

She stopped shoveling and tried to catch her breath.

"Have we really not done anything that's not related to bad guys?" She frowned. "You picked me up from my mom's house when—no, wait. You came because King sent you."

Piper didn't want to think about that night anyway. Her mom with a needle hanging out of her arm and her abusive boyfriend wielding a shotgun as if that is an appropriate reaction to someone wanting to move out.

"We watched all seven seasons of that show," Lou said. "The one with the dragons."

Piper pumped a fist. "Yes. Yes, we did."

"It wasn't very good. Though I liked the fight scenes."

"You would. But worst ending ever."

"We're still watching the one about the killer who hunts killers."

"*Dexter.* Oh, and there's *Killing Eve*! I want to see that one. Wait." Piper's excitement vanished. "Is that all we do? Eat and watch television?"

"We are supposed to leave for the road trip Friday."

"Right!" Piper's enthusiasm returned like a loyal dog. "Road trips are excellent for bonding. There's music and snacks and talking. Wait, what do you mean, supposed to? Aren't you still coming?"

"Yes," Lou said. "But things come up."

"Nothing will come up," Piper said. "We're going and we'll have the time of our lives."

She shoved the end of the spade down into the hole again—and cracked something. "I think—"

"Let me," Lou called, and hopped down into the hole.

Using her fingerless-gloved hand, Lou brushed away the disturbed earth until two black sockets gazed up at them.

3

———————

Lou and Piper stood on the street outside Madame Melandra's Fortune and Fixes with two duffels sitting between their feet. One was stuffed with Piper's clothes, her wallet, and a neon blue phone charger.

Piper was hot. The day had barely started and she could already feel the heat thrown over her like a thick blanket. She just hoped that whatever car Dani chose from the rental place had a working air conditioner.

Staring at her feet, the black bag finally came into focus. Piper frowned. "What's in your bag?"

Lou grinned, her eyes safely guarded behind her mirrored shades. Her hands rested in the pockets of her leather jacket.

How she could wear it in this heat, Piper didn't know.

"Probably guns," Piper guessed. "But hopefully also underwear."

Lou snorted. "What makes you think I wear underwear?"

It was Piper's turn to giggle.

A Lexus rolled up to the curb. From the driver's seat, Dani gave a friendly honk and waved.

Piper pointed at the trunk and it popped open. She threw the bags in and went to the passenger-side window, motioning for Dani to roll it down.

"You didn't have to rent such a posh car. We would've been fine with a compact."

"It's mine," Dani said, and gave a sheepish grin. "My mom wanted a new car, so she gave me her old one. And it's only got ten thousand miles on it, so I thought we could just break it in."

This is the old *car?* Heat crawled up the back of Piper's neck. *Must be nice.*

"What's wrong?" Dani asked when Piper opened the door.

"Nothing," she lied, sliding into the passenger seat. "This is great."

Dani adjusted the seatbelt across her chest. "I'll drive first. I'll be good until at least Houston."

Piper gestured to the I-10 sign. "We need to stop at a gas station for snacks."

"Got it," Dani said, the good humor still seizing her expression.

At least someone is having a good time, Piper thought. They hadn't even started and Lou looked bored as hell, stoic as a statue in the backseat.

When Piper had first thought of the road trip idea months ago, she'd been excited.

Lou had gotten shot and almost died, and as she lay in a hospital for days, all Piper could think about was how Lou needed more good things in her life. It was true they watched TV and went out to eat. They'd been in a bar together a few times. But that wasn't enough.

The road trip was the shift they needed. With music and hours on the highway with only the summer wind in their hair, they could make real memories. Good, drama-*free* memories.

Take that, Henry, she thought. *And this way, if the crime-fighting ever ends, Lou will still have a reason to be my friend.*

Because Piper knew nothing lasted forever. King could close the detective agency or decide to retire for real given his age—and then what? What reason would Lou have to stay in touch with her?

This will be fun, Piper insisted. She wasn't sure who she was trying to convince. *Everyone is going to have a great time, and Lou—*

"Do I just sit back here?" Lou asked, poking her head up between the seats.

Piper pinched the bridge of her nose.

"There's the playlist," Dani offered.

"Good idea." Piper connected her phone to the car's Bluetooth system and turned on the playlist she'd made.

"I added a few NIN songs since you said you liked them. And I've got a lot of Alanis Morissette, some classic rock, Beyoncé, Ludacris, Paramore, and—"

The speakers began to thump.

"What is this?" Lou asked.

"'Imma Be,'" Piper said, adjusting the bass on the stereo. "The Black Eyed Peas."

Lou's facial expression was unreadable.

This will work, Piper told herself. *We'll have fun. We'll make memories. And no one is going to get shot.*

Lou sat in the back of the car, trying to ignore the throbbing ache in her shoulder. She wasn't sure why her body would ache after just sitting. It wasn't getting the workout it would in a firefight or even the taxing movement of pulling a gun.

Dani and Piper sang off-key to "Toxic" by Britney Spears.

Piper looked back at her hopefully, then pretended to extend the invisible microphone she held in her fist out to Lou.

"I'm hungry," Lou said into Piper's fist.

Piper undid her seatbelt and leaned into the backseat. "We've got Doritos, Pringles, gummy bears—"

"Doritos."

"That's my girl." Piper popped open the bag and took a chip for herself. "Mmm, ranch."

But eating the chips only temporarily distracted Lou from the pain in her shoulder and the boring backseat.

As she counted the highway markers and noted the *San Antonio 134 miles* sign, she wondered how she was going to get through this.

"For dinner, I'm thinking about Taco Bell," Piper said.

"Oh god, no," Dani said. "Taco Bell goes right through me. Can we do Burger King? They've got a veggie burger."

"Fine. I like their milkshakes."

"Let's do dinner at seven," Dani said, glancing at the clock on the dashboard. "We can switch then."

"Burger King at seven," Piper confirmed, tearing open the bag of gummy bears. "I'm going to get the Whopper with cheese. And a Dr Pepper."

"Thought you wanted a milkshake?" Dani asked, cracking her window a little more.

"*And* a milkshake. What about you?"

"Probably a Sprite."

Piper nodded as if she'd barely heard this. "How do you guys feel about 'Where Them Girls At'?"

Lou counted the minutes to seven with growing restlessness. When seven passed with no Burger King in sight, she was agitated. 7:20. 7:42. 7:53. 8:23. Her foot bounced in the well behind Dani's seat.

The world darkened and shadows filled the car like rising water. They slithered across her muscles, making her flesh crawl. The gentle pull inside her grew stronger.

She strained against it, willing herself to stay in her seat, the thin beams of moonlight like ropes to salvations.

"We could pick something else?" Dani offered, glancing at the clock. "I don't need a veggie burger. I could go for a—"

Lou felt the shadows around her soften, deepening. *I can't—*

"I'll get it." She exhaled and gave herself over to the darkness. The car, the music, Dani and Piper's soft conversation all bled away.

They were replaced with fresh night air and starlight.

Lou looked up and saw the Burger King sign. It felt good to be on her own two feet. She sucked in a lungful of fresh air. It smelled like garbage, a huge dumpster standing below the lit sign. She didn't care. It was still heavenly.

Inside, she ordered the food, getting three sodas and the milkshake into a carry carton. She gripped the sack of food in her other fist.

She stepped out into the night and wondered if she really needed to go back right away. Maybe she could wander for a bit.

But then they might stop somewhere else for food.

A guy on the sidewalk wearing a Burger King shirt lit a cigarette. "Have a good night."

"You too," Lou said, sidestepping into a shadow between the building and dumpster.

Then she was back in the car.

"Lou!" Piper cried. "Where did you go?"

"I told you." Lou held up the food. "I got dinner."

"No," Piper whined. "We gotta hit the drive-through. We gotta—"

"Thanks, Louie," Dani said. "Can I get that Sprite?"

Lou handed her the soda. "Here's your veggie burger."

"Amazing! And ketchup for the fries! Babe, help me out." Dani was giving Piper a look Lou didn't understand.

Piper rubbed the back of her neck again, accepting the milkshake Lou offered. "Yeah, thanks."

They ate in silence, Piper tearing open little packets with her teeth and squeezing sauce out onto the wax paper.

When the gas light came on, they pulled off the interstate.

"Let's just stop here," Dani said, pointing at the hotel across from the gas station. "We've already done twelve hours today. That's enough. Maybe we'd all do well to get out of the car for the night."

"I didn't even drive," Piper said.

Dani handed her the keys. "You can start tomorrow."

PIPER OPENED THE HOTEL ROOM TO FIND THEIR BAGS PILED AGAINST one wall. On the desk was a note scribbled on the hotel's stationery:

I'll be back in a couple of hours. ;) — L

Dani came up behind her and put her chin on her shoulder. "What do you think the wink face means?"

Piper huffed. "She thinks she's giving us some privacy."

"That's nice of her."

"Is it?" Piper asked, throwing the keys down on the desk beside the note.

"Come on," Dani said with a grin. "This'll be our bed. Lou can have that one."

The look in Dani's eye drew a nervous laugh from her. "Are you implying—?"

"Oh yeah, I'm *implying*." Dani came up onto her toes so that she could kiss Piper's lips.

But Piper broke the kiss first. "I can't. I'm sorry. She could just pop in at any time."

"She's got her compass thingy," Dani said, undoing the button on the top of her shirt. "I think she'll know when it's safe to come back."

Piper liked the look in her eyes. They were dark and hungry. Her hair was cascading over one shoulder as she looked up at her through thick lashes. That look alone was almost enough to undo Piper.

"I can't," Piper said, and this time it was harder to say. "I don't want to be thinking about Lou while I'm..."

She let the insinuation slide.

Dani sat down on the edge of the bed, kicking off one of her boots. She was noticeably colder.

Well, now I've screwed up, Piper thought. *Left and right today.*

"You seemed a little *irritable* today."

Piper looked at the luggage on the floor and then at the note. "Do you think the road trip idea was stupid?"

Dani frowned, shrugging out of her shirt. The sexy look was gone with the clothes as she rummaged in her bag for a night shirt. "No. Why would it be stupid?"

Piper sank into the desk chair and covered her face. "I don't know. I guess I had this big plan in my head that we'd go on this epic adventure and eat snacks, and listen to music and talk, but this whole trip she's just been sitting in the back of the car, *grimacing*."

"Honey, Lou's never been a big talker."

"I know. But I wanted us to bond, you know? I wanted us to have moments like real friends."

Dani unhooked her bra. "What do you mean, *real* friends?"

"Right now we're disaster friends. We hang out when there's a bad guy to hunt or kill or someone to save or if everyone is being held captive by some psycho. What if that's the only reason she talks to me? Out of necessity?"

Dani pulled a Tulane t-shirt over her head and swept her thick hair up into a messy bun. "Listen. You know that Lou is different. A road trip with Lou isn't going to be like a road trip with me. You've got to accept that. Just try to have fun with her the way things are."

The way things are.

But *the way things are* meant accepting that Lou was distant and unpredictable. Unreadable at the best of times. She could disappear at a moment's notice, and what then? Where would that leave Piper?

Disaster friends come and go, Henry had warned.

No. That can't happen, she thought. *I can't let that happen.*

4

———————

The hotel room fell away. Lou relaxed against the shift of the world, feeling points in space realign. She felt it first low in her chest. In the solar plexus, it came as a tug forward, the compass inside her reaching out for its destination. Then her mind dilated, opening like night-blooming jasmine to the darkness consuming her.

But there was only silence, soft shadows, and the smell of water.

When the world reformed around her, she was in a dim bedroom. A man slept beneath a plush green comforter covered in gold fleur-de-lis splattering the fabric. His chest rose and fell softly with his breath as moonlight made the pillows glow. Behind her, the high arched window overlooking the Arno River was open, filling the room with a gentle August breeze. Even though it must be three or four in the morning, Lou could still feel the heat of the day in the air.

She stepped up to the end of the bed and Konstantine stirred.

He rolled onto his back, revealing the pistol gripped loosely in his right hand.

He must've had it hidden under his pillow, she thought. *He pretended to be asleep until he could grab it.*

She pushed her mirrored sunglasses up on her head and smiled. "Bad dreams?"

He left the gun on the bed and sat up on his elbows. His eyes raked her body. "You look good to me."

She arched a brow. "Smooth."

"I thought you were with Piper," he said, careful to inflate the *i* in her name.

"We drove all day." She sounded exhausted even to herself.

Konstantine gave her a knowing smile. "Was it difficult for you? Traveling the way we mere mortals do? I bet when the sun went down it was harder."

"It's a waste of time," she said. "I don't know why she insists on doing it this way."

"It's an American pastime," Konstantine said, lying back against the pillows and putting his hands under his head. Lou noted his bare chest, letting her eyes scrape down his torso, with no attempt to hide her thoughts.

"How's your shoulder?" he asked.

"The same." She wasn't sure why she'd admitted that. It was the truth, but it sounded dangerously close to whining.

Louie Thorne did not whine.

"Do you want to lie down with me?" he asked. "Or do you need to get back?"

She shrugged out of her leather jacket and reached down to unbuckle her boots. She kicked them off onto the floor as she climbed into the bed.

Konstantine moved over, lifting the comforter so she could slip inside.

"I told them I'd be back," she said.

"I'll be sure to keep you awake then," he replied with a devilish grin.

When he moved in, placing the length of his body against hers, warmth radiated through her. Without realizing it, she moved in closer. He placed a kiss on her throat. Then another. On the third, she stiffened, her body going rigid with the pain.

He pulled back, his shadowed face pinched. "Sorry."

Her irritation spiked. "My shoulder should be better by now."

Konstantine arched an eyebrow. "First of all, shoulders are notoriously difficult to heal. Secondly, you were *shot*. The doctor said you would need at least six months. By my count you are six weeks short of that."

"Five," she corrected.

The truth was, it had never taken Lou this long to heal. She'd been shot before, many times. She'd been stabbed, and suffered every other type of injury one could when throwing themselves headlong into battle.

"I've never been so—"

"Bored?" Konstantine offered with a smile. "It's good that things are quiet. You're not as capable as you usually are."

Lou dematerialized, allowing the shadows in the darkened room and those layered by his body over hers to provide the gap she needed to bleed through the world.

She reappeared behind him on her side, her good shoulder bracing her, and put her finger to the back of his head. "Bang."

He rolled over and enveloped her outstretched hand with his. "Yes, you're still fast. And you're still strong. But there is nothing wrong with rest, *amore mio*."

The truth was, Lou had never been one for rest. When Aunt Lucy was alive, she made frequent comments about Lou's restlessness, the way she would pace like a lioness in her cage at even the slightest agitation. At times it felt like a current ran through her, a live wire. And if she didn't do something with all of that energy, that desire, it would tear her apart.

"You could rupture your shoulder," Konstantine said. "Then you wouldn't lose months, you'd lose *years*."

All this talk about her shoulder wasn't sexy. It rubbed against her mind like steel wool.

He must've seen the look on her face.

"I don't mean to lecture you. You know your limits."

Her aunt had often accused her of going too far, pushing too hard and not knowing when to quit. That was great when it came to hunting murderers and mafia kingpins. Less so when it came to the care and maintenance of her own body.

She met his eyes. "I haven't gone *looking* for trouble."

"No," he said, and placed a kiss on the tip of her nose. "But trouble will find you sooner or later."

She grinned. "You're one to talk. I seem to remember pulling you out of a burning villa after Nico carved up half your face."

"*You* set the villa on fire."

Lou didn't remember that part.

"Besides," he said. His voice dropped an octave and a hungry look overcame his features. It was the wolfish way he was watching her lips, relinquishing them only to trace the line of her throat and collarbone. "The sooner you're healed, the sooner we can..."

He bit his lower lip.

"We tried that," she reminded him.

Two months after her brush with death, after the bullet tore a hole in the side of her neck, she'd tried to fuck him. When he'd put his hands on her hips and pulled her forward, the sharp pain shattering that side of her body had rocked her. It was a pain unlike any she'd known before, and few on this planet were more acquainted with pain than she was.

Yet she'd been unable to move for several minutes, while he'd poured apologies into her ears. Of course, that hadn't stopped her from trying twice more.

Now Lou moved to adjust herself on the bed and find a position that didn't allow her shoulder to roll forward, pulling at the weakened tendons there. She settled for lying on her back, her gaze skyward. This left Konstantine on his side, gazing down into her face.

"I must admit..." he began. The hunger was still there in his eyes, but Lou saw the attempt to rein it in. "I'm more than a little jealous that they get to travel with you."

"I took you to New Orleans," she said.

He tilted his head, the ghost of a smile on his lips. "That wasn't a vacation. We went to kill Dmitri."

"There was New York."

He tilted his head. "On our way to kill Nico."

She supposed none of their *travels* could be classified as vacations when one accounted for all the shootouts, hunting, and murder.

"After we get back from San Diego, I'm going to La Loon," she said. "I've been away for too long. I want to check on Jabbers."

"Take me with you," he said, and seeming to hear his earnestness, he looked away.

"Jabbers might eat you," Lou said. "I've never brought..."

She searched for the word. What was Konstantine to her? *Boyfriend? Lover?*

"Anyone," she decided on. "The men I bring are for her to eat. It stands to reason she'd see you and think you're food."

"I'll take my chances," he said with a grin.

Lou arched both brows. "That's because you haven't seen her."

She stopped short of adding, *She's going to scare the shit out of you.*

He considered this for a moment. Then his smile softened. "I trust you."

Her heart clenched as if kicked.

"A trip will take your mind off your shoulder. We can do a proper exploration. I can collect soil and plant samples. We can discover the mystery of La Loon together."

He was searching her face, looking for her answer.

She could admit, if only to herself, that La Loon was a mystery that taunted her. She wanted to know why—of everywhere in the world she could go—she went to La Loon.

It wasn't like she hadn't tried to use her power in other ways. But when she submerged herself in water, it was always La Loon that served as the first stop.

La Loon, with its nightmare landscape of blood-red waters, two moons, and dense black forests. Why should she always slip to that unfathomable place? That said nothing of the monster that guarded the domain.

A beast who Lou was half convinced would tear Konstantine open on the spot.

"I'll take you," she said with a wicked smile. "Don't say I didn't warn you."

5

Screaming ripped through the dark room. Lou came up out of a dead sleep, her gun in her hand.

"No, no," Piper said, holding out a hand toward Lou. "It's okay. She's dreaming."

Piper reached across Dani's writhing form and clicked on the hotel lamp.

"Dani, hey, Dani, wake up. Baby. *Wake up.*"

Dani stopped struggling against her imaginary attacker and grew still in the tangle of sheets. Her heavy breathing continued until slowly, her eyes opened, squinting against the light.

Lou's shoulder burned. She lowered the gun, aware now that she'd pulled it with her left hand, her bad side. Now nerve pain shot up the side of her neck every time a vertebra shifted.

"Was I screaming?" Dani asked, touching her face. When her hands came away wet, she looked at her fingers as if she'd never seen them before.

"No big deal. You okay?" Piper asked, running a hand through her hair.

"I'm so sorry," Dani said, pulling herself up. She pressed her back against the headboard and clutched the covers to her chest. "I'm so sorry I woke you up."

"We don't care about that," Piper said, pushing the hair back from Dani's forehead. Several strands were stuck to the side of her face, plastered there by sweat despite the humming air conditioner.

Dani glanced at the gun in Lou's hand. "I scared you."

Piper made a face over her shoulder. Lou chose to interpret the wide eyes and nod to mean, *Say something nice.*

"I always sleep with a gun," Lou said.

Piper motioned for more.

"In my hand. Like this," Lou added.

Piper rolled her eyes.

"Excuse me." Dani climbed out of the bed. She slipped into her flip flops and crossed to the bathroom. She flicked on the light before closing the door and shutting herself inside.

For a moment the two of them remained where they were, unmoving. Piper stared down at Dani's pillow as if just discovering it empty.

"Does that happen a lot?" Lou asked, putting the gun on the nightstand and trying to roll her shoulder back.

Piper ran a hand down her face. "Yeah. Petrov really messed her up."

Lou imagined that was true. She'd seen the condition Petrov had left the girl's body in after he was done torturing her for information about Lou—information Dani didn't have.

In the hospital, small and broken, Dani hadn't seemed like a formidable investigative reporter capable of destroying Lou's anonymity. She'd seemed like a young woman who'd walked through hell and back, but there had still been steel in her eyes. That more than anything had convinced Lou not to silence her.

"It's worse when she stays over at my place," Piper said, scratching the back of her head. Lou could see the pillow lines cutting across her exposed cheek. "I think she wakes up and doesn't know where she is. But when we sleep at her place, it happens too. She says it happens less when we're together though."

Explains why you sleep together most nights, she thought. She wasn't about to mention how many times she'd appeared in Piper's room in the dead of night just to check on her and in doing so had found Dani asleep in her bed.

Piper continued, the circles dark under her eyes. "I guess I should've realized staying in a hotel might trigger it. New place. New smells, or whatever."

Lou rotated her aching shoulder again. "Some wounds take longer than others to heal."

Unfortunately.

They heard the shower crank on in the bathroom, but it didn't mask the soft crying.

"She'd probably prefer it if we just turned off the lights. I think she's embarrassed," Piper said, and leaned across the bed to flick the switch.

Lou sat in the darkness for two heartbeats. Then she rose from the bed and crossed to the bathroom door and pushed it open.

"Lou—" Piper began.

But Lou had already shut the door behind her. Her compass wasn't always for travel after all. Sometimes it told her where she needed to be, even when she had no need to slip at all.

The bathroom was already half full of steam. The mirror was fogged over and a thin mist was forming on the sink and toilet.

The curtain waved slightly from the force of the stream.

"It's me," Lou said, one hand on the curtain.

"I'm okay," Dani said, her voice thick.

Lou pulled back the curtain anyway.

Dani was sitting in the tub, fully clothed, her back taking the full force of the stream. The water was scalding her skin, turning it red.

Lou crouched down on the floor beside her, the edge of the tub between them.

Spray ricocheted off of Dani's body, splattering Lou's arm and face. She didn't care.

"I saw him ripped apart," Lou said softly. "Petrov is dead."

Dani lifted her face from her knees, her face red with tears. "I know."

"Very dead. Entrails on the ground, head torn off. He isn't coming back for you."

Dani nodded, pushing the wet hair back from her face. "I know. But in my head, I feel like I'm going to wake up and it'll be someone else hurting me. Like there's someone waiting in the wings. Him or someone like him, they're going to come back."

Dani glanced at Lou's arm and frowned.

"You must think I'm pathetic. You've got a million scars. And look at you. You don't fall apart every time you have a bad dream."

Not anymore.

That hadn't always been true. What could Lou tell her about her own nightmares? Of Angelo's face emerging from darkness as he pulled his gun and blew out her father's brains?

Of her father screaming out her name?

How many times had she had that dream, or a variation of it? A hundred? A million?

Yes, Lou knew plenty about bad dreams and the way they hung in the atmosphere long after the dreamer managed to wake. How they burrowed under the skin and crawled along the bones, making it impossible to rest.

Lou followed the girl's gaze down her own scarred arms. Every nick, every cut, every raised scar or puckered bullet hole. She'd been hurt, sure. But she'd never been held down and tortured. She'd never had a finger severed from her hand.

"You're not weak," Lou said, running a hand down her arm, clearing it of droplets.

"Then maybe I'm stupid. Anyone smart would walk away from a job that'll get them killed. Investigative journalists are murdered all the time. Or they're imprisoned, and here I am acting like I can take it, but maybe I can't." Dani sighed. "This is all I've ever wanted to do with my life. Tell the stories that everyone else is afraid to tell."

"Then do it."

"Even if it's stupid? Even if it's reckless and I'm not proving anything to anyone—not even myself?"

"Yes," Lou said, unflinching.

Dani wiped the water from her face again.

"I don't think I could walk away even if I wanted to. Even if it *is* the smart thing to do." Her lips trembled. "God, if it happens again—"

"If it happens," Lou interrupted, "I'll be there."

6

———————

Robert King stepped out from beneath the green café umbrella. Without hesitation, the unforgiving sun beat down on his head and neck. He groaned. The black coffee in his grip immediately felt too hot for consumption.

Iced coffee, the girl behind the counter had recommended, but to King, iced coffee was an abomination. Why would he want to water down his drink when he liked it strong enough to burn an ulcer through the side of his gut?

But standing in the sun with the heat pressing against his mind like a wad of cotton, he was beginning to see the appeal.

King began the slow march back to his office, cutting across Jackson Square, clotted with its pop-up artists and living statues. A girl with a violin played a sad melody beneath the awning of a yarn shop. It hadn't always been a yarn shop, but King was struggling to remember what it was in its previous life.

A souvenir shop? Did they sell t-shirts? It didn't matter to him or the hundreds of bodies cluttered in the square. A young man sat on the curb with a trumpet thrown over his lap. He dabbed at his black brow with a navy handkerchief.

It seemed everyone sought shade where they could find it.

The smell of coffee wafting from his cup was met with something fried and spicy.

He hadn't even fully crossed the square before he felt the sweat pool at his hairline and trickle down the back of his neck. He loved winter in New Orleans, which was much milder than the fierce midwestern climate of St. Louis. But New Orleans in summer was almost too much to bear.

King marched on, noting all of this distantly, counting the steps until he'd be back in his air-conditioned office.

Stepping from the square onto Royal Street, his heart lurched. Even at this distance, he saw the woman waiting on the stoop of the Crescent City Detective Agency. Sweat rolled from his temples. He could feel the dampness under his arms and soaking through the collar of his shirt.

He didn't want to talk to a client right now. He wanted a cold shower.

He wanted to sit in his chair and cool off, sip his coffee, and review the day's objectives. Or maybe he wanted to go by his apartment and change his shirt.

But she'd already spotted him, standing and brushing the dirt from her bottom.

"Mr. King?" the woman called, stepping forward. "Robert King?"

She was blond, blue-eyed, and very pretty. She would've been a welcome sight if not for one problem. King knew immediately who she was.

He forced a smile and extended his hand, inwardly disgusted by its dampness.

"That's me," he said. *Best to play it dumb until I know what she wants.* "Do I know you, ma'am?"

"No, no." A sweet, nervous laugh escaped her. "I'm Abby Smith. I was hoping you could help me find my sister."

Interesting angle, he thought, keeping his smile carefully in place. "Come on in and let's have a chat."

King slid his key into the agency's lock and used his hip to pop open the sticky door. It swelled on warm days like this one and a little extra leverage was necessary to separate it from its jamb.

He entered the office first, looking it over the way one does when an unexpected guest arrives.

Was everything put away? Anything incriminating or too revealing sitting out where it shouldn't be?

The red waiting chairs were empty and dusted. The magazines sat in a careful stack. Piper's desk was clear on its surface, chair unoccupied. He was suddenly very glad that the girls were away for a couple of days. It was good timing. It would give him a chance to figure out what the hell was going on here.

"Can I offer you something to drink?" he asked mildly. "I've got water, tea, coffee, juice..."

"No, no, thank you."

Her eyes were roaming the space as fiercely as his were.

His own desk was not so tidy. Stacks of file folders, a half-eaten sandwich, and his laptop crowded its top. King wasn't worried about the mess, but he was trying to remember which case he'd left open before stepping out.

Sikes, he thought. The burglary case that the local PD had off-loaded to him because they had no leads and no money for another full-time detective.

Was King worried about himself? Maybe he should be, with this viper in his den. But King had a few secrets, too.

He glanced to the back of the office. There were three closed doors. One was a bathroom, one led to Piper's apartment upstairs, and the third—*Shit*.

His first real problem.

King read the name plate mounted there. *Ms. Thorne.*

The labeled storage closet was empty. Nothing in there but toilet paper, paper towels, boxes of unused manila folders, and cleaning supplies. King had also put a few cardboard boxes with tax records in there, on the metal shelves that covered both walls.

He seriously doubted the woman behind him gave a damn about any of that.

But the name plate. Oh, the *name plate* might be worth her time.

Piper had put the damn thing up as a joke because Lou was always using the dark closet as her personal entrance. Lou didn't need a real office. She was an unofficial partner in this agency, sure. Her extraordinary skills helped King more often than not. But Lou came and went as she pleased.

Now would be a terrible time to pop in, he thought. *Don't.*

Lou's possible appearance was only one problem. There was a second, more immediate one.

Was it possible that Diana Dennard, the woman who'd introduced herself as Abby Smith, already knew Lou's name?

If so, that name plate was a dead giveaway.

And her name *was* Diana. Not Abby. King knew that much.

"Thank you so much for seeing me," the woman said, taking the chair opposite King's desk. She'd chosen the cluttered one even before King rounded the corner and sat down in his chair. He was careful to keep his eyes on her face.

Don't look at the door, he thought. *Don't look at the name plate and she won't.*

Because he couldn't exactly go over and take it down now. That would be too obvious.

"You're welcome," King said, fishing a paper napkin out of the drawer and using it to pat the back of his neck and his temples. Once soaked, he threw it into the trash bin under his desk. "So tell me about your sister."

"She went missing back in January. We're from the East Coast."

"Oh yeah? Whereabouts?" he asked, knowing full well they were playing a game. Even in games, sometimes people gave surprisingly accurate information. King had learned this after thousands of interrogations as a DEA agent.

"Philadelphia. She was only a semester from graduating from Temple and then she takes off with this guy, can you believe it?"

"It happens," King said companionably.

"We looked everywhere for her."

"Did you file a missing persons report?"

"Well, no," Diana said, and here her smile faltered.

Oh, she's good, King thought. Her acting skills were superb. She'd been able to, on command, affect the blush of embarrassment.

"We don't want her to get into trouble with the police or anything.

We just want to find her and bring her home. She's always been a little rough, if you know what I mean."

"I see," King said. "If you're from Philadelphia, how did you end up all the way down here?"

How did you find her? King wondered. *What scrap of information led you to us?*

Because there were a lot of cities in the world and Lou could travel to most of them before lunch. What had set Diana on a trail to New Orleans? To King specifically? They'd been more than careful. And not just King and Lou. Konstantine kept a close eye, scanning all channels for so much as a mention of Lou.

"My sister loves this city, so I thought I'd check it out," Diana said. "I've been here for about a month, asking around. A guy I spoke to yesterday tells me that he saw a robbery at the Julia Street station in March. I didn't think anything about it because you know how New Orleans can be. But then the guy described my sister *perfectly*. And he said she was *shot*. Shot! If that's true, I have to find her. I *have* to. Even if it means she's dead."

Her voice broke on *dead*, the lip quaking. And here were the tears. Right on time.

King lifted his mug and took a drink. He slid the tissues across his desk automatically.

Diana took one and dabbed at those big blue eyes. "I've been told you're the best private investigator in the city. You *have* to help me find her. Money is no problem. My parents are well off and they want to find her as badly as I do. We'll pay anything."

King knew she was lying. Maybe she had money, sure. But there were no parents back east. And there was the fact that she'd yet to say her sister's name.

He also knew the secret informant was a lie, because King had been there the night Lou was shot at Julia Street station. He was the one who'd compressed the fabric to Lou's bleeding throat and begged her to go to the hospital. He was the one who'd hidden her guns and vest, and washed the blood off his sleeves in the park's fountain before the paramedics rolled up to the scene.

There had been no one there, not a soul except himself, Melandra, Lou, and Mel's ex-husband, Terry, the deadbeat now in jail.

It's gotta be the blood, he thought. *Someone must've collected it from the scene, run DNA analysis. But what had Diana had to compare it to?* DNA had to be compared to something.

He knew Konstantine ran ruthless checks on the internet for photos, data, and anything pertaining to Lou. He guarded her anonymity more fiercely than Lou herself did.

But it was painfully clear to King that they'd missed something.

Or Diana's smarter than the average bear.

"Do you have a photograph of your sister?" King asked.

"No," Diana said, sniffing. "Unfortunately, my parents suffered a bad house fire last year. A total loss."

"Sorry to hear it. That's terrible. Facebook? Instagram?" he pressed.

"No, we don't have anything like that."

Convenient. Secretly, King was relieved. Diana might've tracked her to New Orleans, but she hadn't done it through video footage or wayward photos. In that way, Lou was still a ghost.

"But I had a sketch artist draw this." Diana reached into her leather satchel and offered a piece of paper across the mess of his desk. "I described her to him and he rendered her perfectly."

King took the drawing and surveyed it.

Yes, he did, King saw. It was a good match. The artist had captured Lou's features well enough that King saw Jack in them. Jack, Lou's father, and King's former mentee—until his sudden and tragic death.

What interested King about the drawing wasn't only the shoulder-length dark hair or the leather jacket. It was the fact that Lou wasn't wearing her sunglasses. Day or night, Lou often wore her mirrored shades.

Diana must've looked her in the eyes, King thought. *When?*

"What's her name?" King asked.

He saw the woman stiffen in his periphery.

"Louise. She goes by Lou. But she might be using an alias."

So she did have a name. Sort of. Louie must've introduced herself as Lou, if she'd introduced herself at all. And she must not have mentioned Thorne. Otherwise, it would have been Abby Thorne, not Smith, wouldn't it?

Again he had to physically stop himself from glancing at the name plate on the closet door.

"Will you help me?" Diana sniffed again. "You have to help me."

"I'm very sorry, Ms. Smith. I'm packed to the brim with cases at the moment." He made a vague gesture to the stacks piled between them.

Anger flashed across the woman's face. It was such a contrast to the blubbering, concerned woman she'd been the moment before, King thought, *Your mask is slipping, Diana.*

Then Diana's face crumpled so quickly King couldn't be sure he'd seen the anger at all. "But you *have* to help me. Please. I need to know where she is."

A personality disorder, he thought. The emotional shifts were too severe and swift. Of course, he was no psychologist.

"Ms. Smith, the first thing I would do is file a missing persons report with the NOPD. I have a buddy there, Dick White. I can put you in contact with him. They can put out a bulletin, look around, and do a far better job than I can do with my present workload. Would you like that?"

"No," Diana said, standing up suddenly, forcing the chair back. "No, I wanted *your* help. The police are useless."

Or is it really you don't want any police involved at all?

"I'm very sorry. I simply can't take on another case right now. I'd be more than happy to put you in touch with the right people who can help you."

"No," Diana said, stiffening. She reached across the desk and snatched the drawing from King. "No, I don't need your help. Thanks for nothing."

And with this, she made a big show of stomping from the agency into the ruthless August sun.

As soon as the door slammed behind her, King's first impulse was to call Lou. To tell her that she needed to be careful, that for whatever reason, Diana Dennard was looking for her. But as soon as this thought came, he shoved it aside, afraid that its very existence might call Lou to him.

He didn't want Lou to come. He wanted her to stay with Piper, heading west, far away from here. Putting her on a collision course with this psychopath—and there was no doubt in his mind that Diana Dennard was a psychopath—couldn't possibly end well.

No, King thought. *It won't end well at all.*

7

Diana pulled a chair up to her desk and opened her laptop. *Lou Thorne, Lou Thorne, Lou Thorne.*

The name had repeated like a mantra in her mind ever since she saw the name plate on the door.

Lou what? she'd asked that night in the diner.

And Lou, with all her damned smugness, had grinned. *Just Lou.*

It seemed a long shot that the PI and Lou had a connection. Yet, she'd seen the detective's face when she'd said, "Her name is Lou."

Then came the refusal to help her. Maybe Lou was Lou Thorne, or maybe not. But the guy knew something about Julia Street station and the woman.

My story was good, she thought. *How did he see through it?*

She bounced her foot impatiently as the computer booted up. She typed the name into the search engine.

She didn't expect to find anything. If Lou was deep undercover, as Diana thought she was, then it seemed unlikely a simple internet search would return much. But she had to start somewhere.

And at first she seemed right. There were no social media accounts. No online photos or work history. No "graduated from such-and-such school."

"Damn," she grumbled at the screen. The room had grown dark around her as search after search turned up nothing.

"Try agencies," the woman leaning against the wall said. She was cleaning her fingernails with a six-inch blade. "These ghosts almost always have law enforcement work histories before they go deep. Otherwise, where do they get the skills from?"

Diana didn't question her sister's logic. Instead, she searched for *Thorne* and every agency pairing she could think of. Thorne because she couldn't be sure what form of Lou was the correct one. Louisa? Louise? Louann? Lora? There were a hundred variations and King's reaction to *Louise* made her think she'd been on the wrong track.

Smug bastard, she thought, her fingers striking the keys.

Thorne and *CIA*

Thorne and *FBI*

Thorne and *police department*

Thorne and *Department of Defense*

NASA. Marines. Air Force. Army. Navy. Coast Guard.

Thorne and *DEA*

An article popped up. *One-year anniversary since decorated DEA agent and wife slaughtered in home.*

Something in her gut kicked. She selected the link and began to read all about Jack Thorne and his wife, Courtney. About what transpired one night over fifteen years ago, in an affluent suburb outside St. Louis. How Thorne and his wife were shot to death by the mafia after Jack arrested and charged the son of a Capo Crimini.

At the bottom of the article, after all the details of the brutal murder had been laid out for public consumption, was a photo of the surviving daughter.

A little girl with brown eyes and brown hair. Sullen. Quiet. Familiar.

Louie Thorne, it read.

Diana wondered if the picture had been taken after her parents' murders. She thought so. There was already something dark and haunted in those eyes.

Diana sat back in her chair, staring at the screen.

"Did you find something?" her sister asked.

"Maybe." Diana pulled up the search box one more time and typed in *Louie Thorne.*

Nothing.

She tried again. *Robert King. Jack Thorne. DEA.*

And there was King's face smiling back at her, his arm over Jack's shoulder.

"An old family friend then," she said. "Looking out for your buddy's kid after he's killed. Guess I walked right into that."

Blair came around the chair and leaned over Diana's shoulder. "Is that what she looks like?" She pointed at the dark, sullen child.

"This picture is at least fifteen years old."

Blair frowned. "Why do you have that look on your face?"

Diana chewed her lip, unsure why the anxiety in her limbs had spiked suddenly. "She's like me. I mean, I already knew she was like me, but I didn't realize how much like me."

Blair gave a crooked grin. "So she's a heartless, obsessive bitch too?"

"Her childhood was destroyed. She coped by fighting back, and she's been fighting ever since."

Blair settled into another chair. "Can I ask you something?"

Diana met her gaze. "What?"

"What do you hope to gain by tracking down this woman?"

"I want what she has."

"And what do you think that is, *exactly?*"

"Money, resources. The things I need to take down Winter."

"And let me ask you this. If you were her and someone showed up and was like, 'Give me your stuff,' what would you say?"

"I'd tell them to go fuck themselves."

"Exactly. Because you work for yourself. You do what you want. Why in the world are we wasting time tracking her down? She's not going to help you. If she's as much like you as you think she is, this will never work. In fact, I'll bet a hundred bucks she won't help you."

"She had no reason to help Jennifer McGrath, but she did," Diana mused. She thought of the night the pervert Jeffrey Fish came to kill the girl. While Diana watched through the window, Fish broke into the girl's house and chased her up to the bedroom with the intention of murdering her.

Once Fish began to rough the girl up, Diana had wondered if she should intervene. It didn't matter to her whether or not the girl ended up dead. Diana had been content to let him wear himself out, and once spent, she'd step in and have her fun. She'd only wanted to make sure Fish didn't see another sunrise.

But before she could decide, Lou had simply appeared.

One minute all Diana could see was Jennifer's wide, kitten eyes and heaving chest. The next, Lou had Fish by the hair, pulling him out of the spotlight of an overturned lamp on the bed.

Lou was good at hiding, at moving unseen.

Diana could use that against Winter.

"If she isn't in it for herself, then she does it for other people," Diana said. "And she isn't hunting mafia bosses, she's hunting serial killers. This isn't about her anymore."

"You don't know she hasn't killed mafia bosses. She could've murdered a hundred of them and then got bored. The point is, you don't know enough about her. Period. You have no reason to believe she'll help you. Why are we doing this, Di?"

Diana had seen Lou in action. She'd seen how coldly the woman had torn Fish from the room. She'd seen the woman's hunger—and her restraint. If anyone could give her what she needed to trap Winter, it was Lou.

"She'll help," Diana insisted, looking at the photo of the kid on the computer screen, the one who'd lost everything but had rebuilt herself into something better, stronger. "We just have to make an offer she can't resist."

8

———————

King spotted Mel at a table before the hostess could pull a menu for him.

"There she is." He pointed at the woman with an Octavia Butler book open in front of her. "Thanks."

He angled his wide body through the gumbo shop's tight configuration of tables, making his apologies as he passed, trying not to bump corners or shake overfilled water glasses. Soft jazz seeped through unseen speakers and the whole place reeked of andouille sausage. Spicy and delicious.

His mouth watered.

Mel looked up from her book and smiled. Her hair was natural, teased out to its full height and pushed back from her face by a soft silk scarf.

"Good evening, Mr. King," she said. The gold bangles on her wrist jingled as she slid a menu across the table toward him. "You're late."

"My apologies." He stooped and planted a kiss on her cheek, French style. "How are you?"

"Fine," she said, unfolding the napkin across her lap. Then she reached up and fussed with the many overlapping necklaces at her throat, gently untangling the strands with her dark fingers.

"And Lady?" he asked, fondly warming at the thought of the Belgian Malinois.

"At home, napping. Do you want to take her with you tonight?"

"No, she's fine with you." This was a lie. King missed the dog when she was across the hall from his apartment, sleeping with Mel. But he knew that the dog brought Mel great comfort and security. And with Dennard lurking around, it made him feel better to know the Belgian Malinois was close by. It was good protection and that dog would die for her.

"Why are you late?" Mel lifted her water glass and took a sip. "I was about to order without you."

"I had to take the long way around." He lowered himself into the chair. He didn't pick up the menu. He knew what he wanted. "I was being followed."

He'd spotted the tail halfway down Royal Street. It moved like a shadow in his periphery. When he'd bent to tie his shoe, he used the dark, reflective surface of his cell phone to search the street behind him. A man with a hobbled gait sharply turned, pretending to look in a storefront window as he rose.

King had cut across Jackson Square, walked through a souvenir shop and out the back, across the alley and into the adjacent street, squeezing past a young man taking out two large bags of trash. It helped that King's own hip wasn't talking to him tonight as it sometimes did. Watching his tail hobble as he did reminded him to be grateful for these rare pain-free days.

Mel straightened in her seat. "Who was following you?"

"A short man, uneven gait, and glasses. And something is wrong with his hair."

Mel snorted, a laugh half escaping her. "What do you mean, something is wrong with his hair?"

King touched his right temple. "I can't tell if he's got a bald spot here or if it's burned short. But something was wrong with it."

"What can I get y'all tonight?" the server asked. It was a woman in a white apron and black tie.

"Chicken andouille for me," King said. The smell of the sausage in the air was making him ravenous. "With a side of cornbread."

"Cup or bowl?"

"Bowl."

"Butter and honey?"

"Yes, please." King would love some sweet, buttery cornbread this very minute.

"And you, ma'am?" she asked.

"Seafood gumbo for me. I'd like the cornbread too, please. And hot sauce."

"Yes, ma'am. Waters, all right?"

"Yes, thanks," King began, then added, "Actually, can I have a Coke?"

When the waitress left, Mel leaned toward him across the table. "Back on subject, please. You've got a guy following you. Do you know why?"

"Either he's with Diana Dennard or he's a different problem."

"Diana Dennard," she said, frowning and placing one hand on the cover of her book. "Where've I heard that name before?"

"Lou crossed paths with her back in March, when they were both hunting Fish."

Last King heard, the serial killer was still behind bars, having admitted to over thirty kills to date. King didn't think that would be the end of it. He was sure Fish would confess to more soon enough.

Every time Lou's restlessness got the best of her and she went out into the night to dig up a new grave, it prompted new confessions from Fish.

"Right," Mel said, shaking her head knowingly. "The other vigilante."

King didn't like that word, *vigilante*. It conjured images of masked avengers blowing up government buildings. Lou—whatever she was— didn't fit that description.

To him, she was an arbiter of retribution. A queen of death. Karma. Payback.

"Dennard came into my office today pretending to be Lou's sister. She was asking about what happened at Julia Street station."

At this Mel visibly stiffened. King understood why. Mel had been the one to pull the trigger that night, and the bullet that was intended to scare her bully of an ex-husband had torn through Lou's neck.

Mel fingered the necklaces at her throat. "You don't think—"

"There's nothing to find," King assured her. "Konstantine and I thoroughly cleaned that scene. But maybe some blood was collected for processing. It could've been collected and processed as part of Terry's case."

Mel grimaced at the sound of her ex's name.

"Maybe they're reviewing all evidence for his trial," King added.

This wasn't anything Melandra didn't know herself. "I'm sure the prosecution is gearing up."

King noted the candle flame flickering on the table, seeing the light dance in her kohl-rimmed eyes.

"You seem okay with that," King said, accepting the Coke put on the table by the passing waitress.

"Terry rotting in prison?" Mel harrumphed. "Hell yeah, I'm okay with that."

Her smile came easy then. Wide and bright. King thought that her smile came a lot easier these days, now that Terry was out of her life.

"And cornbread," the waitress said, placing a large plate on the table beside a small dish of butter and a honey pot. King eyed the mound of soft white cream.

"Thanks," he managed, but the waitress was already gone.

"They're busy tonight," he remarked.

She looked out over the restaurant, eyes falling on a young couple with a baby standing up in its highchair. The mother was scolding it softly.

"It's amazing," Melandra said.

King didn't think she was talking about people having babies, so he kept his mouth shut.

"Absolutely *amazing* how we torture ourselves. All those years of guilt and shame, me believing something that never even happened. And for what? I've lost so much time, Robert."

King reached across the table and covered her hand with his. He gave it a firm squeeze. "You've still got a lot of time left."

And she did. Twenty or thirty years at least. She was healthy and not even old enough to retire, though he couldn't imagine her ever doing so.

"I do," she said with a bright smile, turning back to him at last. "And I'm not going to let anyone else take that away from me. Never again."

"That's the spirit," he said, unable to resist the cornbread any longer. He used his fork to smear butter along the top, which melted instantly. Then he drizzled honey onto it before shoving it into his mouth.

His stomach turned appreciatively.

"Do you think this Dennard woman is dangerous?" Mel asked, moving a piece of cut cornbread to her plate, balancing it on her knife. "To us?"

"I don't know. Her operation is underground. I don't think she would benefit from outing Lou, not with the risk that she herself would be outed. Konstantine said that she was running credit card scams to fund her operation. She stands to face real jail time if she moves out into the open. Whereas Lou would only lose movability. There are no bodies or proof of her crimes, so if she were brought into the public eye, it would just mean that she'd have to work harder to disguise herself going forward."

"No more snatching people from the streets."

"Not without proper precautions," King agreed. "But the question is, what does Dennard *really* want with her?"

Melandra's frown deepened. "You don't think she wants to eliminate the competition, do you?"

King tried to imagine Diana hunting and killing Louie. Louie was the most dangerous and capable person he'd ever met. But she wasn't without her limitations.

"I hope not," he said. "I *really* hope not."

"They're still in the shop," Spencer said into the small communications device clutched in his grip. "I can't believe he slipped me like that."

"You weren't careful," Diana said, whispering into the earpiece tucked into the conch of her ear.

She stood on the stoop outside the Crescent City Detective Agency and pretended to smoke. She hated the taste of tobacco on her tongue and fought down the urge to spit. The passersby talked and laughed with one another, stumbling down the shadowed streets on their way to another bar. Diana hated them too. And this city. It was dirty. Noisy. Crowded. Too many piss-scented drunks wandering around.

And any place with too many people was the worst.

Spencer continued whining in her ear. "Excuse *me*. I warned you that my walk is too pronounced. You should've sent Blair. Oh, their food has finally arrived."

She threw down the cigarette. "I'm going in. Message me when they ask for the check."

Diana inserted two steel pins into the lock on the front of the building. It took a minute to find the correct placement, but once she did, she heard the tumbler move and the door popped free of its hinge.

The office was empty. Moonlight poured through the high window and painted the floor and furniture. Shadows pooled at the back of the shop.

Both desks were clear of all debris. She wondered if King took all his materials home with him each night. He must.

She closed the door behind her and locked it.

In King's chair, she ran a hand over the tabletop, but there was nothing. She wiggled the drawer, but it was locked. She tried to use her pins to open it, but this lock was much smaller. She switched pins.

Once the drawer was open, Diana realized she'd wasted too much time. There was only a notepad, business cards, and gum in the drawer. A few pens were scattered as well. There were names on the cards, and scraps of paper, but none of them meant anything to Diana.

None of them read *Lou*.

She closed the drawer. Her eyes fell on the name plate. *Ms. Thorne.*

Diana crossed to the door, expecting to find it locked. But it opened easily. Diana's heart rose in her throat as she pushed the door wider. She wasn't sure what she expected to find in this room. Another desk. Lou herself, typing away, burning the midnight oil?

And what would she say if she came face to face with the woman now?

But there was nothing. At least, not an office.

There was a row of metal shelves against one wall. Against the other, shelves full of the most banal items. Toilet paper, a box of legal pads.

Diana ran her hand along the shelves, but found no secrets.

Her fingers traced the walls, the dips in the concrete bricks. But nothing.

Is this some sort of secret panel? she wondered.

She pushed against the wall, wondering if there was a way to get it to open. Or maybe there was a secret lair.

Maybe there was a whole *world* under her feet. Questioningly, she tapped the floor with the toe of her boot.

But no matter how she picked at the corners or shoved against the bricks, nothing gave.

Irritated, she pulled the door closed behind her.

The room to her left was a bathroom. The room straight ahead was locked.

Diana was able to use her steel pins to unlock it and found a flight of steps on the other side. They ascended into the dark.

Diana threw one nervous look over her shoulder at the dim office. People passed the large picture windows, but the office itself remained dark.

"They still eating?" she asked into her comm.

"Yeah, the guy just ordered another helping of cornbread. This guy can eat."

Diana mounted the stairs and pulled the door closed behind her. Inside, she found an apartment. A clean, shadowed kitchenette, a living room with sofa, coffee table, and TV. A window that shone with moonlight. The sheer white curtain seemed to glow in the moonlight.

Down a short hall was a bedroom and bath. The bed was made, though not tidily.

Diana searched the side tables. She went through the closet and searched the pockets of clothes. She pulled the luggage down from the top shelves and opened a box that turned out to hold a lot of photographs.

None were of Lou. Most featured a blond girl that Diana didn't recognize.

Is this your apartment? Diana wondered, eyeing the blonde in the pictures with her arms thrown companionably over her friends' shoulders.

At first she thought Lou might live here. But now it seemed that wasn't the case. Or at least, there was nothing in the apartment that suggested Lou's presence. No leather jackets or mirrored shades. No credit cards or paperwork bearing her name.

"They asked for the check," Spencer said in her ear. "Might want to get moving."

"Are you giving me orders now?" Diana said, low.

"N-no, no," Spencer said, too quickly.

"I didn't think so."

If this wasn't Lou's residence, it didn't mean she didn't have a connection to this girl. She simply didn't have the whole story yet.

Putting the bags back the way she found them, Diana crossed to the living room.

She scrawled *Piper Genereux* on a scrap of paper, copying it from the internet bill on the counter, and slid it into her back pocket.

She decided on the upper-right corner of the room as a place to put the minicamera. The microphone bug was taped under the lip of the window, beside the sofa.

She decided to tape another under the counter in the kitchen. And a third in the bedroom, inside the lamp.

"They're getting up. They're leaving," Spencer said. His voice was rising, strident with his fear.

Diana groaned inwardly. Spencer didn't have the stomach for espionage. If he weren't a master with technology and as obedient as a dog, she'd have done away with him ages ago.

"Don't get your panties in a twist."

She could already see Spencer in her mind, in his full leathers, his mouth zippered shut to smother his soft mewling.

Her body warmed.

What a lovely way to spend an evening, she thought, content to have something to look forward to.

Casting one last look at the apartment and making sure it was as she found it, she descended to the office. She stooped under King's desk and pulled another bug from her pocket, fixing it to the underside, deeper than anyone would think to look or reach.

She took the note from her pocket and affixed the top with a strip of tape from King's dispenser.

On the outside of the door, she reminded herself as she stuck the note to the door. *No need for King to know I've been snooping.*

Then she stepped out into the crowded, hot night and pulled the door shut behind her.

9

Lou sat in the back of the car and stared out at the desert. It was beautiful, she had to admit. She loved the dry heat. The tall red rocks growing straight up into the sky. The vast, empty landscape was punctuated only with a passing cactus from time to time, and comically, a tumbleweed. She'd thought they were fake, a made-up comic effect for cartoons. In the distance, a coyote trotted toward the horizon. Its ears lay flat when it caught the sound of the approaching car.

The only flaw was the light. There was too much of it. Lou was a creature of darkness in most ways, and here in the desert, shadows were few and far between.

Piper's phone rang. She dug between the console and seat to find it.

"It's King." She answered it. "*Yo.* I've only been gone for a day, man."

Piper's humor fell away. "What?"

Lou sat up between the seats, regarding her face.

"Yeah, hold on." Piper handed the phone out to Lou.

"Is everything okay?" Dani asked.

"I don't know," Piper said, watching Lou's face carefully.

But Lou knew her expression was unreadable. Her mirrored sunglasses would only reflect Piper's concerns and fear back at her.

"What happened?" Lou asked by way of greeting.

"Diana Dennard walked into my office this morning, pretending to be looking for a missing sister. Can you guess who the missing sister is?"

"Did she see the name plate?" Lou asked.

King hesitated.

"King?"

"I'll tell you, but don't come here now. Don't pop up. She might be watching."

The back of Lou's neck itched. "Okay."

"I think she saw it, yeah, and put it together that we know each other. She must have."

"Why?"

"She left a note for you." He sucked in a breath as if bracing for a blow.

A chord vibrated through Lou's body like a tuning fork.

"How did she know your name was Lou?"

"Because I told her."

"Last name?"

"No last name," Lou confirmed.

"I was worried about that. There was a moment when she turned away, right before she stormed out—I think the name plate might've caught her eye then."

Lou said nothing, sensing that King was warming up to tell her the worst of it.

"She's got something else on you."

Of course she does, thought Lou. *She hunts like I do.* Dennard wouldn't have picked New Orleans out of a hat.

"What led her to New Orleans was the blood collected from Julia Street station, but I don't know how she made a DNA match."

Lou threw her mind back. She thought of the last time she'd seen Diana. They were in an all-night diner in Ohio, not far from the scene of Fish's arrest. Lou had drunk a cup of coffee, refusing to give more than her first name. She thought she'd left a tip, though she had a vague memory of pulling the bills from her jacket and throwing them on the table before leaving.

"Can DNA be pulled from money?" Lou asked. Her back was growing hot against the dark seats. Lou realized Piper had cut the A/C so she could hear the conversation better. "Or a coffee cup?"

"Both," King said. "If the prints were clean, which only happens about thirty percent of the time. I tried to pull prints from the tape she used, but both the note and tape were clean. She must've worn gloves or wiped them."

Lou's irritation spiked. She hadn't expected the woman to pocket her coffee mug after she left. She hadn't even considered the idea that the woman might have access to that sort of technology. And not only the ability to collect and profile DNA but the ability to sweep a police department's private data centers to confirm a match.

Dennard was no amateur.

Don't make the same mistake twice, her father's voice sounded in her head. *You underestimated her once and look how close she's gotten.*

"What can she do with my name and DNA?" Lou asked.

"*What?*" Piper said from the passenger seat. "Who has your name and DNA?"

Lou shook her head, asking Piper to wait.

"I don't know. It depends on what she wants. At first, I thought she'd found out I was at Julia Street station with you. I gave a statement that night, so it was possible she came to me thinking I'd seen something. But she never mentioned that. It's possible she might've come to me by coincidence, hoping to get a decent PI to track you down."

King was being humble. He was more than decent as a PI, but Lou wasn't the type to fluff someone's ego.

He sighed into the phone. "The question is, why does she want you? Did she give any clues when you talked?"

Lou tried to remember the night she sat down with Diana Dennard. The conversation had been interesting. Lou remembered feeling mostly intrigued, that after all her years of hunting and killing, she'd finally encountered someone like herself. Another woman who added counterbalance to the injustices of the world.

"She asked a lot of questions about who I worked for, and what my resources were. What did the note say?"

King hesitated. With a smile, Lou knew he was considering lying. She heard paper rustle and wondered if he was digging the note out of the trash.

"King?"

"She wants to meet. In two days at the po'boy shop on Basin. Across from the cemetery."

Lou said nothing.

"Are you going to go?"

She smiled. "Should I?"

She'd already made up her mind.

King seemed to consider this. "I can't tell you what to do. But keep your eyes open, all right? Be careful about popping in and out of New Orleans."

"All right," Louie said, and terminated the call. She handed the phone back to Piper.

"What's happened?" Dani asked from the driver's seat. She was applying her lip balm a bit too frantically.

And seeing the way she clutched the wheel with her free hand, Lou began to understand why Dani kept insisting on driving even though she could've easily passed the task over to Piper.

She feels more in control behind the wheel. Safer.

"You better start talking," Piper said, wagging her phone at Lou. "What the hell is going on?"

"Diana Dennard is in New Orleans. She came to the agency looking for me and she knows I work with King."

"Dennard," Piper repeated disbelievingly. "The crazy lady we caught stalking Fish? The killer who hunts killers but doesn't give a shit about the women he kills? *That* Dennard?"

"Yes," Lou said plainly.

"And this psychopath knows that you work with King? She figured it out from DNA because you had coffee with her?"

"And because I was shot."

Piper tapped her phone against her chin. "Oh, this is *bad*."

"She wants to meet." Lou tried to consider the situation clearly.

Piper looked at her as if she'd just sprouted a second head. "What? *No.*"

To be fair, this wasn't a one-way street.

When Lou learned there was another woman tracking Fish, she'd investigated her, too. She'd learned Diana's name and history. And then what? Nothing. She'd simply wanted to know who Diana was and what she was after. That was where her curiosity had ended.

Was it possible that Diana was only curious about Lou, too?

Piper's mouth hung open. "You can't be serious about meeting her. She's crazy!"

Lou said nothing.

"Unbelievable." Piper pressed her fingertips into her forehead. "I should've never put up that name plate. It was stupid. Totally stupid."

"You're not stupid," Dani countered, her brow scrunched. But she was grabbing her lip balm from the cupholder again and uncapping it. "Stop saying that."

"I don't like it," Piper said. "I don't like her sniffing around. What the hell does she want?"

"I'm sure we'll find out," Dani said, wringing the wheel again. "I don't think she came all the way to New Orleans for nothing."

10

Piper glanced into the back seat and found Lou...*dead*. Not really. She was sure the woman still had a pulse, but Piper had never seen anyone so miserable-looking in her life.

God, this road trip really was a bad idea, she thought, not for the first time since they'd left New Orleans and traveled west along I-10.

"We're almost there," Piper said from the front seat. "You want some chips?"

Lou, who remained reclined on her back, one arm over her eyes, shook her head. "I'm fine."

"Are you?" Piper asked. "Because you look like you've been murdered."

Lou lifted her arm and met Piper's gaze. "Have you ever seen someone being murdered?"

God, leave it to murder to perk this girl up, she thought. Aloud, "No. And I hope I never have to."

She didn't need to ask Lou the same question.

"Look! There it is!" cried Dani. She was pointing over the dashboard at the blue horizon peeking between buildings.

Five minutes later, they parked the Lexus in an empty space opposite the beach.

Dani popped the trunk and pulled out the three chairs and a stack of large towels, and nodded toward the umbrella. "P, will you get that?"

Lou grabbed the cooler, which they'd stopped at a gas station to fill that morning with ice, water, soda, and beer.

Salt hung thick in the air, seeming to settle on the skin like silt. Waves crashed, adding a blanket of white noise to the scene. Gulls cried out as they swooped low overhead.

Then they were set up and watching the water, as if they'd been there all along.

Piper took a deep breath of ocean air. "Oh yeah, baby. Smell that."

Lou didn't appear to be inhaling. She caught Piper staring at her. "What?"

"*Breathe.*"

"I'm *breathing.*"

Dani squeezed her left hand gently. Piper could either interpret this as *Chill, babe* or *It's okay.*

Piper rubbed her forehead. "Hand me a beer, please."

Lou obliged, opening the cooler and shifting the ice around.

"I don't think you're supposed to drink alcohol on the beach," Dani said.

Piper half-buried the can in the sand. "What beer?"

They spent the morning like that. And when Lou stood up around noon and wandered away, to Piper's credit, she didn't call after her and insist that she sit down and enjoy this beautiful day. She didn't even complain to Dani about it.

She simply sat with the itchy feeling in her heart that this had all gone wrong. It wasn't how she'd wanted it to be. And she felt *not okay* about it.

She doesn't like hanging out with me. This isn't fun for her. I'm stupid and boring and...

Lou returned, with three hot dogs and a pocketful of condiment packets. She tossed them onto a clean towel spread on the warm sand.

"Oh, thanks," Piper said, her narrative cut short.

"They also have soft serve," Lou said, pointing at the food stand halfway down the beach. "Twist."

"I love twist cones."

"I know you do," Lou said with a quizzical brow. "That's why I'm telling you."

This cracked what was left of Piper's reserve. "Lou, I'm sorry."

Lou was stuffing half a hot dog in her mouth. "For what?"

"For this whole stupid road trip idea. I thought you'd have fun, but I can tell you're bored out of your mind. You're in the sun all day, which I don't think you love."

"I don't."

"Right? You're a vampire. And it took forever, when you can just pop to a beach with half a thought."

"I can."

"I *know*." Piper tore open a mustard packet with her teeth and squeezed it onto the dog. "But I wanted you to have the experience. And I wanted us to spend time together. But it was stupid. I'm sorry I insisted we do this."

Lou looked out over the water, placing her elbow on her raised knee. "When I go places, I'm just there. I don't see the in-between. In a car, you see everything. All the parts that connect one place to another. That was nice."

"You liked that?"

"Yeah. I did."

The tight coil in Piper's chest relaxed. They stayed on the beach until the sun reached the horizon. The sky melted red, orange, pink. Piper ate a twist ice cream cone and finished her beer.

"We can drive back without you," Piper said, packing up the beach towels and putting the empty cans in a bag to be recycled. "You don't have to do another two days of this."

"No," Lou said flatly. "I'll ride with you."

"Why? It's a monumental waste of time."

"It's a good habit," Lou countered. "To finish what you start."

Lou offered to carry the chairs and bags up from the car to the apartment. Without waiting for their permission, she put her hands on what she could and shifted from the dark of the car parked in the alley to the apartment above.

Pain sparked in Lou's shoulder as she made a second trip. It wasn't the blinding pain that she felt two months ago whenever she would raise her arm or take too deep of a breath.

Piper's apartment formed around her and she deposited the first round of stuff onto the floor at her feet.

It took Lou four trips to bring all the stuff from the white-gold Lexus into Piper's apartment. Once she was done, her shoulder throbbed so badly she felt unsteady on her feet.

On the last trip, the door opened at the same time and Dani and Piper stepped inside.

"Whoa," Piper said, wrenching her key from the lock. "Sit down. You okay?"

"My shoulder."

"We shouldn't have let you carry all that stuff," Dani said, reaching into the cabinet for a glass. She filled it with water and put it in front of Lou. "Where's your aspirin?"

"Bedside table," Piper said, putting the water in Lou's hand. The good hand, not connected to her overworked shoulder. "But she's right. I wasn't even thinking about your shoulder. I'm sorry, man. I was just thinking I didn't want to carry the chairs up those steps."

"I'm fine," Lou said. She hated being fussed over. It was like a spider crawling up the back of her neck.

Dani appeared, shaking three ibuprofen into her hand. Lou rolled her eyes up and met Dani's. "I'm going to need at least 800 mg."

Dani shook out another pill before handing it over.

Lou took it with the water, finishing the glass in a single go.

Her eyes kept sweeping the apartment. What was this feeling? Like a gnawing in her gut.

"Did you do something different to your apartment?" she asked, assessing the sofa, the kitchen counters, and the gently humming fridge.

Piper followed her gaze. "No. Why?"

The pain in her shoulder made it difficult to think. It pressed against the inside of Lou's skull, obliterating thought. Every breath made the left side of her body throb.

I couldn't fight someone now even if I wanted to, she thought miserably. *Not without trashing half my body.*

She practically heard Konstantine tsking her in her mind. *You should be resting,* amore mio.

Still she searched the dark, expecting to see someone. "No reason."

11

———

Diana stepped into the hot stream of the hotel shower. It had been a long day. Both of the scouts she'd sent out to canvass for Winter had come back with nothing. She was too worried to send any more. If he suspected that she was close, he might move his entire operation, and it would take her months, maybe years, to track him down again.

She couldn't bear the thought of losing the bastard a third time.

At her desk, comb in her hair, she turned on her computer. A furious swipe of the keys brought her to a black login screen. A backdoor login to the dark net.

Diana put in her password for a fake profile she'd created. *Dwayne6669.*

She repeated this until she'd joined all the available feeds.

Box after box appeared, each containing a live video stream. Three, four, five...

Winter had eight feeds running tonight. Each with a different child featured.

It was the one in the bottom right that caught Diana's eye. The girl was seven, maybe eight, with bright eyes. The leather dog collar around her throat was connected to a chain on the floor.

A man, black t-shirt, no pants, stood over her. His erection in full view.

A rough knock came at the door. "It's Blair."

Diana opened the door and found her on the other side.

"Did you see the feed?" Blair asked.

"I'm watching it now."

Blair came into the room, crossing to the desk. "No, not this one. The one from the apartment."

"What—" Diana began, but then remembered the bugs she'd planted.

I need some sleep, she thought. *I'm borderline useless.*

Blair's fingers hovered over the keys. Her face was scrunched up in disgust. "Can I close this? Pedophiles sick me out."

"Yeah."

A few furious punches and a new screen showed the angled interior of the apartment. Diana had researched the place after she'd left it. There was no listed tenant for that address. The detective agency, apartment included, was listed in King's name. But mail she'd seen for Piper Genereux had told her a bit. Piper was a student at Delgado Community College and her official place of employment was Madame Melandra's Fortunes and Fixes, an occult shop around the corner.

Diana had yet to figure out if King had the girl holed up above his office like a live-in girlfriend—a girl fifty years younger than him, a nice lunchtime fuck before getting back to the task of investigation—or if he'd rented her the apartment because she worked for his landlady.

She wasn't yet sure how all these people connected to one another. It seemed clear that Louie Thorne was the daughter of King's long-dead comrade, but what about the others? How did they fit together? What did they do?

And were these lives just covers for a larger operation?

Or was Louie's life, her secret life, a mystery even to these so-called friends?

Diana wanted answers.

"Why are you splitting the screen?" she asked, watching Blair's fingers fly over the keyboard.

"It's the live feed on the right, and the recorded feed on the left."

On the right all Diana could see was two girls sitting on a sofa. One had a mug of something in her hand. She looked Latina, maybe, with thick brown hair and coppery skin. The other was blond, a blanket draped around her shoulders. At their feet was a pile of luggage and... beach chairs? Had they had a beach day today?

Diana wasn't even aware there was a beach in New Orleans. Then again, she hadn't been in the city long.

"Look at the left. I want to show you something. Here." The laptop's fan clicked on. Its soft whirring filled Diana's room.

The feed on the left had been rewinding, and now it showed an empty apartment with bare floors and no girls on the sofa.

"What am I—" Diana began.

"Shh, just wait."

This amused Diana, who enjoyed when Blair's intensity showed. It was good to know she wasn't the only one invested in this operation. To Diana, it often felt that way.

"There!" Blair froze the frame, then let it roll forward at half-speed.

Diana saw it. One minute the apartment was empty, the floor bare. The next, Lou stepped into the frame, arms full, and deposited armfuls of crap onto the floor.

"Is there a door there?" Blair didn't take her eyes off the screen. She pointed at the dark corner of the room where Louie had entered.

Diana stared into the deep pocket of shadow. It took her a moment to review the layout of the apartment, but no... *no*, she hadn't seen a door there.

"Keep watching," Blair said.

Diana did. After dumping three bags on the floor and rotating her left shoulder, Lou disappeared through the pocket of shadow again.

Only to reappear, this time with the beach chairs.

"You're *sure* there wasn't a door there?" Blair asked, her voice high with excitement.

Diana hadn't inspected that corner of the apartment thoroughly. Could there have been a false wall? It had seemed like an *outer* wall, and a story off the ground. Could something have possibly been behind it?

"I didn't look close enough," she admitted. She sat forward. "I want to hear the audio."

Blair furiously punched a few buttons.

"I wasn't even thinking about your shoulder. I'm sorry, man. I was just thinking I didn't want to carry the chairs up those steps." It was the blonde talking.

"I'm fine," Lou said.

The blonde looked up from the pile on the floor and frowned harder. The other was tapping pills into Lou's hands.

Lou threw them back with the ease of a junkie. Hell, maybe she was. Diana didn't know nearly enough about her to rule out a history of addiction.

Lou bent and picked up one of the bags from the mix, a small duffel, as the other two prattled on about nothing.

Diana took everything in about Lou. She looked the same as she had months ago in the all-night diner in the middle of nowhere, Ohio. But she was holding her shoulder differently.

It was Lou's voice that broke the spell. "I'll be gone for a while."

Diana leaned even closer to the screen, until she began to see the pixels of the image in front of her.

"No," she murmured. "Don't go."

The blonde seemed equally unhappy to hear the news. "What do you mean?"

"I'm going to La Loon."

"Alone?"

"With Konstantine."

The blonde pouted. "For how long?"

"I don't know. A few days. But if you try to reach me—"

The dark-haired one laughed. "I highly doubt a page or text would go *that* far."

The blonde sighed, visibly unhappy. "Be safe, I guess. I'll tell King."

Then Lou was gone, again through that strange patch of darkness in the far corner, half cut off by the edge of the screen.

I've got to go back, Diana thought. *I have to look at that wall again—if it is a wall.*

"Show me the feed from now," she said.

A few more furious punches and real-time video feed came into full screen, along with the accompanying audio.

"Babe, you've been going on about this for hours."

"I know." The blonde dragged a hand down her face. "I just worry about her. She's supposed to be resting her shoulder and taking it easy, and she's doing a *great* job."

Sarcasm dripped from the girl's words.

The other one laughed. "You're one to talk. When's the last time you had a day off?"

"Touché."

"And besides, at least she's trying. She did sit in the back of a car *both ways*."

"True," the blonde said.

"And now she's going to La Loon, which is sort of like a holiday for her."

The blonde asked, "Do you need to get home?"

"I thought I'd sleep over."

"Oh." The blonde sat up straighter. "What about Tavi?"

Is Tavi her kid? Diana wondered, always looking for connections and pressure points.

"She's with my parents."

"Do you think we've found Lou's home base or what?" Blair asked.

"There might be a problem with the tech, maybe the camera has a blind spot or something. Otherwise, there's a false wall there that I missed."

"Or maybe she can walk through walls. A literal ghost."

Lou had seemed real enough when she sat across from Diana, drinking coffee.

Her eyes flicked back to the screen.

"Is it okay?" the dark-haired girl asked tentatively, visibly fidgeting with the mug in her hand. "If you're tired, I can just—"

"No," the other girl said eagerly. "No, I want you to stay."

Then she was shrugging out of the blanket and coming across the sofa to kiss her.

"Ooh la la," Blair said. "What do we have here?"

Diana barely noticed the make-out session developing on the

screen. Her mind kept wandering back to Lou, stepping from the shadows into the apartment.

There has to be a door, she concluded. *That building must have a secret passage or something.*

Did Lou have a secret apartment there? Beneath the agency? Or behind a wall? Or perhaps she made her home somewhere else in the city?

Despite the shadows, it had been Lou, unmistakably. Lou in the leather jacket and her mirrored shades. Lou with a duffel in her right grip.

But who the hell was Konstantine? He must be somewhat important if Lou would take off with him for a few days.

"Did you put a camera in the bedroom?" Blair asked hopefully as the girls rose from the sofa.

"Not a video feed, just audio."

Blair pouted. "Shame."

And La Loon...She'd never heard of it. Was it code for a hideout? An island in the Pacific or something? Diana had the impression that wherever it was, it was remote. Isolated.

Blair turned away from the video and regarded Diana's profile. "About tomorrow..."

Here we go, Diana thought, groaning inwardly.

"Are you still going?"

"Yes," Diana said, keeping her eyes on the feed without seeing it.

"Do you think she'll come?"

Did she? She had until Lou'd mentioned this so-called *La Loon*. Maybe Lou couldn't spare the time now. "Maybe. Unless she has to go to La Loon right away."

"And then?"

"Then I'll talk to her."

"And then?"

"Then hopefully she'll give me what I need to take down Winter."

"And *then*?" her sister pressed.

"And then *what*?" Diana snapped back. "Spit it out."

"When will it be enough? If you find Winter, kill him, then *what*? Is it going to be enough for you? Can we quit then?"

"Not this again, Blair. It's late."

"So what if it's late?" Blair sat back in her groaning chair. "You never sleep. You hardly eat. And I'm worried this won't be enough for you. *Ever.* You'll get Winter and then *what*? I want you to tell me what your life—*our* life—will look like after you kill him."

Diana looked at the screen without really seeing it.

"What's going to fix this for you? Can you really let all this go after Winter is dead? Or will it be like this forever? You running yourself into the ground and me watching you do it?"

"I don't know," Diana said, and knew with certainty this was a lie.

12

Lou stood at the window of her St. Louis apartment and tried to understand the queasiness in her gut. It wasn't unlike the feeling she had when someone stood behind her. It was accompanied by an itch in the spine and the impulse to turn.

And Lou kept turning, but there was nothing there. The apartment was bright with morning light. It was quiet, undisturbed. A crow passing her window called out then was silent.

There was no one lurking behind her, ready to swing.

Why do I feel like I'm being watched?

She shrugged in her shoulder holster, noting the two guns press into her ribs. The coffee maker beeped, signaling that her brew was ready. She drank it black, enjoying the sweet smell and bitter taste on her tongue.

She was unhappy. She recognized this distantly, with some cold, detached part of her mind that regarded feelings as strange, inconsistent phenomena.

This comprehending part of her mind also understood it was because she was not hunting. She was not doing what it was in her nature to do, and that made her unwell. Melancholic.

Why aren't you hunting? she asked herself. *Why aren't you out there killing some kingpin or wife beater or—*

She knew the answer. It wasn't the flaring pain in her shoulder which came and went like a tide. It was the terrifying suspicion that everyone was right.

King. Piper. Konstantine.

Everyone who kept trying to remind her about her shoulder, her so-called limitations—that chorus of nagging voices plagued her. But she'd yet to think of a better way to scratch that itch under her collar.

She could still ambush, sure. She could appear behind anyone and simply grab them and put a bullet in the back of their head. She could do it with ease.

But that wasn't *hunting*. It would hold no release for her. No challenge.

Lou took another drink of her coffee before setting the mug on the island counter. Then she pulled a stopwatch from a drawer and laid it beside the mug. She turned the stopwatch over and activated the voice command setting.

She took a deep breath. "Go!"

The stopwatch started its timer at the sound of her voice, and as quickly as she could, she pulled the left gun, the one governed by her good, right shoulder.

0.05 seconds.

She tried again, but this time pulled from her weaker side.

0.2 seconds.

She grimaced. Too slow. And worse, just that one pull had her shoulder throbbing.

She pulled again.

0.4 seconds.

Because pain slows you down, she thought.

Realistically, she suspected she could get only one or two pulls on that side before her arm was useless. Leaving the gun in her hand also posed a challenge. The weight pulled on her shoulder, irritating it.

She wanted to try again from the hip. She took a break, giving her throbbing shoulder a chance to relax.

She refilled her coffee and thumbed through a paperback she'd found at a thrift store that day. In it, the hero hunts the man who betrayed him. When she finished the coffee, she began again. She put on a hip holster, fitting guns into their designated slots.

She pulled from her good side first. *0.03 seconds.*

She restarted the stopwatch and pulled from the left. *0.13 seconds.*

That was better. Maybe because the shoulder wasn't quite as hitched from its starting position.

But what are you trying to prove? To whom?

Lou stepped from her linen closet into the stone casing of a crypt. Startled birds shot from their nests at her sudden appearance. The stone floor scraped against her boots, the walls thick with cobwebs and dust.

A little warm for a nest, she thought, stepping over the broken stone slab that might have once been the door and into the open air. A breeze caught in her hair as her boots adjusted to the uneven ground.

The cemetery spread out in all directions. Coping graves and ledger stones lay interspersed with the vaults and a few crypts. Through the wrought-iron gate, Lou saw the po'boy shop King had spoken of.

She crossed the street carefully, waiting for a white sedan with a donut tire to pass before she approached.

The bell dinged.

Four of the five patrons looked up.

One was Dennard. Her blond hair was pulled back in a severe ponytail, her blue eyes bright with unhinged excitement. Her leg began to bounce under the table as she clutched a basket of fries between her hands.

Behind her a mother pushed battered shrimp into a toddler's mouth as he stood precariously on the seat beside her.

Across the aisle, Lou made eye contact with a man in his forties. What was left of his wispy hair had been smoothed back from his face. His mouth was ajar, as if he'd just heard terrible news. Lou thought he should be wearing a lab coat—something about him seemed...scientific.

The fifth patron had already turned her back to Lou as if uninterested in the new arrival.

A man in a stained apron appeared behind the counter.

"Mornin'," he said with a jovial smile. "What can I do you for?"

Lou walked down the center aisle to the counter. She passed Diana without acknowledging her.

"The fish and shrimp," Lou said after a cursory glance at the menu.

He pulled a pen from behind his ear. "Fully dressed?"

She wasn't sure what that meant, but she was far from a picky eater. "Sure."

"Fries? Pickles?"

"Yes, thank you."

"Anything to drink?"

"No."

He tore the sheet of paper off the notepad and pounded the register keys. "It's cash only here. That okay?"

Lou didn't bother to explain that cash was the only thing she carried. She'd never had so much as a credit card in her name. She simply handed over the bills and thanked the man.

"I'll bring it out to ya," he said, and flashed her a smile. "Sit where you like."

Lou barely noticed the smile. She was watching the parody play out behind her, courtesy of the large mirror stretched behind the register.

The woman in the leather pants sitting alone at a table was making frantic eyes at Diana. Diana waved her off. The man too was watching the exchange, glancing from Lou to Diana and back.

They're all together then.

She suspected the woman with the child and the cook behind the register weren't part of the stakeout, but she wasn't prepared to write either of them off. Should this come to a shootout, or some other altercation, it was better to assume everyone was an enemy.

Dennard had chosen this place. For all Lou knew, she owned it.

Lou pulled out the chair opposite Diana. The screech was terrible and made the woman flinch in revulsion.

She seemed even more shocked that Lou had chosen to sit so close.

The small table between them was an insufficient barrier. It was so small, their knees touched beneath its top.

Dennard pushed her chair back as if this would spare her.

Lou said nothing. She left her shades on. It was easier to keep her eyes on the room when she wasn't expected to look directly into someone's eyes.

The silence stretched between them, Diana's partners growing uneasy. When the child suddenly broke into a wail, pushing back at an offered piece of shrimp, both of Dennard's companions jumped in their seats.

Diana and Lou remained unmoved.

Diana ended the silence first. "I didn't realize how alike we were. *Louie Thorne.*"

Lou waited for her to elaborate. After all, who knew what conclusions she'd drawn about Lou in the five months since they'd last seen each other.

"Did you kill them all?" Diana asked. When Lou didn't answer, Diana pressed on. "The Martinelli family was blamed for your parents' execution. I've got few connections in the criminal world, but the ones I have all say the Martinellis are dead. Even the one your dad put in prison disappeared." Here Diana smiled. "Or did he?"

Lou said nothing.

Diana was undeterred by this. Somewhere in the back a pan flared to life with the hiss of oil against heat. "Then there was your dad's partner. Gus Johnson."

Lou's right hand twitched imperceptibly beneath the table.

"Marked missing, but suspected foul play. There was blood on his recliner and carpet. But no body. His front door was locked from the inside. But you would've been only seventeen or eighteen when this happened."

Lou had still been seventeen when she'd gone to Johnson's house with her father's blade in her pocket. Johnson had been her first kill, payback for giving the Martinellis her father's address in order to save his own skin.

"Did you know King has a missing partner too? Ex-partner? He wouldn't have had anything to do with all of this, would he?"

Chaz Brasso? Sure. Lou had finished him too.

The cook with the greasy apron appeared. His hands were wrapped in surgeon's gloves as he put the basket on the table in front of Lou. He smelled like grease and fried meat.

"There's hot sauce and ketchup on the table. Napkins there. You need somethin' else?"

"No, thank you."

He frowned at Diana's untouched fries. "You don't like yours?"

"I'm letting them cool," she said with a forced smile.

The guy nodded, but he didn't look convinced. "You girls let me know if you need anything else."

Lou started in on the food, intending to leave nothing behind. Lucky for her, the sandwich was delicious, a perfect marriage of sweet smoked meat and vinegar.

Diana continued talking. "If Gus was your first kill, and he's the earliest one I could find, then I'm way ahead of you."

Lou let her talk.

"You've been doing this for eight or nine years, I figure. I've been at it for over twenty-five."

As if this is a competition, Lou thought, taking another big bite.

"I must have a hundred and fifty to my credit," Diana went on, finally putting a fry in her mouth. She left out the word *bodies*, but Lou understood. "Not that I count."

Of course you don't.

"What about you?" Diana asked.

Lou had stopped counting in the high two hundreds, and that was years ago. She was sure she was well over three hundred now, possibly four. Mostly because she'd specialized—no, *thrived*—in large firefight shootouts for a while. Ten minutes of action could put as many as thirty bodies on the ground.

"Well, you got the ones that hurt you," Diana said, as if to cheer her up. Here her eyes took on a wolfish glean. "That's what matters, right? Those are always the ones that matter most."

Here it comes. The pitch.

Diana laughed to herself as if she'd made a joke only she could understand. She put her hands on the table, on either side of her oily food basket.

"It's just *crazy* to me how alike we are. We both saw some horrible shit, lived through some horrible shit, but decided to fight back—good for us. We were both a bit famous for a minute, both disappeared..."

So Diana knew about the first slip. The one that carried Lou from the family bathtub to a pool hundreds of miles away, not without a tangential stop in La Loon.

The manhunt for the missing daughter of a DEA agent hadn't lasted long, but it had hit the local news nonetheless.

"And here we are!" Diana held up her hands as if she marveled at her own assessment.

"Here we are," Lou said flatly.

It was the mania in Diana's eyes she didn't like. She'd seen that look before. In Angelo's eyes before Lou had made him drive his car into the Baltimore bay. In the Russian mob boss Dmitri's eyes when they were finally face to face and he wanted her to atone for the sin of murdering his son.

"The only problem is I *haven't* killed everyone who's hurt me." Diana leaned forward. "I have tried myself, *many* times, to corner this bastard, but he's a snake. But with someone like you, with your resources, I think it'll be possible. *Together*, I think we can take this bastard down."

Lou understood now.

The compulsion to avenge. It was why she hadn't been able to stop after Gus Johnson, or Angelo Martinelli. It was why Lou had torn her way through every man who'd been a part of the wreckage of her childhood, including Chaz Brasso and Senator Ryanson. Even Konstantine had found himself at the end of her gun.

Lucky for him, things turned out differently.

And yet, she also understood something that Diana did not. That once this man was gone—whoever this final target was—she wouldn't be free of the hunger consuming her now.

Worse, something darker, more desperate, would replace it.

Lou had learned this lesson all too well.

"He's the last one," Diana insisted, clutching the basket in front of her. The plastic warped in her hands.

That's what you think, Lou thought. "You weren't hunting him when I met you in Ohio."

Because she'd been hunting Lou's target—Jeffrey Fish. fteen years younger.

"Correction," Diana said. "I'd just finished hunting him. But he got away. He has a habit of packing up and running whenever he smells trouble."

"No," Lou said.

Diana started as if slapped. "No?"

Lou had no problem saying it again for the sake of clarity. "I can't help you."

Diana's cheeks darkened, the red spreading out toward her ears and neck. "Do you think I can't pull my own weight? You don't know the bastard. He's slippery."

What could Lou say? That it wasn't Lou she needed? That Diana could manage the job just fine without her and that wasn't the problem? The problem, Diana would discover, was what happened *after*. When there were no more targets. When there was no way to scratch the itch in a way that truly satisfied. When every makeshift target that followed would seem like the ghost of a meal for a long time to come.

That's when the madness came. A death unlike any she'd known before.

Lou had no interest in shepherding her toward it.

Instead, she stood, pushing back the chair. She took her empty basket to the counter and put it by the register. She slipped a twenty into the tip jar, not foolish enough to leave it on the table for a second time. The cook gave her a solemn nod, which she returned.

"Maybe now is a bad time," Diana said. Her voice was pitched for amiability, but the derision was clear. "When you get back from La Loon, we'll talk then. But think about what I said. Think about it."

There was the hint of a threat to those words.

Lou hesitated at the door, but she didn't look back. She simply pressed forward, stepping out into the bright day.

13

Konstantine stood in his living room, watching the shadows grow long on the cobbled floor. He considered the two bags at his feet. One had a couple outfits, a washcloth, soap, a pop-up tent, and a tightly rolled sleeping bag. The other held slim packets of freeze-dried and dehydrated food, enough to feed them both for four days. There was also his gun, ammo, two lighters, and a firestarter brick as well as the compact sample kit with its little tubes and tools for collection: latex gloves and tweezers.

He wondered if he should bring more than a gallon of water.

Did he want to carry it?

He wouldn't let Lou shoulder any of the burden. He was determined that she rest her injury for the full six months at least, though the doctor who'd put her back together mentioned it wouldn't be unheard of for her to need a year or longer to heal.

And even then, on bad days, the muscles and nerves might bother her all her life.

He wasn't foolish enough to remind her of this possibility, given how much resistance she'd posed to the minimum six months.

He lifted the bags and found they were manageable, one for each shoulder. He hoped the one gallon of water would suffice.

The pressure between his ears popped.

Lou stepped into the room. Her glasses were pushed up onto her head. She frowned at the luggage.

"What's all this?"

"Specimen collection kit and our supplies."

"For what?"

"For La Loon." And now fearing she'd forgotten, he added, "For our trip."

"We enter through a lake," she said.

He smiled. "These bags are waterproof."

"Yes, but you will have to swim to the surface once we get there."

"That's what this is for," he said, and turned one of the packs on its side so she could see the flotation device fixed underneath. "When I activate it, it will rise to the surface."

She arched a brow. "If you get eaten, I'm not bringing any of this back."

He smiled, stepping toward her. She smelled like food, something salty. He kissed the side of her throat.

He moved to her lips.

"I thought you wanted to go," she said, her breath warm against his mouth.

"I do. But I also missed you."

Lou wrapped an arm around his waist. "You have to stop kissing me if you want to go."

"Do I?" he asked. "Have you tried kissing and..." He didn't know the word for what she did.

"Slipping," she offered.

"Kissing and slipping before?" His stomach knotted as he realized he might not like the answer. He didn't want to think about her kissing someone else.

Lou pressed her body against his until he could feel the notch of her hip bone against the top of his thigh. He adjusted the weight of the packs until they felt steady.

She took his mouth with hers.

Then darkness, a shift where all the air left him.

It was as if a belt had tightened across his chest. Or perhaps she was sucking all the air, all the life from him.

When she pulled back they stood at the edge of a lake.

She was grinning. "*Breathe.*"

This startled a laugh out of him. He hadn't realized he'd been holding it. "So this is it?"

"La Loon? No. This is the first stop."

She stooped at the edge of the water and scooped up a small leather backpack that he hadn't seen before.

She saw him looking at it. "I brought it earlier."

Konstantine wasn't sure what he'd expected her dumping ground to look like, but this was quite mild compared to his imagination. For him, it had been built to mythical portions. He'd imagined something like Lake Avernus, an entry into the underworld. The gates of hell.

But this lake was much smaller, placid with a thin mist hanging above the water. Frogs croaked out a hoarse melody. Something with wings buzzed past his right ear.

From where he stood he could see a herd of deer drinking on the other side of the water. Small rings formed where their snouts touched the surface.

A doe lifted her head and regarded him with cautious eyes. The others twitched their ears too, but they didn't seem all that surprised to see Lou.

The water was dark, but held the purple sheen of an approaching dawn. And it was much cooler here than in Italy.

"We're in Nova Scotia," she told him, as if reading his mind. "I have another lake in Alaska."

"Is it this beautiful?"

A rustling in the trees above drew his gaze skyward in time to see an osprey open his wings and glide. Its cry echoed as it soared over the lake, heading in the direction of the brightening forest.

Something moved through the trees off to the right, making a small chirping sound unlike any that Konstantine had ever heard.

"Racoons," she said, smiling.

"Racoons," he repeated, committing the word to memory. He had no image to accompany the word.

"Have you ever been out of the city?" she asked, obviously amused.

"Once," he said. The night he and his mother were dragged from their beds by his father's rivals. The night his mother was executed.

The sky began to shift from purple to pink. She lifted the backpack and strapped it to her shoulder. He caught her wince.

"Let me," he said, extending his hand.

"I can do it."

"It doesn't look heavy. Let me take it."

"I don't need you to carry things for me," she said, her irritation spiking.

Konstantine laughed. "I am well aware. But there is nothing wrong with letting someone help you. You've helped me plenty of times."

When Nico had nearly killed him, putting enough metal into his body to end his life, it had been Lou who had picked his ravaged and bullet-ridden body off the stone floor.

Again in New Orleans, when Konstantine had used his considerable wealth and power to outmaneuver Dmitri Petrov, it had not been for the purpose of saving Lou. In his mind, Dmitri stood no chance against her. He understood that Lou was more than capable of protecting her own life and overcoming such a man.

That aid had been in service of her friends, the ones Dmitri could very well have killed.

"If Piper had a hurt shoulder, would you carry her bag?" Konstantine asked, hoping to shift her view on this.

"I carry her bag anyway."

Konstantine nodded as if his point was made. Then he saw the blank expression on her face and realized it hadn't been made at all.

We take care of the ones we love, he thought. *Because we care, not because they are helpless.*

He couldn't bring himself to say it aloud.

Not when she was regarding him as she was now.

He let it go, giving her a slight nod. He didn't want to begin their adventure with quarreling.

She stepped into the water. The deer on the other side of the lake lifted their heads, watching. But they did not run.

This was the part Konstantine wasn't entirely excited about, but he followed her in.

The water was cold. The chill pressed against his legs and groin. He hissed.

Lou looked over her shoulder at him, smiling. She continued walking backward. "Too cold?"

"No."

"You sure?" she teased, seeming to relish his discomfort.

"I'm *fine*," he said. *I have warm, dry clothes in the bag.*

She stopped when the water was chest high, waiting. She removed her sunglasses and slipped them into the pocket of her leather coat, buttoning the pocket closed.

When he reached her, she slid her arms around his waist.

The intimacy surged through him. He wanted to touch her back. He wanted to coil his body around hers like a snake, but he had all these bags.

"You'll know we're across because the water will turn red," she said.

His heart began knocking in his chest. He felt his pulse in his throat and temples.

"As soon as you're across you need to swim to the surface and get to shore. There are things in the water that will eat you if you linger too long. Or go too far out."

His fear spiked. "What?"

But she was smiling.

"Are you kidding?"

Her smile widened. "I'm not kidding. Get to the shallows as quickly as you can, but let me get out first in case Jabbers is there. If the water things grab one of your bags, let it go. Don't hold on."

His heart was pounding so hard he found it difficult to breathe.

"Just give me a minute," he began.

"Take a deep breath."

"Okay." He inhaled. "How long does this—"

Lou swept his feet. He sank into the water with his bags. The cold dark overtook him, but her hands were still on his body, holding him close. This was a small comfort.

Then, imperceptibly, he saw the waters lighten, turning from black to red. The cold water warmed.

Lou tugged at his shirt, urging him toward the surface. But this reminder was all that she gave him before separating from his body and propelling herself toward the shore.

She was right about the bags.

Immediately they began to pull him down into the water. He sank, groping for the inflation strings on each side.

Then his boots connected with something and his heart jolted. He shifted, near panic, trying to regain his balance.

A car. He was standing on the roof of a *car*.

He pulled the first inflation string and the pillow expanded. He was pulled toward the surface slowly. Then he pulled the second string and really gained velocity.

Ahead of him, a dark shape shifted in the water, revealing a long serpentine body.

Don't stay in the water, she'd warned him. Her grin had made it seem like a joke, but now he suspected that it hadn't been. Whatever he'd seen—or had almost seen—he didn't want a closer look.

He broke the surface. Lou was already in the shallows, shaking water off her leather coat, flapping the front against her chest. She pushed her hair back from her face and turned to see him swimming toward her.

Her eyebrows raised. "You'll want to swim a bit faster."

He followed her gaze and saw four dorsal fins, pointed and black like those of killer whales, cutting the water ten yards away.

He needed no further incentive.

When he was within reach, she bent and grabbed his bags, tossing them onto land before he could object. But she didn't flinch at the task. In fact, she no longer guarded her shoulder as she had moments before. Her posture had improved and her shoulders squared.

He pulled himself from the shallows and looked at the strange world.

It was unlike anything he could've imagined. The blood-red waters. The distant mountains shimmering with an odd yellow haze. Two moons hung in the sky. Close to the water there was a forest, the foliage so dark it was black. Behind Lou, a wide, open plain traced a cliff. The vertical ridge of the cliffs seemed to shoot straight into the sky. He could not see the top of it, lost in low silvery cloud cover.

On her left the water continued until connecting with the ridge. The only way to go was right, away from the lake.

Unless someone wanted to swim across the water to the opposite shore and the mountains there.

But the pod of dorsal fins made Konstantine think that would be a short trip, and the explorer would never see that shore.

"What do you think?" Lou asked, twisting the water out of her hair. She was checking her gun, wiping it down with a dry handkerchief produced from a sealed pocket.

"It's a nightmare," he said.

"Wait until—"

A screech tore through Konstantine's body. The sound raised every hair on his arms and made his insides quake.

"—you meet her."

Konstantine expected Lou to pull the gun, put it up and ready. But she put it away.

"Lou," he began nervously. Something was crashing through the forest, knocking down the limbs as it passed. The enormous shifts of thrashing branches told him the creature must be massive.

"Stay behind me," she said.

"I—" His words were obliterated by the creature emerging from the forest.

It was bigger than Konstantine had imagined. Its long black body, scaled like a snake's, was one massive muscle, contracting.

Its six limbs carved away parts of the earth as it launched itself toward Konstantine.

He knew then that he was going to die.

"No," Lou said, and stepped in front of the creature, her hand out as if that would stop it.

She looked so small compared to the beast. One swipe and it could knock her away.

Yet it hesitated, but only for a moment. It tried to dart around

Lou, its jaws snapping in Konstantine's direction. The muscles in his lower guts loosened. His knees weakened.

He saw that the inside of the creature's mouth was white, and puffy. He imagined how suffocating it would be to go down such a throat.

It screeched again, obviously irritated by this game.

"Konstantine, come here," Lou said, reaching for him. But her eyes remained locked with the creature's.

"No," Konstantine said, finding he couldn't move from the spot. He held one of his bags against the front of his body like a shield.

"I'll remind you that this was your idea," she said calmly. "Come here."

He inched forward until he was just behind her shoulder.

"Give me your hand."

Konstantine wanted to do anything else, but he shifted the bag to his left arm and extended his right hand. Lou took it, moving it toward the beast's face.

"Do you have to—"

His palm touched cool muscle. Large eyes widened, surveying him. Its pupils dilated.

It's very intelligent, Konstantine realized with horror. He could practically see the thinking behind those eyes.

The beast pressed its nose into Lou's abdomen, audibly sniffing her, her neck and chin. Then it sniffed Konstantine's hand again.

"Mine," Lou said, and put her arm around Konstantine. "*Mine.*"

The beast regarded them. The sound it emitted now was more like a cooing.

Lou moved.

Konstantine mirrored her, unwilling to be exposed. "What are you—"

"Let her smell you."

The beast was on him in an instant, easily knocking his bag away.

It bent its head and Konstantine braced himself for the attack, for the searing pain of having his entrails ripped from his body.

But the beast only smelled him. It shoved its snout against his chest and sniffed, then his abdomen, his groin.

"Hey, *hey*," Konstantine said, covering himself with his hands.

Then she was sniffing his neck and ear, his hair.

"I think she can smell you on me. And me on you."

She. Konstantine wasn't sure he could think of this animal as a *she.*

"You've brought other men. Wouldn't their scent be on you?" he asked.

"I don't think it would've been as strong with such short contact. And it's possible I smelled like you then too."

He thought of the nearly two years since the first time he'd touched her. How many kills had Lou brought and dumped in this world in that time? Countless. Had the beast noticed the shift? Was there, in the creature's mind, a *before* and an *after* of Lou's time with him? Had her scent changed for the animal enough that it now recognized the source of that smell?

Lou was placing a hand on the creature's snout. "I didn't bring anything to eat."

It rubbed against her like a cat.

"It—*she* missed you." He found his hands were shaking.

Lou smiled. "Yeah, I think she did."

Lou wondered if her relief showed on her face. She hadn't expected this to go so well. She knew that Jabbers was very intelligent. She had pushed Lou into the water once, when she was bleeding to death, somehow comprehending that the help she had needed was on the other side.

And now, it seemed she understood Konstantine—despite bearing every resemblance to the men she often brought here to La Loon—was not on the menu.

It was more than that. Jabbers seemed interested in him. Curious. She sniffed him and his bags. She dragged her tongue up the back of his neck.

She watched him carefully. Lou couldn't recall Jabbers ever showing as much interest in *her.*

Despite how it looked, Lou kept a close eye, ready for the situation to sour at a moment's notice. Hadn't she seen YouTube clips where a tiger befriended a goat, only to eat it later?

As Konstantine collected samples of the shore's soil, the lake's water, and plucked one of the black heart-shaped leaves from the forest, she kept her eye on Jabbers.

She noted that he didn't entirely look away from her either. Good. It was smart to stay aware.

There were other reasons to be alert.

She'd never been away from the water's edge before. In all the years her power had delivered her to this strange place, she'd only ever stepped onto the shore, and briefly at that.

It had never occurred to her to move further inland and actually canvass the land.

What if there were more creatures like Jabbers, who didn't have their shared history? Would they simply tear her apart—or die trying? And even if Jabbers was one of a kind, that didn't mean there weren't other dangers.

Konstantine must've seen her sizing up the cliffs. "I didn't bring climbing equipment, but we can follow the lake and see if there is a gap at the end, where it seems to connect with the lake."

They walked the plain that stretched between the cliffs and the lake. The grass—if that was what it was—caressed Lou's knees. It was black with a strange metallic sheen to it. When Lou touched it, turning it in the light, it shined like the back of a beetle, iridescent.

Jabbers trailed on her left, seemingly content to follow her guests. Once in a while, she would press her side into Lou's and Lou would pat her hard body reassuringly. To Konstantine, she would sniff his hair, the back of his neck.

It amused Lou. Mostly because Konstantine's terror was thinly veiled.

He bent and opened his case. He snipped some grass and fed the thin strands into a vial. He filled another clear vial with the soil beneath it.

Jabbers stiffened.

Lou pulled her gun.

"What?" Konstantine whispered, staying low in the grass.

"I don't know," Lou said, watching the beast slink forward, toward the lake, her body low. "It looks like she's..."

"Stalking," Konstantine confirmed.

With lightning speed, Jabbers leapt from the shore into the water. Her considerable length disappeared beneath the surface, leaving large rings in her wake.

A moment later she broke the surface with something thrashing in her mouth.

To Lou, it looked like a turtle without a shell for its top half, while the bottom half looked like a dolphin's tail.

Jabbers tore it apart while it screamed.

Konstantine's face blanched.

It occurred to Lou that Konstantine might put two and two together and realize that his brothers died like this, torn apart on the shore by this very animal as Lou fed them to her, one by one.

The look in his eyes said as much.

"She must eat from the lake," Lou said. "When I don't come."

Konstantine put his samples in their carry case and removed a small device. "I wondered. I haven't seen any birds, or small animals. And she's so big. I can only imagine how much she has to eat to survive."

"What is that?" Lou asked, gesturing at the device in his hand.

He followed her gaze. "It's a SUMMA canister. To collect an air sample."

"Is there anything you don't plan to take a sample of?" Lou asked, smiling. So far she'd seen him collect dirt, water, and any plants they'd passed.

"I'd like a sample of her blood," he said with a laugh, nodding toward Jabbers. The turtle-dolphin creature had stopped screaming. Now there were only wet tearing sounds. "And I don't think that will happen."

"No, but you can get some of whatever she is eating before she cleans it all off her face."

Lou smiled, watching Konstantine consider this option as the beast lay on the shore, cleaning turtle-dolphin guts out of the webbing between her paws.

To Lou's surprise, he approached the animal with a cotton pad in his hand.

"If she eats you," Lou began, "it's your own fault."

Konstantine cooed to her softly in Italian and the beast mimicked the sound. Lou snorted.

Show off.

Then, to her surprise, she let him wipe her paw with the cotton pad.

When he returned to his kit, he looked like a kid who just walked out of the candy store with a fistful of free candy. There was a pronounced bounce in his step.

"And there's little bits of flesh in it," he said, stuffing the cotton pad into a jar.

Twenty feet lay between the edge of the cliff and the lake. Beyond was an endless plain. Lou began walking in that direction, interested in seeing the lake from the other side.

"There's a gap. We can pass through here."

Jabbers bounded into her path.

Lou stopped. She tried going around, but again Jabbers sat up on her hind legs.

"She doesn't want us to go this way," Lou said, turning to find Konstantine frowning behind her.

Lou gazed around the animal at the endless stretch of field. More long, metallic grass swung in a low breeze. But the sky was light and unmarred.

What's out there?

"She must think it's too dangerous," Konstantine said.

"For us or for her?" Lou wondered.

"Maybe both."

Lou looked up at the cliffs. "Then let's call it a night."

She craned her neck up to regard the cliff face. It cut from the left into their path. From here, it looked as if the dark mouth of a cave awaited them.

If there was such a cave, she'd much rather sleep off the ground and away from anything that may roam the grasses at night looking for a meal.

It was Jabbers who bounded up the side of the rocks first. Her serpentine body seemed to slide and fold over every obstacle with ease.

Lou relied mostly on her right arm to pull herself up. The incline was very gradual, and a worn path allowed her to ascend without much effort.

Jabbers stopped on a landing a hundred feet off the ground. Lou had been right. It was the mouth of a cave.

"You got a flashlight in there?" Lou asked, staring into the pitch black.

After a short rustle in his bags, Konstantine put a metal flashlight into her hand.

She clicked it on.

The cave wasn't huge, perhaps 220 square feet from its mouth to its curved back wall. Against that wall was a pile of...

She moved closer for inspection, her beam sweeping over the rubble.

"Bones," she said. "There's a pile of bones."

"She piled them so nicely," Konstantine said, his voice still strained from the climb.

Lou snorted.

Jabbers squeezed past Lou to the pile and flopped down onto it. Then she began to roll around like a dog in the grass.

"That's one way to scratch a back," Lou mused.

"Can we eat now?" Konstantine asked, and Lou heard the irritation.

"You're like Piper," she said, tossing her small leather bag against the far wall. "You get cranky when you haven't eaten."

Konstantine was tearing open a food packet with his teeth, rolling his gaze up to hers defensively.

After reconstituting the food with a bit of water and heating it over the small fire he built, they ate their chili mac with beef. Once Konstantine had two packets down, the lines in his face evened out. He was even able to offer her half of his brownie.

Lou took off her boots and shrugged out of her leather jacket. The fire made it too warm to wear it, and she wanted to dry her damp clothes near the flames.

Free of the leather, she stretched her shoulders.

"If this is her cave," Lou wondered aloud, "where are the others? She can't be one of a kind."

The fire threw shadows against the wall, which Jabbers watched curiously until she settled at the mouth of the cave, stretching long and feline against the backdrop of the eternal twilight and placid lake.

"Maybe they are solitary creatures," Konstantine said. "Like jaguars, they spread out and have territories hundreds of miles wide. They only come together to mate."

Lou arched a brow at the word *mate*.

With her eyes on the distant two moons, Lou thought, *There have to be others.* Jabbers couldn't have come from nothing.

"Does it always look like this?" Konstantine gestured at the night. "Are there seasons?"

"I haven't seen anything but this. It's always the same."

"No seasons and the same amount of light? No visible sun in the sky. Well, the tilt of the axis could play a part. And some of the outer planets have incredibly long seasons. Forty years, I believe. But this place has oxygen and life. And it isn't freezing. It can't possibly be too far from a star, can it?"

Lou held her hands toward the fire as he stoked it.

"I honestly don't know enough about planetary systems to guess the conditions where such a place is possible," he continued. "But obviously, this is another world."

Lou had thought of the alien planet idea, though she could not, in her mind, fathom that her ability would take her not only through water but across space.

"I guess I thought it was Earth," she said. "In a really distant future or past."

"Where did the other moon come from?"

She shrugged. "Just the right asteroid came along at the right speed or whatever."

"If this is the *very* distant future, it's possible. But that begs the question, where are the humans? Are there any? Or did they go extinct?"

Konstantine eyed the creature lying at the mouth of the cave. "Did they get *eaten*?"

The fire was cozy and there was something about Jabbers asleep at the mouth of the cave that made Lou feel both safe and uneasy. The creature was guarding them. But from what?

"When we first crossed over, there was a car," Konstantine said. "I stepped on it."

"That came with Angelo," she said, watching his face for any reaction to his brother's name.

"Really?"

She waited, seeing where this might go.

"I didn't realize you could bring an entire car with you," he said.

"I made his chauffeur drive us into the bay. I'd only wanted Angelo, but it brought all three of us and the car across."

She wished she understood the expression he was giving her.

"Has that happened before? Where you've brought entire vehicles or fleets with you?"

"No. I can't do it in the dark."

After a long pause, he flicked his green eyes up to meet hers. "And when he got here?"

Lou said, "She took care of him."

Konstantine laughed. "How do you know she is a *she*?"

"I guess I don't. It's just a feeling."

If Konstantine was horrified by the news that his brother—and most of the family—had been eaten alive by this creature, he didn't show it. But they'd made that bed the night they came to her childhood home and shot her parents.

She relived it distantly, the white snap of the gun going off in the bedroom upstairs and the sound of glass breaking. The gate to their backyard flying open and Lou's father lifting her and throwing her into the pool, knowing it would save her life.

It had taken her years to hunt them all down. Years to discern how all the pieces of that one night had played out, and who had been responsible for what.

All of it had delivered her to Konstantine's door.

His mind ran with questions too. That much was clear. But he said nothing, only looking into the flames.

"That scar on your shoulder," he said eventually, pointing across the fire to her.

"She bit me," she said.

He didn't reply, obviously waiting for the story.

"I was taking a bath and I slipped through," she said plainly, conveying none of the terror of what it was like for her then, trapped in a body with a will of its own. This was long before Aunt Lucy showed her what she could do.

It was Lucy who had given her back her life. Aunt Lucy who'd not only taken her in after her parents had died, but who'd taught her that *Lou* controlled her power. It didn't control her.

"When I crawled out of the lake, she attacked me. I fought back. I don't know if I poked her in the eye or hit her nose, but she let me go and I fell back into the water. I reemerged in a swimming pool in a man's backyard. He was cutting his grass when I just walked out of the pool. Bad day for him."

"Must have been terrifying," Konstantine said.

"I imagine he hadn't been expecting me, no."

"I meant for you."

She looked up and found him watching her.

"You were so small."

"So was she," Lou explained. "Well, small*er*. More like a pony."

Konstantine watched the beast on the ledge sleep, her head tucked toward her tail. As if sensing eyes on her, she peeled open one eye and huffed.

Konstantine looked away first. "She's probably seven meters long now."

"She looks bigger than when I saw her last," Lou said. "It's hard to imagine that she might still be growing."

"How did you become...friends?" he asked.

Lou didn't know how to answer. Were they friends? In a way. But how could she explain the sense of connection she had with Jabbers? How sometimes Lou looked into its eyes and saw herself.

"Slowly," she said to the fire.

Konstantine seemed to sense her reluctance to talk anymore tonight. He removed the two sleeping bags from his pack and laid them beside the fire.

"I don't have pillows," he said, gesturing at the pile of luggage.

She considered making a joke about all the things he'd brought but decided against it. He was the one who was carrying it.

He removed his boots so his woolen black socks poked out the bottom of his jeans. His black t-shirt was tight across his chest. Just in the hours they'd been traveling together, a shadow of a beard had begun to form on his jaw.

She liked the look of it. She wondered what it would feel like to kiss him like that.

He put one hand under his head and regarded her. With the other he patted the sleeping bag beside him. "Aren't you tired?"

Tired was something Lou felt in her mind, rarely in her body. Now, by the fire, her body was relaxed. With a gun and a large knife at the floor by her feet, and Jabbers at the open mouth of the cave, she felt more than safe.

Konstantine was watching her, waiting for her answer.

"No," she said. "You should sleep if you want to."

"You're very beautiful," he said. "I can see the fire dancing in your eyes. Did your mother have brown eyes too?"

"No," she said. "They were blue."

She stopped short of saying, *I have my father's eyes.*

Jabbers lifted her head to regard something in the distance that Lou couldn't see.

Small flaps on the side of her head opened and closed. Lou wondered if those were her ears. Whatever she was hearing was far out of Lou's range.

Truth be told, Jabbers wasn't the most interesting thing in the cave. Konstantine bathed in soft light and looking cozy in his fresh clothes was almost too much to resist.

"Will you lie down beside me?" he asked, his lips looking thick enough to bite.

Lou smiled. She could do one better.

She rose from her place and crossed to him. In a fluid moment, she threw a leg over his lap and settled her weight onto his groin. Her legs squeezed either side of his body, eliciting a groan of pleasure from him.

He searched her face from under dark lashes. "Your shoulder—"

"It doesn't hurt," she said. "Ever since we got here, it stopped hurting."

And strangely this was true.

"But if you—"

"Shut up about my shoulder, or this isn't happening," she said, leaning forward and grazing his chest with hers.

His eyes dilated at the word *this*.

KONSTANTINE NEEDED NO FURTHER ENCOURAGEMENT. HE LEANED up, seizing her mouth with his. His fingers brushed her skin, finding the hem of her shirt.

Yes, yes, yes, his mind chorused.

"Worry about yourself," she said, lifting off of him long enough to pull her shirt and bra off in one movement.

This only excited him more. A low buzz began to tremor along his skin. With a snap of her fingers, she undid the top of her pants. That small motion felt as if she'd unsnapped something inside of him too.

So long. I've waited for so long.

"You want to—" he began, disbelieving. *So long.*

"Yes." She stepped out of her pants, leaving her underwear on.

"Here?" He craned his neck to look at the beast, who was watching them. Desire pounded through him, but so did a tremor of fear. He found, strangely, that one seemed to intensify the other.

"Here," Lou insisted, a smile playing in the corner of her mouth.

She tugged on the bottom of his pants. He lifted his hips to oblige her. The flames threw shadows across her naked chest and stomach.

He thought of the first night he'd seen her.

Then she was just a girl, no more than fourteen or fifteen. She'd appeared in his bed like a dream. Her thick dark hair had been much longer then. It had cascaded nearly to her waist. Her cheeks rounder, girlish. She hadn't yet acquired any of the hardness she'd accumulate over the years. With her lips parted, split like a cherry, wrapped in the nightmares of her father's death, she was the most beautiful creature he'd ever seen.

And those nighttime visits—as far and few in between as they'd been—had only made him want her more.

Fifteen years, he thought. *I've wanted this for over fifteen years.*

She pushed him down against the sleeping bag, sitting astride him again. She began by grinding her body against his. Each contraction of her muscles made something in him tighten deliciously.

Their nipples grazed and he shivered.

He felt her moisture through her underwear and longed to touch her. He traced the edge of the underwear with his finger.

"I want more than that," she said, and the air left him.

"Yes," he said, his desperation high in his throat. "Yes."

That's when she pulled her underwear to the side and slid onto him.

A long, agonizing groan escaped him. His hands found her hips, pinning her onto his lap, her soft flesh yielding in his hands. He wanted to sear this image of her into his mind forever. Her naked, covered in shadows and firelight.

The feel of her contracting around him.

It's happening, it's happening, it's happening.

And she felt even better than he'd imagined. Her flesh and muscles were softer than the hard planes of her body had led him to suspect. Her motions gentler than all the aggression she carried like a shield.

His eyes fluttered closed against the barrage of pleasure. It was a wave overtaking him, drowning him.

"Stay with me," she breathed into his ear. She grasped his chin and squeezed.

His eyes fluttered open. *"Sei perfetta."*

"I don't know what that means," she laughed, low in her throat, before running her tongue along his lower lip. "But I like it too."

14

———

Diana stood at the window behind the thick curtain and watched King work at his desk. He was leaning back in his chair, speaking on the phone to someone unimportant, about a case she didn't give two shits about.

Yet the voice feed was being delivered to the laptop on the table beside her. "If you want her in, you'll have to talk to the DA. I can't subpoena people. I don't have that authority."

His face broke into a grin, his belly shaking.

The laughter echoed through the line a second later.

A short delay then.

It didn't matter. None of it mattered to her, really, as she replayed Lou's words—or lack of them—over and over in her mind.

Her flat refusal. Her borderline disinterest in Diana as a partner. She'd never felt so *dismissed* in her life.

You'll regret that, Diana thought coldly. *Once you realize what I can do.*

And because Diana was busy orchestrating her plan, she couldn't follow King, Piper, or the landlady Melandra personally now. She sent Blair and Spencer, the two most capable members of her twenty-person team, to do that menial task.

Blair was the only one who knew everything. Spencer, more than most. The rest simply believed they were working on an undercover operation to stop a high-profile pornography ring.

Diana wanted to keep it that way.

When she needed additional tails for Daniella and Piper, she pulled from the workers, saying only that the girls were in danger. They were young enough that it could be true. Not children, but young women were always in danger.

Lookouts were posted in the café across from *The Herald*, the newspaper where Daniella Allendale worked, and they also walked Daniella's neighborhood.

King and Melandra were easier to track. They were creatures of habit, their schedules often overlapping, even sharing a Belgian Malinois between them.

It was a beautiful, obedient dog, Diana thought, and she wouldn't mind having it for herself.

Because Diana couldn't be seen, her access to the group was by proxy. She had the cameras in Piper's apartment, but she also had two lookout positions. Adjacent to Madame Melandra's Fortune and Fixes had been an apartment for rent. Diana paid the exorbitant price—not understanding why everything in the French Quarter was so expensive —and could now look through one of the apartment windows directly into King's with the help of a small telescope. She saw the red leather sofa, a large coffee table, and a sparse kitchen with garish black and white tile that hurt the eyes to look at. Below that, she had a decent view of most of the shop. The register and part of the stairs leading up to the apartment.

A second apartment had been rented on Royal Street, providing a view of King's desk inside the detective agency. The view didn't stretch all the way to the door marked *Ms. Thorne*, but that was okay. Diana would make do.

Piper had the most sporadic routine of the three. She floated from King to Melandra to Daniella. She also set up a card table in Jackson Square and read fortunes for hours into the balmy night. Sometimes she went to clubs on Bourbon Street and stayed until closing time.

Diana took all this in about them, about their life, and was disappointed that it all seemed rather ordinary.

No one showed up with suspicious packages. No strangers stopped in for cryptic conversations. They were, on the surface, exactly what they looked like—an eccentric group living out their lives in a tourist district—not a front for a high-powered criminal investigation unit.

Maybe things were simply quiet. Lou was "with Konstantine"—a name that had turned up nothing in Diana's search. Moreover, when Diana had tried to search directly for Louie Thorne, nothing had come up either. There were only three articles that she'd been able to find about her father, Jack, the slain hero, and only in the first one was Lou mentioned, and only as a byline.

The woman was not on social media. She didn't appear in any online photos or public records. She didn't have a driver's license or voter's ID. She—

A rough knock on the apartment door.

"Come in."

Spencer shoved the door open with one hand and shuffled into the room. Under his arm was a manila folder, his smile bright.

"What do you have for me?" she asked, already sensing his excitement.

"Something very, *very* interesting."

She looked at the hobbled man with a scarred face and receding hairline.

In truth, Spencer disgusted her. It wasn't his appearance. It was the way he looked at her, spoke to her, *fawned* over her.

But his work and his loyalty were assets she couldn't bring herself to throw away, not when every choice, every resource had to be managed so carefully.

"Show me," she said, sliding the curtain closed. She didn't want King to look up suddenly and see her face.

Spencer pulled two photos from the manila folder. In one, half of Lou's face was cut by the light of a gas station sign. It was a 7-Eleven, and given the sea of Asian faces around her, she would guess the 7-Eleven was in a Chinatown or maybe Asia itself.

The second photograph was a screen capture of Lou in a cobblestoned alley, the collar of her leather jacket pulled up to hide her neck, her eyes hidden behind those damned mirrored shades.

There was nothing in the photos that Diana could see, except Lou.

"What am I looking at?" Diana asked. Irritation nipped at her ears.

"Look at the time stamps."

Tokyo 6:15. Amsterdam 22:23.

"So? She stopped off in Amsterdam before heading to Tokyo." She was traveling *with Konstantine*.

"Look at the time stamps again."

"An eight-hour difference."

"No." He shook his head excitedly. "An eight-*minute* difference. Considering time zones."

She looked at the photos again and did the math in her head.

"You're telling me that in a matter of eight minutes Lou went from Tokyo to Amsterdam?"

Spencer nodded so enthusiastically that his glasses slid down on his nose. He pushed them back up.

"That's impossible. The time stamps must be wrong. Or maybe these were on two different days."

"It's the same day. I'm absolutely sure of it."

"No," Diana said, thrusting the photos back at him. "There's an error. People don't just travel across time zones in minutes."

Spencer's excitement faltered. He was clearly disappointed by the direction this conversation was going. "Maybe they can with the right technology or—"

"Check again," Diana said.

"But if it's *real*," Spencer insisted. "What if it's tech you could use against Winter."

How thoughtful. His enduring loyalty, his permeating desire to help her fulfill her greatest wish. Something warm stirred within her.

"Spencer," she said quietly.

Her tone alone stopped the blabbering. She slid her hand down the front of his chest to his crotch. There she traced the thin outline of the metal cage with her probing fingers.

"Do you like your new gift? You haven't said," she asked softly, her mouth dangerously close to his. This was the sort of thing he enjoyed, she knew.

"Y-yes," he said. "Very much."

"Do you like the idea of wearing a cage for me?" she asked coquettishly. Her nails tapped against the metal wires encasing Spencer's penis.

"Yes, yes I do."

"Would you like it better if I took it off? If I said *the word*."

He moaned, his eyes rolling closed at the thought. "I'd love that. Yes."

She gripped his chin roughly. "Tonight. If you're a good boy and check the time stamp again. Or better yet, tell me where the hell Lou is now."

"Of course. Of course, I will."

At this she let her hand drop and turned away from him, opening the curtain again on the New Orleans street.

Below, King regarded the open file on his desk, tapping a pen lightly against the tabletop.

Tokyo to Amsterdam in eight minutes. Ridiculous.

"And stop reading so much science fiction. It's rotting your head."

15

———————

Konstantine must've replayed the memory three hundred times before breakfast. As he showered, hot water pounding his neck and shoulders. As he brushed his teeth and selected his clothes—a black button-down, tight pants, and leather shoes. As he shaved, styled his hair, pushing it back from his eyes.

As he walked across the piazza, hands in his pockets, and up the steps of the large stone church that served as the Ravengers' stronghold.

Even as Stefano, his right-hand man, gave him the update for the two days he'd been gone, his mind remained in La Loon, fixed on the sight of Louie's naked body awash in firelight.

"Did you hear me?" Stefano asked in Italian. He sighed. The low light sparked in his dark eyes. Today he wore an Armani suit, his nails gleaming from a manicure.

"No," Konstantine admitted. "Just tell me the last part, about Riku Yamamoto."

"They want more money," Stefano said. He waved his hand. "What has you so distracted today? Bad vacation?"

Again, the feeling of Lou sliding onto him, the wet, slick sensation of her contracting. Her hand shoving against his chest and that look in her eyes when—

Stay with me.

His groin tightened.

Stefano arched a brow. "That well, huh?"

"It had its moments," he said, and the moment he was buried to the hilt inside Lou had been the best of it. He was only glad that he had not climaxed instantly, given how badly he'd wanted her and how the years of longing and waiting had made the desire nearly senseless.

La Loon itself was a nightmarish place. It wasn't only the disorienting landscape, or that all its organisms seemed oil-slicked and iridescent.

It was mostly the creature, which despite Konstantine's reasoning terrified him.

It was unlike anything he'd ever seen—or wanted to see again.

The fear his brothers must've felt in the moments before their death—though deserved—must have been immense. Still, as frightening as that place was, and as alarming as Lou's strange connection to it and its ruler, he was glad that he went.

Lou had shown him a part of herself that she'd shown no other man without also killing him. And that meant more to Konstantine than he could articulate.

His phone rang, spinning out a tune on his desk. Stefano fell back, willing to wait for his master's attention. Konstantine appreciated that about his oldest friend.

At first Konstantine wondered if this was about the specimens. He'd delivered his vials to a lab he trusted for its discretion and longed to hear the results, if only because he thought it might please Lou. But this would be an unusually quick response.

It wasn't the lab. Konstantine knew the number on the screen. In English he said, "Hello, Mr. King."

"Hey. Wait, one second. Let this train pass."

The detective's voice was swallowed by the deafening roar of a passing train. The whistle was loud enough that Konstantine pulled the phone back from his ear.

"Where are you?" he asked.

"I had to come down to the train yard to make sure no one could get this conversation with a long-range device. It's too loud for that here."

The hair on Konstantine's neck rose. "What's going on?"

"Diana Dennard is in town, checking up on Lou. I'm pretty sure she's bugged my office and probably Piper's apartment. She might have gotten something into the shop and our apartments too. I can't be sure without being really obvious. She's definitely got tails following us around. A woman in leather pants and a guy that walks with a pretty pronounced limp."

"To what end?"

"She came in pretending to be Lou's sister, asking me to find her. Didn't Lou tell you about any of this?"

"No." Konstantine thought of the notification he'd received upon returning from La Loon. Someone had duplicated photos of Lou in both Tokyo and Amsterdam before his bots could wipe them. He'd been worried the Tokyo photo was Yamamoto's doing. Maybe it wasn't.

"Since I can't search for the bugs or cameras without them knowing we are on to them," King went on. "I was hoping you could take care of that."

"I can try to disrupt the signals remotely," Konstantine offered. "I need the addresses of all properties you think have been infiltrated and also the name of your internet provider."

He didn't *have* to have this information, but it would make the job quicker.

"Why?"

"I can hack routers, networks, anything that they may be using as a signal for their devices."

King rattled off addresses and the name of his provider, while Konstantine scrawled the information on a notebook at hand. Then King asked, "How long do you need?"

"Give me a day," Konstantine said.

"Better than I hoped."

King thanked him and terminated the call.

"About the yakuza," Stefano began, only glancing at the notepad beneath Konstantine's hand. "Chris Litteri and John Christino just returned."

In the face of Stefano's patience, Konstantine refrained from pulling out his computer and setting about the task that interested him far more than politics.

"Yes," he said, putting down the pen. "I'm listening."

PIPER WAS REFILLING THE COFFEE POT WHEN SHE FELT KING slip the note into her pocket. Her back stiffened as she repressed the urge to ask, *What's that?*

He'd trained her for this moment. *If I ever slip you a note, it's because something dangerous is happening and I can't speak aloud. Don't do or say anything. Don't react. Just make an excuse to leave and read it somewhere safe. The farther away, the better.*

At the time she'd thought he was being a paranoid bastard. Sure, his ex-partner had snuck into his apartment one night and had almost shot him in the head, and they'd also gotten kidnapped by some Russians, but—okay, so maybe he had reason to be paranoid.

Or this was a test.

She checked the time. It was just past noon. "I was thinking about getting some sandwiches."

"I'd love a BLT," he said, without missing a beat. He took his coffee and dose of cream back to his desk. "Let me give you some money."

As he handed over the twenty, Piper was careful to look him in the eye.

His gaze betrayed nothing.

Damn, he's good. "Be right back."

The note felt like a stone in her pocket as she jogged down Royal to St. Peter, catching a streetcar at the edge of the Quarter. She rode it for ten minutes until the two women who'd boarded the car with her exited at a stop in the Garden District.

Only then did she pull the note from her pocket, along with her phone, and unfold it carefully in her lap, pretending to look at the screen.

Agency's compromised. Meet me at Blues Bar at 1:15.

That was enough time to get the sandwiches. And a cookie. Right now she could use a cookie.

BLUES BAR WAS A HONKY-TONK PLACE NEAR CRESCENT PARK. WHEN Piper walked in with her bag of BLTs and cookies, she expected the doorman to stop her and tell her no outside food.

Instead he nodded toward a closed door across the room. "He's down there."

Confused, she entered the bar cautiously, finding it empty at midday.

"Did a guy—" she began.

He nodded toward the door on the far wall again. Piper had to squint to see it in the dim light. A red bulb overhead made the edges of its frame stand out.

"Thanks." She crossed to the door, opened it, and peered down into the darkness. Four white steps could be seen before the shadows swallowed the rest of the staircase.

Oh man, she thought. *If I get murdered over some bacon...*

She descended cautiously. She kept the sandwich bag close, ready to hurl it at an attacker if one appeared.

But at the bottom of the stairs was nothing more than a concrete bunker and three people standing beneath a single swinging bulb.

"Christ," she muttered. "I thought I was going to get murdered down here. What's going on, man?"

Melandra, Dani, and King all turned at the sound of her voice.

"Did you close the door?" King asked. Piper looked up the stairs to be sure she had.

"Yes, now what's going on?"

He was frowning at the sandwich bag. "You actually got sandwiches."

"Well, *yeah*," she said. "You didn't really want one? Well, I got them cut in half so everyone can have half a BLT and a cookie."

King opened the bag. "There are five cookies in here."

"It was five for two dollars. They're Gino's." When King didn't seem to understand, Piper added, "They're *amazing*."

They passed around the bag until everyone was in possession of half a BLT and a cookie. Piper's had M&M's in it. Mel had taken the chocolate with white chocolate chips and Dani the snickerdoodle. King had passed on the cookie.

Piper thought, *Your loss.*

"How do you know about this place? Are you friends with a guy or something?"

"I know the owner," King said, half of his sandwich in his mouth. "She used to be a cop in Washington. She moved here and opened a bar when she retired in '91."

Piper always thought it was weird how old people knew everything by year. *I got my teeth out in '83. I bought the house in '01.*

Piper remembered her high school graduation year, class of 2011, and that was it.

"Why the cloak and dagger meeting? What's going on?" Dani asked.

Piper caught her eye and they shared a smile. Dani looked really cute with half of a huge cookie in her mouth. Piper wanted to kiss her but knew this was a weird moment to start sucking face.

"Diana's been watching us, tracking our movements. I found a bug under my desk at work. I have a feeling that she probably put bugs in other places too, but I can't confirm that yet. And I can't get ahold of Lou either."

"She's in La Loon," Piper said.

She took her boyfriend on vacation. Piper didn't like to think about the Italian stallion if she could help it. Something about him got under her skin. But there was no denying that he was super into Lou and would do anything for her, so she let it slide.

"Did Lou meet up with Diana?" Piper asked cautiously.

"Yeah," King said. "She said Diana wanted to hunt a guy together."

"That doesn't sound too bad," Mel said, finishing her cookie and wiping her hands together to rid them of crumbs.

"Except Lou refused her." King sucked mayo off his thumb and wiped the crumbs off his hands with a paper napkin. For someone who didn't want a sandwich, he sure put it away. "I don't think Diana will let it go."

Dani was rubbing the back of her neck. It was a gesture Piper knew well. She did it whenever she didn't like what she was hearing.

"I just wanted you to be aware about the bugs and to tell you to watch what you say in the office until Konstantine is able to destroy the signal. And I want you to check your place."

Piper realized King was looking at her. "What place?"

"*Your* place," he said. "If there's a bug under my desk, there's probably something in your apartment. Maybe even a camera."

Dani choked on her cookie. "Excuse me?"

Her face was reddening. Piper couldn't tell if it was because someone might have taped them messing around or if she was actually choking.

"You can't say that stuff to her." Piper scowled at King. "You'll freak her out."

"I want you prepared," he said. "That's all. We can't be sure what Diana's next move will be, so we need to be careful."

Dani began wringing her finger. The one Dmitri had cut off.

Mel reached out and placed a hand on her arm. "We're going to be fine, honey. You'll see."

"Exactly. Diana doesn't stand a chance," Piper said, trying to reassure her. "Konstantine's doing his fancy computer stuff, and we're awesome. And we're ready. We're ready for *anything*."

16

———————

Lou stood in the closet of her apartment, breathing slowly, her Browning pistol resting across her chest. She rotated her shoulder but found no pain there. It was tight, but that was it.

She felt good. *Really* good.

Better, better, better, her mind was chanting. *I'm getting better.*

King had paged her twice, but it was no emergency. She ignored it. She had plans.

With a smile, she exhaled into the darkness, trying to hold back her elation and excitement. She let the shadows wash over her like moonlit waves.

St. Louis fell away, and in its place swelled honking cars and the trill of a bicycle bell.

Someone was yelling. And then the veil shifted and Lou slipped through.

Prague sprang to life around her, vibrant and hurried.

Lou stepped out onto Charles Bridge. The city was awash in lantern light with a cotton candy–purple sky. A church, or at least Lou thought it might be a church, was framed against that soft sky with its metallic pale green dome of a roof. Somewhere, a large bell began its toll.

A woman with a cart sold circles of cinnamon and sugar dough that looked like bracelets. It made Lou's stomach knot, but she'd eat later.

For now her eyes remained fixed on her target. A short, muscular man. His leather jacket grazed his hips as he marched away from her. She followed him across the bridge, walking past couples hand-in-hand, students with backpacks, and children pinwheeling, arms outstretched.

His boots clicked against stone and Lou fell into step with him, matching his rhythm.

Jiri Svoboda was a middleman. When a riverboat full of heroin docked on the Vltava River, the drug lord made sure it was delivered to the dealers in the surrounding districts.

It was a warm summer night. She was out hunting like she did back in the day. In her life before Konstantine, before King, before Piper and the rest of it.

A surge of nostalgia overtook her, deepening her confidence.

She followed him through the cobblestoned streets, enjoying the sounds of the city waking up at the promise of night. People stumbled out of restaurants laughing. A bus squealed its brakes in front of a Tesco.

Svoboda cut down a side alley.

Lou was on him a heartbeat later. She grabbed the back of his leather jacket and pulled.

He turned, pivoting as if he'd expected her—and if not her, some kind of trouble.

His elbow swung in an arc as the gun slid out of his jacket. Lou grabbed the back of his elbow, redirecting the energy down the same moment she slid him through the dark.

Prague disappeared. Her lakeside sanctuary formed.

Jiri was not perturbed by this shift.

If he noticed that the city around him had disappeared and in its place stood a nighttime forest, his face showed no recognition. Something splashed into the lake, disturbed by the sudden arrival of unwanted guests.

The swing of Jiri's arm turned him away from her. She released her grip and he stumbled into the shallows. He dropped his gun as water sloshed over the tops of his boots. Without stopping, he pulled another from his low back.

Lou had enough time to slip, sidestepping through the darkness, so that when he pulled the trigger, the bullet bit into the pine tree that had stood behind her, spraying bark like wedding confetti.

She reappeared in time to bring her elbow down hard on the gun hand, knocking it free. It hit the water and disappeared. Ripples radiated across the dark surface.

He threw himself against Lou, checking her bad shoulder.

She cried out and went down, hitting the dirt hard. All the air left her on impact.

He was trying to get his hands around her neck. She was bracing him above her with her forearm, but it was her bad side.

That first ignition of pain incinerated her confidence.

Pain rolled through her body, making her spine go rigid. Red bursts danced in front of her eyes.

She managed to get her good arm between their bodies and cross-pulled a blade from her hip.

She drew it across his throat in one fluid moment. Blood sprayed into her face from the split artery, then began to pour. It hit her throat, cascading over the skin into her hair, pooling at the back of her neck.

He coughed, choking. His body grew heavy and slack against her good arm.

When she was certain her shoulder would snap out of place if she held him a moment longer, she rolled, tossing him to one side.

She sat up, panting.

Her shoulder wouldn't move. The arm was deadweight against her side.

She tried to shrug out of her jacket and get a good look at it, but the movement sent ribbons of fire down her side until her vision darkened.

Svoboda choked out his last on the riverbank then was silent.

The chorus of crickets and frogs that had stopped rehearsing enough for this interlude to play out gradually recommenced their singing.

Lou inched toward the lake. With her good side, she scooped water into her hand and splashed it against her face, wiping away the blood. She didn't want it on her lips. Nothing to do about the viscous globs drying in her hair.

The kill had been sloppy. Pathetic. She hadn't gotten stabbed or shot, which could be seen as an improvement, but now her shoulder was throbbing so badly she thought she might black out.

"I've hurt myself," she murmured, and heard her own disbelief. How was that possible?

Sure, sometimes she was shot or stabbed or thrown into something in the course of a good fight, but she'd never hurt *herself*.

And the emotion she felt now, knowing that if she'd ruptured her shoulder or put herself out of commission for weeks, was that she had only herself to blame.

Anger spiked inside her as she pulled herself to standing. She glanced at Svoboda's body and bent to grab his leg with her good arm.

She'd wanted to take an offering to Jabbers, to thank the beast for not eating Konstantine. But she wouldn't be able to drag this corpse onto the shore. She would do well just to bring it to La Loon and leave it in the shallows for those strange reptilian orcas to eat.

Body convulsing with pain, mind filled with bitter disappointment, Lou slid into the cold water with one thought in her head.

I'm not ready. I'm not ready for anything.

17

———————

Sometimes Diana lamented that her job involved so much time sitting in front of the computer. Tonight she had two monitors in front of her, twice the insult, as sweat trickled down the back of her neck. There was no A/C in this building and the walls themselves seemed to sweat from the heat.

She squinted at the screen, rubbing at her dry eyes. One monitor showcased Winter's feed—nine squares in total, each highlighting a different child.

It was the little boy, maybe six years old, who was getting the worst of it. His abuser kept alternating between raping and beating him, striking the boy over and over across his small back. When the boy bent, vomiting for the third time, she looked away from the grainy image and checked the second screen.

The other monitor was a two-way split feed of Piper's apartment and King's office.

Blair knocked on the door. "Are you going to eat?"

"I already ate."

"What?"

Diana made no answer.

"*What* did you eat?" Blair insisted.

"A sandwich."

"What kind of sandwich?"

Diana scowled at her. "Why does it matter what kind of sandwich I ate?"

"Because you're lying. You've been in this room for seven hours and you haven't left it once."

Diana turned away.

"You're useless to us if you don't eat. And *sleep*."

"You're starting to sound like Mom," Diana said, using a blue bandana to wipe the back of her neck.

"Ouch." Blair threw something and it landed in Diana's lap.

"What's this?"

"A sandwich." She smirked. "Eat it."

She pulled up a chair and sat down as Diana worked to peel back the plastic wrapping.

As Diana ate, her sister watched the screen. When the little boy was thrown onto his stomach again, his mouth visibly mouthing *No, no, wait*, Blair cursed.

"I don't know how you can watch this shit." Blair's throat was tight. "It makes me sick. And furious."

"I don't want to forget what a monster he is," Diana said, forcing another bite of ham, cheese, and lettuce into her mouth.

"Daniel is dead."

Imperceptibly, Diana flinched at the name. *Daniel.* Such a white, suburban name for the bastard who picked her up from school and locked her in a soundproof shed for months. Until she escaped and came back with a gun.

"I'm talking about Winter."

"This isn't Winter," Blair said, motioning vaguely toward the screen. "It's a whole bunch of other sick fucks."

"Winter finds them. He recruits them. Radicalizes them online. He helps them find kids, and worst of all, he circulates this shit across the four corners of the globe. Men all over the world are jerking off to this. These guys are animals, but Winter is the one who feeds them."

"When you disappeared—" Blair began.

"Don't," Diana warned. She didn't want to go down memory lane.

Not tonight, while so much weighed on her mind and every time she closed her eyes she saw Lou Thorne stepping from darkness, from nothing.

Impossible. She wouldn't let Spencer's pathetic mewling get to her.

Blair didn't seem to hear her, or she didn't care enough about Diana's wishes to stop. "It was the longest two months of my life. I thought you were dead. I *hoped* you were dead, because being alive meant—well, you know what it meant."

Diana snorted, shoving another bite of ham into her mouth.

Blair prattled on. "All I can think about is that right now, someone is out there lying awake thinking about these kids, wondering where they are, sick to death about them, wondering if they're ever going to come home. They're lying in their beds, staring at the ceiling and asking themselves what they're going to do if they never find out what happened, if they never see them again. How are they going to move on?"

"No one is wondering about him," Diana said, pointing at the little boy.

Blair looked up, obviously irritated by the interruption. "What?"

"He's not a missing child. That's his father."

Blair swore and took a deep breath. "I answered that question for myself. When I was the one lying in bed, worried sick about you, I asked myself how I was going to move on. And this isn't it, Dee. This isn't moving on. I thought if you got the guys that hurt you, you could move on, but you aren't. You just keep finding new targets."

"These kids—"

"You don't care about the kids!" Blair laughed, high and hysterical. "You go hard because you can't stop. You only do it for yourself. When is it going to be enough? *When?* When do we get to live our lives?"

Lou would understand, she thought. *No one is asking her to give up.*

"You don't have to stay," Diana said. "You can leave at any time. Go get yourself pregnant, pop out some kids, live in fucking suburbia for all I care. Go on."

She stopped short of saying, *I never asked you to be here.* Because that was a lie. She had asked Blair, practically begged her. But that was a long time ago, and Diana wasn't so convinced that she needed Blair anymore.

Not when there was someone who might understand her better.

Blair's jaw was set tight, flexing with unspoken words.

The screen flickered. No surprise.

Sometimes Winter's feed cut out suddenly. If he felt the line was compromised in any way, then he always cut and ran.

Then the second screen went dark too, and they could no longer see into King's office, or the apartment.

"What happened?" Diana said, sitting up and tapping the monitor as if slapping it would get it to turn back on.

Blair threw her hands up in surrender. "Yes, what did happen to your precious videos? I'd hate for you to be interrupted in the middle of such an important conversation."

Diana unplugged the computers, rebooted them, checked the server. Nothing.

"Maybe we just lost signal," Blair said.

Diana stood. "It's her."

"You can't—"

"It's *her*. She's done this because she's back."

"You're guessing," Blair said, in a voice one might use to calm wild animals.

But Diana was already lifting the communicator from the desk. She mashed the button with her thumb.

"Operation Retrie—" she said.

Blair shoved her thumb off the switch. "Dee, come on. Take a breath. You don't know—"

Diana wrenched away from her. "Operation Retrieval activates now. I want all teams mobile in five minutes. Go."

Diana slammed the comm down on the desk and gave her sister a pointed look.

"That's *rash*," Blair said, sitting back in her chair and crossing her arms. "What if you're wrong?"

"You'll see." Diana was already to the door, a spring in her step. She craved action after so much inactivity.

"Diana!"

She turned to find her sister staring at her with an unreadable expression. Disgust? Disappointment? Maybe a hint of fear.

She waited for the accusation.

You know our mother lost her mind like this. You're obsessive like she is. You've got to pull yourself back sometimes.

Blair had said this once, after the first time Winter had slipped through her fingers and Diana had blacked out with rage.

That's what you're for, Diana had told her.

But Diana frowned at her now, her disappointment like an itch in her throat. Maybe she had outgrown Blair. Maybe it was time for someone stronger—and more understanding.

Time for someone who was a hunter like her.

Blair thrust the half-eaten sandwich at her accusingly. "At least finish your sandwich."

18

———————

King woke to the sound of Lady barking. It was a high, strident sound of alarm. Then she whined and fell silent. Where was she? Mel's apartment? The stairwell?

Panic rocked through him.

He sat up in bed and opened his bedside table. There in the shadows sat his .357 Magnum. He pulled it out and balanced it on one knee, searching with the other hand for the ammunition amongst the tissues and a bottle of aspirin.

A cold metal cylinder as thin as a finger pressed into the side of his temple.

"Put it back in the drawer," a man said. His voice was muffled, as if his mouth was covered by a cloth.

When King didn't immediately respond, the gun was pressed into the side of his head hard enough to cock his neck to one side.

"*Now.*"

"All right," King said, sliding the gun back into the drawer and closing it. He left his hands palm up on the coverlet in his lap. "Now what?"

"On your knees, hands behind your back."

King slid from the bed to the floor, knowing that if someone had wanted him dead, they would likely have shot him already, unless their plan was to take him somewhere else and do it.

Lovely thought.

His knees creaked, and without meaning to, he threw a glance at the urn on the side table.

A yank fixed thin hard plastic strips across his wrist. They bit into his flesh. Why were they binding his hands behind his back with *zip ties?*

Black cloth slid down over his head and tightened at his throat with a drawstring.

Black sacks and zip ties, he thought. *This can't be good.*

His old claustrophobia rose.

The panic made his heart pound harder as the cloth flapped in and out against his face with each ragged breath.

But it was what he didn't hear that really frightened him. Lady. She should be raising hell right now. Why wasn't she? *Why?*

Before the terror could fully bloom, the butt of a gun struck him hard against the back of the skull.

Piper woke first. She'd sat up in Dani's bed with a start. Looking around the dim room, she tried to breathe against the pounding of her heart. But it was only Dani breathing softly beside her.

The room was still. The sliver of the hallway visible from the open bedroom door was also dark.

The apartment was silent. Nothing moved.

She exhaled. *That's what I get for watching* A Quiet Place *before bed.* The movie had been awesome, but not for one's anxiety.

Now every creak meant some monster was going to appear and rip her throat out. Still her breathing felt too loud, her heartbeat more like a battle drum played over a loudspeaker.

Then she saw it. A flashlight swept across the hallway wall, sliding over the bathroom's door frame, momentarily lighting the strike plate.

Without thinking, she sprang to her feet and ran to the other side of the room. She positioned herself behind Dani's bedroom door, pressing her shoulder blades against the cool plaster.

Dani sat up in bed, her mouth opening in question.

Piper shook her head furiously, putting a finger over her lips. She waved for her to lie down.

Dani did, but even from the wall Piper could hear her breathing.

Don't cry, Piper thought. *Please don't cry.*

She saw the end of the gun first, its slender black barrel emerging like a snake from the tall grass. As soon as Piper saw the gloved hand, she struck.

She grabbed the butt of the gun and yanked. Bullets sprayed into the bedroom floor.

Who the hell carries a fully automatic handgun?

Piper's elbow, cocked, slammed into the attacker's face. She felt something give—a nose? Lips splitting over teeth? Something hot smeared across the back of her arm.

She didn't know what she was doing, only that she couldn't let go of the gun. Not until it clicked, signaling that it was empty.

"Duck!"

Piper reacted to the sound of Dani's order, dipping her head low. An aluminum bat swept overhead, connecting hard with a body.

The attacker dropped like a sack of bricks and the emptied gun clattered to the hardwood floor.

In her mind, a mantra: *Lou! Lou, we need you! Lou!*

That's when electricity struck the back of her neck. Her body seized, every nerve in her body on fire.

The blackout was a mercy.

MEL WAS AT THE REGISTER, WRITING DOWN A LIST OF THINGS THAT needed to be done the following day.

Buy paper towels and receipt paper

Restock the love candles

Search the August catalog for new tarot decks

Call the distributor about the bead shipment

Send newsletter about Back to Ghoul sale

She'd come down into the closed shop with Lady when she realized sleep wouldn't find her tonight. Sometimes making lists helped to quiet her mind enough that she could finally settle down.

And the shop was a comfort to her. It was the smell of incense and wax and the gentle *scratch scratch scratch* of her pen pressing into the yellow notepad.

Lady snarled, jumping up from where she lay at Mel's feet.

Mel lifted her head only to find five guns pointed at her. Large ones, assault rifles by the look of it.

The soldiers holding them stood in full head-to-toe body armor. Her own face, with its ridiculous look of surprise, was mirrored back to her in their dark visors.

"This is a lot of firepower for an old woman," she said calmly, placing her hands on the glass case in front of her nice and slow.

Lady snapped, barking and darting toward the closest soldier—if soldiers were what they were. He—or she—turned their gun and thrust the butt down at the dog.

Lady was too quick, and the hilt slammed into the floor, gouging the wood.

Mel knew how this would end.

She knew that while these people might want her alive—for now—they likely didn't give two shits about her dog.

"*Assez!*" Melandra commanded. "*Restez, ma grande.*"

Lady whined, her ears lying flat against her head.

It was clear that her instincts differed greatly from the words spoken by her mistress, and because of that, a small war waged inside the canine. She snarled, but didn't lunge again.

"*Assez,*" Melandra repeated. She wanted to pet her, give her reassurances. *Je t'aime, ma grande.*

But she would rather save Lady's life than comfort her.

"You leave the dog alone," Melandra said, stepping around the counter, hands up in surrender. No need to give them a reason to shoot her outright. "I'll come just fine."

Tail tucked, Lady returned to her side, sitting down beside her. As she pressed the side of her body into Mel's leg, Mel felt the animal shaking.

"*Restez*," Mel said again.

Lady's ears twitched, but she was too well trained to disobey.

"*Restez*," she whispered over and over as they forced her onto her knees, tied her wrists, and slipped the black bag over her head.

LOU HAULED HER BODY OUT OF THE LAKE, HER SHOULDER screaming. The Alaskan night breathed cricket song around her. She needed pills. She needed anything that would quiet the raging burn of her wounded side.

The cooling La Loon waters had helped, but not enough.

I did too much, she thought. *I did too much too soon and I'm going to regret it.*

But she'd killed the Czech drug lord and had carried his body to the shores of La Loon. Jabbers had seemed all too happy to see that things had returned to normal.

Now Lou longed for a hot shower, a good night's sleep, and a fistful of painkillers.

Until the alarm bells rocketed through her. Like a fishhook in the gut, she was jerked forward.

Dani's terror was the strongest and loudest. It was so strong that Lou found her arms shaking with it.

Lou pulled her gun, able only to fully command her good side, and checked the bullets. They would have to do.

19

———————

Piper came to on the wooden floor of an empty apartment. Or maybe a house. It was the light socket with a white plastic cover that came into focus first.

They were still in the Quarter. She knew the sounds of this neighborhood the way one knows the sound of their parents' voices. She'd been running these streets as soon as she was old enough to hop on the streetcar alone. There was the trumpet music from Jackson Square and Ariana Grande blaring from a nearby bar.

A sudden swell of bluegrass music fought with the Ariana Grande remix, which made her think they were on Bourbon Street, or close to it.

Piper pulled herself to sitting, groaning. The room spun like the time she smashed two hurricanes on a dare.

You never drink liquor sweeter than Kool-Aid, Henry had warned her. And he'd been right.

She groaned. "The hell, man."

"You were tased, by the look of that scorch mark on your neck," King said. He sounded perfectly calm beside her. His legs were stretched out in front of him, his arms behind his back. Beside him was Mel, looking equally serene.

"Really?" Piper murmured. "Some asshole *tased* me?"

And why did they look so calm? Were they really getting so used to these attacks that they could just roll through them now? True, this cozy apartment, though empty, was better than the garage Dmitri Petrov had holed them up in. This place had none of that torture dungeon feel to it.

Only they weren't all perfectly calm.

Someone whimpered beside Piper. She turned and saw Dani on the floor in the fetal position, tears running down her face.

"Oh shit." She scooted across to her. "Baby. Hey, baby. Look at me."

Dani didn't look up. Her whole body was shaking.

"Hey, shhh. Baby. Look at me. Look at me."

"We tried that," Mel said calmly.

Dani rolled her eyes up to meet Piper's.

Piper forced a smile. "See? You're okay. I'm okay. Everything's fine."

Dani's breathing thinned out even more.

"God, why is she breathing like that?" Piper asked.

"She's having a panic attack," Mel said.

"Baby, you've got to slow down. Slow, deep breaths."

Someone snorted, an aborted laugh, and this dismissive sound made Piper look up.

It was Diana. Her sleek blond hair was pulled back in a ponytail at the nape of her neck. Her big blue eyes were round. She looked like a soccer mom with an unhinged gleam in her eye, especially with the gun in her hand.

A woman in tight leather pants leaned against the door to this small room, regarding the scene impassively. Something about their faces looked similar. Maybe the nose or chin. The brow? Piper couldn't be sure.

The room was hot and growing hotter with the six bodies crowded inside it. With the floor and walls bare and Piper's hands tied behind her back, there was nothing that could be used to defend herself.

Piper spotted a gray box on the wall and thought it might be a cabinet, but upon closer inspection, it was only a breaker box.

"Pathetic. I haven't touched her." Diana's voice was surprisingly melodic for a freaking crazy person.

"She has PTSD, you piece of shit! Untie her."

"Please," Dani said, between gasps. "*P-please.*"

Diana rolled her eyes. "She'll live."

"That's more than you're going to do," Piper spat, forcing herself onto her knees. She was trying to position her weight so she could stand. It was harder than she'd thought it'd be. Some distant part of her mind thought, *If we get out of this, I'm going to need to do more squats.*

"When I get out of this I'm going—"

The slap was hard and fast. It rocked Piper off her feet, costing her the ground she'd recovered.

"You'll *what?*" Diana laughed into her face. "You won't do sh—"

Diana disappeared.

One minute she was leaning over Piper, her face glowing with that murderous rage that Piper had seen somewhere before but couldn't place. Then she was gone.

Piper's gaze adjusted to the low light in time to see Diana slammed against the wall, her feet three inches off the floor. She was pinned by the strong hand holding her. She was choking as her boots scuffed black marks against the plaster in their thrashing.

It was Lou who had her pinned against the wall. Lou, dripping wet, her hair, jacket, and shoes all soaked. Small droplets fell from her matted strands onto the floor beneath her.

The gun was in her left hand, but Piper thought it looked like an afterthought. She didn't like the way that arm hung loose at her side.

She couldn't lift that thing if she tried.

The woman in the leather pants pressed a gun to the back of Lou's head. "Put her down."

Lou lowered Diana three inches so her feet touched the wood, but she didn't take her hand off her throat.

"I didn't hurt them," Diana said, clawing at Lou's fist.

"Liar," Piper said.

"I swear," Diana said. "I just wanted you to come. I told you I could—"

Lou shifted her grip on the gun, before opening the power box, revealing a network of circuitry.

"What are you—"

Once swipe and the lights went out. Someone pulled a trigger and a bullet bit into a wall, spraying plaster across the room.

"Christ!" Diana screamed. "Don't shoot!"

Then Piper felt hands on her, and the familiar shift of the world rearranging itself to Lou's will.

When it reformed, she was in King's apartment. There was the oversized red sofa. There were the worn records leaning slanted against each other, smelling like the old man's weed. Party lights from the fourth of July still hung on the balcony.

King, Mel, and Dani were all on the floor, trying to right themselves. But they were alone. They were safe.

"I've got scissors in that drawer," King called out, nodding toward the kitchen. "No, not that one. The one on the end."

Lou opened and slammed drawers until she produced a pair of blue-handled scissors. She snipped their zip ties one at a time.

Mel was up and out of the apartment. "Lady? Lady!"

The door slammed shut behind her.

When Piper's hands broke free, relief hit her like a wave. In the next instant she had Dani in her arms, holding her, rocking her.

"It's okay," Piper said, pushing back her sweat-soaked bangs. "It's over, it's over. Lou is going to kill that stupid—"

King spoke as if Piper hadn't. "She took us but didn't hurt us—why? What point is she trying to make?"

"Because she's crazy," Piper said. "And you're going to kill her, right?"

"I've never killed a woman before."

"Yeah, well, first time for everything." Piper wished she could read that look on Lou's face. She didn't understand it. Lou was a killer. She killed the people who threatened her friends—why wouldn't she just finish Diana already?

"Is she going to be okay?" Lou asked, pushing her wet hair back from her face. Her left arm remained immobile at her side.

"She'll be fine," Piper said, still rocking the woman in her arms. Dani was finally starting to quiet, but her shaking was worse. "When you *kill* Diana."

Then Lady was there. She bounded into the apartment and nosed her way between Dani and Piper.

"Hey!" Piper said.

But Dani took to the dog like a bird to air. She wrapped her arms around Lady's neck and sobbed. Piper decided not to take this personally.

"Go," King said, nodding toward Lou. "Find out what this is about and end it."

Lou stepped back into King's dark bedroom and was gone.

DIANA FLIPPED ON THE LIGHTS. SHE TURNED A FULL CIRCLE IN THE empty room, not understanding what she was seeing.

"Are they out there?" she called.

Spencer stood in the doorway, his gun shaking in his hand. "No one came this way."

"Give me that before you hurt yourself." Diana tugged the gun out of his hand.

She pulled open the closet door and ran her hands along the walls. "No. No."

"She disappeared," Blair said plainly. "And she took them with her."

"People don't *disappear*."

"*She* did."

Diana didn't like the fear in Blair's voice. It made her uneasy. The pop of a gunshot made them both turn.

Pop. Pop. Pop.

Something crashed to the floor hard enough to make the house shake. A window blasted open and brassy bluegrass galloped into the room.

In the doorway, Spencer turned.

"No!" Diana stepped around him and into the path of Lou's aim. But this time, Diana had her own gun lifted.

"I'm sorry," she spat, seeing the cold, empty stare that greeted her. "Okay? I'm *sorry*. I took your friends to get your attention. I wanted to show you that I wasn't some incapable loser. I have resources. I can run an operation. And I want your help. That's it. I didn't hurt them. And I think I made my point."

Lou didn't move. Her expression remained unchanged.

Diana's heart knocked in her throat. She swallowed against it. *What can I say? What would I say to myself?*

Blair's breath came in pants beside her.

She thinks I'm about to be shot, Diana noted distantly.

Before she could say anything, Lou whispered, "Why me?"

Diana hadn't been expecting this question. *Why not you?*

She thought Lou understood her own power.

"Who else?" Diana said. "Seriously, who else can do what you do?"

Lou lowered her gun.

Diana tried to seal the deal. "I hate bad guys. You hate bad guys. And my guy is the worst. He's not just a pedophile, he runs a billion-dollar child pornography business underground."

Diana dared to take a step toward her.

"I read about your parents, about your dad," she ventured. Lou's eyes seemed to darken, fill up with black. Diana took a breath and pressed on. "You know how I feel, Louie. I can't eat. I can't sleep. I can't—I need this. I need *you*."

She looked down for dramatic effect.

Then she flicked her eyes up, hoping to see some change in Lou's expression. "You'll *enjoy* hunting him. I promise."

Blair shifted nervously in her periphery, but Diana held her smile. It wasn't easy in the face of that cold stare. She'd never seen anything like it. It was wind blowing across the tundra, as if Lou was made of snow and ice herself.

At last Lou lowered the gun, but the cold fire didn't leave her eyes. "Tell me about him."

20

Dani shook on the apartment floor. Her matted hair was stuck to her face. She looked feverish, red-cheeked, eyes glassy. They'd covered her in King's comforter, stripped from his bed. But her teeth still chattered as if it were the dead of winter.

"What can we do for her?" Piper asked, pacing nervously. She wrung her hands.

"I'll be back." Mel rose from her crouch and left through the kitchen door.

King remained on the floor beside Dani, a mug of hot tea in one hand, a cup of water in the other. "You want something to drink?" he asked hopefully.

She didn't even look at him.

Piper ran her hand down her face again. She'd never seen Dani like this before. Her fears and anxieties would rise up suddenly, sure. Sometimes when they were in a club or a bar, she would get this look on her face, and Piper knew it was time to get some air. Or she'd move a little closer on the sofa during a movie. The movement wouldn't be tinged with sweetness or desire—there was a desperate need in it. And there were the dreams from which she woke up screaming.

But this...

She tried to remember the things she'd read about PTSD and what *not* to do.

"Baby," Piper said, trying to get those dark eyes to look into hers. They wouldn't. "Dani, listen."

Dani continued to shake.

"You've gone through this before and you can get through this again. And we're going to sit right here with you, me, King, and Mel, for as long as it takes."

Lady whined.

"And Lady. We're not going to leave you alone until it's over. You're safe. I promise."

Dani looked up, meeting Piper's eyes for the first time. But they were still unfocused.

Melandra appeared with a prescription bottle, orange with a white plastic cap. "Here."

She opened the bottle and shook a round blue pill out onto her hand. "Dani, open up."

"Are you just going to give her a Valium?" Piper asked. "Is this consensual?"

"If we take her to the hospital, they will sedate her with or without her permission. I don't see how this is different."

Cursing inwardly, Piper held the water glass, flinching against the way Dani automatically drank it down.

Someone could take her onto the balcony and tell her to jump and she would. Piper didn't like this checked-out version of Dani.

She's somewhere else. She's somewhere very, very far away.

Come back, baby.

"Did any of you try to contact Lou while Dennard had us?" King asked suddenly. He stretched his neck to one side but didn't try to get up.

Piper loved him for that. She knew that sitting on the floor must be really hard for his old bones, but he stayed right beside Dani like he'd said he would.

"I did," Piper said. "A million times."

"Me too," Melandra said.

"But she didn't come right away," King said. "You know what that means?"

No, Piper didn't know what it meant. All of her attention was on Dani. She wondered how long it would take the Valium to kick in.

"She can't hear us when she's in La Loon," he said.

"What is your point?" Piper said, chewing on her thumb.

"Lou has her limitations. Her shoulder was the first warning. Tonight was another."

"It's hard to forget she's human sometimes," Melandra admitted, pushing Dani's hair back from her face so she could rub her forehead and neck with a warm cloth.

"But she is," King said. "And she won't always be able to step in and handle a situation. We need to get serious about our own security."

The light returned to Dani's eyes. She looked up and sighed. She stopped trembling.

"That's better," Melandra said, encouraging. "You like the hot cloth? I'll make you another."

Mel's knees popped as she rose. At the sink, she rewarmed the rag with the running faucet.

"Let's move her to the sofa so she can lay down," King said. Piper lifted her torso and King grabbed her legs. They moved in tandem, placing her limp body on the red leather. King put a pillow under her head and repositioned the blanket.

Lady looked up at King imploringly.

"All right," he said. "Just this once."

Lady hopped up onto the sofa and draped herself over Dani. She laid her head on the girl's stomach.

Mel placed the warm rag on Dani's forehead. "Her breathing is better."

"Yeah," Piper said, noting the same. "Is she going to be okay?"

"She'll be okay," Mel assured her with a squeeze. "She just needs some time."

"Are we going to talk about why you have a prescription for Valium?"

Mel gave a crooked smile. "Dani isn't the only one who gets panicky."

The pressure between Piper's ears intensified. Lady's ears flicked and her tail began to thump against the sofa.

Piper turned and found Lou emerging from King's darkened bedroom. Her hair was still wet, her cheeks red. She had a gun in her right hand and Piper was pretty sure that was blood splattered on her face.

Mel made a small sound of surprise, her eyes roving Lou's body. "I'll make another rag."

"Tell me that psycho is dead," Piper said.

"Dennard's alive."

"*Why?*" Piper hissed.

"Shhh," King said, raising his hand and waving at them. "She's finally dropped off to sleep."

Piper looked down at Dani, her dark hair framing her face. Her eyes were closed and her breathing a slow, steady rhythm.

Restraining her voice to a whisper, she said, "*Why* is she alive?"

"She wants to destroy a pedophile."

"Who cares what she wants?" Piper raised her fingers and pressed them into her temple. "Do you have any idea what she put Dani through tonight?"

Lou's brow creased. She looked the sleeping girl over. "She hurt her?"

"Not physically, but Dani had a freaking panic attack because some *psycho* kidnapped her, and you're just going to give her a pass for that?"

"Back up," King said. "Tell me about the guy she's hunting."

"Goes by Winter. He runs a child pornography ring on the internet."

King shrugged. "I've never heard of him? Does he work alone?"

"No, he finds and recruits abusers through the internet and pays them to live stream the attacks."

"Why live stream? Why not pictures and video?"

"Harder to trace. No agency can track it. Once the feed is terminated, it's gone."

"Sounds smart." King rubbed the back of his neck. "I prefer my criminals stupid."

"I want to get the children first."

King snorted in disbelief. "There are thousands of kids being raped every day. I'm not saying it's a good thing, but you're not going to be able to move them all in a night."

Lou's eyes darkened. "I'll start with the ones Winter broadcasts. Then I'll take out the abusers and move the kids."

Piper put her hands on her hips. "Okay, fine. There's a worthy cause here and we can help. But then what?"

"Then I'll kill Winter," Lou said.

"And *then?*" Piper pressed.

When Lou didn't seem to understand, King said, "She wants you to kill Dennard."

"Why?"

"Why?" Piper squeezed the bridge of her nose. *Because she kidnapped us. Because she slapped me. Because I took one look at that woman and realized how crazy and how dangerous she is. And if we don't shake her she's going to hurt us,* really *hurt us.*

Did Lou really have no sense of self-preservation? Couldn't she tell when there was someone in the room that you didn't screw with?

Maybe not, if you usually are that person.

Piper exhaled. "Because she's not our friend, Louie! She's not a good guy."

"She wants to destroy a pedophile. Why should I stop her?"

"Easy now," King said, raising his hands. "Everyone take a breath. Piper..."

Piper's jaw was clenching and unclenching, but she managed to roll her eyes up to meet King's.

He leveled her with a soft look. "What happened to Dani scared us, but she's going to be okay. And so are we."

Piper shook her head. "We can't be buddy-buddy with this woman. We can't have another psychopath hanging around. One is enough."

She hadn't meant to say that. She was angry, and tired, and Dani's condition *had* scared her. It'd scared the *hell* out of her.

Piper looked at Lou. She saw nothing. No recognition. No reaction to her words. Her heart plummeted into her stomach.

"No psychopaths," Lou said coldly. "Got it."

And disappeared.

21

Lou wasn't entirely sure where she was going when she stepped from the dark of King's apartment into nothing. She welcomed the compression, the escape.

She shouldn't have been surprised it was Konstantine's apartment that formed around her, his living room with its uneven clay-tiled floor and a large desk set off to one side. An archway showcased the open kitchen.

His desk lamp was on and he was typing away at his laptop with a steaming mug of something within arm's reach.

He looked up and frowned. "You have blood on your face."

"Do I?" she asked. She could smell his shampoo and cologne from where she stood. His hair was still wet from a shower.

His frown deepened. "Is it yours?"

She wiped her face. "I don't think so."

Something in him relaxed. "The others?"

"Everyone's alive."

Here his lips twitched with a smile. "The blood on your face says otherwise."

"King, Piper, Melandra, and Dani are alive," she amended. She shrugged out of her leather coat, but had a hard time doing it.

He hissed when he saw her bare shoulder. "That is swollen. Badly."

"It hurts," she admitted.

He raised an eyebrow, rising from his seat and crossing to her. He inspected it without touching it. His frown only deepened. "It must be nearly unbearable for you to say that. It looks really bad. Come on."

He led her up the stairs to his bedroom above. He stepped into the bathroom and turned on the shower. On a hook, he hung a fresh towel.

"I don't need you to take care of me," she said.

"We've already established this." He gave her a forced smile. "Can you indulge me?"

She stepped out of her pants easily enough, but when it came to pulling the shirt over her head, she found her arm wouldn't move.

Konstantine was frowning again. "Did this happen in the fight with Diana?"

"It was already...irritated."

"How?"

She didn't want to talk about Jiri, about the hunt in Prague. She only rolled her eyes up to his, daring him to press her on it.

He didn't. "You must have compounded the injury. I have something you can take, after your shower, if you want it."

"Something legal?"

He laughed. "Yes."

She gave a slight nod.

"May I cut this?" he asked, pulling scissors from the vanity.

Lou didn't care. The shirt was already ruined with the blood caked into its fibers. So she let him cut it from her body so that her arm didn't have to move. Then she stepped into the steaming stream and closed the glass door behind her.

Konstantine gathered up her clothes and disappeared. She was left with only her thoughts.

Traitorously, they ran on a loop.

Piper's angry face. Dani, sweaty and panting on King's sofa. Even Lady's look of admonishment. Who knew a dog could scold with her eyes?

Lou felt like she'd done something wrong. And she couldn't recall the last time she'd had this feeling. When her aunt Lucy was sick, dying, maybe. There'd been a hint of this feeling, of *not okay*, that had permeated everything then as well.

But that look in Piper's eyes.

Piper. *Yelling* at her.

Had Piper ever yelled at her before? No. Piper was a cheerful person. Lou had seen her cry a few times, usually when it came to her drug-addicted mother, but those unhappy feelings had never been directed at Lou before.

She'd never looked at Lou as if somehow Lou had *betrayed* her.

Lou exhaled and scrubbed her face with a cloth. She washed her hair and body and made slow work of it, given her one able arm.

After she stepped out and wrapped herself in the soft towel, she found a comb in Konstantine's medicine cabinet.

In the bedroom, he'd laid out a pair of his black sweats and a large, loose white shirt.

She put them on and sat on the edge of the bed to brush out her hair.

When she heard a noise, she turned and found him standing there, a glass of water in one hand and a small sauce cup with two pills in the other. He was watching her with a strange expression.

"What is it?" she asked.

He started as if remembering himself. "My mother used to sit on the end of my bed and brush out her hair."

"This bed?"

"No," he said, his smile widening. "It was a long time ago. Here."

He handed her the water first. She had to set down the comb so she could take it with her good hand. Her bad shoulder felt better after being pummeled by the hot water, but it still throbbed. She'd done too much too soon, and that was painfully clear now as the night was moving in on her, as the adrenaline was leaving her and her muscles were stiffening.

"What is this?" she asked, opening her hand for the pills.

"It's your Vicodin, which you stopped taking." His voice held a hint of playful challenge. It reminded her of Lucy's *I told you* voice.

She remembered leaving the hospital with a prescription for it after she was shot. She'd taken it for a week, when the pain was at its worst, and mostly slept because she was so tired. But after that she hadn't liked feeling dull in her mind or in her body. She hadn't realized Konstantine had kept the rest of the pills.

"I doubt I can convince you to see a doctor. I'll settle for immobilizing the arm and treating it until the swelling goes down. And if you *rest*, your shoulder should feel okay in a few days."

"We're going to go after Winter," she said.

He stood and placed the water on a small desk against the wall. "Of course you are. And who is Winter?"

"It's a fake internet name."

He gave her a patient smile. "Yes, I know what a handle is. What do you know about him?"

Lou did her best to recount what Diana had told her.

He positioned himself against the headboard. "I'll see what I can find out. I hate those who prey on children. When are you moving against him?"

"That hasn't been decided. But King is on board."

After a pause, he said, "I heard that Jiri Svoboda went missing tonight. Any chance you've been to Prague?"

She met his gaze. "Was he one of yours?"

He laughed. "Yes. Would you have spared him if you'd known? Did you know?"

"No," she said. It was a blanket answer to both questions.

He smiled. "I didn't think so. He can be replaced. But you do love causing trouble for me—and yourself—don't you?"

He was so beautiful there, relaxed, his hair framing his deep green eyes.

She kissed him. She hadn't known she was going to do it until her lips were pressed against his.

"Hello," he said, a laugh in his voice, as she settled her weight against his lap. "*Buonasera.*"

When she began to rock her hips, just slightly, he stopped her.

"As tempting as you are," he said, his face flushed. "Do you want to make your shoulder worse than it already is?"

Piper's face flashed in her mind again. Why? Why did it keep haunting her like that? When was the last time anything had haunted her?

"What's wrong?" Konstantine asked. When she didn't answer, he said, "If you really want—"

"No." She sat up.

"Was it something I said?"

"I was thinking about Piper."

His brow arched. "Do you often think of lesbians when you are in bed with me?"

His joke fell flat. Lou was too far away, deep in the recesses of her mind. "She's mad at me."

"For what?"

"I don't know."

He snorted, settling back against his pillows. "It is true I am not an expert on women, but what I do know is that they're usually only mad at you if you've done something wrong."

Wrong.

There it was again, that feeling of *not okay*. It made her itch under the collar. It made her want to hold a gun.

"What did she say?" he asked.

We can't have another psychopath hanging around. One is enough.

"She doesn't want me to work with Diana."

"But you agreed to anyway."

"Yes."

"Why?"

When she met his eyes, he flinched. "I'm not questioning your judgment. I'm only asking your reason."

"They're hurting children."

"Okay. But do you need to work with her to save them?"

Lou turned the question over in her mind, but it blurred out, grew fuzzy. She felt her eyes fluttering.

"The Vicodin is working. You should sleep." He patted the bed beside him. "All of this can wait."

He said it as if she had a choice.

But even as the darkness reached out to take her into its arms, it was still Piper's hard, accusing face that she carried with her into the deep.

22

———————

King wasn't sure Lou would come. He sat at his desk sipping coffee, his eyes straying to the door labeled *Ms. Thorne* every few seconds. He'd even made the coffee himself, using the small coffeemaker in the office, lest he should miss her by going down to the café.

He was trying to get some work done, but it wasn't easy. He kept thinking of the night before, of Dani's panic attack, of Piper's anger. He'd known about Mel sometimes taking Valium. She'd turned down his offer to smoke weed once or twice because of it.

"You're too late," she'd said. "I already took a pill. I don't chase my downers with downers."

And drama aside, there was something irresistible about Diana's offer. It was a great case, busting a large pornography ring.

But he wanted to go over the plans for the move against Winter. And he wanted to make it absolutely clear to Lou what she had to risk by working with someone like Dennard.

Only one concern plagued him. When Lou had left, she'd been too quiet. *More* quiet, he thought. It was the sort of silence that unsettled him. It usually meant that Lou was about to do something he wouldn't like.

He glanced at the closed door, leaning back in his chair. He wondered if he could step out for lunch, albeit quickly. He was getting hungry again.

That morning, during a tech blackout, King—with Konstantine's assistance—had been able to find and remove the cameras and bugs.

"We have an uneasy truce with Diana," he said to the urn on his desk. "We'll see where this gets us."

His heart ached. He missed his wife. Not just her smile, and her laugh. He also missed her brain. She would know what to do about Dennard—about Lou.

You forget I came to you for help, her distant voice reminded him.

His eyes flicked to the closed door again. Nothing.

Come on, come on, he urged. This time he even sent a page, hoping it would be picked up by the GPS watch Lou often wore.

Piper's door was also closed, but the girl wasn't home. King and Mel had both given her the day off so she could stay with Dani. King had offered to let Dani keep Lady until she felt better, but there was something about a cat named...Taffy? Tabby? He hadn't caught that part.

Lady stayed with Mel.

The door creaked suddenly and King jolted.

Lou stepped into the office, complete with leather jacket and mirrored shades. Her hair was pulled back in a low ponytail today, but a few dark strands hung around the sides of her face.

"Hey," King breathed, wondering if his relief was too obvious. He held back from saying, *You came*.

"I got your page." Her eyes fell on Piper's empty seat and her shoulders sagged.

"She's off today," King said. "It's just us."

Was that relief he saw flicker across her face?

"You okay?" he ventured.

The stiffness returned.

"Never mind," he said. "Let's talk about Winter. Do you know anything about him?"

"Not yet. Konstantine's searching."

King decided to go for sunny and see where that got him. "That's okay. We'll learn what we need to know."

She hadn't lifted her shades yet, so King couldn't see her eyes. Not a good sign.

"I placed a call to Sampson this morning and he's going to see if Winter is in the system at all. But before we get to that, we need to talk about you."

Lou scowled. "Me?"

"How are you going to protect yourself from Dennard?"

"With a gun."

King laughed. "I mean your abilities. It's one thing to have Konstantine wipe footage or destroy cameras. He's not going to be able to do a damn thing if Diana sees you in action with her own eyes."

"I'll be careful."

Like you were last night? He thought of the room going dark.

"I don't think that'll be enough," King said. "Not for someone like her. People like Dennard are observant, meticulous. She's going to try to figure you out. Hell, she's already trying."

He worried he was veering toward a lecture. Nothing would send Lou running like a lecture. He ran a hand through his hair.

"I'm just saying she can't be trusted with that information. If you're not going to kill her."

"Why should I?" Lou asked.

The genuineness of the question surprised him. It was as if she was looking for a legitimate reason.

"When that reporter from *The Herald* tracked you down, you shot him, didn't you?" It was a rhetorical question. "And if she finds out, would you kill her too?"

"I've revealed my gifts to people without killing them before. Women," she amended.

So it's about the fact that she's a woman.

Damn. King had hoped that wasn't the case. He understood that one day they would find Lou's weakness, whatever it was. He knew she wouldn't hurt children, but children rarely hunt you down and try to shoot you.

This Dennard woman was a different problem. She wasn't like the women Lou was used to saving. If Lou didn't wrap her head around that, she might end up dead for it.

"She doesn't have your abilities," King began, looking for an opening, "but Dennard is very dangerous. Would you shoot preemptively, if someone like you was on your trail?"

She didn't have an answer.

King sighed. He was beginning to feel old again. The feeling was coming on more and more frequently these days, making his mind ache as badly as his body.

"All I'm saying is that we need a plan. It's too dangerous to let her know what you can do."

"She might have already put it together," Lou said.

"Because of last night? I doubt it. She probably thinks you've got tricks. Escape rooms or tunnels in every French Quarter building. I guarantee by the end of the day she'll have convinced herself that you came through a trap door or something. You'd be surprised the bullshit people peddle to themselves when they can't understand something. In the 1700s, they'd had no problem believing in witchcraft. Today? No way. People are too *sensible*. It'll be worse for someone like Dennard, who prides herself on her sensibility."

Lou watched his face for a long moment. Finally, she pulled up the chair to the other side of King's desk. "How do we take down Winter without letting Dennard know what I can do?"

His excitement spiked. He couldn't help it. His love of a good challenge had driven him toward law enforcement in the beginning. Playing by the rules and still winning the game—that was something he understood.

"First, we need to know her plan. She must have one if she's been obsessing about this guy for a while. Once we talk to her and see where she's at, we can build our sham operation around hers. It'll be brilliant, actually."

Famous last words, he thought, glancing at the urn.

He wanted it to work. He wanted to keep his promise to his dead wife, Louie's aunt, that he would keep Lou safe.

"How do we build a sham operation?" she asked. "There's only six of us. And you're not a cop anymore."

A knot loosened in his chest. "I've got a plan."

DIANA STEPPED INTO THE HOUSE EXPECTING...SOMETHING ELSE.

When they'd brought the detective, the shopkeeper, and those two whimpering fools in, the townhouse had been pristine. Now it looked like a Halloween attraction.

She stretched on the latex gloves, scowling at the blood pooled on the kitchen floor. Bending down to inspect the damage, she wrinkled her nose.

The smell of it was heady, fruity to the point of intoxication, and it made her skin crawl.

Diana had selected the building because the bottom level was protected by a secluded garden. This meant that neighbors and passersby couldn't see the entrance or what happened past the town-home's high gate. It had helped that it was only a block from King's office. It had made it easy to bring them in without arousing suspicion.

But it might not have been only to her advantage.

Had Lou relied on this entrance?

Diana had done a headcount that morning and could account for only five of their original crew—including Spencer, Blair, and herself. That either meant Lou killed fifteen people or some of them ran off.

Steph and Sarah Zink—Diana's favorites—had stayed. But everyone else was gone.

Maybe after meeting Lou's gaze down the barrel of her gun, she should be running too. But here she was, mopping blood off the floor.

The stairs creaked and Diana stood, looking into the hallway.

It was Blair, with a knit brow and her own pair of black nitrite gloves. "No bodies. Where the hell are all the bodies?"

"Maybe Lou has a cleanup crew."

Blair snorted, stepping into the kitchen. "Shitty cleanup crew. There's blood everywhere."

"Any idea on how many she shot?"

"If each of the big puddles counts as a body, then fourteen."

Maybe she took them all. Somehow that was better. Diana hated nothing more than cowards.

"But maybe someone ran off," Blair offered. "Can you blame them?"

Diana scowled at her. "Don't tell me you're a chickenshit too."

"I'm just saying, the woman dropped fourteen people in less than a minute. She was in and out of this building and took four people with her before we could get the lights back on. If you aren't concerned, then you're stupid."

"Stupid? No." Diana wasn't stupid. Diana was pissed.

She wanted to know how Lou did it. How did she get in and out so quickly? How did she kill so quickly? *How, how, how?*

The admiration only carried so far. Then it soured, hardening into envy.

There was much more to Louie Thorne—she *knew* it. She only had to crack her code.

"She's dangerous," Blair said, stepping over a puddle of blood. "*Too* dangerous, frankly."

Diana gestured at the room, at the house. "Look at what she can do. Think of what *we* could do with her help."

Diana thought herself magnanimous for the use of *we.* In truth, it was an *I* that framed her fantasies.

I'm going to kill Winter. This time I'll pull it off.

"What we're doing is fine," Blair insisted. "You don't need her to bring down Winter. You don't."

"You don't understand."

"I do!" Blair exclaimed. "You're the one who can't get your head out of your ass and see what you're doing. Take the blinders off, Dee!"

Diana's face hardened. "If you're scared, you can leave."

Her irritation chewed at the back of her neck, nipped at her earlobes. Blair never broke rank with her. Why would she do it now, at such an important moment, when they were so close?

Lou had agreed to help them, hadn't she?

Winter was within her reach.

But if you're being honest with yourself, it's not only about Winter anymore, is it?

"I'm not leaving. I promised that I'd see this to the end with you and I'll do it," Blair said, her jaw tight and face red. "I just want you to tell me where the end is."

"I don't need your doom and gloom today, Blair."

Her sister took a deep breath. "What *do* you need then?"

"Manpower."

23

"Here you go," Piper said, bringing the hot tea to Dani's bedside and placing it on the end table. "And a little saucer for you to put the tea bag in so it doesn't oversteep. I know you hate that."

"Thanks." Dani's voice was gruff. Her face was still puffy and her eyes red. She'd slept for almost twelve hours, but she looked far from refreshed.

Dani caught her staring. "Do I look that bad?"

"You're beautiful," Piper said without pause.

Dani gave her a weak smile. "My chest hurts."

"I think that's from the panic attack." While Dani had slept and Piper had kept watch over her, she'd read what felt like a thousand articles about PTSD on her phone. It was common for people who had had a panic attack to feel sore the next day from the barrage of contracting muscles.

A Valium hangover could also leave someone feeling subdued, tired, and out of it. Between the two, Piper had a good sense of what Dani might feel like right now.

Meow.

Piper glanced at her leg and saw Octavia, Dani's cat, rubbing against her legs.

"You're trying to kill me," Piper said.

"She knows you're allergic," Dani said, lifting the mug and blowing the steam. "She wants you to love her anyway."

"I do," Piper said, sniffing and rubbing her nose. The fluffy British Blue was beautiful and mostly sweet, though Piper had seen her sassy side a few times in their months together.

Oh god, her eyes were already starting to water. "But I still can't pick her up and put her by my face if I want to keep breathing."

When Piper looked up, smiling, she saw Dani was nearly in tears.

"What? What is it?" Alarm shivered through her. "Babe, I love Tavi."

"No, it's not that," she said, her lip trembling. "I hate you seeing me like this. I can't believe—"

"Hey, *no*." Piper rushed to the side of the bed and sat down in the small space between the edge and Dani's covered legs. "Don't do that. Don't beat yourself up. What happened was bullshit. It shouldn't have happened. But we're fine. We got out of there. You're okay. I'm okay. Everyone's okay. Except Lou, who is out of her damn mind, but I'm hoping that will pass."

Dani's gaze was a million miles away, but at least the tears were holding off. Piper hated it when girls cried. It never failed to leave her feeling helpless and inadequate.

"I suppose I asked for this," Dani whispered, sniffling.

"What? No."

"I'm the one who keeps insisting that I be an investigative reporter. I'm the one who keeps asking King for cases even though things like this are going to keep happening. I knew it'd be dangerous and that I'm not as—not as *together* as I used to be, but I keep doing it. What's wrong with me?"

"We could always quit our jobs and open a cat café. Everyone loves cats and coffee. We'd be billionaires. Except, you know, I'd die of anaphylactic shock."

Dani didn't laugh. She pressed the heels of her hands against her eyes.

"Hey," Piper said, taking her hands. "Listen to me."

When Dani looked up her eyes were rimmed red.

"Something terrible happened to you. Some absolute *bullshit*, and instead of giving up on your dream, you're still chasing it. That's *amazing*. Seriously, do you have any idea how incredible that is? You're not backing down, you're not quitting. You're going to have bad days, but you keep getting up and kicking ass and that's what matters. Daniella Allendale, you're *incredible*."

"There were a lot of compliments in there."

"Yeah, well, how many do you need before you believe me?"

"A billion," Dani replied, and then she smiled.

Tavi jumped up onto the bed.

"Hey, not mine!" Piper cried, taking the pillows on her side of the bed and pushing them under the blankets. "Seriously, your cat has it in for me."

"She just likes women who play hard to get."

"Am I playing hard to get?" Piper asked with a smile. She leaned in, putting her lips in range for a kiss.

Dani grinned, an honest-to-goodness grin. "No. Not really."

Dani's lips were warm and swollen, sticky to the touch, but Piper didn't mind. She'd take any kiss from this girl, however it came. She reached her hand into Dani's hair and pulled her closer.

"You're okay," Piper said, pressing her forehead to Dani's. "You can do this."

"What happened?" Dani asked, her breath warm on Piper's mouth. "After I passed out."

Piper gave her the rundown of Lou's rescue and the aftermath in King's apartment. The only part Dani remembered was Lady comforting her. Piper didn't mention that Diana had slapped her. She wasn't sure that Lou even realized it had happened. She thought she might have appeared a second after the fact.

If she told Lou that it happened, what would she do? Would she finally kill Diana on the spot or shrug it off? And if she shrugged it off...

Piper's heart clenched. "I don't get why she doesn't just finish her off. She's a bad guy. She kills bad guys. Period. Full stop."

"Didn't she tell us once she'd never killed a woman?"

"Who gives a shit if she's a woman? Women can be evil too."

Dani sipped her tea. "Maybe she's just curious."

"What do you mean, curious? About *what?*"

"About someone like her. There's another woman out there, hunting and killing these guys, and I don't think she's ever encountered that before. She's got to be curious. It's like finally seeing her own kind or something."

"Diana is not her kind."

We can't have another psychopath hanging around. One is enough.

Piper flinched. "Though I might have implied that she was."

Dani lowered the mug, her face pinched in confusion. "What do you mean?"

Piper replayed the conversation, embarrassment heating her cheeks.

When she finished, Dani squeezed her hand. "You were upset. You didn't mean it."

Piper ran both hands down her face. "I still shouldn't have said it. I practically pushed her into the woman's arms."

Way to prove you're not disaster friends, she thought bitterly.

"What do you want to do about it?" Dani asked.

Piper pulled herself out of her thoughts. "What?"

"We have a psychopath on our hands. What are we going to do about it?"

"I don't know. I'm used to Lou being the one who handles the psycho parts."

"That's our problem," Dani interjected. "We rely too much on Lou's abilities. And in times like this, when she makes the wrong call or when she's hurt, what are we supposed to do?"

Piper saw the color returning to Dani's face. Her eyes were clearer, brighter. She didn't think it was the tea working that magic. It was action. Dani was always at her best when there was something that had to be done.

"We're a team," Dani said. "Me, you, Lou, King, Mel. That Italian guy."

"Konstantine."

"We need to work together. If one of us is out of commission, or has a bad day, the rest of us need to step in and pull our weight. We have to stop thinking that Lou is invincible and is just going to solve all our problems. She's *human*. An exceptionally talented, ruthless human, but she's human."

"King said something like that," Piper recalled. "He said we need to get serious about protecting ourselves."

"Not just protecting ourselves," Dani said. "We need to be in control of the situation. If you're not someone who makes the things happen, then the things will happen *to* you."

"I thought today was supposed to be one of your bad days," Piper said. "You're supposed to be the one resting and I'm the one pulling the weight, right?"

Dani didn't seem to hear. She chewed her lip, her eyes cast down in concentration.

"It'll take me a minute to find my Diana Dennard story. Do I want to expose her? Get her arrested or just force her underground? I'll need to think about it. But that's my plan." Dani put the mug on the side table and lay back against the pillows. "That still leaves you."

Piper crawled under the covers, pressing herself into Dani's side. "Me?"

"Yeah, what are you going to do about her? Lou is curious, so she's playing with fire. King is going to be too seduced by the idea of busting a child pornographer to bow out. Melandra has a shop to run and is dealing with her ex's trial. And Konstantine is probably trying to get Lou to chill out and rest like you are with me right now, but he'll offer her whatever she asks for. That leaves you, baby. What's your move?"

That leaves me, Piper thought. She saw Diana's face, the twisted rage in it when she'd brought her hand across Piper's face.

My move, she thought. *What's my move?*

"She's funding her operation with credit card scams," Piper said thoughtfully. "What if we outed her for that? I can make some calls, talk to the local PD."

Dani cupped her cheek. "Sounds like a good place to start."

24

Lou crossed and uncrossed her legs, staring out at the bustling square. It was getting hot under her leather jacket. The coffee on the table in front of her was growing cold. It was King's idea to meet Diana at Café du Monde. He was insistent that Lou guard the extent of her gift as closely as possible.

Lou thought that was pointless. People either believed in the supernatural or they didn't. If Diana was the sort of woman to rewrite the universe around her to suit her world view, she could have seen a ghost on one of the infamous New Orleans tours and talked herself out of it.

The chair opposite her scraped against the concrete loudly, making Lou's teeth vibrate.

Diana settled into the metal chair with a hint of a smile.

"You like coffee?" she asked, eyeing the Styrofoam cup. "You ordered it at the diner too."

"When you took my coffee cup," Lou said. "I remember. Was it the money or the cup that you pulled DNA from?"

Diana's face smoothed out, removing itself of emotion. "I'll tell you if you tell me what happened in Julia Street station."

"I was shot," Lou said simply.

Diana's lips quirked. "Does that happen to you a lot?"

"More than average."

Diana snorted. "Is that what's wrong with your shoulder?"

Lou waited. She was used to playing the staring game. It was why she liked to wear her mirrored sunglasses. People found it harder to look at themselves. As expected, Diana looked away first.

"I used both. The money and the mug. I like to be sure." She ran her fingers through her ponytail. "Winter is in Springfield."

"Illinois?"

"Missouri." Diana shifted in her seat, her excitement showing. "He has a fourth-floor apartment in a commercial district. Red brick, flat roof. With a coordinated attack we can get him on all sides."

She must be expecting me to bring this manpower, Lou thought. She'd shot nearly everyone Diana had brought to the townhouse with her. "Do you want Winter alive?"

"Yes," Diana said with a smirk. "I don't need to tell you why, do I?"

No, Lou thought. Sometimes it was fun to vent a bit of steam.

"Are the children in Springfield?" Lou asked, trying not to rotate her shoulder. It was throbbing again. The eight hundred milligrams of ibuprofen she took that morning were wearing off. But having strapped her arm to the side of her body had helped.

"Not necessarily," Diana said, twisting a paper napkin between her fingers. "He finds and recruits his rapists online, pays them online too. They're located all over. But I expect that some are on-site."

She said this as if annoyed by the interruption. Something about it unsettled Lou, made the muscles along her spine itch.

"How soon can you get to Springfield?" Diana asked. "He's been there for two weeks already. He's never in a place long, so I don't want to wait."

Now, Lou thought. *I could be there right now. I could close my eyes and just—*

"Three days," she said.

Diana frowned. "Three days?"

Lou couldn't tell if Diana thought three days was too short or too long of a wait.

"It's...far away," Lou said, forgetting what King had told her to say. "We need to get everyone in place."

These words were strange on her tongue. She should've asked King for a script. How long did it normally take to mobilize large groups?

"How many can you spare for this operation?" Diana asked.

Lou looked out over the square. "Enough."

King's voice sprang to mind. *Ask misleading questions so she doesn't get a sense of how you work or what you can do.*

"Do you know what he looks like? Do you have a photo?"

"No photo," Diana said. "He's been careful to keep his face hidden. I only know where he is by his internet trails, and I can only establish those while he live streams."

Lou didn't need a photo. Even now, her compass was searching the dark.

Where are you...the one she wants.

Something clicked inside her. On the other side of the darkness, a man took shape. And Lou could feel that it was a man now. He smelled like cologne, something cheap and alcoholic, and body odor. The hiss of a grill was nearby. For some reason, Lou had the impression he was in a restaurant. A small one where the patrons sat quite close together. She pushed further, she caught the smell of fried potatoes and meat.

She supposed even monsters had to eat.

"What?" Diana asked.

Lou blinked.

"Where'd you go just now? You looked like you were a million miles away."

"I was in Springfield with Winter."

Diana laughed, mistaking this for a joke.

"I'll bring manpower. What will you bring?"

"I can offer technical support and a bit of muscle, but I'll be relying on you to surround the buildings and take Winter down. After you extract him, he's mine. Are we clear on that?"

"I want the children," Lou said honestly. "I don't care what you do with Winter."

Diana smirked as if amused by the answer.

Was that what it was like, Lou wondered. When one had to rely on large coordinated efforts to achieve an aim. Lou thought their small operation of six was cumbersome at times. She wasn't sure she could work with more people than that, not when she preferred being alone.

"You don't have anything to say to me? No 'I'm sorry I lost my temper and killed your entire team'?" Diana pressed. When Lou said nothing, she harrumphed. "Yeah, okay. I guess I deserve that. I kidnapped your pets. And you're going to make it up to me anyway. Give me Winter and we'll be more than square."

Lou wondered why talking had to be a part of this. Conversations were taxing on the best of days, but like this, when it felt more like a dance, an exchange of double-edged blows and parries, it was particularly exhausting.

Diana rubbed her nose. "I have to say, when it came to your crew I expected a little more steel."

The hair on the back of Lou's neck rose.

"The cop and the black woman, they're stone cold. I like them. I'd recruit them if I thought they'd ditch you. But the two girls...*whew*. Where did you find those crybabies?"

Lou found her hand opening and closing under the table. It itched for a gun.

"You must be more lenient than I am." Diana wrinkled her nose as if she disapproved. "I don't tolerate any weakness on my team. If I'd heard even one *second* of that sniveling, I would've dismissed her. Or put a bullet in her head."

She must've seen something in Lou's face that frightened her. The sneer evaporated. In its place, there were only wide eyes.

"Don't give me that look. We're partners now. I won't touch your people," Diana said, though her grin had too many teeth. "What's good for you is good for me."

Is that right? Lou wondered. *We're about to find out.*

25

───────────

Konstantine stood and took a turn around his living room again. He regarded the sofa pressed against one cream wall. The large red rug on the stone floor. The desk, the painting, the pristine kitchen that he'd spent an hour cleaning. The smell of espresso in the air. He glanced at the stairs but knew that was ridiculous. They wouldn't come through his bedroom. The living room was largest. She'd bring them here, to the heart of his home.

"Close the drapes," Lou had told him. "Make the room as dark as you can."

He pulled the curtains together and stood in the dim light, trying to decide what to do with his own body. Did he want to be behind his desk or on the sofa when they arrived?

He decided to sit at the desk, affecting a pose that didn't convey the unease in his stomach.

He caught himself drumming against the arm of the chair and forced himself to stop.

The pressure rose between his ears suddenly and popped. Then his living room wasn't so empty.

In the center of the room stood four figures that hadn't been there a second before.

Lou was the first to meet his gaze. The others seemed to just be getting their bearings.

He found his voice quickly. "Can I offer you something to drink? Coffee? Water?"

"Whoa," Piper said, breaking ranks first, stepping away from the huddle and toward Konstantine's desk. "This is where you live? God, what smells so good?"

He wasn't sure what question to address first. "Espresso. Would you like one?"

"*Yes.*" She looked around, appraising the apartment. "Nice place."

"Can I offer you a seat?" he said, motioning to the sofa. Only then did he realize that it would only seat three of them comfortably, and he had no other chairs in the room but his own.

It was clear now that he never entertained here. Stefano had been to his apartment, and little Matteo, who often followed Konstantine around with a dog-like reverence.

He motioned toward his seat as he stepped into the kitchen to make a fresh espresso. Lou waved him off, crossing instead to the window. She pulled apart the drapes, letting light fill the room again.

As he made the coffee, he took her measure.

Her left arm was still strapped to her chest, immobilizing that shoulder. He wasn't sure if this was a good sign, that perhaps she was finally taking her self-care seriously, or if it warned of a greater vulnerability.

"Where is the other one?" he asked, tamping down the grounds. "Mel?"

He didn't even attempt to say her full name. Just the nickname felt strange on his tongue.

King answered, looking relaxed as he reclined on one end of the sofa. "She's with Lady, the dog. They're running the shop. Truth be told, she's preoccupied with her husband's trial. The court date is in a couple weeks, so she has enough to be getting on with."

"She won't be involved in this operation?" Konstantine asked as the moka began to burble.

"Operation," Piper snickered. "You sound like King."

Piper's spirits seemed high at first glance, but now Konstantine saw the puffiness under her eyes. She wore makeup to hide it, but the swelling was still noticeable.

But it was the other who looked truly pained. Dark circles sank deep beneath her eyes. Her skin was sallow. Konstantine wondered if she'd slept in days.

He caught Lou watching him. She arched a brow.

He smiled, bringing his focus to the detective. He'd begun speaking again.

"Our objective here is to hide Lou's abilities from Diana. I think we can do that," King said, tapping his knee. "What do you think?"

He was speaking to Konstantine.

"Aren't you worried that by helping this crazy person at all, we'll never get rid of her?" Piper asked. She sat between Dani and King. "What if she shows up every time she needs help with something? Is this the sort of behavior we actually want to *encourage*?"

"No," Konstantine and King said in unison.

Konstantine handed her the espresso in its little cup. "Would you like sugar?"

"No, thank you." She sipped it and scowled. "Oh, it's *bitter*. Maybe I should've said yes to the sugar."

"Give it to me," the other one said. She downed it in a single go.

"Have you considered killing her?" Konstantine asked. He was watching Lou. She stood at the window, watching the courtyard outside, her arms crossed. He wondered how her shoulder was feeling. She wore dark cargo pants and a tight black tank top.

"She hunts predators," she replied without looking away from the window. "Why should I stop her?"

Konstantine saw movement in the corner of his eye and turned his head ever so slightly to better track it. Piper was taking the other girl's hand in hers. Her jaw was furiously working. The emptied espresso cup was placed on the table beside the sofa.

"And if she hurts someone? One of us, for example?" Konstantine asked.

"Then I'll kill her."

She said this plainly. And perhaps anyone else listening to this statement would believe it. Lou's ice-cold exterior was terrifying. It made such declarations easy to believe.

But Konstantine heard the slight drop in her voice. He saw the miniscule shift in her body weight. She might kill Diana if the woman crossed her in some way, but she didn't *want* to.

How interesting.

"This man that Dennard wants to find—"

"Winter," the dark girl interjected.

There was a bit more light in her eyes now. Konstantine wondered if he should offer her another espresso.

"Correct. If they wanted to arrest a man like this, what's the lawful protocol?"

They were looking at King.

"I assume that you mean without all the red tape. Because when someone does a sting like this legally, it's all about warrants and probable cause. Bureaucracy prevails."

"And we don't want this man to be put on trial?" Konstantine asked him.

"I always try to get the families justice if I can. Peace of mind is priceless, you know? But in cases like this, I'm not sure it matters," King said. "Sometimes the families are the pimps themselves. Or if they aren't, an arrest doesn't undo what happened to the kids."

"I can take him," Lou said calmly. There was no boast in it.

Konstantine knew better than to point out the obvious, but he did so anyway. "Your shoulder isn't a hundred percent, *amore mio.*"

King almost looked relieved. *Better you than me*, that face said.

This amused Konstantine, the idea that he wasn't the only one trying—and failing—to take care of Louie Thorne.

"I second that," Piper said. "You were supposed to rest for six months. I don't see how this is *resting.*"

"I'm with Lou," Dani said. "I can't think about those kids enduring one more night of that."

King held his hands up when everyone's eyes fell on him. "I can't tell anyone what to do with their own bodies. But we should be sensible here."

Konstantine stepped forward. "Assume that the red tape has been cut and the operation to capture Winter was approved. What would a police force do? We can't pretend to be such an operation if we don't know what it looks like."

"That's the problem, isn't it?" King laughed. "We don't know what Dennard thinks we are. An off-grid organization of some kind?"

"We'll pretend to be whatever you think is most believable," Lou said.

King shrugged. "A privately funded enforcement agency?"

"And what would they do?"

"They'd go to his last-known location, surround the place. Extra points if he's home and apprehended, but they'll go in regardless to collect as much evidence as possible."

"And how many people are needed for such an operation?"

"A ten-person SWAT team is standard for a small city, but there's as many as sixty for an urban area like Chicago. If there were multiple locations, such as a home and a workplace, they would move on both at once. Usually there's a bit of a stakeout to see if he shows up, so that the likelihood of apprehension is higher."

"Diana wants to move against him once he gets online and starts a feed. She says she can confirm he'll be in the building if he starts streaming from it."

This is true, Konstantine knew. He knew it was possible to track a person's location in such a way, if they remained connected long enough. There were ways to disguise one's exact location as well. For a man such as Winter, Konstantine suspected he knew how to do that.

"We need to be prepared for the possibility of a second location," Konstantine said. "Or it is possible he will not be in the building. He can mask his location."

"Not from me," Lou said.

"True," he acquiesced. "But if you're at a raid location with Dennard and she is convinced he's there and you know he's not, how will you explain your knowledge? You cannot disappear. That's what we are trying to plan around."

"Why do some criminals have to be smart," Piper bemoaned. "Why can't they all be dumb?"

After brief eye contact, Piper's face reddened and she looked away.

"Could we put Lou on an earpiece so that Diana thinks she's there and involved, but that frees her up to move if necessary?" King asked. "It would also explain any information that comes in."

"That would be ideal," Konstantine said. "Perhaps a large team as well, a show of force, enough to give her pause in moving against Lou in the future, and then a second, smaller support team in case Lou needs to pivot."

"I'm fine," Lou said with a tone that brooked no argument.

"We know, babe," Piper said. "Everyone here is aware that you'd tear your own shoulder off rather than lose your new BFF."

Dani squeezed Piper's hand.

Lou frowned.

"Would it be possible for you to get fifty or sixty people together in two days?" King asked.

"Yes," Konstantine said plainly. "But you realize that I cannot hide what they are. They will not look or act like police officers. If you want Dennard to perceive you in a certain light—"

"I don't care how she views us," Lou said. But she was looking at King to see if he objected.

King only shrugged. "I don't think it's a bad thing if she thinks we run with rough people. I wouldn't mind instilling a bit of fear in her."

"Have you ever managed a coordinated operation like that before?" Konstantine asked, watching the detective pick something out from under his fingernails.

"With the DEA? Sure. We did drug busts all the time. I can figure out the schematics of the building, the entrances, exits, electricity, and all that. Who moves where and when. I just need a team who can follow directions and a good communication system. We can have a contingency plan for the presence of any children in the building versus if he's alone. What would be more impressive, though, is if we can coordinate a cross-country attack where all the streamers are taken down and arrested simultaneously. They busted a ring in South Korea and made over three hundred arrests all over the world. In the US, UK, Canada, and Saudi Arabia. That would really scare the shit out of her, if she thought we were everywhere."

"I'd need more than three days for that," Konstantine said. Did he have people everywhere? Yes. But well-executed plans still took time.

"You're right," King relented. "It would be cool, but unimportant at the moment. Let's just dispose of Winter, rescue the kids, and placate Diana. Then if Diana is stubborn enough to stick around, we'll deal with her too."

Piper was watching the other girl, whose name Konstantine finally remembered. Daniella Allendale. She was the newest addition to their inner circle, and what Konstantine had learned about her wasn't much except that she was an investigative reporter who helped expose the killers Lou had tracked down. Her mother's ancestors were rich sugar barons from Cuba who'd emigrated to the US when Castro seized their homeland. Somehow, they'd maintained their considerable wealth despite those first, uncertain years. But more interestingly, he knew that Dmitri had tortured her almost to death—yet here she was. She hadn't run.

She must be much stronger than she looks, he thought. Though she didn't look it today. Not with those dark circles and a face drained of color.

"Would anyone like gelato?" Konstantine asked.

"Hell yeah," Piper replied, leaping to her feet. "Babe. We have to get gelato. We're in Italy."

"Where is it?" Daniella asked, as if the idea of a walk troubled her.

Konstantine stood, crossed the living room to a window, and pulled back the shade. "Across the courtyard here, under that archway. The gelateria will be open for another hour. Stella makes delicious tiramisu and limoncello gelato."

"Stracciatella is my favorite," Piper said. She pulled Dani to her feet. "It's basically chocolate chip. Come on."

Konstantine didn't think this was the time to argue that American ice cream could never compare.

Dani wiped invisible dust from the front of her jeans. "But I don't have any Italian money."

"Tell Stella I sent you."

"No," Lou said, and fished her wallet out of her cargo pants pockets. She produced a wad of euros, handing them over. If Konstantine's eyes weren't deceiving him, that wasn't the only foreign currency she was carrying. At a glance, he also saw pounds and yen, tucked in beside the euros and American bills he recognized.

"Right," Piper said. "We don't want your gang people recognizing our faces, and if I walk up in there saying Konstantine said give me some gelato, that might send the wrong message."

Konstantine smiled. "The gelato will be worth it. I assure you."

The two girls were down the steps and halfway across the courtyard when Lou said, "I want to go with them."

"I'll wait here for you," King said. "Go on."

Lou seemed to need no other encouragement. She closed the apartment door behind her, leaving the two men alone.

King rubbed his chin. "Can you really assemble fifty or sixty trustworthy men in two days?"

"Yes," Konstantine said. He crossed to his kitchen and turned on the espresso maker. It was almost too late in the day for it, but he wanted it nonetheless. Just the smell of the ground coffee freshened his mind. "Can you really lead them with only a set of walkie-talkies?"

King laughed. "Yes. But to be honest, it's not the operation I'm worried about. I'm worried about Lou."

Konstantine refilled the moka, but didn't interrupt.

"It's not just her shoulder, it's Dennard."

"I haven't had the pleasure of meeting her," Konstantine said. "What's your assessment?"

"Like Lou on steroids. Determined, focused, doesn't know when to quit, but it's more than that. She's like a rabid dog. She doesn't have an ounce of Lou's self-possession or control. She isn't as hard to read as Lou, there's that. Her anger and coldness are all over her face, and there's..." He seemed to consider his next words carefully. "I don't know. There's an unsteadiness. An unpredictability. If I didn't know better I'd say she's crazy. Clinically out of her mind."

"That sounds like a very dangerous woman. But Lou can defeat her easily." And he believed it.

King laughed. "I don't think she wants to. That's what worries me."

Konstantine wondered if it was more than seeing a kindred spirit in Diana. What if Lou was unable to kill a woman? Women, children, animals—Konstantine had a sense that Lou never raised a gun against those weaker than herself. Perhaps it violated some unspoken inner code.

And what would she think of him if she knew the truth? That he held none of the qualms she did, if the end prevented unnecessary bloodshed in the future.

"We could take care of it," King said quietly. He pitched his voice low, as if he was afraid someone might overhear them. "There will be a lot of commotion. Something could just go wrong at the operation."

Konstantine smiled ruefully. "If I kill Diana for her, she'll be furious. At the very least, she will kill whatever man I gave the order to."

King was watching him with a strange expression, and Konstantine wondered if he'd gone too far. The relationship between the two of them was an odd one. King represented the law, having invested over thirty years in an organization that actively worked to disassemble the power of men like Konstantine.

Yet here they were, working on another case together and sharing a concern for the woman standing between them. Did it matter that King lived by and respected the law while Konstantine violated it at every turn?

"Lou is better about letting Piper help. Or was," King added, glancing out the window.

Konstantine felt a twinge of jealousy at that.

"Maybe because she's a woman. I don't know. But I think Lucy would support us in this."

Konstantine reluctantly pulled himself from his thoughts. "In what?"

"In protecting Lou from Diana. She might not want my help, but I promised to look after her. And Lou looks out for all of us. It's fair."

Fair, Konstantine mused, hearing Piper's voice in the courtyard and knowing the girls were almost back.

When was anything in this world fair?

26

———

Piper sat in her bed with her laptop open on her lap. Her purple comforter was pulled around her and the A/C clicked on in the living room. She stared at the blinking cursor.

Lou, Konstantine, and King had their plan for the Missouri operation. Every time Piper thought about it, bees buzzed in her temples. They were playing with fire—didn't they know it?

Diana couldn't be trusted, and if they weren't careful, that viper was going to bite them. She felt like they were already poisoned and she was the only one seeing it.

What are you going to do about it? Dani had asked.

She regarded Dani sleeping beside her, her dark hair spread over Piper's pillow. If she was honest with herself, she liked her there, in her bed, in her apartment. She liked that Dani's soap was in her shower and her makeup was on her sink. She liked that Dani could pull a mug down from her cabinet like it was the most natural thing in the world, that she had her preferred spot on the sofa.

It steadied something inside her.

Piper opened the new desktop folder labeled *DD*. It contained all the information they'd gathered on Diana as far back as March, when they'd first bumped into the woman while hunting Fish.

She scanned the data, opening and closing files at random. When nothing caught her eye, she went online to Diana's forum and began scrolling. Most of the posts were about missing women. Some were about abuse and asking for help in taking down an abuser because authorities had failed to take their complaints seriously.

There were *thousands* of complaints. Maybe even tens of thousands.

God, Piper thought. *Why is the world such a mess?*

A post snagged her attention. It was dated two days ago.

Want to make Earth a better, safer place for women? Ready to work hard for something that matters?

Piper wasn't sure if Diana had created the post herself or if she'd simply seized and repurposed it, but the forum seemed to be her hub for recruiting.

Yeah, you need new people, Piper thought. *After Lou laid waste to your ass.*

Piper took the name from the post and added it to her growing list. She'd added more names every time she found a new admin in the forum. While she couldn't be sure that every admin posting was Diana, she was sure that at least seven of them were her aliases.

"Sloppy," Piper said.

"What?" Dani asked, stirring beside her.

"Oh, sorry," Piper said, closing the laptop enough so that the light didn't fall on Dani's face. "I didn't mean to wake you."

"What time is it?"

Piper checked the computer screen. "Just past midnight. I'm almost done."

It was a lie to buy her time. Hopefully, Dani would drop back off to sleep and she could keep working.

But Dani didn't turn back over. Instead, she rolled toward Piper. "What are you working on?"

Piper closed the laptop rather guiltily. "Diana. I'm making a list of the names used on admin posts. Since it's her site, some of these might be her credit card aliases. Piper wrapped an arm around the girl. "Maybe we can get her arrested for her credit card scams. That's pretty illegal."

"Fraud only has a jail time of ten to fifteen years," Dani said.

"Yeah, but that's fifteen years we don't have to deal with her. She'd be in her fifties when she got out. Or maybe she'll get shivved in prison and save us all some trouble."

Dani gave her a sleepy laugh. "I don't think so. Ask Mel how this one goes."

Poor Mel. Her abusive, homicidal husband had been in prison for twenty-five years, and the first thing he did when released was show up on her doorstep and bully her for money.

Piper sighed. "Possible payback aside, this is the most solid option I've got."

"Why are you so worried about her?" Dani asked, her dark eyes on Piper.

"You mean except for the fact she kidnapped us and gave you a heart attack?"

Dani didn't answer.

"I don't like her. Having her around is screwing with Lou's head." These excuses sounded pathetic, even to her own ears. *I don't like her* wasn't a great reason for conspiring to send someone to prison or wishing them dead.

It was more than that.

To Piper, Diana felt dangerous. Dangerous in a way that Lou, and even Konstantine or any of her work for King, had never felt. Even when Dmitri Petrov was joking about cutting her finger off, she hadn't been this afraid.

Maybe I'm an idiot for that, she thought, but she didn't think so.

She said, "The sooner she's away from us, the better."

"I can help with the research," Dani offered, rubbing at her eyes. "I'm doing it anyway with my story. We'll need someone to officially open a case and charge her. If we can make her a national fugitive, put her face everywhere, that would be a bonus. Journalism can only take us so far. We've got to get someone else involved. Preferably someone with connections to the law."

"Konstantine might help," Piper said hopefully. "He knows good and bad cops."

"Yeah," Dani yawned. "Maybe."

"I could call Sampson, but he's going to want to know why I'm calling him instead of King."

Dani smiled. "Your mind is really working this over."

"I don't like her," she said again. *What am I, five years old?*

Dani snuggled closer. "So you've said. But I've never known you to hate anyone apart from Mel's husband."

Piper shrugged. "She slapped me."

Dani pulled back, mouth open. "When?"

"When I was yelling at her to let you go." Piper felt the heat rise in her face. "It didn't hurt."

A lie.

"But it pissed me off."

Dani came up onto her elbows. "Does Lou know that she slapped you?"

"No. I think she appeared a second or two after that."

"You could just tell Lou that she slapped you, and that'd probably solve all your problems."

What if it doesn't? What if Lou straight up sides with a psycho over me?

Dani's brow scrunched. "You *do* know that Lou would kill her for touching you, right?"

"Hmm. Would she?"

Dani sighed, collapsing back against the pillow. "You don't know. That's why you haven't said something. Piper, what's going on? Ever since the road trip you've been weird about Lou."

The shift in her voice made Piper look at her.

"Spit it out."

Piper tried to articulate this feeling choking her. Nothing came. If she couldn't say *what* was wrong, she'd start with *when*. "I think it started when she hurt her shoulder."

"What started?"

"This feeling." She saw Dani's face and shook her head. "I don't know what to say."

"Walk me through it," Dani said, adjusting the pillow under her head.

Piper sighed, searching an invisible point on the wall. "Maybe this isn't the right way to enter it, but it's the moment that keeps coming to mind."

When Piper didn't go on right away, Dani added, "I'm listening."

"It's like...King was an agent for *decades*. He's got a million cool skills. You're only a year older than me and you're this amazing journalist with a college degree. I don't even have thirty credits yet. I can't fight. I'm not a ninja. I don't have powers like Lou and I don't own half the world like Konstantine. I don't even have my own thing like Mel. I'm just...I'm just me. All I can do is be her friend, but we're not even friends. Not really. We're *disaster* friends."

"What are you talking about?" Dani laughed, disbelieving. "Are you serious?"

"When we first met, you even targeted me as the weakest link for your story. You thought I could get you close to Lou. You picked me because there's nothing about me—"

"Whoa, *wait*. First of all, that was a stupid mistake on my part, and says way more about me than about you. You're not a weak link. I'm sure King, Lou, and Mel would all say that you are very important to them. Everyone relies on you, baby. You're essential."

"I barfed on a Russian guy trying to crawl up the fire escape. That's not what I would call *essential*. There's nothing that I do that makes me critical to this team. You guys could replace me with anyone."

"Piper," Dani interjected. "The work you do for King *literally* puts criminals in jail. Secondly, how many times have you helped me through my attacks on my bad days? My own mother would've thrown me in the loony bin if she'd seen me like that. Mel wouldn't be able to keep her shop open without you. You're in there every day, keeping the shop running, and I see the way she looks at you. You're practically her daughter. And how about the fact that it *doesn't matter* what you do? You're a lovely person to be around. Period. Your very existence makes people happy. It's not about how useful you are to them or what degrees you have or don't have. It's about how you make people feel."

Piper's face must've conveyed her disbelief.

Dani wrapped her arms around Piper's neck. "I guarantee that Lou hangs out with you because of how you make her feel. Not because she needs you to dig up bodies in the dead of night. She had the bodies thing covered long before you showed up. As hard as it might be to believe, she asks for your company because she *likes* it."

"Then why does she have to act like she's got more in common with a complete psychopath than with me?"

"I would tell you to talk to her, but I don't know if Lou is self-aware enough to clarify this for you."

Silence stretched out between them. Piper was listening for Dani's breath to change, to drop off into peaceful sleep, so she could get back on her laptop, though she wasn't sure how she was going to open it without waking the girl nestled into her neck.

But into the darkness, Dani said, "I hate her too."

"Lou?"

"Dennard."

"You didn't hate her before?" Piper asked, sincerely surprised.

"No, it felt like my own fault that I had a panic attack. But now that I know she put her hands on you, *ugh*." Dani growled. "I want to take her down."

Piper grinned, opening her laptop again. "Let's see what we can do about that."

27

K ing found Mel's apartment door open. He stopped at the entryway regardless, raising his fist and rapping on the wooden frame. "Anybody home?"

Lady appeared first, her tail swishing back and forth as her nails clicked across the tiled floor. King took this as a good sign. If something was wrong and Mel's door was ajar for some nefarious reason, surely the dog's behavior would reflect that.

He inhaled, smelling popcorn.

"Come on in," Mel called from somewhere deep in the apartment.

He entered and hesitated. "We expecting anyone else or can I close the door?"

"Close the door."

King shut it behind him. Mel's apartment was a mirror of his own. They had the same counters, appliances, and tile. They both entered through the kitchen and beneath an arch, a spacious living room spread out beyond that. Both their living rooms ended in a door leading to a balcony. Both connected to a single bedroom and bath.

There were some differences, of course. Mel's furnishings were lighter, pale lavenders and pinks. Instead of a large armoire doubling as a TV cabinet, she had a simple TV on a stand opposite her sofa. By the balcony door, where King had his record player, she had two armchairs and a potted plant that fanned out against the wall almost like feathers. In the small corner between the kitchen wall and bedroom door, she had an antique rattan chair with a peacock back. King's mother had had one of those chairs. But that one didn't have the bright orange pillow that Mel's had.

Mel came out of the dark bedroom and closed the door behind her.

She checked her watch then crossed to the television. "We've got five minutes. Will you grab the popcorn off the counter? And the soda is in the fridge."

He did as he was told, grabbing two cans of Coke with one hand and the large bowl of popcorn with the other.

They settled onto the lavender sofa together, the bowl between them. He handed her one of the Cokes.

"Who do you think will be eliminated this week?" King asked.

"It's hard to tell," she said. "I think it should be the one who rapped. She should've been eliminated last week."

King laughed. "What do you have against rappers?"

"Nothing," Mel said, bringing a handful of popcorn to her mouth. "When they can actually rap."

"I think the rabbit might go."

"Kalynda Kicks?" Mel asked, surprised. "I thought she was pretty good with the song she sang."

"Me too," King said. "But the judges have been giving her a hard time for three weeks now. I think they're going to toss her soon."

"Or they're building us up for a comeback story."

King shrugged, shoving another fistful of popcorn in his mouth.

"How's the Diana bullshit going?" Mel asked.

King snorted. It always amused him when Mel swore, because it was such a rare occurrence.

"Still mad at her for tying you up in the dead of night, huh?"

Mel harrumphed. "She didn't even buy me dinner first."

Coke went into King's nose as he sucked in air to laugh. "See what you made me do?"

He rose, went to the kitchen, and grabbed a napkin. He dabbed at his jeans, which had taken the worst of it, and a small spot on his shirt.

Lady lifted her head from her paws to watch the show, before deeming him boring and putting her head on her paws again.

As he settled back down beside Mel, the program started. They watched it without speaking. It was an unspoken agreement between them.

But once the first commercial break aired, encouraging them to switch insurance companies, King turned to her.

"Are you sick of us?" he asked, his face serious.

She frowned at him. "What are you talking about?"

"You know what I'm talking about," he said, turning the Coke can on his knee. "First it was Chaz who broke in and put a gun to your head."

Just the idea of it made King's blood boil.

"Then it was Petrov and now Diana. Aren't you sick of it? Aren't you afraid one night it's going to end with you getting shot?"

Mel looked at her hands for a moment, as if considering each of her gold rings carefully. Then she met his eyes and said, "If I get shot, I'll know I had it coming."

"Lou didn't die."

"I still shot her," she said. She sighed, letting the silence rest between them. "When Terry was still around, I used to have a lot of trouble sleeping. I was scared he would come home, knowing if he did, he'd hurt me. And scared that he wouldn't and what might happen to me if he didn't. I know what it feels like when your home isn't safe. That's not what we've got here. You, me, Piper, even Lou and Dani. It feels right. It feels like we're supposed to be together, all five of us, here, in this place. It's why I haven't hired another person to run the shop. It's not that we couldn't use the help. And I've got the money put back for it now if I change my mind, but no. It's because we're all here now. Do you understand? We're all here."

King took her hand and squeezed it.

She squeezed back. "If some bastard comes up in here and makes trouble once in a while, fine. Let 'em. But we're together and that's how it's supposed to be. I feel it deep inside. That this is how it's supposed to be."

When Terry was still around, King thought, remembering the lean man in the bone choker and denim, the crow feather sticking out of his hat.

"When's the court date?" he asked.

"The twenty-first," she said. "I've already gone over my testimony with my lawyer several times. I feel like I could testify in my sleep at this point."

"Nothing wrong with being prepared," King said, watching her face carefully. He saw the strain there, the worry. "They're going to put him away."

She turned and gave him a weak smile. "I know. And I can't wait to see it."

28

———————

When Lou appeared in Konstantine's apartment, he was standing at his bedroom window. The window's high arch was laid bare, the shutters pulled open to reveal an unfettered view of the Arno River. He stood there with his back to her, and her eyes traced the planes of his shoulders, his bare neck. The back of his exposed arms and the tattoo peeking out from under his sleeve.

Beyond him, the river glittered as the light from the lamps shone on its surface. Laughter carried up from the street below as a warm breeze pushed past him.

His heady, dark scent washed over her.

"What are you thinking about?" she asked.

Something in his back relaxed. "I was thinking about your world. *La Loon*. It's very different from ours."

"Miss it already?"

He laughed, turning to face her. "No. But it would be nice to get out of the city. Even if only for a night."

In the soft light from the lamps outside, she could see the dark circles under his eyes. This gave her pause.

Bad day? she thought. She didn't ask.

She suspected running one of the largest criminal organizations in the world had its fair share of stress. And this was the thin line they walked. She the destroyer of the criminal world. He its benevolent manager.

Lou stepped toward him, wrapping her arms around his waist. Before his hands could fully envelop her in return, everything shifted. His sensuous touch tightened in reflex.

When all resettled, the scent of a forest swelled around them. Thick green pine sap and packed earth.

"Wish granted," she whispered.

They were at the edge of a clearing, the tall grass connecting the woods at their back with those on the other edge of the circle.

At the far end, something moved through the trees. Moose? Wolves?

"It's beautiful," he said, stepping forward to behold the moon.

Though not as quiet, she thought, noting the swell of crickets, frogs, katydids, beetles, and all the other voices vying for their part of the night.

She shrugged her shoulders in her leather jacket. It was too warm for it. It made her long for fall and winter, her preferred seasons. Summer was always too bright, too hot. But it was almost over. She could taste it on nights like this, that first crisp shift in the wind.

Soon the nights would run long again.

"How does your shoulder feel tonight?" he asked.

"Fine." She would have said this even if it was torn in half and hanging limp from her body.

He smiled as if he knew this, the moonlight collecting in his teeth and the whites of his eyes. "Of course it is."

Lou didn't want any more questions about her shoulder or whether or not she felt well. Instead, she shrugged out of her leather jacket and laid it on the ground.

"You can sit if you want," she said.

He laughed. "How chivalrous of you. But what about your jacket?"

"I'll wipe it down later."

He looked reluctant to sit on the packed earth even with the jacket.

Lou suppressed a laugh. He was fussy about clothes. It wasn't only that she often caught him wearing expensive brands that hung off models on the runway, but also how he cared for them. Her own wardrobe was much less luxurious. When every other night ended with her covered in someone's blood—not to mention the sweat—it didn't pay to waste money on nice clothes.

Lou got most of her t-shirts and jeans from thrift shops. She had only a few items she really cherished: her father's two flannels and his bulletproof vest. She didn't wear those when she hunted. She also loved her leather jacket, but it was far from irreplaceable. She could have another one if she wanted it.

"Are you thinking about tomorrow?" Konstantine asked, looking up at her from the ground. "Everything has been prepared. My men will meet King at the rendezvous point he's chosen."

"I was thinking about your clothes," Lou said.

This surprised a laugh out of him. "Why?"

"I was wondering if I could take them off without you objecting."

"Yes," he said, too quickly.

She knelt in front of him, bringing her eyes to his level. "Are you sure? Because they might touch the ground."

He laughed harder. "I'll make the sacrifice."

"Lay back."

He did, his eyes roving her body.

"You're very beautiful," he said. "Do you know it?"

Did she? Sometimes. When she caught her reflection in the mirror, there was nothing there that pleased her, but there'd been hints in the way others regarded her. The way their eyes lingered on her face or her body. It was something she noted, distantly and only in context.

She didn't answer the question. "Is that what you're thinking about when you look at me like that?"

"I'm thinking about a lot of things," he said, his eyes sparkling with starlight. "About you. Tomorrow. Diana. The yakuza. My mind often rehearses before the actual event."

"And you're rehearsing for tomorrow?"

"Yes," he said. "Do you wish you could read my mind?"

She hesitated.

"Would you trade your ability to be anywhere at any time to know what people are thinking?"

Lou considered this, placing her hands on his chest. "No. I don't think I want to know what people are thinking all the time."

"Will you lie beside me?" he asked.

He sounded small. Sad.

"Why?"

"I want you closer."

She lay down beside him. The earth was cold despite the warmth of the day. They were in Tennessee, quite close to the eastern mountains, and it had been nearly a hundred degrees all day. Yet the earth was cool on her bare arms.

He turned to face her. "What are *you* thinking about?"

"The weather," she said. "You."

He smiled. "What about me?"

"Do you know that you're beautiful?" she asked with a mischievous grin.

He took her hand and pressed her index finger to his cheek. "Even with this?"

He forced her to trace the rough ridge of his scar. It was long and vertical, bisecting most of his cheek.

Lou remembered Nico pressing the blade into his flesh, the way the cheek had hung open, bleeding, a mask of blood covering half his face.

He'd had at least two surgeries to improve the scar's appearance and to repair the muscles cut beneath. While they had returned the muscle function, it hadn't been enough to completely remove the surface damage.

"I like you better with this," she said, and meant it.

It surprised another laugh out of him. "Really?"

"You were too pretty before."

"I am more attractive to you now, with the scar?" he asked, his voice deepening.

"Yes."

He rolled onto her then, holding his body above hers, careful not to add any weight. That heady scent pressed against her.

"I should thank Nico then," he said.

She slid her fingers around the back of his neck and into his hair and pulled him down into a kiss, forcing his body against hers. Her muscles rolled instinctively, and his body tightened in response.

She deepened the kiss, forcing her tongue past his lips and holding him in place. He didn't object. He relaxed into her, opening his mouth wider, meeting her tongue with his.

It was easy to slip her free hand, the one not wrapped up in his dark hair, under his shirt. She lifted the fabric and he broke the kiss just long enough to let her pull the shirt over his head.

His skin pricked with goosebumps as she put the shirt on her jacket for safekeeping.

Her fingers traced the tattoo from his shoulder to his elbow.

"Do you like it?" he asked. "Some women do not like tattoos."

Lou arched an eyebrow. "No woman has ever told you she didn't like this tattoo."

"No," he admitted. "But I'm asking you."

"I like it."

"What else do you like?" he ventured. He was smiling down at her.

"You want me to inventory the things I like about you?" she asked. It made her think of Piper suddenly. Hadn't she asked similar questions?

Lou hadn't known how to answer her, any more than she knew how to answer Konstantine now. What did she like about him?

Physically? His green eyes. His thick dark hair and its tendency to curl. The scar and the tattoos, but also his stillness. Every move he made seemed deliberate. He was very comfortable in his skin.

She liked the look that filled his eyes when he regarded her. The way his voice dropped, softened, when he spoke to her.

"Why do people need assurances from me?" Lou asked softly.

Konstantine pulled back, looking into her face. "For me, because you're difficult to read. Who else?"

"Piper."

He didn't look surprised by this answer. After a while he said, "You have nothing else you like about me, besides the tattoo and the scar?"

"Your eyes," she said. "Your voice."

She thought harder.

"The way you smell."

She came up onto her elbows and placed her face into the crook of his neck. She ran her mouth along the line of his throat up to his jaw. She had an urge to bite his throat, so she did, pressing her teeth into his skin until he shivered.

"The way you taste."

When she released him, pressing her back to the ground again, she saw his eyes were heavy with desire.

She grinned and reached beneath him, unclasping the button on his pants and sliding her hand between his legs.

KONSTANTINE SAW THE LOOK IN HER EYES EVEN BEFORE HE FELT HER hand tug at his pants. He knew what was coming. He supported his weight on one side, thinking, always, of her shoulder and the dangerous day they had ahead of them.

When her fingers found him, cupped him, sliding over his skin warm and smooth, he hardened. His desire, which had already begun to form as soon as she'd removed his shirt, mounted to an uncomfortable high.

He found himself squirming, pressing harder into her palm.

He couldn't decide if he would accept this, if it was enough just to be in her hands now that he knew what she felt like.

He wanted to be inside her, buried to the hilt. His face and neck felt like they were on fire, and the throbbing between his legs had grown unbearable. He rose up suddenly and began tugging off his pants. He freed one leg, then the other, until he was completely naked on top of her.

He waited, looking for any objection, but she was unhooking her own pants and lifting her hips to remove them.

He helped, tugging the fabric down to reveal long, muscular legs. He wanted to remove her shirt, but she was already reaching for him, pulling him back down onto her.

He settled for pushing it up enough that their bare stomachs touched.

Skin on skin.

He probed her first with his fingers, found her soaked. He moaned into the hollow of her throat.

"We didn't use a condom in La Loon," he said. "And I don't have one now."

"I'm clean."

So was he. "But there's still the matter of *bambini*."

"I take birth control," she said, her hand already on him, guiding him in.

He sank into her, enjoying that first rush of warm, wet sensation. She wrapped her legs around him, locking him into place, making it hard to pull out more than a couple of inches before driving in again.

When she moaned, his whole body shivered, something in him relaxing.

His mouth was on her throat, at her ear.

I love you, he thought.

Don't say it.

I love you.

Don't say it. Don't say it.

He remembered their conversation in the hospital. He'd replayed it in his mind many times since. She'd woken from her brief coma. She'd said, "I didn't want you to fall in love with me."

He confessed, "I'm already in love with you."

"Don't. People in love want to get married, they want kids. I don't want any of that."

It had hurt to hear her say it, to hear all his desires laid bare and dismissed. But he was also prepared to love her on her own terms. To respect her own desires. He had dreams, as many as any man. But what he wanted most of all was her.

If this was all he could have, moments like this, losing himself in the feel of her, he would take it.

She came first, sand he was grateful because he followed a second after. He moved to pull out of her, but she wouldn't let him go. The heels of her feet pressed into his lower back.

"Not yet," she panted in his ear. She was shivering.

For a terrible moment, he worried he'd hurt her shoulder.

"I'm not finished," she said, as if anticipating his question.

She rolled him onto his back and began to slowly rock against his hips.

After a minute, maybe more, she shivered again, collapsing onto her good side.

He lay on his back, looking up at the stars. Something bright and streaking crossed the sky. Konstantine tried to remember what it was like three years ago. Five. Ten.

When he'd wished for this woman in his arms, when he'd longed for her so badly that it left a raw and burning cavern within him.

And here she was.

After so much dreaming, here was her weight against him, her breath hanging in the silence of their collected pleasure.

"Will it always be like this?" he asked into her hair.

She stiffened.

Don't ruin it with romance, he thought.

"Outside. On the ground," he said with a forced smile. "Do you have something against beds?"

She relaxed against him. "You said you wanted out of the city. You didn't say anything about a bed."

29

___

Dani, Piper, King, and Lou stood in the middle of the Crescent City Detective Agency. King thought they looked like a rather somber bunch despite the sunny summer day pressing through the front windows.

"Don't die," Piper said, frowning at them. Her arms were crossed over her chest as she looked from Lou to King and back to Lou again. "You look too relaxed. Take this seriously, okay? Diana is crazy. Be on your guard."

"Sure you want to sit this one out?" King asked. It wasn't like Piper to insist she stay behind during the action.

"I'm sure," Piper said. She glanced in Dani's direction. It was such a quick micro movement, King wasn't sure she realized she'd done it. But it told King a lot. Maybe Piper was staying behind for Dani's sake. Maybe because Dani didn't want another encounter with Diana.

"We've got plenty of work to do," Dani said, taking Piper's hand. "But you guys be safe and let us know as soon as it's over."

Piper was watching Lou closely.

King wondered if it was the guns. Lou had a shoulder holster with two Browning pistols and a hip holster with two Berettas. Her arms were covered with Kevlar sleeves. The body armor on her chest made her look battle ready. That and the fact her hair had been pulled back from her face, in a ponytail.

"Be careful," Piper said, stepping forward. She looked like she wanted to give Lou a hug but wasn't sure how to manage it with all the guns.

To King, Lou said, "Let's go."

Piper's face fell.

They haven't made up.

"Sure." He stepped into Lou's office, the broom closet with her name on the door, and she followed him in. She closed the door, leaving them in pitch darkness.

"Did Konstantine tell you where he assembled the men?" King asked into the dark.

"There was an empty office building across the street from Winter's apartment. That's our first stop."

Before King could ask more, the room shifted around him. The darkness rolled over him, squeezing him, and the floor dropped out. His stomach turned, and then the gravity shifted again and he was on his feet in the middle of a large lobby.

King would never get used to it, the feeling of being compressed, pinched, and stretched out in turn.

"Shit." The man closest to his left elbow jumped, bumping into a dusty plant. A cloud puffed into the air.

King took this moment to right himself and take the room's measure. The men were spread around the dusty, forgotten place, standing in small huddles or leaning against the sheet-covered furniture. The buzz of conversation died upon their arrival.

Silence stretched out between them.

The man they'd startled hung over one of the sheet-covered armchairs as if ready to throw himself over its back and run if necessary.

"Damn. He wasn't joking," someone said. "It's her."

All eyes were on them now. No, not *them*. Lou.

They tracked her movements with keen interest—and perhaps more than a little fear.

Her shades were down, her weapons in full view.

No one wanted to move closer. When her mirrored shades passed over them, their gazes flicked away.

This gave King ample room to make his own assessment.

At first glance, they didn't look like gangsters.

A few had tattoos across their exposed hands, but that didn't mean anything. One had some writing sticking out from under his shirt collar. But mostly, they looked the part of operatives. Head to toe in black, bulletproof vests, earpieces, and guns.

"Good evening," King said, finding his voice at last, despite the nausea from Lou's slip lingered. "Before we get started—"

"He said we answer to her," one of the men said, motioning toward Lou. "Not some cop."

No need to ask who *he* was.

"Sure," King said. He was a little miffed that despite his hard work over the years, he still emitted a cop vibe. He thought he'd done a pretty good job of eliminating it, *thankyouverymuch*. "Do you have anything you'd like to tell them?"

A few stiffened, their backs straightening.

"Listen to him," Lou said. She grinned. "Or we're finished here."

More than one shifted nervously at the implied threat. Someone muttered, "Fuck," as if only just realizing what they'd gotten themselves into.

"Any other questions?" King asked, eyebrows raised.

No one spoke.

He hated his hard-ass voice. He hadn't had to use it in years, rarely since he'd trained recruits at Quantico. But it was a necessary evil tonight. These men had to follow his lead if they hoped to fool Diana and take down Winter.

I'm the only one here that knows what an operation is supposed to even look like.

"Good. Now we're going to split into two teams of twenty, and a third team of ten." When no one moved, he added, "Now."

The men separated into two groups. King made a few adjustments, asking men to switch sides until he had an even mix.

"Okay, Team A, that's you." King pointed at the cluster on his left. "We're going to position you on the ground, surrounding the building.

Team B, we're sending you into the building. Do any of you Team B-ers have experience clearing a room?"

Most indicated they had.

"Team C, you'll stay close to—" He'd almost said Lou's name. "Her."

"She's here," Lou said, her eyes fixed on the parking lot.

King turned and saw two black cars swinging into the cement lot. Diana stepped out from behind the driver's wheel into the gloomy day. Her entourage exited the two cars and came toward the office building's entrance and its two glass doors.

"And now," King said as Diana reached for the door handle, "pretend we've known each other forever."

LOU BARELY LISTENED TO KING AS HE PRATTLED ON ABOUT THE instructions for the raid. Even after Diana entered the building and explained how her team would be overseeing the technology and monitoring of the operation, Lou couldn't hold her interest.

Her eyes kept straying to the apartment complex across the street. Its faded brick exterior seemed watchful, as if it was waiting for this moment as much as she was. But it was also what she was feeling.

Or *wasn't*.

She reached out for Winter again, trying to get a lock on his location.

Close, she thought. But it wasn't fixating on either of the two apartment buildings. The compass kept circling.

Lou tried to remember the last time her compass had done that, been unsure of a target's location. Even if they were in cars or airplanes, somehow their bodies in motion, it was still enough.

"We good?" King asked her suddenly.

She turned and saw that most of the eyes were on her. Not just King, who was waiting for an answer, but Diana, the silent, leather-clad woman beside her, and the short man with the hobbled gait. Lou noted the bruising on his neck.

All of the others too, watching her carefully as if waiting for her to say something.

Lou motioned King close.

His brow furrowed. "What's wrong?"

"I can't get a lock on Winter," she whispered, keeping her voice too low for the others to hear.

King was careful to keep his voice low too. "You don't think he's in that building?"

"He's close," she said. "But I can't get an exact lock."

King rubbed his jaw. "Has this ever happened before?"

"No."

King shook his head. "We'll work with what we've got."

"Anything you want to share with the class?" Diana called. This earned a few snickers from her own people.

Those who belonged to Konstantine said nothing.

What stories did they hear about me? she wondered. She understood that she had some notoriety in the underworld. She'd killed too many of them to not loom in their imaginations larger than life.

"What are we waiting for?" Diana asked, her arms crossed.

"Dark," Lou said, and the men around her stiffened, reacting to her voice.

Someone murmured the word *vampira*, but Lou didn't catch the source. She considered smiling mischievously, fueling their fear, but her eyes kept sliding toward the buildings across the street.

"Sundown is in twelve minutes. We'll need another thirty minutes after that for full dark," the woman in leather said.

She must be the sister. Lou watched how close she stood to Diana, almost protective.

Her eyes fixed on Lou and didn't waver. Unlike Diana, who often dismissed the people around her, this one paid attention. No detail seemed to escape her notice.

"Plenty of time to get ready," King said. "Now let's run through the plan again. I want to go through the scenarios. Scenario one, if there are children in the building..."

Lou only distantly noted King's instructions as he drilled the men again and again about the situations they might encounter.

When Diana began to issue her own orders, Lou learned some names. The woman in the leather pants was Blair. The hobbled man with the fresh bruises on his throat was Spencer. From the corner of her eye, she watched Diana affix technology she didn't recognize to their clothes.

Sitting on a sheet-covered sofa, Diana opened her laptop.

"He's streaming," she announced. "Just give me a couple of minutes to confirm his location."

Which is more than I can do, Lou thought, her insides tensing.

The streetlights grew brighter, the night darker, and Lou began to see lights in the building across the street. She focused on each one, wondering which one might be Winter, but again her compass only swirled and swirled.

Was she concentrating too hard on the building?

Lou felt the moment the sun slid behind the horizon. The itchy heat in her body cooled instantly.

Sometimes it was like that. The second the shadows took control of the world, she felt a surge of energy, something inside her waking up.

"He's there," Diana said, speaking up, her face lit with excitement. "The building on the right."

She was vibrating like a tuning fork.

King motioned toward the glass. "All right. Into positions. Remember, we're surrounding the building on all sides first. He might try to bolt the second he sees us setting up formation, so be prepared for that. Let's go."

Everyone followed him out of the building into the cooling night.

Lou considered slipping from the dusty office building straight into Winter's room, but since this whole charade was to fool Diana into thinking Lou was a normal woman with abundant resources and nothing more, she restrained herself.

It surprised her how quickly they had the building surrounded.

Those who weren't part of the raid, including Lou, King, Diana, Blair, and Spencer, stood under the row of manicured trees expertly arranged along the side of the road opposite the apartment complex.

Diana didn't like being in the proverbial backseat. Every time King issued an order she looked ready to speak over him and rewrite his command.

Somehow she held herself back. Perhaps it was because these were not her men, and she had no guarantee that her order would be heeded anyway.

Whatever it was, Lou watched her struggle with amusement, aware that while she watched Diana almost everyone else watched her.

Konstantine's men stole sly glances, as did Diana's remaining team. The sister in particular seemed to be reconciling something in her mind.

Meanwhile Lou's attention kept returning to the apartments.

No, she thought. She wasn't drawn to *both* of the buildings. It was the façade on the left that drew her. The twin to the building now surrounded.

Are you in there? she wondered, tracing the windows with her eyes. *Have we chosen the wrong one?*

"Go!" King said.

Men pushed through the doors on all sides. On Diana's monitor, Lou could see them moving silently, snakelike through the bowels of the place. They filled all the stairs, corridors, and doorways.

"Come on, come on, come on," Diana said, urging them on.

"Any change in the signal?" King asked.

"No," Diana said. "It's good that your people are going in quiet. He probably doesn't realize we're in."

Then Lou realized that King was looking at her, not Diana. The question, *any change*, was about her inability to get a lock.

"I need to check something," Lou said, retreating across the parking lot and into the office building as if she'd left something inside.

When she turned back, looking through the glass front, she saw that Blair had followed her halfway across the parking lot, standing beneath the orange lamplight.

Lou couldn't worry about that now.

She stepped into a hallway off the main lobby. It was more than dark enough in this space. Already she felt the thin gossamer curtain of the world shifting around her, threatening to pitch her through.

Winter, she thought. *Winter, where are you?*

Again, she got only a strange doubling in her mind that seemed unable to settle upon a single place.

The one Diana wants, she thought. *Come on. The one she wants.*

At last the dial shifted, her focus sharpened. The dusty office building around her fell away. In its place, a hallway with scuffed red carpet materialized.

Near the end of the hallway, a child was crying. Lou walked toward the sound.

"Shut up and put on your coat," a gruff voice said.

Then a door was opening, and the child was shoved out into the hallway, her feet tangling beneath her. But she didn't get far.

It was a little girl, seven or eight years old. She had on a pink coat that was dirty at the elbows with a smear of something at the throat. Her hair hadn't been brushed in a few days at least. Both cheeks were tear-stained.

A squat man with a bald head stepped out after her, yanking the door shut behind him.

"Stop crying. We have to get out of here. In five minutes *here* won't even exist."

As soon as the girl saw Lou, her eyes doubled in size. Lou pressed a finger to her lips, urging the girl to stay silent as she crept forward.

But even the smallest invitation of salvation was too much. The girl took off at a run, bolting for Lou as if she were the gates of heaven.

"Hey!" the man screamed, releasing the door handle and turning until he came face to face with Lou.

His eyes roved her body, took in the leather and the body armor, the guns.

That's when he pulled something from his pocket.

Without thinking, Lou grabbed the girl and stepped back into the shadows, the world falling away.

This new apartment was like a movie set, with lights and a camera set up over a stage.

"No," the girl murmured. "No, not here."

And on the stage, a child-size bed.

"Please, please," the little girl begged, her hands tightening around Lou's neck. An ice pick of pain ran down her left side. Lou sharply inhaled, but didn't let go.

"Please don't leave me here," the girl said.

"I won't," Lou said.

She wanted to kill that man. She wanted to tear him apart and handfeed what was left of him to Jabbers.

But Lou couldn't fight with a kid hanging from her neck.

"Okay," she said. "It's okay. I've got you."

Lou listened to the feet on the stairs, noting their growing distance. Instead of giving chase, she stepped away from the shining movie set and back into the dark.

When the dusty office building sprang up around them, Lou carried the girl out of the building into the night.

"King!" she shouted, trying to cross the parking lot as quickly as she could. He turned, pulling the headphones off his head.

"We've got the guy!" King said, his face lit up and bright. Then his eyes fell on the kid.

"No, you don't," Lou said. "Get everyone out of the buildings and back up. They're about to blow."

His face fell. "What?"

"They wired them to explode. Get everyone out."

"There are kids in there," King said, panic growing on his face.

Lou tried to pry the little girl off her neck and the girl squealed. She didn't want to be handed over to King.

"I'll take her," a voice said. Lou looked up to see Blair, hands open.

The girl finally released Lou.

"Go," Blair said, eyebrows arched, and Lou had the distinct impression Blair meant *go. Slip.*

"Go on," King echoed. Then, into his headset, "There's a bomb in the building. Both buildings," he amended. "Clear out now. Pronto, chop-chop! Back to the admin building!"

Lou glanced toward Diana and saw that she was poring over her laptop footage, cursing to herself.

"Where is he?" she hissed, scrolling furiously. "Where is he?"

Lou ran toward the apartment building. Once she was around the side, in the shadows thrown by the trees, she slipped.

Kids, she thought. *I want the kids.*

Lou materialized in a dingy room and immediately realized the problem. A boy was shackled to the floor. A thick iron chain was latched to the floor, connecting to the collar around his throat.

He was crying and naked, trying to cover himself.

"We can't get it open," one of Konstantine's men said, real panic in his voice. His eyes were round, his jaw working.

The apartment door burst open. "I've got them!"

The incoming man stuttered when he saw Lou, the bolt cutters coming in front of him like a shield.

Lou snatched them and put the chain between the blades. She snapped the handles together. The fire in her shoulder intensified, but she pushed past it.

The chain broke and the freed boy collapsed with relief.

"How many kids are in the building?" Lou asked, scooping him up.

"Six," he said. "That we know of."

Lou threw her mind out, searching the dark.

"There's a bomb in the building. Get out of here," she said, and with that scooped the boy into her arms and disappeared.

It was the night that formed around them again. An alarmed bird startled in the tree above her.

"You see those people?" Lou asked, putting the boy on his feet. She pointed at King. "Run to them. Go on. Get away from this building."

She pushed the boy forward and he ran on unsteady legs.

Lou reached out for the next child and found her on the second floor. Another snap of the bolt cutters and Lou pulled her through the dark.

Each child that she delivered to the patch of darkness took off over the uneven grass as if their life depended on it.

"Over here!" King called, waving them forward. "Hurry!"

Lou had just managed to get the seventh kid out of the building when King screamed, "Forty seconds!"

They must've found the bomb, she thought. Either on video or while still canvassing the building. Lou dematerialized again. The room that reformed around her was a nightmare.

Two men with their pants around their ankles lay face down in their own blood. A girl no more than twelve years old stood over them. Lou didn't recognize the men as either Konstantine's or Diana's.

The girl was naked from the waist down, with a dark crust of blood spread on her inner thigh. Her hair was matted to her face with sweat, her chest heaving.

Lou didn't know where she'd gotten the gun, if it was given to her by one of Konstantine's men or if she'd taken it in the commotion.

But she stood there heaving, crying, unable to move. Unable to lower the gun. Her whole body trembled.

When she saw Lou, she raised the gun instinctively and fired. Lou shifted through the dark and felt the bullet graze her good arm, ripping a hole through her leather jacket, a second before she reappeared behind the girl and grabbed her.

She thrashed in Lou's arms, screaming, crying beneath the large evergreen above them.

"It's over," Lou said into her ear. Her voice was strained with the pain of her shoulder. "It's over."

The girl went soft in Lou's arms, and Lou scooped her up.

She was in the parking lot when the building blew behind them.

30

There were seven men and two women cuffed face down in the grass median between the admin building parking lot and the street in front of the apartment buildings—or what was *left* of the apartment buildings.

Sirens wailed in the distance.

"Go on," King said, waving the men away. Konstantine's men cast one look at Lou as if to make sure she wasn't going to follow them into the night.

"Go," she said.

They fled like kitchen-fed cockroaches when the light comes on. They dispersed in any and all directions, across parking lots, into the trees, down the streets.

Diana rolled one man onto his back. "I don't understand."

"Get out of my face, bitch," the guy said. He was thin and mean, his face etched with deep scars.

Diana yanked up the sleeve of his jean jacket and scowled. "Give me a light."

Blair produced her phone's flashlight, which Diana used to inspect the man's bare arm.

"No," she screamed, shoving him back down. "No!"

"What's going on?" King asked, leaning toward her.

"There were two men," Lou said.

"No, I saw them on the feed before she shot them. They weren't him."

"I'm not talking about the men in the building." Lou could feel the heat wafting from the burning buildings from here. Sweat beaded at her temples. "There were two men using the handle Winter. The man you actually wanted and this one. They ran the operation together."

Lou toed the lean, mean bastard with her boot. "You're Winter, aren't you?"

"Who's asking?"

"No, he's not," Diana said, kicking the man in the gut.

King's eyes lit with recognition.

"And you saw him, the other guy?" Diana asked, chest heaving. "He was here tonight?"

"He left."

"Damn it!" She kicked the man a second time. "Where's your buddy, asshole?"

"Long gone," the man cackled.

Diana brought a foot down on his face, splitting the nose.

"We're going to have to explain any damage to the authorities," King said.

"The hell we are. Spencer, get him in the car." Diana hauled the guy to his feet and thrust him toward the man with the hobbled walk.

Spencer managed to get Winter across the parking lot and into one of Diana's cars.

Then she pulled her gun.

"Hey!" King said.

But Diana was already firing. One bullet into the back of every head lying in the grass median. Those toward the end of the line, realizing what was happening, began to scream, to rise up. The children also began to scream, huddled behind Lou as if she could protect them.

Brains splattered across Lou's boots.

When Diana's gun clicked empty, she met Lou's gaze, her chest heaving.

"A lot of help you were!" Diana shouted, shoving the emptied gun into her waistband. "You let the bastard get away!"

"He can't escape me," Lou said, and now he couldn't.

Not now that she understood why the strange doubling had happened, when her compass had warred with itself to reconcile the difference between the man named Winter and the one Diana was really hunting.

"He wasn't for you! He was for *me*!" Diana said, throwing herself off the curb. "We're leaving!"

Her team broke and ran for the vehicles. In one movement, Blair dropped the girl she was holding and snatched up the computer.

The girl let out a small, startled cry.

Lou pulled her close, and the girl rested her head against Lou's thigh.

"Shit," King said, watching them go. "That wasn't how we were supposed to wrap this up."

Red and blue lights illuminated the trees at the end of the street. Any second, the police would turn onto the road and see the devastation.

A bunch of dead bodies, two blown-out and burning buildings. And the children.

"We have to go," King said. "*Now.*"

"What about them?" Lou asked, pointing at the children sitting huddled together on the grass.

King bent down to talk to the kids. They shrank away from him.

"I'm not going to hurt you," King said tenderly. "I want you to stay right here until the police arrive. When they get here, I want you to give them your names, okay? And they'll make sure you get home to your parents."

One boy visibly flinched at the word *parents*. He looked past Lou to the man lying face down in his own blood.

"Was that your dad?" Lou asked, her insides boiling.

The boy nodded.

She reached out to him and he climbed into her arms. Even in the orange streetlights, she could see the bruises along the side of his face.

Her anger rose so intense it obliterated all thoughts in her head.

"You're okay," Lou said into his ear as he tucked his face into her shoulder. She wasn't sure if she was speaking to the boy or herself. "You're okay."

"What about us?" the little girl squealed, the one Lou had rescued from the hallway, from the real Winter Diana sought.

"What're your names?" King asked.

"Mitchel."

"Katie-Jo."

"Raelara."

"Jean," said the one who had first run into Lou's arms.

"Zoe."

"Lea Reynolds. And this is my brother, Lane Reynolds."

"And what about you?" Lou asked, noticing that one hadn't spoken.

A silent girl reluctantly rolled her eyes up to Lou. "Danielle."

"Pretty name." Lou smiled. "I want you guys to stay here and stay together."

"But!" The outcry was immediate.

"Stay here," Lou insisted, "and those officers will make sure you get home."

They could see the police now, the cars zooming into view. Before the headlights got too close, Lou reached out and grabbed King's elbow, and the three of them disappeared through the dark.

"How can you do it?" the little boy asked when they stepped out of the storage closet in the Crescent City Detective Agency. "Are you magic? Are you an angel?"

"No," Lou said. When she tried to untangle his arms from her neck, he only tightened them. She relented. "Can I shift you to the other side, please?"

Her shoulder was throbbing and each pulse made red flash behind her eyes.

The boy loosened his grip enough to let Lou adjust his weight.

"What's your name, buddy?" King asked.

The boy didn't answer.

"It's okay," Lou said into his ear. "He's a good guy."

"Shai. With an *i*."

"How old are you, Shai?" King asked, coming around his desk and settling into the chair. He unlocked the drawer with a key from his wallet and fished out his laptop.

"Six," the boy said.

King booted up the computer. "You got a last name?"

"Wilson."

King began punching at the computer furiously. Lou crossed to Piper's empty chair and sank into it.

"Tampa, Florida," King said. "He was reported missing by his mother eight months ago."

"Eight months is a long time," Lou said, and she and King shared a knowing look.

A door creaked open and Piper stepped into the office. "I thought I heard you guys. How'd it go?"

Then her eyes fell on the kid.

"Oh, hey." Tears sprang to her eyes. "Oh gosh. Um, I'm Piper."

"Shai Wilson."

She held out her hand, swallowing hard. "Nice to meet you, Shai."

"I'll take him to his mom," Lou said. To Shai, "Do you want to see your mom? Is she..."

Lou couldn't figure out how to finish the sentence.

"Has she ever hurt you?" she managed.

"Mommy is nice. But she doesn't like it when I leave my trucks on the floor."

"Sounds reasonable," King said. To Lou, "I don't suppose you need the address."

Shai's stomach rumbled loudly. The boy looked embarrassed.

"Sorry," he whispered.

"Don't be sorry," King said.

"I have stuff to make a sandwich," Piper said. To the boy, "Are you a ham and cheese guy or a peanut butter and jelly guy?"

"Peanut butter, no jelly," he said. Then he looked afraid.

"Crust or no crust?"

"Mommy cuts off my crusts."

Piper looked ready to cry. "No crust, no jelly it is. Be right back."

She started up the stairs two at a time. Overhead, Lou heard a cabinet snap shut. A drawer slid open, then closed.

Lou reached out with her compass. She searched the darkness, looking for the mother first. She found her, sensing that she was in a very dark room. Maybe the only light was the television droning on somewhere in the background.

Safe? Lou wondered. *Will he be safe with you?*

Piper reappeared with a sandwich with no crusts tucked into a paper towel.

Shai took an enormous bite, like a dog lunging into a food bowl.

"How'd I do?" Piper asked. "Enough peanut butter? 'Cause I got more."

Shai spared her another smile. "It's good."

"*You're* good, you know that?" Piper said.

The kid was getting breadcrumbs on Lou's jacket.

"We're going," Lou announced. To Shai, "Are you ready?"

"Where?" he asked, squeezing his sandwich so hard that the bread flattened out in his fist.

"To your mom. Is that okay?"

"Can't I stay with you?"

Lou shook her head dolefully. "You can finish your sandwich first."

What commenced was the slowest consumption of a sandwich that any of them had ever seen. And when there was nothing left but the barest sliver of bread, Piper took the paper towel and wiped the peanut butter and crumbs off his face.

"It was nice to meet you, Shai. Be safe."

"Thank you," he said.

Lou placed one hand on his back. "Ready?"

"No."

Lou stepped back into a pocket of shadow in the corner office.

"Come back when you're done," King said. "I need to—"

That was all Lou heard before the darkness rolled over them, pulling them through.

The office was replaced by a small house with its porchlight on. The bungalow sat on a street with many identical houses, and an identical concrete walk linking them.

Lou stood outside the soft circle of the porchlight, regarding the house. "Is this your mom's house?"

"Yeah," he said, sliding out of her arms for the first time.

She wanted to believe it. She wanted to believe that he would be safe here with his mother.

"Mom!" Shai called, running up the walkway. "Mommy!"

Lou walked up the sidewalk, casting glances up and down the quiet street. A black cat sat at the end of a driveway, watching them with interest, its tail flicking against the warm concrete.

A breeze rubbed the palm trees, the large fronds lifting.

"Mommy! Mommy!"

The door opened. "Shai?"

The woman looked dazed, as if half dreaming. Lou wondered if this was the first time she'd opened her door calling her child's name.

"Shai?"

"Mommy, it's me!"

Recognition dawned in her eyes the moment she put her hands on the boy's shoulders.

"Shai! Oh my god, Shai!"

She cupped his face and cried out, "Oh my god, baby. My baby! What happened to you?"

She fingered the collar of his shirt, yanking it down to reveal his slender, bruised throat.

"Oh god, oh god, oh my god."

She crushed Shai against her, collapsing into her sobs.

Then her eyes fell on Lou. On the body armor, on the guns. "You! Did you do this? Did you hurt him?"

She launched herself at Lou, fingers hooked into claws as she swiped at her face.

Lou sidestepped easily, catching her wrist and twisting it.

The woman screeched.

"It wasn't me," Lou said calmly, ignoring the pulsing pain in her shoulder.

"She's an angel, Mommy! She saved me!"

The woman yanked her hand away.

Lou turned, intending to walk to the trees across the street and disappear in the shadows between the two palms.

"Don't go!" Shai seized her leg. "Please don't go. *Please.*"

Lou turned. "I can't stay." She cut her eyes up to the mother.

"What if I need you?" Shai said. "What if—"

Lou placed a hand on his chest. "I'll be around. If you need me."

"Can I pray to you?" he asked. "If I pray like this, will you hear me?"

Shai closed his eyes, pinching them tightly shut.

Lou felt her compass spin inside her, responding to it. It reminded her of Piper, who also used calls of help to get Lou's attention.

"You can do that," Lou said. "But only if you're really in trouble. Don't waste your prayers."

In this life, we learn how to save ourselves.

The boy nodded solemnly.

"Who are you?" the mother asked, pulling Shai back as if Lou were the dangerous one. And between the three of them, Lou supposed it was true.

"No one."

"She's my angel," Shai said. "She saved me."

"An angel?" the woman asked, frowning down at her son. "Is that..."

Her question died on her lips. When she looked up, Lou was gone.

31

———

It wasn't hard to find Diana. Lou simply had to think about her and the compass did the work. It spun around in the dark, orienting itself in time and space, before locking in on her.

Stalks swayed in the breeze. The smell of corn silk hung in the air. As the stalks parted, Lou saw a barn, with a single light in the darkness.

Lou moved through the corn, her boots crunching on fallen stalks.

"How the *hell* did you find us?" a woman cursed.

Lou turned and found Blair standing, legs apart, gun cupped in her hand. She aimed at Lou's head.

"I knew you were a freak." Blair laughed, but there was no humor in it. "I told her to believe what we saw, but *no*. My sister has to be the rational one."

"Lower your gun," Lou said. She thought she was being rather polite about it.

"No, thanks. I know what you can do."

If you already know... Lou thought. She sidestepped through the shadows, reappearing behind Blair. She took in the woman's long, slender neck before bringing her elbow down hard on the back of it.

Blair collapsed, falling face down onto the dirt. This was when Lou heard the others, moving through the corn, drawn to the sound of the commotion. The hobbled man would be here, of course, with the others who served Dennard.

Get me closer, she thought, and the swaying stalks and stench of packed mud and corn silk fell away.

Then she was at the back of a barn, a rough red door under her hand.

She pushed it open.

In the doorway, Lou hesitated. She smelled hay, but also something electric and burning.

Winter was tied to a wooden chair in the center of the room. Three utility lights were strung overhead, beating down on the man. Cinderblocks were latched to the bottom of each chair leg as if to hold it in place.

His chest was bloody from throat to bellybutton. The light hair covering most of his stomach was matted. Lou suspected the source was the three thick gashes along his collarbones and chest.

His white-gray hair was mostly untouched except for a crust of blood on the right side, the side facing Lou.

The scene reminded her of her early hunting days. How she would find one of the Martinellis and string him up, hurt him until something inside her, a long-festering sore, broke open and oozed. In this letting, she'd find a momentary relief from that unquenchable ache within her.

Had she looked like Diana did now? Her sleeves rolled up, a knife twisting in her fist, her face all business and fury.

"Has he told you where he is yet?" Lou called from the doorway.

Diana looked up, her eyes still glazed.

"He will," she said. "If he knows what's good for him."

"You're going to kill me either way," the man said, turning his head and spitting blood on the ground. "Just fucking do it already."

"No," Diana said, pressing her boot onto the ground. The man convulsed, twitching wildly in his chair.

At this distance, it looked like Diana was stepping onto a block. Lou edged closer and saw it was a peddle connected to wiring wrapped around the chair.

Pushing the peddle down ignited an electrical charge which then coursed up the wires and into Winter's body.

Diana was watching her face instead of the convulsing man. "It doesn't bother you?"

What should bother her? The smell of burning hair? The pitiful mewling? She'd seen—caused—worse. "No."

"You are *cold*." Diana smiled. "But you still fucked up tonight."

"Because the other one got away?"

"He's not the *other* one," Diana hissed, pulling her boot off the switch and wiping the bloody knife on her pants. It left a smear across the top of her right thigh. "He was *the one*."

"Why?" Lou asked, leaning against the doorway, arms crossed.

She tried to piece together Diana's story. She remembered most of it from the diner, the night they spoke for the first time.

Her father's friend had picked her up from school and taken her home to his house, locking her in a soundproof shed. She hadn't gone into detail about what had happened in the shed in the weeks he'd held her captive, but Lou could guess. When she'd escaped, she came back with a gun and shot the guy. If the one who'd hurt her was dead, who were these two men to her?

Where did they fit into her story? Lou was ready to believe that there was more than one villain.

For her, there hadn't been just one either. Not really.

Her *one* had been Angelo Martinelli, because he'd pulled the trigger. But there'd also been Gus Johnson, her father's partner, who'd given the Martinellis their address in exchange for sparing his own life. There'd been Chaz Brasso, King's old partner, who'd sold out Jack and Gus as the ones who'd busted Benito Martinelli for drugs.

There'd been Senator Ryanson, who'd been lining Brasso's pockets for years and who'd given the order to take her meddlesome father out of the picture once he'd gotten too close to the source of the corruption. Not to mention Angelo's father and brothers, who'd executed the ambush of her childhood home and the murder of her parents.

No, not one man. It was rarely *one* man responsible for a woman's accumulated pain. Lou understood that.

"Who is he to you? Really?" she asked, blinking past the irritation of her shoulder. She needed another Vicodin, but it could wait.

It didn't look like Diana would answer. Then she surprised Lou.

"Do you know that these photos and videos that end up on the internet stay on there forever? *Forever.* Unless someone actually takes them all down, but even then, sometimes copies will resurface."

She wiped her nose on her sleeve.

"The internet was a new thing when I was taken," Diana said. "It had only been around a few years, but it was sophisticated enough. My rapist didn't just screw me. He filmed himself doing it. Never his own face, but my face? *Sure.* My face was everywhere. You see, these sick perverts get off on the crying as much as the raping."

Lou waited. She knew the story was only getting started.

"What you don't realize is that people can *recognize* you. Once you're in the system, once a hundred or a thousand assholes have jerked off to your crying face, they *remember* you. Remember this, you piece of shit."

Diana stepped on the switch again and the man resumed convulsing. It wasn't until he slumped unconscious that she took her foot off the pedal.

"One night, when I was fifteen, a couple of years after that nightmare in the shed, I'm walking home from the library with one of my friends. I notice that a guy is following me. I can't get a good look at him, but I'm ready for any bullshit. After what I did to Daniel, I stayed ready."

Lou assumed Daniel was her original kidnapper. She wasn't about to interrupt the story to ask.

"This guy waits until my friends and I split up, and of course he follows me. He follows me three blocks, and I know he's looking for the right time to grab me. So I make it easy for him. I cut across the playground. It wasn't a nice playground. It had a busted swing and the grass was overgrown, and it sat between two abandoned houses. I thought about going into the houses, but I wanted someone to hear me scream if my plan didn't work out."

Lou shifted against the door.

"He grabbed me by the back fence, before I could get to the gate. When he threw me on the ground, you know what he said to me?"

Lou didn't answer.

"He said, 'I *knew* it was you. Look at you, my good girl. My good little slut.' That's what Daniel was always saying, 'my good little slut.' He kept saying it while getting his hand under my skirt. He kept saying it until I cut half his fucking arm off."

She slammed her foot down on the switch but nothing happened. The man's muscles twitched but he remained unconscious. White foam bubbled at the side of his mouth.

"You were looking for a scar," Lou said, remembering the way Diana had yanked Winter's sleeve up. "Of where you stabbed him."

"That's what they do," Diana said, more to herself than anyone else. "These sick bastards. They come back."

She met Lou's gaze at last, and Lou knew the look in her eyes. She'd seen it in her own.

"Don't wear yourself out," Lou said, taking a step back into the darkness. "You've got one more coming."

32

———————

Lou's wrist buzzed.

Are you okay? the message read.

Lou sat up in bed, trying to shake the sleep off. She'd needed it, and the pill she'd taken after Diana's raid had given her long, uninterrupted hours of it.

Even with two days of rest behind her, her body ached. She wasn't sure which act had actually exacerbated her shoulder, but it was still speaking to her in low, threatening tones.

Two days and two nights in her apartment, alone, sleeping and eating and standing under the pounding stream of hot water. All of it had helped, but it hadn't erased her discomfort entirely.

Amore mio?

Lou looked at the watch face and sent a simple return text. *I'm fine.*

All other explanations would have to wait. She had a date with a man with a scar.

She might need more rest, but two days was the most she could manage before her restlessness overcame her again.

She rose, kicked off her comforter, and stretched. She particularly stretched her shoulder, until it moved without hitching in its socket.

She ate the second half of a burger she'd procured the night before.

She'd only eaten half of it before the Vicodin had kicked in and her desire to sleep outweighed her desire to keep eating. But now the hunger was in full swing. She chased the burger with two apples and a banana from the glass fruit bowl on her kitchen island.

She washed it all down with water, wishing instead for about half a gallon of coffee.

She settled for a pot of it, which she drank as she stood by her large picture window overlooking the Mississippi river.

Her eyes were on the shimmering waters, the way they sparked with the fading embers of the lowering sun. Outwardly she was relaxed, ready. Inwardly, her compass churned. It whirled, searching the darkness that connected every point in the world for her target.

She didn't use the word *Winter* now, since it hadn't been accurate. She used the face, the one she'd seen in the hallway as he stepped out to lock the door behind himself.

That was what she locked in on. That was the face her compass searched the dark for.

And found.

Something inside her clicked, jerked into place, and she felt a slight tug forward, like river water pushing at the backs of her knees.

As she drained the last of the cup, the sun descended, tucking itself beneath the horizon for the night. And with each passing moment, Lou's limbs grew stronger. Her hands steadier.

Good.

She'd need her strength.

MICKI JAMES STAYED ON THE MOVE. SINCE SPRINGFIELD TWO nights ago, when Murf got himself caught, Micki had known better than to stop his car for more than a few hours. He gassed up, grabbed a cold sandwich from a case beside the soda fountain, and got back on the road.

This car smelled like cigarettes whenever he rolled up the window, so he kept it cracked while he drove. The breeze hit his eyes, encouraging them to stay peeled.

He took speed from those little packets found on gas station counters and named after insects—wasps, bees, whatever—that kept him awake long after his brain begged for sleep.

He understood why the drugs were named this way now. After four pills, it was definitely like bees were in his brain, buzzing, bouncing off the insides of his skull.

He thought of Murf again. They'd been partners a long time—Micki and Murf. They'd had a good thing going. But he'd known this day was coming. What did his mama use to say? All good things come to an end?

And where had she heard that? From her Sunday morning preachers over the radio or the old biddies with whom she crocheted sweaters for the war veterans?

It didn't matter. His mother had been dead for twenty years.

And now Murf—*Winter*—was dead too.

You got caught 'cause you're careless, his mother said from the backseat.

There she sat in her curlers, a cigarette hanging from between her lips, her Coke-bottle glasses so thick he couldn't actually see the eyes behind them. *You've always been a careless boy.*

"Shut up, Mama," he said, and his voice, gruff, echoed in the car.

That cigarette smoke smell made his stomach hurt. He rolled down the window more.

Micki realized he was tired, maybe too tired to be driving, if he was having conversations with his dead mother.

But he couldn't stop, not now, when it felt like someone was still following him.

Welcome to California.

He turned in his seat, following the sign as far as his eyes would allow.

He planned to stop in San Diego, maybe Tijuana. Yes, Tijuana was better. That's where he'd regroup, assess his situation. That's where he'd get some sleep. When he woke with a clear head, he'd figure out who had found him and where he'd gone wrong. He had plenty of cash on hand and more stashed away in a few accounts, and even two computers locked in the trunk.

He'd be up and running in no time.

He reached into his plastic cup holder and fished out another packet of speed. He tore it open with his teeth, his sweaty fingers sliding off the steering wheel as he grabbed for his drink. He tore off the red cap and downed it in several deep gulps.

The car hummed, groaning as it slipped over the rumble strip on the side of the road.

He pulled the wheel left, getting back into the lane.

He threw the drink back into the cup holder with a sudden rage. He was pissed about losing the girl. She was such a sweet little cherry. Just the thought of her little hands on him was enough to get him hard.

That bitch with the guns and the mirrored shades. He'd make her sorry for taking away his girl.

Bees bounced off the inside of Micki's skull, lulling him with their rhythm. The Coke in the back of his throat stopped burning and the white line in the middle of the road swayed, seeming to be playing a song. A bass line.

Da dum da dum da dum.

You were always a careless boy, his mother said again from the backseat. *Remember when you fell off that little wooden bridge into the river. You weren't watching where you stepped and you got your nice shoes, your best Sunday shoes, all wet. Tore a hole in the seat of your pants, too, if I remember.*

"Shut up, Mama," he said again, wishing he'd grabbed a bag of chips or something he could have mindlessly shoved into his mouth. Something for his hands to do.

He turned on the radio, but a touch too loud, and it made his head hurt. He turned it off and opened the window, all the way down now, and angled his head out into the fresh air.

That was better, as the frigid cold pulled tears from his eyes. The sleepiness receded.

With his head back in the car, he blinked away the tears and saw a woman in the backseat.

"Go away, Mama," he said. "I told you to shut up."

"I'm not your mama," a voice said.

His bleary eyes snapped to the rearview mirror again.

She was right. It wasn't his momma in her Coke-bottle glasses and tight gray curls. There was no cigarette smoke rising thin and blue toward the car's roof.

It was the shades he remembered.

The woman in the hallway, the one who'd taken his little cherry pie. She leaned forward and grabbed the steering wheel. She yanked it hard, veering his car off the road, over the rumble strip and into the grass.

Here Micki thought to hit the brakes, but at first attempt his foot slipped off the pedal. The second attempt sent the vehicle into a slide but didn't actually slow it much. He was going too fast, the pillar was too close.

He began to scream.

The concrete barrier rose in his vision, doubling, tripling in size until all else was blotted out.

His heart hammered, beating furiously as he waited for the impact that never came.

LATER, AS THE EMERGENCY CREWS HOSED DOWN THE FLAMING CAR, they'd wonder where the driver was, and if he—or she—had taken off on foot. All agreed that whoever the driver had been, they must've rolled from the vehicle before it slammed into the overpass barrier.

They sent a search party to look for the driver. If they'd survived, they might be hurt, disoriented. But after three hours and no sign of life except the coyotes hunting rabbits under the large moon, they called it a night.

They believed the driver would turn up eventually.

Cars didn't drive themselves.

Diana emptied her Smith & Wesson .45 into the wooden target at the far end of the dirt path. Once the gun clicked empty and the trees lining the path stopped their rustling, an optimistic cardinal let out a shrill chirp. However, Diana was just getting started. She reloaded and went for another round.

Again, her mind railed. *He escaped again. How could it keep happening? How?*

There was nothing special or gifted about Winter. He should've folded like a house of cards under all her efforts by now.

A tap resounded against her shoulder. Blair held a folded piece of paper between two fingers.

"I told you not to bother me," Diana said, turning toward the target again and raising the gun.

"Spencer's gone. I think Lou killed him."

"No, she didn't." Diana gestured to the heap of dirt beneath a nearby sycamore. "He's over there."

She managed to empty the gun before her sister recovered from the news.

"*You* killed him?"

"I thought you hated him," Diana said, unable to hide her irritation.

In truth, Diana hadn't meant to do it. She'd said *the word*, giving Spencer permission to plunge himself inside her after roughly four weeks of refusal. Before she'd had a chance to orgasm, he came, abruptly ending her rhythm and her pleasure. The next thing she knew she had her hands around his throat, squeezing, grinding her hips into his, until an orgasm finally shivered through her.

She'd thought he'd liked it, the squeezing, since he'd resumed thrusting. It wasn't until she unzipped the leather mask and saw how blue his face was—she would never forget the bulge of his eyes—that she'd fully realized what she'd done.

I didn't mean to do it, she told herself.

Are you sure about that? a colder voice asked. *Or did you know exactly what you were doing? Will that be your next craving? Find a guy, enslave his cock, and kill him once you get bored? Sounds promising.*

"It had to be done," she said simply. "He wanted to go to the police. I couldn't let him do that."

Blair gawked at her, unblinking. "You're lying. He did everything for you. He was—he was the best—"

"Don't exaggerate." Diana wanted to change the subject. "Why did you think Lou killed him?"

Blair produced the folded piece of paper she'd first waved to get her attention. "She left this taped to the bathroom mirror. She was *in* our house. Surprise, surprise, it didn't even trip the alarm."

With a huff, Diana applied the safety to the gun and slipped it into her waistband. The warm metal bit into her flesh, chafing the bones beneath.

She unfolded the note. There were jotted coordinates, and then below them, *Get there before he wakes up.*

Diana's heart skipped a beat. "Have you checked it out?"

"I don't like it, Dee. She's shown up at our house *twice*. And in the cornfield, she just slipped past me like I was nothing. One second she was there, and—"

Diana was sick of these ghost stories. She raised her voice. "Did you check it out?"

Blair shifted. "Yes. You'll want to see for yourself."

Diana took off for the waiting truck at a steady jog. At the end of the dirt path and adjacent lot, her beat-up truck sat parked in the shade of an old-growth maple tree. She hauled herself up into the beast.

Hanging from the window, she called to her sister, "Coming or not?"

Blair climbed into the passenger seat, her jaw tight and working. Dust swirled around them as the truck reversed and sped out of the lot. It was almost a mile of packed dirt before concrete finally rose up to meet them.

The coordinates on the note were a short drive from Diana's worn farmhouse in Kansas. She was trying not to be bothered by the fact that Louie had found her so easily. The land and farmhouse and its two barns had been her hidden sanctuary for over six years. It was off grid and buffered by wild, overgrown land on all sides. The idea that Louie could find it only hours after they parted made her mind run wild with possibility. Had she put trackers on their cars? On her, somehow?

The coordinates took them to a service road marked only by a number. Diana drove the beat-up truck down it slowly, letting the oversized tires gently roll through the dips, creaking.

It seemed like an hour before they found a small, leaning shack at the edge of a dirt field.

Diana pulled the truck around back into the heart of the thicket so that it couldn't be seen from the road, and the two women hopped down into the long-overgrown weeds.

Someone was crying inside the shack.

The deep, rolling sobs could barely be heard over the rushing water of the river coursing behind them.

Diana pulled her gun from her waistband, removed the safety, and inched toward the shack.

"You won't need it," Blair said.

Diana paid her no mind. The door was rough under her hand and felt wet.

It's rotting, she noted. One more good rain or storm and this shack would go down. She wondered if this was what was left of a garage, perhaps the house long obliterated by the elements. Or perhaps a boathouse for the river behind them.

A man lay in the middle of the concrete floor. Naked and shackled.

Not just shackled, but in the way the children were often chained in his videos, with iron-like collars clamped over their throats and thick, unyielding chains drilled and hooked into the floor.

He was pulling on the chain, but it wouldn't give.

When their boots hit the concrete, the scuffs muffled by the wooden walls, he jumped. His cries escalated into panicked yips.

Then he seemed to see Diana.

"Please," he said. He shuffled toward her on his knees. "Please help me. Get me out of here before she comes back."

Diana knelt down and took his arm, turning it in the light to see the scar.

"Wha-what are you doing? What are you looking for?"

It was an old scar, at least twenty years since she'd carved it, but she'd recognize the hooked mark of her savage blade anywhere.

This was her man.

This was her Winter.

"Please," he begged, his face red and covered in snot. "Please, before it gets dark. She moves in the dark."

"I'm not here to help you," Diana said, dropping his arm.

The shack stank of his body odor and sweat. She thought he'd probably pissed himself too.

Even so, her pleasure uncoiled inside her. Her excitement doubled, then tripled, until her chest felt ready to explode with it.

"I'm here to *hurt* you."

The wind blew and the wooden sides of the shed groaned. He flinched, his eyes darting toward the blackened corners pressing in on them.

"Please," he cried, inching toward her. "*Please*, before it gets dark. Sh-she could come back."

Diana yanked hard on the collar.

His hands shot out instinctively to catch himself. Seeing him on all fours reminded her of Spencer. "Did you hear me?"

"He can't hear anything. He's scared out of his mind," Blair said.

There was a sound in her voice Diana didn't like. Awe? Fear? Or some unnamable emotion halfway between the two?

And Winter *was* scared out of his mind, that much was clear.

But he wasn't scared of her. He barely registered Diana's presence at all.

No, she thought. Her fist tightened on the chain. *No, he should be afraid of* me.

She *deserved* that much from him.

His eyes kept darting to the corners of the shack every time the wind rolled along its delicate sides. Each creak and moan intensified his fear. Diana could almost taste it, like battery acid on the tongue.

He made himself smaller and smaller. He folded and compressed himself in the medallion of sunlight shining from the hole in the roof above, as if the light was his last chance at salvation.

He's terrified, but not of me.

34

"Questions loom around the suspected raid in Springfield, Missouri. Police have identified two of the men as registered sex offenders connected to an internet pornography website known as—"

"Turn that up!" Piper stepped out of the bedroom with her toothbrush in her mouth and pointed at the television.

"In the eight hundred apartment block of Henderson Street..."

Dani, wrapped up in a thin summer blanket on Piper's sofa, reached for the remote. She turned up the volume with a mash of her thumb.

"We've found evidence in the building behind me that this was a shooting location for child pornography videos," a man was saying. He stood in the camera's spotlight with the smoldering building behind him. Even though the firefighters had been working on the building for days, it seemed the smoke wouldn't quit.

"Several children, all identified and returned to their families, were rescued from the scene. The only bodies present were the suspected pornographers, shot execution style in the back of their heads."

Piper spit into the bathroom sink. "Can they say that? Can a cop just say that on television?"

"I think he's in shock," Dani said. "Look at his face. Maybe he's not thinking about what he's saying."

Piper wiped her mouth and turned off the bathroom light behind her. The man on the television did look shocked. His eyes were too wide, the visible white nearly eclipsing the color. His mouth had a slack look to it, as if it were incapable of fully closing.

Piper suspected that if he took his hands off his hips, there would be a tremble to them.

A rough knock on the door made both girls jump. Dani pulled the blanket close. Piper reached across the counter and pulled a knife from the butcher's block.

"Who is it?" she called, her voice an octave too shrill.

"It's me." King's gruff voice was muffled by the door.

The tension in the room evaporated.

"Come in."

King entered with a cardboard box in one hand, the other on the knob he was turning. "I'm heading out for the night. I thought I'd see if you guys wanted the other half of this pizza. I'm not going to eat it."

Stepping into the living room, King stopped. When he saw the knife in Piper's hand he frowned. "Did I miss something?"

"No," she said, sliding the knife back into the block.

His gaze flicked from Piper to Dani. "You okay?"

"I'm good, thanks," Dani said automatically.

"Sure," he said with a snide laugh, as if he didn't believe anything either of them was saying. He lifted the cardboard box to show his half-devoured sausage pizza. "Do you want this?"

"What do you think, babe? Pizza?"

Dani smiled a bit too brightly. "Sounds good. Thanks, Robert."

"My pleasure." He placed the box on the island cabinet and headed back toward the door. "I'll lock up on my way out."

He hesitated when his eyes caught the news report.

"Is that—"

"Yeah," Piper interjected as she slid a slice from the box. "It looks like a mess."

"It was," King said as the story faded to black and the next tragedy cued. "Diana made a real mess of it. Trigger happy, that one."

"Authorities are searching for a woman by the name of Diana Dennard. The suspect, white, female, thirty-eight years old—"

King, who'd been turning toward the stairs, froze and whirled back. "What did she say?"

"Oh yeah." Piper spoke around the pizza in her mouth "Here we go."

Diana's picture appeared, covering half of the screen while the report prattled on.

"—responsible for at least thirty fraudulent scams across the US. Credit card bills exceeding two million dollars have been attributed to her seven known aliases..."

"Shit." With his hands on his hips and mouth ajar he looked like the police officer who'd reported on the raid. He turned to Dani. "Did you do this?"

Dani pursed her lips, ready to speak.

"It was me." Piper sucked in a deep breath. "Before you get mad, let me explain."

She took another slice of pizza from the box in case King decided to rescind his gift.

"What'd you do? Why in the world would you provoke her?" King ran a hand through his hair, clearly trying to compose himself.

"Aren't you tired of it?" Piper threw up her hands. "Bad guys are always coming after us, kidnapping us, telling us what the rules of the game are."

"If we were confrontation adverse, we would find new jobs," he said.

"I don't want a new job. But I'm not going to be the prey either. *Nope.* No more waiting around to be rescued while Lou does all the badassery. I'm taking control, damn it. Those jerks are going to start worrying about *me.*"

"Huzzah." Dani was smiling as she took her slice from the box and began picking off the sausage. "That's the spirit, baby."

King, however, looked far from optimistic.

. . .

DIANA WAS SCRAPING THE DIRT AND BLOOD OUT FROM UNDER HER fingernails with a metal pick when she saw someone step into her periphery. She met their eyes in the mirror, finding Blair, her body tense and face drawn.

Diana wanted a shower. She wanted to fuck Spencer and sleep for two days. Maybe then the dull ache in her overworked shoulders and back would go away.

You killed Spencer, she reminded herself. *I suppose you could dig up his corpse and fuck that. And when you're done with him, why not Winter too?*

Diana sighed. She thought she'd feel better. Energized. Overwhelmed with triumph or at least relief.

But she didn't. Winter was dead and she felt—nothing. It was an anti-climactic end to a long and arduous search, and what did she have to show for it?

You're just tired. You need to rest, and then you'll feel it.

What she didn't need was whatever lecture Blair was mentally rehearsing behind those sullen eyes.

Diana sighed. "Before you ask, *yes*, I buried him deep. No coyotes are going to drag him out like the—"

"We have another problem," Blair said. Her tone was flat, nearly devoid of emotion. When Diana only continued to wash the dirt from her hands, Blair added, "A *big* problem."

"Don't be so dramatic." When she looked up, Blair was gone, her lithe form halfway down the narrow hallway connecting the bathroom and living room.

Wringing her hands with a towel, Diana followed her deeper into the converted farmhouse. It wasn't luxurious. She'd spent little money on renovating it. Only enough to get water into the pipes and electricity into the wires and a furnace strong enough to beat back the long fingers of a Kansas winter. Even so, wind blew through the place as if there were holes in the walls.

In the living room, a small television sat on an overturned milkcrate. A battered futon rested in its view with a strip of silver duct tape keeping the stuffing inside.

Blair pointed at the screen, turning the knob to increase the volume.

The blown-out and smoldering buildings filled the screen as a team of firefighters combated the flames. They struggled with the large hoses, looking small and comical in their raincoats.

"They found the bodies." Diana shrugged. "So what?"

"Keep watching," Blair insisted. "They've played this story on a loop for an hour."

"Diana Dennard"—her heart stuttered in her chest, plummeting into her stomach, and her arms and legs felt suddenly weak—"has run credit card scams for over two million dollars across the US."

The world shifted on a tilt as her face appeared, blotting out the rest of the screen.

"What we know about Diana Dennard results from an alleged kidnapping over twenty years ago. She has only one living relative, a sister. The whereabouts of her sister remain unknown, but seven known aliases have been uncovered in an attempt to—"

"Do you think Lou did this?" Blair asked, her hands cupping her elbows.

"No," Diana said. Lou couldn't be bothered with such a menial task.

Her mind sprang back to the night in New Orleans, to the bait lying on the floor of her townhouse.

Diana had dug deep into all of Lou's associates and had learned that Daniella Allendale, the simpering, pathetic girl who had fallen apart over a little zip tie, was a reporter.

Not just any reporter. An *investigative* reporter from a rich and well-connected family. No doubt an entitled and spoiled brat who thought she was above everyone and everything.

No, Diana didn't need to wonder how her story had been thrown to the press.

Was this payback? Had the little bitch decided to grow teeth?

"Wanted in connection with at least thirty-five cases of fraud," the television droned on. Diana's own face continued to look back at her accusingly.

Her face. Her face everywhere. And now her financial backing was compromised along with her anonymity.

Her freedom. Everything. Gone.

And it was a terrible picture of her.

Anger unfurled in Diana, so rich and full-bodied she was nearly drunk on it.

Lou. How could you do it?

Lou might not have pulled the trigger on this betrayal, but she must've known it would happen. And did she stop it? Did she defend Diana?

No. She let her take the bullet.

"What are we going to do?" Blair asked.

Diana wrung the towel in her fist. "Kill her."

35

L ou was perched on the edge of her sofa, lacing her boots, when her watch buzzed. She rotated the digital face, turning it in the light to better read it. It was King.

911

She'd told Konstantine she'd be there tonight. She could feel his restlessness like a tight wire in her gut. It set her own teeth on edge.

The watch buzzed again.

911

"Coming," she grumbled. *Konstantine will have to wait.*

She stood and crossed to the island, grabbing her Browning pistol off the countertop. It was still light outside, so she stepped into the linen closet and shut the door behind her, the most complete darkness she could offer herself at this time of day.

The shadows rubbed against her body like a cat against a leg. Cool and needy. Her internal compass spun in the dark, seeking out King on the other side. When it clicked into place, she let go of her hold on this part of the world and slipped through the thin veil separating the two points of their respective space.

She'd expected the office, or maybe King's loft apartment. Either way he was more than likely poring over papers. He was a chronic workaholic, not unlike her.

What she found was something else altogether.

She was in a concrete bunker. Overhead, honky-tonk music blared and the rhythmic thumping against the ceiling conjured the image of line dancing and leather fringe. She could smell grease, maybe fried pickles, and the sharp tang of alcohol.

Lou raised her gun.

"It's just me," King said, stepping into the spotlight of a low-hanging bulb.

Lou lowered the gun. A chill ran up the back of her spine. It was cold down here. Where were they? A basement? "What's the emergency?"

"Did you see the Dennard story?"

"What Dennard story?"

He rubbed his forehead with his fist. "Christ. Don't you have a television?"

"No. You can get me one for Christmas," she said, her tone light. "If it bothers you so much."

His lack of reaction made her stomach harden.

"Spit it out," she said.

"Piper dug up some charges on Dennard. Her credit card scams, her disappearance, the sister, all of it. Then she sold it."

"What do you mean, sold it?"

"To some of Dani's connections, to some of mine. Names I had floating around the office. She broke Dennard's story wide open. Diana's face is all over the news. Her cover is blown."

Lou was having a hard time understanding. "Why?"

What did she have to gain by going after Dennard?

"That's what I asked," King said with a bark of surprised laughter. "Now that Dennard had her man, I was hoping she'd slink off into the sunset."

Lou had thought the same. She hadn't expected to see Diana again, at least not for a long time.

"She said Dennard had it coming. That she didn't want her thinking she could do whatever she wanted with us."

Lou thought of Winter, the way he'd cried when she'd clamped the metal collar around his throat and welded the chain to the hook in the floor.

"Diana might not have seen the news yet." Lou holstered her gun. "She might still be working on Winter."

Or maybe not, a little voice said. *How long did you play with Angelo? Twenty minutes?*

Would Dennard be able to resist ripping the man apart, swiftly and brutally? And no matter how much the punisher may enjoy it, the human body can only withstand so much.

Her man would give out on her, sooner or later. Lou knew that better than most.

Then Diana will discover the worst of it. That her hunt had been a distraction, a lie. It had promised relief, complete satisfaction.

But nothing would satisfy again. Not really.

"You know she's going to retaliate, right?" King ran a hand through his hair. "She's going to think we did this, and she's going to come after us."

Lou wasn't sure what to do with the mild panic thrumming through him. He seemed to need some sort of reassurance from her.

"It'll be harder to get to New Orleans now," she offered. "If her face is all over the news, it's not like she can walk around in the open."

"Please," King laughed, clearly exasperated. "She's blond, blue-eyed, clean cut. There are hundreds of her in the French Quarter alone. If she's careful, she'll blend in. And she wasn't working alone, remember? She has people she can trust. If she were a true loner, this would be easier. But she's not. She's a master manipulator. They're far worse."

King's irritation, his borderline hysteria, nipped at the back of her neck, made her shoulders inch toward her ears.

"What do you want me to do?" Lou asked. Because it was clear he wanted something.

It wasn't the secure location or the 911 page or even his tense body language. It was the look on his face, the desperate, pleading look that said, *Please. Please, Lou.*

But whatever the request was, she needed him to spit it out.

"I want you to take Piper, Dani, and Mel somewhere safe. Drop them on a deserted island for all I care, but don't leave them here."

Lou laughed.

"This isn't a joke."

"They aren't going to let me take them anywhere."

"Take Dani at least," King said. "Diana probably thinks she's the one who ratted her out. She must know she's a journalist and has the contacts to launch a story like this. If Dani goes, maybe Piper will too, but they need to disappear, you understand that? Diana *will* kill them."

The hair on Lou's arms rose.

"She won't stage another pretend kidnapping to get your attention. There's only one statement she'll want to make."

You were supposed to understand, Lou.

"Her rapist took something and she killed him. Winter took something and she hunted him for years, and now we took her freedom, her anonymity. She's going to feel especially betrayed by you. You move like she does, hunt like she does. You're supposed to understand. The only difference is that if she comes for you, you can handle yourself. Piper and Dani can't."

King ran his hands through his hair.

"You could take her out, end it before it begins. Give Dennard a one-way trip to La Loon."

Lou snorted.

"What's funny?"

"You make me jump through hoops to nab someone like Fish, and now Diana comes along and you just want me to 'take her out.'"

"She will retaliate," King insisted.

"When?" Lou asked. "Tomorrow? In six years? Mel, Dani, and Piper have lives. You can't ask them to go into hiding forever. And it's impossible to know when she'll make her move."

And what about me, King? Will you try to eliminate me one day? Will I cross some unseen line and suddenly be too much of a liability to you? Will you be asking someone to "take me out"?

"I'm just saying it'll be easier if you kill her."

"No," Lou said, jaw clenched. "You can't sell me on this idea that the system matters, that the process matters, and then ditch it the first time someone scares you. Either I kill whoever I want, whenever I want"—*And I will anyway*, she thought darkly—"or we play by the rules. Which is it?"

King clasped the back of his neck.

Lou didn't want to point out the obvious. Holding Diana accountable for her work seemed hypocritical. Why should Lou hunt as she pleased while Diana must be restrained?

"I don't want any of you to get hurt." King rubbed his fist across his forehead. "But you're right. I can't tell you to back off on Fish then ask you to go hard on Dennard. That's..."

Wrong.

"Inconsistent," he said with a grimace. "But she's dangerous and she's going to blame us for the exposure. Because it *was* us. It could only be us. I don't think anyone else knows who she is."

The music overhead renewed and the pounding feet changed their rhythm, increasing the tempo.

"What about moving the girls?" King asked, still hopeful. "Maybe Konstantine knows somewhere they'll be safe."

"I'll ask," Lou said. But she already knew Piper's answer.

"What? No." Piper scowled at her over a bag of tortilla chips. She took a handful, put them on a plate, and covered them with cheese. Then she put the plate in the microwave for thirty seconds. "I'm not scared of that psycho."

Maybe you should be, Lou thought.

"King wants us to leave?" Piper asked incredulously. "Or are you just mad that you can't hang out with your friend anymore?"

Lou noted her irritation distantly. *What now?*

"Listen to her," Dani said, sitting on the stool at her kitchen island. She took a chip from the bag.

Lou liked the color in her cheeks and the steadiness in her eyes. She was doing better.

A cat meowed at Lou's feet, rubbing its head against her boot. It reminded her of Jabbers.

Lou bent down and scooped up the feline, scratching her ears. The cat began to purr, cradled against Lou's chest.

Piper moved around Dani's kitchen as if it were her own. She knew where all the plates and utensils were. Where the ingredients were stored.

Piper opened the bag of shredded cheese wider. "Why should we run? Diana can't do anything. The French Quarter is full of cops. It's not like she can walk up to the shop or King's without someone seeing her."

Dani spread her hand on the countertop. "She could wear a disguise. Or she could send someone else after us."

Lou noted her bouncing knee and the way she pulled her lip into her mouth and pinned it there with her teeth.

Piper rolled her eyes. "She was dumb enough to walk into King's office and pretend to be Lou's sister. We're light years ahead of her, babe."

"She kidnapped us and zip-tied us. Like hogs."

Lou watched this exchange with a growing sense of unease.

The microwave beeped. Piper lifted a pan from the stove and scraped veggies onto the chips. On top of this, she spooned out generous dollops of sour cream, avocado, and salsa before pushing the plate toward Dani.

"Thanks," she said, but didn't touch the nachos.

Piper forked raw hamburger into the pan and continued. "That was before Lou killed like ninety percent of her men. She's not stupid enough to come at us empty-handed. She's a survivor. Survivors don't make futile moves."

I've made plenty of them, Lou thought. In the heat of a hunt, when led forward more by her hunger than a self-regard for her own life, she'd been more than careless.

Piper must've seen the disagreement on her face. "Do you want nachos or not?"

Lou sank onto a bar stool, still holding the cat. "Yes."

"Beef like mine or vegetarian like hers?"

"Beef."

Piper began arranging another plate. Once it was in the microwave, she said, "Even if she wants to come after us, and she scrounges up enough people to do it, *and* she's dumb enough to risk being murdered or arrested, there's still the question of *when*. We have no idea when this will happen. We can't just drop our lives and go into hiding indefinitely."

Here she turned to Dani, giving her a questioning look.

Dani took her first tentative bite of the nachos, and audibly swooned.

"You can't take any more time off work," Piper said. "And my semester starts in ten days. I need to be buying my books, not packing my bags."

Dani traced shapes on the countertop and sighed. "My job performance hasn't been a hundred percent lately."

The microwave beeped and Piper pulled the steaming plate from the machine. "We can't screw up our lives because of one crazy person. Not when we've worked so hard to rebuild them."

"What about you?" Lou asked Dani. She placed the cat on the floor. "Do you want to leave?"

Dani didn't speak. She eyed her nachos, fingering the edge of a cheese-covered chip.

Piper added sour cream and salsa to her own plate. "Babe, if you want to go, go. I'm not telling you to stay. I just don't think Dennard will risk getting caught."

Dani dragged a chip through a dollop of sour cream thoughtfully. "I *really* can't miss any more work."

Piper cut open and destoned a second avocado. After spooning the green mush onto the plate, she slid it across the island to Lou. "The beef will need ten minutes."

Seeing Dani's expression, Piper frowned. "Hey."

Dani looked up, and Piper reached her hand across the island. Reluctantly, Dani took it.

"Don't worry about this. Diana doesn't deserve an ounce of your stress and worry." Piper squeezed her hand. "We've got this."

Lou thought of Angelo Martinelli bursting through the back gate of her parents' home, a leather-clad nightmare of rage, and the white-flash pop of his gun going off. The sound of a wine glass shattering and her back hitting the surface of the family's moonlit pool.

"This comes with the territory. But we're tough. We can survive anything."

It came with the territory, yes.

But Lou didn't think Piper understood what that meant. Not yet.

36

She found Konstantine in his bedroom, his legs stretched out in front of him and a book open in his lap. His ankles were crossed as he sipped from a glass of red wine.

He looked up from his book, touching his ear as if it hurt.

"I felt you," he said, placing the wine glass on the bedside table.

"Did you?" She crossed to the bed and sat on its edge.

"Sometimes I can," he said, pulling his ear lobes. "It's like a popping in my ears."

"Dani says that too." Lou wasn't sure if she should take off her boots and leather jacket. Was she going to stay? He looked cozy and occupied. She pushed her sunglasses up onto her head as if in question.

"I was starting to think you wouldn't come," he said.

"King pulled an emergency call."

Konstantine nodded. "He must've seen the news."

"I'm guessing you did, too."

He took a bookmark from the back of the book and slid it between the open pages. Then he snapped the book shut. "I am well versed in the news. Published and unpublished."

She was sure that was true, and how much news there must be in the world that never reaches the filtered content packaged prettily for public consumption.

"And something interesting happened," he said, laying the book face down and open on the bed.

"What?" Lou asked, reading the cover of the book.

Buonanotte. The author's name was Liane Carmi.

"Is this a romance novel?" Lou asked, surprised. The cover definitely looked romantic.

"I like romance novels," Konstantine said with a wicked grin. "They have happy endings."

She picked up the book, unbothered by the fact she couldn't read the words. Some of them looked familiar, like they might be words borrowed into the English language, but she knew enough about foreign languages to understand that false cognates were common.

"Someone has been trying to expose you," Konstantine said, taking up the wine again.

She put down the book. "What do you mean?"

"Your name and picture have popped up on a few websites. Two news outlets that I own published stories about you. I made a few phone calls and they were taken down. George, one of the editors, says that it was a young woman in leather pants who sold him the story. Maybe the sister?"

"King said they would retaliate," Lou said. "Clearly they're trying to." And in truth, she didn't mind. She would rather Diana blame her for the exposure than Dani or Piper. It felt safer, with herself as the target.

"Are you worried?" Konstantine asked, placing a hand on her thigh. His thumb traced the crease in her jeans.

"I think Diana is more dangerous than Piper realizes." Lou stood, shrugged out of her leather jacket, and tossed it across the foot of Konstantine's bed.

Then she bent down and undid the laces on her boots. He seemed pleased by this and moved over to make space for her. He even peeled back the covers in a more obvious invitation.

"I must admit, I am surprised you haven't killed her yet," Konstantine said. "But I understand why you haven't."

Lou snorted, sliding in beside him. "Do you?"

"You don't believe you can hunt and kill every monster in this world. Here is another woman who can help. You also value your freedom above all else. You can't imagine stopping someone with the same drive."

Lou wondered if that was it. She had a feeling it might be something more. She searched Konstantine's face. "Are you afraid of her?"

"No," he said, finishing the wine and returning the glass to the opposite table. "She is no match for you."

"You'll jinx me." She pressed herself into his side as he used both his free hands to envelop her. She liked his scent, heady and all-encompassing.

"That's the danger, isn't it?" He retrieved his book and opened it to the bookmarked page. "Even beginners get lucky."

She put her head on his chest, listening to him turn the page every so often, his fingers playing absently in her hair while he read.

Lou was almost asleep when something occurred to her.

"The editor you spoke to, where was he?"

"Hmm?" Konstantine asked, looking up from his book. She felt his warm breath on her face. "The one who spoke to Diana's sister?"

"Yes. Where was that?"

"Oklahoma," Konstantine said. "Why?"

Oklahoma was south of Kansas, where Lou was fairly certain Diana's secret farm was hidden.

"Would you..." She didn't even know how to finish the request. She'd never directly asked anyone for help before.

"Anything," he said without pause. "What do you need?"

"Do you have someone you trust in New Orleans? Maybe four or five people that can follow Dani and Piper around until this is over. It wouldn't hurt to have eyes on Melandra and King, too."

Anyone to buy time, in case I'm too slow to reach them.

"When?"

"Now," she said, lifting up from her warm and comfortable position in the crook of his arm.

Konstantine put the book face down and retrieved his phone without another word.

She stretched out on the bed and watched him make the calls.

The compass inside her was spinning, trying to settle on a location that Lou couldn't yet see, only feel inside her.

Had Blair simply driven across the state line into Oklahoma? Had they hoped to sell the story and settle the score? Or were they already heading south, perhaps as far south as New Orleans?

37

———————

Piper read her class schedule from her laptop while Dani turned a mug of tea in her hands. Piper was trying to decide if she wanted to make herself a cup of mint tea, too. Those nachos were turning in her stomach riotously. If she didn't take measures, it might be a long night of indigestion to look forward to.

"Since I have to go to campus for the lab class on Fridays, I was thinking I could stop by your work after class and we can do lunch before I head to the Quarter. What do you think?"

"A regular Friday lunch date?" Dani asked, taking a sip of tea. "I like it."

Piper got a whiff of the peppermint and her stomach turned.

"It's the only class I couldn't get online." Piper frowned. "But I like science, so I'm not too pissed about it. But a three-hour class every Friday, *gah*. It'll be nice to recharge with you."

She closed her laptop and pushed it onto the coffee table.

"How are you feeling?" she asked.

Dani smiled. "Better."

"Even though Diana is still out there."

Dani looked out over the living room as if it were a vast horizon. "Yeah. I think it's because I made my decision."

Dani snuggled closer, lifting her tea up as she settled in to make sure it wasn't bumped.

"I was having such a hard time because it felt like everything I was doing was losing. That I wasn't good enough. That I was failing to hold it together. But I've changed my mind about that."

Must be nice, Piper thought.

"All those feelings are still there, but I've decided they're bullshit. The only way I can really fail is if I let Petrov and Diana or whoever else comes along take away what I love. I love writing these stories. Uncovering the truth. That's my passion. And if I have to suffer nightmares or convulse on a floor once in a while to make it happen, then that's just how it'll be. But no one is going to take it away from me."

"I'm proud of you," Piper said. She thought this was the better thing to say, though part of her wondered if Dani was being masochistic by clinging so stubbornly to her dream.

"I'm proud of you, too," Dani said, tucked into Piper's side.

Uncomfortable heat spread up the side of Piper's neck. She laughed. "For what?"

"You work so hard. You have your two jobs and you're going to school. You're amazing."

Piper shook her head, as if this would volley the compliment away. Receiving compliments had never felt comfortable, but coming from Dani it was even worse. Part of her retracted, shrinking from the words as if they physically hurt. The other part, as thirsty as a desert plant, stretched forward.

She didn't like that part very much.

"If I'd stayed on track, I'd have a master's degree by now. Or I'd be studying for the bar instead of Biology 201."

"Everyone's life is different." Dani's voice was drowsy with sleep. "You've had a lot you needed to take care of. We're lucky to get a chance at education at all. In some countries—" Dani gasped, bolting upright. "Octavia! No!"

Piper craned her neck in time to see the cat squatting in the kitchen, pissing beside the potted fern.

"Oh geez." Piper took Dani's tea and guided it safely to the coaster on the coffee table, so Dani could leap up and assess the damage.

Dani unwound a wad of paper towels from their dispenser on the wall. "Her litter box is probably full. She's fussy about that."

She's fussy about a lot of things.

Piper was fairly certain Tavi refused to use her litter box if there was *one* turd in it.

"I'll change it." Piper threw back the light blanket and got up.

Dani was already on her hands and knees with the cleaner, spraying the floor and the side of the planter. "Would you? That would be a huge help. Everything is in the closet."

Piper found the pan liners, scooper, and fresh litter in the hall closet outside the bathroom. Not one for scraping or inhaling the scent of cat piss, she gathered up the whole pan liner and double bagged it closed. The pungent smell burned her nose, and she gagged before dumping the fresh litter into the pan, holding her breath throughout.

Octavia meowed from the bathroom door.

"All for you, you princess." She carried the bag past the cat to the front door. She slipped her feet into plastic flipflops, calling over her shoulder, "I'll run this out to the trash. Be right back."

"Thank you so much," Dani said, turning from the kitchen sink, where she was washing her hands. "I'll have a big kiss for you when you get back."

Piper had more than a kiss in mind. She supposed her eyebrow wag said as much.

Dani's face turned red and a little nervous laugh escaped her. It brightened the dark mood that had hung over them most of the day. Something was weighing on Dani's mind. She hadn't brought it up to Piper yet, so they were in limbo.

In their six months together, Dani had sometimes gotten dark like this, discontent, unpleasant. Piper hadn't known her long enough to know if these moods were part of her natural temperament or if they were the result of her PTSD. Either way, there seemed no remedy for them except to let Dani share—or not—at her own pace.

I don't have much to offer, but I've got time, she thought.

And nothing said "I love you, you're going to be okay" like carrying a bag of cat shit to the dumpster outside.

When Piper stepped outside, she found the night hot and balmy. A sheen of moisture formed along her hairline and the back of her neck before she even reached the dumpster at the edge of the parking lot.

Damn, NOLA, she thought. *Why you gotta be so hot?*

She tossed the bag over her head and listened to it crash into the bin. Up and down the street, soft lamps burned.

She took her first big breath of air.

It smelled like sun-soaked trash, but it was still better than the piss-stained litter box.

Most of the houses in the Garden District had wrought-iron fences enclosing their yards. Half a block up the street, a woman—or man—paused to let their shih tzu piss on the iron rods.

The wind changed and she caught the scent of something sweet. Oleander, maybe.

On the other side of the street a trash can crashed and a group of kids broke into laughter. A flash of metal sparked in the dark.

What were they swinging? An aluminum bat? A lead pipe?

Whatever it was, it struck the side of the can, spilling the trash. Their laughter rose as they ripped open the bags and kicked trash into the street.

She considered calling after them. *Punk asses.*

But since they had a weapon and she didn't, she decided it was better to go back inside and make out with her girlfriend.

Something slammed into her back. Her skull hit the pavement, ears ringing.

She rolled on her back, her hands going up to protect her head.

Her fear spiked. Her mind vacillated between screaming for Dani or calling out to Lou. Dani might be closer, but Lou would be of more use.

Someone grabbed the front of her shirt and hauled her to a sitting position.

The person wore a ski mask—in this weather, Piper marveled—and head-to-toe black on black.

"Show your face, coward." Piper spit gravel out of her mouth. She thought her lip was busted. She could taste blood as she dragged her tongue across her teeth. All were present and accounted for. "Tired of trash cans already?"

She thought she was talking to one of the kids. Street kids could turn like that. Anything for a laugh or to show off in front of their friends.

"Okay," a mature voice said, and the black ski mask was yanked up.

It wasn't one of the punk kids whacking trash cans. It was Diana. Her face was colder and more ruthless than those kids could ever manage.

"Tell Lou I'm waiting," she said, and slammed her fist into the side of Piper's face.

38

Lou woke to a buzzing sound. Then a light clicked on.

Her eyes opened, squinting against the soft glow of the lamp. Konstantine sat on the edge of the bed, the phone pressed to his ear.

"I understand," he said. "Thank you for calling."

He terminated the call, tossing the phone onto the bed. He opened a drawer and pulled out dark jeans. "We need to go."

She sat up, her compass reaching out. But she felt nothing.

"What's happened?"

"Someone, presumably Diana, attacked Piper, and took Daniella."

Lou was out of the bed in a heartbeat. She laced up her boots and threw on her leather jacket.

Konstantine grabbed her arm. "Take me with you. I want to speak to my people."

"Your guys were there?"

"Dani's apartment building was blown up."

Lou's body iced.

"They found Piper unconscious in the parking lot outside. She is still unconscious, but alive."

"Dani?" Lou asked, her voice thick.

"I don't know."

"Your people in New Orleans called you?" She felt her mind trying to complete the scene, understand what was happening.

"No." He released her long enough to pull on pants and a black t-shirt. "There is a chain of command. I usually speak only to the boss of their boss."

Why can't I feel you? Lou thought of Dani. Her heart hammered in her chest. She had a sense of her location, but not her emotions. No fear. No need. She reached out to Piper and found the same.

She hoped they were both unconscious. Not dead.

"Okay. I have my wallet and—"

Lou was already pulling them both through the dark before he finished. She exchanged Italy for a hot, humid night in the New Orleans Garden District. The scent of flowers bloomed bright and instant, mixed with the smell of hot, putrefying garbage.

But both were overshadowed by the tremendous spike in heat.

She stepped away from the dumpster's deep shadows and was hit by a wall of it.

Piper was in the grass, between the street and parking lot. It made Lou instantly think of the pornographers that Diana executed during the raid.

A young girl, no older than sixteen, stood guard over her with an aluminum bat propped against her shoulder. Three guys jumped back when Konstantine stepped into the light.

"Whoa. Dude. Where'd you come from?"

Their eyes shifted to Lou instantly. "Shit."

But Lou didn't care about them. She wanted to see Piper with her own eyes.

She dropped to her knees and pulled Piper up to a sitting position. Her head lolled.

"Piper."

Her face was purple and swollen in two places. It looked like she'd been struck in the forehead and in the eye, which was swollen shut. And her lip was split and bloody.

Lou's anger began to well up inside her, threatening to overtake her senses.

"Piper. Wake up."

"I already tried that," the girl said, pulling a red lollipop out of her mouth. "I think they drugged her."

"What happened?" Lou asked. She saw unflinching eyes and a mischievous grin.

"We came by to check on things and saw this one"—she pointed the bat at Piper—"get jumped. But it was the other girl they wanted. Saw them carry her out and throw her in a truck before the building blew. The cat followed them out. Lucky cat."

Lou looked up and saw Octavia lingering near the dumpster. Meowing uncertainly, as if unsure she could come forward.

The girl snorted. "She's cute now, but don't be fooled. I tried to pick her up and she scratched me."

Konstantine was shoving money into the guys' hands.

"Don't you want to know what direction the truck went?" the girl asked, eyebrows arched. She ran the lollipop along the bottom of her lips.

"It doesn't matter," Lou said.

The girl laughed. "Sure. Whatever you say. Hey, is this girl important to you? I've seen her around the Quarter a lot. For the right price, I can keep an eye on her for you. Make sure she doesn't run into trouble with psychos anymore."

Lou didn't answer.

"Alice," Konstantine said, and shoved a wad of cash twice as thick as the boys' into her hands. "Thank you."

"I go by Bane, actually," she said, flicking the sucker between her teeth. "As in 'bane of your existence.'"

Konstantine's smile twitched. "Bane."

She looked at the wadded-up bills in her fist again before flicking her eyes back up to Konstantine's. "Anytime, boss. Let's go, boys."

She took off across the street with the guys obediently in tow. She swung her bat one more time, knocking a trash can into the street. The boys behind rolled it for good measure.

"She won't wake up," Lou said. She heard the fear in her voice and hated it.

"She will," Konstantine said, kneeling beside her. "Let's get her somewhere safe."

Meow.

They turned to see the British Blue inching tentatively toward Piper.

Meow.

"Grab the cat. It's Dani's." Lou lifted Piper into her arms. Her shoulder protested, but she ignored it.

Konstantine crept toward the animal, speaking sweetly to it. *"Vieni qui, micia-gattina. Vieni."*

ALICE BAINES STOOD IN THE DARKNESS, ROLLING THE LOLLIPOP IN her mouth. She watched the woman pull the blonde into her arms while Konstantine coaxed the cat forward. And it *was* Konstantine. She didn't care what Micah said about the boss of all bosses being too important to mess with pissants like them.

He'd told the boys his name was Georgio. That he was just here to settle the account.

Bullshit.

Because it wasn't about them being pissants. It was about the woman, the boogeyman, the *strega* Bane had heard so much about. The Ravengers passed stories about her like they passed joints. And threaded through every story was the same theory: Konstantine and the woman were linked. Maybe she was the devil. Maybe he'd sold his soul for all the power and money he has. Whatever the reason, where you found one, you found the other. And Alice wanted to know if there was something to all those stories.

"Bane—" Micah began.

"Shhh. I told you, not a word."

"But—"

She shoved the head of the bat into his stomach. *"Shut it."*

Silence.

Alice squinted harder, trying to keep the woman and Konstantine in clear view.

As soon as Konstantine's hand was on her shoulder, they disappeared.

One minute they were at the edge of the streetlight. The next, nada. The grass was bare.

No Konstantine. No mysterious woman in black. No blonde. Even the cat was gone. And it didn't matter what direction Alice searched, there was nothing to be found.

And it wasn't like there wasn't enough light. The burning building made it as bright as day. People from the adjacent houses were trailing out into the night to see what had happened.

A fire truck wailed in the distance, coming closer, drawn to the blown-out building like moths to a flame. And a burning building was all they'd find.

Not the woman who could disappear in the dark and be anywhere she wanted with a simple thought. Woman. *Strega.* Devil.

"Badass," she whispered with a sigh.

She wished she could do shit like that. Some people had all the luck.

39

Piper was stretched long on her sofa, a blanket thrown over her legs. Lou sat on the floor beside her, staring at her as if this intense gaze would wake her up.

The British Blue wandered from room to room, meowing indignantly to anyone who'd listen. She was obviously displeased with the surroundings and the sudden displacement.

It looked like she was searching for Dani.

Dani.

Lou opened and closed her fists.

"I should go."

"They'll be expecting that," Konstantine said. He stood in Piper's kitchen, searching the cabinets for a mug. He found one to the left of the stove and filled it with fresh coffee. He placed this on the table for Lou. "She wants you to come unprepared."

Hold on, Lou thought. *Hold on, Dani.*

"Drink this." When Lou didn't take it, he put the mug in her hand.

"I thought this was for her," Lou said.

"Do you often pour beverages down the throats of unconscious women?" His lips quirked with a smile. "How strange Americans are."

"What if this is a coma?" Lou placed the untouched coffee on the table. "What if she's going to die from this?"

"Her heart rate and breathing are fine. She might have a concussion and an ugly black eye. But I don't think she will die from a punch in the face."

She didn't need to say the obvious. They'd probably hit Dani too. Knocking her unconscious would make sure they could get her out of the building without a fight.

If they'd left Piper conscious, she could've called Lou, alerted the authorities. Or possibly she could've gotten a plate number or vehicle description.

But why leave Piper alive at all?

A knock came at the door and Konstantine rose to answer it. Melandra and King entered the apartment.

"Me first," Melandra said, seeing Piper on the sofa. She elbowed her way past King.

"What is that?" Lou nodded toward the syringe in King's hand.

"Ask me no questions and I'll tell you no lies." He slipped the capped syringe back into his pocket.

"Adrenaline," Konstantine wagered. "By the look of it."

King shrugged, as if to say *maybe*.

Mel knelt in front of the girl and uncapped a small tube. She waved it under Piper's nose.

Piper's eyes fluttered, lazily. She groaned.

"Hey, baby. Welcome back." Mel touched Piper's cheek and cooed. "Ouch. Look at your face. I'm going to get some ice for that. Lou, open that window and get some air in here."

Lou opened the window as instructed.

Piper blinked, sitting up. She groaned, placing one hand over her eye and hissing. "Oh god. I'm going to puke."

Konstantine produced a trash can. White plastic with blue birds painted on the side. Given the tissues inside, Lou suspected it came from the adjacent bathroom.

Piper locked eyes with Lou, holding the trash can but not using it.

"Would you rather have this?" She offered Piper the coffee, but she shook her head.

"I'm really dizzy. What happened?"

"What do you remember?" King asked.

Piper looked at her couch as if she'd never seen it. "I...I don't know. I paid for my classes. For the fall. I have a biology lab on Friday. It's three hours long."

"After that," King pressed on.

Piper searched Lou's face as if the answers were written there. Then, when those features told her nothing, she looked from Konstantine to King.

Mel reappeared with a towel-wrapped ice pack and held it against Piper's face. "That's going to hurt tomorrow."

"It hurts now," Piper mumbled through her fat lip.

Meow.

Piper twitched at the sound, seeing Octavia wander into the living room, tail flicking.

"Hey, Tavi," she said.

Then her face pinched.

"Wait. What is she doing here?" Piper's face screwed up with concentration again. "I took out the cat litter."

The ice fell from her hands. "Dani! Where's Dani?"

"Diana took her," Lou said plainly. There was no way to blunt this truth. "And I'm assuming she's the reason your face looks the way it does."

I'm going to kill her.

Piper stood on wobbly legs. She fell forward and Lou caught her by the arms.

"Is she, oh god is she—" Piper began.

"They took her. Presumably alive."

Piper seized her wrist. "Please, go. *Now.* You have to go get her."

Lou stepped back, ready to do just that.

Piper's hold tightened. "No, wait. Diana said something." Her face screwed up in concentration again. "She said...she said she'd be waiting for you."

"Of course she is." King was leaning into the kitchen island, jaw working. Lou saw and understood his fury.

"This is my fault," Piper said. "If I'd said yes to going into hiding, if I—"

King shook his head. "It's too late for that now."

"Robert." Melandra scowled at him. "Self-righteousness never helped anybody."

"Yeah, all right."

Piper held on to her like she was flotsam in a large and raging sea. With Konstantine's help, they got her back onto the sofa, but she wouldn't let go.

"It's not your fault," Lou said.

"Whose is it? Yours? You said you'd protect her."

"Blame won't help either." Melandra adjusted the towel and repositioned the ice pack on Piper's face. "We stick together. That's what we do."

Piper's gaze was fixed on Lou. "Get her back, Louie."

Tears sprang to her eyes. "*Please.* I'll forgive you for choosing that psychopath over me if you just get Dani back."

She finally released her, and Lou stepped back into the shadow-soaked corner of the room.

Konstantine caught her wrist before she could slip. "I won't ask to go. I know I will only distract you and slow you down, but she will be ready for you. She might have the building rigged to blow. Or she might place a sniper on an adjacent roof. You have to be ready for anything."

"I don't think she would blow up two buildings in one night."

"That is not a bet I would take," Konstantine whispered, his face drawn. "Be careful."

"Keep them safe," Lou said. "For all we know she planted explosives here before taking Dani."

Konstantine's lips quirked. "I've already checked."

"Post guards outside to watch the streets."

Konstantine's smile deepened.

"You already did that, too."

Then the smile was gone. "I'm not worried about them. I'm worried about you. It's you she wants, really."

"How can you know that?" Lou asked. It seemed to her that Dani was the target.

Konstantine sighed. "Because a woman like Diana, I can understand."

40

———————

Once Piper's apartment bled away, Lou found herself in the hidden armory beneath her kitchen island. The smell of sawdust tickled her nose as she took stock of its shelves. She decided on a shoulder holster with twin Berettas and a hip holster with twin Brownings. She pulled Kevlar sleeves up onto her arms and fixed a bulletproof vest snug across her chest.

Not that that helped much last time, she thought. Being shot in Julia Street station had made her very aware of a vest's limitations.

Pulling on the jacket, her shoulder ached. A throbbing stab shot up her neck into the base of her skull. She considered taking a Vicodin, but immediately decided against it. She wanted her mind sharp for this fight.

Lou took a breath and pulled the string, extinguishing the overhead light.

The darkness pressed in against her as she exhaled, slowly, the sound of her breath filling her ears.

Then she was outside. The wind was cutting across her cheek and pulled tears from her eyes. When she blinked, she saw the city skyline. She gazed out over the lights, trying to place the view. She didn't recognize it.

"I knew you'd come," a voice drawled. At the edge of the darkness, a form shifted, stepping into the light. "Do you know where we are?"

"No," she admitted.

Diana inched forward, light cutting across her cheek, showing only the right side of her face. "We're on the Plaza building. Funny that your headquarters should be in New Orleans and yet you don't know this building. *Is* New Orleans really your headquarters?"

Lou said nothing. She was trying to find Dani. Her compass said she was here, that she was close, but Lou couldn't see her.

"Where is she?"

"It's dark up here, right?" Diana laughed. "I made it that way just in case Blair is right. I want to see what you can really do."

Lou searched the top of the building, but the dark was absolute. She saw no shapes, no shifting bodies. Only that bare sliver of concrete lit by the single lamp.

"Blair said that I'd be giving you the advantage," Diana whispered conspiratorially. "Because she believes you can move through the dark like it's a doorway. And I thought Spencer was the one with the imagination."

Diana snorted at her own joke.

"But you can't see in the dark, can you?"

Diana stepped back into the darkness, disappearing.

Lou froze on the spot, closing her eyes. There was no point in leaving them open if this was the game Diana wanted to play.

She searched the dark with her compass.

Dani, Dani, Dani, Daniella Allendale.

She felt the air shift on her right, knew the attack was coming on that side, but it would be too slow. Lou was already releasing her hold on the darkness and sinking through.

The night disappeared for a moment, like passing behind a brick wall, a blessed reprieve, and then broke open again.

Diana laughed. "Oh, you're good."

Heat swelled on Lou's back and she turned at the last second, seeing the glint of a blade before the darkness swelled again.

This time icy fire sliced through her upper arm, drawing blood.

Another slash crossed her Kevlar sleeves. She took this opportunity to rotate her wrist and seize the hand holding it.

She yanked them forward, but it wasn't Diana. It was the leather-clad sister, Blair.

Her eyes were hidden behind night vision goggles, the mechanical eyes comically large and insectile.

Blair yanked herself out of Lou's grip and sidestepped into the dark.

Something slammed into her bulletproof vest, making her pivot her body. Fabric ripped. She reached out to grab the attacker but her hand swiped air.

Another cold flash of a blade sliced across the top of her thigh. An icy, electric fire preceded the warm welling of blood. She felt it gush up between the flesh and fabric, soaking her pants.

Diana laughed.

The laugh was too far away for her to be the one who'd cut her. There were at least three of them up here.

A foot slammed into Lou's torso, knocking the air from her. She went down to one knee.

"I'm disappointed in you," Diana said, her voice disembodied and echoing. "I thought you'd understand how important my work is. You were supposed to understand. You were supposed to *get* it."

Her shoulder was engulfed in pain. Lou struggled to draw a breath.

"And what's worse, I tried to expose you, yet somehow, every story I leaked, every picture I showed, just disappeared. Why?"

Lou managed to get to her feet again, but red crowded her vision.

"Why do you get to keep your name, your secrecy, but I can't have mine? Doesn't the work I do matter too?"

"Yes," Lou said, thinking of the little boy who'd held so tight to her neck.

"Then how could you? Not one of them, King or those wannabe sleuths or my sister, or Spencer. None of them understand what our work means to us. No one but you. How could you?"

Diana stepped into the light, pushing her own night vision goggles up onto her head.

And she wasn't alone. She held Dani close to her chest, pinning her with one arm. But Dani's eyes were closed, her expression slack.

She's dead, Lou thought, fear ripping through her. "You killed her."

"No," Diana said, rolling her eyes. "She's just very, *very* sleepy. I didn't want her flailing around on the roof, you know? It wasn't safe."

She snorted, laughing at her joke. But it was cut short by an explosion of anger contorting her features.

"You let her expose me." Diana yanked on a fistful of Dani's hair. No reaction. "You did this."

Lou didn't bother to explain that she hadn't given the order. She didn't control her people—and now she realized, with fear banging at the base of her throat, they *were* her people—like Diana did.

Her leg was going numb. She was starting to wonder if the cut in the thigh might've gotten her femoral artery.

Diana's face fell. The anger folded into something saccharin. A parody of emotion. "I'm so disappointed, Lou. I was starting to think we could be really great, you and me."

Diana doesn't feel anything. Anger, maybe, she realized. *Frustration.*

But she had none of the fear clogging Lou's mind. She had no one she was ready to take a bullet for.

Diana seemed to read her mind and didn't like it. Her face screwed up with fresh irritation. "Let's find out if you can really do what my sister says. This building is forty-five stories high, five hundred and thirty feet tall. It's dark on this side of it. Look. Go ahead, look down the side. I won't push."

Lou didn't.

"I'm *not* going to push you. *I'm* the trustworthy one here."

Lou glanced over the side.

It was dark, but not completely. Lights from the city reflected off the many windows and ricocheted into the night.

"See, I didn't push you. Yet." She snorted, her delight returning. "Here's what's going to happen."

Lou shifted forward, wanting to put a hand on Dani—just a hand would be enough to get her off this roof and away from this dangerous game Diana wanted to play.

But Diana yanked her back, shoving a gun into Dani's forehead. "You're not faster than a bullet, are you?"

"No," Lou said. When in truth, she thought, *Sometimes.*

But she saw Piper's crestfallen face flash in her mind, and sometimes didn't feel good enough.

Diana trained the pistol on her instead. "Here's your choice. One: I put a bullet in her head and then one in yours. Or two: I push her off the building and you jump off after her."

"You want to kill her."

"Hell *yes.*" Diana laughed, high and hysterical. "Without a doubt. The only question I have is what to do about you. Do I toss her over, or shoot her, and then we fight it out on this roof? I already have two people with guns on you, by the way. Or would you like to go over the edge with her and save me the trouble?"

Lou saw a red dot scurry over her leg, abdomen, and chest. The fact she could no longer see it meant it must be higher. Probably trained at her head.

Diana's widening grin certainly suggested so. "No bulletproof vests for a face, huh? Shame."

Lou's vision darkened at the corners again, another pulsing threat of unconsciousness.

I'm running out of time.

"What'll it be, Louie Thorne?"

Lou had never tried to slip while falling. She wasn't sure she could do it.

She wasn't even sure that the darkness could be collected and used in such a way. Where would it spit her out? Above another pavement?

If they died, if both she and Dani splattered on the concrete below, at least Piper would understand that she'd tried.

I tried to save her, she thought.

Because Lou knew she'd rather die trying to save Dani's life than look Piper in the eyes knowing she'd failed her so completely.

"I'll go over with her," she said.

Diana laughed like Lou had made the best joke in the world. She threw back her head and gave all of herself to it. "Will you?"

"Yes."

"You're serious right now." Diana laughed. "Oh god, Louie. It's a shame you're about to die. It really is. You're the most interesting person I've met in years. Possibly ever."

And if I survive this, I'll be the last person you ever meet, Lou thought. Because it couldn't end any other way. If Diana was alive, they'd never be safe.

Piper, Dani, King, or Mel.

A strange longing fluttered in her chest. She tried to find a word for it, but all that came was *affection*, and even that wasn't quite right.

Lou had known in theory that she'd liked her little crew. It was a dim acknowledgment that if they needed her she would come, without question. But now it was more than that. Diana had put them into sharp relief.

They weren't simply a way to pass the time.

They'd given her a reason to go on.

After Angelo. After all the hunting and longing and anger—they'd given her something to hold on to. The way she'd hung on to her father, his strength, as her growing power to slip threatened to tear her apart.

And here was some asshole trying to take it. *Again.*

That old, familiar ache rose up in her. The one she'd been waiting for.

Diana grinned as if she'd seen the shift herself. "Look at that smile. Are we about to have fun, you and me? You're starting to look fun."

Diana shoved Dani hard, the girl's body bowing as if punched. Her spine rolled over the concrete edge, tipping dangerously into the sky.

Without thinking, Lou shot her arm out. She grabbed a fistful of shirt and felt the fabric rip.

Instead of pulling her back onto the roof, to darkness and safety, they were pitched forward by Dani's weight.

Then hands shoved hard into Lou's back and over the side they went.

The wind was a force, tearing at their faces, their clothes. Lou managed to pull Dani against her, but that drop-sink feeling in her gut multiplied.

Come on, come on, come on, her mind begged. *Give us a soft landing. If we have to fall, give us somewhere soft.*

She knew she had six seconds at most, falling from this height. But she'd never believed herself fully in control of her trajectory. Now was a hell of a time to prove otherwise.

Five...four...

Please...

Three...two...

Oh oh...

One.

Lou expected death. She expected her brains splattered on the business district sidewalk for some unfortunate soul in an ironed suit to find.

But she was slowing down.

Or at least, it felt like she was slowing down. The wind that had been terrorizing her a moment before lessened.

She opened her eyes to see the city of New Orleans was gone. The lights of the business district had been snuffed out. She was in the dark place. *Her* dark place.

In the world between worlds.

But slowing down wasn't the same as stopping, and after this heartbeat pause, the dark broke open again.

It wasn't concrete that slammed into Lou's back. It was water.

It was as if a horse had kicked her. The force was enough to knock the air out of her, even with her vest taking the brunt of the impact. Dani's body was cradled against the front of her torso and mostly spared.

Lou began to sink into dark depths.

She kicked for the surface in a circle, trying to get a sense of what body of water they were in.

Fresh. No salt.

She felt that pull at her leg, the membrane thinning again. An offer to sidestep this world into La Loon.

Lou broke the surface, checking to make sure Dani's head was above the water.

"No," she said, spitting water from her mouth and kicking her legs as if to free them. "Not now."

She paddled a circle, searching for shore.

And there it was. A familiar and welcoming sight. It was the shore of her lake, her place of eternal night.

"Dani, can you swim?"

No answer.

"Dani?" Lou turned the girl in the water, checked breathing and pulse. She was alive, but her eyes were closed and she remained unresponsive. Whatever Dani needed to wake up, she couldn't get it here.

One problem at a time.

Lou lifeguard-dragged Dani onto the muddy bank. This was the first time she'd pulled an unconscious body *out* of her lake, rather than into it.

On the shore, she panted, catching her breath. Her fingers sank into the mud, cold against her palms. A slight breeze chilled the droplets on her neck. Water dripped from her nose, splattering the side of Dani's cheek. Wind whispered through the trees.

She dragged her hand down her face, clearing it of water.

Then she laughed. A high, hysterical sound.

She couldn't stop until her throbbing shoulder made it impossible to draw a breath.

Her body was a buzzing tank of adrenaline—and she needed every drop of it to take on Diana.

Go now, she thought. *Right now, before she has a chance to understand what happened.*

Piper paced the floor, back and forth, until it threatened to leave a grooved trail in the hardwood. Her face hurt. Her body hurt. She wanted to skin Diana Dennard alive.

Every time the woman's face flashed across her mind, a murderous fury consumed her, heating her whole body. But she wasn't angry for herself. She was angry for Dani. The sick truth, she knew, was that if Diana had only hurt her, she wouldn't be mad at all. She'd be terrified.

And she was pissed about that too.

"They'll be okay," Melandra said. She turned over another tarot card on Piper's coffee table.

Piper didn't like that Five of Wands. "Is that what the cards say?" she asked with a derisive snort.

"That's what *I* say," Mel said.

"Lou is very capable," King added, opening the carton of pork lo mein in his hand and dumping it onto a plate. "Would you like some of this?"

Piper shook her head. She couldn't imagine doing something as simple and controlled as sitting down and eating right now. She felt like her skin was trying to crawl off her bones.

Her ears popped and she staggered.

Lou was on her hands and knees, crouching over Dani on the other side of King's coffee table. They were both soaked, Lou's hair sticking to her face.

Dani wasn't moving.

"Oh god, is she—"

"She's breathing," Lou said. "Just unconscious. Where's Konstantine?"

"He stepped outside to make some calls. What happened?" Piper demanded.

"Diana pushed us off a building."

"*What?*" Piper, Mel, and King asked in unison.

Mel left the room before appearing with three large towels. She offered one to Lou, who began to dab at her face and hair, shaking out her jacket.

King sat down on the couch. "Is Diana—"

"I'm going back," Lou said.

"To kill her?" Piper asked. To her surprise, she was suddenly afraid for Lou, her anger completely overshadowed. If Diana was capable of throwing Lou off a building—Lou, her invincible, faultless Lou—what else could that woman do?

Lou flicked her eyes up to meet Piper's.

Piper's stomach dropped.

"Yes," Lou said. "Like you wanted me to since day one."

Before Piper could say anything, apologize or explain, or even hug Lou, Lou was gone, leaving a mess of water in her wake.

"It's not just water." Mel turned the towel in the light, frowning. "There's blood. A lot of it."

They searched Dani but didn't find a scratch on her.

"It must be Lou," King said solemnly. "Something must've happened *before* they were thrown off the building."

Don't you die, Piper prayed. *Don't die and I swear to God, I'll apologize for everything. I'll stop being a whiny little ass and make it all up to you, Lou. I swear. Just don't you dare die.*

41

"What do you mean, she never came down?" Diana spat, whirling on the sidewalk.

The New Orleans humidity made the hair around her face curl. Sweat was beginning to bead in her body's creases, her elbows, knees, pits, and neck. She hated this place.

She searched the sidewalk stretching in either direction, disbelieving. But there were no bodies. There wasn't so much as a drop of blood. The sidewalk was unblemished, as long as one didn't count the crushed paper to-go cups in the gutter and the black gum ground into crevices by passing shoes.

There was absolutely no sign of two women hitting the pavement at all. And she'd had a lookout on the ground the whole time, so it wasn't a question of a cleanup crew. Lou might have a full support team, an organization capable of removing all evidence of her existence if it came to that, but they'd have at least *seen* the bodies being carried away.

People can't just disappear from the air, she thought. *Unless she can fly.*

"I told you," Blair hissed in her ear. "I know what I saw. Now you're fucked."

Blair punched Diana's chest hard enough to knock her back. Her boots stumbled along the pavement before she regained lost ground.

The fear climbing up the back of her neck bloomed into rage. She whirled, ready to throw her own punch until she saw the tears standing out in her sister's eyes.

"What's wrong with you?" Diana asked, deflating. "Pull yourself together."

"She's going to kill you," Blair said, lip trembling. "She's going to *kill* you."

Diana looped an arm around the girl's neck. "She can try."

Blair sobbed against her.

But her words were absent of their usual bravado. If Blair was right, if Lou could appear and disappear at will, then—

I want what she has.

Blair screamed, her shrill cry splitting Diana's ears, setting them to ringing. Her grip tightened on Diana but it made no difference.

She was torn from Diana's arms and thrown. She rolled, tumbling along the pavement before crashing into the side of the building. The wind from her rolling body scattered the trash in the gutter.

Diana already knew who she would see before the hand closed over her throat.

Murderous eyes the color of fire met hers.

Even in her periphery, she saw Blair pulling her gun, her crew lunging forward.

Too slow, she thought.

And they were.

The hot, rank streets of downtown New Orleans were replaced with resplendent pine. It reminded Diana of the Christmas tree farm their parents had taken them to as children each Thanksgiving weekend. Blair balling up a handful of snow and tossing it at her, laughing.

So long ago. Another life.

Diana's knees gave in the shift, the fluid in her ears trembling, contributing to her dizziness. But the hand on her throat held fast, keeping her on her feet before a punch slammed into the side of her face.

Pain bloomed red and fragrant across her cheek. She hit the earth like a rock. Her teeth cracked on stone. Mud filled her mouth.

She spat and held up a hand. "Wait!"

Lou's leg lifted, slamming down on Diana's knee. Something snapped and pain radiated down to her toes and up through her chest. Her heart stuttered and all the air left her.

Thought was obliterated from her mind.

There was no mind, only the body. Only pain.

Some aware, ever-awake part of her knew that the screaming animal in the distance was her.

Fists gathered up her shirt, hauling her limp body up to a sitting position. Any movement in the knee was enough to make her vision blur.

"Is this what you wanted?" Lou shook her until Diana's eyes fluttered open and she was forced to meet that black gaze. "You wanted me to prove what I was? Do you still want to see what I can do?"

Her voice was calm. There was no anger in it. No fury. The pure, impenetrable reserve was like a patina of ice, a tundra extending beneath an empty, starless sky.

Lou slammed her against the ground, once, twice. On the third time, Diana's head hit something hard and it felt like the back of her skull split open. On the fifth slam, she bit her tongue. Blood bloomed in her mouth, spilling over her lip and chin.

"How?" Diana asked, spitting blood. It was warm on her skin. It was filling her mouth so fast she was forced to swallow it down or risk choking. "*How?*"

Her mind raced with possibilities. Government serum, some top-secret program that turned assassins into dangerous, obedient creatures. Fulfilling agendas on some political party's whim.

She suddenly, desperately, wanted to know who Konstantine was. Had he given her this gift?

"It runs in my family," Lou said.

Diana struggled to meet her gaze. But her eyes wouldn't focus. It was genetic?

No. No. "No."

Lou released her. "I thought you wanted to help the children, but this was about you."

The children? Who cared about children? Hurt kids grow up to hurt other kids. Didn't she know that very well? That boy Diana had seen in Lou's arms was just going to be another rapist, another pedophile.

And this bitch had the gall to suggest that Diana was the clueless one?

Diana laughed, a low, throaty sound. She turned and spit blood onto the ground. As she did, she thought she saw a tooth in the mud. A small fleck of enamel. One swipe of her tongue told her all of hers were accounted for.

Someone else's then. Was this a graveyard?

She looked around, saw the dark water and endless forest and what she didn't see. Any sign of civilization. No lights or smoke. No salvation.

She met Lou's eyes.

"Why should you have it?"

"I don't know. My aunt could do it too."

"Family heirlooms." Diana gave herself over to laughter. It sounded hysterical even to her. "If you want to kill me, kill me. Because I won't stop until I have what you have. If I have to slit your throat and drink all of your blood, I'll do it."

"I know," Lou said.

That was when the gun appeared, as if it had always been in Lou's right hand.

Diana had only a moment to register the cool muzzle pressing into the stretched skin of her forehead before even the dark forest blinked out.

42

———————

Diana weighed nearly nothing. It was weird when that happened, when a body with so much weight to it one moment became a husk the next. Lou wondered if the soul, in fact, held all the gravity of a person. Or if humans were soulless, perhaps the weight came from the burden of living.

She walked out into the cold water slowly, Diana floating behind her until the depth was chest high. Her boots sank into the mud with each step. Her teeth were chattering. Her limbs weak.

Sleepiness pressed itself against the edge of her vision.

Almost done, she assured herself. *Just a little more.*

Still she dove, pulling the corpse under with her.

When the purple waters gave way to red and she found the embankment rising, she floated the body to shore. No sign of the reptilian orcas. In the distance, near the yellow mountains, she thought she saw the small cut of a fin. Perhaps that was their choice hunting location this evening.

Jabbers was already on the embankment, sitting on her haunches, chewing her webbed paw like a cat. She rolled those eyes up to Lou's as if expecting her. She was more than a little interested in the body she brought with her.

Jabbers' eyes tracked the corpse as Lou dumped it onto the shore, then turned to Lou. It was as if those eyes said, *This is new.*

Or maybe it was blood-drained Lou's imagination. Maybe she was projecting and Jabbers couldn't tell the difference between a female corpse and a male one.

"I know," Lou said with a tired laugh, walking backward into the water. Blair's and Spencer's faces flashed in her mind. "And there will be more."

WITH WHAT WAS LEFT OF HER STRENGTH, SHE SLIPPED THROUGH THE shadow of a tall, proud evergreen and onto the bench seat of a moving truck.

Ahead of her, the yellow dash of the centerline ticked out the seconds, a headlight painting the black concrete bright. Blair was behind the wheel, one hand resting on it, the other on the stick shift protruding from the wide floorboard in front of the bench seat.

As soon as Lou appeared, her boot came down hard on the brake, pitching Lou forward into the dust-coated dashboard.

She was winded on impact, her chest connecting hard with the plastic casing of the dash. Slowly, she pushed herself back against the seat, but it was too late. Her hand was empty. The gun had fallen to the floorboard and her upper body was numb from the blow.

Breathe, she commanded. *Breathe.*

Her chest remained compressed and unforgiving.

Blair pointed a Glock at Lou's face, her pulse visibly jumping in her throat.

Lou still couldn't breathe. Her limbs were suddenly too cold to move. And the deep shadows pressing in from the corners of her vision, overtaking her sight in undulating waves, were not the kind she could command.

Blood loss, she thought vaguely, her last thought before passing out.

LOU HEARD THE BEEPING FIRST. A SLOW, STEADY *BEEP BEEP BEEP.*

Something was up her nose and she pulled it out, detesting the feel of anything against her face. Plastic tubing came away in her hand. More, she soon realized, was affixed to her left arm.

The blurry lights cleared and her bed, the stiff hospital linens, and the low light came into view.

She thought maybe she'd slipped from the truck into Konstantine's apartment, as she'd done on the brink of death before.

But the nurses outside her room were speaking English. Perhaps it was King, then, who had hauled her to the blood supply she so desperately needed.

Then she saw her, still in her leather pants and studded boots. One leg was thrown over her knee as her unflinching eyes regarded her.

"We're still in Louisiana," Blair said. "If you're curious."

"You could've killed me and left me in a ditch." Lou's voice rasped, breaking at the ends. She needed water.

"I thought about it when you slumped over in my seat," Blair said with a flick of her eyebrow. "I'm still thinking about it."

Lou leaned back against the pillow and mashed the call button on her plastic bedrails. Blair must've seen her do it. If she was worried Lou might call for help, she showed no signs.

"But I don't think I can walk away without answers," she admitted. "And *boy* do I have questions."

"Like?" Lou prompted.

"Is Diana dead?"

"Yes."

"Did you do it?"

"Yes."

Blair didn't look surprised by this. She nodded once, a short jerk as if checking an unseen box.

"Were you planning to kill her from the beginning? Were you just fucking with us?"

"No." It hurt Lou's throat to speak. "She didn't leave me a choice."

Blair's eyes flicked down and to the side. It looked like she was having her own private consultation. "My sister is...*was* like that. She had a way of boxing people into corners they couldn't get out of."

A short black woman pushed open the door, knocking on it as she did. "Good morning, miss. Glad to see you're awake."

"Can I have some water? Please."

"Sure thing. And I'll tell the doctor that you're awake. He'll wanna have a chat with you about what happened. Your hero could only tell us so much."

When she closed the door, Lou arched a brow at Blair. "Hero?"

She shrugged. "I told them I found you on the side of the road."

She didn't speak again until the nurse left her with a Styrofoam cup of water, a straw, and assurances that someone would be back soon.

As the door clicked shut, Blair asked, "Can you really do what I think you can do?"

Lou continued to drink her water, her gaze steady over the rim of the cup.

"Right." Blair laughed, a tired, humorless sound. "You know, I don't think it was the questions or the curiosity that stopped me from killing you. I think it was the blonde."

The hair on the back of Lou's neck rose.

"What's her name? Your little sidekick? The squirrelly one?"

Lou said nothing.

"It was how she looks at you. I know that look. It's how I look —*used to look*—at my sister, before things got bad between us. I couldn't kill you knowing that someone loves you that much."

She rubbed the scrunched skin between her brows.

"When Dee disappeared, I was only eight. She was my world, you know? Everything she did was the coolest. When she started painting her nails, when she started dancing to MTV videos in the living room, mastering the choreo, when she would walk down to the gas station with her friends to buy soda and candy bars. I wanted to do everything with her. Then she didn't come home..."

Her voice trailed away.

"I mean, her body came back. *Someone* came back. My parents put her back in her room and called her Diana, but it wasn't my sister. Somehow she'd been replaced by this other creature. My sister had been funny and *fun* and kind, and the girl who replaced her..."

She searched for the words.

"It was like someone had taken Diana and scooped out her insides. Everything that was her was replaced by this insatiable hunger. And no matter what you said, or did, or gave her, it was never enough. Never."

Blair ran a hand along the back of her neck, massaging the muscles there.

"I think I was hoping that someday she would really be able to put it all behind her and we could build a life. Maybe that life would never be as great as what we'd started with, but it would be a life. But after she finished off Winter, I realized how stupid I'd been. It was in her eyes. One look and I just knew. She'd finally gotten everything she wanted, but the hollowness was still there. And then she killed Spencer. *Spencer.* He'd been so loyal to her. If you can do that to someone who loves you so much—there's no coming back."

She looked up, finally meeting Lou's gaze.

"I guess I'm telling you all this because I want to understand, Lou. What the hell happened? Why couldn't she stop? *Why* didn't she come back?"

Lou looked at her blood-crusted knuckles and scarred arms. She thought of her own losses.

It had been one terrible night, but it'd been a clean break and she'd been saved from the worst of it when her father lifted her from their patio and threw her into the pool, knowing it would save her life. Angelo and his men could have—would have—done more, but they hadn't had the chance.

More than that, her landing had been soft. In the wake of her loss, she'd been folded into her aunt's arms. A kind, loving aunt who knew her and her abilities better than anyone. She'd been able to help her in ways that even her father hadn't managed.

Diana had been in the shed for weeks at the hands of the man who'd kidnapped her—and then Winter had come after her. The prolonged pain of what must've been done to her...

Lou licked her dry lips. "Maybe what happened to her was worse than what happened to me."

"How did you do it?" Blair asked. When Lou said nothing, she added, "How did you move on?"

"I haven't."

"But you have a life. You have people you love and who care about you. You don't push them away or use them as a means to an end. If someone comes for them, you blow them away. You might still go after assholes, but you do it for a reason that's not just about you, right?"

Lou was stuck on the phrase *people you love.*

"You might still be dealing with the shit that happened to you, but you built a life around all that darkness. How? *How?*"

The desperation in Blair's eyes hurt to look at.

Lou thought, *I don't know.* She said, "I'm sorry."

Blair sat back in her chair, tears in her eyes. "I forgive you."

Lou's throat squeezed.

"It was only a matter of time before she lost control and hurt a good person. *Spencer* was a good person. Hell, maybe she would've killed me. I guess I should be thanking you. But you probably want to make sure I'll never hurt your people either. I won't, but I understand if you need to be sure."

"No," Lou said.

Blair nodded, a tight, strangled sound slipping past her quivering lips. "It would've been easier if you just killed me. What comes next will be harder."

A rough knock rapped against the door and a black man in a white lab coat pushed it open. "Good afternoon, ladies. Mind if I come in for a chat?"

Blair stood, pushing back the chair. "I'm leaving, actually."

The doctor and nurse shuffled out of the way, clearing her path to the door.

"Blair," Lou called out to her. "What will you do now?"

With one hand on the door frame, Blair quirked a smile. "What I should've done a long time ago. What I kept begging my sister to do."

She tapped the doorway once, as if for luck.

"Move on."

43

Piper sniffed, rummaging through her dresser trying to find something for Dani to wear and finding it difficult. Her shirts were too small to accommodate Dani's ample chest and her pants too tight for her butt.

Meanwhile, voices warred in her head.

Maybe she can trade the Lexus for clothes. Or get her loaded parents to replenish her wardrobe.

Don't be like that. She just lost everything. Now is not the time to be petty.

At least all Piper had to worry about were the clothes and the cat. King, she knew, was working with the police department to create a decent cover story for the arson. With his connections, he was the most likely to throw suspicion off of Dani and onto Diana.

"We're sticking to the truth," he'd announced before leaving to meet up with Investigator Dick White.

What version of the truth did he plan to sell them, Piper wondered.

Good thing it's August, Piper thought glumly. *She'll just have to wear my night shirts and boxers.*

She wiped her running nose on her sleeve, and the pressure between her ears popped.

Still elbows deep in her dresser, she turned and found Lou standing in the dark corner of her bedroom. Her hair was wet and she smelled like soap.

"Is Dennard dead?" Piper asked.

Of all the things to say. How are you? Are you okay? I'm sorry I was an asshole. Thank you for saving Dani's life and jumping off a freaking building for her.

Lou looked paler than usual but her voice was steady. "Yes."

"Like you saw her *dead* dead? I don't want any of this villain-comes-back-in-the-eleventh-hour shit we get in the movies."

"I shot her and dragged her corpse into the lake. Last time I saw her, she was at Jabbers' feet."

Piper nodded. "Yeah, okay. That works for me."

Lou glanced at the half-packed bag on the bed. "Where are you going?"

"I'm making an overnight bag for Dani. Mel took her to the hospital. They think Diana dosed her with opioids or something. We just want to get her checked out to make sure there's no lasting damage. When she finds out she slept through a kidnapping and a base jump off a building, she's going to *freak*."

"Will she be okay?"

Piper sniffed again, her eyes beginning to itch. "She'll be okay."

Even though King and Mel had both assured her this was true, Piper had a hard time believing it. She wanted to see Dani's brown eyes open and lucid. Then she'd believe it.

Piper took her largest t-shirts from the top drawer, both of which she'd stolen from Henry, and slid them into the overnight bag. She'd have to pick up a package of underwear on the way. Dani had way more booty than she did. Oh, and socks. Dani's feet were always cold, no matter the season.

With the bag packed, there was only one thing left to do.

Piper crossed to Lou, stopping short of her. She wanted to cross her arms but didn't. She forced her back straight and met Lou's gaze.

"I'm sorry," she managed to spit out. "Lou, I'm very sorry for the things I said to you."

Lou shifted her weight to her other foot.

That's okay. No words is a valid response, she reassured herself. *Keep going. Finish the apology like you practiced.*

Piper cleared her throat, which was now itching more than her eyes. "It's my fault. I'm the one who pushed Diana out into the open by exposing her, and you had to clean up my mess. She came for Dani because of what I did, not what you did, but I put that on you. I've been so stupid lately. I've been suffocating you with this friendship stuff and you're clearly not into it. I get it. I'm...me, and you're this super-cool badass way above my pay grade. I should've never tried to—"

Lou's frown deepened. "What are you talking about?"

"The road trip and all that. I know you hated it."

"I didn't hate it."

"You were *super* bored, but I kept pushing it on you because I wanted you to have something normal in your life and I wanted to give you a reason to be my friend when all this is over."

"When it's all over," Lou repeated. Her eyebrows nearly touched.

"King is *old*. He's going to die or retire. And I have no idea what I'm doing in school, if I'll be a cop or a lawyer or whatever, but I can't expect you to hang around if my life goes off in a new direction and I get all suburban or something. I was trying to prove I had something to offer you, and all I did was drive you into the arms of a psychopath who understood you better. And I get why you liked her, I really do, but I want you to know I wasn't trying to change you. I wanted to give you more. You and Diana had more in common than you and me, but I care about you. I really, really care about you, and oh god please say something. Your scowl is terrifying."

Lou looked like someone had shoved a lemon in her mouth.

"*Please*," Piper prompted.

"I don't care if we're different."

"What?" Piper's itchy eyes began to water.

"I murder drug kings and mafia soldiers. Konstantine runs a gang of them. We're very different."

"Oh." Piper swiped at her nose with the bottom of her sleeve. "Oh, right. Wow, why didn't I think of that? But he's still living in that underworld with you. You guys have that. He's got resources and a decent level of badassery. He can hold his own with you."

And he's rich. Which I will never be.

"You hold your own," Lou said, searching her face.

"I mean, I can dig up a body and use a computer and I don't scare easy, but is that enough for you?"

Lou pulled her close. "More than enough."

Piper sniffed.

Lou's hair was cold and clammy, but Piper didn't care. She hugged Lou back.

"Are you sure?" Piper sniffed again. "It's just going to be bad TV and boring road trips and drag shows and pizza. And problems, oh *so* many problems."

Lou hugged her tighter. "It's enough, Piper. It really is."

An emotion so raw and coursing tore through her chest. The muscles in her back softened in Lou's arms and she sank into the embrace. It took her a while to gather enough air and control to speak again, but she managed a whisper.

"You're enough too. I don't ever want you to think I want you to be normal when I make you do normal things. Just because I...because I've never had a friend like you doesn't mean I want you to be like everyone else. You mean so much to me."

"I mean so much to you?" Lou repeated the words as if she didn't understand them.

Piper pulled back, wiping at her eyes. "Yes, damn it, you mean so much to me. You want me to say it again? Or tattoo it on my face, or what?"

"Is that why you're crying?"

"I'm not crying," Piper said, dabbing at the corners of her eyes with the collar of her t-shirt.

"You have tears running down your face. Your nose is red."

Piper was definitely crying, and not just crying but on the edge of a full-on ugly cry. Still, she stiffened her lip and affected a pose of mock offense.

"It's the cat. Don't look at me like that! It is. I'm really allergic and my apartment is so much smaller than Dani's and the air flow isn't as good. I think my allergies are worse because of it."

They regarded each other in uneasy silence. It was Lou who broke into a grin first. Piper felt her relief like a palpable wave. She fell into laughter.

"I'm so glad she's dead," she said. She released her t-shirt, hoping her face was mostly clear now. "You really killed her?"

Lou's smile widened. "I did."

"What about the sister and the minions? Anyone else going to show up and throw people off the building to prove some point?"

"Her sister is alive. But I don't think we have to worry about her."

"That's what you said about Diana."

"She saved my life."

"Diana?"

"No," Lou said. "Her sister. She could've killed me, but she took me to the hospital."

Lou's gaze was suddenly dark and distant. Wherever she was now, Piper couldn't go there with her. *And that's okay*, she thought. *It only matters that I'm here when she comes back.*

She shrugged. "Okay then. You're probably right."

And we're alive, she reminded herself. *We're alive, this is over, and we still have each other.*

Piper wiped at her running eyes. "Hey, how do you feel about cat-sitting?"

44

———————

Italy was often warm in the summer, but on this night, it felt oppressive. Konstantine had taken off his shirt and wore only thin silk pants. Still, he opened the window in his bedroom and invited in the breeze caressing the Arno River. Enticed, the breeze swept through, ruffling his sheets and the book on his bed.

The river itself was beautiful to behold, pulsing with moonlight. The spell was broken by a group of teenagers laughing riotously on the opposite bank.

"Do you still have your medical kit here?" a dark voice asked.

Konstantine turned to see Lou shrugging out of her leather jacket. He hadn't even heard her come in. It had been two days since he'd seen her.

Her hair was down, accentuating the hollow of her throat. She removed her shirt, revealing that she was already braless.

His throat clicked as he swallowed, his eyes tracing from the curve of her breast down to her hip bone. "It's under my bed."

She stooped, hiding the best parts of her. It was enough for him to regain his composure.

The case rattled as it was dragged across the stone floor and into the lamplight. She looked up, met his eyes. "Do you mind?"

He gestured with an open palm, and that was all the invitation she needed to take the kit into the bathroom and shut the door.

The shower ran, then quit. The kit clattered as the lid was thrown open and then she was there again, a towel wrapped around her body.

Konstantine noted the stitches along her leg and knew they weren't Lou's handiwork. He'd seen hers, both on his body and hers.

"Who did those?"

"The hospital."

"You have a story to tell," he said. "Maybe two."

She told him about Diana, Blair, the hospital. Her friends were alive and accounted for. The beast prowling the shores of La Loon was fed.

"It's a good thing I went to the hospital. You don't have the right needles in your kit," she complained, throwing the towel onto his bed. "How do you stock this thing?"

He smiled. "Inadequately. Apparently."

She shot him a look. He crossed to the bed, to what he'd begun to think of as his side, and stretched out on the covers. He watched her arrange the packages in his kit. When her hands faltered, the shadows would shift and she'd disappear, only to reappear moments later with her fists full of sterile white packages, many stamped with red letters and blue trim.

He held up a hand. "Do you mean to tell me that you're appearing and disappearing, *naked*, in some medical supply facility right now?"

She flicked her eyes up to his and smiled. "No. I'm taking it from my kit. I'll restock it later."

"Ah, I see," he said with a touch of sarcasm. "Thank you for making my kit adequate again."

"It was for me," she said. "I don't want to die because you didn't have something I needed."

"Smart move. Anything else?" He was disappointed to see her tug the shirt down over her head and pull on pants.

His eyes traced the last visible stretch of skin between her shirt and hip. "Will you lie with me? I want to tell you what I learned about La Loon."

She crawled into the bed beside him.

. . .

LOU HADN'T MISSED THE SHIVER THAT HAD RUN THROUGH HIM AT the mention of La Loon, and she wondered if he'd ever view the place as anything but a nightmare. To Lou it was a haven, strangely familiar, and yet she understood that no one else would ever feel that way.

"The plants on La Loon, including that strange grass we saw, don't photosynthesize. They likely feed on fungi in the ground, parasitically. And the fungi probably feed on carcasses. Perhaps those left behind by your pet or whatever washes up onto the shore."

Lou said nothing. She watched his face as he spoke, tracing his jaw with her eyes.

"The air is 27% oxygen, 71% nitrogen, 1.4% argon and 0.06% carbon dioxide. There are dust particles in the air, but no pollen. There are some other solid particles but nothing we can identify. The soil is volcanic and rich in iron, calcium, magnesium, sodium, potassium, phosphorous, sulfur, and silicon. I wonder if the cliffs we saw were an extinct or dormant volcano."

"Why?" Lou asked.

"The soil shows no sign of eruption. There would be..." He seemed to search for the word. Lou liked his voice, low and soft like a melody. "Sediments. Maybe there are caves underground, carved by lava. I want to try a GPR."

"I don't know what that is."

"Machines that can send pulses into the ground to show us pictures of what's beneath. There could be miles of caves under there."

Warm and relaxed beside him, she began to feel the effects of the Vicodin she'd taken before coming. She hadn't wanted to take it, but her shoulder needed the relief. And so did she.

After two nights of endless assault, Lou could barely move it at all and the swelling had returned.

She hoped she would fall asleep quickly and wake to find her mobility had returned.

Sometimes, after a hard night, the exhaustion of the fight would take her completely. Other nights, the adrenaline pulsing in her veins would fight against sleep. She hoped it wouldn't be that kind of night.

IIis fingers were in her hair.

"I think the evidence shows your world is not Earth," he said. He said this gently, as if the news might disappoint her.

"You think it's an alien planet?"

"I do. We can never know for sure, but I do."

Her eyes traced the soft, swirling plaster in his ceiling. After a long stretch of silence she said, "I guess that's no stranger than the idea of going forward or back in time."

"No," he agreed. "But are you disappointed?"

He must have heard the hesitation in her voice.

"No," she answered honestly.

"No? Why?"

In truth, Lou's mind had trailed off to other things. "I'm worried about the boy."

"Which boy?"

Lou adjusted herself against the pillow. "The one we saved in the raid."

Konstantine turned on his side so he could look at her face. They lay like that, thighs touching, nearly nose to nose. "Do you think he is still in danger? Do you feel it?"

"No. Not right now."

"But?"

"But..." *Diana said they come back.* Predators remain predators. Their hunger and lust will always drive them to find the kids, the vulnerable and afraid.

Someone out there would love to find Shai, hurt him, and relive their sick fantasies at his expense.

Shai's father was dead, but how many had seen the videos? Who might recognize his face on the street and want Shai for themselves?

"He's so small," she said.

Konstantine pushed the hair back from her face. "You can always check on him."

He was right. She could keep Shai on her radar as well as the others: Piper, Dani, King, and Mel.

Konstantine.

Would it keep extending like this? Her circle?

And why should she prioritize one person above another? One cause above another? Did abolishing the drug trade mean more than saving children from those who'd prey on them?

Was Piper, Dani, King, Mel—or Shai—more inherently valuable than any of the other seven billion people on the planet?

No. But they mattered to *her*.

And that was better than the alternative. The alternative was to be Diana Dennard, or something like her. To care about nothing, no one, but herself.

She had her hunger. She always would. But she also had more.

"You said you understood a woman like Diana?" Lou stared into those green eyes. "Is that because she's like me?"

"No." Konstantine placed a kiss on the tip of her nose. "There's no one on this planet like you."

EPILOGUE

Shai shot up in his bed, his heart pounding in his chest. Whatever dream had been on him the moment before was already fading. What was left was the funny tickle on the back of his neck. Sometimes it kept him awake at night, this tickle. Sometimes when he closed his eyes, he saw his father's face, felt his father's hands on his body.

"Are you there, angel?" He wet his lips. "It's me, Shai."

Shai spoke to the dark, waiting, listening.

As one moment stretched into two, his hopes sank.

She's probably busy. Angels must be very busy.

He'd slid beneath the blankets when he felt a tight pop between his ears. It was like the time he took an elevator to Mommy's work. She worked in an office in a very big building. On the hundredth floor, she'd told him.

His eyes slid to the corner of his bedroom between his closet door and bookcase.

For a moment it was only black. The thick, unyielding shadows were complete.

Then she stepped into the light. The orange haze from the lamps outside his window cut across her face like tiger stripes.

"Angel!"

His elation threatened to erupt from his chest. He suddenly didn't know what to do with his hands or his body. His legs bounced under the blanket as he reached out for her.

She pressed a finger over her lips.

He covered his mouth and stifled a laugh. He wanted her to come closer. He wanted to touch her again and remind himself that she was real.

She did. She sat on the edge of his bed and placed a steadying hand over his jittery legs.

He tried to make them be still.

"How are you?" she asked.

He liked her voice a whole lot. It was lower than his mother's.

"You came."

"Were you afraid?" she asked. "It felt like you were afraid."

She knows how I feel. She knows everything.

"I was. I get scared in the dark sometimes." He wanted to be honest with her. He wanted to tell her everything. He lay back down. "But you like the dark."

"I do," she said, pulling his covers up and draping them across his chest.

"When I was littler, I used to think there were monsters in the dark," he said. Then he smiled at her. "Is that why there's angels in the dark too?"

Her smile faltered. It hurt his feelings to see it, like maybe he'd said something wrong.

"How do you know I'm not a monster?" she asked.

"No," he said, relieved that it wasn't something he'd said. "Monsters are scary. You don't scare me."

"I don't?" she asked, running a hand through his hair.

His body relaxed against the pillows. "No."

"A little bit of fear is okay," she said. "Sometimes, fear keeps us smart."

"Really?"

She tucked the blanket around his chest, placing a hand on top.

"Yes. If we didn't have any fear, we might go too far." She frowned. "Do you understand?"

"Yes," he said. He didn't, but he wanted to make her smile.

And she did. "You're a smart boy."

A door creaked overhead and soft footsteps started down the hall. Shai knew his mother was coming to check on him. The angel must've known it too, because she stood, her eyes sliding between the door and the dark corner of his room.

"Will you always come when I'm afraid?" Shai whispered.

Please say yes. Please.

"If I can," she said. "Close your eyes."

He shut his eyes.

When his mother opened the door, Shai was lying perfectly still under his blanket. Through his lashes, he saw that the place where the angel had stood a moment before was empty now. Now it was bright with hallway light pouring in over his mother's shoulder. It haloed her wild hair and thick robe as she lingered in the doorway, watching him sleep.

With a sigh, she pulled the door closed. A second later, the hallway light clicked off and the thin strip of light beneath the door disappeared. He listened to her steps weighing heavy on the stairs before shuffling down the hall overhead, and heard the slight click of her own door closing again.

In the dark, a cool hand pushed back his hair, tracing his forehead and neck. He knew it wasn't his mother's, but he also didn't open his eyes.

Anything to keep her with him for a little longer.

WHAT COMES AROUND

SHADOWS IN THE WATER BOOK 6

1

———

It was November in Paris. Lou Thorne, in her leather jacket and mirrored sunglasses, strolled alone from one end of the manicured garden to the other, taking in the burnt orange and soft golds of the changing trees. The cool air was a welcome change from the blistering summer heat that had lingered well into fall.

The garden path ended, opening on a little café with a glass front and economical black door. The handle and its hinges were gold, giving it an elegant face.

Lou took a seat at a wrought-iron table outside the café, the legs of the chair scraping along the gravel, and waited for the waitress to appear.

She watched the people in their warm wool coats cross the cobblestone paths, each urgently bent toward their own destinations, and picked at the flaking table with her thumbnail.

The waitress burst through the door a moment later, her long black apron slapping against her thighs as she called out, "Bonjour."

"Bonjour," Lou returned. And then using the little French she knew, added, *"Un café et le journal du jour s'il est disponible. En anglais, s'il vous plaît."*

"*C'est tout?*"

"*Non.*"

When the waitress waited for more, Louie realized this must've been the wrong response. With a disarming smile, she said, "*Oui?*"

The girl laughed and in heavily accented English said, "That's all you want. A coffee and the newspaper?"

"Yes. Thank you."

"*Très bien.*" The girl disappeared into the glass café again.

As Lou sat at the table, waiting for her order to arrive, she considered the cramped street again. Even though tourist season was over, it was thick with passersby.

An old woman walked a black terrier. Her flannel shawl was draped dramatically over her shoulders. A little black hat on her head. It was as if owner and pet were dressed to match.

Two men on bikes passed her carefully, their long hair pulled back in buns at the base of their necks. A slim girl wearing earbuds pulled a pack of cigarettes from her purse, searching for a lighter with a frown on her face.

Why am I here? Lou wondered, not for the first time.

True, Paris had been the first big and beautiful city she'd ever seen, brought here by her aunt Lucy not long after the deaths of her parents. The trip was meant to console her, inspire her to all the possibilities her strange gift had to offer her. And now Lucy was dead, leaving Lou more than a little sentimental toward Paris. No wonder she wandered its streets.

Sometimes she went to the Le Bobillot bistro in the thirteenth arrondissement and the quaint patisserie across from it, both being her first taste of Paris. But if she had been missing Lucy, she would've been drawn to that bistro.

This was different. Something else drew her to the city these days. Some pull that turned her inner compass toward this place again and again.

For nearly two weeks she'd woken to feel a strong pull toward Paris coursing through her, but when she'd followed it, her target was never clear.

Who was she looking for?

No one stood out. It was always too crowded and she'd been unable to fixate on an exact person. Once she'd found herself in a strange room. Its walls were seemingly made of glass but it had been too dark to see out of it. And there had been no one there. No one in trouble. No killer with an axe or gun.

Just an empty room.

It was unlike her compass to have such difficulty locking onto a target, and Lou wasn't sure what it meant. In the past it meant the person she was looking for was dead.

So why did the feeling linger? Why did the undeniable pull remain insistent?

She'd visited Paris four times this week alone, three the week before. Yet her inner compass, that unknowable force that seemed to guide her dark gift, didn't let up.

It wanted her to be here. She only wished she knew why.·

Lou hoped her plan to gather more information would help to narrow down her search.

"*Voilà*," the waitress said, placing a small white cup in front of Lou, the saucer clinking delicately against the table. "*Et le journal en anglais.*"

"*Merci.*" Lou accepted the newspaper, opening it up to find the articles in English as she'd hoped.

Despite her thick American accent and the fact that she'd never made a formal study of a language as Lucy had encouraged her to do, she'd still managed to pick up bits and pieces here and there as she'd traveled. Enough for small functional exchanges at least.

French. Spanish. Japanese. Italian. More Italian than anything, since that's what the Martinelli clan, the murdering mafia whom she'd tracked for years, had spoken.

But for something as complex as reading in another language, the translate feature on her phone could only take her so far.

Who am I looking for? she asked her compass again. She wondered if her questions were too vague.

Give me something, anything to work with here.

Eyes closed, she turned the pages of the newspaper until her hands hesitated. The muscles in her abdomen tightened.

She opened her eyes and read the article title.

Mme. Delphine du Maurier's Death Ruled Suicide

Beloved feminist art historian Delphine du Maurier was found dead in her home on Saturday, October 20, at the young age of 47.

Her body was discovered in the bathtub.

Acclaimed art critic Etienne Martin, her longtime partner, was the one who discovered her in the home they shared. Due to the nature of Mme. du Maurier's injuries, M. Martin was questioned as a suspect but released after more than one hundred eyewitnesses, mainly guests at the FIAC event which he'd attended that night, had placed M. Martin at the Grand Palais during the hours of Mme. du Maurier's death.

"A wound to the stomach is not a common form of suicide," Detective Dulac told reporters. "However, it is also known that du Maurier adored the subject of suicide in art and it is possible that this is some misplaced form of artistic expression."

The couple's townhouse in the fifteenth arrondissement is renowned for its tight security and lack of staff despite the size of the home. No others were home at the time of Mme. du Maurier's death, and no other leads are known at this time.

Lou's compass tugged inside her as she looked at the printed photo of Delphine.

Black hair in a sleek bob and severe bangs cutting across her face. Black glasses framing fierce blue eyes. She wasn't smiling, and the mole to the left of her nose stood out prominently in the photo.

Was she killed? Who killed her?

Lou let her compass spin, reaching out, searching, feeling for a connection on the other end.

But there was nothing. No fixed point. Maybe there was no murderer.

A rich woman kills herself, calls it art. Probably not what I'm looking for, Lou thought, wondering why her compass kept whirling inside her. Like a telephone that rang and rang but no one picked up.

When Lou finished her coffee, she ordered another, which the waitress brought along with Lou's bill.

As Lou flipped toward the back of the newspaper, intent on searching the obituaries, her compass tugged again. She paused, finding a headline halfway down the fifth page:

Algerian Student Remains Unfound

Assia Toumi, 23, has been missing since October 16.

Her roommate, the last person to see her alive, asserts that it must be foul play.

"This isn't like her at all," claims Nada Gaood, University of Paris student and roommate to Mademoiselle Toumi. "Assia was a good girl. A very good girl. She studied night and day and always checked in with me. She told me she was going to the library and never came back. Something must have happened to her. She would have called me if she could."

Ms. Toumi's parents, who remain in Algeria, and a brother who resides in New York City have also not heard from Ms. Toumi.

Both Mlle. Toumi and Mlle. Gaood share an apartment in the Saint-Lambert neighborhood. Toumi is one semester from completing her Master Aire in Life Sciences.

The police remain diligent in their search.

October 16.

Lou looked up from the paper. Wasn't that about when her compass began tugging her toward Paris? If not that day exactly, soon after.

There was no picture of Assia Toumi as there had been for the beloved art historian.

Lou didn't need it.

She folded the newspaper and laid it on the table beside her empty coffee cup. From her pocket, she pulled out the euros needed to pay her bill and tucked them under the saucer to protect them from the light wind cutting across the garden's path.

Then she rose and strode west toward the approaching night.

Slipping easily into the flow of foot traffic and the smell of cigarette smoke and car exhaust, Lou walked until she found a pocket of shadow, folded between two trees at the edge of the path. A woman bent down to pick up her whimpering toddler, but otherwise, there were no eyes.

Take me to Assia, she thought, and stepped into the patch of shadow.

The world shifted, falling away.

The din of voices, the screech of the Métro, and the rumble of incessant traffic were all replaced by cold, dark silence.

Am I in a grave?

She froze in place, unable to see even the hand in front of her face.

Reaching into her pocket, she grabbed a lighter and flicked it twice. On the third strike, orange flame sprang to life.

No. Not a grave.

She was in the world of the dead.

The Paris catacombs.

The tunnels spreading in both directions were lined with bones instead of bricks and stone.

The world above had smelled alive. Food, perfume, and lilacs on the breeze.

This world reeked like a tomb. That cold, damp scent of crumbling bones, the dust of a decaying world.

Yet there was something much *fresher* than old bones down here, and even the momentary smell of lighter fluid couldn't overpower the acrid stench of something chemical.

She took a few tentative steps forward, her boots scraping across the dirt floor. She supposed those bits beneath her feet were either crushed stone or disintegrating bones. Perhaps both.

The powder caked her boots, and as something rumbled overhead, more dust rained down onto Lou's leather jacket. Something with too many legs scurried across her hair, but she hardly noticed. She was too glad that it was at least twenty degrees cooler beneath the city than it had been above.

Lou stopped.

The smell was overpowering now. It clogged her nose like a soaked rag.

She angled the flames toward the wall of bone closest to her, trying to bring it into focus.

Bingo.

These weren't old bones picked clean and half ground to dust by time's patient hand.

These were slick.

Wet. Fresh.

Lou frowned. She was disappointed. She'd hoped to find the girl alive, and hadn't. She always regretted when she wasn't fast enough.

She reached out and placed her finger on the knobbed edge of a joint, the synovial joint maybe.

Assia.

"Found you."

2

Paolo Konstantine opened and closed his fist, watching the blood fill his split knuckles. At his feet was a bare-chested man, his face purple and swelling.

"*Mi dispiace*," he said, over and over again. "*Non lo faccio piu.*" *I won't do it again.*

"*Di questo sono sicuro.*"

Konstantine was glad that he wore the sunglasses today. It hid the discomfort in his eyes. He didn't like doing this. He'd done his best to delegate all corrections, any cause for violence, to men who enjoyed it. And weren't there plenty of such men around him?

Unfortunately, there were times when it could not be avoided. When the message he must send was a strong one.

"We do not hurt those under our protection," Konstantine said calmly, wrapping the cloth Stefano offered around his hand. "It's a cardinal rule."

He pulled his gun and pressed the cold barrel to the man's forehead.

The man began to plead and cry.

"Gianna?" Konstantine said.

"*Sì?*" A woman stepped forward. She'd been lingering by the church's pews. The side of her face was still swollen. She needed to put ice on her left eye.

"Take this," he told her.

She hesitated until Konstantine turned his gaze on her.

Licking her lips, she stepped forward, her thick hair hanging loose over her shoulders. Her eyes wide and panicked.

When the gun was in her hand, it shook.

"Aldo hurt you," Konstantine said plainly. "Didn't he?"

"Yes," she said.

"Do you want to take his life for what he did to you?"

She looked to Konstantine as if she didn't understand.

"I…"

"If you want his life, take it," Konstantine said. "His life is yours."

She looked at the man on his knees as if she'd never seen him before. As if there were possibilities before her she'd never considered.

Her spine straightened. Her hands steadied.

Konstantine thought of Padre Leo. Of all the times he'd been forced to make an example of someone, just as Konstantine was forced to do now. Padre never warned him how hard it would be.

Padre in his black clothes and thin, severe face, more bones than skin. His gray, thinning hair and dark, sunken eyes, which even when very sick had always looked on Konstantine with kindness.

I will name you as my successor, Konstantine, Padre had said. As he'd coughed blood into his handkerchief.

Why in God's name? I am no one, Konstantine had replied.

You are my choice. You are the only one strong enough to protect them when I am gone.

Konstantine remained haunted by his words. Plagued by a belief that he was failing in every conceivable way, to do as Padre had asked. To keep his gang unified, to keep everyone in line. To elevate them above the poverty into which they'd been born, without bringing more pain into the world.

It was a fine and difficult line to walk.

"Please," Aldo begged, crying into his hands. "Please, Gianna. I'm so sorry."

Konstantine braced himself for the whipcrack of the gunshot.

It didn't come.

With a calm face, Gianna lowered the gun and exhaled. "He isn't worth it."

She handed Konstantine his gun and he nodded, dismissing her. Her hands clasped behind her neck, she started up the aisle of the church, heading toward the outer door and the sunlit streets of Florence.

Konstantine bent, placed his lips beside Aldo's ear. "She spared your life, *amico mio*. Remember that. If you touch her, or any woman again, I will do what she did not. *Capisce?*"

Aldo wiped his ruined face on his shirt. "Okay. Okay."

"Stay away from her."

"I will, I will," he stammered as two men helped him stand on quaking legs. "I promise I will."

Konstantine watched Aldo stumble toward the exit. The placid Mother Mary statue watched him go.

Somewhere in the dark cathedral, clapping began.

He turned. Vittoria, in a long, overflowing red dress, came up the center aisle. Her eyes were painted dark, her lips as red as her dress. Stefano was close on her heels.

"*Fratello!* What a show!" She pretended to fan herself. "You really are the son of Fernando Martinelli, aren't you? *So dramatic!*"

She slid into the first pew and patted the seat beside her.

"When did you get to town?" he asked, putting more distance between them than she'd suggested.

"Just now. I came to see you, of course. I hear you're in trouble, little brother."

"I'm honored, but you're mistaken. There's no trouble here."

Her presence made him uneasy. It was true that they were both born of Fernando Martinelli's wanton indiscretions, but their temperaments were quite different.

He heard from her only when she wanted something, and her requests had yet to be *pleasant*.

"I'm so impressed by what you did there." She crossed her legs and leaned toward him. "Is that conflict resolution as Padre Leo taught you?"

"You do it differently in Venice?" he asked.

"Oh yes. I never ask anyone what they want. I simply kill them. I like to do it when no one is expecting it. At dinner. Teatime. A party. Better if there's an audience. Just pull out a gun and *bang bang*."

"They must think you're mad." He softened the words with a smile.

She returned it. "Oh, I hope so. It is easier to rule when people think you're crazy. Then everyone is too busy trying not to provoke you. They don't have time to plan a revolt."

"Still," he said, "I know you're not insane. If you're here, you must have business with me. Tell me what you need."

She laced her fingers and tilted her head. "I've heard that you're having trouble with Erjon Hysa."

The hair on the back of Konstantine's neck prickled. "Where did you hear that?"

Because she wasn't wrong.

"It doesn't matter. Did you know that I am good friends with Erjon? I introduced him to his wife."

"Your good friend seized two of my ships and killed fourteen of my men."

"Yes, I heard." Vittoria affected a pout. "But I've spoken to Erjon and he's willing to broker peace."

"With me?" Konstantine asked, disbelieving.

"No, with *me*. Since we're allies, I can get him to leave you alone. But in order for me to do this, I'd like you to do something for me."

Konstantine tilted his head to mimic her coquettish demeanor. "And what can I do for you?"

"I want your *strega* to kill someone for me. Someone who is giving me a lot of trouble."

Lou's face flashed in Konstantine's mind.

Vittoria mistook his hesitation. "He is a bad, troublesome man that no one will miss. I swear it. And I hear she loves murdering men like that."

"You assume that she's my pet. That she will obey my command," he said.

"Isn't she? She comes when you call her, right?"

When I beg for her mercy, he thought. Pleading to be saved was hardly the same as a command.

And Lou Thorne was many things to him. His lover. His obsession. Part demon, part angel. The first thing he thought of in the morning and the last before he went to sleep. A face that filled his dreams, his thoughts. He ached for her the way addicts ached for the heroin on his ships.

Yes, she was many things, but certainly not a pet.

"I cannot give you what you ask for," he said.

"Fine." Vittoria's anger flashed, but was quickly concealed by another exaggerated pout.

"Is there something else I can give you?" he asked.

She regarded the illuminated statue of Mary behind the altar, with her palms turned out in offering as if she would embrace them, if only they'd run into her arms.

"Because we're family and because you're in a difficult position, I'll make another offer. You can give me one of your boys."

"I'm sure any of my men would be happy to serve you."

"No," she said, ice entering her voice. "One of your *boys*. One of the ones I saw playing out in the courtyard. You have so many and it makes me jealous. I need an heir too, you know."

Konstantine's heart dropped. "Which one?"

The truth was he felt deeply protective of all the boys in his care. He had been such a boy once, relying on Padre to keep him and his mother safe. He saw himself in those young, trusting faces.

"I only heard a few names, but perhaps Nario?"

When Konstantine was about to agree, she shook her head. "No, not that one. Matteo?"

His cheek muscle twitched and her smile deepened.

"Yes, Matteo. If you cannot cure me of my little problem, then give me some comfort. Give me Matteo and I will broker peace with Erjon for you. One phone call from me and he won't bother you anymore."

She wants him only to hurt me, he knew. *This is a test.*

Though what outcome Vittoria wanted, he couldn't be sure. To see if he could command Lou? Or at the very least, if Louie would listen to him? Or to simply see how much power Vittoria could wield over

Konstantine? He might not know the point of this game, but Konstantine still understood it *was* a game nonetheless.

"What's wrong? Why do you hesitate?" she asked with false concern. "I won't hurt him!"

"Matteo has a life here."

"I'm very good to my people. He will be like my beloved child. Perhaps I'll groom him to rule Venice, assuming he is a bright boy. Or perhaps that is the problem. Perhaps Matteo already is your chosen one?"

Konstantine didn't justify this with an answer.

"Well, then I don't see the problem."

"And if I refuse both offers?"

Vittoria shrugged. "Then you can go to war with the entire Albanian mafia and watch how many of your men they kill. They are much better at war than you are. Far more practiced. Perhaps even little Matteo will be killed. War is what it will come to, and you know it."

He did. How many times had it spilled over into his home in just the two years since he'd come to rule this clan? But transitions were always tumultuous. He had hoped the fighting would level out with time.

Konstantine's eyes fixed on the statue of Mary and her sympathetic stone face. "Give me time to think about it."

When Vittoria opened her mouth to object, he pushed his sunglasses up onto his head and leveled her with a glare. It was a trick he'd learned from Lou.

It worked splendidly.

Her brows arched and her mouth snapped shut.

"All right, but my offer stands only for a week. After that, you must deal with the Albanians on your own. Good luck to you."

She stood from the pew and fluffed the skirt of her glamorous dress, brushing imaginary dust from it.

"Now, give me that tour that you promised me."

"Matilda?" Konstantine called, and a cute girl with freckles and a gap in her teeth stopped before him.

"Yes, sir?"

"Please show Madame Rossi around and end your tour at Toni's gelateria, will you?"

"Yes, sir."

Vittoria preferred the company of women, Konstantine knew. He would oblige her, hoping her good mood would buy him time to think.

Matteo. Dear, sweet Matteo. How had she known how to hurt him? No doubt someone had said something, unknowingly arming her.

A bright, kind boy. A good-natured and playful boy. His favorite.

If he could come up with no better plan, wouldn't Matteo be safer in Venice if war with the Albanians were on the horizon?

No, his mind rebelled. *She will not keep him safe. She will be as careless with his life as she is with all the others. I'll think of a better plan. I only need time to think.*

Only he wasn't left alone as he hoped.

Stefano slid onto the pew beside him as soon as Vittoria's birdlike chatter and staccato steps faded into the shadows.

"What are you doing?" Stefano demanded. "You cannot agree to this. She's crazy."

"I'll do what's necessary." He regarded his good friend. Dark hair, hazel eyes. A thick mouth with a non-existent smile. Even as children, Stefano had been a serious boy. As an adult, it seemed his face had only one job, to convey his constant state of displeasure to the world.

And yet he was handsome.

"Just ask *La Strega* to kill the bastard. She'll enjoy it."

Of that Konstantine had no doubt. Lou often enjoyed the kill. But that wasn't the point.

"How many times must I tell you that I do not *own* her. She does not obey me."

Or anyone, for that matter.

"But—"

Konstantine interrupted him. "Padre left *me* this empire. He expected me to make these hard decisions and I will make them. Just as he did. I will solve our problems. That is my duty."

I don't know how, but I will find a way.

3

———————

Robert King scraped his heel against the curb outside 777 Royal Street. Through the glass window that read *Crescent City Detective Agency*, he could see Piper behind her desk. The top of the desk was covered with its usual mess of papers, and her open laptop. Sleeping in the patch of sun just beyond her door was Lady, the Belgian Malinois King had gotten them over a year ago for protection.

Piper and Lady weren't alone.

King pushed open the front door. "What are you doing here?"

Melandra looked up at the sound of his voice and smiled. "Good afternoon, Mr. King."

Mr. King. Despite his urging to call him Robbie, or even Robert, Mel had persisted in calling him only Mr. King.

"Good afternoon, *Ms. Durand.*"

Mel harrumphed.

"We're doing the schedule. Do you have any say where I go next week? If you do, speak now or forever hold your peace." Piper twirled a blue ink pen between her fingers. The silver rings on her fingers caught the fading light and sparkled. He caught a glimpse of the crow-in-flight tattoo on her inner wrist.

King gave Melandra's shoulder an affectionate squeeze as he leaned over the desk and regarded the calendar. He noted the hours, running the math in his head against the cases he knew needed his attention in the coming days.

Then he shook his head. "Looks good to me. Though don't you think you're working too much? That's forty-five hours."

Piper scowled. "I like having money, man. Shoot me."

Melandra made the sign of the cross. "Don't say that. Don't even joke about getting shot."

Mel had been superstitious on this subject since accidentally shooting Lou in the shoulder and nearly killing her.

Piper wrinkled her nose. "My bad."

"You know your limitations better than I do." King slid behind his desk and opened his own computer.

"Damn right I do."

The bell above the door rang. A bike messenger stood at the entrance with a large bouquet in her hand. Piper visibly straightened.

King assumed the flowers were for her, given that Piper was the only one around here with the semblance of a love life. But then the messenger said, "Robert King?"

King regarded the red lilies in clear plastic. "That's me."

The girl handed the flowers over. "I need you to sign here."

While he signed the document, she pushed her bicycle helmet back on her head. Then she left, the bell signaling her departure.

King had two pairs of eyes on him.

"Is it your birthday or something?" Piper asked, now visibly deflated.

"His birthday is in September."

"September!"

"The thirtieth," Mel added.

"Why didn't you tell me! We missed it."

"It's not a big deal when you're old," King said. But the truth was, Lucy had died close to his birthday. Now, the entire month had soured on him. He didn't think he'd ever be able to enjoy a birthday again.

"Let's not get off subject," Mel said, her own grin wicked. "Who sent the flowers?"

King rummaged through the foliage until he found the card. "Beth Miller, the DA."

Mel and Piper exchanged a look.

Piper clapped her hands together. "Yeah, buck those gender norms. Men deserve to receive flowers, too."

"It's not like that." With the lilies in King's arms, he felt dizzy from their heady floral scent. "She sends them to everyone when they close a case."

Piper snorted. "I doubt that. Have you seen her send anyone else flowers?"

King admitted that he had not.

"Next thing you know she'll ask you to dinner," Melandra said.

King wanted to wipe that grin off her face. "Joke's on you, because she already asked me to dinner. We're meeting tonight, actually. Seven p.m. at Jim's."

Piper and Mel exchanged another look, their amusement barely contained.

"She sent you flowers and asked you to dinner? Man, come on. She's not even trying to hide it."

"You two are ridiculous."

"Is she married?" Mel asked.

"No," King replied. "Divorced."

"Likes men?" Piper asked.

"I don't know. I've never asked!"

"Children?" Mel asked.

"One, but he's grown. Lives in Orlando."

Piper shook her head. "Sometimes the gays breed too, so that doesn't give us much." To King she said, "Ever seen her date anyone?"

"Yes, she was dating Phil Roper last year. But now he's engaged to someone else."

Piper slapped the desktop. "Bingo. Interest in male species confirmed."

"You're both wrong. We only talk about work." King closed down his laptop, packing up for the day. He couldn't work in these conditions.

"Where you going?"

"I need to shower before dinner." And he didn't have a vase for the flowers here. They would wilt if he didn't get them into water.

"Yeah," Piper said, leaning back in her chair. "I like to smell good for my bros, too."

The storage closet opened and Lou Thorne emerged. Mirrored shades hid her eyes and her dark brown hair grazed the top of her shoulders. Her leather jacket was tight across her shoulders.

She saw the flowers and hesitated. "Did someone die?"

"They were a gift," King said.

"Is it your birthday?"

King exhaled slowly through his teeth. "No. They're just a gift— why are you here?"

"There's a murderer in Paris."

Now all eyes were on her.

"How do you know?" King asked.

"I found fresh bones in the catacombs. Not in the public part. It must be a section not included in the museum."

King had to admit it was a good place to hide bodies. "There are a lot of those tunnels. It's possible that someone found a separate entrance. Though how they're getting a body in and out without anyone noticing is the question."

"It was only the bones," she said. "Cleaned."

"Easier to transport clean bones in a backpack, I suppose."

King couldn't tell if Lou was looking at the flowers or not. But that slight tilt to her lips made him suspect so.

"I don't have contacts in Paris." He adjusted the flowers in his arms. "If you think there's a killer, you should just take them out."

"I would if I could find them."

"What do you mean?" Melandra asked. Her bangles clanked against the desktop as she sat up straighter.

Piper had forgotten the flowers too and was now straining forward. "You always find them."

"I can't get a lock. Maybe I'm asking the wrong questions."

"Explain, please." Piper waved a hand impatiently.

"I go to Paris whenever I get the urge, but no one stands out. I kept slipping to parks, squares, places with a lot of people. So I went through the paper and searched for missing people. Deaths. I found a story about an Algerian student. When I asked the compass to take me to her, it took me to the catacombs, which is where I found her." Lou cut her eyes to King. "But when I said, 'Take me to her killer,' I got nothing."

"Nothing." Mel touched her throat.

"It's happened before, when I was trying to find someone who was dead."

Piper frowned. "So the killer is dead?"

Lou shrugged. "Maybe *Assia's* killer is. Her bones are the first concrete thing I've found. I'm going to follow that and see where it gets me."

"Her name was Assia? Pretty name," Piper said, her face crestfallen. "How old was she?"

"Twenty-three."

"Oh man." Piper pressed her fingers into her forehead. "I hate it when they're our age. Or younger. Younger is even worse."

"I also wondered if there were two killers," Lou said. She turned to King. "I had a problem getting a lock with the two Winters, remember?"

King nodded. "But you don't think there are two killers now?"

"Nothing is coming up."

King considered Lou's predicament. "I can't imagine the police will ever go down there. The paperwork and red tape that would have to be cut in order to get permission to search the entire tunnel system based on a tip alone."

He whistled.

"You could move the remains to a central place and see if that kickstarts an investigation, though if they're cleaned like you said, they won't get much forensic evidence from the bones. Examining the original site would be better, but if you've already been there, it's polluted."

"At least if you give her back, her family will get closure," Piper offered. "It might be worth moving her just for that."

King tapped his pen against the desk. "It's possible they can't even get to the section she's in. I don't know if all the tunnels are accessible.

Were there entry points of any kind? Anything to suggest how the killer got down there?"

"No," she said. "It was pitch black and the walls are mostly bones. I think it's a very old section of the catacombs."

He shrugged. "I'm sorry. I don't know what to tell you. Maybe Konstantine knows someone. Europeans are a bit more friendly with their neighbors than with us."

King saw the time. "I have to go."

Piper snorted. "King has a *date*."

King felt Lou's ice-cold eyes slide over him.

"It's *not* a date," he said too quickly.

Lou said nothing.

"It's not," he insisted.

"Come on," Melandra said, rising from her chair. Her bangles clinked together as she moved toward the door. She pulled the shawl tighter around her shoulders. "After you, Mr. King."

When they were gone, Piper looked to Lou and snorted. "It's *totally* a date."

"Is it?"

"Oh yeah. But good on him. He hasn't even looked at a girl since Lucy died. And that was over two years ago."

"Right," Lou said, her eyes still on the door. "Two years."

It was 6:54 when King crossed the threshold of Jim's Jambalaya, a Cajun restaurant positioned on the edge of Jackson Square, adjacent to the stoic white cathedral serving as the centerpiece to the square. King had been to this restaurant a few times since moving to the city, both for the food and for the Thursday night poker. Tonight, he was looking forward to enjoying a delicious New York strip with a side of red beans and rice and garlic mashed potatoes.

A bright-eyed hostess greeted him and asked if he was a party of one.

"Robert!" a voice called out.

King looked up and saw Beth at a table halfway back.

She looked amazing in a maroon pantsuit that hugged her curvy frame. Her long braids hung over one shoulder, the strands adorned in beautiful gold beads. The hair near her scalp was gray, matching the silver she'd painted on her long nails.

"No," King said to the hostess. "I'm with her."

The hostess gestured to the path stretching between the tables. "After you then."

King reached the table, pulled out the chair as the hostess put a menu down on the table in front of him. "Enjoy your meal."

"Thank you."

Beth smiled, settling back into her own chair. "I'm glad you could make it."

"Thanks for inviting me. I love this place."

She laced her fingers on the tablecloth. "Do you? It's got great food."

"It does," he agreed.

She leaned forward conspiratorially. "I always feel bad for people who have to eat at *chain* restaurants. I'd rather *die* than eat like that. Where did you like to eat when you were in St. Louis?"

He rattled off a few restaurants.

Beth wrinkled her nose. "Now you know better."

He laughed. "I do."

"What do you plan to get?" She gave the menu a cursory glance. "It's the blackened catfish for me."

King told her of his plans for the New York strip.

She lightly touched his hand. "Good choice."

King hesitated at the touch. He supposed southern women were far more touchy than their northern counterparts. Reaching out and squeezing a hand or an arm was as common as a smile down here, and Mel had told him as much.

"Thank you for the flowers," he said cautiously, folding the menu and returning it to the tabletop. "They were beautiful."

"I'm glad you liked them. I saw them and thought of you."

Thought of me.

Immediately King saw Melandra's and Piper's mischievous grins in his mind. He shoved them down.

They're wrong, he thought. *They're absolutely wrong about this.*

And yet the seeds of doubt had been planted.

Before he could test his theory, the waitress came, took their orders, and delivered their drinks.

A full ten minutes had passed before King was able to say, "You must have a hell of a flower budget."

She looked up from her menu. "What's that?"

"You've closed a lot of cases lately. It must be hell on your office budget."

She laughed. "Nah. I only buy flowers for the cute ones."

King's face flushed, and when his steak arrived, he cut it with a little more vigor than necessary.

A commotion at the door made King turn in time to see Piper walk through the entrance and say something to the hostess. Then she spotted King and waved.

Don't come over don't come over don't come—

"Hey!" Piper bounded to a stop beside their table. "Good evening, Ms. Miller. You guys look *cozy*."

Beth turned her wine glass in the light. "What's the point in working hard if you can't play hard too?"

Piper's smile stretched wider. "I hear you there."

"I hope you're having fun, or does your boss work you too hard?"

"Oh no," Piper said. "He's a great boss."

Piper patted him on the shoulder. "That steak looks great. Good choice." Then, for his ears alone, she said, "But the potatoes have *a lot* of garlic. Better grab one of the mints on your way out."

King plastered on a smile. "Aren't you late for something?"

"Yes!" Piper said. "Yes, I am. But I didn't want to be *rude* and not say hello to y'all. Okay then! Bye."

With a little wave, she was off. Beth watched her go with a relaxed smile.

"She seems like a good girl."

"She is. Very good," King choked out, though he was feeling less than generous with his praise at this very moment.

The sentiment only deepened as their meal progressed. After Piper's appearance, it became impossible for King to miss even the smallest of flirtations. Beth's glances over her wine glass. The brush of her feet against his under the table.

As they were exiting the restaurant, King saw the little basket of mints on the podium. Defiantly, he marched past it without grabbing one.

Outside, Beth's eyes were a rich, deep brown in the streetlight.

"Thanks for a lovely meal," King said.

"My pleasure. Though I have to say..." She reached up and tucked one of her braids behind her ear. "Robert, I'm worried you might not be getting the message, and while I prefer a more nuanced and natural approach to these things, it seems I'm simply going to have to state the evidence for you."

His heart kicked.

"I find you very handsome and I'm interested in seeing if there's more here between us. Romantically."

"Beth, I'm...I'm very flattered by your attention."

"But? Am I not your type?" she asked. Her smile had faltered, but only slightly.

"Of course you are," he said, and immediately wanted to kick himself for the adamance in his voice. "My wife just died."

Beth put a hand over her heart. "Oh my Lord. I'm sorry. I had no idea. How did she pass?"

"Bone cancer."

"I'm so sorry to hear that. Were you married a long time?"

"No." He shifted his weight. "No, actually we married just before she died. A sort of send-off, but she was in my life for a long time."

This wasn't *exactly* true. When Lucy had left him to raise Lou after Jack died, they hadn't so much as spoken for twelve years. But Lucy had never been far from King's mind, before or since.

"It's been two years since she passed," he added. "I don't know if I'm ready to..."

"Right. I see." Beth considered this, fingering the necklaces at her throat and nodding. "I understand. Well, I want you to know two things."

King recognized this attorney voice, the unmistakable final-remarks-before-a-ruling tone.

"First, I want you to know that this will in no way affect our working relationship."

King relaxed. "I'm glad to hear it."

"I am a professional and so are you. Regardless of what may or may not transpire, I think we can both agree to separate these aspects of our lives, can't we?"

"Sure we can," he said.

"Well then." She rolled her lamplit eyes up to meet his. "Should you prefer a no-strings-attached sexual relationship instead of something so *severe* as dating, I want you to know that I am amicable to that idea as well."

King must've looked as dumbfounded as he felt.

"Sex." She smiled. "Robert, I'm suggesting we just have sex."

A suppressed snicker drew King's attention.

There, twenty paces away, was Piper at her card table, with a half-finished tarot reading spread between her and an emo kid, his skateboard propped against his knee, black eyeliner thick around his bright blue eyes. They were both looking at him, but it was Piper's grin that made his face burn.

4

―――――

Lou pulled a can of cat food from the cabinet and set it on the counter. Before she even removed the can opener from the drawer, four soft feet landed on the stool beside the kitchen island. A pair of golden eyes watched her over the lip of the counter.

Lou peeled back the lid on the metal can.

Meow.

"Yes, this is yours." She pulled a fork from the drawer and scraped the meat into the little dish Dani had given her, the word *Octavia* written in an embellished script across the white porcelain.

Lou pushed the dish toward the cat, who made the last jump between stool and island countertop to eat it. When she was finished, she pressed her head into Lou's hand, purring.

"You're welcome." She scratched her ears, enjoying the feel of the British Blue's soft fur against her fingertips. Lou had to indulge in these moments, considering that after feedings were the only times Tavi showed genuine affection.

The cat reminded her of another golden-eyed beast. One who required far less maintenance than this princess. At least Dani had kept to her promise of keeping the litterbox clean so that Lou didn't have to touch it.

Once the cat grew bored of Lou's attention—which was quickly, Lou noted—she hopped down and returned to Lou's bed. She curled herself into a ball at the end of the mattress, soaking up the last of the fading sunlight.

It would already be night in Paris.

Lou grabbed her leather jacket off the arm of her sofa and slipped it on. She put the two Browning Hi-Power pistols, gifts from Konstantine, into her holster.

"I'll be back later," she said to the cat. This was a strange and nonsensical exchange that had developed since Lou had agreed to take Octavia when Dani lost her apartment.

But she hadn't been able to stop herself from declaring her arrivals and departures.

Lou stepped into the linen closet.

It was pitch black in the small space. Only a strip of light shone from under the closed door. Lou adjusted her weight against the bare wall, taking in the scent of the lavender sachet she'd hung from the ceiling. The wall notches, which used to hold shelves, scraped against her jacket as her mind searched the dark.

Take me to Assia's killer, Lou asked her compass again.

Nothing.

Well, almost nothing. Lou felt the cold north wind of a barren wasteland blow through her. It was a sensation she always felt when trying to locate the dead.

Take me to the one responsible for her death, Lou tried again.

Here the compass moved. It warmed, whirling to life inside her. As it sifted through all the possible coordinates in time and space, Lou breathed.

This pull was stronger, but still not an exact match.

Take me to someone who knows something about her death.

Delphine crossed Lou's mind and the pull clicked into place. A tug through Lou's navel drew her forward. The closet fell away. The scent of lavender and the compressed air of an enclosed space were replaced by the light breeze of open air. Lou stepped out of the shadow of an enormous tree and into the twilight of a manicured park.

She recognized it as the Jardin du Luxembourg because of the iconic Medici fountain stretching before her. The dark pool shimmered in the moonlight. At the far end of the pool, the outline of the lovers entwined, the moment before they're ambushed by Polyphemus.

Ten paces east brought her out into the open, a yard from the stone benches lining the path. A man had his face in his hands, sobbing softly.

Is he the one I'm looking for?

She was still trying to decide how she would initiate a conversation when a shadow moved in the corner of her eyes and her compass seemed to redirect its attention.

She turned and found a girl, no more than sixteen or seventeen, with a dustbin, sweeping cigarette butts off the gravel path.

She wasn't alone. Five yards away was a second shadow, tracing the edge of the hedges. As the girl moved, the shadow moved. More than that, it was *closing* the distance. Getting nearer and nearer, the deeper into the park that she went.

Lou stepped through one patch of darkness and emerged through another, so close to the pair that she could smell the cologne wafting off the hidden man.

Now that she was closer, Lou realized the girl wore earbuds, humming to a tune under her breath.

Lou waited. If he made a move, so would she.

She wanted to make sure she wasn't about to kill a friend who only wanted to jump out and scare someone in jest. Yet Lou got her answer when the girl propped the dustbin against the trash and reached into her pocket for her phone.

The man leapt from the bush and grabbed her arms.

But instead of laughter, instead of a hand across the chest in the universal *oh god you scared me* gesture, the girl cried out. It was cut short when a large hand was clasped over her mouth. Her arms went up to shield her, the forearms crossing one another in defense.

As soon as the woman's back hit the ground, the man was on top of her. Whether he wanted to rob her, beat her, or rape her, Lou would never know. She was already yanking him up by his hair before any real progress could be made.

Hauling him between the trees, Lou felt the gravel of the Jardin du

Luxembourg shift into the wet, marshy land of her private lake. In exchange for the manicured foliage, miles of Nova Scotian wilderness sprang up around her. The toads, which had been indulging in song a moment before, paused in their rehearsing. Geese resting on the lake after a long day of migration took sudden flight.

It was beautiful, this wilderness, saturated in the late afternoon sun.

But Lou's true sanctuary, her Alaskan stronghold, wouldn't be available for a couple more weeks, when darkness would descend over the arctic.

Lou would settle for this for now, sunlight and all.

The man lost his balance and was pitched forward. His arms went out to break his fall, hitting the water's surface and sinking. On all fours, his knees remained on the muddy shore. His arms were submerged in water up to his chest.

Lou could only guess that the stream of words pouring from the man's mouth were the typical mixture of disbelief, anger, and indignation. Conveyed by generous use of profanity.

When he saw Lou, he definitely swore.

"I don't speak French," she said calmly. "If you want to insult me, you'll have to do it in English."

"Who the *fuck* are *you?*" He managed to pull his hands out of the muck with a defined sucking sound. He tried to right himself, shake the mud off, but his arms went out to balance himself on shaking knees.

Lou didn't answer his question. Why should she? In two minutes, he would be dead.

"Why did you hurt Assia?" she asked.

"Who?" he spat.

"Assia," she said again. "The missing Algerian student. Do you know anything about her death? Did you hurt her?"

"I haven't hurt anyone. I would never hurt anyone."

"The woman in the garden would say otherwise."

"We were just talking. We were friends." He was looking around, taking measure of the trees. The terrain. If he was looking for help, he was out of luck.

The nearest town was at least thirty miles away. There was nowhere he could go that Lou couldn't follow, and no one to hear him except the coyotes and deer.

"She didn't look happy to see you. Your *friend*," Lou said.

"What do you want from me? Why did you bring me here? *How* did you bring me here?"

She chose to answer the first question. "I'm looking for Assia's killer."

"I don't know who that is, but I swear, I haven't killed anyone."

His eyes were wide and shimmering in the dark. When Lou pulled her Browning and pointed it at his forehead, those eyes only widened.

She didn't understand the stream of French that followed, but she suspected that he was praying, maybe begging. The way he pressed his palms together and turned his face to the sky suggested as much.

If this man really is innocent, if he's never hurt anyone, tell me where to take him, Lou thought.

She inched forward, closing the distance between them.

Except her compass didn't respond to the request. No home coordinates were sent.

Not so innocent then.

The man rose suddenly, throwing all his weight against her, knocking her back.

As she was falling she folded her arm so that he came down on her bent elbow.

On impact he cried out. He rolled onto his side, winded. Before he could regain his breath, she had him by the legs, pulling him into the water.

"You fucking bitch," he said.

She yanked hard, pulling him under at the same time that she sank herself.

He began to writhe, trying to untangle himself from the anaconda-like limbs holding him beneath the surface. But the water was already changing from pale blue to deep red. The temperature change was palpable, the cold Nova Scotian lake fading to a memory. When Lou broke the surface she was in La Loon once again.

The nightmare landscape of her childhood.

Its strange purple sky, twin moons, and smoky yellow mountains greeted her. As she climbed the embankment to the oil-black shore, she stared out over the red waters she hadn't seen in weeks.

The air smelled like sulfur and the taste of ash was on her lips.

A screech ricocheted through the eternal twilight, and Lou smiled.

The branches of the waterside forest bent and twisted as a beast cut through the undergrowth, barreling toward Lou at a speed that had always astonished her, no matter how many times she saw it.

As Jabbers broke through the trees, the beast barked twice in what Lou could only guess was unrestrained glee. The black, muscular body contracted as it circled Lou twice. Serpentine skin the color of tar and six legs with scaly feet that cut deep rivets in the earth. Her yellow, forward-facing eyes dilated at the sight of Lou, as her nose was shoved into Lou's belly, pushing her back.

Again, she thought of the little cat in her apartment and wondered how two creatures—infinitely different in their physical traits—could remind her so much of each other.

Lou placed her hands on the large, cool head. "I haven't been gone *that* long."

The creature cooed another frightening sound, temporarily revealing the inside of its cotton-white mouth and rows of sharp teeth.

The man spoke from the water, a surprised, choking sound.

"Your mistake," Lou said. "If you'd remained quiet, maybe she would've overlooked you a bit longer."

The plates that ran down Jabbers's back rose, erecting in a line of tension from the base of her long neck to the tip of her tail.

"Too late," Lou said as the beast leapt into the water.

LOU WAS STILL WET WHEN SHE STEPPED OUT OF KONSTANTINE'S closet. He was on his bed, his ankles crossed and a book open in his lap. She turned her wrist until the GPS watch lit. It was almost eleven p.m. in Florence.

He lifted a mug to his lips. "Good evening, *amore mio*."

"Bedtime?" she asked.

"I would ask you to join me, but not in that condition." He regarded her dripping body and his wooden floor.

She followed his gaze down to her soggy boots. "I'll clean this up."

She stepped into his bathroom, stripped, knowing full well his eyes were on her back. She didn't mind. There wasn't anything he hadn't seen in their time together. And if she was being honest with herself, she liked his eyes on her. Liked how clearly his hunger mirrored her own.

She made quick work in washing the otherworld out of her hair and off her skin.

When she stepped into the bedroom again, a pair of Konstantine's black sweats and a white t-shirt lay across the foot of the bed. And a comb lay beside them.

He remained in the same reading position, as if he hadn't moved at all. As if these items had simply appeared for her.

The moment she reached out for the clothes, he pounced, trapping her face down on the bed, his body braced above hers.

"*Must* you wear clothes to bed?" he purred into her ear.

She felt the warmth of him through the towel. "Then why did you put them out?"

He kissed her ear, her neck. Slowly, she rolled onto her back so she could look up into his face.

He remained above her, bracing his weight so that she could position herself as she liked.

Keeping her eyes locked on his, she opened the front of the towel.

"Is this a game?" he asked. "To see how long I can stop myself from looking down?"

She grinned and wrapped her naked legs around his waist.

His eyes slid from her face to her chest, trailed between her breasts and over her abdomen.

"You lose."

He gripped her hips and grinned. "Do I?"

He placed a kiss on her throat, her collarbone. Electricity skittered across her skin. She slid one hand into his hair, felt his dark locks curl around her fingers.

When he looked up and met her eyes, he said, "A successful hunt tonight?"

"How did you know?"

"There is still the hint of sulfur on your skin. You only have that if you cross over. You only cross over if there was a body to bring."

"You want me to shower again?"

"No. I want to stay right here." He grazed her ribs with his teeth. "But am I right?"

"I took a man from Paris," she said.

And mentioning the city caused her to recall the park in its twilight splendor. The way the hedgerows had stood in tight formation like soldiers holding a line. The way it had been quiet, nearly deserted, with the smell of the city pressing through the thinning branches, which were quickly losing their leaves.

"Hello. Where did you go, *amore mio*? Back to Paris?" Konstantine purred, biting her ribs a little harder.

"Yes."

"If it was a successful hunt, why do you look so displeased?"

"My compass isn't working," she whispered.

He stopped teasing her with his teeth. "Really?"

She frowned harder. "Or it might be working but my questions aren't getting me anywhere."

He seemed to consider this, and when Lou fell back into her thoughts, he came to lie down beside her on the bed, putting his head in his hand.

"What have you asked?"

It was true that no one—not King, nor Piper, or even Konstantine —would understand what it was like to use the compass inside her, but Lou thought that Konstantine might understand this much.

She repeated the questions she'd asked thus far. Who killed Assia? Take me to her killer. Who hurt her? Take me to Assia. Where was she before she died? Who is responsible for her death? Who knows what happened?

She took him through the last two weeks of her searching, ending with her night in the Jardin du Luxembourg.

"I'm sure the man I took was going to hurt the custodian," Lou finished. "But I don't think he was the one I'm looking for."

"Maybe it was the man who was crying, or even the young woman herself."

"Or someone I didn't see," Lou said. "As soon as I saw the man stalking her, I homed in on him. It's possible that I didn't look around well enough."

"Is there anything I can do to help you?" he asked.

"Do you have contacts in Paris? Official ones. Police? Detectives?"

"Yes."

"Find out if they will go into the catacombs and get Assia's body."

He considered this. "Anything else?"

"Yes," she said, and hooked her thumbs into the waistband of his sweats and tugged, sliding them easily down, exposing his backside. She loved the feel of her hand sliding over those muscles. "Help me fall asleep."

He was *more* than happy to oblige her.

5

───────────

The anxiety coursing through Piper's body made her feel like she was covered in ants. She checked herself in the bathroom mirror for the third time, adjusting her suit jacket on her shoulders, brushing at her lapel. Did she need to take her makeup off? She'd skipped the eyeliner and had gone for fresh-faced, but was it too much?

She couldn't remember the last time she'd fretted over her appearance like this.

Calm down. You're sweating, she chided herself. *You'll be a mess before you even get across the river if you don't get ahold of yourself.*

Dani appeared in the hallway, a tight blue dress hugging her curves. It was the color of the sea at night and it suited her.

She brushed her long dark hair over a shoulder and pushed a small diamond earring through her right earlobe. "Wow. You look great."

Piper exhaled the air from her puffed cheeks. "Why am I meeting your parents again?"

Parents were not Piper's forte. Nor were rich people. And apparently she was about to lunch with both.

"Because they want to meet the woman who saved my life. And you generously agreed to that," Dani said.

"They should be meeting Lou then, right? If I recall correctly, I was unconscious by the dumpster when Diana kidnapped you."

It was Lou who saved Dani's life, not Piper. When Diana Dennard had kidnapped Dani from her apartment and had blown it apart, it was Lou who had chased Dennard down, fought her and her minions, and even jumped off the side of a building after her.

Piper, on the other hand, had been knocked out with one punch.

Of course, they hadn't been able to tell any of that to the authorities.

The official story was that there had been a gas leak from an unattended stove in the adjacent apartment, causing the explosion. Piper had come over for a late dinner, had smelled the gas and forced her way into Dani's apartment. As far as they knew, it had been Piper who had dragged the unconscious Dani to safety.

No mention of Lou or murderous psychopaths was made. No one even asked why Piper's nose was twice its usual size.

Dani snorted. "Can you imagine Lou meeting my parents? They'd die of fright at the sight of her."

I'm going to die of fright, she thought.

Dani must've seen something in Piper's face, because she reached out and squeezed her shoulders. "Hey, it'll be fine. I mean, they're boring snobs, but they don't bite. It'll be a quick lunch, an hour or two tops, and we'll head back. The whole thing won't take us more than four hours."

Piper took a big breath. "Okay. Fine. Let's do this."

Dani drove. It was easier since of the two of them, she was the one who actually knew where her parents lived. Piper tried not to squirm and feel out of place, which she already felt every time she was in Dani's luxury SUV. It was the leather seats, the automatic buttons, and the fact that this was also the first car she'd ever ridden in where the car *talked back* to you.

It didn't help that Dani looked like a million bucks in the driver's seat. All calm reassurance and the perfect poise of good breeding.

By the time they arrived in Mandeville forty-five minutes later, Piper had chewed both her thumbnails down to the nubs.

"Oh my *god*," Piper groaned as Dani's SUV slowed to a stop in the circular drive. "You're *kidding* me."

"I know. It's a bit ostentatious."

Ostentatious didn't begin to cover it.

The two-story plantation house stood surrounded by old live oaks and acres of perfectly manicured lawn. The windows shone, gleaming as if they had just been washed that morning. Black lanterns hung from the ceiling of the balcony, with what Piper hoped were flameless candles flickering in their glass casings.

As the SUV rolled to a stop outside the front door, a man stepped off the porch. Dani let him open the door for her, and she climbed out, all smiles, placing a kiss on each of his cheeks.

He was short, only a few inches taller than Dani, with dark eyes like hers. Gray hair encircled his bald crown. He spoke beautiful, fluid Spanish, which Dani returned with equal ease.

In a natural pause in the conversation, Piper reached her hand toward the man. "Hi. I'm Piper. It's so nice to meet you, Mr. Allendale."

Dani and the man froze, exchanged looks, and burst into laughter.

But the man shook her hand. "It is very nice to meet you, Ms. Piper, but I'm not Señor Allendale."

Laughing, Dani said, "This is Juan. Our butler."

"Oh god, sorry. Right." With the Spanish and the kissing, and the door opening, Piper had just assumed this must be Dani's father.

"He just wants to park the car," Dani added.

Her face was burning. "Valet parking. Of course there's valet parking."

Dani's smile faltered as she handed the keys over to Juan.

The front door opened and a woman stepped out into the bright afternoon sun. As soon as Piper saw her, she knew it was Beverly Allendale, Dani's mother. They looked nearly identical except in the shape of their bodies. Dani was curvier from the waist down, and Beverly more slender.

But looking at the older woman's face was a wonderful preview of what Dani might look like in thirty years, and Piper wasn't a bit disappointed.

"Piper," Mrs. Allendale said with a bright smile. The jewelry on her wrists and fingers caught the sunlight and sparkled as she reached her hand out to take Piper's. "It is so nice to finally meet you."

"You too," Piper managed, trying to recover from her blunder. Fortunately, Juan was driving the SUV away. "Thank you for inviting me."

"Of course!" She touched her throat and laughed. "How could we not invite the hero of the hour?"

Piper flashed a shy smile.

"Daniella, why don't you show Piper around while I check on lunch. I think Margot is almost ready."

"Where's Papa?"

"Where he *always* is. In his office."

Dani took Piper's hand and pulled her into the house. "Come on."

The inside of the house was even more breathtaking than the outside. High ceilings with large windows, white marble floors that echoed as if they were walking through a museum rather than someone's actual home.

Dani rattled off the names of opulent rooms as they passed. Names for rooms that Piper had never considered. The *salon*, which was somehow different than the *lounge* and the *parlor*. The *family room*, which was different than the *den* and the *sitting room*. Though in Piper's opinion, all six of these rooms looked like a living room.

These people had *six* living rooms.

The bathrooms, at least, were all called bathrooms, though Piper had seen seven and counting. One for every day of the week.

When they were halfway up the grand staircase, Piper's hand tightened on Dani's arm.

"Is this a joke? Did you really grow up here?"

Dani wrinkled her nose. "Yeah. It's weird, right?"

"I feel like I should be in a maid uniform." She affected a fake British accent. "Will the miss have her tea in the *salon* or the *sitting room* today?"

Dani elbowed her. "Be serious."

Except that Piper was being serious. The deeper into the house they went, the smaller and more insignificant she felt.

I could never compete with this.

They stopped in front of a carved white door, Dani resting her hand on the golden handle.

"Are you ready for this?" she asked with a nervous grin.

"Probably not," Piper returned, pulling on the collar of her shirt as if she could undo it. "But here we go. Is it another living room? Because I don't think I can handle any more settees."

"No settees. I promise." Dani pushed open the door and revealed a bedroom. It was soft pinks with a creamy white border and trim. In the center was a four-poster bed with hibiscus flowers on the comforter. Three large teddy bears rested against a heap of pillows.

One wall held a mound of ribbons and medals. There were so many that they were pinned overlapping one another, four layers deep.

There was a bookcase full of books arranged by color, and a gleaming white desk with photos.

"This is my room," Dani said. "*Was* my room."

"That's a huge violin." Piper looked through the glass window of the display case. "You played the violin?"

"It's a viola. And yes, I did, for nine years. I wasn't very good at it."

On the opposite wall Piper peeled back the ribbons, inspecting each.

"First place in barrel racing. What the heck is barrel racing?"

"Horses," a voice called from the door.

They turned and found Beverly in the doorway, one hand gently resting on the doorframe. "You should take Piper out to see Buttercup. She'd be so happy to see you."

"No wonder Dani has such great posture." Piper backed away from the wall of achievement as if it might bite her.

"Yes, between that and the orchestra, Daniella should! Play something for us, *mi querida*."

"Oh no." Dani waved her off. "No one wants to hear me play. I haven't picked that thing up in over a year."

"*Daniella Vivienne.* I didn't buy you a Cecilio just for it to rot in a case. Play us a song."

"Mother, it isn't even tuned."

When Beverly only stood in the doorway, one hand on her hip, making it clear no one was going to leave this room until Dani played that instrument, Dani sighed and pulled it out of the case.

"Don't blame me when your ears start bleeding," she muttered.

She twisted the end of the bow until the hairs tightened. When she ran the bow across the strings it released a horrible screech. "I told you."

But after a moment of turning the pegs, she tried again, and the sound that came out was a beautiful swell of music. The notes were lower and richer than the violin music Piper so often heard from buskers in the French Quarter, but still very beautiful.

"Play something elegant." Her mother clasped her hands under her chin. "Play that sonata I love."

Piper didn't know classical music, but what followed was a very serious and somber piece that she could imagine echoing through the *parlor*.

Watching Dani sway gently to the music, her eyes closed, Piper's heart sank.

Look at her. Just look at her.

She'd never felt farther apart from another human in her life. Worlds apart. Galaxies apart.

Dani's dark eyes fluttered open, met Piper's, and she smiled.

The song folded from its aristocratic tenor into a robust Irish folk tune. Which Dani began tap dancing along to.

The sudden shift made Piper burst into laughter despite herself.

This only seemed to encourage Dani more, and she threw herself into the folk dance with her whole heart.

Piper felt like clapping along and began to until Mrs. Allendale's eyes fell on her. She clasped her hands together instead.

Dani finished with a defiant arms-out *ta-da* pose. And let out breathless laughter.

"Incorrigible," her mother said. "If that's how you're going to treat such a beautiful instrument, you might as well put it back. I hear Regina's daughter wants to learn to play. Maybe I'll give it to her."

"Oh, Mother, don't be so serious. We're just having fun."

Piper saw the wrinkled nose and half-formed sneer on Beverly's face, and had a pretty good idea of what Beverly's opinion of *fun* was.

"Have I missed the party?" a man asked from the doorway. Unlike Beverly and Dani, he had an accent.

Dani went to him and kissed his cheeks. "Hi, Papa."

"What's that wonderful tune you were just playing? It was fun."

Beverly scowled at him. "Don't encourage her."

"It's an Irish folk song," Dani said, her face still flushed from the excitement. "Papa, this is Piper. The one I told you about."

Mr. Allendale came into the room and reached out both hands for Piper's. Before she knew what was happening, he was placing kisses on her cheeks.

"I thank God every night that you were there," he said kindly into her ear. "And now I thank you."

He kissed Piper's hands before patting them affectionately. "Such a blessing."

Guilt filled her. *I didn't do anything. I don't deserve this.*

This guilt only multiplied under the soft gaze of his dark eyes.

A voice called up from downstairs and Beverly replied in Spanish. To their little party of four she said, "If everyone is done being *silly* up here, Margot says lunch is on the table."

The table couldn't be more grand if the king and queen had shown up for lunch. The place settings were fine china, with cloth napkins beside them. The water glasses were crystal.

When a woman appeared with a little basket, Piper was expecting bread. Instead it was a steaming towel.

It wasn't until Piper searched the table and saw Mr. Allendale wiping his hands that she understood what she was supposed to do with it.

"Thank you," she said, and cupped her hands to receive it.

The entire meal was like this. Watching Dani's every move so she could understand what fork went with which course. How to ask for more water. Where the napkin went after it went to her mouth. She thought she was doing a pretty good job, but given the eagle-eye glare from Mrs. Allendale, Piper was sure that she was falling short by the woman's measure.

"I read your piece on the city council corruption," Dani's father said across the table as he lifted his water glass to his lips. "Very good. *Very*, very good."

Dani was obviously pleased to hear this, sitting up taller in her seat. "Thank you, Papa."

"Yes, we're all very proud of your accomplishments," her mother said, forking a bit of salad from her plate. "But I think it's time you stop experimenting with this hobby and come home. If you intend to be the CEO of a Fortune 500 company by the time you're forty, you really need to get going."

Dani's face pinched. "I don't want to be the CEO of a Fortune 500 company, *Mother*. We've talked about this."

"You're wasting a wonderful opportunity. Both your father and I could offer you executive positions in either of our companies. And with a bit of experience you could—"

"Mom, *please*. I don't want to run a business. I want to tell stories."

"Stories!" she harrumphed. "Be serious. You have to think about your future."

"I do think about my future. My future in *journalism*."

Piper took another drink of water, and over the rim locked eyes with Dani's father.

Aloud, he said, "My loves. We're here to celebrate our good fortune."

"If Dani hadn't *been* in that ridiculous apartment when it *exploded*, there would be nothing to celebrate."

"She wasn't in it when it exploded," Piper said, and one look from Mrs. Allendale made her regret opening her mouth. "Technically."

Dani put her silverware down. "There was nothing wrong with that apartment. It was very nice."

Beverly arched both of her brows, as if this was retort enough.

"I don't see why you left the one I picked out for you. It was in a much nicer location."

Dani's face began to turn red, her jaw working.

Hoping to spare her, Piper said, "Actually, there were several break-ins and *two* armed robberies in that neighborhood. One just next door."

This was a lie, of course. But it was the kind of lying that Piper could do well, lying that defended and protected her friends or soothed hurt feelings.

And Piper was more than certain Dani didn't want her mother to know the real reason she'd moved out of that apartment. That it was because Dmitri Petrov, a ruthless Russian mob boss, had attacked her there. Had tortured her and hurt her there. That even though she'd survived, and had her severed finger reattached, Dani hadn't been able to sleep in that place without having panic attacks.

Beverly reached up and touched her throat. "How would you know that?"

"I work as an assistant to a private detective. We track crime in the area very closely. That neighborhood was a target because it was so nice."

"You work with a detective?" Beverly asked. Her eyebrows stayed up this time. "And Daniella too, I'm assuming, helps with these cases. How many criminals do you come into contact with when you do this work? *Dangerous* criminals, I'm sure."

She sneered these words as if they left a bitter taste in her mouth.

"Actually—"

Dani kicked her foot under the table and Piper swallowed her response.

"No," Piper said instead. "Though she would be a great resource if she ever chose to help us solve a case. She's an awesome journalist."

Mr. Allendale smiled. Beverly, however, looked ready to choke.

To her husband she said, "I told you. I told you it was too dangerous."

There was a rapid exchange between them in Spanish which Piper didn't follow. And then Dani was in it, all three of them speaking louder and louder over each other until Mr. Allendale held up his hands in surrender. He fell silent, but Dani and Beverly charged on.

This must've gone on for five full minutes, a long time to silently bear witness to an argument.

Finally, Daniella switched to English again. "Father, if you don't end this we'll never make it through dessert."

"Beverly," he said. "*Por favor, mi amor. Te lo ruego. Como tu marido.*"

Her mother sighed and lifted her wine glass to her lips. She drank deeply but said nothing.

To Dani, he said, "What will you two do after this?"

Dani took a moment to compose herself and then replied, "I want to take Piper out to meet Buttercup. Then we'll head back. We both have to work tomorrow."

Her mother huffed as if no one at this table but *her* knew what the notion of *work* was.

Everyone ignored this, including Mr. Allendale, who reached out to pluck a toothpick from a little metal dish on the table.

After a tense and silent dessert featuring lemon meringue pie and coffee, Piper followed Dani out into the back garden.

The manicured space with its splash of color and topiary was just as impressive as the rest of the estate. A light breeze rolled through the trees and the windchimes played a soft, melodic tune.

Juan waved as he passed them with a shovel in one hand.

"So this was your backyard, huh?" *Of course it was.* "Did you ever climb that elephant?"

Dani's body was still rife with tension. She only threw a cursory glance at the elephant-shaped shrub to the right of the pool. "No, I didn't."

"Are you okay? That was pretty intense back there."

"I just need some air. Come on." They took five steps toward the stable in the distance. "Wait. Let me grab a snack for Buttercup. She'll be disappointed if I don't show up with at least a carrot. Do you want to try feeding her?"

"Sure?"

"Okay. Be right back." Dani disappeared back into the house, leaving Piper alone in the garden. The light from the pool hurt her eyes, and she wished she'd grabbed her sunglasses from the car.

I don't even know where the hell the car is, she lamented. She collapsed on the last step between the house and grass and put her face in her hand.

Piper closed her eyes, listening to the windchime music.

"Are you sleeping with her?"

Piper started, turning to find Beverly on the top step, looking down on Piper in the grass.

"I...I'm sorry?"

"Are the two of you together like a couple?"

Piper wasn't sure what to say. She and Dani weren't exclusive, and Piper had never asked if she was out to her parents. What was she supposed to say?

"We're..." She searched for a word that didn't sound so vulgar as *hooking up*. "We're taking it slow."

Oh my god, why the hell did I say that?

"I'm sure you, like my *husband*, think my expectations for Daniella are too high. But I love her. Do you understand?"

"Of course." She was sure there was no other acceptable response to such a question.

"I want what's best for her. Can you look me in the eye and tell me that living in the French Quarter, surrounded by *criminals* and *vagrants*, is the best thing for her?"

Did she just call me a vagrant? What the hell is a vagrant? Isn't that like a hobo?

"Tell me that you really think that's the life my Daniella deserves."

"She deserves to be happy."

"Happy? What's happy? Getting attacked? Getting hurt? Getting her *finger* cut off?"

Piper stilled.

"Oh yes, I know about the attack. I have eyes and ears everywhere," she said, pointing in all directions around them as if these eyes and ears were going to pop out at any moment.

"It's true that I don't know exactly what happened to her, if it was a mugging or—heaven forbid—*rape*, but I know she was hurt. The nurses told me what condition she was in and when she came home, and to be honest, I thought, *Good. Thank God! Thank God all this insanity with the little newspaper is over*—and yet here we are. Now she's right back in that shithole, living with *you*, and I'm supposed to be happy about it?"

Piper felt as if she'd been socked in the gut.

"And I'm supposed to believe *you* or this detective of yours is going to keep her safe? That you can make sure the other nine fingers stay attached to her beautiful hands? *Please.* Look me in the eye and tell me nothing bad is going to ever happen to her again."

Piper looked her in the eyes and said nothing.

She thought of how many times bullets had ripped through Lou's arms or shoulders. How many times she'd been stabbed. How closely they stood on the heels of killers and deranged lunatics. After Dmitri, there had been Diana. And who next? She supposed eventually, if they were in this long enough, another Dmitri or Diana was going to cross their paths. And what, exactly, was Piper going to do about it?

"Well then." Beverly looked triumphant, as if she'd gotten the answer she'd wanted. "If you care about her, if you *love* my daughter, tell her to come home."

6

—————

Konstantine woke first. He marveled at the naked woman stretched long beside him, her breathing rising and falling in a calm rhythm.

How far they'd come in just two short years. Two years since she'd pointed her gun at him and wanted to end his life, and now...

He longed to touch her, to reach out and count the freckles spread across the bridge of her nose. Freckles he could only see because of the morning light spilling through the crack around the shuttered window.

He didn't dare. He knew she was a light sleeper and that she slept as poorly as he did. Instead he lay in the glow of his happiness, his good fortune, afraid that should he make the wrong move, he would shatter the illusion and his dream come true would end.

So he slipped from the room quietly and went downstairs.

As he moved around the apartment, he played two messages from Stefano. Both were bad news. The Albanian mafia had found three of their mules in Athens and had slit their throats, leaving their bodies on the steps of the safehouse Konstantine owned there.

Another had been hit by a car and left to die on the roadside. The car accident could be a coincidence and not a symptom of the war brewing between their rival gangs, but Konstantine didn't think so.

Stefano was asking how he would like to respond.

I could ask Lou to end it. I could ask her to send a message to the Albanians and all our problems would stop, as it had with all the other gangs that had crossed her.

Not one of the gangs she'd hunted had crossed him since. But she'd hunted those men for herself, never for him.

As he pulled the coffee beans from the counter and plugged in the grinder, he considered asking her.

He couldn't imagine himself doing so.

On some days their alliance felt tentative at best. Had they really crossed so much distance that now he could ask such things of her? To *protect* the men that she would rather kill?

Padre's men. His men.

They had crossed an ocean of differences in their short time together, but he didn't believe her so loyal—yet—to do his killing for him. To ask her to do it might only push her away, break their bond irreparably.

The last time he'd pushed her to question her position, asked her to question who she really served, he hadn't seen her for months.

He didn't want her to leave him now. Or ever.

You can broker a deal with Vittoria, he thought. *You need only give her Matteo.*

He exhaled, trying to push these thoughts to the back of his mind.

As the coffee brewed, Konstantine arranged bread rolls and cut fruit on a breakfast tray. He would take it up to the bedroom and leave it on the foot of the bed for Lou before heading to the church to begin his day.

Except before his coffee had finished brewing, he felt a presence over his shoulder and turned to find Lou crossing his living room toward him.

His heart skipped a beat at the sight of her in his clothes, her hair mussed from their love-making. A dark hickey visible on her bare shoulder where his oversized shirt had slipped down.

"I stayed," she said.

He wasn't sure what to make of this statement, given his thoughts the moment before.

She must've seen the confusion on his face. "My mattress is against the window so that I don't sleep in the dark. I always slip if I sleep in the dark, but when I'm here, I don't."

Dare he hope it was because she *wanted* to be with him? He didn't dare suggest it.

"I must really like your bed," she said with the hint of a smile.

"You're welcome to it anytime." He wanted to devour those lips. "Are you hungry?"

She reached across his arm and grabbed the coffee. "I came for this."

He laughed. "Of course you did. Now that you are awake, tell me, where will you take your breakfast, *amore mio?*"

"Where do you eat it usually?"

He nodded at the desk.

She settled into his desk chair, and he put the tray down in front of her. She already had the coffee in her hand.

He was going to be late, but he didn't care. Stefano would have to forgive him.

"How did you sleep?" Konstantine leaned one hip against the desk.

"I already told you I like the bed." She brought the coffee to her lips. "Aren't you going to eat?"

Sensing more than a little threat in her question, he laughed. "Yes, I will."

He poured himself a cup of coffee from what was left in the moka, added cream, no sugar, and plucked a frittole from the pastry bag. They'd been a gift from Vittoria, and seeing it there on his plate made him think of Matteo all over again.

"What's wrong?" Lou asked.

"Nothing."

"You're a terrible liar."

"Am I? I would say I'm better than most."

Perhaps I don't want to pretend with you.

He pulled a chair up to the desk and joined her.

She didn't humor this with a response. She only watched him over the rim of her coffee cup, waiting for an answer.

"It will be a difficult day," he said. "That's all."

Her eyes sparked. "Do you have to kill someone?"

"I hope it won't come to that."

She looked disappointed by this answer, and the urge to ask for her help rose up in him again.

Just ask. It's only a question, he thought.

No. It's too soon, a second voice countered. *You must build your alliance brick by brick if you want it to hold for the long haul.*

And even a third voice, the most indignant of all. *You don't need her to solve your problems for you. Who's in charge here? Can you run Padre's empire or should he have chosen someone else?*

"What will you do today?" he asked.

"Go to Paris."

"Ah, yes. To solve your mystery. I haven't forgotten your request. I'll see who we have in the city, though it will be difficult to get anyone into the catacombs, especially if you believe it's outside the bounds of the museum."

The voices began again. *You help her. Why shouldn't she help you?*

Lou spoke, unaware of this intense silent exchange. "I'll move the bones so that her family can get her back. It'll be better than not knowing."

"If they have been cleaned as you mentioned, it is unlikely there will be helpful forensic information."

"Is there more coffee?"

"Shortly." He rose to make more.

"Don't bother if you need to go."

He ignored this and reloaded the moka. "The girl disappeared on the sixteenth of October? And the art woman died shortly after?"

"Yes."

"So you believe the deaths are connected? Why?"

Lou was at the window, looking down at the courtyard below. "My compass keeps putting them together. Half the time I'm asking questions about one, I'm sent somewhere connected to the other. It could be coincidence, but—"

A rough knock on Konstantine's front door came the moment before it burst open. For a moment, Konstantine thought, *This is it. It's the Albanian assholes and Lou will kill them and all my problems will be solved.*

Only it wasn't the Albanians. It was Stefano. *"Konstantine! Dove sei? Sei morto?"*

He saw Lou at the desk, half of a bread roll in her mouth, and sputtered to a stop in the middle of the living room. Maybe it was seeing her in the light.

Seeing her in the light of day always startled Konstantine as well. At night she seemed ephemeral, more creature than woman. The way she moved with the darkness made him question if she was even real.

But in the sunlight, it was impossible to deny that she was flesh and blood. From her small wet lips, her dark eyes, and the spray of freckles across her nose. The color in her cheeks.

All of these things made her seem *very* real.

Stefano's eyes fell on Lou's bare shoulder.

She made no move to cover herself, eyeing him defiantly over the rim of her mug.

"Sei un vampiro, Konstantine? È così che ottieni il tuo potere?" he asked.

"What do you want, Stefano?"

"Ho capito, ho capito," he said. Then, switching to English, added, "I thought you were dead. I see now you were just being lazy this morning."

Konstantine looked to Lou, waiting to see how she would react to this intrusion, but she remained the perfect image of composure that she'd been when he'd turned to make more coffee.

Only one thing had changed. Her Browning pistol now lay on the desktop.

When had she pulled the gun? How had she pulled it *and* put it down before he'd even turned around?

Stefano crossed his arms over his chest. "I hope this is a *work* breakfast, as the Americans say. Have you asked her—"

"Sta zitto. O ti chiudo la bocca io." Konstantine sneered. *"Non ti voglio far male."*

Stefano only stared at him. *"Chiedo scusa."*

"I'll be in soon. You are in charge until then," Konstantine said.

Stefano looked ready to say more. The color had risen in his cheeks and he was getting angry—Konstantine could see that clearly. But instead of an outburst, he turned toward Lou.

"Vi auguro una splendida giornata." He gave a dramatic flourish of a bow in Lou's direction. Then he walked out the door, slamming it behind him.

There was a long moment of silence.

"Did he just tell me to go fuck myself?" Lou asked, with a hint of a smile.

"He told you to have a great day."

"Yeah." She cocked her head and squinted her eyes. "But was it code for 'Go fuck yourself'?"

"Ignore him. He loves to push the buttons."

"Push your buttons. He couldn't find mine with a flashlight."

"Yes, push my buttons."

"Why do you let him?" she asked, leaning back in his chair.

God, he loved to see her in his clothes, his place, so at ease with him.

"I trust no one more." He thought she might be incensed by that. That perhaps, as most women would, she would take this as an insult. But her face revealed nothing.

"Why?" She held her mug out for more coffee. He poured it into her cup.

Konstantine shrugged. "We joined the Ravengers around the same time. He is one year younger, so he is like a little brother to me. He would give his life for me. And I for him."

She didn't laugh. She didn't mock him for his sentimentality. She drank her coffee and said nothing.

When Konstantine had collected the tray, taken it into the kitchen, and was preparing to excuse himself, she said, "What does he want you to ask me?"

His heart skipped a beat.

Just ask her.

Ask her and lose everything.

"It isn't important," he said.

"It seems important. What does he want me to do?"

You could tell her. You could just try it out and see how it goes.

But as he looked at those golden eyes, saw her standing there in his clothes in his apartment, the smell of him all over her, he couldn't do it. He couldn't risk everything he'd worked so hard to build.

"Don't worry about it," he said, pushing his hands through her hair, and to his surprise, she let him. He placed a kiss on her cheek by her ear. "This isn't anything I can't handle."

THE MISSISSIPPI RIVER BURNED ORANGE WITH THE SUNSET. THE water shimmered pink and gold as a riverboat made its slow approach upstream toward the downtown drop-off point. As she changed out of Konstantine's clothes into her own for the day, Lou pondered how she preferred winter sunsets to summer ones.

This particular sunset still had a bit of autumn left in it, seen in the lingering golds that had not yet been replaced by the frosty blue and lavender of the winter sun.

As she laced on her leather boots and cleaned her mirrored sunglasses, she considered Stefano's face, the way it had looked when he'd told her to have a good day.

Trouble in paradise, Lou thought with a smirk. Konstantine was having a spat with his little wife.

Why should it matter to her if there was more in-fighting within the Ravengers? All of that was drama she had no interest in. She had her own work to do.

Then again, hunting serial killers was slow work. She couldn't kill as quickly or efficiently as she was used to when hunting mafia and their mules. On those nights she'd had as many as twenty bodies to drag onto the shore of La Loon.

If he's in danger, he'll tell you, she thought.

"Like hell he will," she muttered to herself.

But it didn't matter. If he was in danger she would know either way. That drop-kicked feeling would ricochet through her guts as it always did when someone needed her.

As she pulled her leather jacket onto her shoulders, she marveled at how easy it was to dress these days when her shoulder wasn't a torn, ruined mess. It had taken seven months to fully heal, and while it was true that serial killers might be slower hunts than the extravagant bar burners she preferred, they were also less strenuous on the body.

Lou gave Octavia a pat on the belly and was rewarded with a swift, sharp bite on her fingers. Lou tolerated this, enduring the furious kicks of her paws against her palm. To Octavia's disappointment, Lou withdrew her hand and stepped into the dark closet.

It would be almost two in the morning in Paris when she arrived.

Perfect.

She leaned her back against the rough wood and listened to the dark. She had a new question to try tonight, since her others had proved unfruitful.

Who am I supposed to find in Paris? Take me to who I'm supposed to find.

Lou's compass whirled inside her. Then with a definitive *snap* it locked into place and jerked her forward through the dark.

A bedroom materialized around her. In the dim room, a man was sitting up in his bed, his head in his hands. He was crying.

She must've made a small sound or cast a shadow against the wall, because he looked up suddenly.

"*Delphine,*" he whimpered. "*C'est vraiment toi?*"

"I'm not Delphine," Lou said, recognizing the man at once. It was Etienne, Delphine's partner. He looked like Steve Jobs, with his thinning hair and the gray in his beard. At this late hour, with the deep bags under his eyes, he also looked utterly broken.

"No," he said. "Of course not. I see her ghost everywhere."

She moved to leave but his hand shot out.

"Please, stay. It's so difficult at night. It is when I miss her the most."

Lou lingered in the shadows, unsure of how she must look to him. Like the ghost of his dead lover? She'd been called a ghost before. A witch. A vampire. Even an angel.

People saw what they wanted to see. Lou knew this.

His lip shook. "Where did you come from?"

"The darkness," she said. Something about bedrooms at night, the intimacy of it, demanded truth.

He laughed, a small, sad sound. "I pray for an angel and dream of an angel of darkness. *Bien évidemment.* But you speak English. What a strange little dream this is."

Finally the crying quieted. He wiped at his eyes.

"I miss her," he said again.

"Delphine?" she asked. She remembered the photograph of the art historian in the paper. Her severe black bob and fierce eyes. The unsmiling portrait.

"*Oui.* The love of my life. My muse. My artist. She's gone, and all I have now is her art. Her beautiful *boîtes de lumières.* But there will be no more of them and these will not last. Nothing lasts." He looked up and locked eyes with Lou. "How can I go on without her?"

"Why did she kill herself?"

"She didn't! She would *never!*"

"She was murdered."

"Of course!" he snarled. "My Delphine could never hurt herself. Not when she had so much work left to do. *We* had so much to do. Together."

After she'd read those newspaper articles, Lou'd asked her compass to take her to Assia, but perhaps that was a false trail. Assia might not have been the reason why Lou had been drawn to Paris over and over again in the passing weeks.

Perhaps Delphine was the one she was meant to avenge.

Would finding her killer give this man peace?

"I can't believe she's gone. Why? Why would God take her from me?"

"I'll help you," Lou promised.

He looked up, eyes wet and red-rimmed. "Really? Will you?"

"Yes," she told him. "I will."

7

Dani slipped into bed and wrapped her arms around Piper's waist. Piper tensed.

Dani pulled back, frowning. "What's wrong?"

"I'm just tired. It's been a long day." And now there was a *viola* in the corner of her bedroom.

"Hey." Dani pressed on Piper's shoulder until she turned over and faced her. "What's going on?"

Piper kept thinking of the horrible conversation she'd had with Beverly Allendale in that ridiculous garden. "Your mom knows about Dmitri Petrov."

Dani's eyes widened. "What?"

"Maybe she doesn't know *exactly* what happened, but she knows you got your finger cut off. Probably why she insisted you play the viola, to see if you could."

"I told them I was in a really bad car accident." Dani searched her face. "Did *you* say something else?"

"What? No." Mostly because Beverly hadn't given her a chance to say anything. "She's the one that said, 'Yes, I know about the attack. I have eyes everywhere, yadda yadda.' She said she spoke to someone at the hospital."

Dani swore in Spanish. "No wonder she wouldn't shut up about the CEO stuff. She always brings it up, but usually it doesn't devolve into an actual argument."

Look me in the eye and tell me nothing bad is going to ever happen to her again?

Piper licked her lips. "Do you think—"

"No," Dani said. "Don't even say it. If you and Lou get to run around and chase bad guys and get beat up, I have every right to chase my dream of being a Pulitzer Prize–winning journalist. So whatever the hell she told you in the garden, forget it. It's not happening."

If you care about her, if you love her, tell her to come home.

Did Piper love her? She didn't know. She had feelings, that was for sure.

Despite the flash fire that had flamed through her eyes, Dani relaxed. "Is that what's been bothering you? Ever since lunch you've been quiet, and I thought maybe you hated my parents."

"Lunch was fine. I liked the pie."

"Oh wow. You only say 'fine' when you're trying to be nice. Was it really that bad?"

Piper thought of the wall of ribbons and the way Dani had looked playing the sonata in the middle of her monstrously large childhood bedroom.

Now that Piper knew where Dani had come from, what she was used to and expected in life, she felt an uncrossable ocean spreading between them, a gulf that couldn't be bridged no matter how hard Piper worked to close it. There wasn't enough overtime in the world to give Dani a life like that.

"Earth to Piper." Dani's eyebrows were arched, her gaze laser-focused.

Piper knew that look. Dani wasn't going to let it go until she understood what Piper was thinking. Because she was stubborn and insistent, she wouldn't table the conversation until whatever needed to be said was said.

"I just..." Piper searched for the words. "I just wish you would've better prepared me for today, that's all."

"Prepared you for what? My mother?"

"*Everything.* That house. Your *mother*. For a lunch served on lace *doilies* or whatever the hell those things were."

"Mulberry silk placemats."

"Ugh, *god.*" Piper grimaced and sat up in bed.

"What?"

"The fact you even know what it's called."

"Of course I know what it's called. My mother mentions it every time we have company."

"She didn't say it to me. Probably would've been bad taste to bring it up in front of Little Orphan Annie."

Dani's lips parted. "What? No."

"Maybe just a street rat then. What does that make you? Jasmine?"

"Stop it." Dani's face burned. "My mother was perfectly civil."

"The hell she was. She made sure I knew I'm not good enough for you. Between the ribbons and the horses and the *viola.*"

"I thought you liked music!" Dani looked on the verge of tears.

Piper's cell phone went off. She slipped out of the bed and grabbed it off the charger even as Dani reached out to her, but Piper stepped away.

"Hello?"

"Is this Piper Genereux?" a man asked, his voice gruff.

"Yeah."

"Can I have your mother's name, please?"

"What?"

"I need to verify you're next of kin. Please tell me your mother's name."

Piper's heart plunged into her chest. *Next of kin. Oh god.*

"My mother's name is Nadine Crenshaw."

"Thank you. Ms. Genereux, we have your mother here at New Orleans General. Can you please come down as soon as possible? Just enter through the emergency room reception area and give your name at the check-in desk. We'll be waiting."

"Now?" A pounding headache was forming behind Piper's eyes, and it was already after midnight. "You *want* me to come now."

"Yes, as soon as you can."

"Okay, I'm on my way."

Piper pressed the phone to her forehead and released a slow, tight breath through her clenched teeth.

I need you, she thought, hoping that despite time and space Lou would hear her. *Please come get me. I need you.*

"What happened to your mom?" Dani asked in a quiet voice. The tears had pooled in the corners of her eyes but hadn't spilled over her cheeks.

"I don't know. They told me to come down to New Orleans General. She's probably..."

Dead.

"I'll take you." Dani pushed back the covers.

"No," Piper said.

"What? Why? Piper, why are you so mad at me?"

"I'm not mad, I'm just..." *I can't spend another minute in your luxury SUV or I'm going to kill myself.*

"I can get there by myself."

Dani threw up her hands. "Don't be ridiculous. It'll be faster if—"

"No! I don't want to ride with you, okay? Just...just don't..."

Lou stepped from the shadows. Her leather jacket was open over a white-t-shirt and green flannel, her eyes hidden behind mirrored shades.

Lou's face was already hard-set. "What happened?"

"I need you to take me to the hospital."

"Are you hurt?" Lou asked.

Piper checked her coat pocket for her wallet and keys. "No, I just need you to take me there. Now. Please."

Lou reached out a hand for Dani but Piper snatched her arm, stopping her. "Just me."

Without another word, Lou hooked an arm around Piper's waist.

Then they were gone.

GIVEN THE UNNATURALLY BRIGHT CONDITION OF MOST HOSPITALS, Lou delivered them to the shadowed walkway around the corner from the entrance. They walked in together, Lou making sure her jacket remained closed to hide the two Browning pistols she wore.

Piper exhaled slowly before speaking to the receptionist. "My name is Piper Genereux. You asked me to come down here to see my mom."

"Please take a seat over there and I'll let them know you're here."

Piper chose an empty chair in the middle of the waiting area. Lou took the red plastic chair beside hers.

"You don't have to stay," Piper said, fidgeting in her seat. "I know you hate hospitals."

Lou didn't deny it. "I'll stay."

"You don't—"

Lou lifted her shades and leveled Piper with a look. "I'm staying."

Piper nodded, her eyes on her lap, her shoulders collapsing.

Lou watched a man hold his wrapped arm with a bloody rag. He made a kiss face in Lou's direction and she opened her jacket enough for him to see her guns.

His eyes widened and he shrank back from her. Then she returned his kissy face, and he looked like he was going to be sick.

"It's finally happened," Piper murmured.

"What's happened?" Lou closed her jacket, already bored with the man.

"She's dead."

"They told you she's dead?"

"No. Not yet. But they're going to. It's not like I didn't know this would happen. I just thought—"

Lou pressed a steady hand into her back. "Breathe."

Except that when the doctor came to the reception desk and spoke to the nurse, Lou saw his face. And her suspicions were confirmed as he took a moment to adjust the lab coat on his shoulders before approaching them.

Piper's mother was definitely dead.

"Miss Genereux?" he asked, stopping in front of them.

Piper lifted her head from her hands. "Yeah. That's me."

Lou could feel her muscles tightening under her hand. *She's preparing herself for the blow.*

"I'm sorry to tell you that your mother passed at eleven forty-eight this evening."

Piper was nodding, but her lower lip quaked.

The doctor continued in a low, practiced tone. "She was unresponsive when she arrived, and we tried to clear her airway and administer Naloxone, but she was too far gone, I'm afraid. We won't know until we get the toxicology report back which narcotic it was, but given the track marks on her arms and the results of the preliminary tests, we suspect it was heroin. When we have the official results we will let you know."

Piper was still nodding, pressing a fist against her mouth.

"We can release her body to you whenever you're ready."

Piper lifted her head. "Her body?"

"Typically the body is released to a funeral home, where they will prepare the remains for burial or cremation. Just let us know which funeral home you will be using and we will take care of everything on our end."

"Do I need to identify her? You're sure it's her?"

"There was identification on her body when it was found. Her face matches the ID."

"Where was she found?"

"Outside."

"God." Piper made a choking sound. "Oh god. He *dumped* her outside?"

"You'd be surprised how often that happens," the doctor said. "Especially in cities as large as ours."

Lou squeezed the back of Piper's neck. The movement drew the doctor's eyes.

"How long before she needs to be moved?" Lou asked.

"There's no rush. She will remain in our cold storage until you make arrangements." When they said nothing, he added, "I'm sorry for your loss."

"Cold storage." Twin streams slid down Piper's cheeks. "She's in *cold storage*."

Lou pulled her up from her seat and walked her out. They made it into the shadows at the edge of the parking lot before Piper began to sob.

"Oh god, oh god, oh god." She had her hands clasped over the back of her head. "He just *dumped* her on the hospital steps to *die*. Oh god, that bastard. That fu-fu...Oh god, get me out of here. But don't take me back to my place, please."

Lou didn't wait. She pulled Piper through the dark, then from the closet into Lou's moonlit living room.

While Piper paced, Lou turned on the lamps, drew the shades.

"Sit here." Lou eased her down on her purple sofa. "Put your head between your knees. Deep breaths."

Piper was dangerously close to hyperventilating.

Lou was trying to decide if she should steal some oxygen when Piper tumbled into her bed and began to cry in earnest.

Lou let her, kicking off her boots and climbing in after her. She pulled her against her body and held her tight, the sobs strong enough to shake the both of them.

This is what Konstantine did, she thought. *When Lucy died, he held me like this.*

Her throat tightened.

For a long time it was only tears. Only the deep release of her grief. Then the words came.

"I knew this was going to happen. I *knew* it. I don't even know why I'm crying when I knew this was going to happen."

"She was your mother." Lou pressed her cheek against Piper's hair.

Lou hadn't had a great relationship with her own mother. The woman had been cold, critical. But Lou had still cried when she died. Still dreamed of her, longed for her.

"It'll get easier," Lou whispered.

She held Piper until she fell asleep. Piper had been still for about thirty minutes when the watch on Lou's wrist buzzed. She turned its face until she found the page. It was Dani's number.

Quietly, she slid from her bed. When she was sure Piper hadn't woken up, she stepped into her dark closet.

"Oh thank God," Dani said as soon as she saw her. "Is Piper okay?"

"Her mom died."

"Oh no. How?"

"A drug overdose."

Dani's eyes widened. "Oh wow. I...I had no idea."

"She'd been an addict for a long time."

"Where is she now?"

"In my apartment, sleeping."

"But Octavia's there. She's super allergic."

"I'll clean the apartment."

"Why? Just bring Piper back here."

"She told me she didn't want to come back here."

"So she'd rather go into anaphylactic shock than be here with me?" Dani clasped the back of her neck. "What did I do? I only asked her to have lunch with my parents."

"Maybe she didn't want you to see her upset."

Dani's anger collapsed in on itself as she pulled the comforter to her chest. "Is she really upset? What am I saying. Of course she's upset."

Dani put her head in her hands.

"Okay. Fine. Maybe it's not personal. Maybe it's just bad timing. Does she need to plan a funeral? Was there a will? Does she know what cemetery her mom wanted to be buried in? Or if she wanted cremation?"

"I don't think she knows."

"Have you planned a funeral before?" she asked. "I haven't."

"I was only twelve when my parents died, and King handled Lucy's death."

"Okay. We'll figure it out. If Piper isn't in a state to handle it, we will. I'll talk to King in the morning and ask him what needs to be done."

Lou, sensing the end of the conversation, stepped toward the darkness.

"Wait," Dani called out.

Lou turned back.

"She...she might not want to see me right now, but she needs someone. Stay close to her, okay? I've never lost a parent, so I don't know what she needs, but I'm sure you do."

Yes, Lou thought. *I know what she needs.*

8

Lou found Konstantine in the basement of his church. He sat behind his mahogany desk, a mound of papers spread out in front of him and the blue light of his computer screen illuminating his face. Behind him the fireplace crackled, adding a delicious warmth to the chilly room.

She stepped forward from the dark corner of his office, but he didn't look up.

She made it all the way to the edge of his desk without earning so much as a glance.

"Did you sleep well?" he asked coldly without looking up.

She tried not to smile. *Jealous much?* "I haven't slept."

This earned her a look. He was searching her face, her body, for injuries.

"I brought Piper back to my apartment."

His brows lifted. "Did *she* sleep on the sofa or in your bed?"

"My bed."

Color rose in his face.

Lou pushed her mirrored glasses up on the top of her head. "I didn't sleep with her. Her mother died."

The jealousy evaporated in an instant.

"I'm sorry to hear that. How did she pass?"

"A drug overdose."

His expression darkened. "Have you come to punish me for that?"

Lou understood that Piper's mother had made her choices. Just because Konstantine sold drugs to the four corners of the earth didn't mean he'd injected it into her veins.

More than that, she'd seen Nadine hurt Piper with her own eyes. When Piper had begged her, pleaded with her to leave her abusive boyfriend, she'd shoved Piper away.

Lou didn't need any other reason to dislike the woman than that.

"No." Lou pressed her cold cheek to his warm one. "Unless you're in the mood to be punished."

He laughed, but she still sensed tension in him. In the tight way he held his body. If it wasn't jealousy, then what was bothering him?

She glanced at the paper on his desktop, looking for a clue, but understood none of it.

"Problems at work?" she asked.

"A few." He rubbed his jaw. "Have you always been so efficient at your work? Was it always easy for you?"

She snorted. "No."

She thought of Tito Rubio, the drug mule she'd paid $70,000 to in order to find information on Benito Martinelli, when she could've just popped into Benito's cell and taken him. She'd stolen that money to pay him and had told herself that the family had needed it.

And there had been a hundred other things she'd gotten wrong in the early days of her hunt. Left trails that others could follow, walked in front of cameras without her glasses on, asked the wrong questions. Her carelessness.

Then there was her first kill—Gus Johnson, the partner who'd betrayed her father. The clumsy way she'd struck him with her father's knife, nearly breaking her back trying to drag him to La Loon.

She told Konstantine these stories, enjoying his laughter.

Finally, when the amusement died away, he said, "Even a deadly lioness must begin as a cub."

She pushed her fingers through his hair. "Why do you want to know about my mistakes?"

He closed his eyes, clearly reveling in her touch.

"I'm struggling with a difficult decision."

"About?"

"I want to avoid death and violence, but in order to do that, I will have to give up something I don't want to lose."

"What don't you want to lose?" she asked.

Instead of answering her, he brought her fingers to his lips and kissed her knuckles.

"I spoke to my contact in Paris. She'll help you and King conduct your interviews the day after tomorrow. I assume you'll be available."

So he isn't going to tell me.

"Assuming Piper can be left alone." She leaned forward, placing a kiss on his neck, once, twice, until he pulled her into his lap. She allowed this, letting him wrap his arms around her and hold her close.

Only when she allowed him to hold her did most of the tension release from his body.

With her lips on his ear, she whispered, "Is this a bad time to ask you to babysit a cat?"

PIPER WOKE TO SUNLIGHT CUTTING ACROSS HER FACE. FOR A moment, she only looked at the white ceiling and wondered where she was. Her face was puffy and her throat was sore, but she didn't recognize the bed.

She smelled the sheets and immediately knew who they belonged to. *Lou.*

Then she remembered.

The temporary ignorance of her confusion was replaced by the weight of her grief. The closet door opened and Lou stepped into the room.

She'd changed clothes. Now she was wearing black cargo pants, with a black t-shirt under her leather jacket. Her mirrored sunglasses were pushed up on her head.

She offered Piper a cardboard box with two slices of pizza inside. Piper recognized the name from the pie shop in New York that they'd discovered a couple of months ago.

Lou sat down on the bed beside her. "Can you eat?"

"I don't know," she admitted, looking at the pizza. It smelled amazing, but her mouth felt like it was full of ash.

"Take this." Lou pulled allergy medicine out of her pocket and handed it over to Piper along with a can of soda from the plastic bag between her feet.

"Oh shit. Where's Tavi?"

"Konstantine took her for a few days. I'm going to vacuum, but I wanted to wait until you woke up." She shook the box at her again. "Take this until I can get rid of the cat hair."

Piper cracked open the soda can and took two of the allergy pills. "Where's my phone? I need to check my classes. I think I missed a paper."

Lou pointed at the wall where a charger connected to Piper's phone. "Melandra spoke to your professors. She got a note from the hospital and sent it to the school. They're giving you a two-week extension on everything. King said they'll give you more if you press them."

Piper's heart flopped. "Everyone knows what happened to my mom? How she died?"

Lou nodded. "They want you to take a couple of days off. I told them you'd be here."

There was a stack of Piper's clothes and a few toiletries sitting on Lou's couch as well as her laptop and backpack.

Lou followed her gaze and said, "Dani helped me pack that."

The pizza soured in her mouth. "What did she say?"

"About you staying here? She understands."

Does she?

Piper seriously doubted it. God, why did she have to start that fight at the very worst moment?

Lou took a huge bite of her own pizza slice. "She wants to know if your mom had a will."

Piper laughed. A tight, choked sound. "No. She wasn't very *future* oriented."

"Do you know what her wishes were?"

"We never talked about it. My dad is buried in Greenfield. I guess I should put her there."

Lou reached into the bag and cracked open a soda for herself. "Is there anything else you need from your apartment?"

Piper couldn't think of anything. She shook her head. "Thanks for the pizza."

"You've only eaten half of your slice."

"My stomach hurts and my throat hurts. I can't tell if that's from the cat or the crying."

Lou took the food from Piper. "Take a shower and I'll air this place out."

Piper untangled herself from Lou's sheets and padded to the bathroom at the end of the hall. She found a towel and washcloth already laid out for her beside the shower stall. She turned on the water as hot as she could stand it and stepped into the steam.

After she'd got out, dried off, and dressed, she found Lou in the living room, hard at work. The vacuum stood in the middle of the living space with the cord trailing along the floor. One of the windows was cracked, letting in a chilly November wind.

The bed had been stripped, the pillowcases and sheets rolled up into a wad in the corner of the room. The fresh sheets Lou was tugging on were a soft sage green.

Then Lou gathered the old bedding up and shoved it into the laundry basket in her closet.

"How do you feel now?"

"Better," Piper admitted. "But these allergy meds are serious."

She was worried she would fall asleep before she could brush her hair.

"Lie down. I put the food in the fridge for when you want to try again." She turned and saw Piper's face. "What's wrong?"

Tears stood out in Piper's eyes. "I told you I was going to be a great friend, but you're the one who keeps taking care of me."

"You threw me two birthday parties."

"That's not the same and you know it."

Lou considered the river outside the window, letting the silence stretch long between them. Then she said, "Lucy would say friendship isn't about keeping score."

Not about keeping score.

But if Piper wasn't useful to someone, would she even be important to them?

"I have to take King to Paris," Lou said. "But I'll be back tonight."

"You're going to leave me alone here?" It came out needier than she'd meant it to, but almost as soon as she'd said it, she was relieved. Time alone meant she could cry, fall apart, and not embarrass herself in front of Lou.

"I'll be back in a few hours."

"Okay." Piper crawled under the covers with her phone, not failing to notice that the tissue box was already beside the bed, along with two bars of chocolate. "You think of everything. Thank you."

Lou pushed her sunglasses down over her eyes and grabbed her leather jacket off the arm of the couch. "You're going to be out in thirty seconds."

It was true—Piper's eyes were heavy. The allergy meds were working very well.

Piper pulled the clean sheets up over her shoulder. She felt safe and warm in Lou's bed.

She was almost asleep when she heard Lou say, "Call me if you need me."

9

———

King braced against the wall that appeared in front of him as the uneven cobblestones formed beneath his feet. He sucked in a breath and swore.

"I hate traveling with you," he admitted.

Lou stepped forward, separating herself from the shadows. "We wouldn't have made this appointment if you'd booked a flight."

He adjusted the duster jacket on his body and straightened. "Which museum are we going to?"

"Museum of Modern Art. Du Maurier had an office there. Konstantine's contact is supposed to meet us at the entrance so she can flash all the proper credentials."

"Hopefully Delphine's colleagues speak English. My French is shit. Yours?"

Lou shook her head. "I can order things. That's it."

"How far away is the museum?"

Lou pointed up the road. "It's close."

They stepped out of the cramped side alley and into the flow of foot traffic. King didn't get far before he was pulling gum out of his pocket.

"Paris always makes me wants to smoke," he said. "They really relish it here, don't they?"

"That's gum in your hand."

"It's for the cravings." He unwrapped two thin minty sticks and put them into his mouth. "Hey, we should bring pastries back for Piper. How's she doing?"

"She ate half the pizza I brought her. That's all I've seen her eat."

King's stomach knotted. He knew that feeling. How hard it was to force yourself to eat, shower, *breathe* when someone you loved died.

Lou was watching a small group laughing at a bus stop. When one of them, a young woman, threw her head back, King wanted to snatch the cigarette out of her hand and take a long drag. "We made arrangements with the funeral home to collect Nadine's body. They found Piper's father's grave in Greenfield. They said he'd prepaid to have his wife buried with him, so that's one less thing to worry about."

"Tell me how much money you need. I'll pay it."

King wasn't surprised to hear Lou had money to spare. Lou's living expenses were low, and the principal balance of the money her parents had left in trust when they died had remained largely untouched in the years since. Her monthly payout likely far exceeded her actual needs.

More than that, King suspected Lou wasn't the kind of woman who wanted *things*.

Guns, maybe. But she probably stole those. Paying for them left a paper trail.

Lou rolled her shoulders. "I don't want her to worry about money, on top of everything else."

King couldn't help but smile. It touched him to see how much Piper had grown on her in the years they'd known each other. *Your wish came true, Lucy*, he thought.

"Me either. I'll go halfsies with you." They passed a boulangerie, and King was hit with the tantalizing smell of warm bread. "I want to stop here on the way back."

Lou barely acknowledged him. She was watching their surroundings. She looked a little out of place in the sunlight. He'd come to think of her as a creature of darkness. Nearly a vampire.

But now, in the sun, he saw she had freckles.

Like Jack.

His heart kicked.

"You need to ask Piper what she wants to do about her mother's estate. Because there's no will, it'll go into probate. There's probably nothing of value except for the house, if there's any value left after back taxes. You can search the place for important documents and see what constitutes the estate. It needs to be done sooner rather than later, but I can't imagine she's feeling up to it."

"I'll take Dani tomorrow," she said. "Watch out."

King had been craning his neck to look through the glass into the bakery, counting the cakes and breads on display. He turned back just in time to dodge a guy on his skateboard.

"Sorry," he muttered, angling his broad body to let him pass.

"This is the museum." Lou nodded toward the large building coming into view. King let her lead as they walked past the burbling crystalline fountain and lines of tourists trying to get inside.

"Monsieur King!" a woman called, and King turned in time to see a petite blonde with thin lips and narrow eyes waving him down. He returned the wave, changing his trajectory.

When they were closer, King extended his hand. "Bonjour. Are you our contact?"

"Bonjour," she said, returning his handshake. "And yes, I am the one you are looking for. I'm Uma Bernard."

Her eyes cut briefly to Lou, but after a polite smile, she turned her attention back to King.

"Is it just the two of you?" Uma asked.

"Yes."

"Good," she said. "Our appointment with Director Mercier is in seven minutes. Shall we go?"

She didn't really wait for an answer before she pulled open the glass door to the museum and marched inside.

Lou followed her with King on their heels. As workers stopped them at the turnstile, their escort showed her badge and had a short, seemingly fierce exchange in French, before they were allowed to pass.

They walked past patrons and art galleries, King enjoying the high ceiling and sacrosanct feeling he usually got in large museums. On the second floor they came to the administration wing, and after another exchange, were allowed into a locked office, opened only by the guard's keycard.

King found himself in a reception area, a young man with neat, slicked black hair typing away furiously on his keyboard.

"*Bonjour!*" Director Mercier called, doing up the lowest button on his suit jacket and stepping toward them. He was tall, like King, with salt-and-pepper hair and thick black spectacles. He'd shaved that morning and bore a small cut on his right cheek. "*Il est agréable de vous rencontrer.*"

"They would like to speak in English," Uma announced, and the man immediately switched languages.

"Ah, of course," he said. His words were not nearly as accented as King was expecting. "Please come into my office."

When they were seated comfortably in the little office with a large window overlooking the courtyard, they were asked if they would like coffee or tea. Both King and Lou declined. Uma accepted.

"What can I do for you today? I understand that you have questions about Madame du Maurier."

It was clear from Lou's position beside him that she didn't intend to speak unless absolutely necessary. Her posture was alert but relaxed, her gaze carefully hidden behind her sunglasses.

King was fine with taking the lead, though he had only the information that Lou had given him on the historian's death and what he'd been able to find online.

"Yes, did you know Delphine du Maurier well?"

"*Bah, oui*," he said. "She has worked in this museum for over twenty years. Of course I knew her."

"Do you think she committed suicide?"

He leaned back, lacing his hands over his lap in a perfect poise of contemplation.

"Had you asked me a year ago, I would have said it was impossible. Delphine seemed very happy with her life and her work. But all artists are temperamental."

He gave a noncommittal shrug.

King pulled a notepad and pen from his pocket. "When you say 'her work,' are you referring to her articles?"

"No, her art."

"I wasn't aware that she created art as well as studied it."

"But of course," he said with an exaggerated nod. "It is true that she was known for her opinions. If a piece was misogynistic or hyper-masculine in any way..." He pulled at his collar as he released a nervous laugh. "She would...*écarteler?*"

"Tear it apart," Uma offered.

"*Oui.* Tear it apart."

King looked at his notepad and read the title of one of Delphine's articles. "*La beauté des femmes mortes.*"

The director laughed. "Not a good translation, but yes, that was a popular feminist piece. Did you read it?"

"I tried," King said with a friendly smile. In truth, he'd only been able to find the abstract in English. The rest had been in French, and all the translation apps he'd found had failed to render the ideas into something understandable.

If the director thought less of him for this, he didn't say so. "It was an argument that women were more beautiful when dead than men."

Lou shifted beside him. King made a point not to look over.

"She meant this figuratively, I hope," King said. "In some artistic sense, you mean."

"She was talking about how when artists paint men in the arms of Death, it is dramatic, sensationalist. It shows vigor. Courage." He balled his fist and shook it for good measure. "However, when *les artistes* paint women in such ways, it is *sucré*. Beautified. They rob the women of their moment of transformation. Their deaths deserve to be as glorious as a man's."

"I see. Inspector Dulac, in his official interview, also mentioned Delphine had an interest in suicide. I assume she also wrote about this?"

"*Oui, c'est vrai.* She argued that women were rarely depicted as subjects in art about suicide. Suicide is often portrayed as power over oneself, one's destiny. But women are not given such power over their bodies in life or in art. This was Delphine's belief."

King jotted some notes down before asking, "What can you tell me about the art she made?"

"I can do you better," he said.

King arched a brow. "Do me better?"

Not the offer I was expecting today.

Their guide said something in French, quickly under her breath, and the director lit up. "Ah, yes. Sorry. I can do you *one* better." He rose from behind his desk. "One moment, please."

For an awkward moment, the three of them sat in the silent room saying nothing.

Then the director returned with a handful of small black boxes. He placed them on the desk in a single row.

"Delphine made these," he explained, his hair falling forward into his eyes as he arranged them.

"Black boxes," Lou said skeptically.

The director laughed and pressed a button on one of the boxes. It lit up, illuminating the contents.

In this particular box, it was a beautiful butterfly. It was wing-pinned in place, suspended to give the impression that it was in the throes of dying, transfixed forever, in that moment before complete death. The main part of its body was cut open as if to reveal its inner workings fighting to keep it alive.

"She was trying to dissect the two layers in the wings. But they were too delicate," the director said with a touch of sadness in his voice. "She had better luck with the caterpillar."

He turned on the light and the second box revealed a similar display. A caterpillar, curling in agony, on the brink of death but with one portion of its torso dissected and on display.

The third box contained a mouse, its mouth open in a silent scream, one of its legs cut open to reveal the workings beneath.

"How many of these do you have?" King asked, trying to write a description of the light boxes on his notepad.

"Oh, we have nearly a hundred here. She had been fighting for years to get the work on display, but it was always denied."

"Who refused to show her work?"

"Albert Kavanaugh. They did not get along and he is Head of

Collections. He decides what we display. I have final authority on the matter, of course."

"And you never sided with Delphine?"

"*Non*. To be honest, to me this is not *true* art. Not because it is macabre but because it is too scientific. They are very skilled but there is no feeling. No heart. For me, art is about revealing what is inside the artist's heart. I see none of Delphine's heart in this."

King considered the vivisected creatures. There was a coldness to the light boxes, that was true. A clinical style in the way the creatures had been frozen, broken open, and their misery put on garish display.

"Can you think of anyone who might want to hurt Delphine?" King asked.

"Being stabbed in the stomach is a crime of passion, *non?* Perhaps it was an accident."

King waited for his question to be answered.

"I can think of many who would be pleased to know that Delphine du Maurier was no longer in this world. But I can't think of anyone brave enough to confront her. She was...*effrayant?*"

"Terrifying," Uma said.

"Yes," the director said, peering into the light box with a considerable frown on his face. "She was terrifying."

As King went into the boulangerie to order a baguette for Mel and cakes for Piper, Lou stood on the sunlit street outside and replayed the meeting in her mind. There was something about the director's interview that had bothered her.

It wasn't the director, she decided. There had been something about those light boxes.

They had made her think of the room Nico, Konstantine's nemesis, had tried to trap her in. Every inch bathing her in relentless, inescapable light.

And there was something about the dissected creatures that had troubled her. What had the director said? The animals had to have been alive when Delphine had begun her work. In order for those expressions and their fear to be preserved for all time, she'd had to capture them at the right moments.

But those light boxes...

Where did I see something like that before?

Her compass whirled inside her, but before it could click into place, King came out of the bakery carrying two plastic bags. "Do you fancy a coffee? They didn't have any in there."

"I want to check something," Lou said. "Are you ready?"

King was not, as evidenced by his face. "Sure. It's cold out here. The cakes will keep for another pitstop. But hey, before we go, I need to tell you..."

King's sudden blush made Lou stiffen. "What is it? Are you sick?"

Sometimes King got nauseated when he traveled with her.

"What? No." He frowned.

"Is someone dying?"

He puffed out his cheeks. "No one is dying. It's about what Piper said about my date."

"I thought it wasn't a date."

"It wasn't," he insisted. "I just wanted to make sure you *knew* it wasn't a date."

"Piper said she offered you casual sex instead."

King threw back his head and sighed at the sky. When he was ready, he spoke slowly. "All I'm trying to say is that I'm not ready. I loved—*love*—your aunt very much. I don't want you to think I'm in a hurry to replace her."

Aunt Lucy. Lucy with long hair and bright eyes. Her penchant for yoga and vegan food. The fact that she tried every day to be a good person and still swore like a sailor and hated people half of the time. That she'd never wanted nor asked to raise a child, but when Lou's parents had been murdered, Lucy had shown up and taken Lou into her life without hesitation.

More than that, she'd shown Lou the beauty of her gift, the power of it. She helped her to let go of all her fear.

And Lucy and King? What did she think of them?

Lou knew that Lucy and King had something in the past, and that they'd rekindled it in the last few months of her life. Otherwise, she knew nothing about what they'd meant to each other.

And it was none of her business.

Yet here was King, concern filling his face. The way he was waiting for her to say something, anything, as if her opinion on his dating life mattered.

"I don't think Lucy would care," she said finally. "She would say you don't have anything to prove to me, or anyone."

King looked away, up the street toward the river, as if the answer were out there somewhere. Then he said, "Sometimes I have dreams about her. She's always telling me to relax."

Lou snorted. "Sounds like her."

"I'm *not* ready to find anyone else," he said again. "But I'm glad you wouldn't hold it against me if I did."

Lou simply stood there, eyes hidden behind her shades, and let King assume whatever he needed to assume about her thoughts.

"All right, let's get out of here," he said finally, nodding once, sharply, as if they'd agreed upon something.

They walked until Lou found a shadowed alleyway. There was a couple locked in a kiss beneath the awning of a boutique, but they didn't even look up as Lou took King's arm and melded into the darkness.

When the world materialized again, they stood beneath a shady canopy of trees. Tombs rose around them in every direction. Many of the stones were stained black by time and acid rain.

"Where are we?" he asked, looking unsteady on his feet.

"Père Lachaise, by the look of it."

"What were you hoping for?" he asked.

"I wanted to know if Delphine was really dead. I had a thought during the interview that maybe she'd faked it as an art stunt."

King's brows shot up. "Good idea. But we're in a cemetery."

"And there he is."

Lou pointed at a man kneeling in front of a gravestone. The grave marker was large, made larger by a sculpted angel, a weeping angel, her face hidden by her folded arms, wings drooping down her back.

"That's Etienne," she told King. "Her partner."

"She must be dead then. Doubt he'd be crying over an empty grave."

"Unless it's for show," Lou said. But when she asked her compass to take her to Delphine, she was tugged forward toward the grave. She didn't think Delphine had faked her death. She was fairly confident that the woman was in the ground.

"Does he speak English?" King asked, adjusting the sacks in his arms. "I can interview him if he does."

"He spoke it the other night," she said. She didn't elaborate that in his grief, Etienne had also spoken French, calling her Delphine, clearly mistaking Lou's appearance in his darkened bedroom for the ghost of his dead love.

Lou took the cakes from King. "Go talk to him."

"Where are you going to be?" he asked.

How to explain that she didn't want Etienne to see her in the daylight?

"I'll be right back," she said.

King didn't seem perturbed by this. He was already pulling his notepad from his pocket and walking toward the crying man.

Lou watched for a moment, sticking close to the thick shadows.

Take me to Delphine's killer, she thought, hoping her compass might work this time.

But it settled on the cold, desolate nothing again.

There was no killer. Could Etienne be wrong? But he'd seemed so certain. Maybe he'd already killed the killer.

Would he tell her if he had?

King's low voice rumbled through the cemetery and the man turned, his eyes bleary from crying. He pulled his glasses off his face and wiped his tears.

Then he looked up suddenly and met her gaze.

Can he see me?

She was deep in the shadows, barely more than an outline beside the crypt resting between two old-growth trees.

Can he even see me?

She thought, by the small smile she saw cross his face, that he could.

10

Ten boys sat in a tight circle. Knee to knee, they spoke in low tones beneath the covered table, the statue of the Virgin Mary watching them from above.

Matteo held a flashlight under his chin, illuminating his round face, as the other boys listened raptly to his story.

"*C'era una volta...c'era La Strega*," he whispered. "This witch cursed the Martinelli family."

"Why?" Franco asked. He was the youngest of them, only four years old.

"*Sta 'zitto*. Do you want me to tell the story or not?"

Crestfallen, Franco fell silent.

Matteo liked it when the others listened to him, paid attention to what he said as if it mattered.

Matteo wasn't the oldest. Both Monte and Nario were two years his senior, but they all listened to him the same when he told these stories.

Perhaps that was why he couldn't resist when they asked him to do it, usually at the end of the day, after their schooling and their work, here in their own little hideout.

"There was a curse on the Martinelli family," Matteo began again. "The *capo di capi*, Fernando Martinelli, made a deal with *La Strega*.

Martinelli promised to give his soul in exchange for power and money and girls."

"Why would he want girls?" Franco asked.

Nario shushed him with an elbow. "*Idiota. Non sai nulla.*"

Matteo continued. "*La Strega* agreed. She would give the *capo di capi* everything he wanted as long as he handed over his soul when she wanted it. But when the day came for Fernando to pay up, he tried to cheat her. He didn't want to lose his soul. So he betrayed her."

"Who? The devil or the witch?"

"Shut up, idiot. They're the same person."

"How did he betray her?" Brando asked. His big ears cast even larger shadows than usual in the flashlight's beam.

"He sent his son Angelo to kill her and her family."

"Did it work?" Monte asked, chewing his thumb mercilessly.

"*Sì,*" Matteo said. "Her family died, but the strega didn't. So she cursed them."

All the boys' eyes grew bigger, doubling in size. Many stopped blinking.

"One by one," Matteo said gravely, "she hunted the Martinellis down and killed them. She took back the money, the power, and the girls."

Monte elbowed Nario. "*Chissa' che avra' fatto con le ragazze.*"

Matteo ignored this. "All the Martinellis died until there was only one. *Il nostro Konstantine.* And she came for him too."

Several of the younger boys gasped. Nario was leaning forward as if to hear Matteo even better.

"But Konstantine is smarter than any of those guys. He was ready when she came."

"What did he do?" Franco tried to sit up taller, adjusting himself on his knees.

"He knew he couldn't kill her, so he made a new deal. He asked *La Strega* to spare his life. And to make him *even richer* than the Martinellis. And when he dies, she can eat his soul."

"We're going to be richer even than the Martinellis?" Brando asked. "*Voglio un paio di scarpe nuove!*"

Nario nudged him. "Konstantine didn't sell his soul so you could have Air Jordans, you idiot!"

"So now, because of Konstantine's promise, *La Strega* protects him and only kills our enemies."

"Not true—she killed Calzone and Vincente. They were Ravengers."

"They weren't loyal. They sided with Nico!"

Monte said, "I wonder how he got her to make a new deal?"

Monte thrust his hips as much as the tight space would allow before puckering his lips at Franco.

"*Cazzate*," Andre said, rolling his eyes. To Matteo he said, "You're making all this up. You've never seen *La Strega* in your life."

"I have!" Matteo cried, shoving him. "I'm friends with her."

Here the boys laughed.

The fabric lifted suddenly and a head appeared, large and disembodied. The features were distorted and monstrous in the bouncing beam of the flashlight.

"Who's under there?" a voice boomed.

All the boys screamed.

KONSTANTINE HAD HEARD THE HUSHED WHISPERS COMING FROM THE Virgin Mary and had stopped halfway through the cathedral. He'd been heading out for the night, longing for his bed after a long day in the basement office, sorting through his holdings and considering which strategic moves he would make next, before the idea of dinner called to him.

What do we have here? he'd thought, crossing to the statue and bending down until he was sure that the voices were coming from beneath the covered table behind it.

Only he hadn't expected to find hysterical boys screaming into his face when he lifted the cloth.

"*Dio mio.* What are you doing?" Konstantine waved his hand. "*Fuori.*"

The boys filed out one by one.

He spotted Matteo instantly, looking the most shamefaced of the group. His flashlight hung limply by his side. "Matteo, I need to speak with you. The rest of you, it's late. Have you all eaten? Done your homework?"

A chorus of "Sì, sì" resonated through the church.

"Then wash up, get to bed. You'll worry your families. Do you want to make your mothers sick? *Vai, vai.*"

The boys fled in all directions, leaving only Matteo, small and worried beside him.

"If it's about the story I was telling—" the boy began.

"What? No." Konstantine moved to the pew and beckoned Matteo to join him. "I have to ask you about something else."

Matteo reluctantly sat beside him, his legs too short to reach the floor.

He will be a handsome man, Konstantine thought, and the tenderness he felt in his chest was almost too much to bear.

"Have you ever been to Venice?" Konstantine asked.

"Venice? *Sì.* Nonno took me for Carnevale."

"What did you think of it?"

Matteo shrugged. "I like the canals. They have more pigeons than we do."

Konstantine smiled, but he couldn't keep the expression on his face. "Matteo, I must ask you to do something for me."

"Me?"

"Yes. Did you see the woman that visited us the other day? The one in the red dress?"

"*Sì.* Signora Vittoria." His big eyes searched Konstantine's face.

"I want you to go to Venice and live with her."

His face folded. "Did I...did I do something wrong?"

Konstantine's heart clenched. "*No. Certo che no.*"

"Then why do you want me to leave?"

Konstantine considered the lies he'd constructed for this moment. The many stories he'd conceived for why he would have to ask this small boy to leave his home, his friends. But now that he was looking at those large brown eyes and the innocent, trusting expression, he couldn't bring himself to lie.

"The truth, Matteo, is that I need her to do something for me. I want her to make an agreement with a difficult man so that we do not go to war with him."

"War," the boy repeated. "Like what happened with Nico."

"Yes, exactly. We can avoid another fight like that, but she has told me I must give you to her. That was her price."

"Why me?" he asked.

"Because she knows you are my favorite."

He hoped this praise would soften the blow but still expected him to cry. Perhaps beg.

Matteo sat up straighter, his back erect with pride. "I'll go."

"You will?"

"It is like a mission," he said. "I will be undercover for you. I'll learn her secrets and bring them back for you."

"No, don't do anything she might hurt you for." Konstantine kissed the top of his head. "She will be good to you or I will kill her. And you will not be there forever. Only until I can come up with a better plan."

"Don't worry, I will make you proud of me."

Konstantine placed a hand on his head. "I am already proud of you. *Sei un bravo ragazzo*, Matteo."

A shadow moved and Konstantine turned. He'd expected to find Lou there. Anytime something moved in the shadows, he expected Lou now.

But it wasn't Lou. It was Stefano.

He was watching them silently, his eyes dark and unhappy.

11

———

Piper jolted awake. She couldn't be sure of what she'd been dreaming, but it must've been awful. Her heart rabbited in her chest, beating so hard it hurt. The only fragment she could recall was something about dishes falling out of the cabinets, breaking and cutting her as they piled up, blotting out the world.

She sat up and found the apartment quiet. "Lou?"

Her voice ringing through the sparse apartment was her only answer.

The space buzzed with silence, shadows washing it in swaths of gray. Light through the venetian blinds cut stripes across the sofa, the coffee table, the bed, her exposed arms.

When she'd woken that morning, Lou had been lying beside her, her chest rising and falling in an easy rhythm as sunlight poured through the wall of windows at her back.

Now it was night again, and the shimmering river no longer sparkled like fish scales in sunlight. It was scrunched, black silk reflecting the stars above. The arch was lit, on display for all to see.

I slept the whole day away. Again, she thought, and felt bad about it.

King and Mel were carrying on without her, she was sure, but it must've made their lives harder.

I'm failing them. I'm letting everyone down.

She pressed the heels of her hands into her eyes and breathed. Her body ached. Her head felt fuzzy, unclear.

Piper untangled herself from the warm sheets and stretched. She walked around the apartment, turning on the lamps and getting herself a glass of water from the kitchen sink. She pulled one of her sweaters off of the clothes piles that had overtaken Lou's sofa and tugged it down over her head.

But her hands and feet were still cold.

God, I wish I had a hot drink. Cocoa. Coffee.

More food—a basket of fruit and French pastries on the island's countertop—had been added to the leftovers filling up Lou's fridge.

For the first time, Piper thought she might actually be able to eat something. She found a plate in the cabinet and filled it. Lou didn't have a microwave, and Piper didn't want to go through the trouble of heating up the stove, so she ate the pizza cold. And when, surprisingly, she found she was still hungry, she ate a pear cut in half with a slice of swiss cheese.

When she noticed her lower back hurt, she refilled her water glass and drank it down. She recognized this particular pain. She often felt it if she was drinking too much soda, or went out drinking too many nights in a row.

The kidneys were always the first to tell you they were unhappy.

Once she'd finished eating, she searched the covers for her phone and found that she'd missed three messages from Henry and one from Dani.

She opened the one from Dani first.

Hi. I hope you're okay. I miss you.

Piper's stomach clenched. She didn't want to think about Dani now or the difficult conversation they would have to have the next time she saw her. She was going to ask Dani to move out. She'd decided that almost as soon as she'd seen the viola sitting in the corner of her bedroom.

This was better for everyone, really. Piper had already felt horrible that she was so allergic to cats that Dani had to give up her beloved British Blue, Octavia, just to stay with her. And now that she'd seen her parents' estate, and knew just how much Dani was conceding in order to slum it with her in the Quarter—no. Just *no.*

Piper couldn't bear it. The guilt. The feelings of worthlessness. It would be better for everyone if Dani found a place of her own. A big, luxurious place where she could be comfortable. Happy.

Next time I see her, I'll just tear the bandage off, she thought. *Get it over with and done. It'll be fine. She'll be happier.*

Who was she kidding? It was going to be terrible. It would hurt like hell.

Piper loved living with Dani. She loved waking up beside her, smelling her perfume on her pillows, seeing her socks in the drawer beside hers. She loved it when Dani came through the agency door at the end of the day with takeout in her hand, looking beautiful and windswept from her walk home. The fact that her face always lit up when she saw Piper hard at work.

The way she would flirt with her if King wasn't around.

I'll see you upstairs, hot stuff. How she'd lean over the desk and give her a kiss.

Piper groaned, feeling especially defeated, and opened her texts from Henry.

P! Where the hell are you?

Seriously where are you? Your detective boss and the psychic queen are both giving me the run around.

I swear to God if you don't answer me I'm going to cut a bitch.

Piper responded to the third text with a quick swipe of her thumbs.

Mom died. Overdose. I'm hiding out.

Da hell, P, why didn't you tell me? Where are you? I'm coming over.

I'm out of town, she replied.

You damned liar!!!

Piper went to Lou's window and angled her phone's camera lens until the illuminated arch was clearly framed behind her. She took the picture, holding still so that it could adjust for the low lighting.

She reviewed the selfie and considered deleting it. She looked like shit. Her hair needed to be brushed and the circles under her eyes were as purple as bruises, probably made worse by the long shadows in the apartment.

She sent the photo anyway.

Fine. You're in STL. Do you want to talk? I can call you.

Piper didn't and said so.

Okay. But you better let me know the minute your ass is back in town. I mean it.

She sent the salute emoji, and that was it.

It was easy to fall into an internet spiral after that. She doomscrolled the news and her social media, and when that led to her hating herself and her life, she signed into her online classes. She had messages from all three of her professors, offering their condolences and promising extensions on her assignments.

She assured them she would complete the work as soon as possible and thanked them for their patience. When there was nothing else to check on, nothing else to distract her mind, she had a choice between showering or streaming a movie through her computer.

Maybe I'll have it in me to bathe later, a voice said.

Gross. Lou is going to think you're disgusting, lying around in her sheets, stinking them up with your BO.

If she loves me, she'll forgive me.

The idea that Lou might be able to smell her and judge her for it was enough to get Piper into the shower. That and the fact that she was still cold.

So into the shower she went. She thought she was doing great until sometime between conditioning her hair and washing her back, she began to cry. And once she'd started, she couldn't seem to stop.

It seemed like an eternity before the tears ended and she was able to get out of the shower.

By the time she'd dressed, she was thoroughly exhausted. She fell back into Lou's bed, her eyes fluttering closed as soon as her head hit the pillow.

The nightmares began again.

. . .

WHAT STRUCK DANI FIRST WAS THE SHARP, CLOYING SMELL OF cigarette smoke, followed by stale body odor. On its heel was something acrid. Piss? Rotting food? She couldn't tell.

She covered her nose with her hand reflexively. If Lou was bothered by the smell she didn't show it. Her hands remained in the pockets of her leather jacket as she surveyed the cramped living room, nudging strewn pillows and trash with her boot.

As Dani's eyes adjusted to the dim light, aging furniture riddled with cigarette burn holes, a scuffed coffee table, and windows covered with blankets came into view.

There were unwashed dishes piled on the end tables. The coffee table itself was laden with empty beer cans, and a tray with a dirty spoon and syringe. There was white powder residue all over the table. An empty pizza box had been left open and had served as an ashtray, crumpled butts littered amongst the rock-hard crusts.

"This is where her mom *lived?*" Dani was unable to hide her shock.

"Yeah." Lou was looking for something. She'd pushed her mirrored shades up onto the top of her head and was peeling a painting from the wall.

"God," Dani murmured, and tucked her hair behind her ears. "I had no idea."

"She didn't tell you that her mom was an addict?"

"No. She'd told me her mom was sick, but I assumed it was cancer or something."

Why didn't you tell me?

"Was she always like this? Did Piper grow up here? In this house with..." She wasn't sure how to finish the sentence. *All of this.*

She hoped her open palm sweeping the room delivered the point.

Lou was scowling at something. "I think it was different before her father died."

"How long ago was that?"

"She was fourteen."

Dani ran a hand through her hair. "She's been dealing with this for over a *decade.*"

Now that Dani saw the house, things began to click into place. Why

Piper never talked about her family. Why she worked so much and always seemed to worry about money. Why she was so sensitive about how she looked, the cleanliness of her apartment, or how far she'd gotten in school.

Why she would sit up suddenly at night, listening to a sound Dani's ears couldn't even register.

Always on the lookout for trouble.

Why didn't you feel like you could tell me?

Dani wanted to help in the search, but she was terrified of touching anything. She'd done so much research on the opioid epidemic raging across America right now. If any of this was Fentanyl, it could be absorbed through the skin and kill a person.

"Don't touch the white stuff," Dani said as Lou bent toward the coffee table in order to inspect the lower shelf.

Lou's grunt could be taken for agreement, or acknowledgment at least.

"Why did she tell you and not me? You guys aren't even—" *Having sex.*

Lou's eyebrows arched as Dani bit the sentence in half.

Lou was lifting the last painting in the room. "She didn't tell me. I saw it when I was here."

"Oh. Why were you here?"

Lou pulled back the rug, checking the planks beneath. "King asked me to check on her. I did."

So, King suspected too. And probably Melandra. Dani was the last one to know. Why? Because she hadn't asked. She hadn't pressed Piper for answers or even suspected that maybe something worse, something horrible, was lurking in Piper's life.

Dani had assumed the story about the sick mom had been true and had left it at that.

Some freaking journalist I am.

The way Lou wouldn't look at her, the way she turned slightly away, made Dani feel worse.

She knew all this. *She thinks I'm a spoiled idiot because I couldn't even imagine where Piper came from.*

Worse than that, the other issue made sense. Why Piper had

freaked out when she'd lunched with her parents. At first Dani had simply thought Piper had been overreacting.

She hadn't understood why she'd been so uncomfortable and embarrassed in that house. It was a little over the top, Dani knew, but it was hardly a palace.

But it must've seemed like a palace to her.

Her eyes scanned the dark, stench-soaked room again.

Her family's wealth, the extravagances, must've seemed like such a slap in the face after everything she'd been through, after everything she'd been asked to do without.

Dani pinched the bridge of her nose. "At least I know why she got upset about lunch."

"Because you're rich."

"*I'm* not rich," Dani said reflexively, feeling the heat rush to her face. "It's my parents' money. Oh god, that's something rich kids say."

Lou's lips twitched in a would-be smile.

Dani pointed an accusing finger at her. "You're far from poor. Why isn't she mad at you?"

"Do I look rich to you?" Lou asked. "I don't even have a car."

"So I'm supposed to wear thrift store clothes and drive a horse and buggy? *What?*"

Lou looked under the sofa. "You should be asking her, not me."

"Fine. You're right." Dani clasped her hands at the back of her neck. "But I wish she would've talked to me. I'm not a psychic or a mind reader like Mel. How the hell was I supposed to know what the problem was?"

Lou tossed the rug back down.

"I don't think there are any papers down here. I'm going to check upstairs." Lou jerked her chin in the direction of the doorway behind Dani. "Look in the kitchen."

She was halfway up the stairs before Dani could form a rebuttal. With a sigh, Dani found the kitchen. It was just as bad as the living room. Peeling tile and stained countertops. The fridge was silent and warm, apparently out of order. When Dani flicked the light switch nothing happened.

She used her phone light to search drawers and cabinets. She lifted an ashtray overflowing with cigarette butts to get the stack of mail beneath it. She went through it slowly, meticulously. Most of it was junk mail, political flyers, coupons. Then she found the bills. Most of them had menacing *PAST DUE* stamps on them, including one from the IRS.

Dani gathered these up and put them into the inside pocket of her wool coat.

The photograph on the fridge of a preteen Piper sandwiched between her parents made Dani's throat clench.

But most of Piper's face had been burned out with a cigarette, a black hole with seared edges where it should have been.

"What the hell?" Dani murmured.

"Come up here," Lou called.

Dani took the narrow stairs, which creaked so loudly under her heels that she half expected the wood to give way and cave beneath her. At the top of the stairs she had a choice of three doors, the bathroom straight ahead and bedrooms on either side. Lou poked her head out of the right-side bedroom and waved a piece of paper.

"I think this is what King wanted."

There was a bare mattress on the floor with clothes piled on top of it, more on the floor surrounding it. Lou had a steel lockbox open, papers overflowing from inside.

"I found a copy of Piper's birth certificate, her parents' marriage license, and a note where Nadine refinanced the house."

"Bring the whole thing," Dani said. She lifted a framed photo of Piper off the nightstand. Piper, eight or nine years old in a red-and-gray softball uniform, her smile bright and cheerful. This one, blessedly, had her face intact. "Piper can go through it and decide what she wants to keep. Do you think the room across the hall is hers? *Was* hers?"

"It was."

Another pang shot through Dani's chest.

"Should we see if there's anything important in there? Anything she might want?"

Lou was trying to get the papers into the box and latch it closed. But now that it had been opened, no configuration seemed to get the accordion of documents back into the box. "We took most of it when she moved out. But sure, go look."

Dani wandered across the hall with the framed photo still in her hand and pushed open the door slowly, almost as if she expected someone to jump out at her.

But Lou was right. It was mostly empty.

There was a small twin bed in one corner of the room, a bed barely big enough for a child. Gray light filtered from the single small window in the upper-right corner.

Dani reached out and touched the covers, surprised to find them coarse and pilled. The pillow was flat and stained, without a cover. The closet was empty as well as the drawers. There was a box of toys under the bed, most of them things only a small kid would play with, but Dani pulled the box out anyway, inspecting each one in turn.

A stuffed rhino. Half-full coloring books. A set of markers. A murder mystery board game. A ball that one could shake and get a yes or no answer. A paddle with a ball tied to it. A ukulele with two busted strings.

She made sure I knew I'm not good enough for you. Between the ribbons and the horses and the viola, Piper had said.

Dani's eyes welled up with tears as she looked at the broken ukulele.

No wonder she hates my viola.

A presence loomed behind her, and Dani turned. Lou was in the doorway, the unruly lockbox tucked under her arm. Her sunglasses were over her eyes again, her face relaxed and unreadable.

"Do you think she would want any of this?" Dani dabbed her eyes with the back of her finger. "Should I bring it back to the apartment?"

Before Lou could answer, the front door creaked open. They both froze, listening to the intruder enter the house, the screen door slamming shut with an angry *thwap*.

The box of toys shifted in Dani's lap and slid to the floor.

"Who's up there?" a man called out. "Piper, is that you, you dumb bitch? Trying to steal shit when I ain't home?"

"Take this." Lou handed Dani the lockbox. "I'll be back."

12

—————

Konstantine took Matteo to Venice himself. As they flew in his private jet, he spoiled the boy with a meal of Fiorentina steak and bolognaise served on fine china. He tucked a cloth napkin into the boy's pressed collar and poured the glass of water himself.

When he asked for a sip of Konstantine's prosecco, he obliged the boy. Then Matteo ate his weight in chocolate truffles, commenting again and again on the niceness of the jet, his leather seat, the view of Italy below.

He thinks this is an adventure.

This alleviated Konstantine of some of the guilt he felt.

Throughout all of this, Stefano remained silent in his seat, careful to keep his hazel eyes averted from them, pretending to look out the jet's window. But Konstantine saw how his fists opened and closed in his lap and his expression remained dark. Even as boys, Stefano had been like this. When something had not gone to plan, he would brood.

Konstantine tried to elevate Matteo's sense of adventure by giving him the window seat in the car as they traveled from the Venice airport to the boats. As they glided over the water, he pointed out the churches he knew, the fountains and monuments. Matteo cried out with laughter when a dolphin leapt up in the distance.

But then all too quickly they'd arrived. The boat rolled to a stop outside of Vittoria's cream-colored villa. Her gleaming windows were shut tight against the chilly November morning, which had just begun to warm.

As soon as the boat docked, the doors opened, and two young women and a man came out. One of the women dashed back inside as soon as she saw Konstantine step onto the ramp and pull Matteo up onto the street.

He had a terrible moment when he imagined Matteo falling into the canal and drowning.

"Do you know how to swim?" he asked the boy suddenly, wrapping a hand around his shoulder and leading him toward the villa.

Matteo frowned, his eyes catching the morning light and brightening. The little lines between his brows knitted. "Of course I know how to swim. What idiot doesn't know how to swim?"

Konstantine made a point not to look back at Stefano, who sank like a rock in deep water.

As they waited on the cobblestones, Konstantine's entourage began to haul Matteo's luggage and trunks onto the road.

"What's all this? Are you going to stay here with me?" Matteo asked hopefully.

Konstantine's heart clenched. "I can't stay. They're gifts from me."

"Gifts?" The boy's eyes widened. "What kind of gifts?"

"You'll find out later when you unpack." Konstantine winked.

I want to give him something to look forward to. Anything to lengthen the magic.

In truth, Konstantine had done this shopping himself and it had taken him days. He'd enlisted the help of some of the other boys, asking about Matteo's tastes and interests, to help fill the gaps in Konstantine's knowledge. By the time day had bled into night, Konstantine had accumulated enough clothes, shoes, treats, books, and trinkets to suit a prince. Not to mention a brand-new gaming system.

He hoped these offerings would make Matteo's separation from home bearable.

Vittoria appeared in the doorway, a flourish of gold today. Her dress billowed and flowed around her, and she stepped into the sun, smiling.

"Arrived already!" Vittoria called out. "My little treasure! Come here."

Matteo stiffened beside him, pressing his weight into the side of Konstantine's leg the way a much smaller child or even a dog would do when afraid.

"It's all right. Go on." Konstantine squeezed his shoulder, pushing him forward.

He watched the boy cross the portico into Vittoria's arms with a sinking feeling in his guts. How would he have felt if Padre Leo had sent him away like this? As if he'd done something wrong. As if he were unwanted. He could only hope the gifts, and their little adventure, would work against whatever voice might whisper such things to him.

It's only for a little while, Konstantine told himself. *Until I find a better solution.*

Vittoria pulled Matteo into her arms and kissed him.

"*Bel ragazzo. Mia piccola bellezza*," she cried. She pinched his cheeks. To Konstantine she said, "Aren't you coming in for lunch?"

"No," Konstantine said. "I have to get back."

In truth, Konstantine was afraid of what might happen if he lingered. If Matteo's courage might fail him, and Konstantine's too.

"Well, then." Vittoria affected a pout. "Wave goodbye, *il mio piccolo principe*. Who knows when you will see each other again."

Konstantine lifted his hand even as his stomach clenched. "*Ciao, Matteo. Essere intelligento. Stai attento.*"

Be smart. Be safe.

Please don't let him cry, Konstantine thought. He couldn't bear it.

And there was a moment when Matteo's eyes seemed bright, his lips quivering. But then he waved, his upper lip stiff.

"Ciao, Konstantine," he called. "Thank you for my gifts!"

He's putting on a brave face for me.

Good boy.

Then they were gone, closing the door on him and leaving Stefano and Konstantine in the chilly morning. Clouds had moved over the sun. Rain was imminent.

Konstantine turned away, motioning for his entourage to return to the boats and prepare for their departure.

When Stefano and Konstantine were alone in the last boat, Konstantine said, "Your face is so red, I think you will burst, *amico mio*. Say whatever it is before it kills you."

"I can't believe you're doing this. Matteo today and who tomorrow? Will you send me to a Turkish brothel tomorrow?"

Konstantine tried to push the image of Matteo's uncertainty, that silent pleading, out of his mind. He'd made his choice and had done the best he could to soften the blow. "Vittoria won't hurt him." *I hope.* "It's done."

"Is it?" Stefano asked, cursing beside him. The gloomy shadows of the canal suited his stern face, the pale waters churning around them. "I'm not so sure."

PIPER STARTLED AWAKE. SHE SAT UP AND FOUND HERSELF IN THE dark, heart hammering so hard that she thought she would die. It had never beat so fast in her life. She didn't know her heart *could* beat so fast. She sat there for a moment, in the tangle of Lou's bedding, unable to draw a full breath. Her throat felt tight and constricted. She was cold again, but this time covered in sweat.

She reached out for Lou and found she wasn't there.

The pillow was unoccupied, the sheets empty.

Maybe she'd gone out for food or to check on King or Mel.

What if she never comes back and I die here and they find my dried-up corpse mummified in this apartment, her mind whispered.

Shut up. This is nothing. I was just having a bad dream.

Once Piper's pulse began to slow, she reached out for the glass of water by the bed. She drank it down, touched her forehead and found it was damp too. Her clothes and the back of her neck as well.

I need another shower, she thought. *That's all I seem capable of lately.* Sleeping. Eating. Showering.

And the nightmares, of course. Piper was getting really good at the nightmares.

Dreams in which her mother was crying somewhere in their house, but no matter where she looked, in what rooms, closets, behind curtains or furniture, the attic, she could never find her. She just heard that unending, relentless crying, which grew more desperate the longer Piper searched.

In other dreams, Willy was beating her. Hitting her mother hard across the face, breaking open the skin, and her mother kept twisting away from him, trying to get away, but couldn't. When Piper would dash forward to stop him, to protect her, she would find that she was in a glass box, trapped on all sides and unable to do anything but beat on the glass and scream her mother's name.

In one particularly horrible dream, she'd heard her mother locked in her bedroom, crying, begging. But no matter how hard Piper slammed her shoulder against the door, she couldn't get it to open.

"Please. I don't want to," her mother had cried behind that door.

And a man would only laugh.

That time, Piper woke sweating with the sound of his laughter in her ears.

She's dead. She's dead and no one is hurting her. No one.

Piper placed her head in her hands and tried to breathe.

Was this what it had been like for Dani? Had every panic attack she'd had after Petrov had tortured been as intense and unrelenting as this? If so, Piper had a newfound clarity of what she must've gone through each night that she'd wrestled with her own fears.

It wasn't fun. That was for damned sure.

Piper wasn't sure how long she'd stayed like this, her head in her hands, half disgusted with herself, trying to build up the energy to get up and take care of herself.

The closet door creaked open and Piper lifted her head to find Lou stepping into the room, her mirrored sunglasses pushed up on her head, her leather jacket hanging loose from her shoulders.

"Hey," Piper said, hoping she didn't look as bad as she felt.

But if Lou thought she looked like shit, she was amused by it. Why else was she smiling?

"I have something for you."

Piper laughed. "I don't think you're the kind of girl to give flowers. Is it food?"

"No. Get your coat on. It's cold where we're going."

Piper's laugh soured. "I don't think I'm in any state to be in public. Look at me."

"We won't be in public. In fact, this place is the opposite of public."

Piper was more than a little intrigued when she slipped from the warm bed and put on socks, her shoes, and her puffy black coat. She hated how shaky her limbs felt.

She probably just wants to take me somewhere cool to cheer me up, Piper thought. Maybe the top of a tall building for a beautiful view.

Just try not to throw yourself off, that dark voice whispered again.

Of course, Piper should've known what a "Lou gift" might look like.

When they emerged from the closet again, she did find a beautiful view. It was the Nova Scotian wilderness at night. Stars brighter and more beautiful than Piper had ever seen, a river of them twinkling above her, seemingly close enough to touch.

The trees were covered in snow and glowed spectral with moonlight. It was a gorgeous, magical landscape.

Until she saw the man propped against the tree, his head cocked to one side in his unconsciousness.

"Willy?" she asked. She looked to Lou. "You kidnapped *Willy?*"

"I thought you might want to kill him."

"Kill him!" Piper took a step back. "How in the world can I kill him?"

Lou opened her jacket. "I've got a Browning and two blades. If you want me to get a grenade or a flamethrower, they're back in the apartment.

"A *flamethrower*, Louie? *Jesus.*"

Piper covered her eyes with her hands, then opened them again. She did this a few times, but the landscape didn't change. She wasn't dreaming. This was real life. Lou had kidnapped her mother's druggie boyfriend and had brought him to the middle of nowhere.

To kill him.

Then again, if that wasn't friendship...

Piper looked around, realizing where they were. "Is this where you bring the people you kill?"

"Yeah." Lou pointed at the placid lake, shimmering with moonlight. "La Loon's through there."

"I can't believe you just offered me a grenade." She burrowed deeper into her puffy coat. "How am I supposed to kill him?"

"Aren't you angry?"

Piper threw her hands up. "Of course I'm angry. Sometimes I'm so pissed I think my head is going to explode."

"Then kill him."

Kill him. It was an idea that Piper hadn't even considered. Had she wanted to beat the hell out of Willy? Yes. Had she wanted to maybe choke him with her bare hands? Absolutely.

Yet, look at him. He was nearly bald on top with graying hair. Slumped against the tree, he looked frail with his pale, track-marked arms and potbelly. He was sick. He was abusive. But ultimately, he was just an old guy with a life barely worth living.

And really, it came down to the fact that Piper didn't think she had it in her to kill someone.

Lou offered her the butt of her gun. Piper took it, looking at it as the strange foreign object that it was. It was heavier in her palm than she'd been expecting. Colder, too.

Piper didn't think she'd ever even held a gun before. Had she?

Willy began to stir, no doubt roused by their voices. When his eyes opened, they fixed on Piper immediately.

"You fucking bitch, I should've known—"

Then his eyes slid to the gun and widened to tea saucers.

For a delicious moment, Piper understood everything. She knew exactly why Lou loved this so much.

Willy tried to get up, shoving himself against the tree as he staggered to his feet. "Oh god. No. *Hey.* I'm sorry. Okay. I'm sorry. I told her not to take so much but she didn't listen. She got into my stash and double-dosed."

"Yeah right." Piper felt something roll through her, something like a winter breeze, and for a moment the gun didn't feel like cold, dead metal. It was warming in her hand.

It was coming alive.

Willy held his hands up in front of her, palms facing them as if this would keep them back. "I swear to God, I tried to save her. I tried CPR. I even took her to the hospital!"

"You dumped her on the curb like some trash," Piper replied.

"That's just because I didn't want to go to jail. It didn't mean I don't care. I do care. I cared about your momma so much. And now she's gone. And I'm...I don't have anybody."

He began to cry, his shoulders shaking with the effort. To Piper it was more than pitiful. It was pathetic. He slid down the tree onto his knees again, covering his face with his hands.

Piper raised the gun. Pointed it at the sobbing man.

On the count of three.

One...

Two...

Three...

Nothing happened.

The crickets chirped. An owl hooted. The breeze caressed Piper's cheeks, chilling them.

But no gunshot sounded.

"I can't," she whispered, and lowered the gun.

Lou's fist slammed into the side of Willy's head and he slumped unconscious against the tree.

Piper covered her mouth. "Why did you hit him like that? That was so hard."

Lou shook out her hand, opening and closing the fingers. "It knocks them out. I hate it when they cry."

"He's going to have a concussion."

Lou only looked at her. "No, he won't."

Piper gave her back the gun. "I'm sorry. I can't kill him."

"Even after everything he did to you and your mom?"

"I know." Piper sighed.

"He *wants* to hurt you."

"I know, but—" Piper searched herself for the anger, for the fury that had made her want to hurt this man a thousand times before. Yet in this moment, she couldn't find it. All she found was her grief. That cold, desolate sadness blowing through her like snow on a winter's night or the river of tears that seemed hell-bent on flowing through her.

"I guess I don't have it in me," she said. "Are you disappointed in me?"

"No. Why?" Lou shifted her weight. "Are you going to be disappointed in me?"

"What? Why?"

Instead of answering, Lou grabbed Willy's leg and dragged him toward the lake. He slid easily over the freshly fallen snow, slipping into the water behind Lou and sinking.

"Are you going to *drown* him?" Piper didn't think she could watch someone be murdered either. "Wait, what is happening right now?"

"I don't want to take the chance he's going to come after you later."

Before Piper could consider whether or not she was okay with... whatever *this* was, Lou was already disappearing beneath the water, tugging Willy down with her.

For a moment, Piper just stood there, regarding the endless night-time wilderness, her mind empty for the first time in days.

Her cheeks were cold. Her hands were cold, but mostly, it was that stone inside her stomach that was cold.

She lay down on her back, pulling her coat around her. Snow began to melt through her sweatpants and dampen her legs, but the rest of her was decently warm.

Above, the stars twinkled, reminding her that this world, this existence, began long before she'd arrived on this planet and would continue on long after she was gone.

Her situation had been far from ideal, but it wasn't everything. Piper could move on. She could get past this. She just didn't know what the hell the next step was.

And another thing had occurred to her—the heart of the matter was that her fear and anxiety over her mother's safety had consumed so much of her energy and mind that now she didn't know what to do without it.

What could her life look like when she didn't lie down every night wondering if this was the night the call would come?

The call came. It was done. Now what?

What was Piper going to do next?

Lou appeared above her, her hair and face dripping. She shook out her leather jacket before lying down in the snow beside Piper.

"I don't know how," Piper began, feeling the tears slide out of her eyes as she looked up at the endless stars. They began to freeze almost instantly against her skin. "I don't know how to move past this. It's just —it's just so much and—"

She exhaled a shaky breath.

Lou reached out and grabbed Piper's hand. She held on tight.

13

———————

Lou stood in her apartment, her hair freshly washed, watching Piper sleep. She'd managed to get the girl to eat dinner, clean up, and tumble back into her bed before she passed out from exhaustion. She hadn't been sure what would happen at the lake. She'd guessed, accurately, that Piper might not be able to pull the trigger. Her aunt Lucy would have said that some souls are just gentler, kinder. That no matter what happens to them, the darkness will never eclipse their light.

Lou had known that Piper was this way.

Yet it still surprised her sometimes, how generous the girl could be with her forgiveness.

But she hadn't truly realized how tenderhearted she was until she'd seen her expression when regarding Willy. There was none of the hatred Lou'd expected. None of the blind fury that had caused Lou to chase Angelo Martinelli to the ends of the earth.

Piper had looked at him and had felt sorry for him.

Sorry.

She has a good heart, Lucy would've said.

Maybe I'm more like my mother than I thought, Lou mused.

Courtney Thorne had been cold down to her bones.

And Lou had felt nothing when she'd dragged Willy onto the shores of La Loon and watched him stir, awakening to the sound of Jabbers's death screech, having only a few seconds to comprehend what might have been happening before those powerful jaws snapped shut, dealing the killing blow.

She'd felt nothing when the beast had torn him apart, ripping through his abdomen the way children tear through presents on Christmas morning.

And now it was done. The threat eradicated. Piper safe again.

Lou ran the comb through her wet hair one more time before placing it on the kitchen island beside Piper's half-eaten sandwich. She watched the girl's chest rise and fall one more time, no hint of nightmares now, and stepped into the linen closet.

She waited in the dark, listening to it, conjuring it.

When it opened up to her, she stepped through into a church centuries older than she was.

Konstantine was sitting on a pew, his head bowed between clasped hands as if in prayer. Lou might have thought that was an intimate, spiritual moment if not for the blood.

There was a pool of it on the stones ten feet from Konstantine's nice Italian leather shoes, and it had smeared in the direction of the hallway, as if something had been dragged in that direction.

Konstantine, too, had blood on him. It was slicked up his arms, soaking the ends of his sleeve. A splatter across his shoes. A smear across the side of his neck.

She touched his shoulder, half expecting him to collapse or his head to lull.

But he looked up and met her gaze. *"Buona sera."*

"Are you okay?" she asked.

He leaned back in the pew, seeming to take note of the blood on his hands, on his shoes.

"Sì. Not my blood."

"Bad day at work?" She could tell from his voice alone that he was in a bad place. Something had been bothering him for days now, and she wondered if he would ever tell her what it was.

"Sometimes it is difficult for me to do what must be done." He opened and closed his fist, the blood cracking along his knuckles. "When the person is not a *complete bastardo*."

Lou regarded him, but said nothing. She wasn't sure he'd finished talking.

He met her gaze. "Do you think less of me, *amore mio*? I am not as—"

She wondered what he would say. Ruthless? Single-minded?

"I'm not as strong as you are."

That was twice tonight that someone Lou cared about was asking her if she thought less of them. And why? Didn't they know she was the broken one? The one so corrupted with darkness that she could become one with it?

Don't say that about yourself, a voice said. It was Lucy's voice. Stern and certain.

Lou stretched her arm across the back of the pew. "Strength has nothing to do with it."

She thought of the way Piper had looked on the banks of her lake, gazing up at the stars with her coat pulled tight around her. Piper was one of the strongest people Lou knew, and she hadn't been able to kill that asshole. Hadn't wanted to.

Lucy, too, had been strong. And her father.

None of them were killers.

Lou sank onto the pew beside him and told him all of this, finishing with the story of capturing Willy Turner from Nadine's house, carrying him to Nova Scotia, and making Piper the offering of his life. How she'd refused.

He considered all of this silently. Then after a stretch of silence said, "I want to be like Padre Leo. But I fear I'm more like my father."

"I considered fucking Angelo once," she said.

Konstantine's face visibly reddened as he turned to her. "Excuse me? Why would you say this to me? And why are you changing the subject?"

"I'm not changing the subject." Lou noted the jealousy and tried not to smile. "I'm saying that I knew I'd rather blow my own brains out before I ever had sex with a Martinelli."

He didn't seem to understand. Fine. She would spell it out for him.

"You're not like your father," she said. "You're nothing like any of them."

His face pinched in confusion until she slid across the pew and put her face quite close to his. Then she kissed him, slow and deep, enjoying the taste of blood on his lips.

"*This* would never have happened if you were."

LOU AND KONSTANTINE MADE LOVE TWICE BEFORE HE FINALLY FELL asleep beside her. But his dreams were not easy. She could tell by the crease between his brows. Lou noted this, intrigued by the idea that for once, she wasn't the one plagued by nightmares. After Lucy had died, and Lou had found killing impossible, she'd been the one unable to sleep, unable to eat. For that reason alone she could never fault Piper or Konstantine their troubles.

But Piper's pain, Lou understood. Grief and loss, she'd met.

Konstantine—*What's going on with you?*

The Florentine apartment was chilly with the early morning pressing against the wooden shutters. A thin beam of light traced the edge of the window's frame.

The compass inside her whirled, and for an exciting minute she thought was going to get an answer, a clue to the secret he was bearing so poorly. But then the compass locked on its destination and she knew at once it was Paris.

Lou slipped quietly from Konstantine's bed, laced on her boots and still damp jacket—*I need to reproof this soon or get a new one*—and stepped through the welcoming shadows.

She knew at once that she was back in the catacombs. The damp smell of old earth rose around her, reminding her of the Meramec Caverns her father had taken her to when she was a child. Only instead of stalagmites and stalactites collecting the moisture from the air, dripping, it was the bones of the long dead.

Lou wasn't alone down here.

She heard movement ahead, perhaps ten or fifteen feet further down the path. Feet scuffling over the crushed bone fragments.

How can they see anything?

She didn't flick on her lighter, even for a chance to see their face. Instead, she crept quietly forward, seeing if she could close the distance between them.

All she needed to do was get her hands on them. Then a hop and a skip to the lake and all her questions would be answered.

Yet she'd taken only one step before the sound of bones clattering into place on top of one another ceased. There was a sharp intake of breath.

Then someone charged toward her. She felt the forward movement, that rush of shifting air, a heartbeat before she heard it.

Without thinking, she faded through the pitch, collapsing into and through the shadows, only to appear again in the catacombs further down the line.

But she still couldn't see.

Lou couldn't understand the murmured cursing in French either, but she knew it was a man.

Did he think I was a ghost? I must've seemed like one, disappearing in front of him.

Was he wearing night-vision goggles?

She thought he must be.

The bones rattled faster now, and Lou suspected he must be stacking them on top of each other hastily, anything to finish his work and get out of here.

If she could just get close enough to grab him…

Another gasp of surprise, and she expected him to rush at her again, but this time the footsteps fled in the opposite direction, down a dark corridor that Lou knew was there but couldn't see.

She ran after him anyway, stretching her arms out until she thought she was close, only to swipe empty air.

A creak. A slam.

The footsteps stopped as quickly as they'd come.

Lou froze, listening, waiting for an ambush. She itched to pull her lighter and turn on the light, but she knew that her strength and advantage lay in the darkness surrounding her.

That if he did manage to hit her or cut her in the dark, it would only work to her benefit, as she could take them both the moment he put his hands on her.

But there was no ambush.

And while the footsteps were gone, in their place was a muffled noise. Climbing? Digging? She couldn't be sure, except to note that it was definitely moving away from her, growing more distant by the second. Behind the left-side wall, perhaps?

Damn it. She pulled the lighter from her pocket and struck it twice. Orange flame and the smell of lighter fluid sparked into the passage around her.

She stood alone on the earth-packed path. She retraced her steps, running her hand along the walls, trying to look for an exit, a sign of where he'd gone. Then she tried the other wall. Both were mud, caked earth that stuck to her fingertips.

No doors. No hatches.

Then she searched the floor with her boots, shifting the crushed bones and years of dust back and forth but finding nothing. The only thing she couldn't inspect with her hands was the ceiling. She lifted the lighter as high as she could and examined it.

Nothing. No outlines of a hatch or door. No hint of light.

She swore. Retracing her steps, she went back down the corridor.

Just before a bend in the path, bones spilled across the walkway. Some of them were still inside a black canvas bag. The skull had cracked, the jawbone hanging loosely to one side. The other bones lay on top of one another like a fortune teller's palette.

Lou shoved the bones into the bag and zipped it closed.

Where is he now? The one I just saw.

The shadows morphed around Lou, shifting, swelling. They offered her passage through that momentary pause of infinity, in the space outside of time.

Then she was at a park. Large ornamental trees lined a path ahead of her, bearing a strange resemblance to the city of the dead below her feet.

Maybe she really was traveling between the city of the living and the city of the dead.

Lou searched the sea of faces. A crowd had formed despite the hour. She rolled her wrist and checked her GPS watch for the local time. It was just past ten in the evening.

Why were there so many people here?

A fountain splashed and burbled beside her. A woman bumped into her and apologized.

Then the band started up and the cheering began.

As she scanned the grounds she couldn't decide which was her attacker. She hadn't gotten a clear look at him. He could be standing right in front of her, looking at her, and she would have to rely on her compass to tell her who it was.

She scanned the crowd for a second time, widening her search to the houses that surrounded the park, their windows dark and watchful.

No click from her compass. No confirmation that her eyes had lain on the one she was searching for.

With irritation nipping at the back of her neck, she stepped between the trees, through the thick shadows, with the duffel still in her hand, and was gone.

14

When Piper's eyes fluttered open the next morning, Lou said, "Do you want to go to the agency with me?"

"Sick of me already?" she asked, her chin still tucked beneath the covers.

"I thought you'd like to help us with the Paris case. I have a bag of bones here."

Piper's eyes, which had been fluttering closed, open wider. "Excuse me, what?"

"My target dropped a sack of bones in the catacombs. Not everything is there—I think he got some of it into the wall before he took off—but I want to take what I've got to King to see if he has any ideas."

"You're going to take King a bag of bones." The sleepiness that had been pressing against Piper's brain dissipated like mist in the noonday sun. She threw back the covers. "Hell yes, I want to see this."

Piper put herself together the best she could, but little could be done about the purple bags under her eyes. That would likely linger for as long as she continued to cry her eyes out every night. She did manage to get down the bagel that Lou offered, already toasted and spread with thick cream cheese.

Once she'd finished it, Lou offered her a pair of mirrored sunglasses.

"Bless you," she said, and slid the glasses over her eyes. "Oh god, it's so dark. How do you wear these all the time? Do I look nuts?"

Lou opened the closet door. "You look fine."

It was a tight fit, the two of them and a bag of bones.

"What's that weird smell?" Piper wrinkled her nose.

"I think it's the chemical he used to clean the bones."

Piper felt the weight of Lou's hand on her hip and relaxed into it the second before the darkness compressed and the world dropped and reformed around them.

Then she was pushing open the storage room door and stepping into the sunny detective agency.

King had his back to them, humming some classic rock song that Piper thought she recognized as he loaded a coffee filter with several scoops of coffee.

"Please make enough for me!" Piper called out. She'd been seriously yearning for some coffee since she'd eaten the bagel.

"Hey!" Instead of adding coffee to the filter, he stopped what he was doing and reached out a large, steady hand and placed it on Piper's shoulder. "It's good to see you. How are you holding up?"

Piper felt tears threatening to form. *God, I'm not even back two minutes and I can't keep it together.*

King nodded as if he understood what the sunglasses were for. "I'm sorry about your mom, kid. That's a tough break. But you're going to be okay."

Am I okay? Am I okay?

He gave her a quick, firm squeeze before returning to the coffee pot. "What about you, Lou? Do you want any?"

Lou shook her head.

The sight of him relaxed Piper. She'd been afraid he'd be drowning under heaps of work and blaming her for it. But his desk was orderly. The paperwork manageable.

The belt around her chest loosened.

"Where's Lady?" Piper asked.

"With Mel," he said, adding water to the reservoir.

Too bad. Piper could've used a bit of canine therapy.

King looked from her face to Lou's and back again. "What brings you in?"

"I work here," Piper said.

"Not for another week you don't. You need the time off." He pressed the start button on the machine and returned to his seat.

"What about the funeral?" Piper asked, resting her weight against the desk.

King leaned back in his chair, lacing his hands behind his head. "Lou gave us the paperwork about your father's burial and the prepaid invoice for your mother's burial plot. I just spoke to them this morning, actually. I was going to call you after lunch."

Piper scratched her elbow, resisting the urge to wrap her arms around herself. "What did they say?"

"They spoke to the hospital and agreed to pick your mom up on Tuesday. They wanted to know if you wanted to see her or—"

"No," Piper said, her throat closing on itself. "No, I don't want to see her like that. Can't they just do the cremation or a closed casket or whatever?"

"They can. I'll tell them that's what you want. Do you want a visitation? Did she have friends or anyone who might want to come say goodbye?"

Only two minutes into this conversation and Piper felt exhausted and sick.

"No. She didn't have anyone. Willy sort of alienated her from her friends until it was just the two of them. And now he's—"

She looked to Lou.

"Gone." Lou's face gave nothing away, but King's brows still rose.

"Okay. But to be clear, you'd rather just say your goodbye at the funeral?"

It would be weird to be back in the cemetery. Piper went every year on her father's birthday, but that wasn't for another four months.

"Yeah. If that's okay."

"It's more than fine with me. Since you don't want anything but the burial, they'll take care of it and give us a time and date. I'll pass it along as soon as I have it."

"Thank you," Piper said. "I'm glad you're helping me. If I had to—" She didn't even know how to finish.

"No problem," he said with a kind smile. "You're too young to be planning a funeral anyway."

An awkward pause bloomed and stretched between them, and Piper wanted the conversation to change but she couldn't figure out how to do it.

Then Lou dropped the duffel onto King's desk.

King immediately frowned. He began unzipping it, talking as he did. "What do we have—*Shit.* A little warning next time."

Lou smiled, and despite her sorrow, Piper laughed.

This only encouraged King more. He pinched his nose, pretended to gag and sputter, even though Piper was one hundred percent certain that he was more than okay with a bag of bones in his face.

"What do you want me to do with these? Dare I ask where you got them?"

Lou pulled two of the red waiting room chairs over, pushing one toward Piper. "What do they tell you?"

"Nothing," he said. "I don't have a forensic background. And if you're looking for a bone reader, she's four blocks east. But she takes long lunches."

Lou wasn't giving up so easy. "What *questions* do they make you think of?"

The coffee pot beeped.

"Wait, I'm going to need coffee for this," King said.

"I'll get it." Piper hadn't even relaxed into the chair before she was up again. She made King's coffee first and put it on his desk before making one for herself, adding the cream, sugar, and vanilla syrup that she liked. Now was hardly the time to think about a diet.

King sipped his coffee and smacked his lips dramatically. "I missed the way you make the coffee."

He's being extra nice to me. I must seem really pathetic right now.

"Well." King considered the bones. "I'd check out the bag. Who made it? See if I can find a serial number or a tag that can tell me where it was purchased, where it came from, how many of them there are. How old is this one? Can I narrow down a purchase date? I would definitely get the bones to a lab, find out what I could about the victim. Age? Sex? Any identifying marks such as old wounds, broken bones, or dental records. I'd cross-reference these against any known missing persons."

King took another sip of coffee.

"Once I knew who they were, I'd try to reconstruct the timeline leading up to their death. Their last known movements before they disappeared. This would tell me who they came into contact with, give me a list of people I should interview, maybe even a time of death, but that's really hard to determine, especially since it seems chemicals were used to strip off the flesh. You smell that?"

He sniffed the air above the opened bag.

"I'd see if they could tell what chemicals were used to clean the bones and see if that gives me any leads. If it's unique in any way then I'd try to trace it the same as the bag."

He considered the sunny street outside before saying, "I'd see if I can make any connection between the victim and someone who had access to the chemicals."

"Damn," Piper said, enjoying the rush of sugar hitting her bloodstream. "That's a lot of work."

"It is. Your way is way easier." King placed his mug of coffee on the desktop and cut his eyes to Lou. "Can't you just pop up and grab the guy instead?"

"He's been sticking to public places," Lou said. "It's hard to pick him out of a crowd."

"And you think the person who killed Delphine is the same one melting down people and putting their bodies in the catacombs?"

"I don't know. Maybe not. She didn't get melted down."

King considered this, flicking the duffel's pull tab. "So we still don't know if we're hunting one killer or two. What about the boyfriend? I didn't have a good feeling when I talked to him."

"Etienne?" Lou arched a brow. "Why?"

"He answered all of my questions fair enough, and I only got the impression that he'd lied once."

"When?"

"When I asked if he had any idea who'd hurt Delphine, he said no. I'm not sure I believe that."

Lou rolled her shoulders inside her leather jacket. "A hundred people put him at an art event at the Grand Palais."

King shrugged, unconvinced. "People fabricate alibis all the time. He could've wandered around just enough to make sure everyone saw him. Left, killed her, and returned as if he'd never escaped at all. The Grand Palais is a big place, right? We should check and see if there's security footage for the entrances and exits for that whole night to see if he did just that. But even if we find it, it's possible that he knows a secret exit."

"I don't think he killed Delphine." Lou took a letter opener off of King's desk and used it to scrape her nails clean. Piper wondered if that was blood she was cleaning out. "I've specifically asked my compass, 'Did he kill her? Is this Delphine's killer?'—and both times I got nothing."

King arched his eyebrows. "I'd still like to look at that event footage."

"I'll see if I can get—" Lou's words were cut off by the ding of the door as someone stepped across the threshold into the agency.

It was Dani, looking gorgeous in her white wool coat, her long hair sleek and beautiful over her shoulder. Piper's heart took off like a shot.

She wasn't sure why, but she stood up.

What am I going to do? Run away? She's blocking the door. If I go upstairs, she's going to follow me. I can't escape through the closet without Lou. Maybe if I just go in there and hide, Lou will know I want to—

Dani wrapped her arms around Piper and hugged her tight. Against the panicked ranting of her mind, she found herself softening, relaxing into the embrace. It helped that Dani smelled so nice, her hair and skin fragrant. Her cheeks were chilly from the November wind blowing through the Quarter.

"I'm so sorry about your mom," Dani whispered. Her hold tightened. "I can't even imagine."

Piper wanted to say something. Maybe *thank you* or *it's okay*.

But she looked up and saw that both King and Lou were trying not to look at them. King had suddenly taken a deep interest in the bottom of his coffee mug and Lou kept cleaning her nails with the silver blade of the letter opener, but her back had turned slightly, further blocking them from view.

"Sorry." Dani stepped back, releasing her. "I just missed you."

"It's okay." *I missed you too.*

All the warm feelings from their hug evaporated when she remembered what she'd vowed to do the next time she saw Dani.

I should just ask her to move out now. No need to drag this on, make it diffi-cult. It'll just be worse if I wait any longer.

"Um, can I talk to you upstairs for a minute?" Piper asked. Dani nodded. To Lou, "Are you good down here?"

Lou looked like she had all the time in the world. "Yeah."

King, suddenly jolted back to action, said, "We can talk about our next steps for the case."

Dani already had her key out and was opening the door that would lead up to the apartment.

Piper took a deep breath and followed her.

15

———————

Matteo lay on his bed, his stomach churning. He was homesick.

His room in Venice was nice, especially once he'd begun to unpack all of the lovely gifts from his luggage. Inside, he'd found brand-new shoes with clean soles. Pristine clothes that still had the tags on them. Packages of sweets, comic books, and movies.

And Venice was interesting. The gentle lapping from the canal outside his window lulled him to sleep each night and cheerful sunlight woke him each morning.

But it was colder here and he didn't know anyone. Despite his forced cheer and determination to make Konstantine proud, he found himself longing for his friends. For the sight of Konstantine crossing the piazza and lifting his hand in greeting before stealing their soccer ball with a few swift kicks then returning it with a smile. For stories and rumors shared in whispers each night beneath the Blessed Virgin.

Konstantine and the other boys who hung around the church were Matteo's first feeling of family after his nonno died, the last family he had in the world.

So he wanted to help Konstantine.

But Matteo had the distinct impression that no matter what he did to please her, Vittoria didn't like him. After the warm greeting, she'd largely ignored him. When she caught sight of him in passing in one of the villa's many hallways, she regarded him not only with a cold eye but with a certain irritation. As if his very presence annoyed her.

Then why had she asked for him? *If she doesn't want me here, why ask me to come?*

To distract himself, Matteo focused on his mission. He'd listened to the adults talking at mealtimes. He'd picked up rumors on the street when traveling with the house maid to complete errands, carrying packages and shopping bags for her. He'd pretended to get lost in rooms and stairwells so he could eavesdrop on phone calls and whispered conversations in the corners of hallways.

There had been much internal debate about whether or not he should record the information in his Bible or in his comic books. If it was the Bible, Vittoria might read it. Or perhaps, under the guise of piety, she might ask him to read her a passage or page some night after dinner or before bed. The comic books, he reasoned, she'd have no interest in at all.

So there, in the white spaces between panels, he etched the secrets he learned, placing only one or two on a page to make them far less noticeable at a glance.

It had become a ritual for him. Each evening after dinner, when he was excused to his room for the night, he would spend the hours before bed recording the secrets he'd collected that day by lamplight.

He had been writing in a Deadpool comic when someone knocked at his bedroom door.

Quickly, he closed the comic book, shoved it into the middle of a stack of others just like it, and sat up.

Vittoria appeared in the doorway, not waiting for permission to enter. That was fine, Matteo thought, if a little rude. It was her house, after all.

Tonight, she wore a black silk jumpsuit cinched at her waist by a thin leather belt. Her hair was pinned up off her shoulders, with only a few ringlets framing her face. Her lips had been painted bright red to match her long fingernails.

She'd changed since dinner. Standing in the lamplight of his little room, she looked smaller, her eyes darker.

"What have we here, little prince?"

She closed the door behind her, shutting them up in the room together.

"I'm just reading," he said. Matteo kept his body still, his eyes on her face.

He didn't fidget or look at the stack of books.

"*Just* reading?" she asked with a hungry smile. "Because a little bird told me that you've been writing things down as well. Letters to your friends, perhaps? Maybe to Konstantine?"

His heart beat faster as he considered what lie he might tell, which one she would believe.

"Won't you tell me what you've been writing?" she asked.

Her face was menacing, painted half in the lamplight and half in shadows. And the dark flowing around her seemed to dance and move.

"*Niente di importante*," he said. "Just stories."

"I want to see them." She opened her hand and extended it toward him.

He shifted on the bed and it creaked. "I'm a little bit shy."

She tilted her head at that, but her hand remained opened, waiting.

Matteo pulled the first book from the pile of comics and handed it to her. Now he did fidget in place, the bed creaking as she opened the cover and regarded the first page. Then a second.

His fidgeting was for show, of course. There was nothing dangerous in this comic. It was what Konstantine would call a diversion. In this one and several others he *had* written stories. Sometimes he changed the character's dialogue or drew on their faces.

"I like to imagine the stories differently," he said, looking up at her through long lashes, hoping he seemed embarrassed. "It's fun."

"Clever boy." She closed the comic book. "I can see why he favors you."

Matteo smiled.

Vittoria didn't return it. "Unfortunately, this means I must hurt you for no reason. I'd really hoped you'd give me a reason, but you've been such a good boy. Too good, really."

The nervous sputter of Matteo's heart slid into true panic.

"You're going to hurt me?"

Vittoria sighed. "Yes. I'm sorry, but it can't be helped. I see no other way."

"What—" Matteo searched for the words. "What did I do wrong?"

Because if it wasn't the eavesdropping, what had been his sin?

She looked at him then, searching his face. "You like to get what you want, don't you, Matteo? It feels good when you get something that you want?"

"*Sì.*"

"Well, you see, I asked Konstantine for what I want, and he *didn't* give it to me. He gave me you instead. You can understand how that's made me very unhappy, can't you?"

His heart was pounding so loudly in his ears he could barely hear her. He was measuring the dimensions of his room with his eyes. The distance from where he sat on the edge of the bed to the door.

It wasn't a big room, but he definitely couldn't reach the handle without passing her. And she would certainly grab him before he ever escaped the room. This close to her, he could smell her perfume. Something sweet. Too sweet. It made him nauseous.

She tossed the comic onto the bed. She began undoing the leather belt around her waist.

No, he thought. *No, please.*

"This is what's going to happen," she said, wrapping one end of the belt around her hand. "I'm going to whip you. Hard. And when I believe you've cried enough, I will have you call Konstantine. Perhaps a video call would be best. When he sees your beautiful little face stained with tears, how absolutely *pitiful* you look, he will feel terrible for sending you here. Then he will give me what I *really* want."

"I can call him crying now," Matteo said. "I'm very good at pretending."

Vittoria tilted her head, smiling. "He's no fool, Matteo. I want this to be *real*. Now, take off your shirt and kneel."

"Please," he said. "Maybe tell me what you want and I can get it for you."

She clucked her tongue. "Such a good boy. But no, you cannot give me what I want."

"But—"

Her hand struck him before he'd even seen her move. It was a sharp slap that caught his ear, making it ring. His jaw throbbed from the impact of it and his mind blanked with the shock.

She hit me. She actually hit me.

No one had ever hit him before.

His friends, especially Nario, got a little rough and shoved him sometimes, but that had been play.

Tears welled up in Matteo's eyes.

Vittoria's smile spread. "Yes, that's a good start. Now kneel down in front of me. Look at the wall."

Please, he thought. *Please don't let her hurt me.*

He thought of the strega. With her cool leather jacket and guns, and sunglasses. The way she moved through the dark as if she was made out of it.

He slid off the bed until his feet hit the cold tile floor. Slowly, he grabbed the bottom of his shirt, his brand-new white polo shirt from Konstantine, and pulled it up over his head.

Please come. Please.

He balled up his nice new shirt and held it against his chest, offering Vittoria his bowed, bare back.

"Yes, like that," she said. "We will hurt your back and spare that pretty face of yours."

The leather belt hit the floor in the ready position with a soft *thwap*.

Matteo drew a breath, bracing himself for the pain.

16

Piper felt like an idiot. She was standing in the middle of her living room with the most beautiful girl alive and she was about to ask her to move out.

If only my heart doesn't explode first, she lamented. She placed a hand over her chest and felt the knocking.

"Are you okay?" Dani reached down to slip off her heels one by one and threw her coat over the back of the island's stool. Then she rolled her eyes. "Of course you're not okay. Your mother just died. I just meant, what's wrong? You look upset."

"I think—" Piper searched those big brown eyes. Her beautiful full lips. *Just say it, you idiot.* "I think you need to move out."

Her stomach clenched so hard she thought she might puke.

Dani, on the other hand, looked as if she didn't understand. "What?"

God, don't make me say it again. It's so hard already.

"I think you might be happier if you didn't live here." Piper rubbed her sweaty hands against her pants. "You could get Octavia back and find somewhere with more space. I bet you could find a nice place closer to your work."

Dani's brow furrowed. "It's a twenty-minute walk from here to *The Herald*."

"I just think it would be easier for you if you found a different apartment."

Dani eased herself down onto the sofa and pressed her palms together in front of her face. "If you need more space because your mom died, I can—"

"No, that's not it," Piper said, coming around to join her on the sofa. "I just think you'd be more comfortable if you lived somewhere else."

"What are you talking about?" Her eyes rapidly searched Piper's face. "I want to be here with you."

"You can't mean that."

Dani's eyebrows shot up. For a long pause she said nothing, clearly trying to calm herself. "It's true that we moved in together very quickly. Had my apartment not blown up, I probably would've waited for at least another year, possibly two."

Piper's hand shot up. "See! You wouldn't have moved in with me if you'd had any other choice."

"What are you talking about? That's not what I just said."

"But it's true that you moved in with me because you didn't have another option."

Dani frowned. "Of course I had choices. I could've lived with my parents or gotten another apartment. It's not like I had to be here or on the street."

Piper considered this. Piper wouldn't have been able to find another apartment in the area because she didn't have as much money as Dani did. But with Dani's resources, it was true—she could've gone somewhere else. She could've rented any of the hundred furnished vacation rentals in the city until she found a more permanent arrangement. Hell, she could've gotten a hotel room.

Dani licked her lips. "If this is about the viola—"

"It's not about the viola," Piper said quickly.

"Then what is this? I know your mom died, but this conversation started before that. I'd ask if you were trying to break up with me, but you never actually asked me out, so it can't be that." And here Piper heard the first notes of bitterness in her voice, and Dani must have caught her own tonal shift too, because she added, "Not that I blame you. You had plenty of reasons for not trusting me and taking it slow. I get it. But this whole move-out-because-you'll-be-more-comfortable thing is bullshit. Tell me what's really going on."

Piper could barely think over the thunderous pulse in her ears. How in the world was she going to explain that Dani was too rich to live here? It sounded stupid in her head, so she could only imagine what it would sound like if she said it aloud. Rich people can do whatever they want. Hadn't she just been reading about a Silicon Valley billionaire who lived in an airstream trailer or something?

"Do you want me to pay more rent?" Dani asked.

"What? God, no." Piper pressed her fingers into her forehead. She was getting a headache.

"Then what is it? Explain it to me. If it's not the viola, it's not what I pay in rent, what is it?"

"I just—I just don't think this is going to work out."

Dani pulled back as if slapped. After a moment she managed to ask, "To be clear, *what* isn't going to work out? Us living together or *us period?*"

Piper took a breath. "Both. Neither. We're too different."

"Says who?"

Piper's blood pressure hit the roof. "Your mother! The world! *Me!*"

"Wow. Okay." Dani looked away, turning toward the opposite wall and regarding it with a distant stare. It seemed like an hour before she said, "So you want me to move out."

"I think it would be best for you."

Dani stood and glared down at Piper, her hands fisting in her own hair. "Don't tell me what's best for *me*, Piper. Not you, or anybody else, gets to make that decision for me. If you want your space, *fine*, but don't pretend that you're doing it for *me*. I want to be here. I gave up my *cat* so I could be here. I'm happy here. In this apartment. And with you."

Piper threw up her hands. "You shouldn't have to give up your cat to be with someone. I feel *horrible* about that!"

"Octavia is fine! She doesn't even like people. It's hardly like she's attached to me. My mother got her and then didn't want to take care of her. Now Tavi only wants someone to keep her bowl full. And it's not like I gave her to strangers! I can see her whenever I want."

"You kind of did," Piper countered. "She's in Italy right now, and you don't even know Konstantine."

Now they were both standing only inches apart, their faces red, their chests heaving.

Piper thought maybe they would kiss, and she wanted to kiss those lips. *Badly.*

But Dani had begun to cry, bright tears standing out in her eyes.

Oh god. Are these anger tears? Anger tears were dangerous.

"I'm sure she's fine," Piper was quick to add. "I don't think Lou would let Konstantine watch her if he didn't know how to take care of a cat. She just did it because I couldn't breathe."

"This isn't about the cat." Dani clasped her hands behind her neck and groaned. "Are you really this dense?"

What was going so wrong here? Whenever Piper had had to distance herself from girls in the past, they might've cried or been bummed out, but they'd never told her that she was *wrong*. They would talk it out, Piper would present her evidence, and then they were able to move into the friend zone.

This conversation didn't feel like it was moving in that direction at all. In fact, it felt like Dani was going to refuse to move out.

Dani blinked and the tears began to dry. In their place was a hard determination. "I want to ask you a couple of questions."

Oh god, Piper thought. *I've activated journalist mode.*

"Okay," she said reflexively.

"Question number one: Do you like me?"

"Of course."

"Romantically?"

Piper didn't think she could convince her otherwise, as hot and heavy as they'd been in the bedroom. "Obviously."

Dani took a menacing step toward her. "You think I'm beautiful? Smart? Attractive? Long-term partner material?"

What game was this? "...Yes?"

"Which one?"

"All of the above."

"Do you have a good time with me?"

"Of course I have a good time with you." The truth was Piper hadn't laughed with anyone so much in her life—not even Henry.

"So there is no problem with me or our chemistry?"

"No."

Dani threw her hair over her shoulders. "Question two."

"We are way past question two. That was like ten questions."

"Fine, *part* two. Do you like *living* with me?"

Piper thought of their lazy mornings, smiles shared over warm mugs and kisses as soon as her eyes were open. Walking into the bathroom and finding Dani in the shower, the beautiful curve of her body framed by the opaque glass.

"Yeah, I like living with you."

Dani's brow furrowed again. "So when did that change? At lunch with my parents?"

Yes. "No."

"You're lying."

"I'm not lying, I just—" *I just what?* Piper's resolve was deteriorating. The more questions Dani asked, the more confused she felt. She *did* like Dani. She *did* like living with her. But she still couldn't stay here because—because—

"Listen." Dani ran a hand through her hair. "I think I get it. When I went to your house—"

Piper's blood iced in her veins. "When you *what?*"

"When Lou and I went to your mother's house."

"Lou!" Piper screamed. "Lou, get up here right now!"

Oh god, oh god, oh god. She must think—Oh god, oh god.

"Why? What's wrong?" Dani's eyes widened. "We were just looking for the papers we needed for the burial and to work out what needs to happen with her estate."

Oh my god, oh my god, oh my god. Piper collapsed onto the couch, her head in her hands.

"Lou!"

"Why are you so upset?" Dani tried to sit down beside her, but Piper flinched away. "It's just a house. It doesn't mean anything."

"Except that I'm hella poor and you're like a freaking duchess."

"You're not poor."

Piper looked up from her lap only long enough to yell again. "Lou! I swear to god, if you don't show up right now I'm going to—"

"What?" Lou pushed open the apartment door, her free hand resting loosely in the pocket of her leather jacket.

"Get me out of here," Piper demanded. The blood in her face was throbbing.

Dani's mouth fell open. "Piper, wait. We need to talk about this."

"No. I can't. *Lou.*"

"Piper!"

Lou's hand was cold on her arm as she pulled her toward the darkness.

LOU HAD NO CHOICE BUT TO STAND IN HER LIVING ROOM AND LISTEN to Piper rant for thirteen minutes. As the girl paced and whined and expelled more energy in this one moment than she had in days. Just when she thought Piper might run out of things to say, she would fix on a new tangent and begin again, rehashing the argument from a fresh angle.

At its essence, it boiled down to, *Why didn't you tell me you'd taken her there? How could you take her to my house? God, now she must think the worst things about me.*

Lou knew better than to interrupt this before it ran its course.

Finally Piper fell back onto Lou's bed and covered her face with the bend of her elbow.

When one silent moment had stretched into three, Lou said, "You're embarrassed."

Piper lifted her arm. "Hell yeah, I'm embarrassed. How could I not be? Why didn't you go to my mom's place alone? At least you've already seen it, and hell, drug dens are nothing new to you anyway."

"King asked me to bring her."

"I'm going to kill him."

Lou watched Piper fold in on herself, the energy that had overtaken her moments before quickly draining away. She wasn't sure what to say to her, to reassure her that Dani didn't see the way Piper thought she did. That no one cared about this the way Piper herself did.

She hadn't finished considering her options when a sudden jerk through Lou's navel tugged her forward.

Someone was calling for her. Someone needed her *now*.

Someone...small?

"I have to go," she said, moving toward the linen closet.

"Fine, abandon me," Piper called out from under her arm. "If you're gone, at least I can cry in peace."

17

———————

Vittoria's heels tapped on the cold tile behind Matteo. "I'm thinking twenty or thirty lashes to start, and we will see how you are then, all right?"

Her voice was far too happy for the topic at hand.

Before Matteo could answer, the belt came down. It whistled through the air before one swift snap licked his skin.

He cried out. The pain and surprise scraped along the inside of Matteo's mind, heightening his fear.

"*Per favore. Mi dispiace!*" he shouted.

But the belt came down for a second time.

He bowed further forward, trying to tighten himself into a ball.

It will end, he told himself. *She cannot hurt me forever.*

He braced himself for the third strike. He waited. And waited.

He was worried that he would turn and she would hit him in his face, but a choked gurgling piqued his curiosity.

Slowly, he turned, and gasped.

There she was. *La Strega*.

La Strega had Vittoria against the wall by her throat. Her feet kicked and scraped along the floor as a pale hand held her suspended. The belt tumbled from her grip as she tried to claw at the hand holding her, but there was nothing to grab. The jacket's leather sleeve was impenetrable.

Then someone was beating at the door, pushing it open.

La Strega pulled her gun with her free hand and shot the man opening the door. He fell back as if punched, crumbling onto the floor outside the room.

With this new space, *La Strega* turned and shoved Vittoria out of the room, slamming the door shut after her.

Then it was just the two of them in his little room.

Matteo's heart raced like a rabbit's.

"Do you want to get out of here?" *La Strega* asked, her eyes invisible behind her sunglasses. "*Vieni con me?*"

"*Sì, sì!*" Matteo scrambled to his feet, tugging his shirt down over his head.

She reached out for him.

"Wait!" he cried, and leaned across the bed to grab his stack of comic books. Then in his unsure English he said, "Okay. I is ready."

She extended her hand and he took it, noting the size difference between hers and his own. Then, and he wasn't sure why, but she reached out and clicked off the lamp.

ONE OF THE CUTS ON THE BOY'S BACK WAS BLEEDING, AND IT FILLED Lou with rage. She wanted to put a bullet—maybe three—between Vittoria's eyes. Instead, she focused on getting him out of there. Once he was safe, Louie would come back for the bitch.

The only problem was she wasn't sure where to take him. Lou had a feeling that this was connected to the situation Konstantine hadn't wanted to talk to her about, and if he still wasn't ready to talk to her, who would?

As the boy scrambled across the bed to grab a stack of comic books, gathering them clumsily into his arms, she thought of Stefano.

Stefano would be all too happy to tell her what the hell was going on.

And while it was easy to find Stefano with her compass, it was harder to tell if he was alone. It'd be quite awkward if Konstantine was with him, and she had to explain that he wasn't the Italian man she was looking for at that particular moment.

But when the light clicked off and the darkness softened around them, she stepped through without hesitation.

In place of the villa's small bedroom was a shadowed courtyard. At the edges, lush trees grew, obscuring the stucco wall encompassing it. At its center, a lit fountain burbled softly. Stefano was at a little wooden table, one knee crossed over the other in the picture of ease. His face momentarily lit as he struck a match to light the cigarette between his lips. Then he was taking his first long drag and exhaling up toward the sky.

Konstantine was nowhere to be seen.

When he saw her, Stefano's ease evaporated. He sat up, shaking out the match.

He crossed the courtyard in three strides, dropping down in front of the boy. *"Matteo! Che ti è successo? Stai bene?"*

"Sto bene, sto bene! Mi ha salvato!"

When he saw the blood on the boy's shirt, he pulled it off, and swore.

In English he said, "That bitch. Did you kill her?"

"No," Lou said. "Should I?"

Stefano stood, motioning toward a door at the edge of the courtyard.

"If you did, it would cause more problems than solutions." When the boy objected he said, *"Non discutere con me! Entra dentro."*

He pushed the boy forward and thrust him into the room despite his protests.

It was Konstantine's office, Lou realized. She'd never walked into the room using the door, so she hadn't realized where it was located in the space. She thought it had been like Padre's office, in the basement of the old church, rather than a one-room annex surrounded by a lush courtyard.

Yet there was the large desk in front of the fireplace. The high-back leather chairs and adjacent bathroom.

"Where is Konstantine?" she asked.

"He went home an hour ago. Were you looking for him?"

"No. I was looking for you."

Stefano arched a brow. "For me? Why?"

"Because he won't tell me what's going on, but I think you will. At least you want to."

Stefano laughed, a high, bitter sound. He opened two drawers before finding a small first aid kit and throwing it onto the desktop.

He asked the boy to turn but he refused.

"Come on," Stefano said. "Do you want it to get infected?"

The boy jerked his chin at Lou and slammed his comic books down on Konstantine's desk.

She didn't follow the rapid exchange that followed. Italian was harder to understand when the speakers spoke quickly and the voices rose as the emotions escalated, but after a short tussle, Stefano threw up his hand and handed the boy the kit.

"Matteo won't let me help him. He wants you to do it."

Matteo. So that's his name.

Matteo crossed to her with the kit in front of him, his smile suddenly shy. He held it out to her.

"Please," he said in English.

Stefano rolled his eyes.

Lou tried not to smile. "Turn around then."

When he didn't seem to understand, she made a spinning motion with her finger.

"*Sì, sì.*" He offered her his back.

Lou sat down in the leather chair and regarded the broken skin carefully. Stefano turned on a separate lamp.

"Thank you," she said without looking up.

"*Di niente!*"

There were two stripes crossing the narrow plane of his back. One was red and raised. The other had broken the skin.

"Are you going to tell me what's going on?" she asked Stefano as she opened the kit and found an alcohol wipe.

She tore the corner off with her teeth and fished the soaked towelette out of its tight wrapping.

"Yes," he said. But then added no more. Lou took this to mean they would talk once the boy had been sent away. "Tell me what happened with Vittoria."

"I found him kneeling on the floor and she was hitting him with a belt. I stopped her."

"How?"

"I choked her. Threw her out of the room."

"Did you kill anyone?" he asked, his eyes remaining dark.

"There was a man who came to stop me. He's dead."

Stefano exhaled. "How did you know she was whipping him?"

"*L'ho pregata! Come la Madonna* ," Matteo said.

Stefano's brows arched. "So you can hear prayers?"

Lou's hand stilled above the cuts. Was that what had happened? The boy had prayed to her. She wasn't surprised. Praying wasn't so different than what Piper or King did when they needed her, basically demanding her attention with their minds.

Actually, now that she thought about it, this wasn't the first time. It had been the same when she'd saved Shai, a little boy trapped in a child pornography ring. Hadn't he said she'd answered his prayers?

Still, it made her wonder. Was that what was happening in Paris? In those weeks when she'd kept getting pulled to the city, had someone been praying for help? Maybe not to her specifically, but a desperate plea for anyone, anywhere, to intervene? Assia, maybe?

A lot of good it had done her. Lou had been too slow.

"Matteo," Stefano said gently. "What did Vittoria say to you before she hit you?"

Matteo spoke in soft, flowing Italian, of which Lou understood nothing.

Halfway through, Matteo hissed. Then he muttered, "*Freddo.*"

"Liar," Stefano said. "Go on."

He finished his story while Lou worked.

Once she'd wiped each line and left them wet and gleaming, she searched the kit for bandages. She found a roll of gauze and tape and covered each wound.

Then she pulled the shirt back down and placed a hand on his head. "All done."

"Grazie." Matteo leaned forward and kissed her cheek before she could react.

Stefano swore again. *"Esci di qui bastardo, prima che dica a Konstantine che hai baciato la sua donna!"*

Lou was smiling as the boy fled the office.

Stefano slammed the door behind him and ran a hand through his hair. "To answer your question, we are on the brink of war with the Albanian mafia."

Lou settled back into the chair, lacing her fingers over her lap.

"Vittoria is on good terms with them, but the price she wanted for helping us was you."

He clearly wasn't as confident in his English as Konstantine was, but his words were perfectly clear, if thickly accented.

"Me?"

Stefano nodded once. "Konstantine refused. So she asked for Matteo instead. But Matteo just told me that it was a trick."

Lou frowned. "What was a trick?"

"Before she hit him, she told Matteo that she was only hurting him so that Konstantine would feel guilty and bring him home. Then she could get what she really wanted. I can only assume that meant you."

"What did she want with me?"

"To kill for her. She has a, uh, what is it called in the American movies? A list of people she wants to die?"

"A hit list."

"Yes, she has a *hit list*," he said. "You kill for her. She makes peace with Erjon and we don't go to war with the Albanians."

Lou considered this, opening and closing her hand as the cooling alcohol dried on her fingers.

"Why didn't he ask me?"

Stefano sneered.

"Because you make him weak. He will cross an ocean for you, spend a fortune on you, risk his life for you, but he can't bear to ask you to do the same. *Why?* Because he *loves* you?" Stefano's anger was immediate and explosive. He slammed his open palm on the desk. Matteo's comic books bounced. "It's stupid. No. It will get him *killed*."

Stefano's anger didn't bother Lou. But his words had struck a chord because they were true.

Konstantine *had* crossed an ocean for her. He'd protected her anonymity from the cameras of the world, including, most recently, those in Paris, where she'd wanted to put bones.

He had stepped in to save her friends when Petrov had taken them hostage. When it came to cases and information, he'd helped her more times than she could count.

In truth, she owed him far more than he'd owed her.

So why had he not asked for her help?

Stefano rolled a matchstick between his fingers. He was composed again, pushing his dark hair off his face. "When Padre Leo named Konstantine as his successor, I knew he would do well. He was the best of all of us. The smartest, surely. The bravest. But he has one terrible problem. When it comes to you, he does not make good decisions. He doesn't do what needs to be done, do you understand? *L'amore è cieco.*"

And was it true? Did she make him blind? Would he avoid an easier solution if it meant inconveniencing her?

She had to laugh at the irony of it.

King not wanting her to kill if there was another way. Konstantine wanting her to kill but refusing to ask.

"He hates it when I smoke in this office. But sometimes I like to piss him off. A little."

Stefano struck the match on the desk and relit the cigarette he'd extinguished.

You really are like brothers, then, she thought.

"So tell me." Through the thin blue smoke, he asked, "Are you *La Strega*? Are you the witch of our nightmares or no?"

"I'm not a witch."

"You certainly don't die easily. If I thought I could kill you without breaking Konstantine's heart, I would have already done it."

She smiled even though she knew he wasn't joking.

"If you don't really care about him, tell me."

"Because you do," she said.

"*Sì*," he said without pause. "*Sì*, I care for him. I swore to Padre that I would keep him safe, and I will die for him. I know this. I don't know the day or the hour, but I will die for him."

Lou had no need to question this. She saw the devotion in his eyes.

Stefano pointed at her with the cigarette. "But will *you* protect him? I need to know if I am fighting alone."

It was hard to overlook the earnestness in his face. For a moment it reminded her of Piper, of the night when she'd said, *I'm going to be your best friend, Lou-blue. Just you wait.* And how much she'd meant it when she'd said it.

"I'll take care of the Albanians," Lou said. And just the idea of it set her skin alight with energy. She wanted to do it. She ached for it. It had been a long time since she'd been able to use her gifts in such a way. Serial killers and pedophiles were a pleasant challenge, true enough. But they couldn't compare to the delicious mayhem of a twenty-or-thirty-against-one fight to the death.

And the truth remained. If someone had threatened her with war, or had threatened Piper, King, Melandra, or even Dani, Konstantine would help without even being asked.

He would do what needed to be done without question or hesitation.

Now Lou had a chance to do the same.

"What of Vittoria?" Stefano asked. "Will you kill her for her little manipulations?"

"I want to. But his enemies will have a reason to unite against him."

Stefano nodded once. "*Sì.*"

"Then I guess she and I will *talk.*" The way she smiled made Stefano shift nervously in his seat.

Lou stood. "Anything else I need to know before I go?"

"Matteo is waiting for you in the courtyard. I've seen him look into the window three times already."

"I won't keep him waiting." Lou turned to go.

"Strega?" Stefano said, standing and running a hand down the front of his suit jacket.

"*Sì?*" she said mockingly.

"Should I need you in the future, only on behalf of Konstantine, of course, should I...*pray* to you as well? Does it really work?"

Lou smiled. "It couldn't hurt to try."

"*Strega?*" Matteo stepped forward timidly, his head bowed slightly in a picture of humility.

Lou couldn't suppress her smile. "What do you want?"

Stefano stepped out of the office behind her and closed the door, locking it with a key from his pocket.

Matteo spoke in rapid-fire Italian, looking to Stefano for interpretation.

"She already knows *that*," Stefano said. To Lou, "He doesn't want you to tell Konstantine that he was whipped. He's worried Konstantine will be upset."

"Not bad," Matteo said in shy English. "It's okay."

But this didn't seem to be all. As the boy lingered, his eyes searched her face.

Stefano groaned. "Spit it out."

Another rapid stream of Italian, this time punctuated with a flourish of hand gestures. But whatever the request was, Stefano clearly disapproved.

"*No.* No, Matteo."

Matteo took this to mean he should ask again, and again, louder and louder until he received the answer he wanted.

After Stefano refused for the tenth time, Matteo turned to Lou. In exasperation, he cried out, "I want to go! I want to *go*. Back. With you."

Lou laughed. "I already have a pet."

And yet the little boy searched her face, waiting, begging for an answer.

Stefano pinched his brow. "He wants you to take him to the church where all the boys are. He thinks if they see you deliver him, it will be *cool*. I told him not to be silly."

It *was* silly. Yet Lou understood.

Once she'd lost consciousness in a confessional. The priest got her to a hospital before she bled out on the cathedral's floor, but he'd kept her guns and her bulletproof vest. So she'd had to go back and retrieve them. When she did, he'd rambled about God, and angels, asking Lou to explain what she was. Why she had the power to do what she did.

She didn't have an answer for him. Yet that hadn't stopped her from melding with the shadows of his office, performing a rather dramatic exit for no reason except to feed the old man's superstitions.

It had been fun. Sometimes you just wanted to *look* cool.

She reached out to the boy. "Okay."

He ran into her arms nearly squealing.

Stefano huffed behind them. But when Lou turned and he saw the boy in her arms, something in his face softened.

Or she thought it did. It was hard to tell. His grumpy, perpetually inconvenienced expression had returned already.

Lou didn't care. With a knowing grin, she slid her shades down over her eyes and stepped into a pocket of shadow cast by the low-slung roof of the dark office.

MATTEO'S HEART FLUTTERED IN HIS CHEST AS HE CLASPED HIS ARMS around *La Strega's* neck. He felt something hard press into his ribs, and knew at once that she held a gun under her leather jacket. If she emerged through the darkness holding him in one hand, a gun in the other, Nario and Monte would never doubt his stories again.

He only wished he knew better English.

Konstantine had insisted they all learn and take their studies of the language seriously, but Matteo hadn't felt the deficit of his education as keenly as in this moment.

"Gun!" he said. "Gun!"

"It's okay," *La Strega* replied. "The safety is on."

He sighed. She hadn't understood, and now they were stepping into that strange nowhere again. It was a breathless place, and though the transfer lasted only a moment, it felt longer.

When they emerged they were in the church, near the pews.

Please let this work, he thought. Every lash on his back would be worth it just to see Nario's and Monte's faces when he arrived with *La Strega*.

The boys were standing behind the Blessed Virgin. This was their meeting place. The last check-in of the day before they went home. Tonight, they were talking loudly over one another. Nario and Monte shoved each other, and Matteo's heart leapt.

They're here!

Lou stepped forward and all eyes pivoted toward her.

The chatter died immediately, their eyes doubling then tripling in size as *La Strega* carefully set Matteo on his feet and urged him toward his friends.

"Thank you, my friend," he said with all the grand pomp and circumstance he could muster. It was difficult with the barely contained hysterical laughter building in his throat.

"Until next time, Matteo," *La Strega* said, and with a slight flourish became one again with the dark.

The slack-jawed boys began screaming, grabbing him, shaking him, demanding to understand what they had just seen.

And for a long time, they didn't stop.

18

Piper exhaled one last shaky breath. There were no more tears to wring from her eyes and her abdomen was sore from its convulsing. She'd cried her heart out. It was done.

"Get up," Lou said.

Piper pulled the comforter off her face and found Lou beside the bed, hands in her leather jacket, a small, smug smile on her face.

"Why do you look so amused? Did you just choke a bunch of guys or something?"

"Get up."

Piper moaned. "Why do you hate me? What have I done to you?"

Lou ignored these questions.

Piper burrowed deeper into the covers. "But I'm not done feeling sorry for myself."

"Too bad." With one hard yank, Lou pulled the cover away. Carried on a draft, it slid across the hardwood floor out of reach. "I have something to show you."

Piper didn't think she could put quite enough disdain in her eyes to properly reflect her blanket-less feelings, but she tried.

Nothing. Lou's smile only deepened. "If you don't get up I'll bring Dani here."

"I can't talk to her. I'm peopled out for the day."

"Then you should choose option one. No talking to people."

There was really only so much resistance Piper could manage when she was the guest in someone else's apartment, so reluctantly she reached out her hand and let Lou pull her to standing.

"What do I need to wear? A coat?"

Lou thought about this. "Yeah. Just in case."

Piper slipped her feet into her sneakers. "Where are we going?"

"It's a surprise."

"I hate surprises! And my birthday isn't until March."

Lou opened the linen closet.

"*Fine.* But I hope this ends in a delicious sugar-laden coffee." Piper stepped into the closet and pressed her back against the far wall. "Or a burger. I'm in the mood for a burger."

Lou stepped in after her and shut the door tight.

"Is this about your Paris murderer?" she asked. Hearing her voice in the compressed dark was intimate, cloying.

"No." Lou's hand was gentle but firm on her upper arm. The closet disappeared instantly, replaced by that flash of nothingness before a new world formed around them.

Piper's weight shifted and she was pitched forward, her feet trying to find steady ground.

Lou held her upright until she did.

When the world disappeared and rematerialized again, Piper found herself on a busy street corner. The night was punctuated by street-lights and neon signs running up and down the boulevard. The streets looked wet, though no droplets fell from the sky. Maybe there had been a hard rain shower earlier and that had left this version of the world iridescent.

At first Piper wasn't sure what she was supposed to be looking at. Her searching eyes must've said as much.

"Her," Lou said, nodding toward a girl on the opposite corner. "In the pink skirt."

Piper knew at once why Lou had chosen her. Not because they dressed anything alike. Piper liked baggy pants and crop tops and this girl was in a neon skirt and a see-through fishnet top. Her black bra was visible even from where Piper stood. Her nails and lips were painted bright pink, and it was probably good that they matched because she kept chewing on her nails nervously as she looked up and down the busy street.

They were about the same age and had a certain similarity in their appearance.

"What about her?" Piper asked.

"Her parents didn't have much money. Her father died when she was young. Her mother is an addict. She started college but couldn't finish because life got in the way. She's like you."

"How can you possibly know all that?" Piper asked.

"We crossed paths when I was hunting Angelo. Her name is Adrienne."

Adrienne.

A man walked up to her, said something, and Adrienne plastered on a reflexive smile. But when the man turned, the smile was waning at the corners, even as she took his arm and began up the street.

"Do you think she's worthless?" Lou asked.

"God no!" Piper cried. "Of course not."

"She's had every opportunity that you've had, but this is her life," Lou said. "She lives in an apartment with a few other girls, and if we went there now, I bet she'd be just as embarrassed as you were."

"Why? She's doing the best she can. It's not her fault."

"But it's *your* fault that you're not a millionaire and your mother died of an overdose."

"That's different." Piper felt like she'd been socked in the guts.

"So I can go put a bullet in her head and throw her in a ditch because it's different? Her life is her own fault."

"*No.*" Piper covered her face with her hands as if this would block out the world. "Ugh. I get it. No more. Get me out of here."

She thought she would be taken back to Lou's apartment then, but instead they appeared outside one of Piper's favorite burger joints in Chicago, a little place that she and Lou had discovered a few months before. She knew it at once by the smell and the sound of fifties music coming through the speakers.

Lou opened the door and held it for her. "Come on."

They chose a table by the window. Lou put her back to the wall, her eyes on the doors.

Piper slid into the opposite seat. For a long time she said nothing. She didn't know what to say.

It was Lou who broke the silence.

"Money is just something that happens. Some people have a lot of it. Others barely any at all. It's not fair how it moves around. People like the Martinellis shouldn't be sitting on piles of it while girls like Adrienne have to choose between giving a blow job or going hungry that night."

"I hear what you're saying." *I don't like it, but I hear it.*

Piper pulled a menu from the carousel at the table's edge even though she knew what she was going to order. The waitress motioned to them, giving the universal sign for *I'll be right with you.*

Lou didn't seem to care about any of this as she draped one arm over the back of a chair. "More money doesn't mean you're worth more. Fish had more money than you and he also tortured, raped, and murdered women before masturbating into their graves."

Not the image Piper wanted front and center of her mind as she searched the list of burger toppings, but Lou was right.

"You're feeling very philosophical tonight," Piper mumbled.

Lou shrugged. "I had a good night."

"If this is a sex thing, don't tell me."

"No sex," she said, the mirrored sunglasses rising as she smiled. "But you need to get over this money thing."

Piper understood this intellectually. Her mind could comprehend the words, see their meaning, but it didn't eradicate that horrible feeling of worthlessness still alive and well inside her. Maybe nothing would ever make that feeling go completely away.

"Okay, fine." Piper sighed. "I'm not worthless because I don't have a degree or a car or a house."

"And Dani isn't worth more just because she comes from money."

Piper groaned. "Okay, but she can speak foreign languages and play bougie instruments and it's hard to not feel like an underachiever around her."

The waitress came and took their drink orders before disappearing again.

When she was gone, Lou said, "I can't play an instrument and my Italian is shit."

Piper threw her hands up. "Yeah, but you can do the shadow thing and the water thing and you're a freaking warrior badass with guns. Come on! I just have a Netflix account, man."

"I love Netflix," Lou said with a grin.

"Look, I get it. Okay? I really do. Those people who have to live in the trash heaps, or people who lose all their stuff in earthquakes and mudslides and hurricanes, they're still worthy. Most people on the planet can't play sonatas or buy a car and they're still worthy. *Everyone* is still *worthy*. I hear you. And I even agree with you up here." Piper touched her head. Then she touched her heart. "But somewhere in here I feel like everything that happened to me is my fault. That I'm where I am today because of the mistakes I've made, and I'm never going to be better than this."

Lou's good humor was gone. "It's not your fault."

Once the drinks came and they'd ordered the burgers and fries, Lou said, "Besides, you are rich."

Piper blew her straw wrapper at Lou, hitting her in the cheek before shoving the straw down into her water. "If you hit me with some platitude about how the gods created everyone equal and I'm just as precious as a malamute or something, I'm going to choke you."

Lou ignored this threat. "You're rich because your friends are rich."

Piper pressed her hands into the tabletop. "Excuse me? I thought you were trying to make me feel better about myself. Because if so, you just took a wrong turn."

Lou pushed her sunglasses up on top of her head, and the song changed from a slow love song to a trumpet-filled bop. "You've got King and Melandra, and you've got me. We aren't going to let you starve or live in a box. We aren't like your mother."

A fist clenched around Piper's heart.

Lou must've seen the pain cross her face.

"I'm dead serious. You might get threatened by murderers, criminals, or even the mafia, but not one of us is going to let you miss a meal or sleep under a bridge. You know that, right?"

Piper held up a hand, silently begging her not to say more. It hurt. It hurt to hear it. "I know, I just—"

It was the shame, wasn't it? The shame hurt. Because she would absolutely go lie down under a bridge before she could bring herself to ask someone for help. Before she'd let anyone see the ways in which she was utterly and totally failing.

Letting other people look out for her made her feel...*bad*. It had never occurred to her—*ever*—that the people around her might look out for her simply because they loved her.

Piper tried to swallow the lump forming in her throat. "I hear you, so please stop talking. You are literally killing me."

Lou stopped talking.

Piper dabbed at the tears in the corners of her eyes. "But seriously, what the hell happened tonight? Why are you in this wise-woman-on-the-mountain mood? Are you channeling Lucy or what?"

They remained silent as the waitress put their burgers and fries on the table, informing them the ketchup was in the carousel.

By the time she'd stepped away, Lou was grinning. "I'm going to kill some Albanians."

"Of course you are. With that much *glee* on your face, it's probably a lot of them. Is it a gang thing? Your Italian stallion ask for your help in settling a turf war or something?"

"He needs my help, but he didn't ask for it."

"Oh, he has a problem asking for help too, huh?" Piper snorted. "Who does that remind you of?"

19

fter the fourth phone call in a row, King was getting a headache. He wondered if this was what getting old was like. He remembered a time when he could spend a whole day updating case files, working on the computer and doing back-to-back calls like the ones he'd just completed without so much as a dip in energy. Now that he was in his sixties, he felt like his battery was perpetually in need of a recharge.

"Maybe I'm just hungry," he said to the dog whose tail thumped against the floor. "Should we quit for dinner?"

King reached down and gave Lady's ears a good scratch. The dog continued wagging her tail. Overcome by the cuteness, King fished a treat from his pocket and fed it to her.

He gave his to-do list one more look and realized he was at a good stopping point for the day, but he needed to give Lou an update on everything he'd learned before heading out. It was moments like this he wished the woman would just get a cell phone.

"How can someone so young be such a luddite?" he lamented to the dog.

Then King remembered that Piper was with her. Or hiding out in her apartment, anyway. At first he'd assumed this was because of her mother's death. But now, given the way that Dani had been moping in and out of the agency, King wondered if there was something else going on. A lover's tiff, maybe.

Not my circus, not my monkeys, he reminded himself.

And he didn't have the time or energy to worry about it anyway.

He would call Piper, leave a voicemail for Lou—or hell, maybe even catch her—and give the update. Then, within twenty minutes, he'd be home, shoes off, pants undone in front of the TV with his leftover barbeque on his lap.

Better yet, he remembered the St. Louis Blues were playing at seven. Maybe he'd smoke a joint and watch the game.

With a significant uptick in his energy levels, King scrolled through his contacts, found Piper's number, and dialed. It went to voicemail, but that was fine. His aim could still be achieved.

"Hi, this is Piper! I can't come to the phone right now, but you know what to do!"

Beep.

"Hi, P, this message is for Lou, so just hand it over the next time she's around." He paused for the presumed handoff before saying, "Hey, Lou, I just got off the phone with the lab tech Konstantine referred us to. The bag is useless. Turns out it's a major brand found in just about every department store in France, so all they could tell us from the serial and batch numbers was that it had in fact been shipped to Paris, but they couldn't be sure which Monoprix it had ended up at, let alone where it was purchased or a time frame. As for the chemical the perp is using to dissolve the bodies, it's mostly lye. There's some other compound that they're not quite sure what it is yet, but it's the lye doing the work. This is no good for us because lye is in all kinds of things. Soap. Cleaning products, drain cleaner, food preservation, you name it. But in its liquid form, it's very toxic and harmful if you breathe it in, so if you come across someone with a breathing problem, that might be our guy, or, er, *gal*."

Smooth, he thought.

"I also spoke to the director again. I wanted to take a stab and see if maybe there was a connection between Delphine and Assia." Mel passed by the window and King waved. Lady, however, jumped up and ran to the door. King stood from his desk and opened the door to let Lady out. He watched as the dog trotted happily after Mel, following her up the street.

It occurred to him then that they could've asked Mel to help with the French interviews, since she knew more French than either Lou or himself, but he suspected that French and French Creole weren't a direct translation.

"I showed him photos of Assia and asked if he'd seen her around the museum, or if he could check the security footage for her. He freaked out about that, something about"—and here King tried to do a terrible French accent—"'Do you know how many girls her age wander through this museum each hour? Let alone days, weeks, months? And you can't even tell me when you think she was here?'" King dropped the accent. Doing it made his throat hurt. "He also said that they *do* have lye in their restoration department. Something about needing it to fix Roman pottery. I thought that was weird for a contemporary art museum, but then he went on about juxtaposing styles for adding meaning, and honestly, I missed all of that, but the point is, if Delphine and Assia were killed by the same person, there might be a connection to the art museum."

The light was fading through the large glass front windows. King needed to wrap this up.

"Anyway, I just thought you should know that there might be a— albeit thin—connection between Assia and Delphine. Maybe Delphine was an outlier, something happened and the attacker wasn't able to take the body away and dissolve it like they usually did, or maybe—"

The voicemail beeped. "If you're happy with your message, press two. If you'd like to re-record your message—"

King pressed two. Then called Piper again.

"Got cut off there. Anyway, if he attacked Delphine at home, I don't know why he'd run away unless she fought back and the attacker was injured. But good luck calling to see if anyone turned up in the hospital injured that night. A city the size of Paris must see wounds like that every hour of every day. Still, maybe we can check the hospital closest to her house on the night of the attack and see if anything hits. Otherwise, I don't know why he would take off without the body if dissolving them is his MO."

King wasn't even going to try to pronounce the name of Delphine's partner. Instead he said, "The boyfriend didn't come home for two more hours. Oh, and the footage did show him at the Grand Palais. He's on camera almost the entire time except for a three-minute bathroom break around nine. So he probably didn't kill her. Three minutes is a tight fit."

The door to the agency opened again and Dani crossed the threshold with her heels in her hands and her handbag thrown over her shoulder.

King said, "Hey. I'm leaving Piper a message. Want me to pass anything along?"

She gave him a small smile before bending over his desk and scrawling a note on his blank notepad.

He turned the yellow legal pad toward him so he could read it.

"Piper, Dani wanted me to tell you that she's looking for another apartment like you wanted."

King didn't bother to add that Dani had underlined the *you* three times.

He turned to Dani for confirmation, but she was already trudging up the stairs to the apartment above, the door closing behind her.

Definitely trouble in paradise, he thought.

"Well, that's all I've got. Lou, let me know what you want to do next. Piper, I hope that you're doing okay. I haven't heard back from the funeral home yet, so nothing to report there, but when I do, you'll be the first to know."

He terminated the call, pressing the phone into his chin thoughtfully.

This rift between Dani and Piper was putting a kink in King's plan.

He'd been going to offer to host Thanksgiving dinner at his place for the five of them this year—Lou, Piper, Mel, Dani, and himself. He didn't think that Piper had had a good Thanksgiving with her mother in years, but more than that, he knew from experience that holidays after a loss were particularly hard. The lack of someone was keenly felt around a time where the national propaganda pushing *togetherness* and family cheer could drive a person mad. The Thanksgiving dinner was going to be the first of many efforts to make sure that Piper didn't feel alone this holiday season.

But now, maybe he should check with Piper before he invited Dani? It would feel weird to exclude the girl, given how she'd become as entrenched in their team as Piper and Lou. They were a set, the five of them—and as much as he hated the idea of being cozy with a crime boss, Konstantine was also becoming a permanent fixture.

But he needed more time with that idea.

Then again, Dani had family in the area, parents and extended, from what he'd gathered, so maybe she already had plans.

One problem at a time, he chided himself.

Right now, dinner.

King tidied up his desk and shut down his computer for the day. He checked to make sure the coffee pot was clean, turned off, and gave the place one appraising look-over before stepping out into the sunny street and locking the door behind him.

"Robbie," a voice called.

King pulled his key from the lock and turned toward the voice.

It was Beth. Today she wore a deep purple pantsuit with golden hoop earrings. Her smile was bright as she looked over the rim of her glasses at him.

"Why, hello," King said reflexively, noting distantly how a dizzy sensation flooded his head. "What brings you down here?"

"I was three blocks away at the precinct for an interview and I thought, you know what I'd like? *A muffuletta.* And there was a sale, buy one get one free, and I thought, now who would I like to eat this with? Why, Robbie King, if he's available."

She smiled, and King's plans for leftover barbeque evaporated.

"How do you feel about hockey?" he asked.

"I love to watch sports as a general rule. Basketball is my favorite, particularly the WNBA, but there isn't a good game on tonight, so hockey will do."

"Come on then. Here, let me carry that."

King took the sandwich bag and watched Beth fall into step beside him. It wasn't lost on him, the way his stomach fluttered as they continued down Royal Street in the direction of the shop.

"Do you live far from here?" she asked. "I knew you walked so I assumed it was close."

They turned a corner to find a pack of unwashed hipsters with a set of pots and an accordion, remixing a song by The Strokes. He could smell the alcohol rolling off of them from here.

"Very close," King said, placing one hand on the horse-head post to inspect his shoes. "My apartment is above Melandra's shop."

Beth's eyebrows rose. "Oh. How interesting."

As they crossed the threshold into Madame Melandra's Fortunes and Fixes, the chandelier overhead moaned eerily, giving the impression that a ghost had swooped down from the ceiling and was circling over their heads. The air was saturated with incense, a deep, earthy sandalwood permeating everything. Mel was clearly close to closing up for the day, with all the candles restocked and figurines in order.

She was sweeping the floor when they entered, bending to scoop the dust into the white pan she held in one fist.

"Good evening," King called out.

"Good evening, Mr. King," she said without looking up.

When she did straighten up, she saw Beth.

Her eyebrows rose a little. "Why hello there, Ms. Miller. What brings you here? Candles? Fortune-telling, perhaps?"

Beth only smiled. The overhead light caught on the gold beads in her hair and sparked.

"I've come to watch hockey," Beth said. "But I must say, your shop is beautiful. Very well put together. I can tell you've worked hard on it."

Melandra's smile beamed a little brighter. "Thank you. I have."

"And I was so sorry to hear that your bastard of an ex-husband went missing in prison. I hope you don't mind me saying, but after what he put you through, I hope he turns up dead."

Mel and King exchanged a quick look.

Neither of them were worried about Terrence showing up unannounced and causing any more havoc in their lives. The man had earned a one-way trip to La Loon, and had left the prison in the company of Louie Thorne. They knew he wouldn't bother anyone ever again.

"Yes, well, let go and let God." Mel dumped the dust into the waste bin and tapped it against the rim for good measure. "Who's playing tonight?"

"The Blues," King said.

"Ah, your hometown. Well, you two enjoy yourselves then."

And if King didn't know better, Melandra's devilish wink was directed at Beth and not him. But Beth was giving Lady's ears a good scratch—whether she saw this wink or was hiding her face, King couldn't tell.

"Thanks, you too," he said cautiously, and crossed to the stairs.

As he approached his door, King ran a mental checklist of whether or not his apartment was fit for company. No dirty socks in the living room or dishes on the countertop. Had he made anything smelly to eat? No. He hadn't cooked in at least two days.

With a deep breath, he opened his door and motioned for Beth to step inside.

Over her shoulder, he made a quick, panicked appraisal. But the kitchen was clean and the living room tidy.

As he put the sandwich bag on the island counter, he peeked into his bedroom to make sure his bed was made and there was nothing embarrassing to be found, like his underwear on the floor.

He was in luck. All clear.

"Oh, this is nice! I wasn't sure what to expect. French Quarter apartments can go either way. They can be really nice, or really *not*," Beth said. "But this is very well done. And it's the perfect size for you."

"Yeah, I really like it," King said, and he did. The large living room with its red leather sofa and enormous coffee table. The checkered kitchen and gray countertops. The bedroom big enough for his king-sized bed. It was true that the bathroom was a tad small for a man of his size, but it was clean and had a shower, tub, and sink that all worked. What else did he need?

"It's the balcony I love," he told her.

Without waiting to be asked, Beth crossed the living room and opened the balcony door. She stepped outside and cooed her appreciation as King fished out two plates from the cabinet and arranged the sandwiches and chips onto them.

"Do you want to eat out here or inside?" she asked.

"It's a little chilly to eat outside. Let's eat in the living room if that's fine by you," he called. "Do you want water or a soda? I'm afraid I don't have much else in the house."

"I'll have whatever you're drinking."

She came back into the apartment and shut the door.

"Robert King." She sniffed. "Do I smell ganja in here?"

King froze, his hand on the handle of the refrigerator.

He considered lying to her, but he knew instantly that would never work.

She continued sniffing the air, reminding him for a horrible moment of Lady.

"I definitely smell—ah, yes." She bent down in front of his vinyl collection and began thumbing through them. It wasn't until she found the Bob Dylan record did she whistle.

She opened it up, and there was his small, very old, very stale stash of weed.

"Am I going to go to jail for that?" King sat the sandwich plates down on the coffee table.

She arched a brow. "For less than a gram? You've got one, maybe two joints here? Do you think I have time to prosecute someone for two joints?"

He was well aware of her case load. "No. No, I don't think you do."

She sniffed the plastic bag again. "And by the look of it, you've had this for a *very* long time. I'm guessing that you don't smoke often."

"No, I don't. But you're very knowledgeable about weed."

"I'm the DA," she said. "And I raised a teenage son."

She closed the vinyl and slid it back into the stack with the other records.

"Oh, you have Cooke's *Ain't That Good News* and *Portrait of a Legend*."

She slid *Portrait of a Legend* out of its sleeve and put it on the player.

The music whined to life just after. She began to dance slowly to its rhythm, and King sank onto the sofa.

Watching her dance, one hand on her belly, the other held up as if in testament as she swayed slowly back and forth, he realized he'd missed having company. A woman's company.

More than that, he liked Beth very much.

"I like it when you look at me that way," she said, finally sitting down on the sofa beside him.

"I like to look," he admitted.

"Do you? That's nice to hear." Her braids clacked as she gathered them in her hand and slid them over one shoulder before leaning forward and grabbing her sandwich plate. "To be honest, I was worried I'd scared you off the other day. When you'd said, 'Thanks for the offer, let me think about it,' I thought that might be code for 'Get me the hell outta here.'"

King laughed. "I don't usually speak in codes."

"No, you don't." She smiled at him again, this time over her plate as she ate another chip. "I like that about you. You're direct but you're also kind. A lot of people call themselves blunt when really they're just jerks. You're no jerk."

His face was growing hot.

She wrinkled her nose. "And you're cute as can be when you blush."

"Thank you." King shoved half of the muffuletta in his mouth to prevent himself saying anything.

"Did you have a chance to consider my offer?" she asked, slipping another chip into her mouth.

King didn't know what to say. Should he tell her that yes, he had? It had crossed his mind, on and off again in the days since they'd last talked. And when he had let his mind run through its daydreams, its fantasies, he couldn't deny that Beth was a beautiful woman.

He respected the hell out of her, and he'd believed her when she'd said that should this sour in any way, it wouldn't affect his work.

"I can't promise anything," he said. "I'm not at my full...emotional capacity."

Her brow furrowed. "Yes. I remember you telling me about Lucy."

King started. "Did I tell you her name?"

"No," she said, and pointed at the urn on the edge of the coffee table. "She's right there."

Dear God. King hadn't even seen it. First he'd been concerned with not spilling their plates and then he'd been watching Beth dance slowly, sensually, in his living room.

I was watching her, while Lucy was right there.

Because in the far corner of the table was the silver urn with Lucy's name etched into the shining metal.

Lucy Catherine Thorne.

An invisible belt tightened around King's chest, and on its heels, an undeniable wave of guilt. *How can I even think about this, about moving on, when she's—*

Don't be stupid, a voice said. *Lucy doesn't give a shit about that. And that's not even her. That's a pile of ash.*

He wasn't sure how long he'd been staring at the urn when he felt a warm hand on his knee and a gentle squeeze.

"I'm sorry," he said, tearing his eyes away. "I don't mean to kill the mood."

She shook her head. "Nothing to apologize for."

"This can't be what you had in mind when you came over with sandwiches."

She smiled. "If you think I'm put off because you have an actual real-life beating heart, Robbie, you're mistaken. I'm still interested, though not tonight. And not here because I suspect this was the last place the two of you were together, am I correct?"

She was.

She nodded, silently considering something. Finally, she said, "My place it is, then. Tomorrow night when you get off work. You bring the dinner this time."

She gave him her address.

"But—"

She held up her hand. "It's an open invitation. If you want to come, come. If you don't, I'll know perfectly well why. There'll be no hard feelings. I swear it."

King let this thought settle in.

"What about tonight?" he asked, as the first Sam Cooke song ended and the second began to play.

She reached for the remote and turned it to the sports channel. "Tonight, let's watch this hockey game."

20

———————

Lou stood in the space beneath her kitchen island and surveyed her arsenal. The room smelled of sawdust and plywood. And it was warmer than the apartment above. The shelves held guns, ammo, grenades, blades. A machete the size of her arm was propped up in a corner. Hooks screwed into the wall held a flamethrower and two bulletproof vests.

As she looked over her options for the night ahead, she couldn't remember the last time she'd been *excited*. The promise of a fight, bloody violence, and even the possibility of death made her limbs itch.

She shrugged on a tactical vest with throat and bicep protectors. This would be her first time trying it in a fight, since usually she went with as little coverage as possible to keep her movements loose. When Melandra had accidentally shot her through the shoulder and Lou almost died, she'd quickly grown tired of listening to Piper, King, and even Konstantine complain about her need to upgrade her gear.

So she'd try the new guards tonight, but if it was too hard to move with them on, they were coming off. She added Kevlar sleeves to her forearms and an extra layer of protection to rest across her quads. But she decided against anything for her lower legs. The thick leather boots that went halfway up her calves felt like enough.

After the armor was in place, she chose the Brownings from the shelf, loaded them, and slipped them into the holsters hugging her ribs. Twin Glocks went into her thigh holsters.

She thought about packing more guns, but the truth was, her targets would have guns, and if she needed to, she could take them off their corpses. What she couldn't materialize from thin air was ammo. So instead of adding another holster, she wrapped two ammo belts across her torso. On each hip, she added grenades and enough .40 S&W cartridges for the handguns.

Lastly, she pulled her new Benelli M3 Super 90 off the shelf. This was also a new gun that she'd gotten only because Konstantine thought she'd like it. She would've ignored this assumption if not for two facts. The first was that Konstantine was one of the few people who'd seen her fight and lived to tell the tale, so perhaps he did know something about her tastes. Second, he'd been right about the Brownings, which she'd been favoring over her Berettas since he'd given them to her.

So fine. She'd take the Benelli shotgun tonight and see how it did.

This is enough to get started, she thought. If she ran out of guns and ammo, she could always come back. That was one of the many advantages that she had. A quick sidestep through darkness and she could grab more guns or ammo. Though she admitted, if only to herself, that she hated leaving the heat of battle once she was in it.

With her arsenal locked away again, the hidden latch on her kitchen island secured, she stood fully armored and ready in her apartment. The orange-pink hues of sunset spilled across her wooden floors as she gave the St. Louis skyline one last lingering look. The high-rise buildings and metal arch looked golden in the last collected light of the day. The water shimmered, sparking white and blue as a small speed boat pushed north against the current.

Lou was happy. She felt steady. At peace.

Lucy sprang to mind. Aunt Lucy as she'd been on the Hawaiian beach just hours before she'd died, with her long hair spilling over one shoulder.

I just want you to be happy, Louie. At peace.

Probably not what you had in mind, Lou thought with a smile, knowing that Lucy was far beyond caring what she did now. *But I am happy.*

A crow flew past her window, calling out.

Lou took this as a good sign.

She took one more deep breath.

Her lungs found resistance from the body armor, but she liked the compression.

With a smile, she shut herself up in her empty linen closet, the shotgun pointing upward to fit in the space.

For a moment there was only the sound of her breath in the softening dark. The slow exhalation of moist air from between her lips.

Erjon Hysa, she thought. *Where are you?*

Because while Stefano had referred to them collectively—the Albanians—there were in fact more than twenty crime families that controlled organized crime throughout Europe, the Americas, and Asia. And even if Stefano hadn't used his name, Lou knew exactly which of the families were on friendly terms with Vittoria.

Lou had made it her business to know. The way that some grandmothers followed the lives of soap opera characters, Lou had made a study of the world's crime factions for years.

Erjon Hysa's clan, the largest and most dangerous family clan, had crossed Lou's radar before, when she'd been looking for Angelo. Lou had passed him by at the time because instead of trafficking drugs, Erjon's crew focused on humans and human organs.

Luckily for Erjon, until very recently, Lou'd had other interests.

Her plan for tonight was simple. She would destroy Erjon's clan and anyone that might take up his cause against Konstantine when he was gone.

Revenge killings, after all, were a given unless Lou made sure there was no one who could seek revenge.

Erjon was the most important target, given that he was kyre, their patriarchal leader, but Lou would kill the kryetars, the underbosses, too, if she had the chance.

Erjon Hysa. And anyone who poses a threat to Konstantine, she told her compass. "All of them."

The compass responded in kind, whirling, clicking, searching the other side of the ocean.

It snapped into place, a sharp tug, a certainty recoiling through her.

The shadows swelled, shifted, and with one step toward a closet wall she'd never reach, Lou found herself in an enormous house.

The ceiling was at least sixteen feet above her head. She looked up, noting the stained glass. The dark, silent staircases.

From an adjacent hall, a man in a bathrobe pattered slowly across the marble floor with half a sandwich—or something that looked like a sandwich—in his mouth.

She thought he would simply walk by without noticing her, but then he did.

He looked once, then again in shock, his eyes doubling and tripling in size. He opened his mouth to scream but choked on his own midnight snack.

Lou didn't wait.

She pumped the shotgun once and fired, blasting a hole through the man's side. He hit the floor, dropping hard and fast.

The food—Lou could see it was a fried pasty now, and it made her think of calzones—splattered across the marble floor.

Blood pumped out of him at an alarming rate, spreading in a rapidly growing pool. But the man wasn't dead.

Lou crossed the floor and bent over him, giving him a good once-over. It wasn't Erjon. An underling then, because Lou never questioned her compass.

She pumped the shotgun again.

"No—" he began, but she pulled the trigger, spraying his brains across the floor.

Where is he? Where is Erjon?

Someone was yelling upstairs. The voice carried down to Lou, words she didn't understand.

Lights in the house began to click on, bright and infuriating. The shotgun blast had been too loud. But if she was being honest with herself, she'd wanted to wake the house. She wanted to spur them all to action. The bigger, the better.

Sneaking through each room, quietly dispatching her targets, wouldn't have been fun at all.

Where's Erjon?

A sharp tug to the right, toward the staircase leading upstairs. A bullet whirred past her head, biting into the wooden door behind her. She looked up to find four men on the balcony above taking aim.

She pumped the shotgun and fired three times. Three men tumbled over the railing and crashed to the floor below.

She realized that if she really wanted to fight a large group at once, the Benelli's pump setting was too slow.

Let's speed things up.

She converted the gun to its semi-automatic setting and reloaded it with as many shells as she could fit into it.

Footsteps rushed toward her. *A lot* of feet.

She smiled. *Much better.*

She chambered a round.

She couldn't stay here, where she was exposed. She could be shot from all sides, even from above. Not to mention that now that the lights in the house were turning on one after another, she was losing precious ground.

Lou stepped into the shadow cast by the staircase and slipped. In place of the staircases and foyer, Lou was above now, looking down.

No sooner had she settled onto the landing above did six men run into the foyer from the right doorway and eight from the left. A few stepped into view from beneath the balcony's landing, but she couldn't see them clearly without stepping into the light. But there must be more footmen beneath her. She could hear them, if not see them.

Still, she had plenty of targets to be getting on with.

She pulled the trigger again and again and again, moving from right to left, her aim to kill fourteen new targets.

Her excitement grew as each new head split open, throats spurted, and men doubled over as if socked in the gut.

The semi-automatic setting was *definitely* better.

But her gun clicked, empty. She needed to reload.

Resting the shotgun against a shoulder, she pulled a Browning and fired. The first two bullets blasted through one man's cheek and out the back of his head, splattering the front door with brains. The next three bullets caught two men in the back, between the shoulder blades, as they began to flee. They hit the ground face first, unmoving.

She stepped away from the railing and reloaded the shotgun as a fresh shower of bullets blew apart the wooden bannister. Then the landing was assaulted, holes punching open in the floor at her feet and the wall by her head.

They were shooting through the floor from below, trying to use it as cover for her return fire.

A bullet blasted through the front of Lou's boot, tearing a hole in the leather, barely missing her toes.

She swore and stepped into the room behind her. A bathroom, dim and vacant.

She leaned across the bath and turned on the water, letting it run into the plugged tub.

Just in case, she thought, should she need an exit to La Loon. Perhaps with the infamous Erjon in tow. Though climbing into tubs with corpses wasn't her *favorite* thing.

She shut the bathroom door loudly, hoping to give them the impression that she'd retreated inside, cornered and helpless.

Yet in the thin patch of shadow behind the bathroom's door she asked again, *Erjon Hysa, come out, come out, wherever you are.*

She stepped forward.

When the world reformed again, she was in a closet. Albeit the largest closet Lou had ever seen, the size of her living room perhaps, with clothes running along two opposing walls. Lou's compass clicked, and it wasn't mistaken.

He was here.

She crept forward, looking for feet beneath the hanging garments. But many of these had shoes stacked neatly beneath them, and discerning an empty shoe from one containing a foot wasn't so easy.

Come on out.

You know you want to.

More gunfire spattered in the distance. After a short silence, feet pounded up the stairs, the shouting growing louder. Then there was banging on a closed door.

They hadn't realized she'd left the bathroom yet. Good. That gave her plenty of time to deal with Erjon. And it wasn't lost on her that he probably wanted to cry out, to tell them that she was here in his closet, not in the bathroom, but to do so would sign his death warrant.

Lou kept her eyes on the clothes, every item perfectly still, betraying no movement.

She passed silk shirts and pants hanging in plastic wrappings.

Her navel contracted suddenly, and at the same time, a metallic scraping screeched over her right shoulder.

She dropped, turned, and fired.

The shot missed, punching a hole in the back wall.

Erjon shouted and kicked out. She moved, and instead of a foot to the face, the hit landed hard on her left shoulder. Her weight folded on that side, the shotgun clattering to the floor. Without thinking, Lou kicked out her right leg and struck his charging body. His knee folded, bringing him down into a crouch.

Then she was on her feet again, thrusting the butt of the shotgun up, connecting with his chin.

He fell flat on his back, and Lou could've ended it right there. Just bent over and shot him in the face.

But she was enjoying herself. Relishing the way her whole body felt alive with adrenaline.

So she let Erjon sit up, only watched him with the shotgun propped against one shoulder as he touched his mouth tenderly and rolled his eyes up to meet hers.

He was shirtless, with his hair hanging in his face, his chest heaving.

"It's you. It's really you," he panted, blood running from the corner of his mouth. His eyes widened to the size of half-dollars. "I thought you were a bullshit rumor that he spread to protect himself."

"Nope." Lou repositioned the shotgun.

"No, please." Erjon came up onto his knees, holding his hands out in front of him in a defensive posture, as if this could hold her back. "Please. Tell Konstantine that I won't—"

Lou pulled the trigger and blasted a hole through Erjon's chest. The man was blown back onto the floor of the closet, crumpling against the far wall. His wide eyes rested open and unseeing on the closet's ceiling.

A door banged open and Lou turned in time to find two men crowd the doorway to the closet. Cries rang out as they saw Erjon's bloodied corpse spread out on the floor.

Lou shot each, knocking them back, before shoving aside a line of silk shirts and stepping through the dark.

When she found footing again the upper hallway was cleared. The door to the bathroom she'd used now stood open, water still spilling from the faucet into the tub, overflowing onto the floor.

She listened. But apart from the running water, the house was quiet.

Almost quiet.

Somewhere, a child was crying.

Lou took the opposite hall, slowly checking corners and nooks as she passed. It wasn't until she found the bedroom at the far end of the hallway that the crying grew clear.

She pushed open the door and found a little girl's bedroom, all pinks and soft whites. A canopy bed drowned in stuffed animals.

Lou opened the closet and inside found a woman clutching a crying girl to her chest.

The woman took one look at Lou with the shotgun and began to plead.

"Please. Please, no."

Will they come after Konstantine? she asked her inner compass.

The compass remained still, quiet. Lou was more than a little relieved by that.

"I won't hurt you," she said, and disappeared without firing a single shot.

Lou found six more men on the estate and shot them dead. The two she'd left unharmed in the closet were the only survivors.

She considered going back for Erjon's body.

It seemed like a waste, not to use Erjon's big, beautiful tub to take at least one body to La Loon, but her whirling compass told her that her job wasn't done.

This house had been cleared, Erjon's immediate entourage extinguished. But there were others.

Extended members of the Hysa clan that would take up his work now that Erjon was gone.

Lou took a moment in the silent house to reload her guns and survey the carnage of the half-destroyed mansion.

Then she asked, *Who's next?*

The shadows swallowed her.

One man was halfway through a blow job when Lou stepped into his dark bedroom and pressed the shotgun into the side of his head. His eyes didn't even flutter fully open before she pulled the trigger and disappeared.

A second had been standing on his patio, smoking a cigarette and drinking coffee.

Lou's first bullet exploded the cup. The second split his skull in half, his bathrobe falling open to reveal his corpulent body as it hit the paving stones.

Who? Who? Who? she asked the compass inside her. And each time it delivered her.

One man was bent over his breakfast table, shoveling eggs into his mouth, a newspaper spread in front of him, when Lou stepped out of his pantry and pressed the gun to the back of his head.

Another had been out for a morning walk with his dog, spouting orders into his cell phone as a cigarette bobbed between his loose lips.

Lou stepped out from a hedge to meet him.

The moment he saw her, the cigarette fell from his lips.

She pulled the trigger and the shotgun clicked empty. No problem. The Browning worked fine.

The dog, scared by the shot, had taken off across the park, tail tucked between his legs, without looking back.

She caught two men in a car together, and here she began to feel *really* nostalgic. She'd finally caught Angelo in a car like this, blowing out his driver's brains as the car sank to the bottom of the bay.

So now a small laugh escaped her as she materialized in the front passenger seat and found a startled driver gripping the wheel.

The two men in the back sat up straighter, coming alive with the alarm ricocheting through their bodies. Lou's compass snagged as she turned the gun on each, so she put a bullet in each of their heads. The driver was trying to find a gun under his seat, but driving the vehicle and reaching for it wasn't proving possible. Lou ended his struggle with a quick *tap-tap* from her Browning, knocking his head against the window. It shattered, creating a spiderweb pattern on impact.

She was out of the car before it crossed the road's painted lines and slammed into a road sign.

One more, she thought as her compass snagged for a final time. *There's one more.* Her compass was sure of it.

But when she materialized this time, a spray of bullets hit her.

Four, five, six, seven.

Click. Click. Click.

Lou's chest hurt where the vest had absorbed the force of the bullets. When she opened her eyes she found an older man, perhaps King's age, reloading his pistol with shaking hands.

Lou aimed the shotgun, but another wild, panicked bullet cut through her forearm. Then one slammed into the bicep cover and a third clipped her hip as she moved to evade the shots.

When his gun clicked empty for a second time, he was screaming.

She didn't understand all the words falling rapid fire from his lips. Either he was begging, swearing, or cursing her name.

It didn't matter. Her bullet went through his brains just the same, knocking him back over a desk to the floor behind it.

When the room rang silent with the report from her shot, she waited.

But the compass was still. The urge to move fading within her. She went around the desk to check that the man was truly dead, and he was.

He lay on his stomach, his head turned to the left, the eyes open and unseeing. The gun had fallen from his hand and lay a few inches away.

Lou waited for the compass to whirl again, to tell her who the next target was.

It remained still. There was no pull, no longing.

The job was done.

21

"*ì, sì. Grazie.*" Vittoria terminated the call with shaking fingers. Her hand clenched and relaxed around her cell phone compulsively.

What should I do? Cosa faccio adesso?

"What's happened?" Alessandra came to sit beside her on the sofa, the fireplace lighting up half of her face. "*Dimmi cos'è successo.*"

Vittoria forced herself to set the phone down. "The Hysa clan is dead."

"Erjon is dead?" Alessandra's eyes searched her face as she took Vittoria's hand.

Vittoria pulled away.

"Erjon. Dren. Guzim. Ilir. *Everyone.*" Even the bastards who were sixth and seventh down the line. *La Strega* did good work. She'd left no one. "Only Yeta and Afrodita survived."

Alessandra fell back as if struck. "Who would do such a thing?"

She grabbed a pillow from the sofa and pulled it against her hair.

"*Dio mio.* Do you think it was *La Strega?*"

"Of course it was *La Strega.*" *You idiot.*

Vittoria usually loved Alessandra's eyes. For their warmth, for their bright innocence. But now, doubled in size, she looked like a cow-eyed moron.

No, she thought. *I'm the one who has been stupid. Very, very stupid.*

She'd miscalculated.

Why had she thought that she could use the woman as Konstantine had?

Why had she thought that Konstantine could simply ask her for help and that his refusal to do so was merely possessiveness? A reluctance to share his power.

He had an asset, an ally, and wanted to keep it to himself.

And all that bullshit about *I don't own her, I don't command her* was just some diplomatic way of telling Vittoria no. Or perhaps even that the rumors of Konstantine's style were true.

That he was kinder to women, more respectful than most of the men in their profession.

None of that mattered now.

What mattered was that Hysa's clan was dead and Yeta and Afrodita had clearly described a wraith of a woman with a shotgun and mirrors for eyes.

Erjon threatened Konstantine, and *La Strega* destroyed him completely.

Will she see me as a threat too? How will I convince her otherwise?

Vittoria threw her phone onto the table and it landed with a crack.

Alessandra gasped.

"Don't be dramatic," Vittoria said, pressing her fingers into her temples. She was getting a headache. "It didn't break."

But when Vittoria lifted her eyes, it wasn't Alessandra staring down at her.

It was her. *La Strega.*

She was already here, and she was pulling Alessandra over the back of the sofa by her hair.

"*Aspetta! Aspetta!*" Vittoria was on her feet, clearing the table and chairs to meet Lou where she stood. The living room was softly lit with morning light, but even as the shadows receded, there was still enough darkness to give *La Strega* the advantage.

Responding to her voice, both Giuseppe and Flavio rushed into the room.

She didn't release Alessandra as she turned and shot both men through the head before refocusing her attention on Vittoria.

More footsteps immediately pounded down the stairs. The cavalry was coming, rushing from the rooms above to Vittoria's rescue.

"Do you want anyone else to die?" *La Strega* asked in English. "I will kill everyone who comes into this room if you don't give me a choice."

And you and you and you. Vittoria's mind snagged on that phrase, repeating it again and again.

"*State tutti fuori!*" she screamed. *Everyone stay out!* "*State tutti fuori!*"

The footsteps faltered. Murmured concern rumbled in the hallway.

"Vittoria," Alessandra whimpered, her hands clasped over those pulling her hair.

"Hush," Vittoria said. To *La Strega*, "What do you want from me? Why are you here?"

Vittoria wished that the woman would lift her mirrored shades so that she didn't have to look at her own scared face. She looked too old in that reflection. Old and helpless.

"I came to give you a message," she said.

"I am listening," Vittoria said. She stood up straighter, trying to return some of the dignity she felt she'd lost.

"If you ever try to manipulate Konstantine again, ask too much of him or—"

"We're family," Vittoria said, raising her chin a little higher. "Our father—"

Lou shoved Alessandra away and grabbed Vittoria by the throat. She had her against the wall, choking, before she could even blink.

Vittoria kicked, clawing at the woman, but it seemed to do nothing. *How is she so strong? She can't be a woman. She can't be.*

Vittoria knew women.

"You look a little like your father, especially when I'm close to you like this. Do you know what I did to your father? Your brothers?"

How could Vittoria forget the reports of the Martinelli curse? As one by one her half-brothers were killed, their bodies never recovered except for Benito's, which had been thrown at her father's feet bloodied and battered.

And then her father, killed.

"Do you want me to show you what I do to a Martinelli when I find one?" the witch asked.

Vittoria wanted power, of course. But she wanted to live long enough to wield it.

"No," she spat out, even as her throat ached under the ruthless grip.

"If you try anything like this again, you won't be his family. You'll be *dead*."

Here the witch smiled, and it sent a sickening shiver through Vittoria. *Satana in persona. È venuta a mangiarmi viva.*

"Did he send you to tell me this?" Vittoria asked.

"He doesn't know I'm here."

"Then why come? You've killed the Hysa family. Why come here and—"

The fingers around her throat tightened. That was answer enough.

La Strega wanted to make it perfectly clear that Vittoria had overstepped. She'd crossed over into the witch's territory, and if she did it again, she would not survive.

Vittoria understood perfectly now. This woman didn't belong to Konstantine. She'd never belonged to Konstantine.

Konstantine belonged to *her*.

"Okay," Vittoria choked out. "I understand. I will not hurt him again. I'm not a threat to him, I promise."

For a moment she didn't move. Then, slowly, she loosened her grip and stepped back.

Alessandra remained on the floor, softly crying.

"Don't give me a reason to visit you again," she said quietly, but before Vittoria could muster a reply, Lou drew her fist back and slammed it across Vittoria's face.

Vittoria cried out and collapsed, catching herself on her hands and knees.

"That's for Matteo."

When Vittoria looked up, cradling her face, the witch was gone.

22

———————

Konstantine sat back in his chair, a frown on his face. It wasn't even noon and the day was shaping up to be *very* strange. The phone in his hand was warm from the back-to-back calls he'd been receiving for nearly an hour now.

Konstantine was still like this, considering the news, when a knock came at his door.

"*Entra.*"

Stefano pushed the door open with one hand, balancing a tray in the other.

He placed the tray on Konstantine's desk, twin espressos on white saucers and a bowl of red grapes in a bowl between them.

"Why are you frowning?" Stefano slid one of the coffees toward him.

"I just received *three* very interesting phone calls," Konstantine said, lifting the little espresso cup to his lips.

Stefano took the other coffee and settled into the chair opposite the desk. "From whom?"

Konstantine took another drink before speaking. "The first call was from the Peçi family. They wanted to know if I *needed* anything?"

Stefano arched a brow. "Was it a threat?"

"No," Konstantine said, returning the cup to its little saucer. "They were very adamant. They want us to know that we're not on bad terms and they look forward to working with us soon. The second call was from the Hoti family. They wanted to know what they could do to broker peace with us."

Stefano was unable to hide his smile behind his espresso cup.

Konstantine cocked his head. "What happened?"

"The Hysa family is dead."

"The *entire* Hysa family?" Konstantine rose up in his seat.

"She spared Erjon's daughter and the girl's mother. Otherwise, yes."

She. Konstantine didn't need to ask who *she* was. Lou.

"Why did she kill them?" *How did she know I had a problem?*

Stefano shrugged. "Maybe she was bored."

"Or maybe you told her our situation."

Stefano said nothing to this. Instead he asked, "Who was the third call from?"

"Vittoria."

Stefano snorted. "What did she want?"

"To tell me that she hopes Matteo is doing well and to apologize for hitting him."

Perhaps Konstantine had not been hallucinating as he'd crossed the palazzo that morning and called his usual hello to the boys playing soccer out front. For the briefest of moments he'd thought he'd seen Matteo, running and laughing amongst the group.

When he'd looked a second time, he had not been there. In fact, the whole pack of boys had run from Konstantine's sight.

He'd thought this was strange, but children were often wild and erratic. He thought perhaps it was a new game, or maybe even they'd done something mischievous, and he would discover what petty offense they'd committed later. But he hadn't considered that the brief sight of Matteo had been anything other than melancholy for the missing boy.

"Also, that his things will be arriving this afternoon." Here Konstantine met Stefano's eyes. "Matteo is here."

"*Sì,*" Stefano said, throwing back the rest of his espresso. With a smack of his lips, he leaned forward and put the empty cup on the tray.

"Did you bring him home?" Konstantine asked.

"No," Stefano said. "Your woman did."

The *snap-pop* of air resounded in Konstantine's ears. When he looked up, Louie was emerging from the dark corner of the office.

As soon as she stepped into the light, he knew exactly what had happened. Blood was splattered across her face and drying across her hands. She still wore her tactical gear, and all the holsters but one were empty. Whatever guns she'd used were either returned to her apartment or ditched in the heat of the moment.

"What's the emergency?" She looked to Stefano first. "I was about to take a shower."

Konstantine opened and closed his fist. "Did you really kill the entire Hysa family?"

Lou shrugged. "I was bored. The case in Paris is taking too long."

Konstantine couldn't hide his skepticism. "How convenient for me that you killed the ones most troublesome for me. I wonder where you got the idea?"

He cut his eyes to Stefano. The bastard didn't even have the decency to hide his smile.

A little head peeked into the office through the window in the door.

"Hey! *Vieni qui adesso!*" Konstantine called out.

The door handle turned slowly and Matteo stuck his head inside. "*Sì?*"

Konstantine motioned him forward. "*Vieni qui.*"

Matteo looked like he'd rather do anything else, but slowly he passed between where Stefano sat and Louie stood to arrive before Konstantine.

"Where did she hurt you?" he asked.

Matteo threw an accusing look at Stefano.

"*Stronzetto. Non ho detto niente.*"

"Liar," the boy said in English.

Stefano threw up his hands.

"He didn't tell me," Konstantine assured him, realizing not for the first time how big his hands were on the boy's arm. *He's still a child. A child.* "Vittoria called this morning to say she was sorry."

Matteo whirled to look at Lou. She returned his smile and Matteo laughed.

"Show me," Konstantine said again.

Slowly Matteo turned and lifted his shirt.

On his back were two long welts, red and angry. There were also tape marks. Someone had cleaned him up, and he was glad for that.

One welt had begun to scab. Clearly Vittoria had broken the skin. The other was puffy and turning purple with a forming bruise, but the skin was unbroken.

A quiet rage filled him as he pulled the shirt back down.

"Did she pay for this?" Konstantine asked, cutting his eyes up to Lou's.

"I killed a few of her people."

"How many?"

"Three, I think. And I punched her in the face."

Stefano snorted.

"It wasn't enough, in my opinion," Lou said.

Konstantine agreed, and yet he was glad that she hadn't killed Vittoria. Despite the problems between them, maintaining a unified front helped him to control the older, more powerful families in Italy, those who still respected the Martinelli name.

Konstantine turned Matteo around to face him.

"I'm sorry that—"

"*Questi sono per te. Guarda! Guarda!*" Matteo pointed frantically at the stack of comic books that Konstantine had pushed to the corner of his desk when arriving that morning. He hadn't had long to contemplate them before the first of those bewildering phone calls had come through.

"What is it?" Konstantine accepted the book Matteo thrust into his hand.

He watched as the boy flipped through the pages, looking for something. Then he was pointing at the cramped writing filling the white spaces between the comic panels.

"*Ho scritto tutto, tutti i suoi segreti,*" he said proudly.

Lou placed a hand on the boy's head. "You have a spy."

Matteo visibly preened at her touch.

"Is this what she whipped you for?"

"No, she whipped him because she wanted you to send me," Lou said.

Konstantine put the book down and pulled Matteo into his arms. He squeezed him, hard, before placing a kiss on his cheek. "Bravo il mio ragazzo. Sono così orgoglioso di te." *I'm proud of you.*

And Konstantine remembered the first time Padre Leo had held him up like this, squeezed him tightly and said he was proud. It was a different office, many years past, but he hoped it comforted Matteo as much as Padre's kind words had comforted him.

Then he released him and patted his cheeks.

"Now both of you, get out of here." Konstantine pointed at the door. Stefano rose and motioned for Matteo.

Before the office door closed, Stefano turned to Lou.

And bowed.

Shock vibrated through Konstantine's mind. *What the hell—*

Then the door closed and they were alone.

"I—" he began, and didn't get far.

A blade pressed against his throat. He stopped breathing.

Louie Thorne stood over him, a knife in her right hand, her gaze bare and cold.

"The next time you send a child instead of me, it will be the last thing you do." She tilted her head. "*Capisci?*"

When he didn't respond immediately, the blade cut the skin under his jaw. It burned, warm blood welling up to meet the steel.

"*Ho capito,*" he said.

She took the blade and stabbed it into the desktop.

Then her lips were on his throat, licking, kissing the wound.

He slid his hands into her hair, pulling her face up to his.

"I'm sorry," he said, and fell into the kissing, a collision of lips and hunger. His fingers couldn't work at the armor fast enough. All that Velcro ripping apart as he removed layer after layer from her body, until he finally found her bare skin beneath.

It excited him to taste his blood on her tongue, electricity sparking along his skin.

Then she was leaning her weight against his, forcing the chair farther and farther back.

He resisted, rising up instead and seizing her. One shove and he sent the coffee tray skittering off the desk and onto the floor. The comic books followed.

Then her legs were hooking around him where he stood, pinning him against her.

"Why did you do it?" he asked. He kissed her throat, her neck.

"Why do you do it for me?" she asked, pulling off the holsters, the Kevlar sleeves.

"Because I—" He searched her face. *I love you.* "I always want to help you."

Down to her t-shirt and pants, she looked up at him. "I only did what you would've done for me."

A swell of relief washed over him.

"They're really dead? All of them."

She smiled. "Very, *very* dead."

No war. At least not today.

And Matteo was home with him.

He was glad that Lou had disciplined Vittoria in his place. He wasn't sure he'd have had the restraint to stop from really hurting her.

He was furious, and yet...*yet* he couldn't hold on to it.

Not with Lou kissing him, pulling his shirt over his head, running her hands down his bare chest. Not when she was pulling at the belt around his hips.

He pulled her shirt off and pushed her back onto the desk so that he could remove her boots.

"I'm covered in blood," she said.

"I don't care."

"And probably brains."

"I. Really. Don't. *Care*," he said. "And I took off my shirt."

This made her laugh.

"What?"

"As long as your clothes are clean."

He seized her mouth with his, swallowing her laugh.

Then he was inside her. She contracted, then relaxed, her legs wrapping around him, pulling him deeper inside and holding him there.

He was suddenly very glad this desk was large and sturdy, given the abuse it was now withstanding.

Her nails raked up his back and she pressed her face into the side of his throat.

She moaned into his ear, causing his rhythm to falter.

"Don't you fucking *dare*," she whispered.

Konstantine flicked his eyes up, remembering for a moment the window in the office door. Blessedly, Stefano had pulled the shade on his way out.

Good friend.

Lou's rhythm changed suddenly. She grew very still, her hold on him tightening and the breathing in his ear closer to a pant.

He felt her contract a moment before a flood of heat and wetness washed over him.

Then she bit him, hard. That was enough to send him over the edge.

But she didn't let him go immediately. He was forced to stand there, still inside her, supported only by his unsteady legs.

"You can always ask me," she whispered against his neck.

He kissed her forehead, resting his weight against her for support.

"You don't owe me anything," he said.

It might be true that he had stepped in to assist her several times over the years. That when it came to protecting her friends in New Orleans, or protecting her anonymity, he'd done all he could without question. But how could that compare to what she'd given him?

Even now, just to be with her, to look on her face, into those golden eyes full of mischief and slaked lust. To kiss her flushed, warm cheeks.

"Maybe I like it when you owe me," she said. And began to gently rock against him again.

23

───────────

Piper woke to the sound of Lou singing in the shower.

Lou.

Singing.

"What is happening?" she murmured to the pillows as she squinted through the light—*God, why is there so much light in this room?* Had Lou never heard of curtains?

Lou kept humming the happy tune that Piper couldn't quite place, even after she'd dressed and had come into the living room to dry and brush her hair.

Piper sat up on her elbows in the bed. "Seriously, what is going on?"

Lou paused with the towel in her hair. "What?"

"Are...are you in a *good mood?*"

Lou smiled.

"Did you just get laid or did you catch the Paris killer?"

"No to the Paris killer."

Piper didn't miss that she'd avoided the sex question altogether. "Okay, if you didn't catch the killer, who did you kill?"

"Some mafia."

"Ah, okay." Piper stretched her hands over her head. "Big firefight, lots of bodies. No wonder you're cheerful. I'm going to need coffee before I join this revelry."

Lou pointed at the Styrofoam cups on the countertop.

Piper practically purred as she leapt out of the bed and seized one. Since one was black and the other the color of caramel, Piper didn't even have to ask which was hers.

"Oh yes. Yes, *very* nice." She took a big drink, and that pleasant tingling sensation washed over her body, warming her from the inside out. "Mmmm."

She took another sip, closing her eyes to fully enjoy it.

"Do you want to look for bones with me?"

Piper peeked one eye open to find that Lou had abandoned the comb in favor of two pairs of night-vision googles. She was examining the lenses and adjusting the head straps.

"Of all the weird things you say to me, man." Piper rolled her neck, and it cracked up each side. "But yes, I'd like to dig up dead people with you. Why not? I have nothing else planned today."

Piper had been filling the quiet hours in Lou's apartment with her homework and was nearly caught up. She just had one paper left for her psychology course, and that one wasn't even technically late. It was due tomorrow.

"Not dead *people*," Lou corrected. With the goggles tightened around her face she looked alien and insectile. "There are only bones left."

Piper chose to continue sipping her coffee rather than split hairs with her over what constitutes a dead *person*. "What are we going to do with the bones once we find them?"

"Drop them in public places so they can be found. I've already done this twice, and that went well. At least, the police were notified. The story hasn't broken publicly yet though, so I need to bring more up to the surface."

"How many?"

"As many as it takes to get them moving on the case."

"Wait." Piper choked on her coffee. "Aren't there like thousands of CCTV cameras in Paris?"

"Konstantine is going to hack the system at certain times so we can dump them without being recorded. Our first drop is in an hour, so we need to get moving."

Piper arched a brow. "And *when* did you guys work out this plan?"

"This morning."

Piper snorted. "I bet you did."

Lou's face might've been impossible to read, but Piper definitely thought she saw a hint of a smile before Lou had fully turned away.

She definitely got laid. And probably after her killing spree. No wonder she's singing showtunes.

"Of course I'll go with you," Piper said, finally satisfied enough to pry her fingers off of the coffee and set it down. "But it's cold in Paris, right? And we'll be underground?"

"You'll need a coat."

"And I'll layer up." Piper began pulling a t-shirt and sweater out of her clothes pile. "What about breakfast? Oh, can we get crepes first? Pretty, *pretty* please?"

Because Piper seriously doubted that she was going to be able to eat after digging up *not*-bodies all morning. Or at least, she'd definitely lost her appetite the last time she'd helped Lou dig up one of Jeffrey Fish's corpses. Then again, that had been gooey and decomposing.

These would be just bones. That might still be freaky though.

"If we make it quick and go *now*. Otherwise, we'll miss our drop-off times."

"I'm going to get a dessert crepe and a savory one. What about you?"

"Ham and cheese." Lou pulled the goggles off her head.

"And for dessert?"

"I don't need dessert."

"God, come on. Your gift is totally wasted on you if you aren't using it to eat fancy French desserts."

"Fine. I'll get an éclair."

When Piper had first arrived, Lou ate maybe once or twice a day. Now she was getting her into dessert. She'd come so far.

Piper sighed with pride. "That's my girl."

. . .

LOU'S FINGER WORKED THROUGH THE DIRT, TRYING TO GET A GOOD grip on the bone buried there and pull it out. The killer really liked to pack them in. Most of them. Perhaps when the fear of discovery was still alive in their mind, they hoped to make the bones look like the others—ancient relics that had become one with the earth around them.

By the time they'd dumped their latest kills here, as with Assia's bones, their confidence had grown significantly. The newest ones were barely covered with dirt. They were just tucked into the wall, piled as one might pile stones, relying on their natural shape and compression to hold them in place.

Lou grabbed the exposed end of the bone she'd been working on and pulled. It was a sternum, she thought, knocking some of the caked mud off. She put it in her black garbage bag.

The garbage bag wasn't as nice as the canvas bag the killer had been using. But though it was far from the most attractive option, it allowed her to carry several bodies' worth of bones to the surface at once.

And it went with her idea of placing these bone-filled bags near garbage bins around town. It was probably the least conspicuous drop-off she could manage.

They'd filled two bags already, and made those drops in the two-minute window that Konstantine had given her. Now they were working on the third round, both Lou and Piper filling their own bags as efficiently as they could.

"There is an uncomfortable number of spiders down here," Piper said. "I mean, I *like* spiders, but there are *a lot* of them. Do you get what I'm saying? And why are they so big?"

"Just concentrate on filling the bag."

"With spiders? Because I'm absolutely sure there are going to be spiders in this bag."

"Don't fill them heavier than you can carry."

Piper's throat made a sound like a swallowed scream. It was the fifth or sixth time Lou had heard it. "Okay, I'm done with this one. Maybe we should go up now, yeah?"

"You're done?"

"I think these other bones are older. Actually, I might've grabbed one of the old bones by mistake. Should I put it back?"

"No," Lou said. "It won't hurt if they know these bones are coming from the catacombs."

Dirt, old bones—King had said that any of it could lead them down here, and that's what Lou wanted.

Lou turned to find Piper in her night-vision goggles, gathering up her bag and hobbling toward her. She dropped the bag halfway and swatted at her hair, swearing.

The night-vision goggles had been a good idea. Lou felt a little stupid for not having thought of them sooner. It gave her vision in the pitch black, but didn't rob her of her advantage in the dark.

"One more each," she said. "And we'll go up."

Lou dug the last bone she wanted from this part of the wall and watched the dirt cave, filling in the gap she'd made.

It trickled out onto her hands and shoes as she shook the bone clean and put it into her bag.

Then she moved on.

They'd been at it all morning. This was their third round, their next drop-off with Konstantine was scheduled in twenty minutes, in a dumpster between a pharmacy and coffeehouse in the eighth arrondissement.

By Lou's count, they'd already carried the remains of at least seventeen victims to the surface, and they probably had at least five more already bagged.

"I need another victim then," Piper said.

Lou set her sack down and began trailing her hand over the packed earth. Her fingers snagged on small rocks, bone fragments, or the ends of bones themselves as she passed. She followed the bend in the path, Piper now in view with half of her face hidden behind the oversized goggles. She was standing between her filled bag and a mostly filled one, one long bone protruding from the top of the second.

Someone recent, she told her compass. *A victim who—*

About ten steps from where she'd been, the compass in her gut snagged. She froze, inspecting the area where her hand hovered.

These were clean, fresh, not packed into the dirt at all.

"Here," Lou said. "You can get this one."

Piper saw it and pumped her fist. "Yes. I love it when they're just sitting here like this. They're easier to pull out."

A sound caught Lou's ear, something as slight as a shifting of rocks, and she slammed a hand over Piper's mouth. Turning, slowly, she looked up the path.

"Grab your bag," Lou whispered.

Lou would be able to grab one of hers as it was within reach of Piper, but the other would have to stay where she'd left it.

Piper, to her credit, bent down and grabbed the tops of each of her bags as quietly as she could, her hand slowly wrapping around the plastic so as to not make any sound.

Lou's eyes remained fixed on the path, trained at the part where it bent, listening to the footsteps as they approached.

The footsteps echoing through the catacombs had been quick, certain, at first. Now they slowed. Lou's half-filled sack of bones was just two feet in front of the spot where the path bent. Could they see the bones?

Lou wished she had a gun. She hadn't bothered to wear her guns given the purpose of this trip, but if she'd brought one, she could've put a bullet in this guy's head and been done with it.

No more murders.

But without a gun, she had only one course of action. Get out of there without being seen.

Lou kept one hand on Piper's upper arm, ready.

She saw the shoes first.

The black boots inched into view. In the night-vision goggles, the person was little more than a shape, a shadow born of the tunnel walls themselves.

But he bent down to inspect Lou's half-filled garbage bag of bones —and Lou was almost certain it was a *he* now, from the slope of his shoulders and the angular build of his body. Those large hands concealed in leather gloves.

The only problem was that Lou couldn't see his face.

Not only was he covered head to toe in black, not only did he have a ski mask over the features of his face, but half of it was hidden away behind night-vision goggles, as large and cumbersome as the ones she wore on her own head.

He can see us. If he looks this way, he will see us.

Piper must've realized this the second after Lou did, as the sharp intake of breath behind Lou's hand told her so.

Then he was looking up, his head pivoting in their direction.

Lou slipped without waiting.

But in her reactivity, she hadn't thought of a destination, hadn't decided where she would rather be, only *away, away from him.*

So when the world opened again, they were tumbling into Konstantine's living room. Piper was pitched forward, the untied sack falling open and bones spilling out onto the stone floor.

Konstantine was behind his desk, his laptop open in front of him, an espresso halfway to his mouth. He started, frowned at the dirty bones now littering his living room.

After a beat of silence he asked, "Was there a problem?"

"No, we're just here to decorate for the party." Piper rose and dusted herself off. "Hell yeah, there's a problem."

Konstantine's eyes were on Lou, his frown deepening. "*Amore mio?*"

"Yes," Lou admitted. "We have a problem."

Konstantine listened to their story for the second time before speaking. "He had night-vision goggles as well?"

"Right," Piper said.

"If he was wearing them when I ran into him the last time," Lou explained, "then he's seen my face."

Konstantine settled back into his chair. His eyes trailed to the CCTV Paris footage rolling on his screen. He noted that they'd missed their last timed drop-off, but no matter. They could catch the one after, and Lou would be able to dispose of the remaining bags.

After they cleaned them up off his floor, that was.

But that still left the problem of one sack in the catacomb and a man he did not know aware that Lou was hunting him.

"It's dangerous that he knows who you are but you don't know who he is," Konstantine said, scratching at his jaw.

"And you shouldn't just pop up and be like, 'Hey!'" Piper added. "Because if he saw you before, then he also knows you can do the shifty thing. He saw you do it, right?"

"Slip," Lou corrected. "I call it slipping."

"Whatever. He'll be waiting for you. He might just shoot you in the gut if you pop up or something."

On his laptop a woman walked her dog past an alley, pausing long enough for it to piss on the side of a garbage can.

"This problem may take care of itself," Konstantine said. "It may not be necessary for you to confront him."

Lou turned toward him.

"Once the bones are discovered, and they will be *quite* soon"—his contacts in Paris would see to that—"then the authorities will begin hunting for this man. This may force him out into the open."

"What about the bag in the catacombs?" Lou leaned her weight against his desk, and it brought back delicious memories of that morning. "I have to get it. My fingerprints are on it."

She must've known what he was thinking because a hint of a smile played across her lips.

He would've suggested they christen this desk as well, if not for the blond girl stuffing bones into a garbage bag.

"Move it to the surface if you want. I wipe your prints whenever they're stored, so don't worry about that."

"Is that why you asked to ink my fingers?" she said.

"We're going to need a vacuum for the dirt," Piper said from the floor. "You have one, right?"

"It's in there." Konstantine pointed at the closet behind his front door. "How many people do you think he killed in all?"

"High forties," Lou said. "Maybe the fifties or even sixties."

"Then he has been at this for quite some time. And Paris must've been quite the feeding ground."

"Found it. Whoa, what kind of plug is this?"

He reached out and took Lou's hand. He thought she might refuse him with the girl here, but she let him take it and run a thumb over her scabbing knuckles.

Had she split these knuckles on Erjon's men or Vittoria's face?

"The next drop is in six minutes. That will be our last for today, don't you think?"

"Yeah," she said. "Hopefully it'll be enough."

24

King spent the morning calling his clients, informing them that he would be out of the office for the next few days. Most of them didn't care, since he wasn't a doctor's office with strict appointment schedules and what they needed from him could be provided by an email or phone call. But also because none of the cases in his current workload were approaching their deadlines. A simple stroke of luck, that was. Otherwise, none of this might have worked out.

He'd chosen to do his calls on his cell phone while walking instead of in the office. Part of it was the crying. He'd heard soft crying coming from the upstairs apartment on and off since Dani had left that cryptic note on his legal pad about moving out. King found it nearly impossible to do even the simplest of tasks—such as fill his electronic calendar with important dates—with a soundtrack of pitiful tears in the background.

It broke his heart to hear her like that. He liked Dani. In fact, after she pulled through Dmitri Petrov's torture and Diana Dennard's mind games, he'd come to respect the hell out of her. She was tough, but still kind. He only wished he could help her. More than once he'd considered knocking on the door and asking her if she needed anything.

But he also didn't want to embarrass the girl by letting her know that he'd heard her.

So instead, he'd locked up the agency and completed his morning calls while walking the lazy streets of the French Quarter. No one was really out at this hour, and because they were easing into the pre-holiday slump, he found the streets cozier, friendly, despite the chilly morning air.

He'd just gotten his coffee from Café du Monde and had stepped off the sidewalk to watch a young Asian woman juggle three blazing batons when his cell phone rang.

"Mr. King, this is Randall from the Greenfield Funeral Home."

"Good morning. Thanks for getting back to me."

"My pleasure, sir. I just wanted to let you know that the cemetery finally got back to me with a time for the excavation. They can get that grave open at ten for you, and give you an hour for your niece to say her goodbyes."

Okay, so King had lied and said that Piper was his niece and that he would be making all the funeral arrangements on her behalf. Randall hadn't questioned this, since the plot was already paid for and they'd collected Nadine's body from the hospital directly.

"We've got the remains in a little wooden box that Miss Genereux can place directly into the grave, by way of a little cere-mony, if that's all right with you? The box is completely compostable, of course."

"That should be fine," King said. "So we'll meet you at the ceme-tery at ten?"

"Yes, sir," he said. "The priest will say a short prayer for Ms. Cren-shaw's soul, as you requested, and read Psalm 23. No other scripture shall be read."

King thought he detected a slight hint of judgment in the man's voice when he said *no other scripture*, but since King was the one writing the check, he didn't say anything else.

"All in all, I think it shouldn't be more than ten minutes, and then you'll have the rest of the hour to yourselves."

"That's perfect. Thank you."

King ended the call as the girl with twin braids caught all three of her batons and bowed. King clapped with the other few spectators and threw a twenty-dollar bill into her upturned hat.

Then he was walking again. As he did, he sent Piper a text.

Funeral at ten in the morning tomorrow.

Then we have a reservation at The Praline Connection at eleven.

He watched his screen but didn't get a reply. This was strange because Piper was usually so prompt when it came to texting.

Then he had an idea.

Lifting his coffee to his lips, he opened his news app on his phone and searched for Paris. Sure enough, the headline read, *Paris Panic! Bones Found All Over City.*

They've been busy, he thought as he read the details of the case. How bones from nearly twenty corpses had been discovered sprinkled—their word, not his—in various dumpsters and trash bins around the city. No suspects had been named, so Lou's face wasn't splashed all over the news with menacing *wanted for questioning* subtitles beneath.

Konstantine must've taken care of the surveillance. Good on him.

King was almost done with the article when Piper replied.

Thank you sooooo so much. Thank you for everything. I'll make it up to you, I promise.

He sighed and made a silent prayer that one day this kid was going to realize that just because someone was kind to her, it didn't mean she owed them. There was no score to keep. At least not when friendship was the currency.

King placed his hand on the horse-head post and wiped his feet on the mat outside Melandra's shop.

When he entered, he found her lifting glass candles from a box, stickering the bottoms with her sticker gun and then placing the candles in an opposite pile.

"Good morning," he said.

"Good morning," she returned.

Lady rose to greet him, her tail thumping against Mel's long skirt as he scratched her head.

"Funeral's at ten tomorrow. Do you have someone who can watch the shop for you?"

He stopped short of suggesting Dani.

"No need. We haven't had five customers today. I can stand to close it for a few hours."

King waited, expecting to see the usual tension and worry that Mel radiated when the dip in sales came. When the uncertainty of her income and business were brought into stark view.

But her face remained relaxed, the muscles at ease.

"Are you worried about the dip in traffic?" he asked cautiously, taking up a sticker gun and mimicking her movement.

"No," she said with a small shrug. "Lou's got a ghost night coming up. Things will pick up after that. And we're always a little slow before Thanksgiving. It doesn't mean we won't have a good holiday shopping season."

What a difference a year makes.

Back when Mel's husband had been threatening her, harassing her, extorting her for money, her financial concerns had eaten up a great deal of her energy and peace of mind. Now it seemed that Mel felt more than confident that whatever happened, she would be just fine.

He'd always believed that, of course. But he was glad to see that she saw it now too.

"So you and Ms. Miller?" Melandra asked with a sly smile as she lit another St. Jude candle embellished with the saint's face from the open cardboard box.

"What about her?" he asked, his eyebrows raising.

Mel smirked. "Don't play dumb with me. Are you dating or not?"

"Where'd you get the idea she even wants to date me?"

"Do you think I'm blind? That I don't have two working eyes in my head?"

King snorted. "I didn't say that."

"Well? Answer my question."

"I don't know," he said. "It feels a little strange after Lucy."

Mel nodded, watching his face while her hands did the work. "I can imagine."

"But I don't think Lucy would care," he said, scratching his jaw.

"Of course she don't care. Why would she care?"

"I don't know. In case she can see me."

Mel rolled her eyes. "She's got better things to do than watch us all the time. I'm sure of that much."

King looked at the candle in his hand, at the hallowed saint with its halo of light.

When he didn't speak for a long time, Mel said, "As far as women go, I think Ms. Miller is a good match for you."

"Yeah? How so?" King placed the candle on the glass counter and grabbed another from the box.

"She's as smart as you. Takes no shit like you. And that means that she also won't let you play any games."

King was offended. "I don't play games with women. I'm very honest."

"I'm not talking about cheating or anything like that. I'm talking about head games, emotional games."

King's scowl deepened. "I don't play those either."

"Maybe not on purpose. But this whole 'I like you, you're an amazing woman, but I'm not going to entertain the idea of dating you because I'm worried what my dead wife will think' thing—I doubt Ms. Miller will stick around for that. She'll probably give you time, but if it turns out that you aren't ready, she'll move on. She's not going to lose any sleep at night over it, if you get what I'm saying."

"I'm too old for someone to be losing sleep over anyway," King said. But he was more than a little happy to hear this assessment. Something about it eased the worry in his chest. It was good to know that Mel thought Beth could—and would—take care of herself first, unlike some of the other women he'd dated in the past.

"Mmhmm. Keep on thinking about it," Melandra said, her smile deepening.

Lady's tail began to thump against King's shoe. Mel scratched her ears.

"She's a wonderful woman." *Who made me an offer.* "Of course I'm thinking about it."

"Don't think *too* long," Melandra said, pulling the emptied cardboard box from the glass case. "That's all I'm saying."

. . .

Piper's apartment was empty when she showed up to get ready for the funeral. She was grateful for this, because she didn't think she could handle the sight of Dani right now without falling apart. But alone, she managed to find a black dress and white sweater in the back of her closet, put them on, and clean herself up.

She noticed little things about the apartment, too.

The viola, for example, was gone. And while Dani's clothes and toiletries were still visible, other belongings had gone into cardboard boxes, stacked up neatly in an unused corner of the living room, close to the front door.

It hurt Piper to see them. It hurt her more than she'd expected, her chest compressing.

But this is for the best, she thought. *Dani will be so much happier when she's living the life she deserves.*

In the full-length mirror in her bedroom, she took one more look at herself, and sighed. "This is as good as it gets."

Someone knocked on her apartment door. She opened it to find Lou in black dress pants, a black buttoned-up shirt, and a new leather jacket. The mirrored shades were pushed up onto her head.

"When did you start using doors, you freak?" Piper asked, stepping back as she adjusted one of the hoops in her ears.

"I wasn't sure if you were ready."

"I am." Piper threw up her hands. "How do I look?"

"Good."

"So do you. Is that a new jacket?"

"And boots," she said, coming into the room. "Mel and King are downstairs. They want to ride over together."

"First you knock on doors and now you're going to ride in a car? For *me*?" Piper put a hand over her chest. "Who died? Oh right."

She did finger guns at Lou.

But then Lou's arms were around her, hugging her tight, and tears flooded Piper's eyes.

"I'm sorry this happened," Lou whispered.

For a moment, Piper couldn't speak. She was too choked up by the hug. Then she said, "Yeah, I got that when you killed Willy."

Lou stepped back and pulled a tissue from her pocket.

"And you have tissues? Who *are* you?"

The corner of Lou's lips tilted up in a smile. "I carry tissues when I interview women about their dealer boyfriends. Sometimes they cry."

Piper dabbed at her eyes. "You're just full of surprises today."

"Everything okay up there?" Mel called from downstairs. "We're going to be late."

"We're coming!" Piper said, and grabbed her wallet off the counter and her jacket off its hook.

One more glance at the packed boxes in the corner made her heart clench.

Not now, she thought. *Deal with that later.*

It took them about fifteen minutes to get everyone into the car and over to the Greenfield cemetery. It was already five after ten, so the priest was standing over the exposed earth. The concrete grave cover that usually kept her father's bones from rising with the water table had been pulled back to expose only churned earth. Fortunately, Piper didn't see her father's bones. Maybe they'd already disintegrated, or someone had thought to carefully tuck them out of sight.

Either way, now there was a small box-shaped hole for Piper to put her mother's remains in.

"I'm sorry I'm late!" Henry called, rushing toward them in a long black coat, his hair slicked back away from his face, an enormous bouquet of red roses in his arms. He was about to hand Piper the flowers when he saw that she was holding the wooden box.

Instead, he threw his arm around her and squeezed her so hard she thought she might pop.

"Fuck." He placed a kiss on the top of her head and said, "I mean, *fuck*."

"I know," Piper said, trying not to look at the frowning priest. "I know."

Then he looped his arm through hers as King motioned for the priest to begin.

While the priest prayed for her mother's soul, Piper held the box between her hands, surprised by its weight. How could all of her mother be reduced down to this five or so pounds?

She thought of how many nights she came home and found her mother passed out on the sofa, her drugs strewn across the coffee table. How she would pull a thin blanket off the arm of the chair and cover her mother's frail body with it, tucking it in tight and placing a kiss on her cheek.

Good night, Momma, she'd thought then. And now.

She began to cry.

As the tears ran down her face, King, Mel, and Henry all moved in closer, surrounding her, placing their hands on her. And despite her best efforts, the tears flowed harder, until she could no longer hear the priest's prayers over her soft whimpering.

Then she was asked to come forward, put the box into the ground, and push the dirt over it. The caretaker or funeral director—really Piper had no idea who the bone-thin man with the frizzy gray hair was —offered her a shovel.

Piper didn't take it. She pushed the dirt over her mother's grave with her bare hands until she couldn't see the box at all.

Then arms were around her. Holding her, telling her she would be okay.

And somehow, she knew it was true. She *would* be okay. Her mother wouldn't be. But she would be fine.

And this terrible truth broke her heart a little more.

She wasn't sure how long she stayed like this, crying in the circle of her friends. But when it began to rain, she looked up. Found that it was mostly Henry who held her, while King and Mel in their black clothes and somber faces remained close. Lou had stepped back a bit, watching the machinery roll into the cemetery to close the grave again.

What she was thinking behind those mirrored shades, Piper couldn't guess. But she seemed nonplussed as soft raindrops splattered onto the shoulder of her new leather jacket.

Piper caught sight of someone over her shoulder. Dani, her hair pulled up in a bun off her slender neck. Her black dress and black pumps were wet with rain. In her arms was a full white bouquet, interspersed with soft pink blossoms.

"I just wanted to leave this," Dani said. She was offering the bouquet to Lou, as if the very idea of approaching Piper was out of the question.

Lou just looked at the flowers. Piper almost laughed.

"Stay," Piper said, pulling herself up to standing as the rain began to fall harder. "At least for the lunch."

The relief on Dani's face was visible.

"Okay," she said. "Where are we eating?"

Thunder rolled overhead.

THE LUNCH WAS GOING BETTER THAN KING HAD HOPED, THOUGH IT was far from a party. Dani and Piper hadn't sat together, and Lou was between them. All the faces around the table had a depressed and dour look about them. Even Henry, who could usually be counted on to carry the conversation with his high energy.

Now, no one seemed to manage more than one-word responses.

Yet they got through, despite the rain pouring down outside and the thunder rolling overhead. Each took their turn distracting Piper. They talked about everything except her mom, the funeral, about what might happen next. King knew that conversation was coming. There was the matter of her mother's estate, after all, but that could hold for a few days.

Piper needed a break. She'd needed one for a long time.

"I can come back to work tomorrow," Piper said. "After this I'm going to finish my paper and get it in tonight. Then I'll be all caught up."

"Too bad," King said, "because I've closed the agency until Monday."

"What? Why?"

"Nothing pressing to be done and I thought we could all use a few days off."

Piper turned on Mel. "I guess it's just me and you then."

"Not really," Mel said. "It's been slow. You know how it is the week before Thanksgiving. I'd say we're fine until the Black Friday rush." Mel slid her gold bangles down onto her wrists.

"That's right. It's Thanksgiving next week," Piper said. "I totally forgot."

"Ugh, don't remind me." Henry rolled his eyes. "I have to drive to Pensacola to see my sister and her kids."

Piper frowned. "You love your sister."

"I do. Yes," Henry conceded, tapping his long nails on the printed tablecloth. "But she invited our shithead of a father, so, say the word. If you need me to stay in town and eat turkey with you, I'm here for it."

"No." Piper scowled. "Go see your nephews, dude. They need a fabulous man in their life. Especially if your dad is coming to dinner."

Henry sighed, running a finger across his eyebrow. "You're right. I know you're right. But I'm going to need a drink or five when I get back, so pencil me in for that Saturday night."

"Done."

"Speaking of Thanksgiving," King added, glad to see the flow of conversation picking up, "I wondered if you'd join me and Mel for dinner that Thursday. And Lou's going to be there too."

Lou arched a brow, a clear *that's news to me.*

"Really?" Piper asked. "Last year and the year before you were busy."

King gave Louie a look that he hoped she could interpret as *This is important, you better show up for this.*

"I love turkey," Lou said in a flat monotone.

"Do you? It's the sides for me. Mashed potatoes, macaroni and cheese, stuffing," Piper said. "Oh god, could we have waited until the food came to talk about this?"

King couldn't pretend like Dani wasn't at the table, he'd decided. He'd invite her, and if something happened between now and Thursday, he'd just have to rely on the girls to work it out.

"What about you, Dani? You going to join us? Mel's table seats six."

"There's a green mole that my mom's cook makes for the turkey." Dani tucked her hair behind her ears. "And she uses piquant cornbread for the stuffing. It's really good. I could get the recipes if you guys want to try it."

King encouraged her with a nod. Piper, he noticed, remained silent.

"All of that sounds *amazing*. You better save me some leftovers."

Henry craned his neck over his shoulder at the kitchen door. "Where the hell is our food?"

King looked out the rainy window and spotted Beth walking slowly past with a black umbrella open above her head. When he turned back, Mel was watching him with a smug look on her face.

"Excuse me," King said, rising from his seat.

"Sure," Melandra said, her smugness deepening.

King rushed out into the rain, trying to stick close to the building, where he remained mostly protected by the balconies extended above him.

"Beth," he called out, but his words were swallowed by thunder. "Beth!"

She stopped walking, turning slowly to survey the street. When she saw him, her face lit up.

"Can I help you, Robbie?" she asked.

This close he could see the rain splotches on her shoulders and the moisture droplets forming on her glasses.

"You're wet," he said by way of introduction.

"Don't worry about it. I'm not made of sugar," she assured him. And when his voice failed him, she added, "*Yes?*"

"I just wanted to let you know that I'll be by tonight. If your offer still stands."

Her smile broke open and King's heart kicked to see it. Why in God's name was he so nervous?

"Of course it stands. You have my address, don't you?"

He did, but confirmed it to be sure.

"That's the one," she said.

He ran a hand through his hair. "Okay. Then I'll see you tonight. Five o'clock. And I'll bring the dinner as promised."

She laughed. "Yes, you will."

Through the window, Melandra smiled over the rim of her glass.

25

———————

Lou sat up in bed, feeling as though she were half in, half out of a dream. She'd been in the strange room again. The black glass on all four walls. The sense that she could see something if she got close enough to the glass, but also a terror that if she did, something bad would happen.

She clasped a hand to the back of her neck and squeezed the tight muscles there.

Beside her, Piper slept, her breath rolling in and out in an easy rhythm.

When Lou had shown up with dinner, hot dogs from a stand in Chicago, she'd caught her crying. But at least the tears had quickly dried once she'd started in on her hot dog.

She'd tried to remember what it was like when her parents had died. The murders themselves were crystal clear. That first *flash-bang* of the gun going off in her parents' bedroom as she stood in the backyard with her father. The sound of her mother's wineglass breaking.

That horrible moment when Angelo had burst through the back gate and her father had lifted her, throwing her into the pool. All of that, she remembered.

But the months that followed. The crying, the grief, the nighttime searching for and not being able to find her father. It hadn't mattered how hard she longed for him, missed him.

He was gone.

Those months were a blur. Bits shone through. Flashes. Of Lucy begging her to eat. To take a shower. To go outside and get some air.

But mostly, what Lou remembered was the atmosphere of her grief. How it was like the air she breathed. Everywhere. All around her and inside her.

It was endless. Until it wasn't.

If Piper was in the same place now, she wasn't showing it. She was sad. Lou could see that. The dark circles under her eyes were pronounced, and Piper hadn't made the effort to hide them.

She's going to be okay, Lou thought. That protective, possessive feeling that first urged her to bring Piper here, to keep her close, relaxed. *She's going to get through this.*

Lou's compass whirled and clicked to life, responding to some silent call she couldn't hear. Paris, she knew, once her navel snagged on those invisible coordinates.

Lou slipped from the bed quietly, careful not to touch or uncover Piper too much. She watched her sleep while she pulled on her boots, but the girl didn't stir.

All that crying seemed to have worn her out.

Grabbing her new leather jacket off the sofa arm and her Browning off the kitchen island, Lou glanced at the pre-dawn river before stepping into her empty linen closet.

The shadows thinned, enveloped her, and when she'd returned to the physical plane again, she was back in the cemetery. Père Lachaise, with its old tombs and enormous trees, an older, grander version of the cemetery where they'd buried Piper's mother that morning.

In moments like this, it was almost possible to believe that Paris was the mother of New Orleans.

Etienne had his back against Delphine's tomb, the weeping angel draped dramatically above his head. One of his hands rested on a bent knee, the other kicked out into the grass.

"I knew you'd come," he said.

Lou said nothing to this. Though if she were being honest with herself, it bothered her how quickly they were figuring it out, how to call her. Piper and even little Matteo knowing how to call her was fine. She wanted them to reach out when they needed help. King, Melandra, and Dani too. She supposed even Stefano, if he had reason enough.

But now Etienne?

It was getting a little ridiculous. Perhaps when she felt sure it wasn't an emergency, she should ignore these calls in the future, just to keep everyone guessing. Keep them from being too reliant on her. She could make mistakes, after all. She wasn't a replacement for self-reliance.

Soft crying caught Lou's ear and she turned. A young woman, perhaps eighteen, nineteen, was on her knees in front of a grave marker. She had one hand on the stone as if praying to it.

Lou didn't understand the French she murmured to herself, not only because of the distance or language barrier but because mostly the girl was sobbing into her handkerchief.

When Lou turned back, Etienne was watching the girl too. Something had changed in his eyes.

Lou couldn't be sure what. Had they always been that dark? Or the pupils that large?

"Are you an angel or a demon?" he asked her.

"Depends on who you ask," Lou said, grateful that he was using English for her.

"You said that you wanted to help me. For Delphine."

"I am helping," Lou said, her hands loose in her jacket. "I'm looking for the one who killed her."

He nodded. "Yes, I thought so."

She expected more questions, something along the lines of *What have you learned so far?* or *How is the investigation going?*

But he seemed to be weighing something in his mind.

"My Delphine was an artist. Her work, her beautiful works, were magnificent."

"I saw them at the museum." Lou shifted and the Browning pressed into her ribs reassuringly.

Etienne's lips pursed. "No, not those. The ones she has at home, her private collection. *Those* were the real art. The little creations she made before were only practice. She had to learn, my Delphine, like all great artists. It takes time to perfect one's art."

Etienne's eyes slid away, tracking something over Lou's shoulder. It wasn't until the girl passed, her face hidden in her handkerchief, that Lou knew what he'd been watching.

"I want to show you Delphine's art. Her passion. I think if you saw them, you would understand my Delphine. My talented, beautiful, *lost* Delphine."

The eyes which had been so dark and hungry the moment before were now soft and sorrowful again.

Did he kill her? Has he killed anyone?

Her compass remained silent, unmoving.

"Where's her art?" Lou asked.

"At our home. Will you come? It must be very soon, I'm afraid. Her creations don't last long. And there are only two left. Please come. Come tonight."

"I'll come," Lou agreed, the Browning again brushing her ribs.

"Will you? Thank you. *Thank you.*" Etienne brightened at this, his eyes lighting up for the first time. "Perhaps once you see it, you will understand her. I just want someone who will understand what I've lost. Such a terrible, *terrible* loss."

"What time?" Lou asked.

"Eleven," he said. "They are best viewed at night. When it is darkest. Sort of like you."

He smiled then, and it was ice cold, his words frozen cubes trailing down Lou's spine.

There were only a few hours between then and eleven that night.

He turned his eyes up to meet hers. "Please don't be late."

KING CHANGED HIS SHIRT THREE TIMES. THEN HE SPENT SEVERAL minutes in his bathroom debating whether or not cologne was in order. Some women loved it. Others found it irritating to their nose and throat. If he put it on and it was too much, it would be difficult to wash it off. He could go into the bathroom and splash water on his throat, he guessed, but only if he didn't get any on his clothes.

Finally he decided he would get ready as he did every day. That's the way he'd been when Beth had seen him and had decided she was interested. So he'd just pretend he was going to work.

Yes to the cologne then.

Mel, blessedly, had been in her apartment with Lady when he'd stepped out onto the landing and locked the door behind him. The dog barked once, and Mel shushed her. He stood frozen in the hall, half expecting Mel to poke her head out and comment on his appearance, but she only called out, "Heading to dinner, Mr. King?"

"Yeah," he said, feeling like a high schooler at the top of the stairs, on the brink of lying to his parents about where he intended to spend the night.

"Take care then," she said. And that was it.

The worse part, by far, was the condoms.

When King went to the convenience store across the street and found the condoms comically opposite the diapers, he grabbed two boxes. No big deal. The embarrassment came when he slipped the packages across the counter to Zeke, the cashier he saw nearly every day.

Zeke only arched a brow at the boxes before running them across the scanner.

Stupid, King thought. He should've picked a gas station or pharmacy he never went to.

"You know," Zeke began, "we have wine in the back, where the beer is, if you want to—"

"No, thank you," King said. But as soon as he'd refused, he reconsidered. "Actually, one second."

"Sure, dude, it's just me and you in here."

King wandered back to the cold cases and found the wine. Quickly, he realized he had no idea what Beth liked. Sweet white wine? A super-dry red?

He decided to skip the alcohol.

"No luck?" Zeke called out as King was walking back to the register.

"Not tonight."

Zeke handed him the bag with his condoms in it as King handed over a twenty-dollar bill. "Well I'm sure you'll still have a good time."

King's Oldsmobile was parked in the alley behind the shop. He tucked the condoms into the inner pocket of his duster, turned the key, and eased out onto St. Peter.

It only took him about ten minutes to find parking outside of Beth's townhouse on Prytania Street. The pretty pink-and-white-brick exterior was beautiful in the orange glow of sunset. He checked the address against the numbers above each door and realized she was in the one on the far left.

Hope her bed is against that outside wall, he thought. Otherwise, he'd be sending an apology letter to the neighbors in the morning.

King didn't even make it all the way up the walk before Beth opened the front door.

"I wasn't sure you were coming in," she said, her smile wide. "You were looking at my door for a long time."

He wasn't sure what to say as he crossed the threshold and stood in her living room. The colors were bright and adventurous. A yellow sofa with turquoise throw pillows. Two red armchairs opposite a glass coffee table. The rug was some sort of cream-colored Indian print with multi-colored elephants repeating for the full length of it. The hard floor stopped at the kitchen, where it gave over to white ceramic tile.

"Don't be shy," she said, offering to take his coat. "I won't bite you unless you ask me to."

"I forgot all about the dinner until I rolled up," he said. "But you can pick the takeout and I'll pay the bill."

"All right," she said. "That's fine with me. There isn't much in this city that I won't eat, let me tell you."

King laughed, shrugging out of his duster and handing it over.

But as soon as he handed over the jacket, he remembered the condoms in the pocket. He reached for the coat.

Beth must've seen something in his face.

"What is it?" she asked. "What's wrong?"

"I just, uh—" His face grew warm. "There's something I need in the pocket."

Frantically he wondered what he should do. Ask to take it into the bathroom? She might think he was a cokehead or something.

And it was too late anyway. Beth's hands were searching the pockets until she found the first, then the second box of condoms and pulled them out.

"Oh," she said. "Oh, I see."

King didn't want to seem like the sort of man who forgot to pick up dinner but showed up with *two* boxes of condoms.

"I'm sorry," he said.

"For what?"

"I..." What was he going to say? *I don't want to seem presumptuous. Or single-minded.* She was the one who'd said she wanted to have sex.

"*Two* boxes," she continued, pushing her glasses up onto the bridge of her nose. "And Comfort XL."

King clasped the back of his neck.

"Well," she said over the rim of her glasses. "I *do* like a man who comes prepared."

26

Piper felt strange being back in her apartment. Lou had told her that she could stay longer if she wanted, but Piper missed her bed, her living room, having her clothes in an actual dresser instead of being piled onto a couch. She could never fully relax when she was a guest at someone else's place, and after everything, Piper was ready to relax.

However, this hadn't prepared her for the awkwardness of coming home to Dani sitting in the living room, arms-deep in a cardboard box.

Piper turned back, reconsidering her decision to come home now, only to find Lou had already gone. *Probably on purpose*, she thought. *She wants me to talk to Dani.*

"Hey," Dani said.

"Hey," Piper countered, knowing her smile was forced and awkward.

Dani looked away first. "I'm sorry I'm still here. I'm just waiting for my parents to show up. They're late."

"That's okay," Piper said. "It looks like you need more time to pack anyway."

Thank God she didn't live here longer, Piper thought. Because the few things that Dani had to pack up were only items that she'd accumulated since losing her apartment in the explosion. That meant that the majority of the things in the apartment—the cookware, furniture, and décor—all belonged to Piper.

And yet, even in their short time together, Dani had accumulated enough to fill five whole cardboard boxes.

Dani's phone pinged. After she read the text, she said, "It's my mom. They're here. They just need to find parking."

"Okay," Piper said. "Do you want me to help you carry anything?"

"No, but is it okay that my parents come up and get boxes? I swear they won't be rude or—"

"It's fine," Piper assured her. Even if Piper felt like a dirty orphan in front of the polished Allendales, it wasn't like they'd be here for long. They could think whatever they wanted about her or her one-bedroom apartment as long as they kept it to themselves.

Dani stood and brushed invisible dirt off the front of her jeans. After a long, mournful look, she said, "I'm just going to go down and open up the agency for them."

"Sure," Piper said, suddenly unsure what to do with her hands. She slid them into her pockets. "I'll be here."

Dani disappeared into the hall, her footsteps echoing as she descended the staircase into the office below. And Piper was left to stand there and look at the boxes, thinking, not for the first time, that maybe she was making a mistake.

Sure, she didn't care for Dani's mother, and no way in hell could she ever go back to that freaking mansion in Metairie, but Piper didn't have to in order to keep dating Dani, did she?

Dani could get her big, beautiful apartment, and they could just go back to having sex and spending time together like they had before the explosion, right?

She's not going to want to have sex with you after you threw her out, asshole! a voice chided.

And you'd only be delaying the inevitable, said another.

What if they fell in love, got married, and had babies? She was just supposed to never return to the Allendales' house again? What about Christmases? What if Dani wanted to buy herself a nice car or go to

Europe or something? Was Piper going to stop her because she couldn't afford to go and she didn't want Dani to pay?

No, I'd tell Lou to drop my ass off there, she thought. No airfare.

Shut up, she argued against herself. *It'll never work. Better to end it now while everything else is already shit. Get it all done in one go.*

A clean break.

"It's up here?" a voice called. Beverly Allendale had arrived. *"Really?"*

Piper took a deep breath and straightened her back.

Beverly ducked into the apartment the way one ducks spiderwebs in a haunted house.

"Hi," Piper said. She made a show of forced cheerfulness. "Come on in."

With her brown hair coiled in a tight bun on top of her head and her hand at her throat, Beverly looked like she'd rather do anything else. She inched into the room, careful to keep her cream-colored suit from touching anything, as if the walls—*hell*, maybe the air itself— were coated in filth and grime.

"The boxes are there," Piper said, pointing to the corner. "And I think Dani has just one suitcase in the bedroom. I can carry that."

"Where is Tavi?" Beverly asked as Dani reappeared, pushing the door open as wide as it would go for the ensuing move.

"I told you, Mom, Piper is allergic. Tavi is staying with a friend of mine."

"God, who *wouldn't* be allergic in this tiny place. You can barely breathe in here."

"Mom!" Dani cried. "This is a beautiful apartment. One of the nicest in the French Quarter that I've ever seen."

Beverly frowned. "Well, honey, that's hardly saying anything. The French Quarter is like one giant bar."

"Can we please just get these boxes down to the street?" Dani asked, giving Piper an *I'm so sorry this will all be over soon* face.

"All I'm saying is that if this place wasn't so small, it would be easier to keep it clean."

"This apartment is *clean*!" Dani cried, promptly dropping the box she'd been lifting from the top of the pile. "I just cleaned it this morning!"

And she had. It was one of the first things Piper had commented on when Lou had dropped her off in the living room. She'd thanked Dani for cleaning straight away.

"You *cleaned?* Why?" Beverly asked. "This isn't even your apartment."

"Because I live here, Mother. That's what people do. They clean their houses."

Beverly snorted, touching her bun as if a hair might be out of place. "I can't believe you lived like this. Next thing I know you'll be renting a room in a drug den. This is hardly a step above."

Piper's stomach clenched. She pinched her eyes shut against the wave of pain crashing over her. The image of her mother, unconscious, unresponsive on the couch. Of Willy shoving her out of the car onto the curb as she lay dying, his taillights fading into the night.

"Piper, oh my god, Piper. I'm so sorry." Dani's hands were on her shoulders, then on her face. "Mother, apologize to her right now!"

"For *what?*"

"For being such a *bitch*! Apologize to her! *Now.*"

"Daniella Allendale, what language! How dare you talk to me like that? Is this the kind of people you're running around with now? Where this sort of language is acceptable?"

Piper didn't understand what happened next. Their heated English had given way to a torrent of Spanish. Somehow, in Spanish they sounded even angrier, the exchange growing louder and more heated until Piper felt like she was going to be sick.

She needed air. She needed to get out of here.

"Excuse me." Piper slipped away out of the apartment and down the stairwell.

Dani called after her, but Piper couldn't stop. She needed fresh air or her head was going to explode. She crossed the sunny office, her sneakers squeaking across the polished floor, and stepped out into the early evening, taking a big deep breath as soon as the agency door closed behind her.

"Yes, yes, I *know*," a man said. "It is *very* difficult to listen to, isn't it?"

Piper turned and found Dani's father standing on the curb.

He wore a Hawaiian shirt and khaki pants. Over the shirt was a thick blue cardigan. He drew deeply on his pipe before exhaling up toward the sky.

"Are you cold?" she asked.

He shook his head. "No, I'm fine. Thank you."

Piper wasn't sure what to do with herself. She could go for a walk. But then who would help them get the boxes out of the house? This guy looked like he was ready to catch a flight to the tropics, not do some heavy lifting.

Mr. Allendale pulled a sleek silver cigarette case out of his pants pocket and opened it. Beside the wrapped tobacco for his pipe were ten dark cigarettes, fragrant even from where Piper stood.

"Oh, no, thank you." Piper only smoked when she was drunk, as a rule, and for that reason, didn't even buy cigarettes or carry them on her.

But given her current predicament, and the miniature war waging in her apartment upstairs—which she could still hear despite *two* closed doors—a cigarette didn't sound half bad.

Mr. Allendale still held the case open for her.

"I don't usually smoke."

"Nor do I," he said. "But sometimes, it's nice, isn't it?"

She couldn't argue, so she plucked the offering from the case and slipped it between her lips. "Thanks."

As he lit Piper's cigarette with a sleek lighter, silver to match the case, Mr. Allendale said, "When Daniella told us she was moving again, I was sorry to hear it."

Piper wasn't sure what to say to this, so she took her first long, deep drag on the cigarette. It was smooth.

Very smooth. They must cost a fortune, she thought.

"You know, I visited her, when she was in the psychologist hospital," he said, exhaling his own thin blue smoke toward the sky.

That wasn't what it was called, the psych ward at New Orleans

General, but Piper didn't dare correct him. No one appreciated that crap.

"Really? She didn't tell me that," Piper said between drags.

"I don't think she knows I came. I'd gotten a call from a nurse who works there. Emmanuelle Perez. Good girl. Good family. Anyway, she told me Daniella had come in, and so I came to see how she was."

"What did Beverly think of that?"

Mr. Allendale laughed. "You think I told her? No, no, no. I enjoy my peace, you know."

Piper smiled, and exhaled blue smoke toward the sky.

"Daniella was sleeping when I arrived. She looked—" He stared at his pipe. "She looked small. Very tired. Like she did when she was a little girl. Always tired, my Daniella."

Piper wasn't sure where this was going, so she took another drag on the cigarette—and *damn* these were good cigarettes. They didn't even burn her throat on the inhale.

"My wife has always been very hard on our girl. Lessons, lessons, *lessons*, you know. All of Daniella's life is full of these lessons. Riding lessons. Italian lessons. Music lessons. Leadership lessons. I tell her, '*Beverly*. She is a child! Let her play. Let her *rest*.' But no, my wife is a very attentive mother. She wants her to succeed, of course. Me? I want her to be happy. And I know that success and happiness are not the same thing."

Our mothers couldn't be more different, Piper thought, putting Beverly Allendale and Nadine Crenshaw together side by side in her mind. An over-attentive mother who planned every minute of her daughter's day, her life, and a neglectful mother who didn't even notice when her daughter came or went.

He sucked on his pipe, the embers glowing red. "That was why I was so glad when she met you."

Piper choked. "Me?"

Mr. Allendale smiled. "Yes, *you*. With you, Daniella is always smiling. She is laughing. She is having a good time, always, when I see her. So I'm sad that she's leaving now. Will you still be friends?"

Piper's heart clenched. "I want to. I just..." *God, am I really going to say it?* "I care about her a lot."

"I know," he said, and reached out to pat Piper's cheek affectionately. "I know. I see it in your eyes. You are both good girls, but sometimes it doesn't work. García women are *very* passionate. She gets it from her mother."

Piper laughed, flicking her ash onto the street.

"Yes," he said with a heavy smile. "But hey, you never know. Things have a way of working out."

A door slammed, and Piper turned in time to dodge the agency door swinging open.

As Beverly spilled out onto the street, she took one look at the pair of them smoking and huffed. "I'll be in the car!"

She marched away from them down Royal Street toward St. Peter.

Mr. Allendale opened his silver cigarette case. "Take another."

"No, really, I wasn't lying. I don't smoke unless—"

"Take it for the next bad day," he said with a wink. "Go on."

"Thanks." Piper slid the cigarette behind her ear.

Mr. Allendale extinguished his pipe and slid it into his pocket. Then he offered Piper his hand. She shook it.

After a gentle pat on the top of her hand, he pulled open the agency door and went inside.

For a moment, Piper just stood on the street, watching the people pass and thinking about nothing in particular. She could still feel the warmth of Mr. Allendale's hand clasping hers. That fatherly pat on her cheek. She didn't think anyone had patted her cheek like that since her dad had died. And that had been a long time ago.

She considered going in and offering to carry boxes, but her phone buzzed.

Are you around? Henry asked.

Yeah, why?

Can you come down to The Wild Cat? I need extra hands.

Piper took one last drag off her cigarette before stamping it out with a twist of her sneaker. Then, with her hands in her pockets, she made her way toward Bourbon Street.

27

Konstantine wondered if this counted as a date. He had never eaten in a restaurant with Lou before. In fact, he was painfully aware of how rarely they were in public together. He had never taken her to a movie, or to a party. He'd never taken her shopping or for a long, slow drive through the country.

Sitting down to a meal with her now seemed almost absurd.

Yet there she was, across from him at the table, a wine glass within reach. Her head was turned, offering him a delicious view of her profile, her pale neck as she looked out over the Piazza della Signoria.

It was full tonight, crowded with people of all ages, despite the encroaching night. They lounged on steps, the fountain's lip, or at dinner tables like theirs arranged at the edges of restaurant terraces. The central fountain lit from within burbled and the street vendors tried to entice both children and parents with lit-up trinkets that could fly, bounce, and dance in the dark.

Cheap plastic things that would be broken before bedtime, or soon forgotten at the bottom of a drawer.

Despite the perfection of the moment, he wanted to tell her something—what he'd learned that day over a brief but intense phone call.

The last test had come back, offering insight into her strange, hellish world. That place she called La Loon.

But there was something in her demeanor tonight that made him hesitate. It didn't feel like the time or place.

"What is it, *amore mio?*" Konstantine asked. He met Lou's eyes over the dinner table, the wine glass sparkling in the candlelight. "Is this too much?"

Lou's lips twitched. "I have eaten at a dinner table before."

He shrugged. "Of course, but when I asked you to dinner, perhaps you were imagining something less formal?"

"This is nice," she said.

Perhaps it was the darkness that suited her, or the open space surrounding them. But she'd seemed comfortable letting him order for her, insisting only that he get her something with steak.

Now she was looking at him.

"What?"

"I like what you're wearing," she said with a suggestive smile.

Muscles in Konstantine's guts tightened. He was only wearing a black turtleneck, soft black pants, and leather shoes. The shirt was pushed up past his elbows to expose his forearms. Had he gone any higher, it would have shown his gang tattoos. So he'd been careful to keep it just beyond the bend in his elbow.

"Thank you," he said with a tilt of his head. "Are you in a hurry?"

"No, why?"

"I am aware that the American notion of dinner is thirty minutes, usually consumed standing or in front of a television. Italians take their time. It might be two hours before all of our courses are served."

"I don't have a TV," she said.

He smirked at her. "Will you be spending the night with Piper again?"

"She went home."

He wondered if his eyes reflected the candlelight as hers did.

He thought again of telling her what he'd learned about that strange world of hers, what, if any, implications it might have for her. But he decided against it. It was such a beautiful moment. Why ruin it with serious talk?

"But I have a date in Paris at eleven," she added.

His jaw clenched involuntarily. *It's only an expression*, he reminded himself. "A date?"

She smiled. "Yes, with a handsome French widower."

He set his wine glass down. "You're taunting me, aren't you?"

She shrugged a shoulder. "Etienne wants to show me Delphine's art."

"I'm sure," he said coolly. "Are you going alone?"

"Why? Should I bring you?"

Yes, he thought. But knew that was more than impractical. "Perhaps not me. I'm not as good at putting people at ease as your detective is. Why did you agree to go?"

Lou eyed him over her own candlelit glass. She took a deep drink before saying, "I don't seem like an art aficionado to you?"

There was a shift in her tone. Had he said something wrong?

"Forgive me. I only meant that you must have another reason for going."

"I want to see where Delphine died."

He lifted the glass again, swirling the wine inside. "King would know what to look for at a crime scene, wouldn't he?"

"He'd probably tell me that there'd be no clues at this point. He'd be right, but I'd still want to see it. If I can see the space, maybe I'll get a sense of how big the person who killed her was." When he said nothing, she added, "If it's a high tub, or if the walls are narrow. Low ceiling. All of it gives me an idea of what size the killer is. I doubt she was stabbed then climbed into the tub while dying, so whoever it was probably put her in there. And I want to compare the space to the size of the guy we saw in the catacombs."

The man who saw you, he corrected in his mind. He didn't like that the killer knew Lou's face. Perhaps he was already hunting for her, planning how to trap and kill her. And what could Konstantine do for her if she got hurt in Paris?

Very little.

He had people there, of course. They could reach her far faster than Konstantine could, but that hardly made her safe.

Don't think of that, he scolded himself. *Focus instead on this gorgeous evening.*

"You're very beautiful," Konstantine said after a beat of silence. "Will you permit me to be a bit...romantic right now?"

It was her turn to tilt her head. "I didn't realize I'd forbidden it."

She hadn't, but he'd seen the way she would tense, turn away, whenever he became too expressive with his affections. When she'd been shot and had almost died, she'd told him, *Don't fall in love with me.* To which he'd admitted, *I already have.*

When she'd heard this, she'd pinched her eyes shut as if to block him out.

But this was a special occasion. Their first normal outing together. He didn't want the moment to pass by unacknowledged.

"It means a lot to me, to have you here. At dinner," he said. He took the wine bottle off the table and bent forward, refilling her glass.

She seemed to consider this.

It was true they almost always kept to his apartment. There were the times when she'd found him in his church, in his office, or in the main sanctuary, but ninety percent of the time, they were in his bedroom. And he'd been to her place only twice.

"Given the prices of the place, it's going to cost you a lot, too."

He smiled, having expected a joke, knowing she would deflect the seriousness of his tone.

"All I'm trying to say," he said, "is that it is very nice to sit and look at you like this." He gestured at the table, the piazza. "I hope we will do it more often."

"Keep dressing like that," she said, "and we will."

He laughed. "So I am not the only one who cares about my clothes."

"After dinner, do you want to get gelato?" he asked.

"Is that what we're calling it now?" She smiled over the rim of her wine glass. "Sure. I wouldn't mind some gelato."

After dinner they ended up in bed. Those clothes in which Konstantine had looked so handsome were on the floor, his body now slick with sweat. She was glad she'd pulled her hair up before they'd begun. She didn't have time for yet another shower before going to Paris.

She ran a hand down his chest. Then she kissed it, licking the salt off his skin.

He purred affectionately.

"Who is the cat here?" she teased. "You or Octavia?"

With one hand on his hip, she moved down his torso. He slid a hand into her hair and fisted it.

"Please," he said. "I beg you."

She rolled her eyes up to meet his. "What?"

"*Sono esausto.* And you'll be late if you begin again."

He had a point. According to her watch, she had only twenty minutes to get to Paris. But she didn't want to go. She wanted to stay in his bed and see how long she could torture Konstantine before he fell asleep.

Octavia chose this moment to jump onto the bed. Perhaps she'd recognized her name.

"*Ciao, bellezza,*" Konstantine said.

The cat bypassed Lou entirely and went for Konstantine's face, bumping her head against the bottom of his chin.

"She's in love with you," Lou said.

"No," he said. "She's affectionate."

Lou wouldn't have used the word *affectionate*. The cat seemed indifferent at best to Lou, except for mealtimes. At mealtimes, the little beast did come alive, and might even reward Lou with a nice headbutt into her cupped palm. Otherwise, she wanted to be left alone to enjoy the sunlight.

"When Dani gets her own place she's probably going to want her cat back."

Konstantine cupped his hands over Octavia's ears. "Don't say such things to her. She will be with me forever. I've already promised her."

The genuinely sad expression on his face made Lou smile.

"Besides," he said, "she makes the apartment so cozy. It won't be the same without her."

"You better hope that Dani and Piper make up then," Lou said.

She glanced at her watch. Fifteen minutes.

Konstantine was watching her when she looked up. "Leaving, then?"

"Why are you jealous?" She stood and crossed to Konstantine's bathroom. "He hasn't even flirted with me."

"You underestimate me, *amore mio*. I am jealous of everyone and everything that occupies your time."

"Maybe you do need a pet then," she said over a shoulder before stepping into the hot stream.

Just a quick rinse, she thought.

When Lou got out of the shower, she found Octavia sleeping in the crook of Konstantine's arm as he read a book. It was hard to deny that the pair were in love with each other. It was an odd complement to what Lou shared with Jabbers, the six-armed beast from the shores of La Loon, with her reptilian black skin and rows of shark teeth.

Lou smiled to herself, thinking of Jabbers curled up and sleeping beside her like that.

"Can I borrow a shirt?" she asked. She could wear her pants and underwear, but her shirt had stayed on the longest and she'd already been sweating before Konstantine had removed it.

"*Sì.*" He pointed at the top dresser drawer.

He watched her pull a black t-shirt from his drawer and pull it down over her naked torso. Then he sat his book open, face down on his lap. "How do you feel about leaving some of your clothes here?"

"If you don't want me to wear your shirt, just say so."

"No," he said. "No, I like to see you in my clothes. But I'm thinking of your convenience."

Lou could step into a shadow and then into her apartment. It was hardly inconvenient to get her own clothes. She'd only asked for a shirt now because—and she'd never admit this aloud—she wanted his scent to linger on her. Wearing his clothes would accomplish that.

"First dinner in a restaurant, now my own drawer?" she teased.

"Is it too much too quickly?" he asked.

This guy.

"Yes, it's all moving so fast, I don't think I can bear to have my underwear in a drawer beside your underwear."

"That is sarcasm."

"Yes," she said, shutting the drawer. "Yes, it is."

Lou slipped her arms through her shoulder holster, putting one of the Brownings in place before shrugging on her leather jacket. She wanted to check the fit before adding the other. This new jacket wasn't quite as loose as Lou wanted, but it would get there. It just needed to be broken in a bit.

"Be careful tonight," he said, clearly deciding to drop the topic of the drawer. He returned to his book.

"Konstantine," she said.

He looked up. "*Amore mio?*"

She tapped one of the top drawers, the smallest one, with the barrel of her gun. "I want this one."

He was still smiling when she left.

28

King lay in Beth's bedroom staring at the unmoving brown ceiling fan with its golden pull strings. Again, for the second time since Paris, he had the urge to smoke. He couldn't remember the last time he'd smoked, having officially quit years ago. But now, as he listened to Beth clean up in the adjacent bathroom, humming some slow, jazzy tune as she did, he definitely wished for a cigarette.

King was pleased with how the night had started. True, they'd gone straight to bed, even before ordering dinner, but he hoped that was a mark of eagerness and mutual attraction more than a lack of anything.

In Beth's bed, she'd been confident, comfortable in her own skin. She'd also been vocal, which King liked very much, and she hadn't been afraid to give directions, which King liked even more. He hated when he had to guess whether a woman was enjoying herself or pretending to.

And she'd been just as interested and invested in exploring his body as well.

She'd discovered early on that he liked his neck to be kissed, bitten, especially just above his collarbone.

King was recalling this, warming to the memory, when Beth's closet door began to slide slowly open.

The happy feelings evaporated as King searched for a weapon in the tangle of sheets.

Attacker? Ex-boyfriend? Secret husband? He didn't know what was coming out of the closet, but he wanted to be ready to meet it, whatever it was.

It was Louie Thorne.

"Christ," he swore, gathering the covers up to hide his bare chest.

"What's that, honey? You say something?" Beth called from the bathroom.

"Uh, nothing. I've just got a work call coming in," he said. "I'll take it outside."

He jabbed a finger at the window, hoping Lou would interpret this properly.

Lou stepped back into the closet and disappeared. King clambered out of bed, pulled on his pants and shirt, and padded barefoot downstairs. Lou was sitting on Beth's stoop when he opened the front door.

"Isn't this more suspicious?" she asked. "You talking to a woman outside."

She was right. "Take me to my apartment then."

She snorted. "Yes, a complete disappearance. Not strange at all."

But her hand was on his arm and she was pulling him through the dark. That drop-sick feeling washed over him—God, he hated that—before his apartment reformed around him.

"Thank you," he said, feeling less than grateful.

"What are you going to do if she looks for you and you're gone?"

"My Olds is still parked outside her place. I'll just tell her I decided to walk around a bit."

Lou slipped her hands into the pockets of her leather jacket.

"So what happened? What's going on?" King put his cell phone away.

"I'm going to Etienne and Delphine's place. I want to check out where she died. I was going to ask if you wanted to come with me."

King thought of Beth's face when he'd shown up with no dinner and two boxes of condoms. And now he'd jumped out of the bed almost as soon as they'd finished having sex. Leaving now would be more than a little insensitive.

"I should stay," he said, rubbing the back of his head. "There's not going to be anything at the house to find anyway."

"You could interview Etienne again," she said. "Or distract him while I search the house. I want to see where her body was found."

Already I'm disappointing her, King thought.

"When you see him tonight, ask him if we can do a formal interview. Tomorrow or the next day. Anytime," he said.

"Anything I should look for while I'm there?" she asked.

King considered this. "Lye. Oh, and hemlock."

"Hemlock?"

"It's a flowering plant that's poisonous. Turns out that the other chemical they got from the bones is hemlock."

"Basically, keep an eye out for weird chemicals," she said. "Anything else?"

He couldn't think of anything, and yet he also didn't want her to go. Looking at her standing there made him uneasy. Was it really about Paris though? Or was he simply embarrassed that Lou had found him in another woman's bed—a first since Lucy's passing.

"I can't think of anything else," he said finally.

"I'll take you back then."

When her hand fixed on his arm, his apartment dropped away. In its place was a cold sidewalk beside a copse of trees.

"Where the hell is this? Oh, wait." After a moment he oriented himself, recognizing the Garden District, and there, Prytania Street.

"To keep up with your 'I took a walk' lie," Lou said, staying close to the shadows. "You better put your phone up to your ear if you're going to sell this."

King pulled his phone from his pocket and did just that.

Lou snorted. "Her place is that way."

"Hey," King said, feeling more than a little silly with the phone against his ear. "Be careful tonight, okay?"

Lou's lips quirked. "You too."

Then she was gone.

King began padding down the sidewalk barefoot. When the town-home came into view, his heart sank at the sight of Beth standing on her porch.

"There you are!" she said. "Out there barefoot! Let me get a towel for your feet."

She had one ready before he reached the step.

"I'm sorry," he said. "It was one of my clients. He can be long-winded so I thought I'd take a stroll. It's so nice out."

It was, in fact, getting very cold.

"I decided on Caribbean for dinner," she said. "I'm in the mood for fried plantains. Do you like Caribbean?"

She held out two towels. One wet, one dry.

He took the wet rag in one hand, cleaned his feet, and then towel-dried them with the other.

"Who doesn't like jerked pineapple chicken?" he said. And hoped that by the time he'd finished eating, this terrible, uneasy feeling would go away.

29

———————

It took Piper and Henry only fifteen minutes to erect the castle backdrop on The Wild Cat stage. Henry really only needed someone to steady the painted wooden set while he snapped the stabilizers into place. It also needed to be just the right height so that Henry could stick his head through the cut square serving as the tower's window to sing the first half of his rendition of "When Will My (Queer) Life Begin?," a satire of the song from the Rapunzel movie.

Once the job was done, Piper wished him luck with the show and headed back toward the apartment to see if Dani or Mr. Allendale still needed help.

She'd just turned off of Bourbon Street onto St. Peter, moving deftly through the thickening crowd, when someone yelled her name. She looked up both sides of the street, but no one caught her eye. No one she knew, anyway.

"Piper!"

She looked again and found a flushed Dani jumping up and down, waving at her.

Piper closed the distance, meeting her on the corner.

"What's wrong?" she asked as the girl came to a gasping stop in front of her. "What happened?"

Dani held her side as if it were cramping. "I...was just...looking...for you...everywhere."

"Sorry, I went to The Wild Cat. Henry needed help setting up his stage set for tonight. Do you need to sit down?" Because she sure as hell looked like she needed to sit down. "If you need someone to move those boxes, I can get them. Just let—"

"No," Dani said firmly. "No, I want to talk to you. I *need* to talk to you."

Piper's heart began knocking in her chest. What was it about a girl saying "I need to talk to you" that dumped adrenaline into her veins?

She rubbed her forehead with her fist. "Okay. Then let's go to the garden."

The garden was only a block away, and there would be plenty of places to sit down. There were steps and benches, and the stone ledges lining the fountain, or even the grass beneath the trees, would be suitable enough, assuming it wasn't still damp from the rain earlier.

As they walked together, Piper watched Dani struggle to get her breath.

"Seriously, how far did you run?"

"I thought you went to Café du Monde or something, so I went that way. Then I circled the square. I ran into one of those girls you know. Black, curly hair. She said she thought she saw you in the French Market."

Scarlet, Piper's ex, could be a bitch when she wanted to.

"I didn't go to the market, sorry. I was at The Wild Cat the whole time."

"I thought you might be. I was heading there next."

"Why didn't you just call me?" Piper asked.

Dani's jaw worked. "I threw my phone when I was fighting with my mother and then I couldn't find it. I think it went into one of the boxes. It was stupid. Anyway, you're here now."

Piper stepped aside so Dani could pick wherever she wanted to sit. She chose a stone bench beneath the statue of Jesus, collapsing onto it with one hand still holding her hip.

"I think I was panicking more than actually out of breath," she said, rubbing the back of her neck. "I was scared I wouldn't find you."

It had been a while since Dani's PTSD had flared up. Piper squeezed her hand reassuringly. "You found me. But seriously, if it's about the boxes, I can—"

"Shut up about the freaking boxes," she said, pulling her hand away.

"Okay." Piper rubbed her palms on her knees. "Then tell me what's up."

"First of all, I'm so sorry about my mom."

"Oh, it's okay—"

Dani threw her hand up. "*Don't.* Don't you dare apologize for her. What she said was terrible and I can't even believe it came out of her mouth. I mean, I've always known that she was a snob, but that was *so* disrespectful. I'm embarrassed for her."

"We don't pick our parents," Piper said, thinking, not for the first time, of her mom. On and off she'd flickered through Piper's mind as she'd moved throughout the day. Sometimes the tears would come, making her throat thick and uncomfortable. Other times, it was only the cool wave of sadness that made her heart heavy. "Your dad seems pretty cool though. We talked before Henry texted me."

Dani placed her hand over her heart. "Oh god, he didn't say anything, did he?"

"No, no! He was super sweet. I like him."

Dani exhaled toward the sky, visibly relieved. "Oh thank God. I mean, he's way better than my mother, but just nothing has gone to plan today so I was prepared to find out he stabbed you or something."

"He gave me cigarettes."

Dani snorted, surprised. "He only shares those with people he really likes. You must've made an impression."

Or I must've looked really sad, Piper thought.

How many times had Henry asked her if she was okay as they were setting up the stage? Too many.

Dani was looking into Piper's eyes, *really* looking.

"What is it?" Piper asked.

"What do I have to do, Piper? Just tell me what I have to do."

Piper's heart kicked. "What do you mean?"

"Do I have to get rid of the viola? My car? Do you want me to give away all of my money or never talk to my parents again—"

Piper drew back. "What? No."

"Whatever it is, please just tell me what I have to do to keep you."

Piper's stomach dropped.

Dani leaned toward her, searching her eyes as if the answers were written there. "I don't care about any of that other stuff. It's just...it's just shit. And if I have to get rid of it for you to be comfortable, I'll do it. I'll make a freaking Craigslist ad for my car tonight."

"I don't want you to do that," Piper said.

"Then tell me what I have to do. I know you think I don't like that apartment because it's smaller than my old one, but I swear, Piper, I *swear* to *God*, I have never been happier in my life. I could live in a freaking cardboard box with you and be happy."

So happy now. Always smiling, Mr. Allendale had said.

"Liar," Piper said. "Where would you put all your fancy skin-care products if we lived in a box? You need electricity for the mini fridge you keep them in."

"Do you really want me to go?" Dani asked. "Look me in the eyes and tell me you really want me to move out."

Piper looked into those warm brown eyes, but found her throat wouldn't cooperate.

Her mind kept saying, *No. No, I want you to stay.*

Dani took her hands and squeezed. "I sent my parents away. I know you *said* you want me out of your apartment, but I'm not leaving. I'm not letting you break up with me when you're not even my official girlfriend. If you want to break up with me and throw me out of your life, you're going to have to ask me out first."

Piper laughed. "You're being serious right now?"

"Yes," Dani said, and squeezed her hands again. "You have to be my girlfriend for at least a whole day before you can get rid of me."

Piper didn't know what to say to this. It was true that she had never officially asked Dani to be with her. Things between them had simply evolved somewhat organically. First when Dani had been in the hospital after Petrov's attack. Then as Dani tried to process her PTSD. When Diana blew up her apartment, it had just seemed really natural that Dani would come stay with her.

And now...

"Piper." Dani gave her a pleading look. "Please tell me what I have to do to keep you."

"Keep me?"

"Keep you. In my life, as my girlfriend. I'll move out if you insist, but before I do that, I want you to look me in the eyes and tell me that you don't like me living with you. That you don't like waking up to this unwashed face, having coffee with me in the mornings, taking showers with me, watching TV at the end of the day, all snuggled up on the sofa. Look me in the *freaking* eye and tell me you want your space, and I'll leave."

Piper looked her in the eyes, but she couldn't say it. Because she loved all those things. And more.

"I mean, I definitely like taking showers with you," she said.

Dani nudged her. "Be serious."

"I do like it. All of it. I like living with you," Piper said. "But we come from really different worlds. You know that, right? I can't live like your parents. I wouldn't know how to act and I'd be stressed out all the time wondering if I was embarrassing you or—"

"Are you kidding me? You could *never* embarrass me. This afternoon you showed ten times more class than my mother did."

"But I won't ever be able to give you those things. I can't buy you a house like that. I can't even afford the insurance on your SUV. You'll always have less with me and it's going to hurt. I'm going to feel terrible about it *all the time*."

"First of all, you're making a lot of assumptions about our not-even-official-yet relationship. Who said you need to provide for me? Are you saying I can't be the breadwinner in our relationship?"

Oh god. Was Piper walking into some sort of feminist trap?

Dani must've seen the panic blooming on her face. "Listen, before we get into all that, let me just say something."

Piper swallowed. "Okay."

Dani looked out over the garden, at the bare trees and swaying grass. Finally, she said, "Do you remember the night I watched you do card readings in the square for the first time?"

"When you were undercover in all that goth makeup, shivering half to death? Yeah, I remember."

Piper missed the black eyeliner, truth be told, but Dani had kept the black nails, which was a nice touch.

"I knew right then that there was something special about you. It isn't just how smart you are, or how hard you work to make other people smile. And it wasn't just that you're a great listener. I mean, you're a *really* great listener. Hell, it's not even our amazing chemistry."

God, yeah, we have amazing chemistry. Piper's stomach muscles tightened just at the thought.

If Dani saw the blush spreading across her face, she ignored it.

"It's that you are so *genuine*. You are the most genuine person I've ever met. You're not artificial, or elitist like my parents. You're *real*. You're a hundred percent real with me and there isn't a single person in my life who has treated me with as much kindness and love and respect as you have. Okay, maybe my dad, but a lot of the time he goes along with my mom, so you're even doing better than him."

Piper's throat was so tight she could choke. Her gaze had slid down to their clasped hands while Dani spoke, but now Dani tilted her chin up and forced her to look her in the eyes.

"I don't need another freaking car or a fifty-room house, Piper Lynn Genereux. I need you because of how you make me feel. Loved. Safe. Happy. And because..."

She searched the park.

"Because what I feel for you is the realest, truest thing I've ever had. Please don't take that away from me."

Tears spilled from Piper's eyes, and Dani wiped them with the cuffs of her sweater.

"I know this is rich coming from the woman who literally lied to you and deceived you just to get to know you, but I mean it. I want to be with you, Piper. And not for anything you can buy me. I want to be with you because I love you."

Piper thought of her mom, dead in her forties, a whole stream of ruined partnerships in her wake. Had her mother ever been happy with anyone? Had she ever felt loved and cared for the way Piper did with

Dani? And was Piper really going to throw it away because she felt like she couldn't give Dani diamonds or sports cars or whatever the hell she was supposed to give a rich girl?

Here was the most amazing girl she'd *ever* met, saying that she wanted to be with her. *Her.* Not for the money or security she could provide but just to be with her.

It was impossible for Piper to believe that anyone could ever like her so much, but even with that aside, there was a simple truth:

Piper loved her. She loved seeing her and kissing her and talking to her. She loved sleeping with her—both literally and metaphorically. She loved spending time with her, and whenever she heard something funny, Dani was the first person she wanted to share it with. She liked having Dani in her orbit, as an integral part of each day. She loved her smile. Her laugh.

And she wanted Dani to stay.

Piper didn't believe she deserved her, but she wanted her to stay. Always.

"Did you hear me?" Dani said. "I love you."

"I heard you."

"If you don't—"

"I love you," Piper spat out. Her face flushed with heat. "I love you too."

Dani's face erupted in the biggest grin as she flung her arms around Piper's neck.

"Then please don't make me leave," she whispered into Piper's hair. She pulled back and cupped her face. "Let me stay and we'll just be together and happy, and argue over who is going to pay for what, *whatever*, but mostly we'll just be happy. Really, *really* happy."

Piper laughed, dabbing at her eyes with her sleeves.

"Please," Dani said. "Please be with me. Be my girlfriend."

It was terrifying, the idea that Piper might have a decent future. Piper wasn't sure she could ever believe it possible, not with all the terrible things that had happened in her life so far. But she also couldn't forgive herself if she didn't try. Her mother hadn't tried, and look where it had gotten her.

At the very least, Piper had to be brave enough to try.

"Okay," she said, and wrapped her arms around Dani too. "Stay and be my girlfriend."

Dani squealed and squeezed her hard again. And when Piper began to laugh, Dani finally let her go, but only so they could kiss.

30

———————

The path leading up to the large house in the fifteenth arrondissement was thick with brush. Shrubs taller than Lou herself crowded the stone path at a black door. For this reason, it was easy to materialize in the shadowed space between two shrubs and step onto the path. But Lou wondered if this was a mistake once she saw the cameras above the doorway.

She pressed the doorbell and felt a sharp prick in her finger.

She yanked it back. A large droplet of blood was forming on the tip of her right index finger.

What the hell?

She bent and inspected the doorbell but didn't see anything. There was a thorny plant growing along the door, but Lou didn't think she'd touched that.

Had something bitten her? Some angry insect who'd felt she'd invaded their home? Lou didn't see any bugs, and besides, it was late in the season.

She sucked the blood off her finger.

Footsteps sounded, and she touched her jacket once to make sure her guns were concealed.

At the last moment, she wondered if she should turn back and get her Kevlar sleeves and her knives.

She decided against it. This would be quick. Only long enough to see where Delphine had been attacked, and then she would leave. Even if Etienne had nefarious plans, he could hardly take her on. He was just one grief-stricken man.

The door opened and Etienne appeared with a wine glass in hand, wearing a black turtleneck that instantly made her think of Konstantine. Except that Konstantine looked very handsome with the candlelight in his eyes and his muscular forearms resting on the tabletop. Etienne, while far from ugly, still didn't wear the ensemble quite as well.

"You came," he said with a breathy sigh of relief. He stepped aside so she could enter. "Please."

Lou crossed the threshold, turning as he moved behind her to close the door. This maneuver prevented her from having to expose her back.

"I am glad you came," he said, his excitement visible. "I wasn't sure if you would."

"I wanted to see where Delphine died," she said. Was this too gruesome or direct? King thought she lacked tact when it came to certain conversations, but she'd always preferred to be blunt with the people she helped. The worst had already happened to them. There was no need to protect their feelings now.

And Lou had had plenty of success before King came along, so no need to doubt her methods now.

Etienne motioned her forward. "Don't worry, it is part of the tour. But first, a glass of wine."

What is it with European men and their wine? she thought.

She trailed behind him as he led the way to the kitchen. As they walked, she took note of where the shadows pooled. Doorways and closets. Large pieces of furniture. Unfortunately, the house was well lit. Dramatic sky lighting from above seemed to cover most rooms from corner to corner. If she needed to make a quick escape, she would definitely need to find a dark room.

There was always the option to shoot out the lights, too. But Lou thought that was rather dramatic. She'd only resort to that if necessary.

For this reason she began to take note of all the closed doors. The pantry, the bathroom, anywhere she could duck inside and turn off a light should she need a quick escape.

There was already a wine glass sitting on the wooden countertop when they entered the kitchen. Beside it, an opaque bottle. Etienne lifted it and filled her glass halfway with red wine.

"Here you go." He lifted the glass from the top, his hand cupped over it as he held it out to her.

"No, thank you," she said. She had no intention of drinking this wine, in case it was spiked.

"Oh, please. Drink with me. I can—"

"I'm fine," Lou said, trying to keep a cap on her irritation. "I don't have a lot of time."

"*D'accord.*" Etienne arched his brows but at least stopped trying to give her the glass of wine.

With his own glass now full, he led the way out of the kitchen and into a large living room featuring many of the same design details. High ceilings and dramatic lighting. Etienne babbled about the interior design and the style of the paintings on the walls as they passed. While the walls were white, the paintings themselves were somber and dramatic. Two in particular highlighted slit throats, and a third showed a man in the throes of dying, his naked torso bent in agony.

Lou regarded these, noticing that the warmth in her hand was spreading through her, transforming into a weight that was settling on her shoulders and upper arms.

After a moment of silence Etienne said, "She kept the real art upstairs. Come."

At the top of the stairs, three of the doors were shut, one was open.

"This is where I found her," Etienne said, gesturing at the luminescent bathroom. "My Delphine."

Lou stepped in, trying to ignore the growing ache in her hand.

The tub was the centerpiece. Deep and set in the center of the room, light seemed to hit it from every angle. Because the walls, tub, and floor were all white, Lou could imagine how it must've looked with the bloody water overflowing from the tub, sloshing onto the floor.

As dramatic as everything else in this house.

Also, because of the width of the bathroom, it would have been more than possible for a man to lift Delphine and throw her into the tub. The man in the catacombs, though on the tall side, would have definitely been able to maneuver in this bathroom.

Delphine, given her shorter stature, would've found it difficult to climb over the high lip of the tub as she was bleeding. Perhaps she'd already been stabbed, then lifted into the tub before the water was turned on.

Or she just fell back into it. Lou imagined a scene in which Delphine, stabbed and dying, turned on the water, let the tub fill, and simply opened her arms, falling into the water.

What a weird idea, she thought, noticing that the weight in her arms was somehow invading her brain as well.

Etienne was watching her out of the corner of his eye. Lou could feel his gaze on her.

"Let me show you her work," he said.

He turned away from the bathroom and crossed to one of the closed doors.

He did not turn on a light when he entered. In the dark, he said, "Come in. Don't be afraid."

Lou wasn't afraid.

While most women wouldn't want to walk into a dark room with a stranger, in the dark, Lou felt the safest. If he tried something, if he so much as put a hand on her, she could shift.

And after wandering these over-lit rooms, the dark space was more than a little welcome.

Then Lou stepped into the room. And her heart began to hammer.

It was the room.

The room.

Four walls of strange black glass. She reached out to touch one to be sure it was real. It was. The glass was cool to the touch, giving the slight impression that her reflection moved like a shadow beneath the glossy surface.

"Let me turn on the light," Etienne said, his voice nearly in her ear.

Lou almost said no, but it was too late.

Light burst into being, the room filling with it.

Not from a fixture overhead, no. The lights were *inside* the walls.

Lou's pulse raged in her ear.

In the glass display before her were two bodies. Two women cut open and arranged like the vivisections from the museum. But these were not insects or plants.

These were human. Human *women*.

One's chest had been opened, the flesh pinned to each side in flamboyant ribbons and the soft tissues removed. The heart somehow remained suspended inside the emptied and cleaned rib cage. Her breasts had also been removed, placed instead in her delicately cupped hands as if the woman had taken them off and were offering them to the viewer.

One of her legs, particularly her inner thigh, had been cut open, revealing the long lean muscle beneath.

But the face. The face was a mask of agony, the features frozen in permanent horror as she stared right at Lou, unseeing.

The second body was not so neatly preserved. Her flesh was turning gray, shriveling up. This face was contorted as well, the head bent back in a silent scream, the jaws gaping to release the force of the sound. Because it was slowly decomposing, Lou realized, the face didn't look as fresh as the other. The graying skin had begun to sag, slide away from the bones, revealing barely contained eyeballs in their opening sockets.

With the lights on, Lou could now see how many squares there were. Twelve in total, including the two the dead women occupied. Had every one of these squares been full of girls? Could Delphine really have displayed as many as twelve mutilated bodies at a time?

"Delphine did this?" Lou asked.

"*Bah, oui,*" Etienne said. "I do not have her gifts or talent."

"Delphine killed them all."

"Of course," he said.

Delphine killed them all. Delphine. That was why Lou's compass could never find the killer. *Take me to the killer*—but the killer was dead. And Assia—was that the same?

Lou struggled to rerun the details through her mind, piecing together the truth. It was far harder than it should've been.

She didn't feel well.

Etienne sipped his wine and said, "Delphine discovered a tree resin which, when heated correctly, can preserve the body for longer, but as you can see, they still do not last. So disappointing. I want to gaze at them forever, each beautiful little creation. *But*, Delphine argued the temporality added to the beauty of the work."

That was why I couldn't find anyone, she thought. Those walls were filled with resin, and thin enough only for the bodies that filled them. The light source seemed to come somewhere from the ground, below their suspended feet, shining up through the gelatinous material. Or were the lights above? Lou couldn't be sure.

Etienne cupped one elbow, wagging a finger at her. "See, you aren't horrified. You are made of different stuff, no? I could tell from the moment I saw you. I can feel the darkness inside you. It speaks to me."

A wave of nausea washed over Lou and she staggered. The lighted images of the women's bodies doubled, tripled, created layers upon layers until she couldn't see.

"What's wrong with my eyes?"

Lou reached out for the wall but missed it. Nothing was there.

"It's the hemlock," he said. "It's affecting you more slowly than the others, which is interesting. But it *will* paralyze you. We used it on all the specimens. It immobilizes the body, so that Delphine could begin before the heart stopped. She liked to feel the heart beating in her hands. She said it was her favorite part."

How had she come into contact with poison? She hadn't drunk anything. She'd been so careful.

"The doorbell was a bit sharp, wasn't it?" Etienne laughed. "We kidnapped a delivery girl the same way."

Lou lunged for him, intending to wrap her hands around his throat, but her palms connected only with the lit glass.

She considered pulling her gun, but shooting blindly was stupid.

The shot would ricochet in a room of this size, possibly hitting her instead.

"Who killed Delphine? Was it one of these women? Assia?"

Etienne sighed. "I told her never to work on the art alone. Without me, it isn't safe. Even da Vinci had his assistants, you see. But Delphine was very particular. She listened to no one. *Artists.*" He laughed at his own joke. "But the girl must have woken up while I was away at Le Grand Palais. Delphine hadn't even given her the hemlock when she began. It was careless."

Was that what happened? Had Delphine, in her excitement, begun something she couldn't finish?

Assia fought back, managed to wound Delphine fatally, but it hadn't saved her.

"You killed Assia?" Lou asked.

"*Non.* They were both dead when I arrived. There was blood all over this room. The bathroom. I cannot be sure, but I think Assia attacked. But Delphine finished her."

So maybe Lou's vision of Delphine turning on the tub and falling back into it to die with all the pomp of one of her subjects hadn't been too far from the mark.

"But you helped her?"

"Oh yes. I would find the beautiful girls for her. Perhaps in a park or when they crossed the street. Sometimes I would invite them in for a glass of wine and they would accept."

"What about Assia? She was a student—she went missing a few days before Delphine died."

"Yes, the last one. Delphine saw her walking by through a window. 'She's so beautiful, look at her bone structure,' she cried out.

"So I went outside, tried to talk to her, but she was resistant. Sometimes they are."

Lou tried to quell the nausea building in her guts.

"I had to strike her here." He touched the back of his neck. "Then I carried her. She was only twelve meters from the front door. But I couldn't stay. I was expected at Le Grand Palais within the hour. I asked Delphine to wait until I got home, but she didn't listen. Oh, *pourquoi, Delphine?* Why didn't you wait for me?"

Delphine killed Assia. Assia killed Delphine.

There was no killer at large. Only Etienne, the dutiful, if deeply deranged, accomplice.

"I had to put the girl's body straight into the wash," Etienne said. "Delphine didn't even get to..." His voice cracked. The grief Lou had seen before reappeared. "I *told* her. I *told* her to wait until I got home and we could do it together. But she didn't. She *didn't* wait."

He threw his wine glass against the floor. It shattered, warm spray wetting Lou's legs.

Lou tried to find the light switch on the wall, the trigger, anything that would allow her to make it dark again, but it was smooth. And because the light streaked in all directions, making details impossible to pick out, she would never find it.

The door, she thought. *I need to get to that other closed room.*

"First I thought you were my Delphine, her ghost. You came to the park that night when I was watching that woman. I almost took her, but you appeared. And again when I dreamt of Delphine you came. 'You are not alone,' she told me. 'You are not alone,' and then you arrived. It was like a gift."

"I'm not your fucking gift," Lou said.

Etienne ignored this. "Then in the catacombs, I was so full of despair, and *again* you came. Whenever I was lonely, whenever I hungered, you came for me. I thought this was all coincidence until tonight. Tonight, I was going to do it. I was going to take the girl in the cemetery, and what happened?"

Lou didn't need to answer this rhetorical question. She knew what had happened. She'd come to the cemetery and had found Etienne sprawled beneath the weeping angel.

What she'd seen in his eyes hadn't been a mistake. She should've never doubted that he was a monster just because he also grieved.

I won't make that mistake again.

Lou's legs were shaking. The heartbeat in her ears sounded strained, erratic.

Fingers brushed her arms, and she tried to grab them but they were already gone.

"Perhaps you are the manifestation of my desire, my thirst."

"Stop talking," she said. *Shut up, just shut up.*

He did not, in fact, shut up.

"Tell me what you are, my strange apparition. You come, you go. You are drawn to me the way I am drawn to you, aren't you? Why have you chosen me? Is it because the catacombs run under this house? Do you haunt me or this place?"

Lou ran her hand along the wall until it broke open. There. The hallway. And beyond that, the closed door.

Her escape.

She just had to make it there.

"Tell me," he begged again. "Are you to be my new artist, or the art?"

When the hand wrapped around her arm this time, she threw her elbow back, felt it connect hard. Etienne cried and fell back. The loss of his body staggered her.

She stumbled out into the hall, willing herself to stay upright on her feet, though her legs were going numb. Her arms were too heavy.

"Where are you going? This house locks from the inside," he called after her. "You cannot open a door or window without my keys."

Something musical tinkled behind her. Was he shaking a key ring at her? *That bastard.*

He laughed, but the sound was thick. Lou hoped she'd broken his nose and that was blood clogging his throat. That was the least he had coming to him.

"If you scream, the walls will only swallow it. We soundproofed everything. The walls. The windows."

Lou didn't need a door or a window. She needed the dark.

She grabbed the handle of the closed door and pushed, but it didn't open. It was locked.

"Stay with me," he begged. "I am not done with you."

Lou stumbled a few feet forward and tried the second closed door, but this handle too didn't budge. The room was shut tight.

"I only want to open you up." His voice was closer now. "I want to see that darkness inside you."

Lou threw her shoulder against the door. It bounced, but it didn't open. She was growing too weak. It was getting harder to breathe.

Definitely hemlock, she thought, believing now more than ever that there must have been the thinnest needle protruding from the wood beside that doorbell.

She was running out of time.

"I cannot turn you into one of Delphine's beautiful creations," he said. "My work will be crude, but I will try my best. I will open you up as...as *gently* as I possibly can."

His voice was close, too close. She thought that was his warm breath on the back of her neck.

With a rally cry, she slammed her shoulder into the door again, and this time, it busted inward. She fell forward into the blessed dark.

There had been a brief sensation of fabric brushing her face, perhaps coats or shirts. It didn't matter. It was enough. If the room had walls or a floor, Lou would never know.

She was swallowed by the shadows before she ever hit the ground.

31

———————

"I suspect we will only need to be there two days, four including travel," Konstantine said, lacing his hands in front of him and steepling the fingers. "Just long enough for me to speak to Antonio, tour the warehouse facility, and perhaps give my regards to the Merrito family. We should think about what gift we are going to present them."

"Am I going with you or do you need me here?" Stefano asked. The man was staring down at his phone, only periodically glancing up to regard Konstantine over the mountain of documents on his desk.

It was late, too late. Konstantine's eyes burned and he longed for his bed. But it had been impossible to fall asleep after Lou had left him. It hadn't helped that he'd found Stefano burning the midnight oil too.

I should just go back to bed, he thought. *She will be fine.*

But first, I will finish what I started.

Konstantine rubbed his jaw. "I think it would be better if you—"

A crash cut his sentence in half.

Stefano swore, his eyes opening wide as he stood, his legs knocking the chair back.

"Konstantine."

Konstantine rose and came around the desk. There on his stone floor was Louie. She was face down and looked as if she was trying to push herself up but couldn't.

"Louie!" he cried, falling to his knees beside her. "Louie, what's happened?"

Stefano helped him turn her over.

Konstantine searched her arms, her throat, chest, legs, looking for bullet wounds or a cut. But there was nothing. She tried to open her hand and Konstantine took it, unclenching her fist carefully to inspect it. There was a dark spot on her index finger, but that couldn't be it. It was tiny. Insignificant. As if she'd merely pulled a splinter from her finger.

"What happened?" he begged her. He pushed her hair off her face and found her burning up.

"P-p—" Her teeth chattered. "*P-poison.*"

Her legs began to spasm.

"Poison?" he asked. "You were poisoned?"

Lou tried to answer him, but her eyes pinched shut.

There were countless poisons in the world, and without knowing what was coursing through her veins, there was no way for Konstantine to know what antidote may help her.

"H-hemlock," she ground out, spitting the word between gritted teeth.

Hemlock. There was no antidote for hemlock.

What will I do? What will I do? What will I—

"What do you want me to do?" Stefano asked, his eyes wide.

Konstantine couldn't answer.

"Paolo," Stefano said, using Konstantine's first name. He was the *only* one who'd ever gotten away with doing that. "Tell me what to do."

Konstantine looked at Lou, shivering—no, *convulsing* in his lap. She was going to die if he didn't do something.

She was going to die.

"Water," Konstantine said. "I need water."

Stefano went into the bathroom and turned on the tap.

"No, I need to put her in water."

"*Cos' è? Una fottuta pianta?*" he cried, turning on the tub's faucet.

It would take too long to fill the tub, and it was too small for him to fit in with her.

In her condition, she would need someone to help her get to the surface. What if her muscles gave completely? Didn't hemlock cause paralysis? He couldn't remember.

"*Non importa. Aiutami!*" Konstantine said, and stood, laying Louie gently on the floor. "I have to put her in the fountain. Help me carry her."

"Help you? She's a *girl. Non pesa niente.*"

"She's much heavier than she looks."

Stefano opened the door to the office and then lifted Lou's legs as Konstantine slipped his arms under hers.

They lifted her together on three and Stefano swore. "Are there bricks in her pockets?"

"Hurry up."

They carried her into the courtyard, and blessedly, none of the children were there. No one had to be sent away. It was only the three of them as they lifted Lou over the lip of the stone fountain and into the flowing water.

It was only three feet deep. Konstantine prayed it was enough.

He climbed in after her, trying to keep her head above water.

Stefano threw up his hands. "*Cosa fai?*"

"This is the only way I know to help her."

"Drown her? And then yourself? *Dio mio.*"

"I can't explain now," he said, hoping that Stefano wouldn't try to do anything reckless, like dragging him out of the fountain.

Konstantine *had* to go. He had to.

There were a hundred things that could go wrong. Lou could die in La Loon, trapping Konstantine forever in that nightmarish place, without the ability to return home. Or that monster of hers, upon seeing him, might devour him whole as she had his brothers, one by one.

Don't think about that, he scolded himself. His fears wouldn't help her.

Konstantine lay down in the water beside her and spoke directly into her ear.

"Louie. We have to go to La Loon. Do you hear me? I am going to dunk us under and you have to take us."

Her eyes fluttered open, and for a moment he thought he saw a flash of recognition.

"Okay. One...two..." He dunked them both beneath the water.

They cleared the surface, their backs resting against the bottom of the rippling pool.

He waited.

And waited.

But the water didn't change from dark blue to red. It didn't warm.

Nothing happened. He waited for a heartbeat longer until he was afraid he might drown her.

He came up choking.

"Louie. You know I can't do it! You have to! You have to take us across."

He shook her a little, hoping to bring her closer to consciousness. He was losing her.

He was losing her fast.

"Perhaps it's the light," Stefano said, his hands gripping the side of the fountain.

"What?"

"The light, in the fountain. Perhaps it's too bright."

Konstantine regarded the light beneath the cherub's face. "*Sì*. Turn it off."

Stefano's feet pounded the courtyard. There was a beat of silence and then the light cut off. The gurgling water fell still.

"Please try," he told her, gathering her into his arms once more, trying to get a good grip on her. "I'll explain everything later, but you have to take us through those waters. *Now*. On three. One...two..."

He dunked them again, their backs hitting the stone floor for a second time.

Then they lay there in the dark.

A terrible panic began to rise up in him, his heart beating faster than it ever had before.

She was going to die.

She was going to die here in his arms and he could do nothing to stop it.

No, please. No, please, not now. Not after everything.

But then the water began to warm, a subtle shift in temperature. Konstantine dared to open his eyes, to find they were much deeper now—the bottom of the fountain had fallen away and its blue waters had shifted to a deep blood red.

Wrapping one arm tighter around her waist, Konstantine kicked for the surface, pushing harder and harder, as fast as he could toward salvation.

32

—————

An eternal purple twilight and hazy yellow mountains formed in the distance as Konstantine burst through the surface of the lake. Twin moons serene in the sky above the blood-colored water stretching off into the distance. And that familiar scent of sulfur, what he'd come to think of as the scent of hell, hit his nose with full force.

But they'd made it. They'd crossed over.

"Come on," he said. "Hang in there."

Konstantine dragged Lou to the shore, only so far as to rest her head on the embankment, safe from the threat of drowning but keeping the rest of her in the water.

He pulled off her coat, stripped her down to only her shirt and pants. He tossed the leather jacket and gun onto the land for safekeeping. Then he inspected the pricked finger again, trying to see the shape of the wound. Had it been a needle? A glass shard?

It was too small to see clearly, especially in this low light.

It didn't matter. It only mattered that he hold it beneath the surface of the water.

He lifted the hand but it looked the same. Maybe the water needed to get into her veins?

Konstantine reached into his soaked boot and found the blade. Sliding it out of its sheath, he adjusted its wet handle in his grip.

He didn't want to cut her hand, something so well used, but he also hated the idea of cutting her.

Would making her drink it work? he wondered.

That's when the monster screeched, and Konstantine's stomach knotted, his bowels threatening to empty themselves right here at the water's edge.

Quickly he slashed Lou's arm. A second, third, and fourth cut followed. All shallow, but enough to introduce the water to her blood-stream. He was about to do a fifth and final cut when the beast burst through the black forest and into view.

As soon as she saw him she shrieked, coming up onto her hind legs, the other four claws in a crooked position beside her pale, scaly stom-ach. The black muscles of her body contracted as she came forward, her head bent, her eyes on him.

"Would you believe," he told her, "that I'm trying to help her?"

She screamed again, showing him her puffy white maw opened wide and the row upon row of sharp teeth contained within.

"Please don't eat me. *Per favore,*" he said, even as his grip on the blade tightened. His voice sounded calm to his ears but inside he knew better. His mind was filled with a single panicked mantra: *please please please please please—*

He tried to keep the air moving in and out of his lungs.

The beast nudged the side of his head with hers, and for an awful moment he thought she was going to open up and snap her jaws shut over his throat.

But then she backed up and turned a circle, coming around to Lou's other side. She did the same headbutting motion, but this time, when Lou's head only lolled, she let out a soft, cooing sound. Almost like a dog's whine.

She did it again.

"I don't know what else to do for her," Konstantine admitted. He didn't put down the knife, but at least the creature seemed more inter-ested in Lou's well-being than severing his spine.

"I thought the water would help," he added.

The beast's long white tongue rolled from its mouth and licked up Lou's arm. The blood left on the surface—or perhaps it wasn't blood but water from the lake—began to dry as pink droplets on her skin.

Lou's eyes fluttered opened.

"Don't give up," he told her. "*Don't.*"

A heartbeat later, she was unconscious again.

The beast lay down beside them, its great yellow eyes fixed on Lou.

It was right. There was nothing else for him to do but wait.

Konstantine began to pray.

Lou woke to a thick, slick tongue dragging across her face. She groaned and tried to sit up.

She felt like *shit*.

Her whole body ached. Either she'd clenched every muscle for the last few hours or someone had run her body through a pulverizer.

"How do you feel?"

Lou turned and found Konstantine sitting beside her. His hair was wet and stuck to his face, no doubt from the trip through the water. But the relief collected in his features shone through.

"Like hell," she said. "What happened?"

La Loon loomed before her, bizarre and sulfuric with its blood-red waters. And this was a fitting setting, considering how she felt. But she had no memory of how she got here, or why it was Konstantine sitting beside her.

Was she dead? Was this a dream?

Konstantine ran his hands through his wet hair. "You don't remember?"

Remember...

She thought of the dinner with Konstantine first. Then the sex. Then...she'd gone to Etienne's. That large house, those macabre paintings. The doorbell that had pricked her.

"He poisoned me," Lou said. "I'm going to kill him."

"The Frenchman?"

"It was Delphine." Lou pressed her fingers into her temples. Her head hurt so bad. "Delphine killed all those girls. She cut them up and displayed them. Assia was the one who stabbed her in the gut."

"That's why you couldn't find your killer," he said. "Your killer was dead."

After a beat he asked, "Did he really use hemlock? That's what you said."

"That's what he told me. And King said they found traces of it on the bones. I should've never rang the doorbell. I'd been so careful about that stupid wine glass and—"

Here Konstantine's concern drained a little. "You were drinking with him?"

Lou was too miserable to give him the look he deserved. "No, I *didn't* drink with him in case he spiked the wine. But it was the doorbell. There must've been a needle too thin to see."

Jabbers pushed her head against Lou's.

Lou reached out and patted her. "I'm not ignoring you. I'm just working out what the hell just happened."

Jabbers began to purr.

"You collapsed in my office. Good thing, because I don't have a bathtub in my apartment," Konstantine said. "I don't know how I would've helped you if you'd followed me there. Perhaps someone is looking out for us."

Lou didn't have it in her to debate the existence of God at the moment. She simply kept her mouth shut and let Konstantine recount her surprise arrival in his office, her condition, ending with, "So, I put you in the fountain."

"You put me in a public fountain? I hope you charged admission for that show."

"No," he said. "We used the one outside my office. I wasn't sure it would work, but I had to try."

"Maybe my head is broken, but I still don't understand why you thought bringing me here was the answer." She frowned. Because if she'd found Konstantine poisoned, the idea of dunking him underwater wouldn't be *her* first instinct.

He bit his lower lip. "I have something to tell you."

"You have herpes?"

He scowled. "What? *No.*"

"You killed one of my friends?"

He huffed. "*No.* I would never."

"You slept with someone else?"

Konstantine pinched the bridge of his nose. "I will never. Do you have any more guesses?"

"No. So spit it out." She sounded more than a little irritated to herself. "What did you do?"

"Do you remember when we came here together the first time and I collected all of the samples? From the soil, from the air, the plants. The rocks."

She did. But not so much for the entertainment value of Konstantine meeting Jabbers for the first time and relishing his barely contained horror as they'd traversed this nightmare landscape together. She remembered it because it was the first night they'd had sex, in the cave hidden amongst the cliffs.

"What about it?" she asked, and wondered if he was thinking about that night too.

"One of the test results was very strange. Very, *very* strange. So I had my lab run more tests."

"Of course you did. *And?*"

"There is something different about this water."

Lou frowned. "What's wrong with the water?"

"It's not exactly water."

"What the hell do you mean, it's not *exactly* water?"

"And it heals you."

She only blinked at him.

"It has the ability to heal wounds. It is full of these strange little microbes that speed up healing."

"Microbes? What kind of microbes?"

"We don't know. We don't have them on earth."

Lou stared out over the red waters. "And you learned this from the sample you took?"

"*Sì,*" he said. "And these microbes are everywhere. They're in the plants, the soil, Jabbers. The air. The water. I want to take a blood sample from you to see if they are in your system, and if they are, how long they live there before they die."

"Are you a mob boss or a scientist?" Lou asked.

He ignored this. "Have you tried drinking it?"

The idea disgusted her. "Do you know what's *in* this water?"

"Didn't you ever wonder why you healed so quickly after a fight? Why you could be nearly *dead* one night and simply sore the next?"

Lou had wondered, but like most things, she hadn't thought about it for too long. She'd assumed it was part of the very weird special ability package that she'd inherited. But now that she thought of it, why wouldn't Lucy have healed? Cancer or no cancer, she would've healed too, since they had the same gift.

Except Lucy only traveled by shadows. Never water.

"It took forever to heal my shoulder," Lou said, trying to force images of her dying aunt from her mind.

Konstantine held up a finger. "But do you remember what you were *not* doing then?"

"I didn't cross over."

"No, after the shopkeeper—"

"Melandra."

"Yes, after she shot you, you didn't hunt for many months."

That was true. And her healing had taken forever.

Come to think of it, it wasn't until she crossed over after her long hiatus that her shoulder pain began to actually disappear.

Lou pointed at the lake. "So you're saying this water heals me every time I cross over and these microbes get into my bloodstream?"

"Yes. That is what I'm saying."

"Do these microbes do anything else? Make me stronger? Faster?"

"That is the interesting part. We can't be sure what all it can do without more tests. It heals wounds, slows the effects of poisons, but does it also slow aging? Cure cancers?"

Lou's heart sputtered at that, the idea that maybe her aunt Lucy could've been saved if only she'd agreed to come here.

Konstantine put a hand on her leg. "I'm sorry. I shouldn't have said that. I only meant that I would like to know more. Wouldn't you?"

"If you're looking to get out of drugs and start selling this fountain of youth water instead—"

"No, no." He shook his head. "I don't want to exploit it. This is why I was worried about telling you. I thought you would be upset."

"I'm not upset," she said. Because no one could come to La Loon without her. It wasn't like they were going to show up and drain the lake when she wasn't looking. She could protect this place from everyone, even Konstantine, if it came to that.

There was only one way in and out of this place, and that was her.

He squeezed her hand. "I'm simply curious. Aren't you?"

"A little," she admitted.

Lou thought of the time she'd almost bled to death on the shores of La Loon. At the last minute, Jabbers had pushed her into the water. One nudge of her huge head had knocked Lou back in.

At the time, Lou had thought it was because the creature understood that Lou came from another world, and that maybe if she went back, she could get help.

Now she wondered if the creature simply understood that the water could heal her.

"You knew all along, didn't you?" she asked, placing one hand on the creature's head.

Jabbers only blinked one yellow eye, then the other.

Finally, Lou said, "I'll let you have my blood. For your tests."

Konstantine brightened at this. "Thank you."

Then his hands were on her face, pulling her to him until their foreheads touched. After a shaky breath, he said, "You scared me."

She pulled back and smiled. "I told you I would."

33

———

Someone was knocking on the door. King rose, placing his soda on the coaster, and crossed the kitchen. When he opened the door, he found Piper on the other side with a bowl of popcorn tucked under her arm.

"Turn it to Channel Four," she said with her mouth full. "You're missing it."

He stepped aside to let her in. "Missing what?"

The girl marched into his apartment like she owned it, and seized his remote from his oversized coffee table.

"The fact you still have cable is wacko," she said. "How do you—Ah, never mind."

The picture stopped flicking.

"Tonight we have a gruesome story of murder," the news anchor said. "The remains of over sixty victims have been uncovered from the Paris catacombs, nearly all of them women between the ages of four-teen and seventy-three.

"Fourteen?" Piper cried. "Assholes."

She fed Lady a few kernels of popcorn.

"Hey, stop that!" King hissed. "She's a working dog. You'll ruin her."

Piper grumbled, but tipped the bowl away.

Etienne Martin moved across the television in handcuffs, his head down as he was put into the back of a police car. To King it looked like someone had broken the man's nose. It was twice the normal size, swollen and purple.

Piper shoved another handful of popcorn in her mouth. "He looks like Steve Jobs except for the nose. That's the guy we saw in the catacombs, right?"

"Yeah."

King looked away from the television long enough to see Lou stepping from his shadowed bedroom into the living room, her eyes fixed on the screen. He hadn't even seen her arrive, looking as she always did in her leather jacket, mirrored shades, hands resting loosely in her pockets.

King jabbed a thumb over his shoulder. "Why didn't you use the door?"

"Ghost night," Piper said around another mouthful of popcorn. "She can't be seen until she does her spooky thing."

King returned to his place on the sofa, Piper taking up the other end. Lou chose to stand.

Piper offered him the popcorn, but he declined. "Dani's bummed out that she wasn't the one who broke the story."

"Where is she tonight?" King asked. For the last two days he'd heard quite a bit of laughter coming from the apartment above his head while he'd tried to work. He was guessing by Dani's acceptance to Thanksgiving dinner and Piper's general perkiness that the girls had made up.

King was glad to see it.

"Her parents went to Houston for the holidays, so she drove home to steal some stuff. I told her to bring whatever she wants. I don't know where we're going to put it all, but whatever. That's a problem for another day. By the way, if you didn't know, she's rich. So if you want to raise the rent on the place, have at it."

King didn't need the money, and he liked having the girls close so he could keep an eye on them. "I'll keep that in mind, but I've no plans to raise the rent on you."

Piper shrugged. "Just letting you know in case your retirement funds are running low."

The fact that King seemed incapable of quitting made *low retirement funds* seem improbable.

The news anchor continued on. "The bodies of the women were brutally tortured before their remains were interred in the catacombs below their home. Officers found that a wall in the basement of the residence had been partially excavated, connecting it to an unused part of the catacombs. This particular portion of the catacombs had been initially excavated in the seventeenth century, but was never fully restored or integrated with the rest of the city's museum. It appears the homicidal couple were using this underground passageway to hide the victims' remains."

"There must've been a false wall," Lou said. "Something they put up to hide the opening between his house and the tunnels."

"Probably," Piper agreed. "They haven't said anything about the dissections."

"They won't put that on TV," King said.

Piper snorted. "Yeah, they'll wait to put that in the book."

King recalled the delicate little creatures splayed open in Delphine's light boxes. Based on what Lou had told him she'd found that night in the couple's home, he could only imagine what it had looked like, those two young women, cut open and wing-pinned like that delicate blue butterfly.

He was more than a little grateful he hadn't been the one to see it.

"The motives for these killings are unclear at this time. More as this story develops." Etienne and wide shots of his Paris home were replaced by a feel-good story of a veteran reuniting with his dog after a year apart.

"I'm surprised you let him live," Piper said, her eyes on Lou now. "If someone poisoned me, I would've had a hard time letting that go."

"I'm not going to let him go. I'm going to kill him."

"Nice. When?" Piper asked, and flicked a popcorn kernel in Lou's direction. It hit Lou's jacket and fell to the floor.

"It'll take them a few months to fully excavate the tunnels. Once they have what they need, he might just…" Lou snapped her fingers. "Disappear."

"Going to take him to La Loon?" Piper asked.

"I'm going to slide a knife between his ribs."

Piper groaned. "*Damn.* Remind me to never poison you."

"You have to stop taking them from their cells," King said, plucking his soda from the coffee table. "It looks like they escape."

"Fine," Lou said. "When I'm done with him, I'll dump him back in his cell."

"Thatta girl," Piper said, and flicked more popcorn. This one went wide, and Lady gave King a longing look.

"All right," he said.

Lady leapt forward, snapping up the two fallen pieces.

"Who is ruining *who* here?" Piper scoffed. "Hey, are we all set for Thursday? Need me and Lou to do any shopping?"

"No, I've got the shopping and cooking covered." King's heart swelled. They'd all accepted his Thanksgiving invitation, even Dani. He was determined that it be a good day for all of them.

Even if that meant not sleeping and doing everything himself.

"Don't be a hog," Piper said. "Let us help you. We know how to pick up groceries."

"What if they don't have something? You won't know what to substitute."

Piper jabbed her hand at Lou. "Uh, *hello*. She can go to any grocery in the whole world, man. You'll get your cream of mushroom soup or whatever."

"Fine," he said. "You two do the shopping."

"And you should designate the sides. Just ask everyone to make something and you can focus on the meats." Piper smacked her lips. "It's the meats that matter."

"Don't ask me to make something," Lou said. "I'd rather clean."

Piper did finger guns at her. "Even better. I hate cleaning."

"I'm bringing Konstantine," Lou said.

King hoped his face remained neutral. "Okay. Mel's table seats six."

"Yeah, you said that." Piper looked down at her watch. "Oh shit, you better get down there and do your thing."

"Be right back." Lou pushed her mirrored sunglasses down over her eyes and stepped into King's dark bedroom.

There was a stiff *pop* between his ears, followed by an ache.

"I know," Piper said, sticking her pinkie in her ear and turning it. She scratched Lady's head with the other hand as the dog rested it on Piper's leg.

A sudden intense screaming came from downstairs. Seven or eight high-pitched wails were joined by a deeper, more terrified one.

Piper snickered. "I freaking *love* ghost night."

Lou surveyed the chaos of the apartment and was quietly pleased. Piper was adjusting the chairs around Mel's kitchen table while Dani smoothed the white tablecloth with her hand. Konstantine was putting a dinner plate in front of each chair as Mel had instructed him to. And Lou remained on guard by the counter, standing between the foil-wrapped dishes that everyone had brought and a very hungry-looking Belgian Malinois.

"Don't try it," Lou said to her, and instead of cowering at such a tone, the dog's tail began to slap the kitchen tile hopefully.

"Does everyone have a wine glass?" Dani asked, placing a handful of silverware on the table. "If not, I can go get some from our apartment?"

Lou didn't miss the look shared between Dani and Piper at *our apartment*, the words punctuated by smiles.

"I think we have enough." Mel put the macaroni and cheese casserole in the center of the table. "But I miscounted the water glasses. Louie, can you grab me one more? It's in the cabinet behind your head."

Lou turned, opened the cabinet, and retrieved the glass.

"Thank you," Mel said, setting it beside one of the empty plates.

Piper was rubbing her hands together in front of the dishes lining the cabinet. "Oh my god, I'm so hungry I could eat the foil. When are we getting started? Everything's ready, isn't it?"

Lou counted heads. Five. Six, if she included the dog. "Where is King?"

"He went across the hall to get tongs for the meat."

"I thought I heard him go down the stairs." Konstantine came to stand beside her, his hip bumping hers as he bent to scratch the dog between her ears.

King burst into the apartment a moment later, and Piper jumped up to widen the door for him. "About time, man. I'm starving. Jesus, that smells good."

King put the turkey on the table and laid a large set of tongs and a carving knife beside it.

"I'm sorry, I got a text from Beth and I had to go down to talk to her."

"I thought she was heading out to have Thanksgiving with her son," Melandra said. "Everything all right?"

"Yes, she just wanted to say goodbye before she caught her flight."

Piper was nudging King with an elbow.

King's face was turning red. "She's just a very polite woman."

Konstantine leaned toward Lou and whispered in her ear, "What is going on?"

"King has a girlfriend." She made no effort to lower her voice.

"I do not," King said, coming to the sink to wash his hands. "We're just—"

"Having sex?" Lou offered.

"Does nothing embarrass you?" King said.

Lou couldn't recall the last time she'd been embarrassed. When she'd screwed up a kill, maybe.

"Man, I wish nothing embarrassed me." Piper moved up to the sink as soon as King was out of the way. Konstantine lined up behind her.

"Yes, everybody should wash their hands," Mel said, her bangles tinkling as she pushed her hair back from her face. She looked warm from the morning's efforts to get the meal on the table.

Dani must've seen what Lou saw. "Everything looks amazing, Mel. Thanks so much for having us."

Everyone said thank you.

"It was Mr. King's idea. I just supplied the dinner table."

No one was fooled by this, given they'd been in her apartment for the last hour, watching her try to get everything in place.

"Let's eat," King said, taking a seat. "It smells so good and I'm starving. I want some of that spicy cornbread Dani brought."

Dani passed the breadbasket over.

Everyone took turns passing the dishes, filling up their plates. Lou almost laughed when she saw the tiny portions Konstantine had put on his.

"Americans do all the courses at once," she told him. "Just pile it on."

"But how will you know what you have and when you're full?"

"This is why he's so fit," Piper said. "Me? I intend to eat like a whale until my metabolism goes bust. And today is not that day!"

She punctuated this statement by plopping an extra spoonful of mashed potatoes onto her plate.

"Now before y'all eat," Melandra began, giving King a look as he shoved a slice of cut turkey into his mouth, "I want to hear what you're grateful for. I'll go first. I'm grateful for this meal and that I can share it with all of you." Then, after a pause, she added, "Also that my ex-husband is dead."

Piper snorted into her drink. "Good one."

Mel looked to King, who was sitting on her left.

King put his fork and knife down. "I'm also grateful for all of you."

"Copycat," Mel said. "Say something unique."

"And for new friends," he said, daring anyone to comment on this.

"Mmhmm." Mel looked to Piper, who sat on the other side of King.

Dani clasped her hands together as if in prayer. "I'm grateful that Konstantine and Octavia love each other so much, so that I can live with Piper."

"*Sì*," Konstantine said. He placed a hand over his heart dramatically. "I adore her. She is so beautiful and soft, and her little face with those whiskers and—"

Lou nudged him, but Dani and Piper were laughing.

"I am grateful for Lady too," Piper said, and her hand went under the table.

"Don't give dogs turkey," King said. "It's bad for them."

"There's no turkey in my hand. It was a macaroni noodle."

"What are you really grateful for?" Melandra asked Piper.

"My new living arrangement? Have you seen her?" Piper leaned over and pinched Dani's cheeks, affecting a terrible Italian accent. "I adore her. She is so beautiful and soft and her little face with these whiskers!"

"Hey!" Dani cried. "I do not have whiskers. I waxed yesterday, thank you very much."

"Lou?"

Lou thought of Lucy, her bright blue eyes flashing across the screen of her mind. And the newfound knowledge of what La Loon's waters did to her every time she crossed. "My health. And that no one here is sick."

"Good one," King said. "Me too."

"Me three," Mel said.

"What about you, Konstantine?" Dani asked, tucking her hair behind her ears. "You're the only one who hasn't said what you're grateful for."

Konstantine looked at Lou.

Don't you dare, she thought.

With a smile and his arm stretched across the back of her chair, he said, "Gelato. I am very grateful for *gelato*."

Did you enjoy this book? Louie Thorne's story continues in *Overkill*, book 7 in the Shadows in the Water series.

GET YOUR THREE FREE STORIES TODAY

Thank you so much for reading the Shadows in the Water thriller bundle. I hope you're enjoying Louie's story. If you'd like more, I have a free, exclusive Lou Thorne story for you. Meet Louie early in her hunting days, when she pursues Benito Martinelli, the son of her enemy. This was the man her father arrested—and the reason her parents were killed months later.

You can only read this story by signing up for my free newsletter. If you would like this story, you can get your copy by visiting ➜ www.korymshrum.com/lounewsletteroffer

I will also send you free stories from the other series that I write. If you've signed up for my newsletter already, no need to sign up again. You should have already received this story from me. Check your email and make sure it wasn't marked as spam! Can't find it? Email me at ➜ kory@korymshrum.com and I'll take care of it.

As to the newsletter itself, I send out 2-3 a month and host a monthly giveaway exclusive to my subscribers. The prizes are usually signed books or other freebies that I think you'll enjoy. I also share information about my current projects, and personal anecdotes (like pictures of my dog). If you want these free stories and access to the exclusive giveaways, you can sign up for the newsletter at ➜ www.korymshrum.com/lounewsletteroffer

If this is not your cup of tea (I love tea), you can follow me on Facebook at ➜ www.facebook.com/korymshrum in order to be notified of my new releases.

ABOUT THE AUTHOR

Kory M. Shrum has published over twenty books including the bestselling *Shadows in the Water* and *Dying for a Living* series. She has loved books and words all her life. She reads almost every genre you can think of.

In 2020, she launched a true crime podcast "Who Killed My Mother?", sharing the true story of her mother's tragic death. You can listen for free on YouTube or your favorite podcast app. She also publishes poetry under the name K.B. Marie.

When not writing, eating, reading, or indulging in her true calling as a stay-at-home dog mom, she can usually be found under thick blankets with snacks. The kettle is almost always on.

She lives in Michigan with her equally bookish wife, Kim, and their rescue pug, Charley.

Learn more about Kory and her work at www.korymshrum.com

ALSO BY KORY M. SHRUM

Fiction

Dying for a Living series

Dying for a Living

Dying by the Hour

Dying for Her: A Companion Novel

Dying Light

Worth Dying For

Dying Breath

Dying Day

Shadows in the Water: Lou Thorne Thrillers

Shadows in the Water

Under the Bones

Danse Macabre

Carnival

Devil's Luck

What Comes Around

Overkill

Silver Bullet

Castle Cove series

Welcome to Castle Cove

Night Tide

The City / 2603 novels

The City Below

The City Within

The City Outside

Jack and the Fire Eater

Poetry (as K.B. Marie)

Birds and Other Dreamers

Questions for the Dead

You Can't Keep It

Non-Fiction

Who Killed My Mother?

You can also support her on Patreon or visit her website to learn more about her work.

www.ingramcontent.com/pod-product-compliance
Lightning Source LLC
Chambersburg PA
CBHW070807190726
48292CB00006B/1919